The Adventures of Elizabeth Stanton Series

Volume 5: Power Plays

Vic Broquard

Published by:
Broquard eBooks
http://Broquard-eBooks.com
author@Broquard-eBooks.com
103 Timberlane
East Peoria, IL 61611

Artwork by Crooked Willow Studios

For Morgan and L. Ron Hubbard

Table of Contents

Chapter 1 Confusions and Postulates

Dopey, yes that is the best description I can give you of me. I remember making the mistake of re-contacting my body way down there, which had been shot in its neck with a poisoned quarrel. As soon as I realized that I had been shot, or my body had rather, I got violently angry and flew off to strangle my assassin attacker. How did I do that? I don't have any explanation; somehow, I, an immortal spiritual being, did it. There was the dead body hanging from the tree to prove it, the assassin's. Yet, just as soon as I did re-contact the body down there, waves of this sticky, greyish-black mass flooded over me, lowering my awareness of myself and the world. I felt utterly dopey and dull.

How long was I so groggy I cannot say? Days? Weeks? Months? God, I hope not. When I finally woke up and became somewhat more alert, I could not tell where I was located either, which complicated matters for me. At least I knew who I was and what my basic purposes and goals were, those had not changed in the slightest.

My name is-was Elizabeth Stanton, originally, and my dearest friends still call me Bethany. When that body died, in my next lifetime I was called Bethany Madelyn Adid, until I married and became the wife of Jes Amir, who was the Great Messiah. I was then known as Bethany Madelyn Amir, and I discovered much later that I was called the Blessed Holy Mother. Most recently, I had a male body known as Ket Bethany. Yes, I have a fetish for the name Bethany and another for long hair, but those are just fleshly body things.

You see, I, like you, am a being — an immortal spirit. I've lived in many bodies and will have as many more as I desire, assuming the world, Tarra, our playground, is not destroyed. It began many years ago. I was part of a group of like-minded people, the druwids. In my group, I was revered as the Wid Bethany — the title that I took nearly nine hundred years ago. As I sit here and look back upon my past, I am Truth and Knowledge. Yes, you may call me a witch, a demon or a heretic, but, in doing so, you mark yourself as just another Blind One. I chose this road — this path I follow — knowingly and willingly. I do it for all mankind, even you.

But I digress; chalk it up to the grogginess still fogging my mind. It was my Ket Bethany body that took the quarrel at the base of the neck. I watched the sun rise and set a few times, but still could not get my bearings. However, more of the dopiness vanished and I did feel better. I've never been very good at looking at the world without using the physical body's eyes; space is somewhat distorted, and I've no proper concept of size or distance.

First, I reminded myself of my basic purpose. My task is to help create a stable civilization on Tarra, keep the strife and war level down, so that Jes Amir, or rather the Guardian of the Anuir as he calls himself now, can work his miracles and free spiritual beings from the need and dependency upon fleshly bodies, gaining near godlike powers and abilities along the way to that freedom. As such, I was leading the Santi del Dio, the Knights of God, an organization composed of the remnants of the Guardians, that's we druwids, the remnants of the Sea Prince Sisterhood, bolstered by many ordinary fighters.

I needed to get back into the game of life quickly. This meant that I needed to pick up a new baby body somewhere. I decided that I would take over the next baby that Jenna Rose Weston had. I had two reasons for choosing her.

First, if the Santi followed my orders, then Jenna would have become the new leader of the movement, taking the place of Ket Bethany. This way, even as a baby, I could keep myself current on all the activities of the Santi. Sneaky, yes. Second, Jenna had just added an eight specialty to druwid training. Normally, druwid trainees in their tenth year of study would specialize in one of seven areas: healing, planning, arbitration, protection, lore, communication (telepathy), or knowing as much as possible about everything. Our titles for these are Healer, Planner, Judger, Protector, Loremaster, Communicator, and Wid. The Wid would lead a Circle of Seven druwids — at least they did in the old days. For three lifetimes, I had been a Wid.

Then along came Jenna Rose Weston. When the evil Holy Paladins of the Megalos Church of Jehosanity took over the Sea Prince sectors after the Megalos Centurions had conquered them yet again, these vile men began instigating new laws, enforcing their perverted version of religion upon the citizens. From their point of view, women were born in sin and had caused the downfall of men. As such, women were held in the lowest possible esteem. Many say that a dog held higher respect than a woman did. These men and their religious priests were vicious and brutal beyond all comprehension. Routinely, men were encouraged to beat their women into submission. Those women who refused to become subjugated were mutilated or killed outright. If a woman had spoken against the Church, her tongue was cut out so that she could never again blaspheme. Yes, women's rights had just suffered a terrible reversal.

In the Sea Prince sector called Zargarb, Jenna Rose ran an inn. She refused to shut it down and the evil priests cut off her hands so that she could no longer work her evil ways. Once her body had healed, her tenacity for life kicked into high gear and she, along with two other women, escaped their prison, called a Nunnery, and settled in the Gnostic Capital of Tarra, Velona. There, she trained under Hank Weston, a Loremaster, and eventually fell in love with him and married.

However, when her tenth year of study arrived, she could not qualify for any of the seven specialties; a lack of hands played a small part in that. Undaunted, she sought out the Guardian of the Anuir, Jes Amir, down in the Red Desert. There, Jes once again worked his miracles. She regained or obtained a tremendous new specialty, the ability to move objects without using a physical body. So new is her specialty that we do not yet have a name for it.

When she arrived home from her training, she performed what the citizens in Velona are calling the Holy Construction Miracle. Elona Po, the benevolent monarch of Velona, was in the process of having an enormous new stone cathedral built. The huge dome was nearly done when the scaffolding collapsed, trapping many workers under tons of stone blocks. From a warehouse across the square from the construction site, Jenna lifted these incredibly heavy stone blocks, block by block, and placed them back where they belonged. She did not stop until she had placed the final stone in place, the top-most capstone, which then heldall the others in place. As a result of this spectacular demonstration of her new found ability, Elona named the new cathedral the Church of the Holy Rose in her honor, only a very few insiders knew that the church was named after Jenna. Only we Guardians know that she was the person responsible for the action. The common folks believe it was an act of God, a miracle.

Now you can see why this is the second reason I choose Jenna to mother my next body, I hope to learn how to do that from her. Okay, I admit this is a self-centered reason for picking her as my next mom, but it is the truth.

Thus, my first action was to postulate, to decide, that I now had a communication line tied to her womb. Once I made that decision, on the back flow, I detected that there was indeed a small body present. Jenna was once again pregnant. I let out a spiritual "Yes!" Problem solved. I knew that as soon as the baby body was born, my thin line down to it would energize, and I would become attracted to it automatically.

Now I could begin to relax and think about the recent events. I realized that I had just lost not only my body, but also my wife Lilly Ann and our children. We just had a baby girl only days before Ket, my body that is, was killed. I'd lost my possessions, my position of leadership, my home, my musical instruments, and all my dearest friends! All these physical things were now gone from me! Lost. I instinctively began looking at my memories of dear Lilly Ann and the twins. All I had now were mental memories. Time passed by me.

For the longest time, it did not even occur to me that I could use telepathy to contact them and visit with them any time that I desired, or that I could move to their location and watch them. However, perhaps this was meant to be part of my spiritual growth. Musing on all this, I suddenly had a realization. Without the actual physical objects at hand, one had a great tendency to forget all about them! Now I could see why the vast majority of beings on Tarra completely forgot about their previous lifetime. When that body died, they lost everything. When they picked up a new baby body, why, all that they had was gone. They were in a new time and location, with new objects around them, new people. Worse still, the baby body lacked mass and mobility for at least a fair number of years before it grew up enough to be used. Out of sight, out of mind! This observation I found utterly fascinating and began wondering how I could make use of this interesting idea.

Naturally, I then speculated on what would happen if a person suddenly found themselves back in the location in which they had lived in a previous lifetime. Would not all their memories of such return? I vowed to test this theory. Perhaps that would be a useful tool in helping to free spiritual beings.

At this point, I remembered that I had a rush of my assailant's mental memories, after I had set him straight. Could the assassin's memories be useful? I must say that looking at another's memories is a very weird experience — no context in which to relate them. Worse, the memories were just a big jumble, as the Rooster had viewed them while he was re-aligning his data realizing that Yazi had played him for a fool. I spent a good deal of time examining them. Several key points presented themselves to me.

First, Pope Yazi had died, and there was now a new Pope who went by the name Pope Amir I. Evidently the funeral had been attended by huge numbers of people on Megalos, judging from the vast number of people along the roadside. I concluded that this religion had now become very powerful and strongly entrenched with the local population of the island nation. This did not bode well for us.

Second, I had images that showed a vast network of tunnels under the church in Constanza City, more of a maze from my point of view. In one isolated section, a special vault had been carved into the bedrock and only the Pope had access to its contents. However, for what it was worth, I now knew where the only key to the vault was kept.

Third, from the Rooster's images, I concluded that Yazi did indeed have a fair number of copies of the original manuscripts written by the ten disciples of the Great Messiah, Jes Amir. Evidently, Yazi had translated them into the language of the Centurions. I would bet anything that he grossly altered the words and meaning to suit his perverted view. A few years ago, the Santi had recovered the complete set of those ancient scrolls. I had been planning to get them translated into Sea Prince dialect and then published using our new fancy printing presses.

I was still analyzing these memories, when all of a sudden I became exceedingly tired, as if I had not slept in ages. I felt weak and I rather doped off once more. All was dark, but somehow I was in motion, a sort of bobbing, rocking movement. I lost track of time. Dark turned to grey turned to dark turned to grey. I lost count. I felt unbelievably thirsty and hungry, but the bobbing continued unrelentingly. What was happening to me? I never felt this way before; naturally, I was very curious, but just had no idea at all.

Now I heard voices. How can this be? The language — it was foreign to me, and that was saying something. I knew ancient Arad, modern Juda Arad, Greenway, Sea Prince, Megalos, the various dialects of Cymry or West Reach, and a bit of Galt and Volksholm. This sounded like nothing I'd ever heard. From the voices, I thought perhaps some were children and some were adult. I was sure some were male and others, female. Where was I?

If this was not enough confusion, suddenly, I heard a different set of voices coming from somewhere else, unconnected to these voices. Yet, I recognized these at once. It was Beth Ann Penton's voice, the Healer from my Circle last lifetime. She was saying, "Okay, Jenna, now push. Yes, that's the way to do it. It's coming. Push hard."

Jenna seemed annoyed, couldn't quite tell, "I'm trying, I'm trying!"

Now more voices joined the other group, still I could not understand a word they were saying. I'm starving! I'm dying of thirst! My head hurts like crazy! I'm freezing! I can feel people lifting me up. No, that makes my head throb unbearably. I'm being moved, yes, jostling left, right, up, down. Yes, they are carrying me.

With a note of excitement in her voice, Beth Ann exclaimed, "One more push, Jenna. It's almost out! Now my head has an entirely new feeling, sort of a massive pressure all over the body, especially my head. Sudden cold sweeps over my body, like standing naked in front of an open door during the dead of winter! Ouch, my butt hurts. I feel upside down. What is happening to me? God, I am starving too. "It's a girl, Jenna. Hank, it's a girl. She's healthy, got all her fingers and toes. Let me wrap her up in the blanket. There you go little lady, snuggle beside your mom."

I heard Hank's voice, "She's beautiful, Jenna, looks just like her gorgeous mother. Still planning on using the name we picked out?"

Jenna seemed relaxed now, but tired. "Yes, your name is going to be Elizabeth Ann Weston, in honor of a very great lady and after all the Ann's that we have around here." She chuckled, and I heard several others join her, as well. "We'll call you Lizzy for short, how's that?"

I wanted to scream "No! Bethany, for short!" but could not seem to make a sound. Ah, well, I could always get them to change that when the body grows up a bit. Lizzy, yuck! I now felt warm; I felt mother's touch on my cheeks. I relaxed; all was well in the world.

These other voices grew louder. I heard a door slam shut. One side of my body is warming up. I hear a fire crackling nearby. I am starving! I'm freezing! I am so dehydrated! My head, no my neck hurts like the devil! I'm being rolled over. I cannot see anything. What is going on? I cannot understand a single word that's being said. Where am I?

Water? Water on my lips? God, give me more! I try to drink as fast as

I can, but it's hard to do while lying on my side. More strange words are spoken. They are doing something to my neck; feels like bugs are crawling all over me.

"Lizzy Ann, why are you shaking so? Aren't you warm enough?" the distant voice of Jenna filled my head. "Beth Ann, come take a look here. Something may be wrong with Lizzy." Her voice sounded very worried.

Hands felt over my body. Other hands moved my neck. God, the neck hurts so. *This is getting really weird! I have two necks!* Now I knew something strange was happening to me. One neck was small, very small. I couldn't get my hands to move right to even touch it. The other neck was big. I tried to move my hands to feel my larger neck, but then other hands forcibly restrained me. The pain, the pain is so great! I blacked out completely. Silence at last.

Hitra, a young girl of twelve, and her slightly older brother Voss were playing stones along the beach late one fall afternoon. Both were dressed in their heavy woolen clothes, which their mother had woven and embroidered with the gay reds, yellows, and browns, typical of the people living here on Eyrarbakki, a small, rocky island that lay far to the north and west of West Reach. Winters came early and stayed late on Eyrarbakki, and the children were playing their favorite game of stones before the ice came. "Mine skipped five times, Voss. Let's see you beat that one," Hitra proudly exclaimed.

Voss got ready to throw his stone, when he spied the strange looking boat with no mast drifting toward their beach. "Look, Hirta, a boat!"

"No one's aboard. How did it get here, Voss?" Hirta asked; both forgot their game. Boats almost never came to Eyrarbakki. She remembered that the last time she saw a boat come here was when she was seven. To her, it seemed to be a huge boat with many big men, and papa traded many furs with them. That's how she got her fancy comb, papa's present to her, which she cherished. Both watched as the boat slowly floated towards them and finally stopped when its bottom hit the sands of their beach.

Instantly both children ran to the boat to pull it up on shore, neither wanted the boat to float away. Together, they pulled hard on its bow and made it secure. Then they looked inside. Hitra screamed, "There's a dead man in there!"

"Let's get papa!" Voss replied, dragging his frightened sister away from the boat. Together, they ran up the beach to their home, screaming for papa all the way. Orebo Lahti was out back chopping wood, getting the chords of firewood ready for the long winter. Already he had ten chords neatly stacked beside their long house. Hearing his children screaming, he came running around the house, while his wife, Vasteri, came running out, wiping her hands on her colorful apron, bread dough still on them.

"Papa! Papa! There's a dead man in the boat!" exclaimed Voss. Hitra merely ran to her mother and buried her face in her apron, crying. Orebo ran down to the boat to see, still carrying his axe.

"What is it, Orebo?" called out a worried Vasteri. "What kind of a boat is that anyway? It sure is strange looking. Where did it come from?"

"Don't know. Yes, there is a body lying in it. Ah, it looks like a funeral barge. Maybe this is someone's dead hero. Yes, rich cloths cover him. Come have a look."

Now that it was pronounced safe, Vasteri and the children walked down to the boat, albeit cautiously. "Children, this is a Hero's Funeral Boat. This man must have been someone's Hero, when he was living. See they honor their heroes much as we do," Orebo began to explain.

"Look at that incredibly long red hair!" Vasteri exclaimed. "Are you sure it is a man?"

"Ah, I recall Lief once saying that the folks in Tewdwr all had red hair. Perhaps this fellow is one of their Heroes." Orebo bent over to inspect the corpse, pulling back the coverings. He nearly got the shock of his life when the corpse moved slightly. "He's alive! Vasteri, this man's alive. Oh, dear God! Kids, don't look. Voss, run and fetch Olaf. Be quick about it. Tell him to being his healing bag." While Voss ran to fetch the village medicine man, old Olaf, Orebo pulled the boat completely on shore. Vasteri took a quick look and saw why Orebo did not want the children to see. The man had a bad neck wound and many worms were crawling in and over the wound.

Vasteri gasped and quickly recovered. "Hitra and I will go get the fire stoked. Olaf will want lots of hot water."

A few minutes later, Voss ran back, accompanied by Olaf and two other men. "Strange boat," one commented. "Never seen the likes of this kind. Wonder where it's from?"

Olaf said, "Voss said someone was hurt?"

"Tewdwr, I think, by his hair. Look at his neck, Olaf. He's still alive." Olaf felt the body and agreed.

"We'd best get him inside, Orebo. Give me a hand with him. Careful now, he's barely alive." Four sets of strong arms lifted the man from the boat, larvae falling off, as they cautiously carried the body up to the Lahti homestead. Olaf had them place the man close to the fire, because the body was deadly cold. Then, he proceeded to examine the wound.

"Can't tell a thing with all this hair in the way. We are going to have to cut it off real short so I can get to the wound properly. Lend me a hand, will you?" Olaf requested. A short while later, he spied the puncture wound at the base of the man's neck. The wound was now very clean, but he treated it, as he would have any wound, finally swabbing his special salve over the wound and wrapping it with a bandage. "His skin feels so dry. Let's try to see if we can get something warm in him. Vasteri, get me a cup of warmish water please." Everyone watched as the man lying on his side reacted to the taste of water on his lips. Reactively, the body tried to drink as if it was dying of thirst.

Finally, Olaf stood up, finished with all that he could do. "Cover him with lots of furs. Give him all that he wants to drink. Probably broth is best. Looks like he's dehydrated and probably half-starved too. Call me if he regains consciousness, but I would not hold out much hope. I think that wherever he came from, he was probably buried at sea, much as we honor our leaders. Come, Orebo, let's see what all they sent with him to the afterlife." Both men left to bring the boat up to the long house.

Besides the excellent cloth coverings, they found an excellent staff and a fine dagger. They also found a black tunic with a large red fleur-de-lis cross emblazoned on its front and back sides. None of them had ever seen such or heard of such heraldry. Still, their consensus was the man was a great Tewdwr Hero of some kind. This could only be his funeral barge, save the man was not yet dead.

For seven days, the man lay on the floor beside their hearth. Every few hours, Vasteri poured healthy broth into his mouth, as much as he seemed to take. On the fifth day since the arrival of the boat, the children had to stay indoors, the first heavy snowfall of the long winter began, a raging blizzard that lasted for five days, common for this island.

"Mama, mama, come quick. He's awake now!" Hitra exclaimed excitedly. She had stopped to look at him and saw his eyes opening. Vasteri rushed over, another cup of broth in her hand.

"Oh my aching neck! Where am I?" I said as I tried to set up, but was too weak to do so. I settled for leaning half up, propped on my elbow.

A smiling woman with yellow hair handed me a warm cup of broth, "Hello, stranger. Here's some hot broth. Drink all you want. There's plenty. How do you feel?" She was talking, but I could not understand a single word she said.

I must have looked rather silly, because a young girl moved into view and "Hello Mister Hero." Still I didn't grasp a word; their language was foreign to me. "Mama, I don't think he can understand us. I heard him talk, but I never heard those words before. What did he say?"

"I don't know, Hitra, I couldn't understand him either. Go get papa, please." I took the offered cup and drank it down, I still felt like I was starving.

Soon a large, burly man with curly, long blonde hair and beard stood over me. At his side was a young lad. All had deep blue eyes and yellow hair. I assumed that I was in some family's home somewhere. "Where am I? Who are you? Thank you for taking care of me. I thought I was dead, or my body was, that is," I explained. However, the totally blank looks on the four faces staring down at me told all. They could not understand a word I was saying. Hastily, I tried every language that I knew, hoping that they might be able to understand one of them. No such luck.

I've been in similar predicaments before. Gesturing at myself, I said, "Me, Ket. Ket. Ket." Then I pointed to the man and said, "You? You?"

"Ah ha," Orebo said, "I get it. He is saying that his name is Ket." Smiles lighted up four faces. Me Orebo. Orebo." He pointed to himself. I nodded and pointed to him, repeating his name. Next, he pointed to himself and said, "Orebo Lahti. Orebo Lahti." Then, he pointed to his wife, saying several time, "Vasteri." Next, he pointed to his son and said, "Voss." Finally, he pointed to his daughter, "Hitra." I pointed to each and repeated their names several time, bringing broad smiles all around. It was a start anyway.

I was starving, so I gestured to my mouth, saying "Eat?" She handed me the broth cup. I shook my head, and made exaggerated chewing motions. Her face lit up as she recognized what I was asking and quickly brought me a slab of dried meat. I chewed ravenously on it. It was meat, but I had never tasted this before. It wasn't deer, cow, pig, lamb, or fish. Nevertheless, it tasted fabulously to me at the time. Later I learned it was dried caribou.

As my strength slowly returned, I had two problems. Only one of these I could do anything about, and that was learning their language. Slowly over the next two months, I learned enough to understand them. The problem I couldn't handle was some numbing and partial paralysis of my left side. The wound had been poisoned; my body ought to have died. I could only speculate that being exposed to the elements and the subsequent invasion of the larvae worms had somehow kept me alive. My walking was awkward, but doable. However, my left arm was nearly useless. Perhaps time would help with the healing.

I learned that I was on an island called Eyrarbakki somewhere in the Vest Sea. Unfortunately, I had never heard of the Vest Sea. Several hundred people lived here in this icy land, most on the other side of the island. Winters were harsh and the snow covering, deep, lasting from mid-September through nearly mid-May. During the winter, the men banded together to go ice fishing and meat hunting, often taking the older boys with them. The women spent the long winters spinning, weaving, and making clothing.

Most of the older inhabitants of the island had been born here, but a few finally were able to help me locate where Eyrarbakki was on Tarra. Their best guess placed the island far north and west of Cymry or West Reach. Worse, sometimes years would go by without a boat visiting the island! I was likely trapped here for a very long time. I could not send word to the Guardians and have them come pick me up. This island was unknown to us all, no way to give a caravel captain sailing directions. Besides, with the heavy ice, a ship could not reach here until at least middle May.

Useless for hunting and fishing, I spent my time helping Vasteri around the house and with weaving projects that I could manage. Of course, they all thought that I was a Tewdwr Hero and insisted that I tell them tales of Great Battles. Whether they thought these were real or just stories and legends, I could not tell, yet they thoroughly enjoyed them.

Mostly, I had time to reflect and plan. What I found very confusing was the fact that I was now operating two bodies at the same time! Fortunately, my new baby body required little of my attention. I'd never heard of any being having two bodies at once. The confusion is just too trying.

I decided against contacting the Santi for several reasons. One of which would be the repercussions: they had pronounced my body dead and given me a proper funeral. Can you imagine the upset if they found out I was still alive? I just could not do that to my sister, Fianna, nor my wife, Lilly Ann, or any of my dear friends.

Instead of looking at this mess as a horrible turn of fate, I chose to look on the positive side. To the rest of the world, I was dead, my body that is. I had complete autonomy to do some key actions that would not have been possible if I were still the leader of the Santi, with all the responsibilities that demanded of me. I looked upon the situation as an excellent opportunity to take some effective action, unknown and unsuspected by everyone. The problem was deciding what that action ought to be.

Late at night, I kept looking over the memories that the Rooster had unwittingly shown me just after I had killed him. "Things happen for a reason," I kept telling myself, and I kept on looking for that motivation. Then it struck me. One time, the Rooster had accompanied Yazi to the Pope's secret vault. Standing to one side of the Pope, Yazi had seen inside the vault, seen the stacks of scrolls, parchments, booklets, and such. He could not read their titles, for they were written in Ancient Arad. However, I could read Arad. I had been a scribe for the prophets of Juda Arad when I was with Jes Amir. One title caught my eye: <u>For the Pope's Eyes Only: Read Only When You Need Control Over the Mano del Dio</u>. For days, I speculated on what this document might contain.

One night, I decided upon my quest: retrieve that document! Whatever leverage the Popes of the future might have over their assassin squads, the Mano del Dio, would be exceedingly useful for our side to have! Perhaps the publication and widespread distribution of that journal might help bring down this evil church. I knew I had to try.

I concluded that the small funeral boat that brought me here could get me there, for it must be sea worthy to have gotten here. It was in excellent shape, except that it needed a mast and sail. If I could somehow make those, when warm weather finally came, I could sail my way back into the known world and down to Megalos, hugging the coastline all the way. After drawing a picture of what I wanted, Orebo volunteered to help make the mast, once warmer weather arrived. Thus, I spent the long winter hours weaving my new main sail. Yet, one gnawing problem greatly concerned me, the paralysis and numbness was slowly getting worse, not better!

On June 1, 637, I set sail. Vasteri and Hitra had made me three water skins and a complete set of fur clothes, all highly colorful and decorated. Orebo packed a watertight box full of dried food, mostly fish and caribou for my trip. I had not words enough to thank them for their kindness. Their view was still that I was a Hero heading off to do battle yet once again. Inspiration struck, I said, "One day, many years from now, another Great Hero will come back to Eyrarbakki. She will come in my name, sailing a huge boat. Elizabeth Ann Weston will be her name. She will repay you for all the kindness you have shown me. Voss, Hitra, you two will probably be married with your own families when she comes, but it will be a story to tell your children and their children."

I climbed aboard and Orebo and Voss gave me a pushing start out into the open waters just off shore from their homestead. Once the sail was set, I turned and waved to them. I was off on yet another adventure. The boat was now rather cramped with the food box and water skins. However, I laid on my back mostly, lowering the center of gravity as much as I could, my one good arm handling the rudder. I had made a rope contraption so that I could lock the rudder in place while I tended the lines.

The first and most critical phase of the long voyage would be somehow sailing back into the known universe. All that I had to go on were the vague notions that this island lay far to the north and west of West Reach. Consequently, I sailed southeast, navigating by the sun during the day and the stars by night. For the first few days, I debated about attempting to keep track of the passage of days. I had no paper or writing implement or ink. I ended up making scratch lines on the port side of boat with my dagger.

Days and nights grew endless, monotonously bobbing up and down in the waves, over and over and over, hour after hour, day after day, night after night. I had little to do; the little boat sailed itself for the most part. Only the occasional squall broke the boredom. When I spied a coming squall, I'd lower and stow the sail and lie down as low as I could in the little boat, riding it out. Days ago, I stopped worrying about what would happen if I never did find land or worse still find unrecognizable landfall. Would I perish at sea like some mariner?

Curiously enough, my attention now shifted to my other body, my new baby body. I took nourishment and comfort from my mother, Jenna, who seemed to dote over her new daughter. It was surreal, me watching my mother snuggling with me in her warm bed, while this body lay on the hard bottom of a small boat far out at sea, bones aching from the cramped position in which I lay.

One day I saw a dark patch on the distant horizon dead ahead. The next day, I made landfall. I'd been at sea for nearly three weeks now. My fresh water was gone and I knew that I had to find water and soon. Yet, where was I? The coastline did not look like Tewdwr at all. Could it be southern Layamon? The land didn't look right for that either. When I sailed as close as I dared to the shore, I saw the red sand dunes. I was just off the Red Desert, having missed West Reach entirely! I found this encouraging, since it meant that I was well on my way.

The sun was just setting when I finally found a tiny cove with a fresh water spring trailing into the ocean. I tacked in to the shore, running the boat hard upon to the sandy beach. I could not worry about damaging the bottom or the keel. I knew that I could not pull the boat on shore, for I had not the strength. Worse still, my left leg now no longer worked, collapsing whenever I tried to put any weight on it. I managed to tie the bow rope to my waist, rolled over the side into the shallow water, and crawled ashore. Once there, I pulled and dragged the boat but still could not get it solidly ashore. Hence, I tied the bow rope to a large rock and crawled to the spring, drinking long of its refreshing, cool, clear water.

Revitalized, I spent another hour filling the three water skins. Most of the time was spent getting them and putting them back into the boat. By now, it was full dark and I decided that I would sleep here on the beach. Paranoid about losing my boat, I tied the bow line to my waist and then fell solidly asleep.

I awoke as dawn welcomed a new day. First action was to search for food. I was craving vegetables and fruit. Half the morning I spent crawling around the area, scavenging what I could find. Although I did find desert fruit trees, I could not climb them to pick ripe fruit. Instead, I had to be content with what I could find upon the ground, piling everything I could onto one of my blankets. My foraging was cut short by a sharp tug on the rope connecting me to my boat. The tide had come in and my boat was now floating free of the beach. Hastily, I crawled back, stowed my precious fruit, climbed in, and set sail once more. With renewed vigor, I was off once more. Now I at least had some idea of where I was at, off the coast of the Southlands.

From my previous voyages down to Megalos, I remembered that there were quite a few large towns with docks for the large caravels, to say nothing of numerous smaller villages along this western edge of the Southlands. Had I had any golden coins, I might have been able to obtain proper provisions, but I had none. In fact, I had nothing at all that I could trade, so I gave up the idea of putting in to any of these villages, giving them a wide berth.

For the next several days, I occupied my mind by attempting to estimate the speed of my little boat. However, without any maps, guessing the distances between points of reference was just that, a wild guess. I gave up the attempt, contenting myself with fishing for food and marking off the days. At least once a week, I would put in at an isolated beach, which had fresh water. There I replenished my water skins and scavenged for fruit, often spending the night ashore.

Probably a month later, I rounded the bend at the extreme southern end of the Southlands, marking a milestone in my trip. Now I would head primarily eastward across the bottom of the Southlands, ending up at Megalos. Yet, I knew that my body was growing steadily weaker. The numbness now completely spanned my left side, and my left arm was now as useless as my left leg! I prayed that I would still have some strength when I reached my destination. What irony it would be to get there and then not be able to carry out my mission!

Three more endless weeks passed before I saw the island of Megalos dead ahead. I had somehow made this incredibly long journey in this little boat. Now I had to find the northern Constanza City, which I judged would be about halfway down the long, narrow island. Should I cut through the narrow firth, where the water was only a few feet deep or take the long way around the backside of the island?

As I neared the decision point just off the extreme southwestern corner of the huge island, the decision was made for me. Hundreds of ships of all shapes and sizes plied the waters in and around the Shallow Firth. I could not risk detection. I would have to go the long way around Megalos. Three days later, after doing my best to fit in with the other small fishing boats just off shore, I spied what had to be my destination. Athos was a small port town, due north of their capital city of Galantas. The Emperor had given the Church of Jehosanity a land grant of a number of otherwise useless acres of rocky ground, just to the south and west of Athos. From sea, I could see the towering cathedral and church complex that was called Constanza City. There could be no mistaking Yazi's complex.

As I rounded the western side of Athos, staying well out of the normal shipping lanes, I spied the small port of the church. A royal yacht lay docked there. From the Rooster's images, I knew where to look for the secret exit. In case of trouble, the Pope could head down into the maze of underground tunnels and exit here, just beside his dock. Yes, it was indeed guarded. I spied two men dressed in blue robes pacing along the small beach and docks. First things first, I told myself. I had to find a place to dock my small boat where it could not easily be found. Yet, it would have to be close. I had limited mobility.

Pretending to be fishing, I sailed around the area for a couple hours before I finally decided that the only hiding place on this rocky, barren coast would be under the dock, beside the yacht! If I took down the mast, the boat would barely fit. Thus, I sailed away for a time to avoid drawing undue attention to myself. At dusk, I sailed back and sat the boat about a half mile from the dock, again pretending to do some evening fishing. Meanwhile, I began to undo the bindings that lashed the mast to the boat. I had a sudden thought and then panic hit me. If I undid the mast and its rigging lines by myself in the current condition that I was in, it would be impossible to re-rig the boat. Even if I successfully retrieved the journal, I'd never be able to get it safely away! Heartsick, I retied the bindings. I had to find another way.

Next, I decided to try sailing in closer, now that full dark had come, perhaps inspiration would strike where it had not done so all day. As I neared the dock and yacht, lightning flashed. A thunderstorm was coming. As I watched, the two guards doused their flame pit and headed onto the yacht, to ride out the storm. This was my chance, I decided to gamble and see if somehow I could manage to swim the short distance. Carefully, I tied my boat up to the backside of the dock, out of sight from the yacht, mostly. Making sure I had my dagger secure and a waterskin, I eased into the warm waters. I could still float at least. Had anyone seen me attempting to swim to the shore, they would have had a good laugh. With my left side not working and the right side going numb as well, I must have looked pathetic.

After an eternity, I reached the stone of the shore and eased myself aground. Now the storm had arrived, rain pelted down like sheets. I did my best to slither to the underground entrance unnoticed. Now came the hard part, finding the vault. By design, these hidden passageways were actually a grand maze, connecting the crypts, their treasury, the vaults, and their escape docks. If one did not know the pattern, he or she would become hopelessly lost in short order. Double worse, it was pitch black inside, and I had no light source.

Ah, a druwid is never without light, we can conjure a dim blue light, though I waited until I had gone a significant distance, not wanting to alert the guards on the yacht. With the dim blue light, I could now see where I was crawling. Mentally, I followed the path that the Rooster had accidentally shown me. The going was slow, but not too painful because the floor was polished stone. It was just exceedingly cold, made even more so because I was soaking wet. Hours must have passed as my shadowy shape slithered along the corridors. Finally, near exhaustion, I found the vault room. I was certain this was it. In an alcove nearby was a small table and chair, along with an oil lamp. Laboriously, I stood up and examined the vault and its lock. Oh, to have Allan, our Planner and expert lock picker here now! I wish I had paid attention to those lessons so long ago.

In the end, I managed to bust the door open, however, doing so also broke the tip off my dagger. At last, I could see the contents. Indeed, Yazi had not been idle. He had found eight of the ten disciple texts written so long ago. Since the Santi already had all ten, plus a whole lot more, these I ignored. Although there were a number of interesting scrolls and documents, I contented myself for that for which I had come, the journal that could be used by the Pope to control the Mano del Dio. Carefully, I placed it in the watertight bag I had brought, which used to hold fresh water.

Now to make my exit. Crawling back the way I had come, I noticed that my right side was now going numb! Perhaps it was the tremendous exertion I was placing upon it, compensating for lack of any help from my left side. The panic thought that I would collapse here in the maze and be discovered pumped more adrenaline into my system. I slithered on, albeit more slowly. After an eternity, I could see the entrance ahead. Luck was still with me, the thunderstorm was still ongoing, though it was lessening.

Thirty more minutes and I slipped into the water near the yacht, being exceedingly careful not to make a sound. I nearly drowned trying to swim the length of the yacht to where I'd left my small boat. That gives you some idea of how exhausted my body had become. I spent another eternity attempting to get back into my boat! With the last ounce of strength I possessed, I managed to raise a piece of sail and rapidly moved out into the bay, heading north. Then, I lost consciousness completely.

Warm rays of sunlight woke me from my daze. I panicked. I could not move either leg, and my right arm barely worked. With great effort, I sat up and got my bearings, sort of. I'd never been in this northern sea above Megalos. However, the continental coast was only about a mile from where I bobbed in the water. The island looked small and tiny to the south. I'd drifted quite some distance during the time I was unconscious. Worse still, I had no idea how much time had elapsed. Was it the next morning or days later? Had the theft been discovered? Was everyone on the lookout for me? What to do now?

With some difficulty, I ate a bit and drank a good deal of water. I really had little choice but to sail back the way I had come, the long way around the island. This time, however, I kept the island as far from myself as possible. The physical effort to sail the tiny boat was almost more than I could do. My whole lower body had no feeling in it, my bowels worked on their own without my consent.

There comes a time when a being just knows that their body is nearing death. Unable to see my wound ever, I could only guess about it. A great tiredness seeped into my body. With all my will power, I forced myself to stay awake and continue sailing. However, I knew that I must find a safe, secure place to stow this hard won journal. Years from now, I could bring a Santi caravel back here to retrieve it, but where was a safe place?

Then, I remembered how my Circle of Guardians had rescued Rea Helios from her estate, where she had been exiled. Her father had built a secret underground chamber, in which she had stored all his and her artwork and inventions. During the rescue, we discovered that he had also built a secret stairs that led down from the underground caverns to the desolate seashore, a secret escape route. I recalled the night that we laboriously carried all her stuff down the stairs, loaded it all onto the dingys, and rowed them out to the waiting caravel. If only I could get to that hidden passage — that would be the safest place to store this journal.

I forced myself to stay awake so that I could sail to that cove. While it was now only a half day from where I was located, my body was beyond exhausted. At last, I began stabbing myself with my own dagger, just to cause enough pain to keep the body awake. It was around midnight when the dingy finally slammed onto the shore near the location of the hidden door. I strapped the precious waterskin that held the journal to my body. With tremendous effort, I got the body out of the boat and onto the shore.

"Good bye, trusty boat. You have served me well. Go now and find your own fate," I whispered to my boat. I gave it a shove as best I could. It slowly drifted out to sea. Next, using what strength I had left in my right arm, I pulled myself towards the concealed door. An hour later, my head banged into the rocks nearby the door. We'd left a key to the door hidden, and I found it right where we'd left it. Another half hour and I managed to get the door open. It took me forever to do the simplest action. Using a numb foot to keep the door open, I turned around and re-hid the key. I looked back at the way I had come. Well, there certainly were no footprints! Drag marks were visible. I did my best to remove them from around the concealed door. Early dawn came and I could at least see that I had accomplished that task. Even if someone followed the drag marks, they seemed to end near the rocky side of the cliff.

I wiggled myself inside the door and let it close. Blackness surrounded me, a cold blackness. I cast my blue light once more and spent an eternity getting the lock to close. Finally, I heard the telltale click as the latch fell into place. Now the door was secure. I collapsed onto the ground, still clutching the waterskin, which held the journal. My blue light faded. I relaxed for the first time in months. I recall deciding never to attempt to have two bodies at the same time again. It is just too confusing.

I drifted back to Velona and awoke in my mother's bed, her arms smoothing my skin, her voice whispering to me. All was well in the world for a time.

Chapter 2 Discovery

"Well?" Silas, now Pope Amir I, leader of the Church of Jehosanity, the largest religious order on Tarra, snarled his intense dissatisfaction. His personal vault, located in a hidden recess within the maze of underground tunnels beneath the large cathedral and complex in Constanza City, had been broken into and robbed of valuable documents. Such had never happened before, of that Silas was certain. According to all reports from his predecessor, Pope Yazi I, such should not ever have happened! Security was the sole purpose of the Mano del Dio.

Silas knew what was missing, only one document, the one that held the incriminating evidence of just what the personnel in the Mano del Dio actually had done, assassinations in the name of the Church. However, he knew also that only one other living man knew about said document, R. Thraxton, who was on assignment in West Reach. This document was the only leverage that the Pope would have over the security arm of the Church. It could not remain "lost." However, he had not told Acting Supreme Prelate Thondakas either the title of said journal or its contents. He would not, unless there was no other way to recover it.

Thondakas carefully inspected the vault proper, while his partner, Prelate Cax, R. Thraxton's other trusted partner, followed other clues. "I will pay the ultimate penance tonight, Your Holiness. That such should happen on my watch is inexcusable! When the Supreme Prelate returns, he can dictate my punishment, which I gladly accept. However, look at this, Your Holiness. A tip of a dagger is embedded in the side of the vault. You have the only key, so it appears that a dagger was used to pry the lock, and it broke." He showed small piece of steel to the Pope.

"Strange tip! It's nothing like we have in Megalos, it's not our make," Thondakas mused, scratching his head. "I've seen daggers like this up in the Sea Princes — no make that West Reach, in the Highlands. I do believe this tip comes from a Highlander made dagger or very short sword."

"How is this possible? Are you saying that someone from West Reach knows the exact location of this vault, knows how to find it, comes to Megalos undetected, enters our complex unseen, breaks into the vault, and vanishes without leaving the slightest trace, except for this broken tip?" Silas fumed. This simply defied all logic. Perhaps if the thief was from Megalos, then it might be remotely possible, but West Reach, total foreigners, total barbarians? Impossible.

Just then, Cax returned in a very ill humor. Thondakas had never seen such an intense frown upon his friend's face. "We've been robbed," Cax explained. "Look for yourselves. See here, something wet has left a path in and out. Never have I seen a plainer trail to follow. I swear the person was sliding his body along on the floor, not walking! I believe I can say with certainty just when the thief came. Two days ago, it rained heavily late at night. Our thief came and went during that time. The fool you call guards that were supposed to be guarding the exit tunnel were derelict in their responsibility; they stayed inside the yacht during the storm! The thief snuck in right under their noses!"

Cax continued, "I cannot say for certain where the thief came from nor went, the slithering marks disappear just outside the tunnel entrance. Thus, I grilled the two night guards; that's why I've been gone so long. I had to wake them. They did report that an unusual looking small fishing boat was out in the sea north of us some hours before the storm came that night. While not suspicious on its own, when combined with what has happened, I think that is a safe assumption that our thief was the 'fisherman' in question. He was casing out our defenses during the day and made his strike under the cover of the storm. However, I have no clue why the thief did not just walk in, choosing to slither along the floor like some serpent."

"There is one other factor worth mentioning. The thief knew precisely the route to travel through the maze from the entrance by the yacht to the hidden vault. He did not make one wrong move! Conclusion: this was an inside job, or at least the thief has had inside help. How many people know the precise location of the vault and the maze, Your Holiness?"

"Inside job? You mean that we have a traitor in our midst?" Silas' anger evaporated. The whole situation took on a very sinister smell!

"There is no other possible explanation for the thief, who is probably not from around here, to have known the precise path to follow, Your Holiness." Cax stood firm on his conclusion. "So I ask again, who knows these two facts?"

"Well, I do, of course, it's my private vault," declared Silas. "Well, your Supreme Prelate Thraxton knows and you two. No other person is supposed to know both facts. Many know the layout of the tunnels, however. That is common knowledge, but only four know the location of this recess and vault. I assure you that I have spoken of this vault to no one."

"Me either," Cax replied hastily.

"Or me, that would be high treason," replied Thondakas. "I'm sure that Supreme Prelate Thraxton would also not reveal it, not even if he were captured and tortured. You know the extensive training that we have all undergone. It cannot be one of us. Perhaps one of the original stone masons who helped construct the vault wagged his mouth off in a pub?"

"That would seem the most plausible," Silas answered, happy at last to have a more reasonable explanation. The alternative was terrifying — that one of the three top security personnel was behind the theft. However, either of the three would have had a good motive, the stolen document described their nefarious activities in detail. Still, of what possible use could this document be in the hands of the barbarians of the north?

"I'm off to see if I can find others who may have seen this unusual boat," Cax said and left at once.

"I believe that the prudent action to take now, Your Holiness, is to find a new location here in the catacombs for your private vault. Hire some outside stonemason, who you trust, to build it. Perhaps the mason might meet with a fatal accident when he is finished. Keep its location very secret."

"Yes, we must change the location of the vault. See to it, Prelate Thondakas," Silas ordered. The two left the vault area, returning to their quarters in the sprawling complex.

Several days passed before Cax came with definitive news. Not only had he been able to find people who had seen the boat off shore, but also he could definitely say that the boat had sailed around the southern portion on one day and then returned the next day. Further, the boat had been found adrift in the ocean. Cax had seen to its recovery and it was now in the church complex. Thondakas and Silas were with him, examining its contents.

"Definitely foreign make," Cax continued. "I queried several sea captains, they agree, the boat probably originates from either the Sea Princes or West Reach. These blankets are well made, perhaps indicating royalty? Notice that there are traces of blood on them, suggesting our thief was injured. Two water skins, a sea worthy box, and the fishing gear suggests the thief did sail here. However, none of the captains could believe that this small of a craft could ever have made the long journey from the far north. They claim that is not possible, though it does have a small sail. Then, there is this," he held up a dagger whose tip was broken off.

"But what of the thief and the stolen documents?" asked Silas.

"His body has not been found as yet. The boat was several miles off our southern shore. There is the distinct possibility that the thief fell overboard and died. I have patrols searching the shoreline looking for his body, should it ever come ashore. Of course, the documents are what really matter. I 'interrogated' rather severely the fisherman who found it and brought it ashore. I believe he is telling the truth when he says it is just as he found it. It is perhaps likely that the documents fell overboard with the thief." Cax sounded hopeful, somehow, this horrible affair had to be put behind them, especially considering the dispatch he had just received!

Silas decided that this was likely what had happened. The document was lost at sea. Already he had been writing a new one, trying hard to remember all the sordid details that Yazi had written down. Unfortunately, he'd only read it once, there being so many other more pressing matters which demanded his immediate attention.

Cax watched the body language of his Pope carefully and saw the time was right. "There is however, some additional news, both good and bad. I've just received a dispatch in code, of course, from our Adept in the Consulate of Bregia, West Reach."

"Let's hear it," ordered the Pope.

"It's about Supreme Prelate Thraxton, Your Holiness. He was successful in his mission, the Evil Witch Ket Bethany, leader of the Santi del Dio, has been eliminated. His plan was successful. However, afterwards, I regret to inform you, he was unable to make his escape. R. Thraxton was killed after he eliminated Ket. His body was buried in the cemetery of Bregia."

Thondakas looked stunned. He never expected his mentor, the Rooster, to be killed. However, perhaps age had slowed him down. "Ah, now the Santi organization will begin to crumble!" cheerily declared Pope Amir I. That was very good news indeed! "I'm truly sorry about the loss of our Supreme Prelate," he added faking a tone of grief for the benefit of the two Prelates standing beside him. As far as he was concerned, he never liked R. Thraxton and did not fully trust him, as his predecessor had. "We should conduct a very special memorial service for him. I will dedicate tomorrow's High Mass in his honor."

"He would have appreciated that, Your Holiness," Thondakas replied humbly. "I believe that it is your duty to appoint his replacement. With all that is going on, I urge you to make your decision soon. The Mano del Dio must have a new leader in place as word of our loss becomes widely known."

"I agree completely. Security is paramount. I do hereby appoint you, Thondakas, as the new Supreme Prelate of the Mano del Dio. And you, Cax, are to be his second in command. Both come with substantial pay raises, I assure you gentlemen. Both men smiled; they both knew that Thondakas was their close friend's choice. The Rooster had told them this many times. Besides, Cax hated being responsible for the entire operation. Too many things could go wrong, and he valued his head.

Silas returned to his quarters to let his Cardinals know the news. He hummed a little ditty as he walked. This was the best news he'd had. Now the Santi was doomed; he expected the troublesome organization to crumble within very short time.

Chapter 3 Exit Florintine Junction

Florintine Junction, Zargarb Sector, Sea Princes is a melting pot of culture and race. Always has been. Located in the extreme northeastern portion of the Zargarb Sector, in the year 637 boasted a population of only some fifty thousand. Originally, the town was built at the crossroads into Juda Arad. In those early days, the Arad was a thriving country and trade was brisk with the city of Zargarb. Originally, seven thousand called the Junction their home. All commodities eventually traveled through the Junction, as the locals call it.

Juda Arad, in those early days, was home to a highly religious, pious people, who worshiped Lord Jehosa, using the Old Ways, as it is now called in 637. The land had numerous prophets, the keepers of the Holy Faith, and messiahs, the enforcers of the faith. However, the Centurions of Megalos had long ago conquered the Arad, holding its population hostage. Undaunted by their overseers, the messiahs waged guerrilla warfare on these Infidels. Their goal was to drive the Infidels from the Arad. Prophets had long spoken of the coming of Lord Jehosa's son, the Great Messiah, who was Jes Amir, and I, his wife. Unfortunately, the prophets mis-interpreted the Holy Scriptures, the Great Messiah's purpose was to free his people, the spiritual beings, not drive the Infidel's bodies from the Arad. In the end, the Great Messiah was crucified upon the cross by the Infidels and never did succeed in his mission, from the Arad's point of view. His ten disciples then wrote down his teachings in Holy Journals and fled the Arad.

Notably, two founded opposing Churches of Jehosanity. Bandar Dero founded the Northern Orthodoxy in the Junction. His church came to the aid of everyone, time and time again, bringing nothing but high praise from all those in the sector and beyond. However, Yazi migrated to Megalos and founded his perverted church in the land of the Infidels. He formed up a group of Holy Paladins, whose initial purpose was evidently to raid the Arad in search of the Holy Relics.

The Barbarian Invasions, the Galts from the Northern Steppes, just to the north of the Arad swept through the Arad. Wanton slaying, pillaging, raping followed unendingly over many years. If that was not enough to make life unbearable, the Holy Paladins continued the unending pillaging and raping, taking what they wanted without recompense. At last, the Arads had had enough. Most migrated from the Arad. Some settled in neighboring Zargarb, while others moved even further from the Arad, some all the way to West Reach, founding new lives and new churches. At that time, along with the blessing of Bandar Dero and the Northern Orthodoxy, the population of the Junction swelled to over one hundred seventeen thousand folks.

However, then came the First Holy Crusade for Religious Freedom, a counter attack against the second invasion of the Centurions from Megalos, who wanted to retake the Sea Princes which they had lost to the Galts some years before. Unfortunately, the Emperor of Megalos, Justinian, made a bargain with Pope Yazi I for his Holy Paladins to take control and rule over the conquered sectors. The Church of Jehosanity destroyed the Northern Orthodoxy church and instigated their own laws and religion. In fact, their first action was to force everyone to attend Sunday Mass, failure to do so resulted in instant death.

Worse, the Official Church now proclaimed that women were born in Original Sin and were thus treated worse than dogs. Their priests proclaimed that men and women had a Holy Ledger kept by Lord Jehosa, who observed their every action on Tarra. When a good action was done, a check mark went in the Good column. Conversely, when a person did a bad action, the Hand of God placed a check mark in the Bad column. When a person died, his soul when to the Holy Gatekeeper, who had a copy of the soul's Holy Ledger. If the soul had more good marks than bad, the soul was allowed entry into God's Holy Realm, Heaven. If the soul had more bad marks, it was sent to dwell for all eternity in Hell, ruled by Lucifer himself, a sentence to eternal damnation and suffering.

The priests claimed that their only goal was to help all souls get to heaven. This formed the basis of their laws and orders and actions. They insisted that they were only looking after the souls of men. However, since women began life with a ledger full of bad marks, theirs was a difficult challenge. Hence, the Church proclaimed a set of rules for women to follow. In their eyes, if those were followed, it would guarantee that a woman would gain nothing but good marks during her whole life, and thus the ledger could be balanced so that her soul could go to heaven.

As you can guess, these "rules" set back women's rights in the Sea Prince sectors back tremendously. Originally, when the seven Sea Princes founded the seven cities, they treated women as chattel, utter slaves to the whims of men. Brutalized, women knew nothing else. However, some of these battered women formed the Sisterhood and became the best fighters in the sectors. They aided and assisted ill-treated women and with the help of the Guardians, became one of the most powerful forces in the land. Over time, women gained back their self-respect and more importantly, the respect of men. All that changed back to something worse than the old ways when the Holy Paladins took over in 625.

Women who spoke openly against the Church, or men for that matter, routinely had their tongues cut out. Prostitutes often had their hands removed. Others, their eyes put out. Men were encouraged to beat and rape women, who clearly were earning bad marks instead of good marks. A man received a good mark if he reported upon the bad actions taken by another. And so it went in the conquered sectors for ten years. During this time, many died and vast numbers evacuated to distant lands, as they had done before.

However, in each of the conquered sectors, the Santi del Dio, the Knights of God, had an autonomous castle fortress and dock. The Santi is composed of ex-Sisterhood members, the ex-Guardians of the Greenway, that is, the druwids, and a number of recruited fighters. In each occupied sector, the Santi worked an underground rescue pipeline, helping battered women escape the savagery and immigrate to Velona, d'Grange, West Reach, or Mont Blanc.

The Holy Paladins and priests of the Church of Jehosanity founded two new institutions in each sector. The Holy Nunnery, run by devout chaste women who believed utterly in this new religion, attempted to care for the mutilated women and for those women who wanted to devote their lives to "doing good." About half of these nuns were true believers and the other half wanted some way to escape the constant ravages of men. The Scholastic Universities, now in every conquered city and most of the larger towns, provided education for men, teaching them how to read and write as a first action. Of course, their education of the world was highly slanted toward religion and its impact. For example, it rains because of God's will. A person gets ill because he has sinned. By repenting in Holy Confession, he may be cured, but only if it is God's Will.

By the spring of 637, Florintine Junction's population had dwindled by more than half, less than fifty thousand remained. Some had been killed or died, but most had immigrated westward, seeking sanctuary in Velona and points further west.

Tara Al Marteh came running into her home, tears streaming down her tanned cheeks. "Papa! Papa! You have to do something. The Butcher has taken Elsa! Papa! You've got to do something. They are going to mutilate her, I know it. Papa!" She begged her father more so than ever before. Elsa was her best friend and companion. Both were about the same age, twenty-four, and as yet unmarried.

"Dear Tara, you know that there is nothing I can do," Ali Al Marteh wailed. "We've been over this countless times. You both know better than to flaunt the Butcher's rules." It was safe to do so only in the privacy of one's home, and then only in whispers. The Holy Paladins and priests were called Butchers. Ali was forty now. He had immigrated some twenty years ago from Jerilum, bringing his new family to a better life. For a number of years, it had been a vastly better life. All that had changed when the Butchers took control of the Junction, some ten years ago.

His wife and two sons had been slain opposing these Butchers. Only Tara remained and Ali spent his waking hours trying to protect her. Yet, she was like her mother, refusing to bow down to suppression. Ali had urged her repeatedly not to be so vocal in her opposition and protests. Somehow, for the last decade, they'd managed to avoid trouble. True, Tara ought to have been married at least six years ago, but she insisted that she loved no man in the Junction, refusing all arranged marriages. In truth, he knew that she could not marry any man who went along with the policies, laws, and rules of the Butchers. That had eliminated all men in the Junction.

Her friend, Elsa, was in similar straits. Both women had watched as their mothers were brutalized and died of their mutilations. Elsa now looked after her two younger brothers and sister; both her parents were gone. She insisted on running her father's business, a small grocery store that catered to the Arad tastes. Ali had told her repeatedly that the Butchers did not like any woman to hold such a position of power, but Elsa had little choice, she had three young siblings to feed; she was their sole provider.

Tara whined, cried, begged her father to help her dear friend, but Ali would not budge. He knew that if either of them protested in any way, they would be next. Ali would not risk losing his last child, the last of his family. He did the only thing that he could do, "Come, Tara, let us pray for them." He took her hand and forced her to kneel with him. He began the ancient prayer chant. Ali's father had been a prophet of Jehosa, and he had learned much from his father before his dad was slain by the barbarians. Now, Ali was one of the few preachers of the Old Ways left in the Junction. In secret, usually one on one, he would hold the Sacred Prayer of Jehosa for those faithful who remained in the Junction.

"Come daughter, let us eat," Ali insisted once the prayers were finished. He led her to their meager table. Tara, still grief stricken, only poked at her food. "Eat, eat," urged her father.

"How can we eat when dear Elsa is probably dying out there? How can we?" she screamed.

"Wait until dark. When it is safe, we will go to her," Ali finally gave in a little.

When night fell upon the Junction, few walked the streets. No one dared frequent the pubs any longer. That was a Holy Sin and punishable by the Holy Paladins. Hence, come sundown, everyone stayed indoors, many holding their own private worship ceremonies as they could. The two shadowy figures snuck cautiously down the deserted streets, avoiding the main junctions, where Holy Paladins patrolled. When they arrived at Elsa's store, they found the door ajar.

"Light a small lamp, while I shut the blinds," Ali whispered, as if the Holy Paladins might hear him. Soon the dim light illuminated the wanton destruction of Elsa's store. Shelves of goods had been smashed and lay scattered over the floor. The two began looking for Elsa and her two brothers and sister. Near the main counter, they found Elsa's bloody body, lying upon the counter, where customers would place their purchases. Tara could only cry, while her father took the lamp and examined the young woman, who could just as easily be his last remaining child.

"She's still alive! All praises to Jehosa," he exclaimed. "Tara, find the others!" Only with great effort could Tara pull her eyes from the mutilated body of her dear friend. Something snapped in her, snapped utterly. Yet, she did as her father asked. Not too far from the counter, half buried under debris from the store, lay one of Elsa's brothers, the older one. His neck lay at a weird angle from the rest of his body. The boy of twelve had tried to protect his older sister. Tara moved on, looking for the other two. She found the other boy of ten not too far from his older brother. He no longer had a recognizable face; he'd tried to aid his older brother. Tara's blood ran cold; she grit her teeth and continued looking for Ankiel, the young sister of Elsa.

However, Ankiel was nowhere to be found. At last, Tara called out, "Ankiel, Ankiel, where are you? It is safe now. I'm here. Elsa is still alive. Come out. Come out." She heard a noise from the trunk in the single bedroom and ran to it. She opened the clothes trunk, and her eyes saw a terrified six year old girl.

"Are they gone?" asked a frightened, timid Ankiel.

"Yes, Ali is tending to Elsa. Do you know what happened?"

"When the Bad Men came in and started beating up Elsa, we were all playing in here. They went to help her and told me to hide. I climbed in the trunk. I heard awful noises. I was too scared to come out. I don't want to be beaten."

"No man will ever beat you, ever, Ankiel, I promise you that!" Tara declared, a note of extreme coldness and resolve in her voice. "Never. Come on, you can stay with us tonight."

Tara tried to shield Ankiel's eyes from the lifeless bodies of her two brothers and managed to get her out to the counter. "Ah, the boys?" Ali inquired.

"Gone," Tara said tersely, "Elsa?"

"We best get her to our house. You bring Ankiel. I'll carry Elsa. Not a sound out of you two when we are out on the streets," he urged them, fearing discovery.

A short while later safe inside their own home, Ali placed Elsa on Tara's bed and began to tend to her many wounds, with Tara's assistance. While Tara first thought the worst, seeing blood covering Elsa's clothes, as they began wiping her clean, she discovered that Elsa had not been cut or stabbed, just beaten to an inch of her life. Her nose was broken, which accounted for the bloody clothes. However, her face was a mess of bruises. Her left cheekbone was broken, and her left eye dangled from its socket. The swelling of her face made Elsa look nearly half again as large. It was awful. Tara slept beside her holding Elsa's hand all night.

The next day, Ali contacted a number of his close friends, believers in the Old Ways. Together, they went to the store, recovered the two bodies, and gave the two young brothers a proper Arad burial. Many of the immigrant men and women witnessed this, and secretly talked among themselves.

That afternoon, Elsa regained consciousness. While Ali looked after her, Tara took their clothes to the open laundry. Here was one of the few places where the women could gather and share their inner thoughts, without fear of the Butchers. No man would ever come within a hundred yards of the washerwomen and the well. As Tara approached, she heard many women discussing the recent attack on Elsa. "They've sunk to a new low, beating up a woman and killing two small boys not in their teens!"

"The Butchers ought to be punished!"

"It was not like this in the Arad in the old days. In those days if someone did this, why the messiahs would eliminate them immediately!" declared an older woman. "Where have all the messiahs gone?"

"I keep saying that we ought to do something. I don't know what — maybe go back into the Arad. I heard all the towns are deserted. Perhaps Jaifur Qa Jahdi would take us in. Some say that he practices the Old Ways."

"Tara, thank Jehosa you found them last night! How is Elsa doing?"

Tara told the women all the sordid details, sparing nothing, that coldness still present in her voice. "We all should move back into the Arad," she said. "I say kill all the Butchers and men who have gone along with these Butchers. Move what's left of our families back into the Arad. Heaven knows that there are towns enough for us all there, empty, just waiting our return. I'd rather go hungry than spend another day around here!"

The old woman replied without hesitation, "You have my complete support! All hail to Messiah Tara Al Marteh! It is time that we women don the robes denied us since the dawn of time. Men have proven completely unworthy. Now it is our turn. Hail Messiah Tara!"

To Tara's compete surprise, some fifty women gave her the long unheard messiah greeting! Her army was forming. "The Wrath of Jehosa shall fall upon this town!" she declared to her followers at the laundry station. "Hence forth, this shall be the place of our meeting. Go forth and begin compiling a list of all men in the Junction." Inspired by her own words, she added, "Make two columns: Good and Bad. Place a checkmark in the proper column for each man in the Junction. Write it in the ancient Arad so the Evil Infidels cannot read it. Bring your lists to me here. One day soon, the Wrath of Jehosa shall fall upon the Junction and that day we leave for the Arad, free women once more. I have spoken!" Tara really was caught up with her own words. She had snapped when she saw the dead boys; such butchery would never happen again!

Slowly word of the new messiah's coming spread among the Arad women of the Junction. Daily, Tara went to do laundry, even though most of her clothes were not dirty. These women knew they had to exercise extreme caution. Not only were many men, some their own husbands and siblings, actively supporting the new regime, but also many women had gone over to the other side. Women ran the Nunnery, for example. Each woman knew that if any of these ever got wind of their conspiracy, they would be brutalized or slain at once by the Butchers. Hence, these women used extreme caution, speaking openly only to those whom they knew were trustworthy. Ten years of Holy Paladin brutality had shown where nearly everyone stood.

A month passed, and Elsa now accompanied Tara to do the laundry. It was her first time out of doors since her beating. She wore a black leather patch over her empty left eye socket; the massive swelling had subsided, though she still found it painful to talk. Her face, still black and blue all over, brought curses to the lips of the women at the well. She received many well wishes and offers of aid and support. However, she explained that Ali had graciously taken over her store, cleaning up the mess and running it daily now for her. "At least they did not mutilate me," Elsa added, "like they did Lara, who lost her hands and later died. It could have been worse. I can still see out of the other eye." She tried to put up a brave front, though she now found herself terrified of all men, excepting those she knew and trusted, like Ali.

Three women came up to Tara and discretely handed her their lists. "This makes the last of them," Tara declared to Elsa. 'We've now got the complete lists. The Day of Reckoning is coming!"

"Hail to Messiah Tara!" the daily chant in ancient Arad began again, although low in volume.

That night, while Elsa called off the names on these lists, Tara marked them on her master list. At midnight, they finished, and Tara counted them up. "All told, we have forty-five hundred men on the Bad List, accompanied by one thousand five women, and that includes the Holy Paladins and their priests. Another thirty-five hundred wish or ought to move elsewhere and will not be coming with us, most are Sea Prince natives. That leaves forty thousand one hundred of us to return to the Arad."

"But how are we going to kill that many?" Elsa replied, completely aghast at the large number of evil men within the Junction. "We don't even have swords."

"Jehosa will provide," coldly replied Tara. "We need no swords to win this battle." Purposely she did not explain further, even to her best friend.

During the next month, Tara began hiking alone around the countryside outside of the town. Each day, she carried large sacks and heavy gloves with her. On the first day of her hikes, she exclaimed, "Ah, there you are!" She found the precise plant for which she was searching. After putting on the heavy gloves, she said, "Jehosa provides," and pulled the green, leafy plant up by the roots. Carefully, she removed all but the roots and placing them into the sack. When she had filled the sack, she then hiked to an obscure rock formation, just north of the Junction. Here, she carefully placed all the roots on the table rock and began pounding them with a rock. Once she had the roots completely pulverized, she left them there to dry, returning home.

Each day she returned to the table rock and carefully scraped the dry power that was left into small containers, which she took from Elsa's grocery store. Then, she would hike the countryside looking for additional roots. After a vigilant month, she had a very large supply of the dry powder, sufficient, she hoped for the task. Would it work remained to be seen.

Tara knew that she needed proof that her scheme would indeed work. Yet, she had no idea just how quickly the powder would do its job. She needed a test subject. Inspiration struck during her next laundry trip. Giovanna was there doing hers. As usual, she sported another black eye. Yes, her husband was on the elimination list. Giovanna explained, "I was trying to get all the loaves baked yesterday and the kids were sick and I forgot to set out Alberto's beer. He came home and well, you know." She flinched and did not say what he had done, though it was more than obvious.

Coldly, Tara handed Giovanna one of the small vials of the dry powder. "Put this in the mug before you pour his beer tonight. Don't say anything about this to him. Your problems should be over. Let me know tomorrow here at the laundry."

Giovanna took the vial and hid it under her blouse. "Will this work? Oh, thank you Messiah!"

"Yes, but I don't know how fast or what effects it will have. This time tomorrow, no man will be beating you again!" Tara said sternly and flatly.

The next day, Tara knew the plan would work, even before Giovanna came to do her laundry. Word of Alberto's sudden death had spread. Giovanna spied Tara and came over to her. "Thank you Messiah! It worked. I and our children are free at last of Alberto's fists and temper."

Tara smiled, "Jehosa helps those who help themselves. Come, tell me what happened."

After making sure no one else was listening or could overhear them, Giovanna explained, "Well, he gulped it down as he usually does, with not even a thank you. Right away, he began to be sick, but he couldn't speak, which I thought was particularly good. He kept bending over, and his arms and fingers just kept fidgeting around. Didn't last long. No sounds, very quiet like. I dumped the rest of his beer outside on the ground. I cannot thank you enough for freeing me from that vicious man! Honestly, there was no other way out of it for me. If I protested at all, the Holy Paladins would attack me or worse. Then what would become of my three children? No, this is the only acceptable solution."

Tara smiled, it was fast acting and she particularly liked the loss of voice aspect, no cries of alarm would be heard. No begging and pleading, no last curses or recriminations. Fast and effective. It was one thing to poison a husband and quite another to dispose of some fifty-five hundred of them.

Unable to deal with such a large problem on her own, Tara at last realized that she needed the assistance of many other women. Her actions and proposals would be viewed as high treason to the Holy Paladins and priests of Jehosanity here in the Junction. If even the slightest hint of what she intended to have happen should leak out, she knew that her life would be forfeited on the spot. Intuitively, she countered these thoughts with the feeling that she alone had now accepted the mantle of protecting her people, those who believed in the Arad Old Ways. If she failed, she felt that she would be betraying over forty thousand others.

After much thought and mental picturing, she decided upon making Pentagrams. That is, she would be at the top with her four most trusted friends with her. Each of those would be the top of another pentagram, and so on down. This way, if one was caught, only a single Pentagram would be compromised, not her entire group. Once Tara reached this decision, she put her plan into action, deciding to give each Pentagram a number. Only Tara would know the actual number of individual Pentagrams and even she would not know who was in those below hers.

Pentagram One included herself, Elsa, Giovanna, Raphaeli, and Elonia. All were about the same age as her. During the next month, the Pentagrams became founded and organized. By the end of the month, some two hundred fifty Pentagrams existed, a thousand women organized for the sole purpose of regaining their freedom from the savagery of these unholy men.

Over laundry, Pentagram One discussed their opening move. Tarra whispered, "The very first action must be to eliminate the Holy Paladins and the priests, all at once. If they are gone, we only face limited resistance from those who have bought into their perversion. Those men are not organized and can easily be handled, even though there are lots more of them."

Raphaeli added, "We've got three cooks on our side. Every day, the Holy Paladins all eat at the same inn. Each shift comes in like clockwork to get their meals. We could have the cooks put it in the day's food."

"Yes, but what about the priests?" interrupted Giovanna. "They never eat there."

Elsa answered her, "I've heard that they have their own eating facilities in their churches. If we could get to all those cooks, we could do it."

Elonia added, "I say we also take out some of the worst other offenders at the same time, like those who turned in their own wives who were then mutilated and sent to the Nunnery. They deserve to die, more so than the wife beaters."

"I agree, Elonia, let's plan on getting those in the first wave," Tara answered. "Stealth is required. We need to eliminate them without raising any alarm flags. Those that are sleeping must not suspect anything is wrong. I urge you to impress that upon every participant. Stealth. I suppose that we will also need some on standby duty in case some of them stagger outside the inn or churches looking for aid or trying to raise the alarm."

"Well, the morning shift eats at the crack of dawn," Raphaeli volunteered. "Hardly anyone else is about the streets that early. The next shift doesn't get to the inn until around noon. That gives us six hours to dispose of the corpses. Just where are we going to get rid of that many bodies?"

Tara pulled her hair thoughtfully, "Well, they die quickly. So we ought to have the Pentagram personnel nearby, but well hidden. As soon as the last one is stricken, one of the cooks can give a signal, and the rest of us can come in and help move the bodies. Stack them in the basements or side rooms, anywhere out of sight. I think it will work."

"By suppertime, the entire lot ought to be gone," Elsa thought aloud. "That means that we could then go after the others that must be eliminated at supper time, ought to be easy to do that."

"Sounds feasible," Tara replied, "and then we issue the ultimatum to those who are marginal or who we know don't want to abandon the Junction. We force them to pack up and leave by morning. That then gives us at least a day to get ourselves packed and on our way out of here, before any of the Butchers in nearby towns can get word of this and ride here to kill us. Perhaps we might have more than one day."

Raphaeli snickered, "Why not get them to pull many of their forces to way down south around the Cedar Forest? You know, invent some 'captured' message that the Arad Raiders are planning to invade in force down there. Let the Butcher leaders order their army of Butchers to ride all the way down south. That would give us more time to evacuate."

"Oh, I like that idea," Tara smiled coyly. "Let's make it a notice from Jaifur Qa Jahdi to his Arad spies in the Junction, calling for their aid." The five women chuckled at this deception. They knew that the Butchers would jump on this with abandon!

"Also, we should take all the dead men's weapons," Elsa added. "We may need them to defend ourselves later on. They may try to come after us you know."

"Not if we burn this town to the ground," Tara countered. "When we leave, we will have set fire to every building in the town. When they come, there will be no more Florintine Junction. We are going to wipe it off the map of Zargarb. Teach the Butchers a lesson they will never forget!"

"Now you are talking!" exclaimed Elsa, who hated these men with a passion. Her face would never look appealing after her vicious beating she had suffered; she was disfigured for life.

Over the last ten years, half of the dwellings in the Junction had been abandoned. Tara stored her large supply of Nightshade powder in one of these near her home. Later that afternoon, she sat alone in the ruins contemplating the deadly details. She felt that the real problem was not the elimination of so many — no that could be accomplished with careful planning. What worried her most was what would happen after the deed was done. How could they coordinate the movement of so many people, mostly women and children? They would need wagons, all the wagons they could possibly find, along with all the horses the Junction had. People would have to pack and load their possessions. Even with all that chaos, how could she lead the huge caravan into the Arad? Tara did not remember the roads or tracks, let alone the watering holes. "I must plan for the future," she declared to herself.

The Day of Freedom Tara set as August 1, 637. The week prior, small packets of the powder were handed out to the various Pentagrams, who in turn handed it out to specific women. Tara had carefully coordinated the massive list of perpetrators and supporters with who had access to them. Wives, aunts, grandmothers, sisters, the list was extensive. The largest bags of the Belladonna went to those cooks who's actions were the most critical and most retaliatory; they were the "feeders" of the Holy Paladins, the Butchers, and their priests. Also, Tara saw to it that the carefully crafted letter was secretly handed to Molly, who worked tables at the inn where visitors often stayed and which always had one or more Holy Paladins in attendance.

The next day, Molly's report came up the line of Pentagrams to Tara. Molly had carried out the subterfuge perfectly. When all was relatively quiet and after a number of men who looked like Arad traders, even though they were not, had left, Molly pretended to find a dropped dispatch. Acting concerned, she went up the highest-ranking Paladin and told him someone had dropped this. She went back to cleaning tables, but kept a close eye on the Butcher. Sure enough, he took the bait, leaving hastily, as if he had just discovered something of extreme importance. Another report also trickled up the communication lines of the Pentagrams. Late that night, a Paladin rider was seen galloping southwards towards Zargarb. Tara smiled and continued working on organization plans.

The night before the big day, Tara could not sleep. Already, she had everything in her home packed and ready to be loaded onto Ali's wagon. Ali had also packed up most everything in Elsa's store. He knew that he had to work fast as well as look after Ankiel; both Tara and Elsa would be busy coordinating the exodus. Tara fretted and sweated all night long. A million things could go wrong. Any moment, she expected the Butchers to come pounding on their door looking for her. At last, convinced there would be no sleep for her this night, she dressed and ate a little. Ali was also up as well. He hugged her and whispered, "No matter what happens, Tara, I love you, and I am extremely proud of what you have done here. Now you had better get going before it gets light out. I'll take care of things here. Go with Jehosa's blessing."

Weaponless, Tara opened their door and peeked out into the early dawn twilight. Seeing no one about, she quietly slipped out and cautiously made her way to an abandoned building close to the inn, which served the Holy Paladins. Already, she could hear the sounds of the cooks making breakfast in the kitchen of the inn. Smoke tendrils rose into the clear blue sky. It looked like every other summer's day about to dawn, only this one would be anything but normal! From the window, she spotted other women from other Pentagrams sneaking to other nearby buildings, some joining up with her. No one said a word. Everything depended upon stealth.

As the cocks began crowing about the Junction, the Holy Paladins, disheveled and unshaven, began stumbling their way into the inn. In this first group would be nearly three hundred of the Butchers! She watched, as their priest was the last to enter. From the stories relayed to her by the cooks inside, she imagined what was happening. What did happen was very close to her imaginings.

These men were forced by their religion into specific rituals. One of these was that none could eat until their priest cast the Meal Blessing upon the food that they were about to eat. Uniformly, once the prayers were said in unison, everyone would drink a toast to Jehosa. Inside, Father Jax finished the usual prayers, announcing, "Join me now with a toast to our Lord Jehosa; may we be worthy of his praise this day. Thankful are we for the bounty we are about to eat." Some three hundred of the day guards raised their mugs and all drank their usual morning ale, and then set to work on the meal already set before them by the cooks.

Tara had been near this inn a few times around this time. She noticed the distinct lack of guffawing that these Butchers made while eating. It was mostly silent. Inside, the cooks later said that they grasped at their throats, made gagging noses, bent over, with their arms and fingers shaking violently. One by one, they then dropped onto the floor. One cook came to the door and gave the simple hand signal.

"Let's move out," Tara whispered. The women strolled over to the inn and slipped inside. Within three minutes, two dozen had entered. Bodies lay everywhere, many still struggling for life. Efficiently the women dragged the dead into the side room or over the stairwell to the basement and let go. Others began stripping the men of their weapons, making a pile of them in the kitchen. One cook stood guard, in case someone unexpected came; none did.

A half hour later the last of the bodies had been moved and all pitched in to clean up the mess and make the huge dining hall look perfectly normal, ready for the next batch, who were due around noon. Satisfied that all was going according to plan, Tara and the women gathered up the large amount of weapons and snuck out of the back door. Quickly, they deposited the weapons in the abandoned warehouse just behind the inn. Each woman took her pick of the weapons, but hid them under their clothing. Women were not allowed to have any weapon, under the Holy Paladin's Laws. As Tara left, she spied other women quietly slipping into this very same building, following her orders to come and find themselves a weapon. So far, so good, she thought to herself. The real test would come during the day. Would the absence of the Butchers be noticed? Would the alarm be raised?

Later the cooks reported that a number of men, usually supporters of the Holy Paladins, dropped by asking about the missing men. Per their instructions, the cooks replied that they had all been at the inn for breakfast, but that they had suddenly left, something about Arad Invaders down by Zargarb. As expected, this satisfied all inquiries.

The noon shift likewise went as expected with no surprises. This time two hundred or so were poisoned. All that afternoon, Tara fretted. She knew the real action would occur at suppertime, the designated time for mass action. If all else went astray, Tara felt good that they had killed five hundred or so of these vile men. A hundred remained, the graveyard shift. She and Elsa passed the long afternoon hours doing final packing, while Ali stacked everything near the front door. Only what was needed for cooking and eating supper was not packed.

Even though both women were so nervous, their stomachs knotted, they forced themselves to eat. Neither knew when they would have their next meal. The plan was for Ali to lead the first group out of the Junction and into the Arad. He remembered the route and was elected to guide the first group. Tara planned for groups of a hundred wagons and horses to travel together as a unit. She'd lined up forty men and women who knew the Arad and would act as guides for a group. Everyone would head for Jerilum, the ghost town that long ago used to be the capital city of Juda Arad.

As she tried to force some food down, Tara again tried to imagine what was happening. In truth, she was not far off. All over the Junction, the designated women were serving the men on the Bad Ones list their fatal meal. At the inn, the last of the Holy Paladins were getting theirs, along with the remainder of the priests. The three men who ran the Scholastic University and taught the children and teenagers were to be spared, primarily because they continued to attempt to moderate the vicious behavior of the priests and Holy Paladins. More than once, they had been publicly threatened with expulsion and being sent back to Megalos to answer to the Pope for their protests against the inhuman treatment they witnessed. That detail was the mitigating factor that spared their lives, though they would be force to flee the Junction along with thousands of others.

Still with the nearly simultaneous execution of thousands would likely be fraught with complications and misses. Tara had anticipated such. With their last meal in this house finished, the two women cleaned up and packed the last of the gear. Now they could only wait.

Per the grand plan, those who had poisoning to do were to report on their success or failure to the designated member of a Pentagram. One by one, the Pentagrams would relay the results of their small group on up the lines, eventually reaching Tara and Elsa, who crossed the various names off the list. By seven o'clock, the last Pentagram reported in to Tara. "We've missed fifty-three men," Tara declared. "Let's make some copies of the ones we are looking for, Elsa." Hastily, the two began making a new list of those that had escaped the initial poisoning. When they had ten copies made, Elsa left to distribute them to the other members of her Pentagram, and they, on down the line.

Meanwhile, Tara's task was now to give the long awaited signal for mass action. Soon massive chaos would break out all over the town, particularly among those thousands who knew nothing of what was about to happen. Tara went to the abandoned building behind her house, carrying her oil lamp. Two minutes later, the building went up in a roaring blaze, the signal fire. By the time she got back to her front door, other fires began dotting the town. Within ten minutes, half of the buildings in the Junction, the abandoned ones, were blazing.

The reason was twofold. First, it was a signal that the deed was done and that everyone should begin harnessing wagons, tacking horses, and packing them. Second, it was the signal for the thousand plus women who formed the pentagrams to drop their concealment and step forth as the leaders of the new society. Their immediate task was to go from house to house, visiting all those who were not going to go into the Arad. Each household was notified that the Holy Paladins and supporters have been righteously slain and that the Junction would be burned to the ground at dawn. They had until dawn to pack what they could carry and leave; if they did as they were told, they would be spared.

Chaos it was indeed, as Tara helped Ali load some packages on the wagon in front of her house. People were screaming and running in all directions. Tara was awaiting the arrival of Raphaeli. Soon, she saw her friend marching proudly toward her, accompanied by about fifty younger men. "Sir," Raphaeli saluted Tara, "The men have been gathered as ordered. All are armed. All have the list of the ones that were missed. They await your orders, Messiah Tara." This was her finest moment in her life; she was ordering men. Tara grinned.

"Well done, Raphaeli." Tara turned her gaze upon the men. "You all know what you are to do? You have the list of the evil men, which have been missed. Go take care of them. Once that is done, return to your families and help them get on their way. We have a long night ahead of us." Surprisingly, all fifty men bowed low to Tara, a gesture normally bestowed upon the messiahs of the old days. Tara knew that she had their respect, and that was enough for the moment. She watched them run off to search out the remaining bastards.

She said farewell to Ali, strapped on her sword, and headed out to her designated coordination point, in the center of the Junction. Elsa and Raphaeli fell in beside her. The others of her Pentagram soon joined them. Just then, a young Arad man came running up to Tara. "Please, I'm told you are in charge. Please, come with me to the Nunnery. I've got to rescue my wife, Aneta!" The man was in a near panic, sweating profusely.

"Calm down. When was she taken?" Tara asked calmly.

"Six months ago," he wailed, tears flowing uncontrollably down his face. "They broke in our house at night, broke my arm, and took her away. I've never seen her since, but they told me she had been placed in the Nunnery. I cannot leave without her, please, please, you must help me break in there and rescue her, please, I beg you with all that is holy, please."

"Okay, let's go," Tara was moved by his plea. Her group headed for the Nunnery. About half way there, a young woman came running up to them.

"Messiah Tara! Oh Messiah Tara! You must come to the Nunnery! It is far worse than we ever imagined. Oh the Butchers! It is so horrid! We don't know what to do!"

Tara and her group ran as fast as they could to the Nunnery, which was a large, converted warehouse. It had three floors of rooms and a basement. When they arrived, four women, who had been assigned to take over the Nunnery, were standing outside, waiting their messenger to return. Vomit covered the ground near the door. All four looked quite ill, but one, the Pentagram leader, promptly saluted Tara. "We've taken the Nunnery per your orders. But, but, but." She gagged.

Quickly, another said, "Come see for yourself." Tara motioned for her to lead the way. Just inside, she found the ten nuns nicely tied up, sitting on chairs, awaiting their sentence. In spite of the fact that the head nun tried to speak to Tara, she ignore her and followed her guide. Inside, she found an empty kitchen and mess hall. Just beyond this was a long narrow hallway, with a stairs at the far end. Dozens of rooms lined each side, doors now open, left ajar by the women. Her guide, holding back tears, simply said, "Look in each one." Then, she began crying uncontrollably.

Ben Hamid, didn't wait. He began yelling out for his Arad wife. "Aneta! Aneta! Where are you? It's me, Ben. I've come to rescue you. Aneta!" He raced from room to room, yelling like a madman. Tara followed behind him peering into each room. She nearly lost her meager supper!

In each room, three or four women sat on the edges of their beds, frightened and scared. Each woman had been carefully placed in each room according to what she could still perform. Some were without eyes; some, without tongues; many were without hands; some had no arms remaining. Many were ghastly ill, infections and the stench of rotting flesh was overwhelming.

Up the steps ran poor Ben, fearing the worst, that his beloved Aneta was dead, though he kept on screaming for her. Elsa gagged and had to leave, likewise Raphaeli. Tara rushed after Ben, but kept on looking into each room she passed. The air grew fresher as she climbed the stairs to the second floor. In these rooms, the mutilated women were not in such dire peril as those below. Tara was thankful for this small thing. She had nearly caught up to Ben, when he bolted up the stairs to the third floor. She thought better of hollering at him. Though a Sea Prince native, he obviously loved his wife. Inwardly, she hoped that he did not find her.

On the third floor, some of the rooms were empty and the air was breathable up here, no rotting stench. These women appeared to have recovered from their various mutilations. None had any bandages, though they were dressed in nothing but feed sacks! Then she heard Ben cry out, "Aneta! Oh Aneta! What have they done to you? I love you! I've come to rescue you." What else he may have said was lost in mountains of sobbing. Tara could not resist peering in the room. She nearly gagged and pulled her head out quickly. Aneta had no arms any more, but Ben was cradling her, both were bawling like babies. Two other women in the room were there crying as well, but they at least had their arms, though only one each.

Hastily, Tara ran back down to the main floor. There her guide pulled her to the stairs that led to the basement. "You haven't seen the worst yet. Brace yourself." They descended into the dimly lit basement. Fifty women were kept in cages. Every night some of the Holy Paladins would drop by to have their way with these women. They were cut, bruised, beaten, and had initials carved upon their chests. Various ropes and belts were fastened to the wooden pillars, where the victims would be tied up, tortured, and raped, while gagged to keep the noise down. Many had all their teeth removed so that they could not even bite their rapers. Many had burn marks upon their torsos, while some had long ago had various appendages removed to make them more docile. All wore steel collars with metal loops around their necks, so that they could be easily hooked up to the ropes. Tara lost it completely, vomiting all over the floor.

She drew her sword and raced up the steps, intent on butchering every one of these vile nuns! With murder in her eyes, she drew back her arm, ready to cut off the head of the nearest nun. Just then two things occurred. One, the nun, tears in her eyes, said, "Mercy. We have been tending their wounds; there are a hundred fifty-two of them; we've only been trying to heal them." Two, her guide asked her, "How can we heal all these women? What are we to do?"

The murder lust evaporated; her tears finally flowed. Tara commanded as best she could, "Untie them. Release them. We are burning down the town. Take what you want and leave this town on foot. For what you have done, Messiah Tara spares thee." With that, she had to leave the building, joining her team outside, still crying nearly uncontrollably.

"What are we to do?" insisted the woman who had brought her here.

The leader in her kicked in once more. Tara ordered her Pentagram, "Go and fetch a dozen wagons from those who we are allowing to leave for Zargarb. Tell them that their wagons are to haul the mutilated women they failed to aid. Raphaeli, go find a man we can trust to take a message to the Santi down by Zargarb. Bring him and his horse to me. I will be here." Raphaeli saluted and ran off. Tara asked, "Has anyone seen anything that I can write a message upon?"

Then, to one of the other women she said, "Go and find some clothing fit for a hundred fifty women. If nothing else, they will look like women when they leave this accursed place!" Tara knew that she had to stay here until all these victims had been safely loaded onto the wagons. Someone brought her pen and ink. She composed a letter, addressed the envelope, and sealed it.

Good timing, Raphaeli came running up with a young man in tow. "Messiah Tara, how may I be of service?" He bowed low to her.

"I have perhaps the most critical of all errands for you to run. I am sending a message with you to the Santi down by Zargarb. You know their fortress there?" He nodded. "But first, I want you to see why I am sending you. Go inside and take a peek into each room on the first floor only, be quick about it and do not scare the women, please." He bowed and ran inside. He was gone for only a minute before he rushed out and puked beside the door. "Now you know why this message must get through to the Santi. I have heard tales that they are great Healers. We need them desperately. We will be on the main trail into the Arad, heading for old Jerilum. Go now with the blessing of Jehosa upon thee. Ride like the wind. Let nothing keep you from delivering this message." Crying, he took the letter, bowed, and mounted his horse, galloping at top speed down the road, dodging the many people, carts, wagons, and horses in his path.

Raphaeli asked, "You think they will come?"

"If they don't we will be burying many of them along the way," Tara replied. "Perhaps that will be for the best. Only Jehosa can say."

Just then, Ben, leading Aneta, his arm securely around her waist, came to the door. "Hold just a little, Ben, Aneta. I want her to leave this nightmare looking like a woman, not dressed in a feed sack!"

Thankfully, one woman came running up with her arms full of spare clothing, the first of many that night. "Oh dear Jehosa!" she exclaimed as she saw Aneta. "We had no idea. . ." her voice trailed off; she could find no words.

Tara rummaged through the clothes and picked a simple dress. "Here, let's put this on her." Tara intended to do it herself, but Ben took the dress from her.

"Excuse me. I'll do it. I am going to have to be doing lots for my beautiful wife from now on." Aneta merely began bawling. They disappeared and reappeared a short while later. Now Aneta looked more like a young woman. She had stopped crying.

Tara forced a smile, "There, that's much better Aneta." Both walked out of doors and up to Tara. Aneta leaned over as if she were going to hug Tara, who realized that was indeed Aneta's idea, although she had no arms with which to make this simple, commonplace gesture. Instead, Tara hugged her.

Aneta said meekly, "Thank you for rescuing me, Messiah Tara. I know that I now a hopeless cripple and totally useless. I'm afraid I will only be a burden to everyone now. Still, I am grateful to be out of that accursed building. Thank you."

Tara could not keep from crying again. What could she say to a woman so mutilated? Her life would be a hell from now on. What would a real messiah say? Tara wondered. "Aneta, you are alive and well. You have a most loving husband and children at home awaiting their mother's return. You are no burden. You should thank Jehosa that you have so much good still alive and around you. There are many who no longer have their wives — children with no parents. Elsa has lost her whole family, except her little sister. Be thankful you have such wonderful people to help and support you. In time, I am sure that you will find many ways to be of use in life. It will just take time and some experimenting." She looked at Tara with her big blue eyes, leaned over, and gave her a kiss on her cheek.

Tara had another thought, "Ben, if you or Aneta need anything, just let me know. In fact, why don't you bring your wagon into my group and join us? We will be the last ones out of here. But I will understand if you want to leave sooner." He thanked her, and Tara could see that Aneta also wanted to be with her messiah and with the other victims with whom she had lived for nearly a half year.

More clothing appeared and several wagons began lining up. Now it was time to begin to confront the horrible mess inside. Tara ordered the top floor evacuated first, since these women were at least healed of their wounds and did not need critical medical care. As each woman came out, Tara had Raphaeli write down their name and the names of their nearest relatives. Later on, Tara would attempt to get them back to their families. There was no time now with all the evacuation chaos going on.

Five wagons pulled out carrying approximately fifty fully healed women. Another five were filled up with those that were partially recovered. Finally, another ten wagons moved into position to handle the remaining fifty or so who were in grave peril. Each was re-clothed as best they could and gingerly placed in a wagon, covered up, and made as comfortable as possible. Finally, Tara had the remaining wagon filled to overflowing with all the medial supplies that could be found in the building.

Finished here, Tara's Pentagram moved back to their original, centralized location. More fires were springing up all the time. When a family had everything they could take packed and were ready to fall into their place in the caravan lines, they gaily torched their old homestead. Now fully three quarters of the Junction was blazing away, providing a surreal illumination on the evacuation chaos.

More reports from various Pentagrams came to Tara. Already, five thousand had left the Junction, and Ali led the very first group. More were lining up constantly. Every available horse, cart, and wagon had been pressed into service. Yet it was woefully insufficient for the task. More than half of the people had to walk, carrying what they could on their backs. However, those lucky enough to have a cart or wagon volunteered to carry as much extra baggage as they could. Tara was pleased to hear that everyone was indeed helping everyone else out as much as possible. It could have been a near disaster with people fighting other people over transportation. Tara concluded rightly that the forty thousand now evacuating were more than thankful to have the opportunity to leave.

Slowly during the night, the chaos died down. At dawn's first light, only the one thousand of her force remained, along with the fifty or so men she had allowed to join her group. All gathered around the central well. Tara spoke loudly. "Spread out. Search every building that is not on fire or burned down. Confiscate anything that we could use and bring the stuff to the eastern edge of town. Once the building is searched, set it on fire. Report to the eastern edge when every building is on fire or destroyed. May Jehosa be with you and guide you."

With that, everyone began running to the remaining buildings to carry out their messiah's orders. Tara walked to the eastern edge where the wagons holding the wounded sat waiting to depart with Tara. She found Ben and his family, and watched as Aneta's children gaily talked to their mother. Tara was touched to say the least.

Since she had time to kill, she decided that a true messiah ought to go say a few encouraging words to all the mutilated, wounded women. Thus, she began to make her way from wagon to wagon. She had not planned what she would say; the words more or less came to her as she spoke. "I am Messiah Tara Al Marteh. We women have now freed all those faithful in the Junction and have burned the Junction to the ground. Not a single building stands. Know this: all the Butchers, the Holy Paladins and their vile priests, are dead, poisoned by us, along with over five thousand others who supported them or turned some of you in to be tortured. We are now a free people and are moving back into the Arad, seeking a new life. You and I, we finally have our freedom. Further, no longer will men be allowed to control our lives. From now on, our leaders will be women only. Those of you who still have family members and relatives, know that I will be locating them and reunited you as soon as we can. I pledge that you will be allowed to become contributing, honored members of our new city. Somehow, I will find a way. We are moving to old Jerilum, at least that is the current plan. Now rest, we have a long, long journey before us."

Surprisingly, when she gave the speech to the wagon nearest Ben and Aneta, Aneta yelled out as loudly as she could, "All hail to the Greatest Messiah ever!" All others within hearing, nearly everyone, took up the hail, chanting praises to Messiah Tara. Tara felt embarrassed.

An hour later, the last wagon left the ruins of the Junction behind. Now mounted on a horse, which she could barely control — Tara had only ridden one a couple times in her life — she gave ten riders new orders. She had the ten ride ahead and begin tracking down the relatives of those women who were already healed of their wounds.

Of necessity, travel was painfully slow. More than half of the people were on foot, and the wagons dare not go fast for fear of causing even more harm to the wounded they carried. However, now Tara found herself on untested grounds. All her planning had been leading up to this point. She'd no time to plan further. Besides, she had often doubted that they would have actually succeeded and been on their way.

Thus, Tara realized that she must place her trust in those who remembered the old tracks and roads and watering holes. Most were men, though a few older women had excellent memories as well. In these hundred or so, she placed the guidance of the caravan, allowing them to advise her on what they thought best. By the third day out, water was clearly going to be their most serious problem.

They had brought along the Junction's two water wagons, which used to be used to fight fires. Each wagon held a monster sized barrel in place of a wagon bed. Accompanied by two Pentagrams and ten of the trusted male fighters and guided by two who knew the land, Tara sent the water wagons on ahead to fetch and return with water. She hoped this would be enough.

Surprisingly, food was not going to be a problem. Many of the older Arad women remembered all sorts of edible plants that grew wild in this desert region. Hence, Tara had them out foraging as much as possible.

No, her real problem lay in the trailing eight wagons, which held seventy-five women who were in very bad, even critical states. Tara had no healing training, none whatsoever. Yet, she did not need to have such training to know things were exceedingly bad, the smell alone told her that. Worse still, no one seemed to really know how best to treat the wounded and the infected. Various opinions flew this way and that, but each voiced opinion seemed to contradict others. In the end, Tara decided to have the volunteers simply wash and dress the wounded, not attempt various proposed treatments. She hoped against all hope that the Santi would come to their aid, though she only spoke of this to the own Pentagram. Midmorning of the fifth day, Tara spied a dust cloud coming from their rear.

Quickly, fearing the worst, she issued orders for the remaining male fighters and the nearby Pentagram members, who were now at least armed, to form up a battle line here at the rear to attempt to protect the caravan's rear. How could the Holy Paladins get here so fast, she wondered, but then their speed was dismally slow.

Jaqua rode like the wind, as his new messiah ordered him. However, he didn't need to be told to do so! After peering into those few rooms and seeing the dire plight of the women, he needed no further encouragement or orders. Jaqua would get to the Santi in record time or die trying. He rode night and day and even traded his worn out horse for a new mount in one of

40

the villages that he passed through. In less than two days and nearly setting a new record for speed, he came galloping up to the Santi fortress, just east of the walled city of Zargarb. Although it was now the middle of the night, he pounded on the gate as loudly as he could. Soon the gatekeeper slid open the viewing window. A light shown in his face. Blinking, Jaqua called out animatedly, "I have a vitally urgent message for the Santi from Florintine Junction. Please, let me in so I can deliver it. It is a matter of life and death!" True, Jaqua was being a bit melodramatic, but it was heartfelt.

The Zargarb Circle and Santi Zargarb Strike Force #1 had just returned to the fortress, having successfully delivered a chest of gold coins from the city to three outlying towns. Banditry was now a rampant fact of life, brazenly striking within just five miles of the city. The Centurion overlords, the Holy Paladins had no choice but to hire the Santi del Dio to guarantee the safe delivery of the funds, without which the small commerce with the city would stop completely.

Officially, Le Ann Weatherby, the Wid of the Circle, ought to have been their leader; however, she routinely allowed Andre le'Gouer, the Protector, to make critical decisions when fighting was involved. He had been stationed here in Zargarb long before the rest of the Circle came here. Indeed, Andre had fallen in love with then Fighter Group Leader, Lenkova Pazzio, and the two had been married before the others ever arrived in Zarbarb some thirteen years ago.

Actually, Andre now referred to their Circle as the Greying Circle, a joke. All of them were showing signs of age. Andre was the youngest, now thirty-five. His wife, Lenkova led Strike Force #1, which was composed of twenty-five ex-Sisterhood fighters, all wearing chain mail. She was approaching forty-seven. She and Andre had two children, twins.

Le Ann was fifty-three, streaks of grey showing markedly. Her husband, Art, was their Judger and was fifty-four. Tom Bridgeport, the Planner, was fifty-two, and his wife, Mary, the Communicator, was the same age. Fred Waterton was their Loremaster and was forty-one, while his wife, Ann, also forty-one, was their Healer.

Attached to these two was one of the many Santi Scout Squads, which consisted of the best trail riders and scouts in all the lands. Scout Squad #5 was led by Felice Bugatti, now fifty years old. She had married Thomasio Farare, a local horse breeder in Velona. These two had the highest respect for each other, and Thomasio had traveled here to Zargarb just to be near his wife, whenever possible. For him, it was a nice vacation. The squad also had twenty excellent scouts in their own right, plus two additional Guardian members. The squad Healer was Jana Heather Batten, thirty-five, and her husband Elmer Batten, their Communicator, was forty-two. Thus equipped, the Santi Scout Squads were entirely independent, but could relay information instantaneously.

The Fortress Zargarb, as the Santi complex became known, was commanded by Tom Whiteheath, a Protector, also in his fifties. His wife, Sally, was his Communicator. Thus, any news could be relayed to the Santi headquarters at Mont Banc instantaneously as well. Additionally and perhaps most valuable was Art Longton, their Judger. Routinely, he used his skills to infiltrate the walled city and carry out numerous activities. His wife was an ex-Sisterhood fighter, Lena, and she was now the Fortress Zargarb Fighter Group Leader. Fully five hundred now inhabited the fortress, more than three quarters were combat fighters. The rest provided support. Yes, it was a greying group indeed here in Zargarb.

The gatekeeper followed the protocol and chain of command this night. He marched to his sergeant and relayed the request. She in turn went to rouse both Lena and Tom, Lena for security and Tom because it was a message for the Santi Leader. Hastily, they put on some robes and followed the sergeant. "I suppose another woman has been attacked," Tom commented to Lena. She did not reply. They hastened down the stone steps and across the courtyard to the gatekeeper, whose sergeant fell in behind them. Seeing Tom nod, the gatekeeper slid back the bolts and swung the gate open, revealing a nearly dead horse and a young Arad man, perhaps only in his teens, holding a parchment.

Jaqua animatedly repeated, "I have a vitally urgent message for the Santi from Florintine Junction. Please, let me in so I can deliver it. It is a matter of life and death! Are you the Leader?" Tom nodded and Jaqua thrust the letter into his hands faster than he could reach out for it.

Lena jested, "You are getting slow, old man." Both chuckled, while Tom opened the letter. It was written twice, once in the Arad language and then repeated in a shaky Sea Prince dialect. He read aloud to the others.

Commander of the Santi

I have heard that the Santi are great healers. We have a critical need for the best healers on Tarra. Let me explain.

We, the women of Florintine Junction, have had enough of the Holy Paladins and their brutality toward women and children. As you read this, know that we women have already rebelled. Every one of the Centurion Butchers in the Junction is dead along with every one of the locals who supported or aided them in their butchery, that is, over five thousand of them that we women have killed this day.

Now, some forty thousand of us are moving in a caravan back into the Arad, heading for the abandoned city of Jerilum, there to live a life of freedom. By the time you get this, the Junction will be no more. We've burned every building to the ground and sent some five thousand locals on their way to other towns.

When we took control of the Nunnery, the horrors that we discovered inside are almost impossible to put into words. We have one hundred fifty-one women who are in dire peril, with eyes put out, limbs cut off, and things far worse. The stench of rotting, decaying flesh is almost too much for any of us to bear. No one among us knows how to heal such horrible wounds. So I, Messiah Tara Al Marteh, do beg of you, if you can heal such horrid wounds, please come at once. I fear that over fifty of these women will not survive without expert healing.

If you need money for your services, I will find a way to pay you. Please make all haste. Just ask my messenger. I had him witness it.

Messiah Tara Al Marteh

"Oh good god!" exclaimed Lena.

"What's up?" said Art, who wandered down to find out what his wife, Lena, was up to at this late hour.

"Just in time as always, Art," Tom replied, handing the letter. "Read and go rouse the Circle, show them this. Lena, go rouse the Scout Squad. Sergeant, take this boy to the mess hall; he looks like he hasn't eaten in days. Gatekeeper, take his horse to the stable and have them walk him before the horse dies. I'll be in the Chamber. Have the Circle and Fel meet me there as soon as possible." The instant compliance startled Jaqua; they acted without any hesitation, a very hopeful sign, he thought. True, he had not stopped to eat since he rode out of the Junction. He wondered how this man could know that.

Ten minutes later, with a leg of turkey in one hand and a roll in the other, Jaqua found his hasty meal interrupted; he was being escorted, food and all, to some meeting. The sergeant thoughtfully carried a pale of mead for him. Lanterns provided the only illumination in the large hall. To his eyes, this meeting hall looked like the fanciest, grandest room that he ever had seen or could even imagine. Fifteen men and women sat around the enormous table, most wearing robes, many wiping the sleep from their eyes.

Tom explained, "They have all read the letter from your messiah. We wish to find out more about what happened in the Junction and when it occurred. You may continue eating; we know you haven't eaten for some time."

Poor Jaqua, he really felt uneasy. He felt that he was now around Gods. "I rode here as fast as possible, been forty hours now, about two days ago." He didn't know much about how so many of the Butchers and their supporters had been killed, but he suggested the women had used poison on them.

"Oh this will never do," broke in Sally. "Dear boy, you are amongst some of the greatest Healers on Tarra. However, it is imperative that we know with what we are dealing. To that end, I would like to look at the images that you saw, according to the letter. It is painless and you might enjoy it. There, see, harmless. Now I want you to recall what you saw when Tara asked you to go into the Nunnery. Yes, just like that." Sally had already performed a Mind Link to all those present. Poor Jaqua, as he relived what he had seen, his greatly needed meal involuntarily came up, spewing all over the table. However, no one even noticed it, thankfully. The sergeant merely began cleaning up the mess quietly without disturbing anyone.

"Could you show us what else you saw that evening before you were called to meet with Tara?" Sally inquired. Jaqua obeyed, and then Sally broke the connection with him.

"Take him back to the mess hall and let him eat his fill. Then, let him get some much-needed sleep. We'll wake him when we are ready to ride, sergeant," Tom ordered. Gently, the sergeant led Jaqua back to the mess hall.

Once the lad was gone, everyone spoke at once. Expletives flew fast and furiously. Tom allowed them to get the revulsion off their chests so that they could become more rational.

"We've seen one, two, maybe three at one time, but a hundred fifty-one? That is utterly inhuman!" declared Ann.

"Ann, you and Jana have seen what we face. Determine what supplies you need to take with you. Lena will see that they are loaded. I'm sending the Circle and the Scout Squad just as soon as you are prepared to leave. Andre, Lenkova, do you see the Holy Paladins attempting to retaliate and go after the fleeing people?"

Andre looked at his wife and they agreed, "No, we don't think so. That is many men lost utterly. Town's gone. They have much to handle there. I don't think that they have enough other men to attempt to go after such a large number of people, even though they are mostly unarmed civilians. Besides, Lenkova thinks that they are basically cowards at heart and would not risk entering the Arad, knowing that the Arad Raiders control that territory."

Lenkova added, "No, water is going to be their big problem. They must be on foot; there cannot have been enough wagons or horses for that many. Crossing the Arad desert on foot, water will become a very precious commodity for them."

Art added, "I saw that there were two town water wagons lining up, there in Jaqua's images. I suspect they will be taking them along. Yet, that's not going to be enough to handle forty thousand people on foot. They are going to need at least three more. We should bring three with us."

"Yes, but heavily loaded water wagons will slow us down horribly," Lenkova replied.

"Bring them up there empty and fill them up when you get close to the caravan," Art suggested.

A lull in the conversation ensued, and Le Ann at last spoke up, "I observed one critical detail. This Tara woman only allowed the boy to see what was on the first floor. From appearances, there should be two more floors and perhaps even a basement. I have a hunch that what we have just seen is only the top of the tree. I saw piles of vomit just outside that entrance door. Many piles. Something in there must be so bad, so awful, that Tara did not allow the boy to see it. Healers, expect something far worse than what we were allowed to see. Go prepared for something much worse, please."

Both Healers promised to do so. Quickly, the group broke up to begin preparations. Time was now their enemy.

At dawn, everyone was saddling up. Andre commented to Lenkova, "You know, I've been thinking. Remember that huge buildup of Holy Paladins that we saw east of here a couple days ago?"

"Yes, we thought that they were heading out for a battle, but we knew there was nobody out there. That's why we have scouts," she replied.

He said, "Well, I been thinking. If the Tara woman is smart enough to have planned all this — I mean you don't go around killing five thousand people without careful planning — and all without raising any notice that you are doing it, why, I figure this woman must be very smart. That said, I think that somehow she managed to send all those Holy Paladins out on the wild goose chase two days ago — probably to make sure they vacated the Junction."

Lenkova chuckled and teased, "See, I keep telling you that women are inherently smarter than men!"

"Of course we are," Fel, who had overheard them, replied coyly. "Doesn't everyone know that?" They roared with laughter. "Better go issue my orders," Fel excused herself. She wanted outriders fanning out ahead of them on both sides; some would be three miles ahead of the main party.

Lenkova positioned her twenty-five fighters encircling the Circle members. Most everyone also would lead a packhorse, whose packs were brimming with what the Healers thought might be needed. A smaller band of a dozen would follow behind bringing the three empty water wagons with them. For once Lenkova was thankful that they would be riding up the north-south track just inside the Arad, instead of following the ridiculously curved roads of the sector. Besides, in the sandy track they could make much better time.

As they mounted up and headed out, Tom took an added precaution. "Jaqua, I want you to also wear one of our tunics. This way, any prying eyes will think that you are one of us." The boy wore the black tunic with the red fleur-de-lis cross with great pride. He felt that he was with the most powerful people on all Tarra.

When they reached the north-south track and began heading north, Lenkova explained to Jaqua, "We cannot ride as fast as you did. We have no spare horses ahead of us. Yet, we will push these hard. A lot depends upon how fast your caravan will be going. Maybe three days till we catch up with them, four at the outside."

"Lots have to walk," Jaqua replied. "I hope they don't die, until we get there." Suddenly he realized how that sounded, and hastily added, "I mean I don't want them to die at all." She grinned.

The scouts had nothing to report until late the second night. Giant smoke clouds still trailed up into the sky from where the Junction used to be. Lenkova was glad that no fighting had slowed them down, although she was itching for a fight. She'd not had one for weeks now.

Late the third day, the scouts reported sighting the trailing end of the caravan ahead. They were now heading due east along the track out of the Junction, which led ultimately to the now abandoned paved roadway built nearly a century ago by the Centurion overlords of Juda Arad. Thus, late on the fifth day since the burning of the Junction, the Circle, the Scout Squad, and Lenkova's Fighter Squad came upon the trailing wagons of the caravan, riding up hard and fast.

They saw a rag-tag line of men and many women, trying to form a defensive line against the riders. Andre said to her, "They don't even know how to use the weapons they are holding or my name isn't Andre."

"The men might," she replied, and then they slowed down and closed the short distance. Just as soon as they were close, the black tunics with red crosses identified them as the Santi. Everyone in the Sea Princes new their colors by sight, as well as those of the Holy Paladins. Lenkova did her flying dismount, mostly because she had a new audience. Landing adeptly on her feet, she proclaimed, "Zargarb Fortress Fighter Group Leader Lenkova Pazzio here. I've brought a large number of Healers. Where is Messiah Tara?"

Clearly impressed with this magnificent woman fighter, clad in shining chain mail, Tara timidly stepped forward. "I am she. I didn't think you would come, but I had to try. Please, save my people."

Le Ann, now dismounted, stepped forward, "I am the Leader of us Healers. I suspect that time is critical for our patients. These are our two best healers, Ann and Jana. Can you halt the wagons and allow them to have a quick survey of what the situation is? Then, we will want to get started. We can all discuss things later on. It's the wounded and injured that matter right now."

Tara sent several ahead to call a halt. "Follow me, but honestly, if you get sick, I understand. It is truly an awful sight to behold." Ann and Jana followed her, while the rest of the Guardians fell in behind them. Lenkova and the others took care of the panting horses.

Ann kept whispering, "Oh my god!" over and over. Jana simply cried as they moved from wagon to wagon, finally ending up at the lead one, where Ben, Aneta, and their children sat.

"Can you save them," Aneta bravely asked. "I am so utterly helpless now. I can't do anything for them."

Le Ann had come up now and overheard Aneta. She knew that the two Healers could scarcely speak, so she did for them. "Yes, you can help them, Aneta; when the time is right, they will need much encouragement. You can help them fight for their lives. It will mean far more coming from you. We'll come get you when you can help us." The smile that flooded over Aneta's face was a wonder to behold.

The three returned to the rear. Ann called out, "Healer conference now!" Jana at last stopped crying. "Le Ann, I just don't see how you figured that it would be so much worse than what we saw, but you were right! This must be in small scale like what Ket ran into with the Crusader army casualties. All right then, here's the plan. Jana and I will sort them into three categories. The ones that must have immediate attention get our top priority. Art, Andre, Tom, and Fred, you four will handle those that need minor work, and you are to inspect everyone that appears to be healed. Check them all over very carefully. Le Ann, Mary, Elmer: you three are on the emergency cases. If you run into something you are not sure about, come get Jana or me. Jana and I are on the worst cases. Fel, Lenkova, you and your people are going to be our go-for-this-and-that's. For starters, we are going to need lots of boiling water and a clean place to operate. So setup our big open-sided tent quickly. As soon as the tents are up, we begin, if not sooner."

The ex-Sisters were a model of efficiency. Within ten minutes, five large tents were setup along with numerous cots and bedding and working areas. Four fires were lit and four water kettles were positioned. Tara asked what they could do to help, so Ann got her to find much larger kettles for boiling water and had her move her wagon of medical supplied between the tents.

Ann and Jana were most efficient in the sorting process. Each had a keen eye for the exact situation of each patient. Another ten minutes and the first sorting was finished. The men had seventy-five patients to assist or to thoroughly examine how their healing had gone. Le Ann's crew had another forty on which to operate. Unfortunately, Ann and Jana had thirty-six women, all in extremely critical condition. Tara and her people moved all the critical patients into Jana and Ann's tent for them. "Let's prioritize them together, Jana. Let's arrange them in order in a line, that way we can go right down the line together."

"Good idea. Let's double-check each other's diagnosis as we go. We simply cannot afford the slightest mistake," Jana replied. Quickly the two set about this next task, ordering their patients. Their helpers quickly moved the makeshift stretchers into the dictated order. "Now for it," exclaimed Jana, and the two Healers began.

Jana's first patient had had her hands removed, rather crudely. The staunching of the wounds had not been effective, and she had lost a lot of blood. She was running a high fever, and gangrene had set in on her stumps. Worse still, telltale streaks of bright red ran from her rotting stumps up towards her arm pits. Jana cried, wiping the tears from her face, she said to Ann, "I've got to remove the rest of them, right?" Ann concurred. And so went the day into the night.

Around midnight, the two women, completely exhausted, covered in blood, finally finished up the last patient, helping each other finish off this one. Together, they staggered out of the tent and collapsed beside the fires.

The other Guardians had long finished their work on all the other women and had been assisting the two as they could. Now their husbands began cleaning up the women, while others stuffed some food in their mouths.

A half hour later, Le Ann finally asked them, "Okay, Healers. Prognosis? Or do you want our reports first?"

Ann sighed, "We've got seven that may not make it through the night. And an eighth that will take a miracle for her to survive. The others will probably survive, but we can tell better in tomorrow's light. Someone's going to have to sit with these eight all night. Wake us if there is any change in their condition."

"Which is the eighth? The one that needs the miracle?" Le Ann asked.

Jana, now too tired to cry any more, said, "Alice, I think her name is Alice. I had to remove the rest of her arms. She's lost so much blood already, I — well, we need a miracle for her." Ann showed the others which ones had to be watched closely all night. Then, the two Healers laid down beside their husbands, who proceeded to give them a relaxing rub down; both fell asleep almost at once. Later, the two men then returned to watch duty.

Meanwhile, Le Ann went to find Aneta. "Excuse me, I know that it is late, but we can use you tonight, Aneta, if you are up to it." Clumsily, she got up and Ben gently lifted her down out of the wagon, as though she was a precious flower. She followed behind Le Ann to the critical tent.

"Alice is her name we believe. The butchers did such a bad job with her that she lost a lot of blood and her arms began to rot. Blood poisoning was almost to her armpits. Another day without treatment and she would have been dead. Jana's done all that she can for her." She noticed Aneta was crying. "We need a miracle here, Aneta. You have suffered as she is suffering. I want you to talk to her during the night. Encourage her, anything you can think of. I know that she appears unconscious, but she can still hear and understand us. Trust me on this point. The other Healers will be checking up on her from time to time, but if you see any change in her condition, let the others know at once. Give it your best shot. We are praying for a miracle. Jana believes that if she lives through the night, she may yet make it. Can you do this for her, Aneta?"

"I've got to try. So many have helped me for so long, and it is something I can do," she bravely said. Le Ann leaned over, kissed her forehead, and then left her, heading off to make inspection rounds of the others.

Aneta squatted down beside the pale young woman, guessing that she might be all of twenty-one. She began to whisper into Alice's ear, "You can do it. I want you to live. You can make it. We now have the best Healers on Tarra here with us. You just have to make it. I know it's going to be hard. It was and is for me. But you have to try." She kept on whispering for a long time.

Dawn came and Tara walked solemnly over to the tents and the Santi camp. She hated to be bringing the bad news, but it was the messiah's position to do so. "Excuse me, Le Ann, but I've got some bad news. We are nearly out of water. Yesterday, we used up nearly all that we had with us, from every other wagon. My scouts tell me that we are still a long way from the next watering hole."

Rubbing the sleep from her eyes — Le Ann had actually gotten four solid hours of sleep — she said, "Don't worry. Our water wagons ought to be here by noon. We brought along three more like the two you have."

Taken by surprise on two accounts, Tara inquired, "But how do you know we brought two water wagons? They are miles up ahead, trying to bring back water to the front of the caravan. I'm so glad that you are bringing more. How can we ever thank you?"

"Oh, ah, well, Jaqua told us about the two wagons," Le Ann fibbed slightly. It was easier to say this than to try to explain about the Mind Link. "I'm sorry that we did not get the chance to talk about things yesterday. Your women were in much worse shape than we originally thought. But come, let's see how the worst of the cases are doing today. Ann and Jana are making their first rounds, now that it is light enough for them to see well."

Jana found Ben at the side of his wife, Aneta, who was still talking to Alice. As Jana began inspecting her patient, Aneta exclaimed, "She's still alive. That's a good sign isn't it?"

"Sure is, well done, Aneta. Look, her eyes are fluttering. I think that she is regaining consciousness," Jana looked most pleased indeed. Her patient had survived terrible odds and was still alive at dawn.

"Alice, it's me Aneta. You are just like me now, but you are alive. I am so glad you are; we have so much to live for now. We are all free at last." Jana knew the woman needed fluids, and helped her sip some water, laced with chicken broth.

"Easy does it, Alice. You can have as much as you want. Today, I want you to drink lots of soup. If it all stays down, then you can have something more substantial at suppertime. You know that Aneta here has sat beside you all night long, praying for your recovery? Ben, you can help her drink as much as she wants. Aneta, you keep on talking to her. I've got to check on the others."

Ben said, "No don't try to sit up just yet. Here, I made this for Aneta. I call it a tube. I put one end in the cup, and you suck on the other end, and the soup comes right up into your mouth. Give it a try; Aneta loves it. Makes her just a bit more independent." He gushed encouragement, nearly as much as his wife had. Alice sucked and it worked well for her. Pleased with this success, Aneta began a lengthy discussion of all that had been happening, with some slight exaggerations, of course. Alice seemed pleased with the attention, especially with Aneta's condition.

A little later on, Jana caught up with Le Ann, and said, "Well, it looks like I got my miracle. Somehow, Alice made it through the night. She's conscious and drinking with no signs of the infection, and the fever is much lower this morning."

Le Ann commented, "I had Aneta talk to her all night long, encouraging her to survive. Ket taught me that trick many years ago. Perhaps there is something to it after all. I wish Ket were around; I'd love to chat with him about it."

Jana gave her a hug, "Thank you, madam Wid!" And she meant it.

"No, it is we who should be thanking you two," Le Ann replied. Jana smiled.

Then, Jana became serious again, "You do realize that over two dozen of the seriously wounded women were being routinely and continuously tortured and raped, over and over, probably for months in some cases? There is just no other way to account for their injuries. One has at least ten bruises on top of older bruises."

"I was not sure, but I guessed that might be the case. I will meet with Tara later this morning as see what I can learn. If it's what we think it is, I will be pressuring for the Santi to take some decisive action over this," Le Ann replied sternly. Le Ann seldom made threats.

Later that morning, Le Ann arranged for a formal meeting with Tara. Normally, she would have just invited her to a tea in the Great Hall. However, they were out in the middle of nowhere in the desert. A campfire would have to suffice. The prime consideration Le Ann had to make was this: How many of them did she dare have sit in on the meeting. Tara would be alone. She might feel very uncomfortable if ten other Santi sat around her. She asked Art, ever the Judger, who replied, "Well why not just ask her?"

"Tara, ten of we Santi would like to hear your full tale, all that has happened. We have no intention of judging you or any actions that you took. We wish to find out the truth of what happened, and particularly what may have been going on in the Nunnery. If you feel uncomfortable with all ten of us surrounding you, it could just be us, one on one."

"I've nothing to hide. You have answered my prayers. We all believe that it is a miracle that none of them has died. I would like others to know the truth," Tara bravely said.

Quietly, without drawing undo attention to themselves, the other Guardians sat down near the camp fire in a semicircle around Le Ann and Tara. "Please, Messiah Tara, begin at the beginning and let us hear your story. Leave nothing out. We will understand." Thus encouraged, and even somewhat relieved finally to be able to safely share her deepest feelings and thoughts openly, Tara began to explain what had happened, beginning with Elsa's recent beating and the slaying of her two younger brothers.

For two hours, she presented her tale, trying hard not to leave anything out. When she was finished, Ann said, "Tara, you have given your people a miracle. Very well done. However, as a Healer, I am most concerned about what was going on in the basement of the Nunnery. I know that none of your people has ever witnesses what went on there. Still, with the Nunnery now destroyed, the best we can do would be to see what it was that you saw when you went through it. Mary, could you possibly explain it to Tara?"

Mary, one of the two Communicators present, Elmer being the other, tried her best to explain the Mind Link. Elmer made the link between the others present and Sally back at the Fortress. Sally in turn made the hook up to headquarters at Mont Blanc, who made the connection to those in Velona. Gently Mary moved into Tara's mind and said, "Please just move through the images in your mind of what you saw. Perhaps, it is best if you start when Ben ran ahead of you into the building. Just look at the successive images and we will be seeing them. Dutifully, Tara did as she asked, ending when she came back outside and vomited.

She looked up to see ten exceedingly pale faces. Andre and Fred both vomited on the spot, looking quite green afterwards. Le Ann spoke softly to Tara, "Honestly, Tara, none of us Santi had any idea that this was going on in the Nunneries. Perhaps as a small consolation to you, please know that because you let us see what you saw, the Santi will act upon this and attempt to do something about such wickedness. You have my solemn word on that! The butchers!"

Art wanted to caution his wife about making such all-encompassing statements about what the Santi organization would do about this, but thought that now was not the time. Fortunately for everyone, the water wagons arrived at this moment. Everyone went out to greet them. Le Ann had one wagon remain here and sent the other two on up the line, allowing them to refill any of those who needed water as they went. In case of trouble, she sent a fighter along with each wagon.

Next, Le Ann met with her entire force. "How soon can we travel?" she asked Ann.

"Not for a week at least," came the reply.

"Okay, then here is the plan. There are forty thousand people strung out like flies across this desert, ill-equipped to make the journey with food and water in low supply. We are going to accompany all of them until they reach their destination, Jerilum. We may be treating viper bites, scorpion stings, who knows what else. Besides, they need our guidance and support. Lenkova, I leave it up to you how best to deal with the water situation, you and your scouts know this land far better than I do. We've only been across here once with Ket, some ten years ago. Any questions?"

Andre simply punched his hand in the air, exclaiming, "Yes!" Everyone else shared his sentiments. Le Ann went to find Tara to explain her decision. Ann and Jana once more made their rounds of the critical patients. Six of the multiple rape victims, for want of a better term, had been so badly beaten and cut up and abused, that all or parts of one or both legs had to be removed; the bones were so badly crushed they could not be saved. Gangrene had already begun its work. Several women who had had their teeth pulled out had massive infections; the infections were so close to their heads, they all were touch and go for the entire week. Both Healers predicted that ten of these women could never again bear children. Yes, the thirty-six were in terrible shape. That not a single life was lost was a testimony to the skill of Ann and Jana.

The next day, having caught up on sleep and recovered from their ordeal, the two Healers expanded their visits and inspections to the middle group. They carefully checked on the work done by Le Ann and the others, just to make doubly sure that nothing was overlooked. Nothing had. At last, they expanded their examinations to all the other remaining women.

"Honest, I am fine," Aneta protested slightly when Ann came to check up on her well-being.

"We just want to make absolutely sure everything has healed," Ann overrode her objections. These women who had healed were being examined in a secure tent, so that any others, particularly men, could not see. They had had enough humiliation to last a lifetime. Carefully, Ann removed Aneta's dress and inspected her shoulders, asking occasionally if this or that hurt. Nothing did. "Now if you will lie down, I want to check your womanly parts."

"What? I don't care about that. I am not going to have any more children. Ben has his hands full with me as it is. I don't want to make further burdens on him," she declared.

Ann looked at her with her stern motherly look, "Since when is a child a burden to anyone!"

"Well," Aneta looked embarrassedly at the ground.

"Yes, you have fared much better than many. I pronounce you fit to have all the children you and Ben desire."

"You think he won't think it a burden?" she timidly asked.

"Why not just ask him? If I know men, I'll bet he'll go for more kids than you are willing to have," she jested playfully. Aneta grinned sheepishly. Ann helped her dress and sent her on her way. After a complete inspection, the two Healers found no new cases with which to deal.

Le Ann suggested that Tara send word to everyone in the caravan that the Healers were here. If anyone needed any doctoring, head to the rear of the caravan. During the course of the next month, they handled several other cases unrelated to the Holy Paladins.

During the week, Tara began to reunite those women who were pronounced fully healed with their relatives. However, before the first were to be reunited, she addressed all the women. "Today, we have located some of your relatives and the reunions begin. However, as many of you fear, you might not be accepted or worse. If any one of you has any difficulties at all with the reunion or what transpires after that, just let me know. My

Pentagrams are all around. Let one of them know and they will relay it to me. I want every one of you to know that I will find a loving place for you to stay, even in my own house with me, if nothing else. We owe you a lot for the suffering that you have endured, the price you have paid for our freedom. I will never ever forget your sacrifices. So if you have any troubles, you let me know. I am your Messiah. I will help each and every one of you, for you women are the true Heroes!"

It was quite a speech. Art took in every word and later commented that, for an untrained person, Tara was indeed masterful and operating from her intuition, not from formal training. In short, Art pronounced her a natural Judger, and that was the highest compliment he could make about his specialty.

What amazed both Tara and Le Ann the most was Aneta. Every time a woman was about to be reunited, there was Aneta doling out tons of encouraging words, convincing the woman that she could do it, that she was worthy, that she was not totally helpless and useless. Invariably, they would look at Aneta and gain the courage to face their relatives.

However, Tara fully expected problems to arise; she felt it in her heart. The day before they were finally to begin moving once more, Elsa and Raphaeli, lists in hand, pulled Tara aside for a private conference. These two were in charge of the list of the wounded and the finding of their relatives, who were now scattered across untold miles of desert track. "Messiah, we have run into a real problem with relatives," Raphaeli began, her voice deadly serious, full of worry and concern. "Twenty-six of the Heroes are of Sea Prince descent, not Arad. None of their relatives is with us. Also, we have six other Heroes whose relatives we have not been able to locate." She, as were many others, now calling the brutalized, mistreated women, Heroes. "Poor Alice, Aneta's friend, she is Sea Prince. Whatever are we to do now?" Her voice trailed off into a pathetic note of sadness. She didn't finish her idea, that these women had sacrificed so much and now had no family at all, no one to care for their needs.

Tara felt empathy for the plight of these women, more so than she had ever felt in her life for anyone, except perhaps for Elsa. "Re-interview the six and expand the list of possible relatives. Before I take any other action with them, we must be sure, be certain."

"Yes, Messiah!" Raphaeli acknowledged. It was what she was thinking, but had not voiced.

"With the Sea Prince women, let's get facts straight. Some may have been turned in by their own families. I won't dare return them to those who have already betrayed them. Probably we have eliminated some of those who turned in their wives and daughters to the Butchers. Let's quietly, without raising the women's alarm, re-interview them and cross check their relatives with the To Eliminate list. Let's be quick about this, put as many Pentagram personnel on this as you can, without drawing undue attention to what we are doing. Report back as soon as you know anything more." The two women dashed off to carry out the revised orders. Still, Tara had a queasy stomach; while she expected a few more relatives to surface, the problem was not about to go away. She knew she had to deal effectively with it.

Unknown to Tara, Le Ann had not been idle during the week. Via her Communicator, Tom Whiteheath, the Fortress Commander had been fully informed, and thus the entire Santi organization. Le Ann's suspicions were backed up by all the Judgers: the survival of these brave people was in dire jeopardy. Imagine forty thousand people moving out into a desert land, bringing only the barest necessities of life with them. They were moving into a long abandoned, ransacked city of adobe buildings with no visible means of supporting the lives of so many people. No livestock, no farms, no firewood. Grim.

During the week while their patients were recovering, Santi telepathic communications flew in all directions. Loremasters were consulted as well as knowledgeable Arad immigrants. What crops would grow best in the Arad? What livestock was best suited? What about the lack of firewood? The Planner's lists seemed endless. Tom and Sally acted as the coordinators for all actions. Once the key questions were answered, all hands tackled the problem of where and how to acquire what was needed. Key to the whole issue was timing; the supplies had to get to old Jerilum quickly, certainly in less than a month. This limited the potential sources of supply.

The one thing that saved the day was the ex-Sisterhood leaders, who used to run the Sisterhoods in the Sea Princes. Non-combatants, these women were expert business personnel, long used to running wide spread organizations. After the Centurion invasion, all had joined up with the Santi, helping to run this new organization. Now that the problem was precisely laid out for them, that is, what was needed, where, and when, they set to work. Pouring over their maps in the Great Hall in their new headquarters in Velona, they began to work out the trading details. One ship would transport a load of wheat from Calgary to Velona, which then allowed a ship of dried fish to be sent to Zargarb, replacing a similar shipload of dried fish sent to the Fortress in New Barq, which replaced the ship load of dried fish in New Barq, which was loaded onto wagons and driven to Jerilum by the south road. On it went, the shuffling of goods, materials, and livestock, from place to place, ultimately allowing the right items to be sent at once to Jerilum. Overall, it was a truly amazing coordination of efforts that saw the huge convoy of wagons moving slowly down the paved Centurion road toward the abandoned city of Jerilum.

Raphaeli reported on the search for relatives that same evening. "Messiah, we have placed four of the six Arad Heroes with their uncles and aunts. Two have nowhere to go; one is blind and one lost an arm. We must handle these two. Elsa has determined that twenty of the Sea Prince women are officially in limbo. Either their spouses or parents gave them up to the Butchers or had officially abandoned them to their own fates. There is no going back for them. Six others appear to have distant relatives in other sectors. Plus, we have six of the twenty-six who can no longer speak for themselves, no tongues. Now what do we do?"

"Sorry I am late," Elsa interrupted. "I think I have found homes for the two, Raphaeli." Tara encouraged her to continue. "Well, I got to thinking about my own situation. I asked each of the two if they had any close friends with whom they would like to live. Both families are eager to take them in. If it is okay with you, Tara, I'll place them right away."

"Excellent thinking, Elsa! Well done. I believe that is what we should also do for the Sea Prince Heroes, ask them. However, since they are not Arad, perhaps it would be best if we had one of the Santi present. They may offer other solutions for the Sea Prince women. After all, they are not of Arad descent. Come; let's find Le Ann."

Tara and Raphaeli found Le Ann and took her aside. Tara carefully explained the situation facing these twenty-six Heroes. She also told Le Ann what she was proposing to do and why. Le Ann replied, "I'm glad you are involving me, Tara. It is a wise decision. I, too, am completely reluctant to put one of these women back into harm's way in another of the occupied sectors. However, as opposed as I am, it really ought to be their own choice. I am prepared to offer all of them sanctuary in Velona, d'Grange, or even West Reach, should they desire it. Come, let's put it to them now."

Together, the three, accompanied by an unobtrusive Mary, Le Ann's Communicator, gathered together the twenty-six Sea Prince women, one of which was, of course, Alice. Interestingly enough, Aneta was sitting beside Alice. By now, she had made herself inseparable from her new friend. Tara began by explaining the situation the women were facing. She finished up by saying, "Those that wish to come with us to Jerilum and begin a new life of freedom here in the Arad are most welcome. I will find loving families that will take you in, no questions asked. Yet, I must warn you, life in the Arad is challenging. It will not be easy, but any of you that want to come with us, we will welcome you with open arms, as the Heroes you truly are."

Le Ann added more pragmatically, "As your Santi representative, I offer you some other alternatives. Many others in the free sectors, Velona, d'Grange, and West Reach, are very willing to take you in and give you a new life of freedom there. In many ways, life in Velona, daily life, is not so different from what you are used to in Zargarb, less of course the suppression from the Butchers. I caution you, it is as Tara says, a much harder life to live in the Arad, though no less fulfilling. Finally, we know that six of you can no longer speak for yourselves. Fear not, once we have listened to the others, Mary here will listen to you. Don't ask how just now." She smiled a motherly smile.

Alice spoke up first, "Can I stay with my friend Aneta, please?"

Unspoken was her terror of moving to Velona, where she knew no one and expected to have everyone staring at her; it was more than she could bear.

"Please, can she?" begged Aneta.

Sternly, Le Ann asked, "Have you asked Ben about this? You realize that you are making his job twice as hard?" From their body movements, she could tell that they had not consulted Ben. Quietly, Raphaeli slipped away to get Ben. "We'll give your request serious consideration, Alice." She moved on to easier cases.

A few minutes later, Raphaeli came back, Ben in tow. She had not explained why she needed him here at the meeting, however. Ben sat down beside his wife and gave her a forehead a kiss as he did. Le Ann looked sternly at Aneta, who slightly embarrassed, asked, "Ben, we are trying to find new homes for all these Heroes. Alice and I want Alice to come and live with us, Ben, if that's okay with you. I know I am asking far more than I ever ought to ask of you, but she needs us and me." A year ago, she would have added all sorts of other pleas, such as we won't be any trouble, she can help around the house, help take care of the kids, and so on. Now she realized none of that could be true. Tears began to form in her eyes as she had these thoughts.

Ben's instant reply took her and everyone else completely off guard, "Wow! Then I would have two flowers in my house! You bet you can, Alice. We'd love to have you come and live with us, wherever that ends up being. I'm the luckiest man in the caravan. I've gone from having no wife at all to having my beautiful wife back and now I get her beautiful sister to brighten up my home as well! Wait til the kids hear about this! I know that they will be very happy to have you around too, Alice. You two can play kick-ball with them so I can get some work done," he jested good-naturedly, having already found things Aneta could do with the children. "Oh," his face suddenly reddened, "er, ah, Alice, are you willing to let me, ah, er, clean your, well you know, privates? Someone has to help you, and our daughter is too young.

For an instant, Alice almost lost all her newfound dignity, as she began to realize the true nature of her plight. So many commonplace things that she now needed help with flooded into her mind. Aneta, who had already long ago been through this herself, recognized instantly what was happening. "Don't worry so, Alice. Yes, we both need all sorts of assistance now, but there is lots of life and help we can give back in return." Coming from Aneta, for Alice the words held a deeper meaning. If Aneta could survive this, so could she, Alice decided.

"Are you sure you won't mind?" she asked timidly.

"Not at all, Alice. For months, I have been praying to Jehosa to get my adorable, loving wife back somehow. I swore that I would do anything to have Aneta back with me. My prayers have been answered. Instead of getting my beautiful Aneta back, now I have another very beautiful woman to care for as well. You are more than welcome to come live with us. Think of me as a big brother." Alice smiled.

"Well, then that is settled," Le Ann took control of the meeting once more. "She must remain under the Healer's care for some time yet. Now, let's see what we can do for the rest of you." Nineteen others thought better of moving out into the desert and opted to accept the Santi's offer to take them to Velona.

Next, one by one, Mary used her telepathy to join with the remaining six women, who could no longer speak. In the process, Mary learned an awful lot about what had happened to these women, the ordeals they had been through. In the end, all six also chose to go to Velona.

The next day, the caravan began moving slowly across the desert track once more. The Healers kept a careful watch on their patients for the first few days. They would take no chances.

About three weeks later, Le Ann met with Tara. "In two days, the front of your caravan should be entering Jerilum. It is fitting and proper that you, their messiah, ought to be leading the first of your people into the city. Besides, we have a little surprise waiting for you there. So today, we'd like you and your group to ride with us up to the front of this long caravan, please?"

The Zargarb Circle, Tara, along with Lenkova and a few of her troops rode swiftly past the long, long line of carts, wagons, horses, and people. Two days later, Tara proudly led the first of her people into the abandoned city of Jerilum, their new home.

To her complete surprise, many other Santi were already there. Twelve wagon loads of food and seed for planting awaited her, along with a very large flock of sheep, a dozen oxen, and a wagon full of chickens. One additional wagon was full of building supplies, such as nails and boards. Tara just stared at the scene, hardly believing her eyes.

Le Ann formally stated, "On behalf of the many free peoples of Tarra, let me extend our hand of friendship in your time of need. Know that many have donated so that you and your people may thrive here in your new home, adding a new free people to Tarra."

"But, but how can we ever repay you?" Tara blurted out. "Such kindness, such thoughtfulness. You have the thanks of forty thousand!"

"Thrive and be free. Later you may be called upon to help others in need. Know this bit of irony, Tara. All the cost for these supplies has been paid for by the Butchers themselves, though they know it not, nor would have approved. The Santi charge them a stiff price to transport their valuables. Thus the price they paid has provided you this aid, ironical yes?"

Tara could not help but chuckle, so the Butchers ended up paying for this! She was pleased with that idea. Le Ann knew that she would be. Le Ann added, "Let me also introduce you to Sam and his wife Matilda. They are Santi and will be staying here with you to help in any way they can. They are assigned here until they are certain our help is no longer needed. If you need anything, they can help you obtain it. The rest of us must return to the Fortress as soon as the last wagons enter Jerilum."

"Please to meet you Messiah Tara," Sam said. "We've already alerted your neighbors to the west of here. Jaifur Qa Jahdi sends his greetings and welcomes you back to your native land. He promises to pay you a visit after you all get settled in a bit."

"Which house do you want?" Raphaeli interrupted. "Everyone wants to know what we do now?" Tara had to put her attention onto this next step of the operation. Thousands were now pouring into the city and there was much to do. All of it was unfamiliar to everyone.

A week later the Santi group rode through the gates of Fortress Zargarb, tired but more than satisfied. They had led a successful rescue mission. More than that, they knew that they now had the ammunition with which to deal the Holy Paladins a nasty blow.

Chapter 4 Rule by Thug

When Zargarb fell around 625, nearly half of their ships had been sunk by the Emperor of Megalos and his fleet of triremes. The people of the Sea Princes made their living via a network of extensive maritime trading with many other lands. Worse, Velona's introduction of the new caravel, which carried twice as much cargo twice as fast as the normal ships in the Sea Prince fleets, spelled doom for the commerce of Zargarb.

Compounding the disaster, Emperor Justinian had nearly all the nobles and their immediate families slain just as soon as his troops entered the main gates of Zargarb. These men and their wealth had owned and operated the merchant fleets. With these men gone, along with so many ships, Zargarb faced a crisis the likes of which it had never seen! Compounding the disaster were the Holy Paladins, who took control of the city, bringing with them new laws and rules to be followed under pain of death.

These new rulers forced everyone to attend Sunday Services, to learn about the Church of Jehosanity, and to follow their rules of conduct, especially with regard to women. They were under orders to eliminate the Sisterhood and put women in their proper place, according to church doctrine. These Holy Paladins were thoroughly brutal in their effectiveness. However, these men were not leaders, at least in the sense of being able to run a complex city as these Sea Prince cities were. Certainly, they were not equipped to handle the massive problems facing Zargarb, after its capture.

General Helas Taxos took control of Zargarb, appointed by the late Emperor to this sector. He slavishly followed the orders of his Holy Pope, Yazi I. First, he was to create a Nunnery, where those devout, chaste women could tend the sick and wounded women, study their religion in depth, preparing the way for their souls to enter heaven when their bodies died. He confiscated the Sisterhood Inn in Zargarb and established the city's first official Nunnery there. Second, he was to create Scholastic Universities, where people could learn to read and write. Of course, they would also be taught many other studies, all from the official church doctrine's slant. Parents were encouraged to send their sons to the university and daughters to the Nunnery. This he accomplished by confiscating the mansion of one of the late nobles. Third, he was charged with getting the city operational again, with yearly taxes being sent back to Megalos.

While the first two were handled within days, the third remained problematical, even a decade later. Knowing that he had to guarantee yearly funds to Megalos and his church, General Helas, no fool, proceeded to search out and confiscate as much treasure as his men could find in the homes of the late nobles. He accumulated a very vast sum, which guaranteed him that the yearly funds to send to Megalos and the tithes to the Church would be paid, no matter what the real situation actually was here in Zargarb. As it turned out, this initial action on General Helas' part proved the wisest move the man ever made.

When they entered Zargarb, well over two hundred thousand people were packed into the walled city. Many had come from the outlying towns and villages, come for protection from the invading Centurion army. The High Council of Zargarb had stockpiled sufficient provisions to withstand a siege of six months. However, with the shipping industry nearly destroyed, the orders from Pope Yazi I were to force many people to take up other professions, particularly farming. Yazi correctly deduced that the production of sufficient food would become the largest problem facing Zargarb. He was right.

The dockworkers, mostly out of work during the past year, save for the occasional Santi caravel that had docked before the city fell to the Centurions, watched as the fleet was sunk in the harbor. While they were physically strong men, they were not stupid. One Unit Captain, Rodrigo Decasas, was particularly adept at grasping the significance of events as they played out here in Zargarb. "Men, our fleet is sunk. We've been wasting our time manning the walls and for what? Nothing, the other fools just opened the gates! They got old Thomasio last night. I heard about it. He was the last of the Noble Houses. I say, who is going to rebuild the fleet? Who is going to run our shipping industry? No one. Men, do you know what that means for us?"

"Yes, I heard we's supposed to become ground hogs, farmers they calls it," one man replied. Rodrigo was meeting with two dozen of his work crew in secret in one of the warehouses. These burly men chortled and laughed, before spitting on the floor.

"It means that we are out of a job, that's what. How are we going to feed our families? We don't know nothing about growing anything. We are all going to starve to death. Worse, men, this whole damn city is going to starve!"

"Yes, but what about all those supplies they's stored up for the siege?" another inquired.

"Stupid, who do you think is going to get that food first? Us or the Holy Paladins and their crew?" Everyone saw his point immediately. Once people began to get hungry, the stores would be doled out, but when that ran out, there would be hell to pay. The bickering and arguing level rose for several minutes. Rodrigo allowed them to get good and angry before he said any more.

When he had them right where he wanted them, he said, "Boys, I got a plan. If we do this right, we won't be lacking for nothing!" Yes, Rodrigo played them like a well-tuned guitar. They all accepted his plan and leadership at once. During the next week, three hundred other dockworkers joined as well.

The Holy Paladins' orders for those that lived in the outlying towns and villages to return home within the week also played right into Rodrigo's hands. Their first action was to secret away all the weapons they could find, before the "Confiscation Law" was enacted. Second, in small groups, they would enter a storage warehouse. Mysteriously, a crate of food supplies would disappear from that warehouse, only to reappear in a secret, abandoned warehouse. During the next month, these men ferreted away nearly half of the extra provisions that the nobles had stored for the siege.

Stuff was stored in a large number of locations. These men knew all the "secret" storage rooms, back ways, and long unused side rooms of the many warehouses surrounding the docks. They had lived, worked here all their lives ,and knew things that nearly no one else knew, not even the nobles when they were living. During the time that food was still being doled out by the Holy Paladin's appointed commissars, Rodrigo gave the blacksmiths some work. In secret, he acquired five hundred steel blackjacks. Each was no more than six inches long, but was heavy and fit the hand well. He knew that in the future few could walk the streets carrying a sword, those had been outlawed. Only the Holy Paladins and the city guards they appointed were allowed to carry openly a sword. Besides, Rodrigo convinced his small army, "Dead men don't trade." Yet their blackjacks would be mighty convincing on the normal person.

Early that next spring, all hell broke out. Everywhere people no longer had any food, the Paladins had used up all the stored crates that they knew about. Yes, this became General Helas' nightmare, but marked the beginning of the Rule by Thug.

Desperate, hungry people sought out food by any means possible. Very quickly, the word spread that you can get anything you want at the docks, for a price. Enter the biggest barter system the Sea Princes ever had, which put to shame the bartering that their mariners used to do in foreign lands. The blackjacks kept the people from cheating Rodrigo's men. He wanted them alive so that they eventually could pay up and settle their debt.

By late summer when grain once again began to arrive from the Greenway in the caravels of the Santi, the dockworkers had amassed nearly everything imaginable. From gem cutter's tools to coal mining picks, from sewing kits to weaving looms, the list of items was endless. Worse still, one out of two citizens of Zargarb was in debt to the Rodrigo, and his "interest" charges were steep, covering the risk that he and his men took.

General Helas always looked the other way, primarily because somehow these burly men had kept the food going when he could find none. In fact, even the General and his staff did a brisk business with Rodrigo! By 637, Rodrigo and his men were in fact the actual owners of Zargarb. Every citizen was in debt to him in some way, and he exercised his power over them ruthlessly, blackjacks always at the ready. In fact, if one needed something or had a payment to make, one merely looked for a man with a blackjack hanging from his belt.

It was late summer 637, Helas had just dismissed the lieutenant who had just brought in the latest harvest projections. He pounded his fist on the table in anger, "Damn these ignorant swine! Never have I seen such utterly stupid idiots! Incompetent morons!"

"Who's a moron? Good afternoon, General," the sweet voice of Father Rolan took Helas by surprise. He had not heard the High Priest enter.

"Oh, these idiot Sea Prince peasants," he replied, his anger subsiding. No need to get the priest upset. This was his problem. "The harvest projections are in; I assigned twenty-five percent more locals to farming pursuits this year, as you know. And what are the results? Can you guess?" He sneered, but didn't wait for a reply. "Down, lower than last year by twenty-five percent! Idiots, they are all idiots. Whatever does the Church see in these people?"

"There, there, General," the covert, soothing voice of Rolan answered. "You must learn to take the good with the bad. On the positive side, we have had a one hundred percent increase in the number of children who are now attending the Scholastic University of Zargarb. All told, we have nearly three thousand young minds learning about Jehosa and the skills to live. That's impressive, don't you think?"

"Well, you *do* house, cloth, and feed them. Did you ever think that's why your enrollment is way up? Parents cannot afford to feed themselves, let alone their children. So what better way than to send them off to school, where at least they won't go hungry?"

"Ah, point taken. Then there are the Nunneries. Do you realize that in Zargarb alone we now have six hundred nuns in various stages of training? The Head Nun predicts that by next year, she will have over a thousand women under her tutelage."

"Well, they get food and shelter. Honestly, they aren't stupid. If you're starving, you'll do anything to eat regularly," Helas shot back. He hated the sneering contempt the priest had for him. He could tell that Rolan though he was an imbecile.

"True, true," Rolan said smoothly. He changed the subject, "And what is the official tax census this year? I know it must be down even more from last year. However, as usual, as long as a gold coin is sent to Megalos for every person you count, I will say nothing." He knew that Helas inflated the population figures and thus was sending back substantial gold. Where this gold came from, the priest didn't know, only speculation, which he could never pin down with hard evidence. The inflated figures had been given for a decade now, and he had long since given up trying to find out where Helas got the funds. Supposedly, the funds came from the gate entrance fees, one copper per person or animal. He'd done the math many times, and always came up wildly short.

"Officially, I will be reporting two hundred thousand people in the sector, but we both know that there's now barely forty-five thousand in Zargarb. It is becoming a ghost town. I remember the day we entered the city. There must have been well over two hundred thousand within the walls. Who knows how many others were still in the outlying towns and villages. Florintine Junction is still the second largest town. I know that there are more people living there than within these walls. It's crazy."

"Well, yes, yes, I understand. Perhaps allowing the migrations was a bad idea, though at the time, we had insufficient food to feed so large a population. If you had not allowed them to move, the graveyard would probably be full. What choice did we have?" Rolan said sympathetically.

"None, and that's the Lord's truth! Perhaps in your weekly sermons you can extol the virtues of being a good farmer, and produce abundant crops so that people can eat." Desperate, Helas was willing to allow the priest an opportunity to improve the situation, though it was probably too late for this year. He thanked his luck stars that he had had the foresight to confiscate all the treasure he could find from the nobles. They certainly did not need it any longer; his men had killed them all. Another benefit, he reminded himself, was that he did not have to deal with those bickering men, constantly hounding him. His father had once been a Governor down here in the Sea Princes, he knew what his dad had to deal with, and he vowed he would never allow himself to be in that kind of position — hence, the summary executions as soon as his forces entered the city. That that also was the expressed wish of his Emperor only re-enforced his justification of the deed.

"Your wish is my command," Rolan replied agreeably. He had another matter to discuss with Helas, which was the real reason for his visit this afternoon. "On another issue, General, I've just come from the Nunnery. It seems that the unholy women that are being cared for in the basement have contracted some unholy disease. It might be wise to tell your men to not come to the Nunnery evenings until the disease has run its course." He was being polite as usual. What he implied, Helas sensed at once and looked up.

"Should I send the men to the physicians?" he asked. He knew that when the disease had run its course, his men's play toys would have to be replaced with new toys.

"That would probably be a prudent action to take," Rolan answered.

"Consider it done," Helas answered, but thought about asking for further details. At last he added, "Mine too?" He was referring to his special toy, one reserved for his exclusive use. "We've all tried our very best to help these women gain 'Good Marks' to counter their ledger of 'Bad Marks.' I hope they've acquired enough for their souls to gain access to Lord Jehosa's realm."

"Ours is not to judge the totality of their ledgers. However, I would think that each one of the women have certainly added a large number of 'Good Marks' to their tally. However, we cannot know how many 'Bad Marks' they had logged before we came. In answer to yours, Helas, she alone is un-diseased. You may continue to help Ariana increase her 'Good Marks,'" he smiled coyly. The General seemed visibly relieved, just as Rolan knew he would be.

The priest thought that Pope Yazi I had been a genius. Stationing so many young, virile men away from home for such extended periods of time created numerous problems, of which monetary pay was the very least. By having certain women gaining 'Good Marks' by meeting the needs of the Holy Paladins was truly an inspired decision. Reported rapes of the local women by the Holy Paladins was nearly non-existent, a notable, remarkable record.

Rolan, with a twinkle in his eye, coyly said, "Shall I tell the matron that you will be by at your usual time tonight?" By having prearranged times for his visits, the matron would see that Ariana was properly dressed to serve the General best.

"Yes, I definitely need some relaxation after this impossible day. Thank you." Helas seemed preoccupied with the figures, so Rolan took his leave. After dropping by the Nunnery, blessing the many Nuns there as was his wont, and notifying the matron to expect Helas later that evening, the High Priest took a leisurely stroll back to his rectory. It had been a satisfactory day, he felt.

Ariana Zar was miserable, more miserable than any person should ever be, she concluded. She was trapped, and though she hoped and prayed for a Divine Miracle, none had come. Her hopes, plans, and wishes for her future had all evaporated, gone in that single instant some ten years ago when the city gates were opened and the murderous Centurions entered her fair city of Zargarb.

At that time, she was only ten years old, the young daughter of the Zar noble family. Ever since she could remember, her father had drilled into her mind the fact that she could trace her roots, her lineage, all the way back to the founder of the Zargarb Sector, hundreds of years ago. She had no pretenses to gaining the power of rule over the city; there were too many more direct descendants ahead of her — if her father was correct, twenty-two. At the time of the siege, her parents had gladly allowed her to go and stay with her best friend, Gina Tortelli, and her family.

Her father was preoccupied with the city defenses, and Gina's family could use an extra hand around the house. The Tortelli's had six children of their own, of which Gina was the oldest, ten as well. Both girls tended the younger children, giving Gina's mother more time to handle family activities, while her husband was off on nearly continual guard duty. For months, the routine had worked to everyone's great advantage. Yet, that single night ten years ago changed everything.

Vivid images of Hermino rushing in that night still haunted Ariana. "Gates have been opened! Centurions are murdering all the nobles!" His words still sent chills down her spine, and her stomach knotted once again. She remembered wildly trying to leave the house to go find her parents. The sweaty smell of Hermino physically restraining her assaulted her olfactory senses, almost as much now as it did back then. "It's not safe. You'll be killed too. You must stay with us. That's what your father would want. Trust me! Trust me!"

Ariana cursed, "Damn you Hermino, damn you to the Fiery Pits of Lucifer's Hell!" She sobbed to herself a while before the memories continued their unstoppable march onward through time. Life had been tough after that, no doubt about that. Yes, she had worked as hard as she could for Hermino, doing everything he had asked of her. Within a week, they heard the sad news that her entire family had been slain that night, her family estate confiscated by the invaders. She knew that her marvelous dowry, her inheritance, was now as gone as her family. Although she kept insisting the Hermino take her to her home so she could get all her money, he did not. He knew the nobleman's treasury was long gone. For her protection, they pretended her last name was Tortelli.

For the first half year, they had managed to get by somehow, but then food began to become scarce. Hermino was a craftsman, a maker of wooden casks for water, ale, or wine. Now he could scarcely find any work; no ships came; orders for new casks were few and far between. Slowly he began to barter off their possessions, trading a bed for a week's supply of grain to feed so many mouths. Then the dressers went, next all the storage boxes in which their clothes were kept. When there was nothing left to trade, Hermino returned with yet another week's supply of food. The Thug had given him credits. At first, this seemed a godsend, but quickly his debts mounted, and his repayments, small. Often, he returned home with massive black and blue bruises from the heavy blackjacks. At last, he traded off all his wood working tools. That was a sad day, because even Ariana knew that without the tools of his trade, he had no hope of making any funds.

Now her memories fixated upon that fateful turning point in her life. Their youngest child, who had just turned six, died in his sleep. Skin and bones, the boy died of starvation. She too shared the family grief. Ariana could not help but wonder who would perish next. All of them were gaunt and perpetually hungry. That's when she learned to enjoy eating rat soup laced with fish. His wife, now frail and distraught over the loss of her youngest child, died in her sleep a week later. Ariana remembered that the guards had come to take the body away and dispose of it. Hermino could not even afford to have her properly buried. The city took charge to avoid outbreaks of disease. Hermino was distraught, out of his mind with grief and despair. "That's what probably motivated him," Ariana said to the walls of her prison, though she only saw the walls of their home.

The next day, Hermino came in with a weird smile on his face. "Come with me, Ariana. We are going for a walk."

Gina insisted, "Yes, Ariana, you go with papa." There was a note of coldness in her voice that Ariana had never heard before. Whatever was about to happen to her, Ariana knew that Gina knew all about it and approved. "I ought to have known something was very wrong," Ariana explained to her walls. Then, the memories swept her away once more. She remembered pleasantly chatting with Hermino as they walked to the western end of the city, but he would not say what they were doing or where they were going.

They arrived at the old Sisterhood Inn, which now had a huge white cross of Jehosanity affixed prominently to its towering roof. Hermino held her hand tightly, forcing her to follow him inside the main entrance of the Nunnery. Her angry cries, her wild protests, her pleading, her begging, all this flashed by in her mind, just as vividly as if it was happening right now. She watched as an older woman handed Hermino a heavy sack of gold coins, and he forced Ariana into the waiting arms of a large, strong woman.

She still heard the woman's words, "You've come to stay with us now, Ariana Tortelli." She cried, she screamed, she protested, she refused to move. The strong hands of the nuns picked her up and carried her to an upstairs room. The only good thing that happened was another nun entered with a large tray of hot food. Oh did that food look good to Ariana, who was half starved herself. She ate with gusto, momentarily forgetting what was happening to her.

For nearly a year, Ariana was a virtual prisoner in her room at the inn. Yes, she ate regularly and well. Her weight increased to what it should have been. All she had to do was listen to the incessant rantings of the nuns, all about Good Marks, Bad Marks, souls, and Eternal Damnation. None of it made the slightest sense to her. However, during this year or so, she was able to ask some questions and learned that indeed all the noble families had been slain, including the children. Although it was now worthless, she knew that this meant that she was now the rightful heir to the rulership of Zargarb.

The only thing that troubled her was the weird, horror-stricken screaming of women that she sometimes heard late at night. The terror, pain-filled cries came from some distant portion of the inn. Whenever she asked about it, the nuns would only say that some women needed some help to stop adding Bad Marks to their ledger. Ariana was left to her own imaginings of what this might be.

When she turned eighteen, disaster struck. One night the Head Matron visited her. "Ariana, you have been given the highest honor possible. General Helas Taxos, the supremely Holy Paladin who rules Zargarb, has chosen you to be his companion. You have been given a Holy Opportunity to earn many, many Good Marks on your ledger, to offset the huge quantity of Bad Marks that your soul was born into." At first, Ariana did not understand what was meant or happening. Several nuns helped her change out of the sacks that they called proper dresses and into a fine silk dress, although they refused to provide any undergarments. Ariana thought this was peculiar, especially since the dress only came down to her knees, very unseemly for a virgin maid.

Next, they led her down into the basement of the Nunnery. At first, she asked about that awful smell, like rotting fish or corpses. As she passed by some of the numerous closed doors, she heard what sounded like moaning women. The nuns simply ignored everything she said or asked. They took her to the very back room, the last one to the west. Inside the door, she saw a dimly illuminated bedroom, replete with nice sheets and pillows. Standing near the bed was an older man, dressed in the familiar sky blue tunic with white cross emblazoned upon its front and back. "Here is the maiden Ariana, General Helas. I hope she pleases you so that she can gain many Good Marks upon her Holy Ledger."

Ariana vividly recalled how he took her hand and forced her to lie down on the bed, while he began to remove his clothes. Suddenly, she realized what he was about to do, and she began protesting, screaming, and tried to escape the room. However, these nuns had obviously had much experience dealing with recalcitrant women. Before she knew what was happening, they had her arms tied to the bedposts. Then they forced her legs apart, tying each to the other posts. Ariana lay there helpless to stop this man. She screamed and screamed, squirming uselessly all the while. Again, one nun then forced a gag into her mouth, effectively ending the loud noise. A short while later, it was over, and she was back again locked in her room.

On repeated visits, she protested and fought the nuns, refusing to participate in this foul, unholy act, but to no avail. Finally, she seized her chance and lashed out with her fingernails, severely scratching the General's face, a small token of her utter loathing of this man. "Yes, that was my mistake," Ariana wailed to the empty walls, though still she saw them not, only the ugly, horrible memories in her mind. She vaguely heard the Head Matron say something about Ariana would need some help to avoid all these Bad Marks that she was tallying up, instead of good marks. She also heard her apologize profusely to the General.

"Notify me when she can deliver no further Bad Marks, ma'am. Good evening," and he left. She remembered wondering what all this could possibly mean. Soon to her horror, she found out. Quickly her nice dress was removed, and the sack-like bag placed over her naked form. Instead of being led back to her room, two men dragged her to the first room by the stair. When she entered, she was horrified by what she saw. Bloody tools lay everywhere; a sole bench occupied the center of the room. The men forced her prone on the bench and tied her securely to it. One put a gag in her mouth, while the other said, "This is going to hurt."

Oh the pain, intense pain. She blacked out. These despicable men had cut off her fingers! After that, the days dragged on, one series of endless pain. Her bloody hands became infected, she realized. Some weeks later, she was dragged back to that awful room for more work. The Head Matron explained that Ariana must have a ledger filled with an awful lot of Bad Marks, because her hands had not healed and would have to be removed. More pain, more unconsciousness. She remembered waking up and seeing red stained bandages where her lovely, dainty hands used to be. She remembered vomiting and passing out.

Endless horrible months had passed, as she slowly healed. Tended day and night by well-meaning nuns, she felt as utterly helpless as she was. When her body had finally healed, she had two nice, rounded stumps where her hands ought to have been. Ariana remembered endless hours and hours of crying to herself.

Then, the Head Matron came to her at night once more. "Ariana, I hope you have learned your lesson. You must earn Good Marks, not Bad Marks. I came to warn you, if you use your feet to kick him, they will be removed as well. If you use your teeth to bite him, like several others have, your teeth will be removed, and you can eat porridge for the rest of your life. Do you understand me?" She was stern and unforgiving.

Ariana succumbed, allowing whatever happened to happen. She was still not a willing participant, her body was not her own to use. She felt like she was just a toy for the General to play with when he desired, which fortunately was only once or twice a week. Endless days and nights passed by in a daze, Ariana was no longer living, merely going through the motions that others forced upon her.

It was early August 637, though Ariana knew it not, nor could have cared had she known. She felt forsaken by Jehosa, men, and the entire world. She moved only when forced to move by a nun. Ariana had no hopes, no dreams, except the nightmares, no will to live, just the passing of endless days. Vaguely, she watched from some dream-like trance while the nuns once again removed her rags, bathed her, combed her hair, which had grown very long by now, and put the nice but short silk dress over her body. "Is that me they are walking down the hall with?" she thought. "It does not seem real. Perhaps this is all that life is, nothing but a dream. Nothing is real. Maybe the dream will end soon."

There was the General, as usual removing his clothes. There was her body, prone on the bed, the awful stench somehow infiltrating even this room. Just as he was about to climb on the bed, someone knocked on the door. That had never happened before. Perhaps that was what brought Ariana back into the present. "General, it's urgent. I must speak with you!" She'd never heard that voice; perhaps it was some disembodied spirit coming for the general. He pulled his trousers up and opened the door.

"Sir, I bring really awful news. Florintine Junction, sir, it has been destroyed, burned to the ground, the whole town! All our men and thousands of our supporters have been murdered!"

"Good god! What happened? Arad Raiders? I thought we had our cavalry in position east of here," the General barked.

"Not the raiders. No, it was the Junction's Arad women. They poisoned all our men. Estimates place over five thousand dead! Another five thousand were forced to flee for their lives, carrying what little they were allowed to save on their backs! The women, they did this horrible deed! How could they? What are we to do?"

"Hell, I don't know!" for once General Helas spoke the absolute truth! "What about the others there? It's our second largest city, must be fifty thousand at last census."

"Gone, sir. All gone. No one knows where, just gone."

"How can that be? Come on; we must find out what happened. Get my horse. Rouse the garrison. We ride for the Junction tonight!" The general grabbed his clothing and left, trying to put on his shirt while running down the hall.

Silence. Eternal silence. Ariana lay there on the bed, waiting. No one came. No one. Time passed. At last, she ventured to sit up. It was the first action she had taken in years on her own decision, her own motivation. No one came. Ariana stood up and walked about the twenty by twenty foot room. There was not much to see, but it was her choice to walk. No one came.

On the far wall was an ornate, huge tapestry depicting scenes of the Sisterhood in the distant past. "Where are the Sisters now when I need someone like them?" Ariana said to the tapestry. These were the first words she has intentionally spoken since her mutilation. It felt good to speak, she thought. "Damn Sisters, I remember mother telling me about how you all cared for battered women. Not me, oh no. No one is here." Ariana got slightly angry and began batting at the tapestry with her arms, a futile gesture, but significant, since she was actually angry and causing it. It felt good to hit something. She had been forced to obey utterly so for so long that it gave her a wonderful feeling just batting at the tapestry!

All of a sudden, her arm hit something metal. Curious, she felt around it. "Some kind of bar?" she said to the tapestry. Now a wee bit of curiosity seeped into her. "I wonder what that is? Some new diabolical trap they have not yet used on me?" Ariana began to move the tapestry aside to see behind it. "A lever? How strange! I wonder what it does?" She looked about. Still no one came or was coming, no sounds at all, except distant moaning. "If I had hands, I could pull you," she declared to the lever. Then she realized that she didn't need hands to pull it down. Locking her arms around it, she used the weight of her body to pull it down. The sound of stone sliding upon stone echoed in the room. "What's this?"

Ariana saw a small secret room had appeared. "I wonder what's in here? Too dark, can't see." She looked around her prison room. Five oil lamps provided the dim illumination. One had a large loop handle at its top. "I can manage that one," she said to herself and proceeded to put the lamp's loop in the crook of her elbow. She walked back to the tapestry, pulled it back, and stepped into the secret room. She noticed another lever on the wall right beside her and pushed it up. She watched as the stone slab slid back into place, sealing her inside this small room.

Ariana began to explore this much smaller room. A dark passage led off opposite the secret door. A few old, rusting swords lay in one corner, along with a large pile of rags. She found a food sack with moldy, rock hard biscuits in it. She even found a gold coin on the floor, although she could not find a way to pick it up and soon gave up trying. "I wonder where this leads? Looks like a tunnel. Oh yes, I remember, this used to be the Sisterhood Inn. Mom brought me here for lunch once when I was nine." That memory brought a flood of grief and tears to Ariana. At last, wiping them on the sleeve of her dress, she took a deep breath and began to look down the long, dark tunnel. "I wonder where this goes?"

Slowly, she began walking barefoot down the narrow tunnel, dislodging spider webs as best she could. After a long time, she found another barrier wall, again a lever was at the side, and there was some kind of sliding window just at eye level. "This must have been a secret escape tunnel exit of the Sisterhood. I wish I could see out. I wonder where I am and what's out there?" She did her best to examine how the window operated. At last; she tried to slide the bar and it moved to one side. She peered out into the world. Fresh air filled her nostrils. It was dark; she saw stars. Now she recalled that she had not seen the stars since she was ten. Enthralled with their beauty, she stood there peeking up at them through the narrow window. She saw no signs of the city.

"Well, here goes nothing," she said as she closed the window and pulled down on the lever. Stone grated on stone, and a narrow doorway beckoned her. She stepped out into the night. She turned around, spied another lever, pulled it, and the door closed. Suddenly, Ariana panicked. The lever now retreated into a concealed notch in the stone surface. One would need fingers to get to it and pull it. She was now trapped outside, for good or ill. She could not go back.

"Why do I want to go back?" she suddenly chided herself for feeling so frightened. "I never want to go back there! But where am I anyway?" Her lantern's dim illumination was swamped by the inky blackness of the dead of night. She was at the bottom of a little hill. Logic told her to climb to the top and have a look see. Carefully, she sat the lantern down and slowly climbed to the hilltop. Before her lay the walled city of Zargarb. She was about a mile from the outer walls. She could also see the limestone tower of Fortress Zargarb, standing taller than anything in the city did. It was on the opposite side of the city from where she stood. "I guess I am west of the city," she said to herself.

For some time she stood there alone on the hilltop, staring at the view before her. Then she noticed that her lamp had gone out, and she carefully moved back down hill to where she had left it. "Rats, it's gone out all right. Must be out of oil. No matter, the moon is rising, so I can see a little. I think I shall sit here and watch the stars. They are so beautiful."

A very quiet male voice, not too far away, said, "Yes, they are indeed, quite spectacular I always say. I like to spend as much time watching them as I can spare."

Instantly, fear flooded over Ariana. She stifled a screech. Wild visions flooded her mind. The man un-hooded his lantern slightly, and she could see the black tunic with a red fleur-de-lis prominently displayed on its front. "Sorry to frighten you ma'am, Santi here. You are in no danger. I am called Art. What's your name, pretty lady?"

Is he blind? thought Ariana. *Can't he see that I am a hopeless cripple with no hands?* Instead, she replied meekly, "Ariana, sir. Where did you come from? I didn't see you before." She didn't finish her thought, feeling that might reveal too much information about her predicament.

"Pretty name for a pretty woman. I came from yonder Santi tower. I was up at the top watching the stars and things. I saw your light here and thought 'how unusual.' And I came to investigate. We don't get many people wandering about outside the city walls, especially in the middle of the night, and especially ones as pretty as you are. Do you need any assistance?"

Before she could reply, he added, "Don't be alarmed. My wife is joining us now." Sure enough, a dark figure stepped out of the shadows. She wore chain mail armor and carried a large sword. Her tunic matched that of her husband's.

She spoke to Art quickly, "No sign that anyone's seen anything out here. It's safe." Art nodded.

"Ariana, I'd like you to meet my wife, Lena, she's an expert Santi fighter. She used to be in the Sisterhood here in Zargarb before the Centurions took over."

Lena moved closer to meet Ariana. "Oh dear god! Not another one! Oh you poor thing! Thank god, we've found you. You are safe with us. We've rescued many women like you who have been brutalized by these vile, evil men."

"I'd lost all hope. I'm afraid that I'm nothing but a terrible burden to you."

"Nonsense, young woman," Art replied. "I suspect that you were housed in the old Sisterhood Inn, the Nunnery it's now called, correct?" Ariana nodded. "They keep that place locked up tighter than a drumhead. Yet, you managed to escape all on your own. Pretty remarkable. I have a very good idea how you got to this particular location. For the security of everyone, I must ask you how you got here to this location all by yourself?"

Ariana hesitated to answer. Did they know about the secret tunnel? Ought she tell them? "I walked down a long, dark tunnel by myself."

"Ah ha. And you came out just over there," Lena pointed to the precise location of the concealed exit."

"Well, yes," Ariana affirmed.

"Well done, Ariana. But tell me: is knowledge of our secret tunnel known widely in the Nunnery? This is very important to us. How many others know about it?" Lean inquired.

"Er, I don't know. I only just discovered it a while ago. Perhaps no one knows about it."

"Wow, and you managed to open the doors all by yourself?" Lena asked, rather surprised.

"Yes, sort of pulled down on them like this," Ariana demonstrated.

Lena smiled, "Makes sense. Are the doors open or did you close them behind you. If they are open, I'll go back and shut them."

"No, I closed them; but this outside one — after it closed, I realized I can't open it again. I got trapped outside, though I never ever want to go back in there." Grief now welled up in her, and she began to cry. Lena hugged her tightly and patted her lovingly on her back.

"I understand," Lena said softly, "my first husband many years ago used to beat me every Saturday night. He beat me so badly, that I can no longer bear children. I got even; I cut his throat open many years ago. Art, we have to get her back into the Fortress right now."

"I don't have any shoes," Ariana began to grasp that she was indeed about to be rescued.

"And you are dressed in this flimsy party dress, well, no matter. We can carry you." Art explained, "Climb onto my back; lock your legs around my waist and your arms around my neck, here we go. Just don't choke me — that's a joke, by the way." She did as she was told and off they went, Lena leading the way, her sword still drawn, just in case.

They headed toward the city walls. Ariana whispered, "We're going the wrong way, don't we need to go that way, all around the walls?" She began to worry that they were taking her right back into prison once more.

"Shortest distance between two points is a straight line, Ariana. Watch and see a bit of Santi cleverness. Just keep really still no matter what happens when we are close to the city." Soon they reached the tall west wall of the city. To her surprise, both waded out into the water a few feet and moved around the wall. "Not much of a barrier is it," Art whispered. He could not resist a criticism of the city designers. Quietly they passed underneath the docks and on past the public beach. After a while, they reached the east wall, where Art once more moved out into the water a few feet, bypassing the edge of the wall.

Now they were east of the city. They kept close to the beach, so that the ridge line kept them mostly hidden from any prying eyes that might be manning the walls at this late hour. Art figured there would not be any, considering the large number of men who had hastily rode out several hours ago. A few minutes later, they walked up to the main gate, which opened at once; no words were spoken. Evidently, the gatekeeper had been expecting them. Art sat his precious cargo down. Winded he replied, "I'm getting too old for this sort of thing. The ground is smooth in here; it's safe to walk barefoot."

They walked up to the tall, impressive fortress tower. Standing by the entrance doors was another couple. The man said, "Welcome to the Santi del Dio Fortress Zargarb. I am the Fortress Commander, Tom Whiteheath, and this is my wife, Sally. Ariana you are now safe. No one will ever harm you ever again, I promise you. Please, let's go inside, away from prying eyes. Sally, will you lead her? I want a word with Lena and Art."

"Please to meet you," Ariana finally remembered long forgotten manners; she spoke as though she were ten years old.

As the two walked inside the Fortress, Sally continued her disarming chat, "I just cannot imagine how much you must have suffered. If we had known about you sooner, we might have been able to come to your rescue sooner. But that is perhaps just wishful thinking. Are you hungry? We ought to get you a proper bath and into some descent clothes that you can manage with better. When did you last have a proper sleep?"

"Yes, a little hungry," then she realized that this woman would have to feed her. Grief once more swamped her emotions.

"I suppose that the nuns had to feed you all the time. How silly of them. I suspect that you can do much more than they ever gave you credit for, but if not, I don't mind in the least. You see, Ariana, we've helped dozens like you. Some were in far worse shape, and some even died of their wounds. Okay, first stop, pantry."

They entered a large room, filled with tables. Only a single oil lamp provided the nighttime lighting. You sit here and I'll fetch something. Have a fancy for anything in particular? Cheese maybe?"

"Cheese? I haven't had cheese forever, not since I was ten! And something to drink, I am suddenly very thirsty, ma'am, I mean Sally."

She brought a cup of mead and a plate of cheese along with some biscuits. The mug had sides, which flared outward. "See, you can pick it up with your arms and drink yourself. Have some, while I cut us up some cheese." Sally cut a number of slices and carefully placed them standing on their edges so that Ariana could pick them up. Then, she began eating some herself, all the while watching Ariana closely.

She could tell at once that this was the first time Ariana had tried to do anything for herself. Carefully, Sally paid no notice to her awkward movements as the young woman tried to help herself. Only when one piece slipped and fell down flat did Sally intervene and stand it back up on its edge. After Ariana had finished her biscuit, cheese, and drunk her fill, she said, "I thought I was completely, utterly helpless. At least the nuns told me so. They did everything for me. Maybe I am not so helpless."

"Of course not. Just a bit more challenged than most folks are. Now how about that bath?"

"You mean a real bath? Like in the public bath houses?" Ariana exclaimed, completely surprised.

"Of course dear. Say, when was the last time you had a proper bath anyway?"

Ariana did not respond right away, as they walked down another hallway. When had she last been in the bathhouse? As they entered the steaming room, she finally remembered. "When I was ten, papa took us all to the bathhouse. That was only a couple of days before I went to live with my friend, Gina." However, mentioning her friend brought back a flood of the horrid memories. She involuntarily began crying once more. Sally ignored that, swiftly removing the skimpy party dress. Her eyes rolled upwards when she also saw that the poor woman had on no undergarments at all. She had her suspicions affirmed now about what this woman had endured.

"Okay, hop in," Sally suggested. Ariana did as she was told, only discovering that she really did want to take a bath. Maybe all that ugliness would wash off her body, all traces of that ugly man.

Just then, Lena entered. "Mind if I join you, Ariana? I need to wash off the Med Sea and all the dead fish heads. If I don't, Art will not let me back into our bed," she jested. She slid into the warm waters joining Ariana.

Bond with her a bit, Sally sent to Lena, who nodded.

"Here, you wash my back and I'll wash you a bit," Lena volunteered.

"I'm not sure I can do a very good job of it though," Ariana defended her awkward attempts to move the washrag over Lena's back. Then she began to see Lena's body. She had some strange boney bumps.

"Bones never did set properly," Lena volunteered, sensing that Ariana was noticing her. "Told you he used to beat me. Broke many bones, and some didn't heal quite right. Doesn't hurt, just looks weird. Art doesn't care, thankfully." Lena chatted away.

Finally, she turned around to wash Ariana. She couldn't help notice Ariana's very full bosom. She teased, "Men are going to sure be goggling over yours, look at mine." Lena was flat chested compared to Ariana, who flushed. She had never had any opportunity to think such thoughts.

When Lena got to washing Ariana's private parts, Ariana went a bit crazy. "Please, wash there really, really well. Wash it all off. Wash. Wash. I'll never get clean. Wash his filth off me, please." She began crying uncontrollably. Now Lena too knew what this unfortunate woman had been through. She complied, doing her very best to make her clean. Finally, when the tears had stopped and both women were clean, they climbed out, and

Lena kept an arm around Ariana's waist to steady her.

Sally threw a towel over Lena's back and took one herself. "Here, you work on drying Lena's back and I'll do yours." This was Sally's way of gently convincing Ariana that she could do some things, no matter how awkwardly. Both women ignored Ariana's continual explanations that she was not any good at this. Once dried, Sally produced a slip-like covering that was open at the bottom. "When you need to go to the bathroom, just pull it up." Then, she helped her slip into a warm robe. "Now then, I think we have all had enough excitement for one night. Come, I got just the room for you to sleep in," Sally said, leading Ariana down the hall and up a flight of stairs. The door on this room had special hinges and no doorknob. It swung in either direction, which Sally pointed out to Ariana. "See you are not trapped inside the room. Here is a special chamber pot with flared edges I think you can manage it. I'll tuck you in and you can sleep as long as you want. When you wake and want something tomorrow, I'll be just down the hall, come and get me."

A little while later, Sally and the other three sat around the large planning table. Tom said, "Well done, you two. Do we have any idea who she is? I've looked over the list we have of missing persons, but there is no Ariana on the list. Do we have a sir name?"

"No, just Ariana. She seemed in a complete childish daze when we found her," Art answered. "Severe trauma, I'll wager."

"Long term trauma," Sally added. "I'll know more later. I believe she was kept as someone's sexual pet. She is remarkably beautiful and my guess she is around twenty. Her fondest memories appear to be from at least a decade ago, around the time when the city fell. I suspect she has been kept in captivity a long time, as well as molested. She's going to be a tough case, probably traumatized for years."

Tom ended the brief meeting, "Okay then, I suggest we get some sleep; this has been a long day indeed. Glad our folks got on their way before the General even got word of the Junction situation. They have a good head start on them." With that, the four retired for the night. Sally kept their door ajar, just in case Ariana should need something.

The next morning, Sally poked her head into Ariana's room to check up on her. The room was empty. She'd heard nothing during the night and began looking for the young woman. As she passed various people, she asked they had seen their new guest. Finally, one woman came up to Sally, "Commander, she is in the bath. You had better come at once. She's been in there a very long time."

Sally found Ariana in the bath, crying and washing her privates repeatedly, muttering something about "Got to get clean." Sally used her telepathic skills to touch Ariana's mind gently, sending calming, soothing vibrations. "Good morning, Ariana. Ready for some breakfast?" she said as charmingly as she could. Ariana snapped out of whatever she was stuck and rather sheepishly climbed out, her skin quite wrinkled and pink. "You dry your front, while I get your back side," Sally requested. Like some docile obedient dog, Ariana complied. Sally did not like how this was going at all.

After a light breakfast, Sally took Ariana up to the planning room, where the others had already gathered. It was time to find out about Ariana. Who was she? Where were her relatives? "First things first," Sally explained for everyone's benefit. "Ariana, the Santi have the best Healers on Tarra. So the first thing we must do is have our Healer examine you to make sure that you are as well as can possibly be expected. She'll be gentle and bring you back here when she's done. Is that all right with you?" Ariana nodded and followed the other woman to a side room. A short while later both women returned smiling.

The Fortress Healer spoke quickly, "Ariana's perfectly healthy. No diseases," she stressed that word, "and no lingering wounds. Quite a remarkable young woman." With that, she left to attend to several other injured women in her infirmary.

"Well, that is a blessing, Ariana. We all feared the worst," Tom began. "We've rescued a number of women who were in terrible shape after similar ordeals to yours. Some did not make it, despite our best efforts. Now come have a seat. We all would like to hear your story. I guess the place to begin is with your full name. Who are your parents? Is there anyone we should contact?"

"Ariana Tor. . ." she stumbled, but saw no reason to continue the decades old deception any longer. "Ariana Zar," she declared, a tiny note of pride arose in her. However, as soon as she spoke her last name, her grief ebbed back into her mind. Parents? All dead. All dead. Tears began dripping down her cheeks.

Art thought for a moment, and asked, "Any relation to Emilio Zar?"

Now bawling, she blurted, "Papa, my father. All dead." The four now knew with whom they were dealing. Sally quickly Mind Linked the four of them, giving Ariana time to recover.

She is a noble's daughter! Art sent.

I thought all the nobles and their families were killed outright ten years ago, put in Sally.

Ariana is the first and only survivor we've ever come across. You know what that means? Tom added.

Art answered, *She's the rightful heir to the throne of Zargarb!*

Right. If anyone's ever going to put Zargarb back on its feet when the Centurions are ousted, it has to be the next in line, Ariana. We have to protect and help her at all costs! Tom outlined. He saw that she had recovered her composure somewhat, so he asked her to tell them all about what had happened to her, starting at the beginning. Like an obedient dog, she began to tell them about papa allowing her to go stay with her friend Gina.

76

As she did so, all the horrible memories, the trauma, the betrayals came back upon her. She could not tell where she was at; it looked like she was still locked away in that awful room in the Nunnery. She did not know it, but four hours had passed by, as she continued to relive those nightmare memories. Then, when she reached the time just after her fingers had been cut off, she became utterly stuck in that time, one of complete and utter apathy, total surrender to all life and livingness. She did not hear the gentle coaching, pleading, and orders that the three Santi Guardians were telling her. She only saw the four bare walls of her prison, her room. Life had come to a complete stop.

"Good god, do something!" exclaimed Art.

"I'm trying, but this is way beyond my skills," Sally protested. "I've got to contact Headquarters for help. Keep an eye on her, will you?" She Mind Linked back to Mont Blanc and to Velona. Eventually, they put her in contact with Alana d'Grange, who in her previous lifetime was known as Willow Windsong, the only person who could handle my temporary insanity that I, Ket or Bethany, encountered whenever I got lost in my casting of lightning bolts.

Try singing or humming a gentle lullaby to her, directly into her mind, her beingness. That should calm her down and then you can nudge her up to the present. She is stuck in the past memories of her trauma. Alana was right once again. Sally began to hum and then gently touched Ariana's mind, bringing the soothing sounds to the person.

Slowly, Ariana began to respond and once more began moving through her memories. She related more of what had happened to her recently. All the while, Sally continued her humming. At last, Ariana talked about her escape last night, and then asked, "Why are you humming?" Sally stopped, realizing that Ariana was now back in the present. It was clear that she had not known that she had given them all a terrible fright by getting "stuck in the past!"

Sally now armed with messages and orders from Velona, took charge. "Ariana, the Santi will help you with everything. You know how powerful we are, don't you?" Ariana had only some vague ideas about the Santi, having been isolated for so long. Sally saw that she clearly did not. "We are now a large organization and are dedicated to helping others who are in need, people such as you, who have lost or sacrificed much. In fact, the leader of our whole organization has asked me to beg you to come and visit her in Velona. There, she may be able to offer you something of the greatest value in your life. She wants to see you just as fast as we can get you there. Are you willing to go?" Sally hoped that Ariana would agree without her having to go into a whole lot of details about the Guardians.

"Yes, ma'am. I will go. When?" Ariana had already dropped back into being an obedient puppy. Then fear grew in her. "But I'm afraid. I'm so alone." Sally knew right then that she would have to go with her.

"Don't fret one pretty hair on your head, Ariana. I'm going to go along with you." She saw Tom's mouth open, but he wisely said nothing. "Now Tom, go make the arrangements. We do have one caravel in dock, right? Commandeer it at once."

"Yes, dear," he replied, a note of sarcasm in his voice. He ought to be making the full decisions, especially with half the garrison forces riding hard to the rescue of forty thousand Arads from the Junction.

A little later, when they were alone, Sally explained to Tom and Art the details. "She is in a dire mental state, bordering on insanity. You've noticed how she keeps slipping into the past and getting stuck there? Alana helped me get her back out of it. I think I can keep her in the present for a while, but the orders came directly from Jenna Rose Weston! She has ordered us to bring Ariana to her as fast as possible. I know this makes problems here, but I will make mental contact with you and Art at least every couple hours, so I can continue my Communicator duties. Jenna's orders do take precedence you know." Tom couldn't disagree with that point. Quite why Ket Bethany chose her to succeed him as the Santi leader still baffled him.

Sally and Ariana began packing the few things that they would need. She discovered very quickly that Ariana, never having been out in public since her maiming, was exceedingly embarrassed about doing so. "No problem, my dear child. We will just use this shawl to cover your arms. See like this. Now you look just like any other woman." It seemed to satisfy her somewhat. Arm in arm the two headed to the dock, Tom followed behind toting two large sacks.

"What kind of ship is this? I've never seen one so big, so different. Is it safe?" asked Ariana. Sally was glad to have something commonplace to talk about while they boarded and were shown to their cabins on the poop deck. Sally had at most a week to help Ariana become more comfortable being around other people before they would dock in Velona. Considering the sheer size of Velona, now boasting well over two hundred thousand people just in and around the city proper, Ariana would need all the coaching Sally could muster.

It didn't work out quite as Sally had planned, however. She forgot to bring along herbs to counter seasickness. The first day out, she became quite green and ill, vomiting all over the cabin. Ariana had two choices, try to beg one of the crew members, probably one of the Sisterhood fighters to come and help out and see just how horrible Ariana was, or she could try to deal with her new ill friend herself. She opted to try herself first. Clumsy and awkwardly she cleaned up after each mess, and helped clean Sally's face, even helping her in and out of the hammocks. In the end, Sally had managed to illicit more self-confidence from Ariana, but not the way that she had planned.

By the time they were tacking into Velona, Sally had recovered and both women were standing on the main deck watching the splendid sight. Ariana still carried her shawl, hiding her missing hands. Nothing could have prepared her for the grand sights that she saw that day! Velona, once the rat hole of the Sea Princes, was now a stellar city, huge and breathtaking. A huge stone cathedral rose high above every other building. The throngs of people on the streets were so completely different from Zargarb that Ariana stood spellbound on the deck. Once docked, Sally took Ariana's arm and led them down the gangplank. One of the Sisterhood fighters assigned to the ship brought their gear, following quietly behind them.

As the two walked across the giant dockside plaza crowded with people, Ariana received numerous whistles and catcalls. Sally whispered, "They act like they have never seen a beautiful woman." Ariana flushed, but was beginning to feel very uncomfortable with so many, many people around her. Jenna had already assumed that would be the case and had a Santi escort with a carriage waiting for them, just past the plaza. Ariana was very glad to climb inside the coach. Now she could look around her and not feel so embarrassed and awkward. She gaped at the sights as they went by, Sally pointing out the key locations.

Finally, they left the outer walls of the city. "Where are we going?" Ariana asked. She had just assumed that they Santi would be in the fortified city.

"Jenna has her own private estate just north of the city. Be there in a couple of minutes. My, has this city ever grown! I remember when it was smaller than Zargarb now is. My, how time changes things."

"Ah, here comes the estate ahead. See, they have a stone wall around it as well. Many guards. Very safe place indeed. I just know you are going to love Jenna. She's one of the finest women I know, very, very wise. Very knowledgeable. She has quite a lot of children too. She just had another one this year, Lizzy Ann, I think is her name. Be nice to see the new addition to her family. I rather miss not having many children at my feet, but then I am getting way too old for all that. Ah, here we are." The carriage came to rest outside the Weston estate house. The two climbed out and began walking up to the front door.

At once, Ariana noticed something peculiar. The large front doors had no doorknobs! Sally, having been instructed to observe Ariana, replied. "Yes, you only need to push on them to open the doors. All the doors in this estate work this way, for a reason. Ah, here she comes now."

Ariana gaped. Walking toward them came a woman, perhaps ten years older than herself, holding a baby in her arms. What shocked her was that the woman had no hands, just like herself! "Hello there. You must be Ariana. So pleased to meet you at last. I'd shake hands with you, but we'd have a slight problem with that, but I can shake with you, Sally. Good to see you. It has been entirely too long." To Ariana's total surprise, Jenna held out her arm; Sally took it, and the two shook a welcome.

"This is our new addition to our ever growing family, Lizzy Ann." She proudly showed off me to the two women. Sally, I noticed, gave me a strange look, almost one of recognition. I purposely said nothing — well a baby cannot say anything anyway. I was not yet ready to announce to the world that Bethany or Ket was back. My new body could not do anything except eat and go to the bathroom.

Sally took me in her arms, leaving Jenna free for the moment. She stuck her arm into the arm of Ariana and led her inside, chatting all the while. "You probably have noticed that none of these doors have any knobs. My husband designed them for me. I can go freely anywhere now and not have to fiddle with trying to get a knob turned. Rather frustrating you know, trying to turn a knob with no hands."

Ariana finally found her tongue. "You, you are the leader of all the Santi? But I don't see how you. . ." her voice trailed off.

"Yes, I am the leader of the entire Santi del Dio. We number something like ten thousand strong, if I remember right, but you probably want to know what happened to me. Well, I used to run an inn in Zargarb. The Holy Paladins cut off my hands, I escaped and came here. The rest is history, as they say. Look Ariana, let's get one thing perfectly clear, just because we don't have hands doesn't mean we are hopeless invalids. Actually, we can do just about anything we set our minds to doing, only sometimes it is pitifully slow in the doing. Hence, no doorknobs. Come let me show you around our home."

An hour later, Sally said farewell and returned to the caravel, which sailed back to Zargarb. This time, however, she remembered to bring along some herbs to counter seasickness. Sally knew that she did not ever want to be a mariner!

The next afternoon, with Ariana now comfortable in her new surroundings, Jenna and Ariana sat on the patio, I was in my baby crib beside mom. Jenna said, "Now I want you to close your eyes and return back to when your father was granting you permission to go and stay with your friend Gina. Yes, that's it. Now I want you to look at everything that happened after that, telling me all about it. What you are seeing, feeling, smelling, everything." Thus began the true healing of Ariana. Actually, Jenna felt that there were two minds observing, working her therapy. I was quietly watching the proceedings, learning her technique better, ready to jump in and lend a hand if needed. That day I stared insanity square in its face and watched it dissolve and evaporate.

Damn is mom ever good! I thought. *She is facing this head on without even the slightest flinching!* I already knew that I could not have done so on my own, face insanity head on.

Back at Zargarb, the day after Sally and Ariana sailed for Velona, Art strolled into the city, paying his copper to enter. He strolled down to the docks and began asking around for Rodrigo. It took an hour of persevering before he was led into a back room of a warehouse, plush with the amenities of home. "Ah, there you are Art Longton!" The big man got up to greet Art.

"You are a hard man to find, Rodrigo Decasas," Art jested, shaking his hand firmly.

"Well, you cannot be too careful these days. You know what I mean." Art certainly did. "And what brings you, old friend to Rodrigo? Got something to trade? Come have a seat. Some wine perhaps?"

"Ale would be better. Thanks. No, not business today. No, I'm afraid that it is far worse than a little trading gone south. I've come to inform you of something absolutely horrible and ask your advice about it." After pouring them both a mug of the finest ale in Zargarb, Rodrigo sat across from Art, prepared to listen. Of all the people in Zargarb, Rodrigo respected Art above all.

"Let me begin by asking you if you know what actually is going on in the Nunnery, the old Sisterhood Inn, especially at night."

"Well, frequently the Holy Paladins go there at night. I suppose it is their religious duty or some such. Frankly, none of us ever paid them any mind, as long as they stay out of our business," Rodrigo admitted.

"Bring the whole pitcher of ale over here; you and I are going to need it," Art said seriously. He then began to relate the truth, as best as the Santi knew at this point in time anyway, of what was actually going on in the basement. The more Art talked, the angrier Rodrigo became.

"Now I don't ask you to believe me on all this. I know it is a wild tale that I am telling you. However, I would like you to station a number of men to watch the Nunnery 24/7, especially late at night. If I am correct, within the next few days, certainly a week at most, you are going to see a lot of dead female bodies being carried out and buried, probably in secret."

"I swear to you, Art, that I will put my best men on it. Nothing shall leave the Nunnery without us having seen it!" Rodrigo declared.

Art spoke softly, leaning close to the big man, "If I am right and you observe a large number of women being buried, then watch out. The Holy Paladins will be kidnaping at least another two dozen of Zargarb's younger women, hauling them off to the Nunnery citing various 'holy reasons.' I don't know what we can do about it, if that happens. I leave that up to you. If you need anything from the Santi, send word the usual way."

"Damn them to Hell! I knew something funny was going on. My father, bless his long dead soul, he used to tell me stories about how the barbarians of the Northern Steppes used to rape our women after they conquered the city. Thousands of rapes, if he's to be believed. Now if these Vile Paladins want their own private brothel, then everyone would find that a much better solution to men's needs. But what you are talking about, the mutilations — now that is going too far, way, way too far! The evil perverts!"

"Well, perhaps I am wrong. Hold judgment until you see the bodies.

If you know any physicians you can trust, perhaps you can dig up one of the graves and see from what they died. That ought to provide you with certainty," Art cautioned. The two chatted a while longer and then Art said goodbye, returning to the Fortress. He knew that he had set into motion events, which may well shake the status quo up considerably.

Five days later, around midnight, two Holy Paladins carried a large bag out of the back door of the Nunnery, loading it onto a waiting wagon. They drove to the cemetery near the park at the northern portion of the city. They dug a shallow grave, threw the sack in, covered it up, and left it as an unmarked grave. Neither saw two shadowy figures watching their excavations and did not see these men recover the sack and refill the grave with the dirt. Neither did they see another cart arrive and take the sack away. Neither did they see these same men return the next night, re-burying the body.

"Aye, Rodrigo, I examined the woman. She was missing her right hand. Her legs had serious rope burns on them, the kind the seamen get from repeated burnings. Her front teeth were missing. I counted twenty-five burn marks on her torso — can't tell what made them."

"Damn. Well, how did she die?" Rodrigo had heard enough, clearly this woman was tortured.

"Her privates were badly infected with a green puss. You know what that means, unclean woman. I cannot say for certain, mind you she was not my patient, but she probably died from the infection. That also very likely means that those who used her are also sick and unclean."

"Thank you for your discretion and observation, Floyd. Here, accept this box of food for your services."

The man smiled, "Anytime, anytime." He just acquired another week's worth of food, invaluable, these days!

Later that night, Rodrigo called a special meeting of all his many lieutenants. It was a deadly serious meeting indeed. He outlined all that he knew about the nefarious activities of these Vile Paladins. He issued urgent warnings to be delivered to everyone associated with his organization in any way: for the next few weeks, keep all their young women safely inside their homes. In no way attract the attention of these men or their priest! Further, he ordered a sharp watch be kept to see if these men actually kidnaped other women from Zargarb. For the very first time, he issued the order for his men to use their blackjacks on the perpetrators freely, even though they were likely the Holy Paladins!

During the course of the next two weeks, at least ten more bodies were dumped into unmarked graves. Rodrigo took a stroll through the area during the daytime and noticed that there were quite a lot of unmarked graves in this section of the cemetery, firming his resolve.

A week after that, two Holy Paladins broke into the home of a family not too far from the docks. They claimed that the young wife had been found guilty of Holy Transgressions and was sentenced to the Nunnery. They dragged her way, kicking and screaming. So engrossed in trying to keep the squirming woman under control, they failed to see two big men move silently up behind them. Both Holy Paladins woke up on the street curb the next day with massive headaches and very large bumps on their heads. The woman was nowhere to be seen.

The same scenario occurred three more times during the remainder of the week. Rodrigo felt that by now the message ought to have reached the general — time to pay him a visit. Thus, Rodrigo, accompanied by a large number of his burly men, walked over to the General's mansion.

"Ah Rodrigo Decasas, I was just about to send word to you, and here you show up on my doorstep. Welcome, come on in," the General tried to sound as hospitable as possible. Events were going wrong far faster than he could handle them. He had a symbiotic relationship with this rogue. Without his support, his control over the city would become a nightmare. He needed Rodrigo on his side. Yet, he suspected that his thugs were behind the recent spate of nighttime attacks upon his men.

Rodrigo refused the offered fine wine. Helas knew that this was going to be a serious talk indeed. The man had refused his wine! "General, I will come directly to the point. I am not a man of many words." He briefly outlined what he knew for a fact was going on in the Nunnery at night. He also could not help notice that the General's face reddened slightly as he spoke. To Rodrigo, Helas had "Guilty" written all over his face.

"General, we, all of us in Zargarb, respect the fact that your conquering army has not raped thousands of our women. You are not the barbarians from the Northern Steppes. That you prefer to use shall we say a brothel to satisfy your needs, is perfectly fine with us. I dare say, the average citizen of Zargarb would fully support that. But the mutilation of those women, the kidnaping of innocent women just because they happen to be pretty and then cutting off hands, legs, eyes, pulling out their teeth — that, sir, no one will stand for. You have gone too far, far too far. If you persist in this manner, I came to warn you that you will likely face open rebellion from every citizen of Zargarb. Yes these past few nights, it was my men that knocked yours out. I sent you a message; they could just have easily been killed. However, we do not want you and your men dead; it's bad for business. Might I suggest that you find willing volunteers and then not mistreat them? I suspect that if you paid them for their Good Marks, you'd find many a willing volunteer." Rodrigo had used Art's very words, Art's suggested solution.

General Helas was in a pickle. He knew that he could not find Rodrigo. He'd tried that many times before in the early days of the occupation. The man was incredibly slippery. He also knew that without this thug's support, he would be forced to ask the Pope for more men, thousands of more men. He had just lost over five hundred up in the Junction. If he asked for more men, so many questions would be raised that his very life would be in jeopardy. At the very least, the Pope would send one of those deadly Mano del Dio security men to investigate. His life would not be worth living if that happened; his long, illustrious career would be over, completely over. The Mano was greatly feared, even by the very priests whom they were protecting!

Smoothly, he replied, "Yes, perhaps my men have been a little over aggressive with their women." He did not mention his own situation. He found himself wondering yet again what had happened to her. He forced his mind to stay on the topic at hand. "I think that your suggestion holds great merit indeed. After all, what is a little payment? I agree with you fully in principle. All that remains is how we might find, say, two dozen volunteers?"

"An offer of a week's food rations for a nights work and I can get you two dozen eager volunteers," Rodrigo laid out his bated hook, knowing that he was about to catch a big fish.

"Excellent. I shall have the posters prominently displayed tomorrow. Have your volunteers report to the Nunnery after suppertime, any night. Mind you, no hags!" Both men chortled.

"No hags, General. It's been a pleasure doing business with you as always," Rodrigo rose and shook the General's hand. Helas saw him safely to the door, greatly relieved. He had just defused what could have brought his complete downfall. He heaved a huge sigh of relief after the burly man departed.

"If all my other problems were this easily solved." He called in his lieutenants and phrased the new orders of the day to be posted around the city. "Now, next order of business: has anyone gotten news of my girl?

One red faced junior officer rose, "Sir, no sir. I interrogated the Head Matron personally today. Grilled her, but she stuck by her story all the way. It seems that the nuns were not notified of your departure and as always did not disturb you. When they went to check on her in the morning, they found the door to the basement room ajar and the girl missing. They have searched the entire complex three times now. No trace of her has been found, she has just vanished. With no hands, there is no way for her to unlock any of the doors, let alone open the doorknobs. She could not get out by herself. All the nuns are accounted for, as you know they sleep in the same large room. All were there the entire night. All the other women's rooms are locked at night, so they could not have helped her escape. She just vanished in the night."

"Sir," another junior officer spoke up, "I have searched the city, and no one has seen her walking the streets. I assure you that a woman with no hands walking the streets at night would have been noticed."

"Damn it, then what happened to her?" Helas was mad, but could do nothing about it. The room was entirely quiet.

Later that night he composed his Annual Report to the Pope.
Your Holiness,

The population of Zargarb remains fairly constant at two hundred thousand souls. Enclosed you will find their gold tithe and tax contributions for 637. The rainfall has been dismal here yet another year. Consequently, the harvest is again much lower than expected. If you could possibly send another ten loads of grain, the people here will bless you for your kindness.

Consequently, most of the people from Florintine Junction have decided to move further west in our sector. The Junction is, after all, right at the beginning of the desert. Crops have been failing badly there. So I have encouraged the mass migration to more tillable lands in western Zargarb. At this writing, many folks are still on the move; hence, the head count will be more accurate next year, as they settle down in their new homes and villages and begin to raise more bountiful crops.

Finally, it is with a sad heart that I must send you this list of your most Holy Paladins who had died furthering the cause of our great church. An epidemic struck the Junction, possibly brought in by the stray, unclean Arad nomads. We lost five hundred brave, good men to this outbreak of disease, which also claimed ten times that number of Junction citizens. Perhaps that convinced the remainder to move to find better, greener lands to till. Please say a blessing for each of my fallen men. They died valiantly defending the faithful. They will be sorely missed.

Yours in Faith,

General Helas Taxos

He wondered if the Pope would take his subtle hint and send him desperately needed replacements for all the men he lost at the Junction. He looked at his remaining horde of confiscated gold and guessed that even if the attrition continued as it had this unfortunate year, he would still have enough money to pay the taxes until he retired. He felt relieved with that observation. He took another long drink of wine and wished he could go to visit his plaything. What had happened to her? He just could not get her out of his mind.

Chapter 5 The Banditos of Solamina

Solamina, the sector adjacent to Zargarb, was also an ardent supporter of Bandar Dero's Church of Jehosanity Northern Orthodoxy. Thus, when the traitors opened wide the city gates allowing the Emperor's Centurions to capture the city without a fight, the average person was furious. When the Holy Paladins and their priest arrived, forcing their perverted brand of Jehosanity upon the citizens, furor rose to new heights.

However, unlike Zargarb whose entire infrastructure had been destroyed, Solamina's fleet of ships was not sunk in their harbor. True, their nobles and households were eliminated much as they had been in Zargarb, but their fleet was still intact. The middle management was still operational, and it was their hard work that kept the wheels of commerce flowing. Upper management made the deals, approved the transactions or not, and did the long range planning. Now that was all gone.

The buyers and sellers continued setting up deals, issuing sailing and shipping orders, just as they had always done. What was lacking, of course, was someone at the top directing the action, coordinating the shipping, and making the plans that would lead ultimately to success. The Holy Paladin overlords allowed these managers to work as they always had and did not intervene with orders and dictates over them.

However, two factors took a heavy toll on Solamina's economy since the takeover by the Holy Paladins. First, the lack of top-level decision making and planning led to much wasted effort. A ship carrying a cargo from point A to point B should never return to point A empty. Yet, in their haste to get ships active and commerce flowing, empty returns became commonplace. Of course, this led to smaller and smaller profits, until eventually the ships and their captains were barely breaking even. The support personnel on the dock side took the brunt of the belt tightening.

The second factor was the new caravels. While Solamina had purchased and received one of these new ships from Velona just as the war began, now that it was over, they still had only the one caravel. The nobles were not there to finance the needed massive new construction of ships modeled on this single caravel. Other sectors did begin to build caravel fleets of their own, starting in 626, financed heavily by the nobles, who expected ultimately to get a sizeable return on their initial investment. In Solamina, the new managers attempted to make up for this lack of financial support by pinching part of the profits from each shipping transaction.

Slowly but surely. this had an impact upon the overall profitability. Five years later, only two new caravels had been built in Solamina. So meager were the profits that there simply were no funds to replace their aging fleet. Thus, their shipping contracts became fewer and of lesser value.

Unable to make a profit and having to take the bottom of the barrel shipping runs, the free, independent ships and their captains moved on to other sectors. About a quarter of all the ship captains in the Sea Princes owned outright their own ship, not counting the new caravels, of course. Thus, by 631, Solamina had lost a quarter of its fleet to neighboring sectors.

Making matters worse, another quarter of the ship's personnel simply quit and signed new contracts in the other sectors, as the demand for more mariners grew because of the increased availability of newly built caravels there. By 637, life was grim indeed in Solamina. Their shipping now consisted primarily of ore runs way down in the Southlands, and the managers were forced to pay hard coin for the grain and produce that they needed to import to support their population. So much for the economics of the day.

Praedo Garcia was a shipwright and planner, had been so all his life, just as his father had been before him, and his father's father. It was the family tradition. When the new sleek caravel sailed into Solamina, he cheered, relishing the opportunity to study this new design, which instantly obsoleted all other ships in the world. He had finally completed the first set of plans, copying every minute detail of the ship when the Centurions swarmed through the city gates that fateful night.

He kept his family indoors for the next few days, fearing for the safety of his wife, Miranda, and his two young daughters, who were close to the marrying age of fifteen. He was only a boy when the Barbarians of the Northern Steppes had sacked Solamina. He had terrifying nightmares dating from that era, fears that still haunted him today as a grown man. His own mother had been raped and beaten, dying shortly afterwards. How could he protect his two daughters? He was not a fighter.

Some say that a being always gets what he puts his attention upon continually. In hindsight, Praedo would agree with that opinion. Constant worry about his daughters kept him awake during the nights. During the chaotic times after the fall, he could not work, even if he had wanted to work. Worse, under pain of death, he had to take his family to Sunday Services. Each time they went his fears for their safety rose higher. At last, it happened, the dreaded knock on his door. Honestly, there was nothing poor Praedo could do but allow the Holy Paladins in their sky blue robes to take away his two daughters, screaming at the top of their lungs. That night, Praedo would never, ever forget. It was the worst night in his entire life.

A month later, someone found their bodies on a side alley. Their bodies had been beaten and tortured. When he brought a cart to bring their bodies home to be buried, he knew that they had suffered a horrible death, a painful death. Although her eyes were red from crying, Miranda pointed out one salient fact that Praedo had missed: both girls had never given in to whatever demands had been made of them! "Praedo, they fought to the bitter end. We cannot give up. They have sent us a message." Something deep within this mild, passive man snapped. He would never be the same again.

Within a week, he and his wife packed up all their belongings into their wagon and rode out of Solamina, vowing never to return to this unholy city. He had spent the last of his life savings to purchase a large supply of dried foods so that wherever they went, at least they would not go hungry. Without even knowing where they were headed, the two somberly rode out of Solamina, up the north spoke road.

The road system in the Sea Princes is a bit unusual. The original layout of the seven sectors centered totally upon the namesake city. All roads led straight into the city from the outlying areas. These are called the spoke roads. Periodically, a semi-circular road whose radius was centered on the city arced around the countryside, from the eastern to the western seacoast. These are called the rim roads. Rim roads are about five miles apart close to the namesake cities, gradually becoming farther apart the further out from the city they were, until the last rim road was twenty miles from the next inner rim road.

Praedo and Miranda rode due north on the main north-south spoke road, passing the various crossroads, which often had small towns and villages at these intersections. They had gone nearly a hundred miles when they stopped at an inn in the small town of Grina. Sad and lifeless, the pair ordered a dinner. Neither said much. Soon they could not help overhearing several men bitterly complaining.

One man yelled, "Aye, they just kidnaped my own wife and daughter. Yes, I know that she was going to marry your Fredio, but that's not going to happen. Damn those Evil Paladins; damn them to the Fiery Pits of Lucifer!"

The other man replied, "Double damn them, if that's possible. There are only two of them; we ought to go get them back and send them vile excuses for holy men to Hell. Fredio will help too, Silvas. Heck as soon as he finds out, I won't be able to stop him from trying to rescue her."

Praedo could not help but add what he knew, "I know what you are going through. They just came and took my two daughters away for no reason. Found them later, dead, badly tortured and molested. Damn all these Evil Men to Hell. Yes, you should try to get them back, if you can."

The two scooted their chair over to join Praedo and Miranda. "So it's happened before. I'm sorry for you and the misses here. Where ya from? Not seen you around these parts before. Name's Silvas Armato. This here's Benito Fuella." Praedo introduced himself and his wife. Before long, he had told them the short story of his life. Both men were very sympathetic but grew angrier about the recent kidnaping.

As Praedo talked, a plan formed in his mind, as plans always did. Until the loss of his daughters, he was never without a plan of some kind to think about. "Say, I'm getting some ideas here. Tell me the details of the kidnaping. In short, the two Holy Paladins had smashed in his door, grabbed the two women, tied them up, and forced them to ride a pair of spare horses. Silvas heard one of them say that they would be taking the women down to Solamina, but first they had to collect some funds from their associates in the next rim road village. "Tell me, Silas, once they have finished their business there, what is the shortest route back to Solamina? Is it back to this crossroads and then straight down to the city?"

"Aye, Praedo, that be the shortest way," Silvas replied.

The barkeeper came over, "You folks be careful. If they see you are from town here, why they will just come back in force and kill us innocent townsfolk. They did it just a while ago. Makes people pretty scared 'round here, if you know what I mean."

"Yes, I certainly do know what you men," Praedo replied. "No, if you want to get your women back, I know just how you can do it." Silvas insisted on hearing Praedo's plan. The four leaned close, while he whispered the details.

When he finished, both men grinned. "Don't that beat all," exclaimed Silvas! "That's mighty clever. It ought to work! You in Benito?" All three men shook hands and the two left Praedo and Miranda to finish their meal.

Instead of heading off to bed, the two climbed back on their wagon and parked it near a building at the crossroads. This village was centered on the crossroads intersection, where the arcing east-west rim road intersected the north-south spoke road. Miranda slept in the wagon bed, while Praedo kept watch. Sure enough, just about sunset, the two Holy Paladins came trotting up the rim road, leading two other horses, which carried the two women. Praedo noticed that not only were they tied up securely and tied to the horses, but they were also gagged. Evidently, they had been yelling for help. *Help is soon coming,* he thought to himself. The riders veered down the spoke road without stopping. However, the men glanced around, making sure that no one lay in ambush for them here in the town. Seeing nothing unusual, they rode on down the spoke road.

Praedo urged his team and slowly his wagon began heading after them, going south back toward Solamina. About five miles south of the town, Praedo had noticed a rather dense patch of forest. If Silas followed his plan, Silas, Benito, and Fredio would already be there, their trap set. Praedo had his horses going only slightly slower than the Paladins. It would not actually do to catch them. He needed to be only a few minutes behind them at most.

Ahead, Silvas and his friend lay in wait. They had bandanas covering their faces. Silvas was hiding behind the trees on one side, while Benito and Fredio were hiding on the other side. They had drawn a line in the dirt road. When the lead horse reached this spot, they would act. Not long now, thought Silvas, he heard hoof beats coming down the road. Although it was getting rather dark here in the dense stand of forest, they could still see to shoot. Silvas aimed his heavy crossbow at the lead rider, hoping that Benito and Fredio were doing the same with the second rider, only a few feet behind him. As the horse got to the line in the road, Silvas fired. Almost simultaneously, he heard two more crossbows fire.

He picked up his sword and raced the short distance to the riders. One Holy Paladin had fallen off his horse and was not moving. Silas ignored him. The other man, quarrel protruding from his sword arm, was attempting to dismount. By the time that the three got to him, he had awkwardly drawn his sword with his left hand. Both Silas and Benito had been trained for fighting and defending the walls of Solamina. Ordinarily, one would have expected the Holy Paladin to have bested all three, but not wounded and not left handed. A minute later, one of Silas's strikes drew blood, while Benito's thrust pierced the man's heart. The body dropped the sword and slumped to the ground. Fredio kept chopping at the fallen man's body until its head was nearly cut off, and then he did the same to the other fighter.

Meanwhile, Silas and Benito untied the women and helped them dismount. Then, they set to work removing the gags, cutting the ropes that held their hands behind their bodies. Just as the hugging and cheering reunion began, Praedo's wagon arrived. He called out, "Well done, Silas, Benito. You must be Fredio."

Silas was beside himself with happiness. "It worked! It actually worked, Praedo! Three cheers for Praedo!" He then had to explain to his wife and daughter that Praedo had devised the plan to rescue them.

"We'd better stick to the plan," Praedo cautioned. "Who knows when another rider will come along?" The two women climbed on the wagon, joining Miranda, while the men searched the bodies, confiscating anything of value, tossing the stuff onto the wagon, and then dragged them off the road into the forest, covering them up with a stray brush. They tied the four horses to the back of the wagon, and got their own horses from where they had been tied up, a good distance from the road. Together, they all rode back to Silvas's home. Few saw them as they passed through nearly deserted streets; it was full dark.

While Miranda helped in the kitchen, the men sat around the table discussing how easy this whole ambush had been. "You know that from now on, it's not safe for you and your family to be here in town," Praedo cautioned. "Eventually, they will be missed and others will be sent to find out what happened to them. It is only a matter of time before they find out that the two men took your wife and daughter. The only conclusion they can reach is that you were responsible for the ambush."

"I know. We have a small shack not too far from here. Dad's old line shack; he used to herd some sheep many years ago. I've kept it up, not as big and nice as this, but it will do. Right Nika?"

"I'd live anywhere as long as those vile men can't get at Rosie or me," she declared.

"I'm coming too! I'll protect you, Rosie," broke in Fredio, proud that he had had a hand in rescuing his soon to be bride. Rosie blushed, but felt very lucky to have Fredio around.

Over a late supper — the women had not eaten since noon — they discussed their futures. One thing led to another. Before they all turned in for the night Praedito's Banditos had been formed. During the next month, more and more men began to join them and their successes grew. With success came more weapons, horses, supplies, and gold.

At first, they operated in the same general area. However, Praedo insisted that they diversify. Disguised as a road maintenance worker, Praedo took his wagon on nearly every road and track in Solamina, but never venturing as far south as the first rim road, some five miles from Solamina. During his travels, he drew sketches of the terrain and especially locations that were most suited for their ambushes. Within a year, he knew every detail of all the roads with the sector.

Meanwhile, Silas and Benito sent other men out scouring the countryside. Praedo had insisted that they needed to find several remote, safe locations where their ever-growing resistance fighters could stay. Solamina had a number of limestone caves in the sides of gullies up in the far north. Slowly, these were made habitable. Food, water, grain, and fodder were ferried to these safe houses. "We are everywhere" was Praedo's group motto.

Indeed, one of their primary thrusts came at tax collection time. When the tax collectors had finished obtaining one gold piece per resident of a town, they and their Holy Paladin protectors were uniformly ambushed on their way back to Solamina. Secretly, the funds were returned to the village from which they had been collected. Per Praedo's orders, after each ambush, the dead men's bodies were dragged some distance from the road and buried; the ambush site was then "cleaned up." The result: the Holy Paladins and tax collectors had just disappeared, vanished without a trace.

In the small villages, which had no Megalos controlled Church of Jehosanity yet, Benito, a mask hiding his face, would visit each house, handing back the required number of coins. With the larger villages that had overlord sponsored and controlled churches, far greater care and caution was needed to keep the Megalos priest from knowing what was going on, that the just collected taxes were being returned. The trick Praedo used was to have Benito, in disguise of course, enter one of the larger pubs when many people were present. He went to the barkeeper and announced loudly so that everyone could here. "Praedito's Banditos is giving every person in the town, man, woman, and child, except the Holy Paladins and priests, one gold coin each. Barkeeper, you are in charge of seeing everyone gets their coins. If you cheat anyone, you will have to answer to Praedito's Banditos, and that will not go well for you."

After this had occurred for several years, everyone in these outlying towns and villages supported Praedito's Banditos one hundred percent, which was exactly what Praedo had planned. The next phase of his grand plan was to establish communication centers in each town where messages could secretly be sent to the banditos. One discrete location in each town was chosen and periodically, one of the banditos would check it for messages. By the third year, nothing that the Holy Paladins or the priests did in any of these towns escaped the notice of Praedito's Banditos. By the end of their third year of operation, the banditos knew about every action their enemy did almost as soon as it occurred. Frequently, well-planned ambushes reaped ever-larger rewards.

Praedito's Banditos did not stop with just recollecting taxes. Every caravan of goods that the Holy Paladins attempted to ship was hijacked. Only when they began escorting their wagons with over a hundred Holy Paladins did a shipment actually get through to the designated area. However, often once they returned home, that location was then robbed, sometimes in broad daylight. One way or another, all shipments were confiscated.

Now among the many shipments were food supplies. While these were confiscated and a portion used to feed the banditos, frequently the banditos once more returned food supplies directly to the needy families in those towns and villages. "A Present from Praedito's Banditos" became a common phrase heard in many households.

Of course, this forced the Holy Paladins to switch to hiring the Santi del Dio to run the vast majority of their shipments. This, however, always cost them a percentage of the value of the shipment. Praedito's Banditos never once molested in any way a Santi escorted group. Praedo insisted on that, explaining that would be like cutting off your own foot. The men grasped the concept and followed that rule slavishly. This did not, of course, prevent them from later robbing the recipient of the delivered goods. Again, if those goods were needed by the townsfolk, the shipment was clandestinely returned.

By 637, the Holy Paladin General of Solamina had lost well over one thousand men and untold supplies along with a fortune in gold taxes. He, however, had no choice but to make up the difference in taxes. General Hecate Lox paced his planning room angrily. "What do you mean the taxes have been lost yet again? How much this time?"

A nervous aide said, "Five hundred, Sir."

Hecate had long since stop worrying about the number of his men that had been lost. He didn't want to know any more. "This has got to stop! What town is next?"

"Amerios, Sir."

"All right, new plan. Listen up. We are going to catch these damn banditos this time. Look at the map. Take notes. I don't want to hear that we lost these taxes!" He outlined his plan carefully, using markers to represent the units placed carefully on the map. "Take the entire Garrison Force 1. They leave tonight. These woods here will be the likely ambush site. Everywhere else is open ground. This will be their ambush site. Place our forces equally on both sides of the road, well hidden and about a half mile into the woods from the road. Send the usual forces with the tax collector, only this time they ride in a wagon. Make very sure that they have a trumpet with them. As soon as these damn bandits attack them, they blow the trumpet see. Our huge force sweeps out of the woods behind them and we trap them all. Leave no bandito alive. Kill every last one of them!"

"Brilliant, positively brilliant!" declared one aide.

"This cannot fail!" added another one.

"We have them this time, Sir!" exclaimed another.

"Then get to it! Send out the garrison now. They need time to get into place." His aides rushed to carry out these new orders, confident that this time the banditos would be eliminated for good.

Later, after supper and just before sundown, a hundred Holy Paladins rode out of Solamina, heading up the spoke road toward the northeast. Resplendent in their sky blue tunics with white crosses, these well-armed men looked totally confident and poised. They knew that many eyes were watching their departure and vanity took the forefront.

No one noticed an old man toss a pigeon into the air. No one paid any attention to the pigeon as it also flew away to the north. At their secure camp hidden in a limestone cave, Praedo was sipping his after dinner wine with his friends, when a man interrupted them. "Sir, this message just came in. I don't know what to make of it." He handed Praedo a small slip of paper.

At once, Silvas and Benito edged closer so they could see. Praedo read it aloud.

"100 HP left S at dusk. NE spoke."

"Do we have any word about future actions involving one hundred of the Holy Paladins?" asked Benito.

"Not that I recall," Praedo replied. "Let me look through the pile we've got here." He rummaged through dozens of papers. "Nope, nothing about this move. Must be up to something. Let's see, what is likely to happen soon? Ah, yes. Amerios hasn't had the tax collector visit them yet. The NE spoke road is a likely route to follow to get there. Silvas, send out the usual scouts. Let's see where they are going and what they are up to this time."

Silvas chuckled, "Up to no good, I can tell you that! I'll send them at once."

"Make sure that you give them a couple pigeons and a quill and ink," Praedo reminded Silvas. He was always double-checking everything, the planner in him.

The next afternoon, they received another message by pigeon.

"TC left S. Dawn, NE Spoke."

"Well, that makes sense," Benito commented. Praedo said nothing, deep in thought. He wondered what the Holy Paladins were doing. Still no news had come.

Late in the afternoon, a pigeon arrived with the answer. Praedo read aloud.

"100 HP hiding in F. Both sides of NE spoke."

"Ah ha! To the maps everyone." Praedo rushed over to the maps that he had compiled. "Yes, it now makes sense. See here is Amerios. All rolling hills along the route, except here, where we have ambushed them several times, this patch of woods. So the Paladins are hiding in the woods."

"Yes, but why? That doesn't make any sense," Benito asked, confused by the information which didn't make any sense. These were fighters and ought to be guarding the tax collector and his gold.

Praedo grinned slyly, "O'l Hecate is trying to out fox us, yes he is. Look, Benito, suppose that we wanted to hijack that gold shipment, which of course we actually do. Where would you place our men?"

"Oh, right there in that woods! Oh, I see, I see. As soon as we do that, they attack us. Ouch. Good thing we found out about in time."

"Rats, I guess we leave this tax shipment alone," Silvas complained. "No matter, we have enough to make it up to the folks in Amerios."

"Ah where's the sport in that," cajoled Praedo. "Give me a minute to counter plan. This is most interesting indeed." He reread the message, "Both sides it says. Probably split into halves."

"Yes, I believe this will work," Praedo finally broke the silence. "Come here; let me show you my plan. We do not want to attack one hundred; too many of our men are likely to get hurt. So here's what we will do." He outlined his countermove. Benito and Silvas roared with laughter when they saw the totality of the new plan. At once, they set off to get it implemented.

"What was that all about?" asked Miranda, when Praedo rejoined her, after refilling his wine cup.

"Oh, just a move-countermove, nothing serious," he replied.

A little while later, two groups of a hundred banditos each rode out of the caves. Benito led one, while Silvas, the other. For a time, the two groups rode together, but ten miles later, at the first rim road, they split and went in different directions. They rode most of the night, stopping only for a three-hour sleep period. At dawn, both groups continued their long ride to get into position. As expected, Benito's group reached the far western edge of the patch of woods several hours before Silvas reached the far eastern edge. Benito's men took advantage of a lengthy break, before they began the second step of the plan.

Just after full dark, both groups entered the woods. Just inside the dark woods, they tied up all their horses. Now stealth was required. Each sent out three advanced scouts ahead of their main parties. On Benito's side, one scout veered to the northeast, one went due east, one veered to the southwest. The main party gave them some lead time and then headed due east. Everyone walked as quietly as possible. No talking was allowed. Stealth was everything on this mission. Partway through the woods, a lone whippoorwill gave its lonely call. Benito gave a similar reply. The scout had found the enemy due east. He led his men in that direction.

By midnight, both parties had snuck up on the Holy Paladin's two camps. As expected, all their horses were tethered on one long dragline. Two sentries stood guard over the sleeping men. The Holy Paladins expected no action at all until the tax collector returned tomorrow late afternoon. Benito signaled two men. Slowly, using extreme caution, the two crept up on the unsuspecting guards. A few minutes later, hands slipped over their mouths, while a dagger slit open their throats. Ever so quietly, the dead were lowered to the ground. Benito gave another signal and more men crept towards the line of horses.

While the remainder of his men kept their crossbows aimed at the sleeping men, slowly and deliberately the horses were led deeper into the woods, back to where they had left their own mounts. It took all of Benito's will power to stick to the plan. His men could fire a round of quarrels and perhaps kill half of these sleeping men before they knew what happened. He hesitated a minute, half expecting to hear Silvas begin shooting at these evil men. However, hearing nothing but the woodland noises, he gave the retreat signal. Just as quietly as they came, they left.

Once free of the woods, ten men from each side were assigned to lead the newly acquired horses back to the caves. Meanwhile, the two groups mounted up and rode north, beginning step three of the plan. They joined forces at the extreme northeastern edge of the woods, along the rim road down which later this day the tax collector should be coming. Leaving their mounts hidden just inside the first line of trees, the men fanned out using the natural cover of the hills, lying prone on the ground. Now came the long wait. Even if the tax men had some way of signaling the Holy Paladins, without their horses, much time would be wasted in running the nearly six miles from where they were at to this location.

Sure enough, late afternoon the tax collector's wagon came lumbering down the road. Six Holy Paladins sat in the back alongside the collector, while two more sat on the buckboard, one driving, and one with a crossbow at the ready. Helping the banditos, the men were engaged in a conversation, which of course the banditos could not understand, wrong language. A whippoorwill called out. Immediately, eighty crossbows twanged. The wagon's personnel had no chance of survival. They had become human pincushions.

Quickly, everything of value was confiscated. The horses were unhitched and taken as well. They left the dead men on the wagon, where they had died. A few minutes later, they all cantered off down the rim road, leaving the ghastly wagon parked at the side of the road. Soon, they estimated the Holy Paladins would arrive on foot to find out where their wagon was at and see the aftermath. Once more, Praedo's plan worked perfectly. Not only did they have the gold, but also had added a hundred and two new horses to their ever growing herd. It had been a fine day's haul indeed.

When General Hecate did not hear news of his smashing victory over the banditos at the appointed time, he sent two riders out to find out what was delaying his men. Sometime later they returned with the news. Several more days passed before his weary men finally reentered the main gates of Solamina on foot, however.

When General Hecate heard the news, he broke his right fist by pounding his table far too hard. Yes, he lost his temper and paid for it rather steeply.

A week later, wrist hurting badly, General Hecate stared at the final figures. The population count said that one hundred twenty thousand lived in the sector. Of that, eighty thousand lived in and around Solamina proper. The rest resided in the many outlying towns and villages. His tax collectors had actually deposited nearly ninety thousand gold coins in his treasury, which meant that he was short thirty thousand gold coins. His problem? Where could he possibly get that much money in a very short order? For ten years now, he had cleverly made up the deficit from the gold he had taken when his men had systematically eliminated all the noble houses of Solamina. Last year, he had used up the last of that horde. Now what? For hours, he paced back and forth in his planning room, hoping the walls would inspire him.

"I can double the gate fees, but it will take eternity to raise thirty thousand. I could increase everyone's taxes within the city, but that is going to be very unpopular. I've lost so many men to these despicable banditos, that if the city gets unstable, I will very likely lose complete control of it, and there goes my head! Maybe I could get a loan from the merchants? Heck, they are in just as bad a situation as I am in; they cannot even afford to build their new ships. They are losing crews faster than I am losing fighters! The damn Santi, I'll bet they could get the funds! Heavens knows I've had to pay them enough, just to get food supplies out, and produce in from the outlying towns and farms."

"The Santi, but what would I use to back the loan?" He could think of nothing at all that he could use for collateral. Nevertheless, he could think of no one else who could possibly arrange for that amount of cash as quickly as he needed it. He had to send in his yearly report and funds within a week. "Hell, there is nothing wasted in at least asking! They can only laugh at me, that's the least of my worries right now."

Late that afternoon, General Hecate walked out of the eastern gate of the city alone. The short mile between his outer wall and the outer wall of the Santi fortress passed rapidly. He approached the main gate. It was shut, naturally. He knocked with his good hand. The gatekeeper slide the viewing window open. "General Hecate Lox to see the Santi Commander," he said briskly. The window snapped shut. He waited for what seemed eternity before he heard the massive iron bars being slid out of their locking position and the doors swung open.

A young man, in his mid-twenties greeted him. He wore highly polished chain mail armor. His hair was long and nearly yellow, as was his elegant moustache. His tunic was black with the familiar red fleur-de-lis cross standing in stark contrast to the plain white cross on the general's tunic. "Solamina Fortress Commander Emil Brighton, at your service, General. Come on in. Shall we take some wine in the Great Hall?"

He seemed pleasant enough, thought General Hecate, who had never actually met this young replacement commander. "Yes, that would be kind of you." He followed the Commander, though his eyes glanced around the complex. He saw signs of numerous fighters, all well armored similarly to their Commander. Many were women, he noted. "Well-built fortress," he commented to Emil, and he actually meant it. The quality of workmanship was clearly visible, while Solamina's stonework left much to be desired.

The Great Hall was well lit, but far too austere for the General's tastes. Two others were already present at the Great Table, which could seat dozens at one time. "Allow me to introduce my wife, Matilda, and my second in command, Saxon Bye." The General nodded to each. He could not remember seeing any woman as homely as Matilda, however. He decided that his taste in women vastly exceeded this Commander's! He took the offered seat facing the three of them. Matilda poured four gold goblets and passed them around.

"What brings you to us today?" Emil wasted no time in asking. Forthright fellow, thought Hecate. Maybe I can reason with him.

"I have a small problem that I hope you might be able to help me with — it's these darn taxes that must be paid to Megalos each year."

"Ah yes, how is that coming along? Nearly done, I expect," Emil commented.

"Ah, yes, as done as we can be. As you know, the Church and Megalos expect every citizen to pay one gold coin each year. Our count of citizens is around one hundred twenty thousand. While the city folk here pay their taxes willingly and without any problems, I am having a good deal of trouble with the outlying towns."

Saxon could not resist, "You mean those people are unwilling to pay their just taxes?"

"Oh no! No. They pay them all right. No it is these darn bandito fellows. They keep on robbing the tax collectors. Only a couple days ago they stole the entire sum that my collector received from Amerios! So it has gone all season. Now that we have finished the collection, because of the thefts from the banditos, I find myself thirty thousand gold pieces short this year. What am I to do, I asked myself. I had several choices. I could double the city entrance fees; I could double the individual taxes within the city here to cover the losses from the outlying areas; I could even double tax the outlying towns. But between us, I don't want to place any further burdens on our wonderful people." He tried to make it seem as if he had the best interests of the city in mind.

Hecate continued, "I know that your organization, Santi del Dio, also has the welfare of the common man as one of your prime directives. I thought that perhaps we could work out some kind of an arrangement, where by the Santi might loan me the missing funds." Well, he had finally said it. They could only laugh at him and that would be the least of his worries right now.

Emil answered just as he predicted he would, "You of course have some collateral that is worth at least thirty thousand gold coins and a plan by which to repay the loan in a timely fashion?"

At least he was being polite about it, Hecate thought, and was responding just as Hecate would have responded had the Santi just asked him for a loan. Before he could answer "no" to both accounts, Emil spoke up.

"General, we will gladly donate thirty thousand gold pieces to your fund, providing a few, simple requests are met on your part."

Hecate was taken completely by surprise! He could not believe his ears or his incredible luck! "By all means what requests?" he found himself blurting out rapidly without thinking of what he was saying.

At this point, Saxon leaned over the table slightly. "We know what is and has gone on in your Nunnery, especially late at night." He proceeded to outline a theoretical scenario, based upon what the Santi had learned was going on in the Zargarb Nunnery. The General's face turned red and then ashen. Saxon knew that he was not too far from the truth.

Emil said, "We will *give* you the funds providing that three conditions are met. First, today, immediately, we are given total, free access to the Nunneries to go and bring out of there and into our fortress any and all women who have been brutalize or maimed or mistreated. They become our responsibility. Second, we are allowed access to the Nunneries or any place else such deeds are occurring at any time, to remove to safety any woman being mistreated or who has been maimed. Third, you and your men will desist in maiming any further women in this sector. For god's sake man, why don't you just hire some women who are willing to trade sexual favors for a week's food supply?"

He could not believe what he was hearing! He half expected they wanted him to leave the sector or something equally impossible for him to do. But just their whores? Never in a million years did he think that their play toys would be worth a gold piece, let alone thirty thousand! "That is all?" he asked in complete and utter disbelief.

Emil answered, "Yes, that is all. Will you agree to those terms?"

"Yes, yes of course, immediately, if not sooner!" Hecate declared.

"I must warn you not to break your word. If we find that your men or priests or anyone under your control have mutilated another woman, then our fees for delivering your precious cargos will double. For each new woman mutilated, the fee will double again." Emil's voice was very stern and commanding. He wanted this man to realize fully that he meant what he was saying.

"Doubled?" Hecate said in wonderment. "No, no, you have my word. Please, give me sufficient time to spread the orders and see that they are complied with!" He had visions of doubling and doubling fees, completely bankrupting the whole occupational force.

"Agreed. If you are ready, I will go arrange the funds, while Saxon and Matilda and a small group of my people will go with you right now to check on the Nunneries and retrieve any women they find have been harmed," Emil replied.

"Agreed! I thank you ever so much," Hecate answered. The two leaders shook hands sealing the bargain. At once, Saxon and Matilda led the General back outside. He was more than a little surprised to see a squad of women Santi fighters lined up ready to march behind them. How could they possibly haven know about this, he wondered for days afterwards?

By nightfall, thirty-three women were recovering inside the Santi fortress, their wounds being examined or attended to by the Healers. Many were later shipped off to Velona to speed their recovery process. No one saw another pigeon take flight from the top of the Santi tower late that night. It flew due north a very long way. A lengthy message was affixed to its foot.

Chapter 6 Two Thieves

Pieta, the sector adjacent to Solamina, experienced an entirely different situation. When the Emperor arrived, Barcarole Occala, the head nobleman of Pieta, argued with the other High Council members. He won the chance to bargain with the Emperor. His bargain saved the city. It is illustrative to recall that fateful day when he dined with the Late Emperor Justinian of Megalos, whose army of Centurions was camped outside the walls of Pieta.

Six of the High Council members, including Barcarole, rode up to his lavish tent. At least Barcarole had listened to the Sisterhood representative, who had insisted on keeping some of the council members safe inside of the city, just in case of treachery on the Emperor's side. "Greeting Emperor Justinian, very pleased to actually meet you," Barcarole exclaimed in his usual jubilant business manner. "All these many years we have been doing business together and yet we have not met." He offered his hand, but Justinian rebuked it. An aide whispered that no one was allowed to shake the Emperor's hand. If it bothered Barcarole, he made no outward sign.

"Come, let us dine," Justinian said in a grand manner, deflecting the awkward moment, gesturing toward the lavishly set table. A luncheon meeting was Barcarole's favorite time to conduct important business, and he was in his prime setting. The other five council members totally deferred to Barcarole in most matters and did so again here, letting him handle the conversation.

After some small talk, he said, "And how may Pieta be of service to you? Long have we been perhaps your best shipping partner. I will freely admit to you that Megalos uses well over half of all our ships. For years now, it is Pieta ships, which bring spices to your land, moves coal and iron ore to your foundries, even grain from the Greenway. In all these years, Pieta has never been blessed with a royal visit of the Emperor of Megalos. Indeed, sire, we are extremely honored and proud to have you come to our fair city. As you no doubt have seen, the gates are wide open to you." Mentally, he ticked off all the key points that he had wanted to interject into his opening remarks, designed to convince the Emperor that they were allies, not warring enemies.

Justinian, taken completely by surprise, tried to look as nonchalant as possible while he hastily thought how to react to this unexpected turn of events. "It is true that a good deal of our shipping is handled by Pieta, although you realize that the precise details are left to those in charge of such affairs. Seldom am I directly involved in these matters." He could not outright say that this war was to elevate him into history by retaking the lands that were lost by his predecessors. He could not say I want all your money and ships.

"Oh, I understand perfectly. A leader leads and shouldn't manage all the details, that is why we have our aides and managers. If we tried to manage everything, we'd have no time to lead. Surely, there is something that Pieta can help you with, shipping, finances, supplies. What can your shipping ally do for you today?" Cleverly, Barcarole shifted the focus to that of an ally and aide that could be given, hoping to deflect any latent animosity that may be behind the Emperor's war against the Sea Princes.

Poor Justinian, he could not just say I am here to conquer you or I want to take back Pieta, which was stolen from us by the barbarian invasion so many years ago. A shrewd politician, he was quick to size up a situation. "Ah, well you see I have a couple little problems in Megalos. My people, particularly the Senate, are demanding that the Sea Princes be returned to our control after we were forced out by the Galts. Between you and me, I think that they are feeling the lost revenues. Worse are the demands from the Church of Jehosanity. I must tell you that the church now has the backing of most of the citizens of Megalos, so I cannot just ignore their requests any longer, which are two. First, they want to be able to establish their churches here instead of the heathen Tur and the perverted Northern Orthodoxy churches. Secondly, they wish me to disband forcibly, if necessary, this association of women called the Sisterhood, which they believe totally perverts the role of women on Tarra. But we are businessmen first and foremost," Justinian added, knowing full well he had almost no interest in commerce, except counting his revenues, "I'm sure that we can come to some agreements on these without the use of force of arms." He added that last to make sure that Barcarole did not lose sight of the fact that he had his army camped on the doorstep of Pieta.

Barcarole stifled the urge to chuckle. Justinian had just given him his fondest desire on a silver platter! Long had he been opposed to the Sisterhood, as his father before him. He found it disgraceful if not utterly revolting and disgusting that women would band together in this Sisterhood and operate outside the boundaries of Pieta society. Money would not be a problem, because he'd just raise the shipping fees to cover any taxation Megalos might place upon Pieta. Further, he cared little for religion, but all of Pieta was tacitly followers of Tur, the God of the Sea, being primarily mariners. "Is that all that this is about? It's hardly worth all the bother. I'm sure that we can work out an equitable tithe to send to Megalos; after all, being shipping allies, what is good for you is also good for us. Your church can build all the churches it desires in Pieta, I don't think anyone would protest in the slightest. Mind you, most follow the sea god here. As far as the Sisterhood goes, why you will find many of us here in Pieta that believes the same as your church does. In fact, I will go so far as to say that you will find strong support here for abolishment of the Sisterhood."

Justinian smiled, knowing that he had just conquered Pieta without lifting a finger. "Well, as far as the taxation issue goes, I am sure that I can convince the Senate to accept a gold ducat per year per person in the sector. That would be low enough so as not to place any hardships on your citizens, am I correct?" He was demanding the same amount from the other conquered cities, however.

Barcarole realized this was the same amount Megalos demanded years ago when they had control over the city. However, he had another compromise in mind. "I am sure that I can sell that amount," he coyly said, adding, "providing we don't have to have all those Holy Paladins riding roughshod over the city and outlying towns. The High Council will monetarily guarantee you those funds each year, providing we aren't threatened by those supposedly holy men. With that compromise, I am sure I can obtain their full agreement. Any deficit between the amount collected and the amount needed would be made up by the council."

"Oh, that is more than equitable, Barcarole, splendid indeed! You have my word that these Holy Paladins will be instructed to only provide church security here, nothing more. However, what can we do about this Sisterhood mess?"

"Leave that to the council, My Lord. It is only a just compromise on both sides. We will meet this afternoon and send you word later today." He looked at his silent fellow council members and added, "I'm sure that we can convince the others of this just and fair agreement." The two men shook hands to seal their pact. With that, the six High Council members left and headed back into the city.

Yes, shortly after that, Justinian made Pieta his key supply base, having lost all the supply depots on the opposite shores of the Med Sea to the Santi. All during the war, Megalos ships ferried their supplies into the docks of Pieta, dock hands unloaded them, goods stored in warehouses, until they were needed by the army. The Sisterhood was disbanded; however, they all quietly walked over to the Santi fortress. From there, many were ferried over to join the others in Velona. A few fighters stayed at the fortress and became Santi.

General Thadeus Tassos took control of Pieta. One of the youngest generals in the Pope's army, he had high ambitions. "The Pope will be watching my every move," he had convinced himself. Unlike the other two generals, his would be a severe challenge. Because the Emperor had made a bargain, now he could not make and enforce the Pope's wishes! Bishop Theophilus was assigned to Pieta to oversee the priests, destroy this pagan Tur worship, and get the peasants converted to Jehosanity. This was a tall order, under the circumstances. Thadeus was not in total control of the sector, as he had been promised. Worse, he had to abide by the Emperor's bargain as well.

Daily, the two men met attempting to work out just how they were to carry out the Pope's orders. Neither man wanted to send a message to Pope Yazi I outlining the unexpected turn of events, asking for different orders from His Holiness. "Donkey's ass, I cannot convert souls this way!" Bishop Theophilus bitterly complained to Thadeus. "Every time I try to convince a man of the merits of Jehosanity, he just ignores me, saying something about Tur is the mariner's god."

Thadeus sympathized with the older priest, wishing he could just issue the ultimatum, attend church, or forfeit your life. "Have you been able to locate a building for your first church?" He wanted to change the subject over to one to which he was not involved.

"No, every time I find a suitable building, the owner not only wants me to pay him for it, but also at double its real value! The swine!" He'd only been able to acquire the ex-Sisterhood inn, and that, because they had evacuated the building. It became the official Nunnery.

"I have an idea, why don't you choose which buildings are best suited to your needs. Once our Emperor has finished conquering the Sea Princes, which should be fairly soon, I will meet with him and explain how things are not working out for us. I'll demand a slight revision in our charter, allowing you to confiscate said buildings," Thadeus suggested, hoping the priest would take the offered bait. If he did, the Bishop would be deeply in his debt. You never can have too many people deeply in your debt — that was Thadeus's motto. Cultivate those obligations and one day, call them in, when you really need the assistance and backup. The Bishop fell for his suggestion wholeheartedly and left to make his survey and list.

Sometime later, news reached Pieta of the death of the Emperor and the near destruction of his mighty army on the borders of Velona. Immediately, General Thadeus recalled all his men that had been stationed in the outlying towns and villages. He concentrated his entire force of twenty-five hundred Holy Paladins within the walls of Pieta. He half expected to have to with stand a siege by the Santi del Dio. Yet, after a time, that did not materialize. His head swelled with the idea that the Santi must think highly of the fighting prowess of his Holy Paladins, because they had not attempted to retake the city by force.

Now was the time for him to make his move. Accompanied by a large force, he visited the head nobleman, Barcarole Occala. "Ah my fine General, so good to see you again," the fat old man covertly greeted the General's grand entrance into his official office that fateful morning. "How may I be of service?" Barcarole mentally checked off all the obligations that the Emperor had insisted upon; all had been satisfactorily handled.

"There are going to be some changes made around here. First, I have a list of buildings that are going to be donated to Bishop Theophilus for his new churches, donated free of charge. Occupants are to be given two days to vacate the premises. Second, beginning next Sunday, all people of Pieta, and I do mean all, must attend one of the Bishop's Sunday Services. Consistent failure to attend results in instant death by our hands. Third, I make all the laws in Pieta now. Your High Council can still run all your trading, however.

I have no intentions of interfering in your commerce."

"But that was not the bargain that I made with Emperor Justinian," protested Barcarole, sweat beads beginning to form on his brow, which he hastily dabbed with his embroidered handkerchief.

"Do I need to point out that Justinian is dead? Now I am in fully in charge of Pieta. I make the rules, I make the laws, and I enforce them as well." Barcarole became very nervous. How could he ever possibly explain these demands to the High Council? Besides, they would not agree to them. He attempted to weasel, "While I might desire to follow your three points to the letter, my good General, I am sure that the others on the High Council will not go along with them, especially stealing so many fine buildings from their rightful owners. Perhaps you should explain this to the High Council. I can arrange a meeting later today." He attempted to side step the issue, hoping others would rebel openly.

"Not a chance. It is your group; you tell them. I give you until suppertime to begin having the occupants start moving out, or face the consequences. That is all." The General left abruptly, without giving Barcarole any opportunity to say anything at all or to try making counteroffers.

When Thadeus returned to his office complex, he asked his aide, "Have you got the locations of Barcarole's children discovered?"

"Aye, Sir. Located them all. Squads await your orders, Sir!" he saluted.

"Excellent. Tell them if they have not heard from me by dark, they are to execute Plan A at once. Are the spies in position, watching the buildings on the Bishop's list?"

"Yes, sir, all in place as we speak. They have orders to notify you at once if any show signs of packing or departing the premises as ordered, sir!"

"Okay, that will be all," Thadeus smirked. He knew that he could now finally show these backwards bumpkins that he meant business, real business, not the back slapping manner of the foolish Emperor. After all, where had that gotten him? Dead, that's where. No, Thadeus was strong and virile. He would never make such ill thought out deals as the late Emperor had. His Church depended upon him, his Pope depended upon him, and he would not let them down. Besides, he missed the pleasures of a young woman or boy, preferably a boy. "It's been too long," he mused to himself.

He ate his diner slowly and deliberately, confident that after putting up these long months with the silliness enforced upon him by the Emperor, he could now do things the proper way. "Matter of days," he said, toasting himself with a red after-dinner wine, "just a matter of days."

Shortly, his aide entered, saluting, "Good news, sir! It's done. Simultaneous strikes on all locations. Targets destroyed, sir, everyone in each home. Also, a couple civilians were in the way, got them too."

"Excellent, excellent. Now we wait a short while. Keep the men alert, dispatch me when you see compliance. I want to see those buildings vacated. That'll be all." His aide saluted crisply and left.

Next morning, another aide brought him further news. "Sir, Barcarole and wife are dead. Caught them trying to sneak aboard a ship, trying to flee the city. He was carrying this," he plopped a large, velvet bag on the table. Curious, Thadeus dumped its contents on the table. Hundreds of gems of various sizes, shapes, and colors rolled across the table.

"Kind of him to donate a fortune to me," Thadeus commented dryly. "Give all the men double rations today and a bottle of wine each, with my compliments." The aide saluted and left smiling broadly. His General always rewarded his men nicely.

Across town in one of the slummier sections of Pieta, the oldest section of the city, two twins sat in their parent's shop, crying. News had just been brought to them of the slaying of their parents, who had been out for a walk, celebrating their twentieth anniversary. According to the messenger who brought them the bad news, apparently, they had been in the wrong place at the wrong time. A mob of Holy Paladins were charging into a noble's house, and they had been cut down just to get them out of their way — a senseless, useless killing.

Telma and Tino Tergio were sixteen year old twins, sister and brother. Both had average builds, with the typical yellowish hair and sky blue eyes commonly found in the Sea Princes. However, Telma was very homely. Tino was also, but it didn't matter so much to him. In fact, growing up, the two had suffered daily taunts by other children, who often called out to them, "Hey look, there goes the UD," meaning Ugly Duo. Telma never had a boyfriend, and now that she was sixteen, she had given up hope of ever having one. Neither of them had any real friends, for who would associate with a pair of UDs? Evidently, no one was their conclusion; hence, they stuck together, supporting each other and their parents.

Their father ran a lock shop from a small ten-foot building attached to their main building, in which their mother ran Tillie's Tea and Vino. This was a small, cozy teashop where average folks would come to sip tea and sample the marvelous breads and wide variety of cookies their mother made fresh each day. A large sign prominently displayed stated: One Cup of Vino Per Person. This rule Tillie adamantly enforced, saying this was not a pub, but a vino taster's club. Both teenagers helped their parents run both businesses. However, the lock smithing business had been growing slower and slower, ever since the invasion. The teashop continued to have loyal customers and really had been supporting them the past year. Their two older brothers had joined the Crusader Army, but neither had returned from the war.

After burying their parents, Tino was forced to sell off much of his father's supplies to deal with family bills. However, both twins moved all his equipment into the back of the teashop where they lived. He put a For Rent sign on the door of the old locksmith shop. If they could just get someone to move in there, that would really help with the bills.

Both twins were experts with locks, having spent long hours with their dad. Both twins were expert bakers as well, having assisted their mother since they could barely walk. The twins now began to concentrate on running the teashop. Perhaps their story might have ended here had other events in life not come their way.

During the day, Tino only would walk openly on the streets, purchasing the various baking supplies, especially the exotic spices used in many of the cookies. Telma refused to set foot outside during the daytime hours. She'd refused to be taunted and teased any more. At sixteen, she felt mortified by her looks and did not even have a mirror in their home any longer. The taunts did not bother Tino much, but he was not expected to "look pretty and appealing." He mostly ignored the catcalls cast his way as he went about his business.

In sharp contrast, the many locals who frequented the teashop did get around during the day and constantly discussed current events over tea and biscuits or cookies. Thus, the twins heard all about everything many times over during the course of the day. Most of the news now centered on all the new current demands and laws that the Holy Paladins were enforcing. Again, the twins could care less about them.

At night, their favorite pastime was watching the stars. They sat for hours on the rooftop of their home. In fact, they had discovered an interesting thing when they were around ten. At night, they could walk from roof to roof without being seen. By sixteen, these two considered the rooftops of Pieta their own private world! They knew this section of the city by rote, but only from roofs. On the streets, the world looked ominous, threatening, and unfamiliar for the most part. One thing that Telma loved to do was to dance to the stars on their roof. "If only I looked like everyone else, I could be a dancer in the theater." Tino had heard her say this a thousand times by now. Frequently to make her happier, he would even be her dance partner for a short while. When he did, he'd see her magnificent smile, but those were the only times she smiled. Seeing her so happy more than made up for his discomfort at roof dancing.

After the devastating loss of their parents, Telma did not want to dance much, so instead they began long roof walking. Actually, they would pass over all the roofs on a block, climb down into a dark alleyway, cross over to the next block, climb back up, and continue on roof walking. To avoid attracting notice, they never spoke. Instead, the two developed a unique set of hand signals. One finger pointing down meant it was safe to head down; if it pointed up, safe to climb up, for instance. Flat hand meant caution; someone was coming. In fact, they could almost carry on a conversation with their hands. Slowly they became familiar with more and more areas of the city.

Because the temperatures were becoming quite chilly at night now, Telma made them a woolen sweater-like suit. Dyed black, their tight fitting woolens completely covered their bodies. She also had a head-stocking hat that pulled down over their faces, with holes for their eyes, nose, and mouths. Now they could scamper about and not get cold. Tino complimented her and added, "We are almost invisible now." This was her main idea; no one could easily see their black forms at night. No one could ridicule or tease her if they couldn't see her. Now she enjoyed their roof top times even more.

One morning while they were working their teashop, she filling orders and he baking more cakes, the gossip turned ugly. One older woman was talking to her usual circle of friends, "Did you hear what happened last night down by the stables? They found a dead boy! Stripped naked he was, some say that he had been, well you know, harmed in the wrong way, assaulted you know what I mean."

"Who would do that to a child?" another wanted to know.

"I heard it was old Jamilio's boy. Went out for choir practice and didn't come home!" a third added. "What's our city coming too when it isn't safe for a young boy to walk the streets of an evening? I won't let my Josine out at night anymore; I'll promise you that. Isn't safe!"

"Well, I heard that the priest said that the boy had left around eight along with all the other choir boys. It must have happened on his way home. Who would sexually attack a boy? A girl, now that I can understand. Women around here have always had problems, though I do admit it had gotten much better when the Sisterhood was here, you know, before the Centurions came. It must be all these foreigners that's what I think."

"Oh I agree," replied the first woman. "It's them Unholy Paladins! Look, they killed all of Barcarole's children didn't they?" She saw Telma listening as she refilled their teapot. "I'm sorry dear child. I didn't really mean to upset you so. I know, they also killed your folks. No justice, that's what I say. They come in here and are above all law. Now there is no real justice around here. Someone ought to teach them a good lesson, that's what I think."

"Yes, oh yes indeed. You have put your finger on it, no justice for Pieta citizens. You think them Unholy Paladins are going to hang those who killed Barcarole, his family, and the Terzio's? No way, I bet their general went and gave them a medal. No justice, that's what we are in for."

"You are right on that, no justice. Someone really ought to make them pay for what they've done, but was that boy really sexually attacked? That is frightening. First, it is we women, and now our boys. Whatever is happening to our lovely Pieta?"

"You think it is all right for us to get assaulted?" protested the third woman.

"Oh heavens no, Beth. I mean, well, you know, we've always had to put up with that. Now we are supposed to put up with our boys too?" the flustered woman countered.

Telma moved away to other customers, "No justice" still ringing her ears. Later, visibly upset, she whispered to Tino, "I think we may have seen them last night. By the stables, dumping that boy's body, we saw it. Oh Tino." He hugged her and let her cry on his shoulder for a minute.

"Yes, sis, there isn't any justice around here anymore. It's all gone, just like our parents, all gone."

Later that night, by an unspoken agreement, the two found themselves sitting on the roof of the dockside stables, not far from where the boy's body had been found. The air was cold and clear; the stars seemed close enough for Telma to reach out and grasp them in her black hand. The sooty smell of home fires, so commonplace, did not distract her from the freshness of the night.

After a while, they heard voices coming from the mow just below them. Perhaps it was the brutal death of the boy last night that caused them to act; perhaps it was just fate. From the roof, they could not see what was happening below them. However, the hayloft doors were ajar and a thin beam of light shone outward. The rope and pulley system used to lift the hay from a wagon on the alleyway below them rocked gently in the sea breeze blowing in from the Med Sea. "Let's swing down and take a peek, shall we?" suggested Tino. Carefully, they tied one end of the lift rope to the chimney. Together, they slid down the rope and peered in the half opened loft doors.

Both were shocked at the sight before their eyes. Telma stifled a scream. A Holy Paladin, his pants down, was attacking a young boy, perhaps twelve years old. The boy had his hands tied together and was hanging by them from a rafter hook. All his clothes had been torn off. Each leg was tied to side supports, exposing his genitals. The remains of his shirt was tied around his head, muffling his cries. The man was running his fingers up and down they boy's exposed torso. His back was to them. The twins snapped at that instant; they had to do something.

A flurry of hand signals followed until they had formed a plan on which they both agreed. They climbed back to the roof. Tino made a noose in one end of the rope, while Telma carefully measured the rope and tied the middle to the chimney, lowering the other end back down by the loft doors. When they were ready, Tino, carrying the noose in one hand, and Telma slid back down the rope and peered in, his back was towards them still.

Quietly, the two crept inside, the hay muffling their footsteps, along with the muffled cries from the boy and the soft-spoken words from the man. In a flash, Tino threw the noose over the man's head, pulling it tight. Simultaneously, Telma kicked the man hard in his groin, doubling the man over in intense, sharp pain. Together, the two pushed the Holy Paladin out of the window. He fell down several feet and the rope jerked hard, either breaking his neck or strangling him, the two did not check which. While

Tino picked up the Holy Paladins gear, Telma released the frightened boy. Tino, disguising his voice, told the boy, "Run, get out of here as fast as you can." He grabbed the remains of his clothes and obeyed, crying and staggering down the loft ladder. Quickly the duo climbed back up to the roof and made a hasty exit onto a rooftop a block away, where they crouched down out of sight, catching their breaths.

"Justice came for the boy," Telma whispered to Tino.

Later that night, the two returned to their home and examined what Tino had confiscated. They now had a short sword and dagger and a money pouch with two gems and coins worth nearly ten gold pieces. Tino used some of the funds to purchase a heavy crossbow and a supply of quarrels.

As expected, the next day's gossip in the tearoom centered on the miraculous rescue of Finian's boy from the grip of a sexual predator, an Unholy Paladin. Everyone was talking about the mysterious two black men who had rescued the boy and hung his attacker, complete with his pants down for all to see. For want of any other identification, the locals began calling them the Black Avengers. Tino actually saw Telma smiling frequently during the day, as she listened to all the gossip. They had done something for justice, he concluded.

That's how the Black Avengers began their long career of doling out their form of justice. Armed with the gossip of the day, they knew who had been robbed, where other crimes had been committed, or who had been wronged by these unholy overlords. By night, they donned their disguise and went about rectifying situations.

Because of their skill with locks, sometimes they merely retrieved someone's stolen funds, taking away a little extra for all their trouble. Other times, when they actually caught an act in progress, they took matters into their own hands. They found an effective method: first fire a quarrel into the opponent's chest or back, while immediately afterwards stabbing with their weapons. Weekly, their fame rose, especially here in the slums of Pieta.

As the years went by, their successes grew. However, one ongoing situation they still did not understand nor have a grasp on. Several times, they had witnesses a half dozen or so Holy Paladins breaking into a home and snatching a young woman, who often had to be knocked out to keep her from wildly screaming. They carried her into the Nunnery, the ex-Sisterhood inn in Pieta. By all accounts, the woman was never heard from again. From all the gossip, they realized that quite a large number of young women had been abducted over the past ten years, though they had seen only a few occur.

Frequently, they spied upon this Nunnery late at night, but it was built like a fortress. The duo could find no way inside, except the usual street entrances. However, most alarming, on more than one occasion from deep inside the building, they had heard women screaming as though in massive pain. They paid particular attention to the hints that the Bishop let drop during the attendance-enforced Sunday Services. One night before they intended to do their rooftop dance, Telma commented, "This Good Marks-Bad Marks thing must be tied in to the women that have been abducted. As near as I can tell, the ones we know about all refused to bow down to the Holy Paladin's silly rules about women."

"You know, maybe we have it backwards. These so called Holy Paladins are actually Unholy Paladins. So maybe women with Bad Marks are doing good things and to get Good Marks they have to do bad things," Tino suggested.

"Well, that makes more sense than anything the Bishop espouses." After a pause, she added, "But why were they screaming? I swear that they were being tortured or something."

"Dunno sis, just don't know. I wish there was some way that we could find out, though." They decided to spend their evening roof time studying yet again the Nunnery. Perched high on the rooftop, they watched the deserted streets below them. Occasionally, a few drunks would stumble along the street heading home, they presumed.

Around midnight just as they were about to head for home, they spied someone lurking in the shadows across the street from the Nunnery. Hand signals flashed, and the duo began to watch this person carefully. The moon appeared briefly from behind some clouds, revealing the man more fully. Hastily, he stepped back further into the shadows.

"He's a Santi. I recognized his face. I've seen him around the city, from time to time. I know he isn't wearing his fancy tunic, but that's him," Telma whispered.

"I think you are right, sis. What do the Santi have to do with this Nunnery? Are they somehow involved?" Tino answered her. "What's he up to anyway?"

They watched even more closely now. Soon the man, after glancing in all directions, began to move away down the street. Hand signals flashed, and the duo carefully dropped to the ground, crossed the street, and climbed upon a warehouse roof. Soon they had regained sight of their suspicious Santi. As far as they were concerned, the man was actually sneaking down the street, darting into alleys, or dropping down behind water collection barrels outside homes to avoid being seen when someone ambled near his position.

"Whatever he is up to, he does not want to be seen. Come on; let's follow him. How did he get into the city at night anyway?" Tino wondered. He knew that the gates were all secured at dusk. An energetic half hour passed for the twins as they went up and down, from block to block, following their secretive Santi man. He appeared headed straight for the docks.

An hour later, the twins, quite out of breath from the haste that they had to use to follow him, perched at the edge of the last warehouse building.

Before them, the docks stretched out onto the water. Five ships were moored, their boards and ropes creaking occasionally. They watched as the man looked in all directions before opening one of the dumping doors built into the decking of the dock. Fishermen used it as a dumping place for the unwanted parts of the fish they had caught. The man climbed down, pulling the door closed over him.

"Now what do we do?" Telma asked.

"I'm game," Tino replied. "Let's see where he went. We've followed him this far. I'm very curious about him. What's he up to anyway?"

"Yes, but that is down in the garbage dump. Are you sure about this?"

"I'll go down. You keep an eye out. Bird whistle if anyone comes," Tino suggested. Minutes later, Telma watched from her roof top perch as Tino cautiously opened the trap door. After a minute, he climbed down, closing the door above him. Telma began to worry and fret. She did not like this at all, but continued to keep watch vigilantly. After what seemed an eternity to her, Tino's head reappeared, and he flashed her some signs. With a sigh, she climbed down to the dock, snuck over to the trap door. Making sure no one was watching, she opened it and peered down. The stench of rotting fish hit her hard. After a bit, she saw the ladder rungs and climbed down to join Tino. She stood around at the bottom for a minute, while her eyes grew accustomed to the near blackness here under the docks. At last, she could see Tino's hand signals again. However, they had no signs for this situation. He whispered, "Tunnel, come on. He must have gone into this drain tunnel."

Cautiously, they crept into a large, brickwork tunnel. It was tall enough for them to walk standing up, for which Telma was grateful. They could hear the unmistakable footsteps of their secretive man ahead of them. Quietly, they followed him, wondering where this drain tunnel could possibly lead and why this Santi was in it in the first place.

The hairs on Telma's neck bristled, but she could not put her finger on why she was so worried. All seemed right. Then, she noticed it, silence. No longer could they hear the man's footsteps. Tapping Tino on his shoulder, she flashed the danger signal, but it was so dark that he could not see her fingers, so she whispered, "Danger. No sounds."

Just then, a strange, blue light illuminated this whole area of the tunnel. Standing before them was the Santi that they were stalking. The strange blue light radiated from his raised right hand. He had no weapons drawn, though the twins were totally startled and reached instinctively for theirs. He spoke softly and calmly. "Peace, I mean you no harm. I have been trying to meet up with you two for years now. I am called Sam Stone, the Second in Command of Fortress Pieta. You are the famous Black Avengers, am I not correct?"

Tino flashed a hand signal that said he would do all the talking; she was not to open her mouth. Trying to disguise his voice, though he knew not why, he said, "Yes, we're those whom the locals call the Black Avengers. What do you want of us and why have you led us here?"

"I have been trying to meet up with you two for over five years now. We have similar goals, helping the people of Pieta deal with this abysmal occupation. Perhaps we can be of assistance to each other. I know that you have been watching the Nunnery for some time now. I suspect that you have been looking for a way inside to see what is going on. I'm sorry for tricking you tonight, making you follow me here. I could think of no other way to tell you how you could get inside without being seen, except to show you myself. Yes, this is the secret tunnel that the Sisterhood built when they constructed their inn so many years ago. It looks like and acts like a drain tunnel. However, just ahead, there is a secret door on the left side that leads on into the inn."

"You have been spying on us? How come we didn't see you before?" Tino asked, that bothered him the most.

"A Santi is seen only when he desires to be seen. Tonight, I desired you to see me. Again, I am truly sorry that I had to bait you to get you to follow me. I am ordinarily a straightforward man." He noticed that Telma flashed Tino a sign with her fingers.

Tino said, "Could you show us this secret entrance that we may believe your intentions?"

"Follow me," Sam said, and led them a short distance further down the storm drain.

Tino spied what must be the unlock mechanism and flashed a message to Telma, who flashed back that she agreed. He said, "We would like to see what's going on inside the Nunnery."

"Actually, you probably do not want to do that," Sam cautioned.

"Well, we do," Tino said somewhat defiantly.

Sam sighed, "Do you have any idea what you will see inside there, especially in the basement?"

Tino had to admit that they had not the slightest idea. However, he kept it simple, "No." Just then, they heard the muffled sounds of what had to be a woman moaning, as if in great pain.

"No, not just yet," Sam held up his hand outward as if to say stop. "At the moment, there is nothing you can do for her. We must devise a foolproof plan. However, I cannot allow you to go inside the Nunnery without first doing my best to prepare you for what you will see in there, well, at least what we Santi believe that you will see in there. We now know firsthand what has gone on in the Nunneries of both Solamina and Zargarb, and it is just horrifying, almost too grotesque for words."

For the next five minutes, Sam outlined what he had learned about the Holy Paladin's nefarious activities in the basements along with the butchery of women ordered by the priests. "Removal of appendages seems to be their way of obtaining unwavering compliance with their orders.

Fingers, arms, legs, tongues, even teeth. Absolutely horrific! All done under the guise of obtaining Good Marks from the women. Actually, it's worse than that." He went on to explain about the sexual mistreatment that went on in the basements. Twice, Telma gagged and once vomited, so revolting were the images she formed from Sam's words.

"Is there someplace that we could routinely meet and discuss matters?" Sam asked at last. "We Santi would like to work with you to find some effective way to rescue these women and more importantly keep other women from replacing those that we free."

Tino wanted to trust Sam, but he was hesitant. There was Telma to consider. He flashed her some signs, and she replied. "When you wish to get a message to us, come and join the gossip crowds at Tillie's Tea and Vino in the slum section of Pieta." That was all he dared say, hoping that he had not revealed too much.

"Thank you. I have heard of the place. Now it is time for us to leave." He led them back out and made sure that they got safely onto the roof of the warehouse overlooking the trap door in the dock decking. Then, he went back under the docks, walked along the hidden seashore, stepped out into the sea briefly going around the edge of the wall that enclosed the city, before walking down the beach to the Santi fortress.

Once home, Telma broke down in tears. The news of what actually was going on inside the Nunnery was more than she could bear. Even Tino was deeply moved. "Those poor women, Tino," and she sobbed again.

After she calmed down, Tino sighed, "You know it is actually a good thing that we didn't find a way in there. What would we have done? Certainly, we'd try to rescue them. But honestly sis, how would we care for them? It's frightening. These Unholy Paladins must be destroyed utterly!"

Telma sighed too, "Yes, yes, you are right. How would we care for a poor woman with no arms or legs or teeth? I haven't the faintest notion. Their lives must be utter hell. I am sure glad the Santi are on our side in this. Maybe with all their resources they can somehow help the women we rescue. Do you suppose that's so, Tino?" He nodded hopeful agreement.

The next afternoon, the teashop was filled mostly with older women, but a few older, retired men were there as well. All were gossiping as usual, while sampling the many cakes and cookies and sipping tea. Sam, disguised as a dockhand, strolled in the door, looked around, and took a table, smiling at the only one wine glass per person notice. Telma recognized him at once, flashing a heads up sign to Tino. From the corner of his eye, Sam noticed the subtle finger motions and began to realize just who the Black Avengers were.

Telma came up and asked, "What will it be, sir? Specialty of the house is our superb oolong tea. You ought to try the pumpkin cakes." Tino kept a sharp eye on Sam, straining to hear from behind the work counter, where he was mixing up another batch of cookie batter.

"Ah, that will be perfect. I came in to relax and enjoy some good company." Telma smiled politely and went to fill his order.

"Well, you came to the right place for that," one elderly gentleman spoke up.

"Sure are," added another women at a nearby table. "The tea is really top quality. You don't find it in this part of the city, only over in the noble's section. Well, that was all before, you know, before they up and killed old Barcarole. He may not have been the most likeable man, so I've heard, but things sure did run a whole lot better with him around."

"That's right. No justice around here anymore, excepting those Black Avenger fellows," another man added. "I heard that Rosalita's oldest daughter got taken away by the Unholy Fellows last night. We've been talking about that before you came in. Have you heard about it?"

"Yes, that's one reason I stopped in here, to relax. I'm usually on the other side of the city," Sam replied honestly. "Had to make a delivery on this side, but after I heard about it, I felt sick. Figured I needed to calm down a spell, if you know what I mean."

"Well as I was saying to the others," the original woman interrupted, "they say that the Unholy Fellow, that's what we've been calling them since the priest outlawed our usual name, they say he was the very same man with the beady eyes that has been spying on us when we go to their," she coughed, "church." Several others laughed at her make believe choke.

"Near as we can tell, he's been involved in the taking of at least ten young women that we've heard about," added the original man sitting at the table next to Sam. He continued, "If he ain't careful, the Black Avenger's will get him."

"Well, I say good riddance and I hope they do get him. We don't need the likes of him around Pieta," the woman replied.

"What I wonder is what happens to the young women once they get carted away," Sam altered the subject slightly. Telma calculated that he wanted to see just how much the average person suspected was going on at the Nunnery.

"Nobody knows for sure," the woman said. "Their families are not often allowed in there to visit their children. Once, though as I recall, old Roscoe, he made such a stink that they let him in to visit with his daughter. According to him, she looked like she had been beaten up, bruises on her arms and legs. She wouldn't say much to her father and after that visit they never let him back inside."

"Well if it's supposed to be a safe place for women only, then I says, what are all those Unholy Fellows doing going in there late at night when they ought to be home going to bed? I've seen them going in there plenty of times as I was walking back here. You can bet that they are up to no good! It don't take no imagination to see what those Unholy Fellows are doing to those women."

"You are probably right," the woman picked up his idea. "I'll bet a ducat that they are molesting them girls! If the Sisterhood were still around, they would never tolerate such behavior. Why once, I saw one of them Sisterhood fighters cut a man's you know what off after she caught him with his pants down, molesting that girl, you know, the one who used to run the 8th street flower stall!"

"Some of those same Sisterhood fighters have joined the Santi del Dio," Sam added. "I've seen some of them around that fortress of theirs east of town. Sure would be nice if our Black Avengers could meet up with those fighters. Maybe between the two of them they could put a stop to all this nonsense." Tino and Telma picked up the suggestion, however.

"Dunno," the older man answered. "There are only two of them and thousands of these Unholy Fellows. How can two do much of anything against so many? Probably it is best if they keep on as they have been doing. Probably not many Santi in the fortress, never seen too many at one time, though I don't often go looking for them, if you know what I mean."

"True," the older woman added, "most of us are not trained fighters. I saw ol' Amalito try to stop them Unholy Fellows that were taking away his wife. Just as soon as he reached for the sword that the High Council gave him to use when defending the walls, they just cut him to ribbons. He never had the remotest chance. They are just mean, wicked fellows. Like we all say, around here there is no justice anymore."

"You can say that again," Sam replied getting up. He'd finished his tea. He walked up to the counter to pay his bill.

"Copper please," Telma said, watching him opening his money pouch. He handed her a coin and slipping a small piece of paper beneath the coin. Their eyes met, and he smiled, bowed, and left. She carefully picked up the coin and the paper. Deft fingers passed the paper scrap to Tino.

Later they both read the message several times. It was short. "Warehouse #5, 10 pm. Meet with Sisterhood."

They debated whether to go or not. At ten, there they were, resting quietly atop Warehouse #5, a largely abandoned warehouse. Commerce was down for some time now. Curiosity reeled them both in; they had to find out more. Again, they saw Sam's head appear at the trap door, the entrance of the refuse pile below the docks. Quickly, they slid down the drainpipes and crept over to him. He motioned for them to descend, which they did. Below, what could only be a Sisterhood fighter stood holding a special lantern that only emitted a thin, narrow beam in the direction she pointed the lantern.

"Glad you could come. Pieta Fighter Group Leader, Alice Augato. We need to talk. Will you come with us into the Santi fortress where it is safe to talk without being overheard?" She had a mellow alto voice that was melodious to hear. Telma nodded to Tino and he agreed. "This way," she said and the slow trek began. A half hour later, four forms slipped quietly into the Pieta Santi Fortress.

Neither of the twins had ever been in the fortress. In fact, they had only seen it from afar. Now they were inside. Their excitement tingled their feelings. Quickly, Sam led them all inside the massive tower gates. Once safely inside, he and Alice uncovered the hallway lights. "This way, we want to meet in the Great Hall."

To say that both twins were impressed with the size and decorations of the Great Hall would be a gross understatement. In their lives, they had seen nothing to which to compare the grandeur of this hall. They gazed about, marveling on the construction, the sheer size, the quality of the enormous table, and all the tapestries and paintings on the walls. They barely noticed the other people sitting at the table waiting for them.

Sam said, "You won't need to wear your masks in here. You are among your best friends in Pieta." Cautiously, the duo removed their masks, revealing their faces for the first time. "I recognized you at once in your teashop," Sam added. From Telma's stare, he added, "I spied your hand signals to Tino and his back to you. While I have no idea what you said, they were the same type of signals you used the other night. Simple deduction. Come, you are all safe here, safer than any other place in all Pieta."

They sat down where Sam indicated. Telma was a bit self-conscious about her homeliness. Tino hoped and prayed that none of these people would say anything about their looks. That would crush Telma. He himself didn't care anymore.

Sitting opposite the duo were four, three women and Sam. He did the introductions. "This is my wife, Willomena, and the Commander of Fortress Pieta. Jasmine Starkey, our Communicator, and Fighter Regimental Commander Alice Augato. She used to be the Pieta Sisterhood Fighter Group Leader, before she joined the Santi."

Willomena was perhaps five years older than Sam was. He looked to be forty; she had shoulder length black hair. Streaks of grey could be seen creeping into her locks. She had a matronly, stern look on her face. Most importantly, Telma saw that Willomena was not particularly pretty, though not ugly. Only Telma and Tino were the UDs. In sharp contrast, Jasmine was barely twenty, if that. She had blonde hair and blue eyes with thin lips. Her complexion was ghastly white. Perhaps she has been ill, Telma thought. On the other hand, Alice Augato, though forty-two, was very beautiful! Her well-developed bosom caught Tino's attention. She had blonde hair, tied back in a ponytail tonight and pale blue eyes. Tino had seldom seen such a beautiful woman. Yet her arm muscles were twice his!

Willomena began, "Black Avengers, welcome to our fortress! Would you care for some refreshments? I know the hour is late, but secrecy is paramount; we feel that we must act quickly." The two turned down the offer for food. However, Willomena sent for some tea all around anyway.

"Long have we Santi admired the good works that have been attributed to you two avengers. Should I keep calling you avengers?" she asked.

116

Tino flushed, "I'm sorry. No, that is just the name the locals picked out to refer to us. Tino and Telma Terzio, please."

"Terzio? Say, any relation to the couple that was killed when the Holy Paladins raided and killed Barcarole's children and their families?" Willomena asked, the name jogged distant memories.

"Our parents," Tino answered.

"I'm so sorry for your loss. They must have been wonderful people," Willomena replied sincerely.

"Well, now things make more sense," Sam added. "Your parents being killed by these bastards and you seeking some sense of justice." He tried not putting his foot in his mouth.

Thankfully, just then a man entered with a tray. He placed teacups before each of them and served Willomena first, and then the guests and the others last. He left without saying a word. Sam sipped his tea and commented, "Nowhere as good as the tea I had at your place this afternoon. Willomena ought to buy her tea from you two," he smiled. Telma took a sip, agreed with him, and smiled.

Tino noticed her smile and rejoiced! She had never smiled in public in front of others before! Willomena began again, "Let me try this again. For years now, we have been following your career from afar. We knew not who you were, although we have tried for five years to find out. I must say you two are very good at keeping your identity secret. My sincere complements. That is no easy task to do. By our reckoning, over three hundred five Holy Paladins have met their end by your hands. Countless others have been forced to pay recompense," she chuckled, "shall we say against their will? We also know that the recompense ended up with their victims. Actually, that is how you first caught our attention. Anyway, Sam finally came up with a scheme to finally meet up with you and just in time I believe."

"Sam has told you what we suspect has been going on in that Nunnery?" Both nodded he had. "I must admit that until very recently, we had no notion either. I was appalled by what we found out was going on in the Nunneries in Solamina and Zargarb. Actually, I threw up when I saw the mutilated bodies of those women. I've never seen anything like it, although I've heard it was much worse during the Crusade ten years ago. The problem we face here is that even if we know these men are doing similar mistreatment of women here in Pieta, the treaty we agreed to ten years ago prevents us from actively attacking the place and rescuing those inside. Besides, there are thousands of them and only hundreds of us. We would be greatly outnumbered."

"First, however, we must know if these men are actually mistreating or harming the young women that they have taken over the years."

Alice pounded her fists on the table in anger, attracting the attention of everyone.

Willomena added quickly, "If they are, Alice will not rest until we do rescue those women." Alice calmed down, her point made; she was a woman of action, not talk.

"Thus, we must find out what is going on inside that place. Here is where we desperately need your help. I'll let Alice explain her idea, since she came up with it. Alice."

"I used to live in that inn. I know it inside and out, forwards and backwards. There is a way inside, but it will take someone with the skills you two have. On the third floor, there is a storeroom with a window. That window does not have any lock on it, for who could get up to a third floor window. However, during the last renovations, that storeroom was sealed off from the new hallway. It's only ten by five. We put a secret sliding panel in the hallway, so that we could get to this space if need be. Well, ok, we used to store valuables in there," she admitted.

"If you can somehow reach that window, you can get inside. I have drawn up a very detailed map that you can use. Find us the evidence that I need, or we need, please, for these women's sake."

"I wish we'd known this long ago," Tino answered. "We've been looking for a way in there for years."

"Had you gone in unprepared for what you would likely be seeing, you very likely would not have made it out," Willomena said sternly. "Honestly, I'm mortified by what I saw there in Zargarb."

"You were in Zargarb?" Telma asked, rather confused.

Willomena found herself having to explain about the Guardians. She gave the twins a detailed outline. "So you see, one of our telepaths joined with the woman who had been inside and we all saw what she had seen while she was a prisoner there. In order to prepare you for what we think you are going to see firsthand, though I hope and pray you do not see there, our Communication, our telepath, Jasmine here, is going to join with your minds and allow you to see her memories that we all saw that night from the poor woman that was rescued."

"Will it hurt?" Telma asked.

"Not at all, rather the opposite," Jasmine spoke for the first time. She had a soft, very quiet voice, bordering on timid.

"Will you see everything in our minds?" Tino asked, more than a little concerned for his sister's safety.

"I will only see what you voluntarily decide to show me. I will not pry or probe; I do not want to know your secrets, if any, nor do I want to know your personal thoughts. Those are yours, not mine. I will just replay into your minds what we all saw in the mind of the poor woman that night. Is that all right with you?" Both nodded. "If the images are too horrifying and you want me to stop, just say so. I warn you, they are as bad as Willomena has said. Yet, you need to know actually what to expect, if and only if these men are doing similar things to their counterparts in the other two sectors. It might not be this bad here, god, let's hope so."

"Oh!" exclaimed a startled Telma, as Jasmine touched her mind. "It's ah, like, er, um. . ."

"Intimate?" Jasmine whispered.

"Yes!" both Tino and Telma said in unison, relieved to have the precise word that described another being joined with themselves and their minds.

Remember; just think "Stop!" and I will. Brace yourselves; this is really awful. Jasmine returned to that night when the massive Mind Link allowed the entire Santi Guardians to see just what had happened in Florintine Junction's Nunnery. Telma and Tino could not distinguish their own moans, groans, curses, and emotional turmoil from vast mixture contained in the awful scenes being replayed for them within their minds.

When she finished, both Telma and Tino were simply sobbing. They had no words to describe how they felt. The torture and mutilation was far, far worse than anything they could have imagined another person could do to another.

At last finding his composure, Tino, grateful that these Santi gave them this period of quiet, said, "You think that's what's going on here? My god. We must act now, tonight. We have to do something!"

"Yes," blubbered Telma, "no matter the cost, we must try to help them somehow."

"Again, I reiterate," Willomena insisted, "we don't know if that is happening here. It might not be so here in Pieta. I doubt it could be any worse."

Timidly, Telma volunteered, "Yes, it could be. It could by very young boys. Tino and I have eliminated quite a few Unholy Fellows molesting boys who are not even teens yet. Why would they do such things?"

"How can they do such things and claim to be holy?" Tino angrily stated. "Two faced liars!"

"It's a matter of viewpoint," Willomena attempted to speak truth, but she quickly realized that neither twin could understand that and dropped it. "Boys, oh dear me. We thought those might just be isolated perverts. I see what you mean. Well, enough talk. I agree, let's get this spy trip going. Alice, will you go over the map with them, while Sam and I see that everything else is all set for action?"

Alice got her detail drawings out and moved between the twins, spreading the drawings on the table so both could see. "I am so glad you are willing to help us! You don't know how much this means to me and the rest of us. We ex-Sisters feel so helpless right now, suspecting horrible things are being done to women and unable to do anything about it."

"They may have gotten away with it for ten years now," Tino declared, "but tonight, they are going to pay the piper, if I have anything to say about it!"

"I'm with you all the way Tino! So is every Santi fighter here! Now here's what you need to do." She showed them the specific window in question, isolated high on the third floor. "I keep telling Willomena and Sam that it is impossible for anyone to get into that window! It's just not possible," Alice declared flatly.

"Oh, that's particularly easy to do," Telma replied. "We've done much harder actions. We could get in that window with our eyes closed, right Tino?"

"Sure thing, sis. Piece of cake to get in through that window, even if it's locked. The tricky part is sneaking around inside a building full of people and us not knowing the floor layout. That's the hard part. We are never seen or don't want to be anyway. Easy to do Alice. We just slip down a rope and into the window. Might take all of two minutes from start to inside."

Alice looked at him shocked, "You, you are kidding me right?" She hoped that he was, for maybe they were playing with her.

"We're serious," Telma spoke before Tino could think of any proper reply. "Three minutes if the window is stuck and we have to force it open quietly. We've done this many times to get retribution from certain of the Unholy Paladins. It's just challenging to move around inside an unfamiliar room in the dark. We don't ever want to be seen, you see. One of us stands guard while the other opens their safes. Sometimes I open them, sometimes Tino does. He's better at it than I am, I have to admit."

Convinced, a broad grin lit up Alice's face. "You two are simply amazing! I could never do that. I'd be frightened of falling. Just thinking about being that high up on that roof and near the edge gives me chills and a knot in my stomach!"

"Oh we love it up there at night. Then no one can look at us and call us the UD." As soon as she blurted that out, she bit her lip, wishing with all her might that she could retract her words.

"What do you mean UD?" Alice asked, never having heard the term.

Tino stepped in before Telma started crying. "Ugly Duo. The kids called us that nearly every day while we were growing up. We try to avoid being seen in public as much as possible. It really upsets Telma, but I've grown used to it. We are both about the ugliest looking people I have ever seen. Up on the roof tops at night, no one can see us and we can be free to express ourselves as we want."

"Huh? Ugly? Well, have you looked in a mirror lately? Me, well I believe that men used to think that I was a knockout blonde or something. Everywhere I went, men would stare at my boobs. Yes, I know that they are rather large, but they are just boobs, you know?" Telma stole a glance at Tino, his face reddened slightly; he had been staring at them, no doubt about that. Whether Alice noticed him or not, she didn't let on, but continued. "My dead husband and I used to get in these fights all the time. One night he actually stabbed me! Can you believe that? Here, right here." She pulled up her chain mail and blouse to reveal a nasty four-inch long scar on the left side of her belly. "I never dreamed anyone would ever actually stab me, such never entered my thinking, only how to deal with all the whistling and catcalls and wanna go out with me's that I perpetually received. Well, after that shock, I returned the favor. Okay, I admit that I was slightly carried away and cut his throat. He had it coming! Scaring me for life. Anyway, after that I joined the Sisterhood, hating men, all men. I'd go down the street and every whistle reminded me of what bastards men actually are. All that finally changed when I met Ket and the other Guardians. Now I have found there are some men I honestly do respect and admire."

"Oh where was I? I know. Ugly? Well, okay two points, Telma. One, some women are born with better features than others are. While I have seen some women who looked very bad, you are not that bad looking, not at least now. That's why I asked if you have looked at your face in the mirror lately. You might not have looked so great growing up, but now that you have matured and your body caught up, you are average looking, if you ask me. I think you are selling yourself short. Two, we are all spiritual beings; we are not our bodies! Any man who desires you solely because your body looks sexy is not worth a hoot! I assure you that, when the luscious babes get old, their bodies don't look all that appealing either! No, you want to cultivate a relationship with a man who appreciates, admires, and respects you for who you really are, one vibrant, dynamite person, that's what I think. Honestly, though between you and me, I will admit that I never thought this way until after I met Ket and the Guardians. He forced me to rethink a whole lot of my notions about men."

"Are you going to philosophize all night or are we going to get going?" Sam teased. He'd entered and overheard her last monologue.

"Just waiting on you slow men," she jested back at him. The four left the room and headed back outside.

Sam explained, "Jasmine is up on the tower's roof and will be watching. As soon as you two are in place, she will Mind Join with you and relay what you are seeing to the rest of us. If any trouble develops, we will come busting in that building to rescue you. Have no doubts about that. We have your backs covered. Already fifty fighters are in that tunnel I showed you, ready for the signal to bust in fighting. Alice and I are going to accompany you to the Inn overland. Once you are ready to go up, she and I will position ourselves so that we can watch all sides of the building. If we see anything, we will give a whippoorwill call. How's that sound?"

They set off at a brisk pace. Within a half hour, the four stood on the dark, deserted street, looking up at the imposing three-story Nunnery. Dressed in their invisible black outfits, the duo was hard even to detect. Both nodded to Sam and Alice and turned to leave. Tino carried the rope that they would need, and the duo slipped quietly around the building until they found the familiar drainpipe that came down from the roof. Alice positioned herself so that she could watch them ascend, while Sam ducked around to the opposite side. Alice stared in utter amazement as the two barely visible forms shimmied up the drainpipe. "I could *never* do that!" she whispered to herself.

Once on the roof, they disappeared for a moment, reappearing with the rope in hand. Tino had secured it to the chimney. She watched as the rope dropped down to just below the window. Still fascinated, she saw both black forms slide down the rope, stopping at the window. From this distance, she could not see what they were doing. Then one of the forms did a flip and disappeared inside. Immediately the other followed. "Amazing, truly unbelievable!" she commented to herself and then steeled herself into guard duty. She swore that she'd let nothing harm this pair of Avengers. Alice felt the gentle touch of Jasmine in her mind. Now she could see what the twins were seeing. If needed, she could relay instructions to the twins, should they be lost or confused.

Alice spotted something of interest to her. She saw that these two used hand signals, just as the Sisterhood had. Although she watched their motions, she could not tell what the signs meant. As expected the storage room was empty. The new tenants had not discovered this concealed room.

Tino found the latch that opened the secret sliding panel in the wall. Cautiously, he peered out into the dimly illuminated hallway. A lone oil lantern, whose globe was quite blackened and in need of a cleaning, provided a nighttime light, should any of the nuns living here need it. Tino flashed a sign indicating "what luck, light." Telma smiled, they certainly made it easy for thieves. The two stepped out into the hallway. Now would come the hard part. They needed to examine each room, in search of the incriminating evidence, should there be any.

If the Pieta Nunnery was operating along the same lines as the one in Zargarb, then here on the third floor, they ought to find those women, who if they had been harmed, would be fully healed of their wounds. The worst cases would either be on the first floor near the nuns or in the basement. The duo crept silently up to the first door. Tino tried to turn the knob. It was locked. Telma moved beside him, her father's lock pick in her hand. A moment later, a tiny click announced she had unlocked the simple mechanism. Tino tried the knob once more and it gave. Ever so slowly, he opened the door, hoping that the door would not creak and awaken the room's occupants. The Sisterhood who had refurbished the inn so many years ago had settled only for top quality products. It opened silently. Tino peered inside.

It was black. A small amount of light from the dim hallway allowed him to make out the sleeping forms of three women, perhaps in their late twenties. They were sleeping in one bed and had warm blankets covering them. How am I supposed to tell if they have been harmed, he wondered. Telma flashed a sign; he backed out, and she ever so slowly crept into the room. She moved close to the bed and carefully observed the sleeping women. One moved a little and her right arm slipped out of the covers. Telma suppressed a gasp! There was no hand on the end of it! She backed out just as quietly as she had entered, then re-locked the door.

They tried several more rooms, but with only one additional certainty, one woman had been blinded. It was just too dark to tell, and they dared not uncover the sleeping women. Hence, they moved down the stairs to the second floor. Here many of the rooms were vacant. However, they did hear soft moaning behind several doors and dared not open those. The occupants definitely were in some kind of pain. Jasmine sent the suggestion to go try the first floor instead.

They calculated that on this floor the nuns themselves were probably sleeping. However, as they reached the bottom step and peered around the corner, they saw two nuns moving about, back and forth from one room to another. The two appeared engrossed in what they were doing and did not even glance in the direction of the stairs. The duo continued to peek. One nun carried a bowl with a reddish liquid out of a room. Another entered carrying a roll of cloth, bandages perhaps. Straining their ears, they barely head one nun say, "There, there, dear. It will be all right. You will heal and then you can really set about your life long task of earning Good Marks. We here all want your soul to go to heaven. You know that. How many times have we told you that? Too many. We warned you to listen, well now you have no choice but to earn Good Marks. You can praise Jehosa that your soul will now find salvation in the eternal bliss of Heaven. There, there, stop your crying. You will be just fine. Now try to get some sleep. We will be right here if you need anything, just call out. Now it's lights out." The nun extinguished some lanterns in that room and left, leaving the door ajar. What shocked the twins the most was that the nun sincerely believed wholly and utterly what she had been telling the poor woman!

Now that the nuns seem to have retired, the twins prepared to walk down this long hall to the stairs to the basement. However, at that instant, Tino heard the far off call of a whippoorwill. Jasmine relayed the warning: a Holy Paladin was walking up to the door. The twins held their position, however, curious about what would happen next. They heard a soft bell clang a couple times, and a large nun, hastily pulling a robe over her nightclothes came out of one room and headed for the main entrance. The twins strained to hear what was said, although the conversation was faint from this distance. They could only make out part of it.

"Why so late?" the woman asked, irritation in her voice.

The muffled sound of the man was hard to make out, something about having just gotten back in town from a long trip or expedition.

"She's not ready; she's sleeping."

Something about taking anyone.

"Well, all right then, come on," the nun said. She led the Holy Paladin down the distant stairs that led into the basement. After a time, she returned, went back into her room, and closed the door. The duo ignored Jasmine's request to leave. Instead, the two crept along the hall silently. They reached the stairs, paused to listen, and then began to descend. At once, an awful stench assaulted their noses, almost causing Telma to vomit. They could hear noises coming from below and continued down the stairs. At the landing, they halted and peered cautiously into another hallway. Many of the crudely built rooms did not even have doors on them. Sounds of activity came from the other end of the building so they began to move out onto the stone floor of the basement hall. Dried reddish-brown substances on the stone appeared here and there. The place was definitely in need of a good scrubbing!

As they passed by some of the open rooms, they peered inside. Several held women who were heavily bandaged and bruised. While not mutilated, these women had been certainly badly beaten and regularly by the looks of their bodies. None looked healthy and most were sleeping fitfully.

The two crept closer to the room with the Unholy Fellow probably having his way with an unwilling woman. Cautiously they peered inside, ignoring Jasmine's now nearly continuous urging them to leave. What they saw appalled them! The man's back was facing them. The poor woman was gagged and tied securely. She was utterly helpless and moaning. Telma did not hesitate. Silently, but swiftly she closed the distance to the man. With all her might, she thrust her long dagger into his back, aiming for his heart! Tino, right behind her, put his hand over the man's mouth and slit his throat, silencing him for good. Blood sprayed all over the poor woman and the contraption to which she was tied.

Hastily, Telma removed the woman's gag, while Tino let the dead man's body slump quietly to the floor. "Shh," insisted Telma. "Don't make a sound." She began untying the woman's arms, while Tino freed her legs.

Now they had to figure out what to do with the body. While Telma searched it, Tino fumbled around trying to figure out how to ask them where the secret door to the tunnel was located. *I will drag his body out into the tunnel.* Two minutes later, he managed to open the long unused secret door. Just outside, he saw many fighters, just waiting for the chance to wreak havoc or rescue the women inside.

"Get her safely out of here," Tino said to the first fighter. He had no idea who was in charge. "Then, get all the others here in the basement out. We just have to get these women out of here tonight!"

Now the telepathic messages came fast and furious! Uncertain whom to follow, the Santi fighters hesitated. Sam took charge, overriding everyone. His orders came through loud and clear. *Do as he says. As soon as the basement is cleared, let me know via Jasmine. Tino, Telma, you two go light a smokey fire on the first floor near the nun's rooms. Make it smoky, but not a real fire. We don't want to burn the place down just yet. Yet it has to be smoky enough to convince the nuns to leave at once with the firemen. Once the firemen have the nuns out, then you Santi get all the other women out through the tunnel. Tino and Telma can unlock their doors for you. Once everyone is rescued, then we burn this place to the ground. Action time!*

The fighter leader smiled, "Thanks for forcing the issue, Tino! Let's do it!" Immediately women rushed into the basement, fanning out into the various rooms, while Tino and Telma gathered up some wadding to use for the fire. Carefully, they crept back to the first floor. With all the oil lanterns on the wall, it was very easy to make a fire. The tricky part was to make a smoky fire, a fire which would not impair the rescue of the women later on. Soon they had the smoke billowing throughout the hallway.

At that precise instant, Sam and Alice came bursting in the front door, crying loudly, "Fire! Fire! Everyone out now!" He motioned for Tino and Telma to join him. When the nuns began opening their doors, they saw and smelled smoke and saw a large number of firefighters.

Immediately, Alice began moving them to the main exit. "But we have to rescue so many women," protested the Head Nun."

"No, our orders are to get you most valued nuns to safety. Once we have gotten all of you to safety, we will go room to room rescuing everyone else. Your nuns are our prime concern, General and Bishop's orders. Now move!" She needed no further encouragement, after all the Bishop clearly ordered it.

Three minutes later, the nuns were all outside, looking at the smoke coming out. Sam said, "Go to the main church and rouse the Bishop. Have him prepare a place for the others we will bring safely out. Please hurry all of you." The ten nuns began running down the street. Sam didn't mention that the Bishop's location was halfway across town!

"How come they thought we were firemen? Are they blind?" asked Tino.

Sam winked at him, "They saw what they expected to see, firemen. Little trick of the mind, eh? Come on, we have lots to do."

Beginning here on the first floor, Tino and Telma went from door to door unlocking them. As soon as a lock was picked, three Santi women entered and began waking the women up, explaining what was happening, and helping them to evacuate to the tunnel in the basement. The women on this floor were heavily bandaged, blood often soaking through the white gauze. Most had to be carried bodily to the tunnel; they were only semi-conscious of what was happening to them.

As soon as the last door on this floor was opened, the duo raced up to the second floor. There were not as many to open here and it went quicker. As they finished up and headed up the stairs, they looked back to see the Santi helping many walk out on their own, though holding on to them to steady the women.

The third floor took double the time as the others. Here many women were kept locked up at night. The only positive aspect was that these women were at least healed of whatever wounds they had been given. Thus, their rescue went faster than the duo could pick the locks! Many had heard the noise and were already up, wondering what was happening. Thirty minutes had now elapsed.

Just as soon as they had the last door open, Sam ordered them to cover the walls with oil and set it ablaze. By the time they ignited the third floor fire, the last of the women were being escorted down the stairs. On the second floor, they repeated their steps, dousing the walls with all the oil they could find. Telma found several gallons in cans in one closet and sprayed it around with abandon! Once they set the second floor on fire, this time the fire really took off in a roaring inferno! Down on the first floor, Sam had already spread the oil around and was waiting on the twins to appear. "Down to the basement now!" he called out and he torched the first floor, with great satisfaction, I might add.

Once there, they ran into a backup of people lined up to enter the tunnel. While the duo waited, they splashed the last of their oil on the walls here and waited to light this last section. A short while later, they threw a lantern against the wall, it shattered and the walls quickly ignited. The duo dashed into the tunnel and Alice shut the stone door, sealing them off from the blazing inn. "So much for our Sisterhood Inn," she commented.

Unfortunately, the four were now at the tail end of a very long line of people. Because of the close quarters and the critical nature of the rescued women, they could not just barge past them. Telma was very worried and wanted to be of more help, but Sam consoled her, "They are in good hands. There are three hundred more Santi outside the tunnel and lined up along the shore. In just a few minutes, everyone will be safely within Fortress Pieta. You've done quite enough for one night, my dear." She flushed, unable to tell if this was a compliment or a rebuff. After all, she had instigated this by not following Jasmine's orders to leave and then killing the Unholy Fellow.

"I couldn't leave her like that, not when I could do something about it," she replied, having decided it was a rebuff.

"Rightly so. I'd have done the same thing had I been there," Sam replied putting her at ease. "Just don't tell Willomena that; she hates it when we act on impulse." He chuckled. "She always wants everything planned out just so. I think that our improvised plan worked just perfectly, don't you?"

"Yes very much so. We got everyone safely out of there, but I wonder if some still might not make it, you know, it sounded like they were in really bad shape," Telma continued.

"They are going to be looked at by the best Healers on Tarra, beginning just as soon as they get safely inside the fortress. See the line is moving now."

When they finally got outside the end of the tunnel, the twins saw the long line of Santi carrying the rescued women along the shoreline. Tino and Telma turned to go home, when Sam said, "Alice and I are accompanying you two. We are under orders to see that you arrive safely home."

Although they tried to protest, Sam would not listen. Since they would walk the streets, they removed their black woolens. As they walked, although it was now near midnight, many people were out and rushing in several directions. Even from the docks, the massive blaze could be seen, lighting up the otherwise dark night. "Won't they be suspicious when the women are discovered missing?" asked Tino.

"Not at all. As far as everyone is concerned, a number of very brave firemen also died in the devastating blaze along with the women they were attempting to rescue. By morning the inn will be ashes."

"But won't they get suspicious when they don't find any bodies?" asked Telma.

Alice laughed, "Everything will have been incinerated and collapsed into rubble. No one will think about being able to find any remains."

As they reached their teashop home, Alice gave Tino a big hug. "Thank you ever so much! Please, we would like both of you to come by the fortress tomorrow evening for supper. Many will want to meet you and to thank you for what you have done. Please come?"

Tino flushed red. No woman, other than his mother and sister, had ever hugged him. He stammered, "Of course, supper time." Telma grinned at her brother's embarrassment. As they shook hands, Alice slid something into Telma's hand, and she and Sam left before Telma could look or say anything. While Tino opened their door, Telma looked at the object in her hand, a small metal mirror. Did she dare look, she wondered.

She didn't until the next morning, just before they opened their doors for business. "Oh!" she exclaimed, "I don't look half as bad as I remember looking, Tino."

"I've been telling you that," he protested.

"Really, I am not so awful looking now, not like I was. Maybe you and I are not so ugly anymore."

"I think that we just grew up, sis, that's all. Come on; they are lined up to get in today."

Indeed, four women were patiently waiting for the twins to open. The talk all day was about the big fire at the Nunnery. Everyone said that it was a Holy Miracle that the nuns were able to get safely out. However, so many brave firemen had perished trying to rescue those women under the care of the nuns, to say nothing of the women themselves. The fire still burned during the morning, and they had fewer than normal customers. Anyone, who could, walked across town to see for themselves. Fortunately, the

Nunnery was in a block all by itself, so no other buildings were actually threatened. Again, it had been the original Sisterhood foresight to build their inn such that they would not be endangered by nearby fires, which did occur with some frequency in a city as large as Pieta.

By late afternoon, their tearoom was filled to capacity. Everyone was telling their views on the fire. Neither Telma nor Tino were paying much attention. Instead, they were thinking about suppertime. At last, they closed their doors and cleaned up. Tonight, they put on their best clothing, which was nothing particularly fancy. Together, they strolled across town and out through the eastern gate.

As they approached the fortress gates, the gatekeeper swung the gate open for them, "Been expecting you. Well done. Come on in. I've sent the pageboy to let them know you've arrived. It'll only take a moment." While they stood looking around at the inside courtyard, they marveled at how nice it looked by the light of day, well dusk anyway. The gatekeeper shut the door and placed the massive bolts into their locked position.

Shortly, Jasmine appeared beckoning them to follow her. They noticed that she looked particularly pale and worn out this evening. As if reading their minds, she explained, "I've been up all night, along with all the other Guardians and half the staff tending to the wounded. We're taking a break soon, and Willomena has asked me to escort you to the Great Hall. First, would you like to visit our infirmary and see how the women you've saved are doing? I know for a fact that many would like to thank you personally."

Both twins fidgeted, hating since childhood to be the center of attention, because it had always been the wrong kind of attention. Yet, they could not refuse and followed Jasmine. As they walked, Telma apologized, "I'm sorry Jasmine about last night. I just could not follow your orders, not when I could do something about it."

"Dear, no need to apologize or fret about it. I might have done the same thing if I had been there. He got what he deserved. Ah here we are. Before we go in, let me explain a bit. We rescued thirty-three women. Five are in critical shape, and our Healers don't believe that they will make it. Another half dozen are in poor condition; we had to do major surgery on them so that they might survive. Their wounds had become infected you see. Gangrene can be a terrible thing. Yet, our Healers believe they will make it. Twelve are doing just fine, their injuries, at least their physical injuries, have healed nicely. The others are on the mend, doing as well as can be expected. Actually, for the most part, the women are in better shape than those in Zargarb. Here we go." The three entered the infirmary.

What a difference. Gone was the stench of rotting flesh, replaced by a clean, sanitary smell that Telma could not place. Thirty-three beds lined a long stone wall. She could see Willomena and several other women working at the far end. Here at the entrance, a few Santi women were assisting the women. The first woman, the one Telma had seen, whose right hand was missing, was talking to the Santi beside her. "I'm not totally helpless, honest. Bellini needs our help more; she cannot see. Oh, Bellini," she said to the woman sitting on the cot beside her, "here they are — the ones who rescued us last night!"

She got up, came over to Telma, and put her arms around her, rather embarrassing Telma. Meanwhile, the blind woman got up, and the Santi led her to the twins. She felt for them and found Tino, feeling his head and face. "Bless you my son, bless you for getting us out of that hell hole!"

"You are more than welcome," Tino said, face turning quite red. Then, the one handed woman, whose name was Benita, led Bellini to Telma, while she then gave Tino a hug, and shook his hand with her left hand, further embarrassing him.

"I heard what you did, climbed in from the roof! I don't know how you did it, but I can kiss you for having done it!" To his complete embarrassment, she did just that!

Grateful for Jasmine's insistence that they continue and meet the others, the twins moved on down the line of beds. Several women attempted to speak, but their tongues had been cut off, and their speech was not very good. However, that they made the attempt pleased absolutely everyone! What pleased the twins the most, however, was the fact that no more than half of the women had been mutilated. The rest had just been raped, tortured, and beaten severely; their bodies still had all the right parts, which the twins felt was the most important thing. They still could see the vast mutilations in their minds, which Jasmine had shown them. Here in Pieta, it had not been so utterly horrid. Still, it had been bad enough.

Near the end of the line, Telma came upon the woman who had been being tortured and raped by Holy Paladin that she had instantly executed. She noticed that the woman's front teeth had been removed. Her arms and legs were nearly continuous bandages. Nevertheless the woman tried to rise up a bit, "Thank you!" she said, and Telma began to cry, giving her a gentle hug, hoping she was not hurting the poor woman. She later learned that the woman had severe internal wounds, and it was iffy if she would survive them.

Willomena was washing the blood off her hands, when they reached the last woman in the line. "Good timing, we have just finished here. She's unconscious, gangrene, lost most of the rest of her arms, poor woman." Telma leaned over the woman, who was as old as she was, and gave her a kiss on her forehead.

"Hang in there, you can make it, you have to," she whispered, tears streaming down her face. Tino put his arm around his sister, pulling her away, so they could follow Willomena.

"Oh yes, I almost forgot. Sam wants me to bring you two into the Santi dining hall first before we go eat in the Great Hall. All the Santi here want to see you and thank you two. I hope it doesn't embarrass you too much." She was preparing them for what she knew was coming.

They walked into the adjoining building, entering one massively large room, filled with tables. Hundreds of men, women, and even a few children were busily eating. As they entered, Sam jumped up and yelled, "Attention everyone. Attention." Instant quiet. "I am very proud and pleased to introduce Telma and Tino Tergio!" To the twins, he said, "The Santi garrison force."

The thunderous applause was deafening, but the yells and cheers were even more embarrassing for the twins, unused to even a hug. After what seemed an eternity to the twins, the noise settled down and Sam could speak again, "I know some of you are dying to meet them personally; however, you can do so after we dine in the Great Hall. Be patient, will you?" Many laughed, and all returned to their meal. Sam quickly escorted them out and into the Great Hall, where dinner was waiting for them all.

In the Great Hall, many places were set, although only the twins, Willomena, Sam, Alice, and Jasmine were currently there. Willomena said, "I hope you don't mind, but I have asked the women who have been pronounced healed to dine with us tonight. It will go a long way in their mental recovery to be part of society once more. I hope you won't find it too discomforting."

"Not at all," said Telma. They were just about to sit down when another Healer entered leading a line of a dozen of the rescued women.

Benita saw Tino and asked, "Can I please sit beside Tino?" No one had the heart to refuse her; she was reaching out to people, which many of these victims might never be able to do again.

"Sure," said Tino, and he helped her sit down, trying hard to remember all the manners his mother had once tried to teach him, which he had long ago forgotten. Belinda, who she constantly looked after, was seated beside her.

Willomena began officially by saying, "Tonight, we are gathered together to honor those brave heroes, those brave women who have sacrificed so much for Pieta." Sam called out "Here, here." Everyone clapped for the women.

Benita whispered to Tino, "We should be celebrating you two; you are the real heroes! I do hope that you don't mind sitting beside me, a hopeless, ugly cripple, who's going to need help with the meal."

"No, you deserve this and much, much more, Benita. I am honored that you desire to sit by my side; really, you have no idea how much. I mean you are not a cripple; you just need a bit of help cutting up your meat, that's all. Besides, you are not ugly. That's reserved for Telma and me." He looked at her; she was not ugly by any stretch of the imagination, but not a model either. She had long, blonde hair, blue eyes, rosy cheeks, and a full bosom. More than that, Tino admired her spirit; she was one spirited woman.

"You don't think I'm ugly this way?" she held up her right arm.

"You are awfully attractive, hand or no hand."

"Well, I think you are about the nicest, bravest man that I have ever known, that's what I think! What do you mean about you two being ugly?" Alas, over dinner, Tino began to explain about their childhood and eventually the loss of their parents. It felt good sharing that with another person.

"I lost my family too, when they came and took me," Benita explained, a note of sadness in her voice. "They were killed trying to keep the men from getting me. I was only twelve at the time. So I truly do understand how you must feel, Tino, and you are so wonderful to have looked after Telma all these years. She has a fabulous brother. I wish I had someone like you, but then my brother died of the colic when he was little."

"Say, I was wondering something," Tino finally decided to ask what had been troubling him since last night. "Those of you on the third floor, I mean, you all are healthy. How come you were not taken into the basement for the, well, you know what I mean, where the Unholy Fellows had their way with the others, hurting them so badly?"

"Silly, you mean why we weren't their sex toys? Simple, those of us who were smart finally figured out we had two choices, pretend to become a nun in training or become a whore to those filthy men. Cost me my hand to figure it out; Belinda, her eyes."

Belinda leaned in their direction and added, "But we figured it out!"

"We played along with their nonsense religious teachings, though I don't know if they would ever have let a blind woman become one of them. Still, it kept us on the third floor and out of harm's way."

"Now that's what I call good thinking! Well done, Benita, Belinda." He meant it; it was impressive to have undergone all that trauma and still had the sense to find a way out of the mess.

She smiled, pleased with his compliment. "We were always looking for a way to escape, Belinda and I and all the others, but we never got a chance. They kept us locked up mostly."

During dinner, Tino decided that he really liked this woman, more so than he cared to say. After the meal, everyone stretched and walked around chatting with each other. Mysteriously, Alice whisked Telma away, to where, Tino had no idea. However, he had no chance to follow, because Benita had put her good arm through his, insisting that he be her escort. She didn't know the Santi and he supposedly did. He tried to explain that he really knew almost nothing about them either, but she insisted he knew more than she did and refused to let him go. Strangely, Tino liked all the attention she was giving him.

Sometime later, Alice and Telma returned. When Tino saw his sister, his mouth fell open! Alice had cleverly found a very nice dress just her size. For the very first time in her life, Telma *felt* halfway pretty. Tino had always considered her wonderful, but it was her own opinion of herself that mattered. Grinning broadly, she danced over to Tino, with Benita still locked on his arm. "What do you think?"

"Stunning, sis. Wow."

"Thought so! Now I can face meeting all the others that we are supposed to meet," she declared with an enthusiasm that Tino had never, ever seen in his sister.

"You look positively radiant," Benita added, which caused her to smile all the more.

Willomena then led them back into the large Santi dining hall. The tables and chairs had been pushed back out of the way. Still quite a lot of people were milling around, chatting, and awaiting an opportunity to meet personally the Black Avengers, of which they had for so many years been tracking, but never finding. When they entered, the crowd stopped and moved toward the two guests.

For over two hours, the twins shook hands, received heartfelt thank you, and even hugs. Many stayed and chatted, asking all sorts of questions. Telma had several young men who insisted they were here to look after her, following her around. Actually, she was rather pleased by this attention, which had been denied a young woman for so long.

One young man named Johnny caught her attention more than the others did. He was quiet, respectful, and above all, he seemed to know what she desired at any moment, assisting her as though he could read her mind. For example, one young man kept bragging about how many men he had killed, hoping to impress her, for he knew that the Black Avengers had killed over three hundred of the Holy Paladins. Yet Telma was anything but proud of having done this and was very uncomfortable listening to him. Johnny merely moved her away from him, gracefully introducing her to another Santi ex-Sisterhood fighter. Repeatedly, Johnny rescued her, and she began to notice this quiet young man. He was about her size, not particularly athletic, not particularly handsome for that matter. Something about him caught her heart as no other person had, except her brother.

Finally, the hour was getting late. As the twins prepared to leave, Sam and Alice were once more assigned to escort them safely home, Benita, who still had not let go of Tino's arm, leaned over and gave him a loving kiss on his lips. "I hope you don't mind a woman who is a bit forward in her desires," she whispered. The bulge in his pants spoke mountains. No woman had ever kissed him like this before. He liked it and leaned over, giving her a farewell kiss as well.

When the twins were finally alone in their home, Telma said, "I think she likes you Tino. I am so glad that you let her be with you. She has so much to live for. I hope she can get over the trauma she has been through."

"I like her too, sis. Really I do. I mean I've never been around so many young women our age before. Yet, what does it all mean? I really do like her a whole lot more than anyone else there tonight. Maybe I am being foolish."

Telma gasped, "Tino! I do believe you are falling for Benita! Tino's in love!" she teased him and threw three pillows at him, before he wrestled her down.

When the two stopped laughing, Tino said, "Maybe I am." She smiled back at him, and Tino had never seen her look so beautiful before.

Two days later, mid-morning, a deliveryman stopped by the teashop. He came in carrying a large bundle of flowers. Of course, everyone in the room stopped chatting and eavesdropped on him. "For a Miss Telma?" Telma's face crimsoned, but she took them from the man, who turned and left. She stared at the bouquet.

"Well dear, who's it from?" one loyal older woman customer asked. "Look at the card, silly!"

She fumbled and found the card, which read, "To the world's most beautiful woman, Johnny." She mumbled, "Johnny."

"Oh, Telma has a suitor! Tell us about him! Is he a handsome fellow?" The gossip flew fast and furious. She found a vase and put them on the counter top, content to let the customers gossip about her. Tino smiled at her and winked, but she tried to poke him in his ribs.

Late that afternoon, the twins were surprised to see Sam walking into the teahouse. He smiled at them and looked around, then gave a hand signal. The twins wondered what he was doing here. Had some trouble developed? Both gave him a rather worried look, which evaporated a moment later when Johnny, with Benita on his arm, came walking in the teahouse.

She immediately let go of Johnny's arm and walked right over to Tino, "Can I have the specialty of the house, please?" In a whisper, she added, "And have you sit with me?" Tino grinned. He wanted nothing better than to sit with her!

Johnny walked up to Telma and said, "I see they came," pointing to the flowers.

Telma blushed, "Thank you." She whispered, "No one has ever sent me flowers before!"

He whispered back, "I figured." Aloud he said, "How about the house specialty?" He whispered, "And have you join me for a while?"

The twins served the three and then sat down with them, all the while, the gossip flew around them, but now they could care less. Johnny explained, "Benita here insisted on seeing your teahouse and insisted that I bring her. Of course, Sam would not let us come alone." Sam smiled, of course he wouldn't. Johnny was only in his sixth year of apprenticeship as a Guardian, Sam's protegee.

"I wanted to invite you two to supper tonight," Benita explained, "unless you have other plans," she added hastily just in case Tino might not want to come.

"No plans. I, we'd love to," Tino replied.

While the gossips gossiped, the twins showed the two around their humble shop and living quarters. It was not much to look at, but it was immaculately clean and well-tended. Finally, at closing time, they did not have to usher their last customers out as they normally did. Rather, they left, smiling and chatting about the twins. Tomorrow they knew that they would be the talk of the teahouse. Ah, but that was tomorrow. Tino took Benita's arm, while Johnny took Telma's. Sam led the way across town to the Santi Fortress.

Once safe within the Santi fortress, while everyone was milling around waiting for the call to dinner, Benita took Tino aside. She had a very nervous look about her. Tino sensed something was wrong. She said hesitatingly, "They, Willomena in particular, says that she is sending all of us to Velona to have their Healers help us recover. We're to leave when the next caravel comes in here. Tino, I don't want to go! I am all healed, see?" She waved her arm in front of his face. "I, I want to be with you. Please, Tino. I won't be much trouble, and I can help lots at the teahouse, really, I can. I am not helpless because of this." Again, she waved her arm in front of his face. "I, I, I think I am in love with you!" she finally blurted out what she had been wanting to say to him all day! She had rehearsed just how she would tell him this, but it had not come out at all the way she had planned.

Tino hugged her close and replied, "So that's what these feelings are all about! Love. I'll be. Benita, I'm in love with you too! Can you believe that? I felt so light that I could fly while we were walking here tonight. Only your arm kept me from floating away." Mutually, their lips met.

"Let me talk to Willomena tonight. I'll try to convince her to let you stay with us. I am sure that Telma won't mind. We can make up a separate room for you somehow." She just kissed him passionately. Tino knew that he wanted this woman more than anything else. Somehow love, love would not, could not be denied him.

After dinner, Tino managed to get Willomena aside to beg for a few minutes of her time. Shortly thereafter, Tino, Telma, Johnny, Sam, and Benita were escorted into Willomena's private study. Scrolls were piled everywhere; he'd never seen so much "education" as he called it. He was impressed with her, if she could read and understand all of this.

"Okay, Tino, you have my full attention. What is it that you wanted of me?"

Her stern countenance almost caused his knees to buckle. "Is it true, what you have told Benita? That she is being ordered to go to Velona for more healing?"

"Yes," she said flatly.

"But she is fully healed and she doesn't want to go," he replied.

"But there are very powerful people there who can help her remove the last vestiges of the horrible ordeal she has undergone."

"But, but, but we are in love! We don't want to be parted; she, I want her to come and live with me and get married in time, if things work out." There, he had at last vocalized it; he felt humiliated at having to blurt out his innermost feelings, but he had to try for his and her sake.

Sam came to his rescue, "Dear, we were young lovers once too, remember?" For the first time, Tino saw her flush.

"Tino, I do know of what I am talking when I say Benita really does need to go to Velona for a time to fully recover. However, I see no reason that you cannot accompany her. Will that be acceptable to you two?"

Benita bubbled, "Yes! Wonderful!"

"Sure," Tino said before he remembered his sister.

"Where he goes, I go," flatly declared Telma.

"Where she goes, I go," Johnny added just as firmly.

Willomena began laughing, "Do I detect a conspiracy among the young folks?" Sam laughed long and hard.

"Sam, are you going to let your apprentice go to Velona for a time? You certainly are *not* going to accompany him!"

"Sure dear, he can get far better training in Velona than I can give him here. Why, you might miss me?" She pitched a scroll at him in jest.

"Okay then you conspirators. You all go. Boat leaves in three days. Twins, I suggest that you temporarily close your shop. Put up a sign saying you are going on a vacation or perhaps a honeymoon trip. That will make your absence plausible to the gossips there. We certainly don't want your cover blown in any way over this." She then wagged her finger at Tino, "Young man, if when you get back from Velona and you then believe that I knew what I was saying by insisting that she go there, and then you, young man, must give me a hug!"

"What should we bring? We have funds. We can pay our way," asked Telma.

"Gracious me, no. You've more than earned a little escape from it all, dear child. Save your money. Just bring along a change of clothes. You may prefer to get new clothing in Velona; it's simpler than carting around a large chest. By the way, you best bring your savings here to the fortress where we can guard it. I don't want you returning only to find your teashop has been robbed.

"All of it?" asked Tino. "Er, I think that we will need some help bringing all of it here."

That night after Sam and Alice had escorted the two home, Tino took Sam into their back room to show him their accumulated savings. "This chest, this cupboard, these sacks," Tino went from place to place, showing him piles of coins and small gems.

Finally, Sam laughed, "We're going to need a packhorse!"

"Really?"

"Just kidding. No we will need a cart at least, plus an armed escort. I'll see to it." When the day for traveling came, Sam arrived along with a dozen Santi fighters, all disguised as local city guards. Indeed Sam pushed a cart piled high with the accumulated coins and gems of the twins through the streets of Pieta and into the Santi fortress. He promised to count it all and convert it into more easily carried and stored gemstones while they were gone.

Sam and Willomena watched as the caravel backed slowly out of their dock, waving to the foursome on deck. As the ship slowly turned about, Sam said, "You know the twins are awfully wealthy and do not even realize it? They've just been saving everything the acquired over the years, spending only what was needed to keep the teahouse in operation."

"I suspected so, dear. Now they may find that they have something very worthwhile on which to spend it. I do hope it all works out for them. They make such lovely couples, don't you think?"

"Yes, I thought so from the very beginning. That Benita sure has a lot of spunk in her, reminds me of you," he squeezed her rump.

She turned to face him, "Not there, silly, higher, no higher, no, ah, there you go," and their lips met.

Chapter 7 Shanghaied

Barcella, the sector adjacent to Velona, was in chaos after the fall of Justinian in 626. To understand the incredible mess that befell this sector, you must know what had previously happened as Justinian's Centurion forces swept into the sector. Seeing that the other cities had not suffered any apparent harm with their bargains for surrendering the city without a fight, the High Council of Barcella also sued for peace. Immediately that became a significant problem both to the High Council and to Justinian. At that time, this sector worshiped Jehosa and the common folk completely rebelled at the notion of having to adopt the Megalos version of Jehosanity. While the council surrendered the city, its population rebelled.

Bands of religious rebels routinely attacked Centurion supply wagons. Buildings were sabotaged; even lone legions were attacked openly. The streets were not safe for travel unless one was very well escorted with numerous fighters. In short, the High Council in surrendering to the same terms as Pieta found itself completely out of control of its population! The real power now fell into the hands of the local Church of Jehosanity and Tur leaders, who continually preached open rebellion against the council and the invaders.

Now Justinian faced a major situation. He could not continue down the line to attack Velona in an orderly manner. Somehow, he had to subdue Barcella. He expected the enemy to form up a battle line, and then both sides would close to do battle. Within a few hours or perhaps days, if the numbers were large, the war would be over. Here, the enemy never formed a battle line. Instead, large bands would suddenly appear, attack a supply column, kill as many Centurions as possible, inflict as much damage as possible, and then disappear as suddenly as they came. The tactic frustrated not only Justinian but also all his generals.

After a month, he had lost over two legions of men outright, with many more on the casualty lists. Valuable supplies had been stolen as well. His entire campaign came to a screeching halt in Barcella. "How in the name of heaven do we put down this rebellion?" bellowed Justinian for the tenth time. He was meeting with his generals once more. Blank stares told him he was wasting his time yelling at his generals. He fumed.

An aide interrupted his meeting, "My Lord, the Holy Paladins have arrived. General Sanchez wishes a word with you about this rebellion. Shall I send him in?"

"Hell yes! Maybe someone can tell me how to deal with this mess!" barked Justinian, highly frustrated. He was open to any suggestion that had remote merit.

In walked a tall man dressed in the familiar sky blue tunic with white cross emblazoned front and back. "General Ali Sanchez, at your service," the man said with a bit of an Arad accent. Justinian wondered about his ancestry, but motioned for him to take a seat.

"You are aware of the situation that we are facing here in Barcella, General Sanchez?" Justinian asked somewhat politely, pushing aside his anger for the moment. He should at least hear what this man had to say.

"I came just as soon as word of the rebellion of Barcella reached me. As you know, due to the chaotic situation in Zargarb and Solamina, I have been forced to leave five hundred Holy Paladins in each city to enforce your laws. However, while we may not agree on your not letting us control and enforce the laws in Vito, Pieta, and Bonilla, I have left only a hundred men in each city to guard the new churches springing up in those cities. The remaining seven hundred fighters I have brought with me. I believe that will be sufficient to put an end to the open rebellion here, My Lord."

"And just how do you propose to do that?" Justinian barked. He already hated this man after hearing these few sentences. The cockiness, the audacity, the air of superiority he exuded nearly forced the angry Justinian to smash in the man's face.

"Sire, we know how to deal with these rebels. Just give us a few days to implement the solution. We'll have the city and the sector under control in just a couple of weeks. These animals, these dogs, must be taught a lesson in a way that they can understand." He saw that Justinian was about to lose his temper, so he explained a bit further. "We will announce in each town and village that, if anyone there attacks or harms any of your men or us, we will immediately execute ten men, women, and children indiscriminately for every one of ours who is hurt in any way. Yes, we will be thoroughly brutal with public beheadings. After one or two of these public executions, you will find that the animals will behave. Give time for the word to spread. Now, if you will excuse me, I must get to work and bring your rebellion under control. May Jehosa be with you and guide you to victory."

He bowed and left quickly before Justinian could formulate a reply. He cared not whether the Emperor approved of his means or not; Justinian did not matter a donkey's ass, only the ultimate success of his church mattered to this man. The priests could not begin their work here until the rebellion ceased, and General Sanchez intended it to end quickly!

Justinian was about to say something, when one of his generals beat him to it, "My Lord, that is heinous, brutal, savage, and barbaric." It was refreshing to hear another say aloud what he thought, and it gave him time to calm down.

During the next two weeks, word that the Butcher had come to Barcella spread everywhere. True to his word, he did precisely what he said he would do. Every time that the rebels struck, his men came into the town or village and slew outright ten for one. Over one thousand men, women, and children were beheaded during those two weeks! He carefully saved the actual city for last, allowing word of his ultimatum to reach fully the city's population. Thus, when he finally entered Barcella, everyone feared this man and the blue tunic men under his command.

Still a few attacks were made on his men within the city walls. After he summarily executed fifty women and children, they too got the point. Finally, when he continued to slay citizens after even minor sabotages, all resistance quelled. Grandly, General Sanchez rode his horse around the city of Barcella, daring anyone to attempt any actions. None did and he pronounced the city ready for its occupation and implementation of the new laws.

Obliged to acknowledge the success of General Sanchez, Justinian was loathed to meet with him personally. Instead, he sent the general an imperial scroll, which merely said "Thank you for handling the situation." That night, Justinian slept poorly. "What have I unleashed upon these people?" he wondered. There was honor and glory standing upon a battlefield and defeating your enemy, but this outright slaughtering of the completely innocent, even women and children, was revolting, and utterly barbaric. It was conduct far worse that the Galts had displayed, and they were the barbarians. Justinian felt sick at his stomach and barely slept at night.

Indeed, the common man in the Barcella sector seethed with utter hatred of these despicable men, particularly the Holy Paladins and the Butcher. One of the Butcher's first actions upon taking control of the city was to begin the systematic killing of all the priests of Jehosanity, confiscating their churches for his own priests and the "proper version" of Jehosanity. However, the priests and their staff were too quick for him. Just as soon as they wiped out the first church, all the priests disappeared from view, apparently abandoning the churches. In fact, they went underground and for a time were hidden away and cared for by members of the church.

Understand also that originally the people of Barcella worshiped the Sea God, Tur. Only in recent years had about three quarters of the population converted to their own somewhat altered version of Bandar Dero's Northern Orthodoxy version of Jehosanity. Primarily the actual mariners still held onto the old ways of Tur, believing their lives and livelihood depended upon the Sea God. Both churches were thus in dire peril, and both had gone underground.

Shortly thereafter when the Emperor had been killed upon the battlefield and his remaining troops routed, fleeing in bunches into the city, the priests of both religions decided to meet to figure out the best course of action to take. Between the two sects, they had the full support of the population, except the nobles and their families, who had sued for peace, seeking profit over humanity.

Little is known of what was discussed at that meeting, those that attended the secret meeting have never been on good terms with the Santi.

Yet, from the events that occurred afterwards, an educated guess can be made on what the two groups did agree. Because of the Butcher's orders that ten innocents would be killed for every one of his men, everyone within the city and all the outlying towns and villages were under the strictest orders to not harm any of the Holy Paladins or their priests. If fact, they were ordered to "be nice and respectful and appear to be helpful" to these men.

However, when they were traveling in small groups far from the nearest village or town, they were fair game. The rules to which they adhered were two: none was allowed to escape, and all bodies buried so no one would ever find any trace of the missing men. This made it difficult for the Butcher. When he and his men went in search of the missing personnel, he found the nearby towns and villages totally friendly, quite helpful pointing out that his men had been here and had been given all for which they asked. No one had the slightest idea what happened after they had left. Some helpful villagers often suggested that with the amount of money that the men had taken, they might had left for home with all that loot. Of course, the Butcher could not and did not buy into these rumors, which began to spread like wildfire throughout the sector.

The next action outcome became obvious over time. The ships in the Barcella fleet were of the old style. Before the war, the nobles had spent a fortune purchasing one of Velona's new caravels, boats that threatened to sink their whole shipping business, their entire livelihood. As a result, the nobles began to hire the shipwrights to make copies of this single caravel. By September, the first shell was ready to be slid from the dry dock into the waters of the bay of Barcella. The nobles and their families held a large christening ceremony for the first new ship of the line, the Grande Barcella. Musicians played, ale, mead, and wine flowed, a gift from the nobles, ensuring a large attendance for this momentous occasion. The nobles were becoming very desperate to regain popular trust and good will, because so many things had been going wrong for them this year, and they counted upon this celebration to be the start of new beginning.

The musicians played a royal march as bottles of wine were cracked upon her hull. Complete with wild yelling and cheering, the Grande Barcella slipped down the slide and into the waters of the bay. Immediately the large ship listed to one side, then rolled over and sank. The sounds of music faded away, mid-tune. Gasps were heard everywhere. For a minute, the nobles and everyone else just stared in complete, utter disbelief! Thousands of gold pieces had just sunk. Six months later, one shipwright finally discovered the cause of the calamity; someone had "forgotten" to put the ballast in her hull. However, this news never reached the nobles.

Later that fall, the nobles had ordered the construction of a new warehouse to replace one older structure whose timbers had dry rotted and was not worth salvaging. In addition, the new one was to be three stories tall, tripling the storage capacity of the old one. Unfortunately, after the first floor had been filled and the new cargos of wine stored on the second floor, the second floor collapsed down upon the first floor, causing major destruction and loss of stored goods. Structural failure was the official cause listed. The Chief Architect discovered that "someone" had used a very soft pine for the support timbers instead of teak wood. He did not relay the findings beyond himself.

Mysterious fires sometimes occurred in the district in which the nobles lived. Somehow, by a freak accident, the water brigades found that the reserve water barrels had rotted; the water had long ago drained out. The list went on and on, a little calamity here, a little one there. Clearly to the Santi, this was sabotage, though for hours, the Santi debated whether the sabotage was deliberate and knowingly done or whether the sabotage was accidental, the result of suppressing a whole people.

Another factor that must be considered within Barcella was that of weapons. During the siege, more than half of all people living in the outlying towns moved into the city. Every available man and teen was given one or more weapons and helped man the walls. However, when the nobles surrendered the city without a fight, these men kept their weapons, refusing to give them up. In 626, nearly every home contained at least one weapon, sometimes several. For the first time in history, nearly every household in a country was armed, although few had any significant training in how to use the weapons.

The final factor that came into play in Barcella was the independent sea captains, who owned outright their own ships. Typically, a quarter of all ship captains in any sector owned their own ship and was not employees of some noble. However, one third of all the captains who flew the flag of Barcella, a sky blue flag with yellow moon in its center, were independent mariners. These men could pick and choose what cargo to carry, when and where. In ordinary times, these independents cut into the nobles' profits by about one percent overall.

These sea captains felt that the nobles had betrayed them and their city. During the first few years of the occupation, one by one, these men took their trade next door to Velona. Not only were they protesting against the Barcella nobles, but also because of Velona's prosperity, their own profits were greater. Yet, with their older, slower ships, the hauls that they received were usually hauling lumber for the massive new ship construction going on in Velona. Mahogany and teak were prized commodities, and these men made numerous trips between Velona and the western coastal regions of the Southlands.

Reggio Diaz, captain and owner of the Portly Pig, had just dropped off another load of mahogany and teak timbers in Velona; it was the year 630. An independent sea captain, this year had been his most profitable yet! The demand for tropical woods had so outgrown the supply coming from Lulu that he'd made more money this year than the last five combined! Now he was on his way from Velona to Barcella, his hometown and port. He'd accepted a small fee to deliver some grain from the Greenway. Now he was all set to put his well-thought out plan to the test. Would it work?

He had not docked in Barcella for some years, five to be exact. Not since his wife, child, and father had been executed, part of General Ali Sanchez's retaliation of ten for one had he been ashore. He could not face the city, his grief too strong. His wife had done nothing wrong, was not involved in any rebellion; she was only trying to raise their first child. Not even his father, a retired sea captain himself, was involved in any nefarious activities. His walking was very wobbly at best. Reggio swore revenge the day he heard the news from a passing ship.

Now, things were going to be different. He had a plan, a profitable one as well. It all stemmed from the tropical port town of Lulu, half way down the western coast of the Southlands. There the logging bosses felled the great mahogany and teak trees, turning them into logs for shipping to other lands far and wide. These logging bosses, who were making a large profit, used black skinned natives as either slave labor or paid them a minuscule wage. However, the tremendous demand for more wood, due in large part to the invention of the caravel in Velona, was at an all-time high. The black skinned natives made poor workers and were often caught talking to the trees, not chopping them.

The logging bosses now had to waste valuable manpower trampling through the jungle to find remote villages from which to steal able bodied men or find ways to entice more into such work. One of these logging bosses, called simply Diggor, was a good friend of Reggio. Together, they had devised the plan, which Reggio was about to execute. If it worked as planned, both men would gain monetarily, and Reggio would begin to extract his revenge.

Flying the sky blue flag with a yellow moon of a ship from Barcella, which he rarely flew these days, the Portly Pig slowly inched up to the dock. Soon the able dock hands had her securely moored and the gangplank lowered. Many hands began unloading the grain. Meantime, Reggio saw faces, which he had not seen for years now. Many recognized him and chatted with him. "Say is old Hermino still around?" Hermino had been a friend and a dockhand crew leader. An hour later, he met with Hermino at one of the local dockhand pubs.

After exchanging news for a time, Reggio asked, "Interested in making a little money on the side?" Of course, this perked Hermino's interest.

"Aye, times are hard. Take anything we can get," he replied, adding in a whisper, "especially if it hurts the Butcher."

"Aye, that it will do, that it will certainly do. Here's what I have in mind," and Reggio outlined his plan. For it to work, he needed the assistance of Hermino and some of his men. The two shook hands, sealing their bargain. Under the table, Reggio slipped a small pouch.

"Put a pinch of this power in their drink. That'll do it, just a pinch, mind you. We are to sail at high tide, which is tomorrow morning. Is that enough time? If not, I can delay until the next high tide. I'll make up some excuse."

"Better make up that excuse. Might take me til then to arrange it all. Have to be extra careful these days; you know what I mean. T'is a grand plan. Just wish you wanted more than two."

"Two at a time, Hermino, just two. I'll make frequent trips here. When you see the black pennant, that will be the signal that we need two more brought on board in the middle of that night. Don't do anything until you see the pennant flying."

"Right, I'm going to love this job! Great seeing you again. Figured with your wife being killed, you'd never set foot here again. Good to see you back, Reggio. Even more pleasure doing business," both men laughed and ordered another ale.

The next day, Reggio raised the small, inconspicuous black pennant. His men smiled as they watched it flutter; they already knew the plan. It meant more coins in their pouches, although they were already wealthier than they had ever imagined possible. Captain Diaz had really come through. Some even hoped that he might be able to buy one of the new caravels one day.

It was eleven at night. The two Holy Paladins sat in the dimly lit corner of the Slap Happy, one of the local dockhand pubs. General Ali had ordered his men to fan out, frequent various pubs, and listen in on the conversations around them. The purpose was to gather information, which might prove useful in tracking down the remaining renegades. Already they had consumed a fair number of ales. The barkeep came by with another round, which they eagerly accepted. "I do like this job," one said to the other after making a loud burping sound. "All the free ale you can drink!"

His companion laughed, "Perks, love these perks. Here's to the General, long may he live." They clicked their mugs and downed the contents, very large burps followed. A short while later both men were asleep. They did not notice the strong hands, which quietly pulled them up out of their chairs and out the back door. The barkeeper was being occupied by a minor scuffle at the other end of the pub, a scuffle carefully arranged. Once outside, a pair of dirty, worn out blankets were thrown over the forms. Four strong men secretly carried the two onto the Portly Pig, laying them down on the deck. At once, a money pouch changed hands, and the crew members carried the blankets below deck.

At dawn, the Portly Pig sailed quietly out of the bay of Barcella, bound for Lulu and another load of valuable timbers. Once at sea, mid-afternoon, Reggio went to check on his "passengers." He had built a secret compartment in the bow of the ship, just big enough to hold two men. He slid open the secret door, revealing the two Holy Paladins. Both men had been stripped of their clothing, wearing nothing but meager underwear. Their clothing and possessions had been safely ditched far out at sea. Both men were heavily chained, both wrists were fastened close together; both ankles were similarly tied. Further, both men now wore a metal neckband, and a chain held their necks securely to a support mast. Both men were tightly gagged.

Reggio removed their gags. "What's the meaning of this? We are Holy Paladins. Wait until General Sanchez hears about this! You will be drawn and quartered in the square!" one man bellowed, defiantly.

Smiling at his accomplishment, Reggio quietly said, "Oh I think not. I thought I would tell you where you are headed. You are now members of the chain gang of Lulu. You will be wearing these chains for the rest of your lives, however long that is. I hear it is not very long. Cutting down teak trees takes a lot out of a man. You two are now and forever more logging slaves of Lulu. Enjoy the trip. Your work begins in a couple weeks. Until then, the crew will bring you some rations twice a day. We want the slaves to arrive ready to go to work, now don't we? By the way, you can yell all you want to, we are far out in the Med Sea. Bye bye." He shut the sliding door, leaving both men in total darkness.

Two weeks later, his crew led the chained men off the Portly Pig. They were docked in Lulu for another load of timbers. Diggor was waiting for him, along with his top slave driver. "Ah, I see you have new workers for me. These look like strong, able men indeed. They will be at least twice as effective as the ignorant natives are. We should make a very handy profit. Please send more," both men laughed. The two Holy Paladins looked positively terrified. Their slave master cracked his whip and ordered them ashore. They disappeared out of sight. "Come, let's share a drink." The two men toasted the success of their plan.

During this time, Lyle had been observant. Every Santi fortress now had one of Niccolo Helios's inventions, the Far Seeing Eye. Lyle loved to sit on the rooftop of their tower and observe the city close up. He likened his view to that from a caravel crow's nest. He spotted the tiny difference in ships while they docked. The Portly Pig often flew a tiny black pennant. No other ship did. Subtle inquiries brought no information, just the notion that these independent captains often flew their own flags. Unsatisfied, Lyle continued to watch the Portly Pig whenever it was in dock.

One night he found what he suspected. Four men carried two long bundles on board very late one night. A few inquiries the next day convinced him. Two Holy Paladins had once more disappeared. This information, the shanghai of Holy Paladins, was relayed to the other Santi fortresses in the Sea Princes. Sure enough, Lyle received further reports of shanghais in many of the other Sea Prince cities. After some consultations with Velona,

Lyle was able to conclude that these hostages were most likely being used as slave labor in the logging industry somewhere along the western coast of the Southlands. Lulu was a likely location, because the Portly Pig made very frequent runs between Lulu and Velona, bringing much needed timber for the ship construction industry. While the numbers were small in comparison to the total number of Holy Paladins operating in the Sea Princes, every man lost was beneficial.

By 637, seventy more Holy Paladins had joined Diggers work crews, compliments of Captain Diaz. His total output of timber tripled. Both his and Reggio's profits soared even higher. Poor General Ali, men continued to disappear. He could find no pattern in their disappearance whatsoever! The only common thread was that normally a pair turned up missing at a time. Never more. No one, not even those he drilled or tortured had the faintest idea what had happened to the men. They had simply vanished while drinking in a pub! Unfortunately, he could not order his men to stay away from the pubs. They would likely mutiny. By 637, he gave up worrying about the mysterious loss of fourteen men each year. He had far more serious problems with which to deal.

Back in the spring of 628, General Ali Sanchez paced his command post. "Damn these infernal barbarians. Another patrol has gone missing! How many does that make now?" He was fuming, his face red.

Wiping the spray of spit with which his General had just blasted him, the aide replied, "One hundred forty-nine all told, Sir. Should I order another twenty people executed? If so, from what city?"

Just then, Bishop Lex Turthios walked in, "I just heard about the loss of another patrol, General Ali. I will pray for their souls. How did it happen?"

"Missing, just missing," Ali tried to calm himself down. It would be bad to show weakness before his Bishop. Word would certainly reach the new Pope Amir. "They were in Augar and left at noon. Got a hundred witnesses all saying that they left, even got a good meal before they departed. They were to be here by nightfall. No sign of them or their horses anywhere between here and that town! Vanished without a trace. Bishop, how can this be?"

"I don't know, my son, I truly don't." The bishop scratched his head, he really didn't. After a pause, he said what he came for, "I was wondering if you are going to continue your policy of executing another ten for one?"

"It's supposed to be twenty heads this time," Ali replied.

"Here or in Augar?"

"Heck I don't know! It doesn't seem to make any difference at all," he complained bitterly. "When I first came to this rebellious sector several years ago, killing ten for one completely put down the rebellion. Now, my men are disappearing like flies! No matter how many I kill or where, they just keep on disappearing! I don't suppose that you have had any word from Megalos that my men have been showing up back home have you?"

"No, no. No such word. I'm sure if your men betrayed you, they would have headed for home and their families. The Church has made discrete inquiries on your behalf, but none of the families has heard anything. I really think their desertion is just a local rumor. You know how rumors go; once they get started, they are impossible to quell or even disprove."

"Yet, I did come to warn you, General Sanchez, the Church can no longer support such a wanton loss of life in this sector. You've reduced the population considerably, many thousands. That translates to a loss in revenue to both the Church and Megalos. I am warning you: both are keeping a close eye on the reports. What with all the immigration to Velona and your extermination campaign, Barcella's head count has reached an all-time low. Barely a hundred thousand remain. This year the revenues from Barcella are down fifty percent from two years ago. That does not look good on your record, General."

Ali recognized that he had just been reprimanded, unofficially thankfully. He decided to pander to the Bishop a little. "How is your Scholastic University faring and the Nunnery?"

"Oh, our head counts show a steady increase. The boys are learning well and will one day become priests and missionaries in their own right. Admittedly, we do not have all the nuns that we had expected to have by this date. However, thanks to your work, we do have all the facilities that we need. This is, of course, a good mark on your record, General Ali. Just find some other way to retaliate, please." The general glared at him. The Bishop smiled, knowing that he had him right where he wanted the general.

He coyly suggested, "I have some news that might be of some assistance in helping you figure out just how to retaliate for the missing men." As expected, Ali looked up sharply. "We have just heard some news that one of the Deacons that was slated to be executed before he disappeared, is now living in Augar with the Rodrigo family, Deacon Azir, I believe." The deacon had fled Barcella right after the first church had been taken over and its entire staff executed.

Ali's face brightened up. "This is the best news that I heard in a month! Leave it to me. I will see that the sentence is finally executed!"

"Thank you, General. I must leave you now. I have a mass to deliver." He bowed to the General and left. Neither of the two men saw the serving woman leave a moment before the Bishop. They had not seen her all the while they were meeting, although she had twice refilled their wine cups. Serving wenches were not supposed to be seen. Jovanna was extra careful to follow all the rules set down by the Bishop and his enforced religion. Women were never to speak unless directly spoken to by a man. They were meekly to do their subservient tasks, quietly and without disturbing the men in any way. Before the Bishop had even gotten back to his church, a lone rider galloped out of the north gate, heading towards Augar.

When the fifty Holy Paladins arrived in Augar in the early evening, they found the Rodrigo home ablaze. They townsfolk claimed that they discovered the renegade Deacon was being given sanctuary by Rodrigo and his family. The town had taken matters into its own hand, or so everyone said, and burned them all alive. No matter who was asked, man, woman, or child, they all told the same story; they were all inside when the fire was lit and no one had come out. The renegade Deacon had perished in the inferno. That Rodrigo, his family, and the Deacon had moved out hours ago into one of the many abandoned homes left behind by immigrating townsfolk was not mentioned.

Shortly after this episode, the Green Crosses began appearing, quite suddenly in fact. The Santi, ever vigilant, were the first "outsiders" to observe them. In the cemetery of Barcella, hundreds of wooden crosses began appearing. Painted green or dyed green, made of various scraps of wood, each cross bore the name of a person. The Santi discovered quickly the names were those who had lost their lives to the Butcher's retaliation. Soon, thousands of the Green Crosses adorned the cemetery in the city as well as in every other town and village! The Deacons and High Priest of Tur had made martyrs out of all those innocent people whom the Butcher had slain. Ironically, neither Bishop Turthios, his flock of priests, or the Holy Paladins recognized these crosses for what they really represented. None could read Sea Prince dialect. It certainly bolstered the morale of the oppressed people.

Now it was 637, just a few years after the crosses appeared and the common folk needed all the help they could get. A man dressed in black robes with a white cross emblazoned across his chest stepped off a Megalos yacht onto the docks of Barcella. Hooded, his features could not be easily seen. Yet, cold fear radiated from those who approached his vicinity. He watched as his black coach was unloaded and his team of two black stallions were lifted from the cargo hold and harnessed to the coach. A white cross was the only marking, one on either door. Finally, five other similarly dressed men left the ship. One climbed into the driver's seat, while the first one and four others climbed into the coach. Thus, Prelate Silas Manos of the Mano del Dio arrived to set things straight in Barcella. A hundred years later, the commonly used phrase "You better be good or Silas will come get you!" was used by parents to get their children to obey. The coach sped off toward the central Church of Jehosanity in Barcella. One dockhand noticed three tiny drops of blood where the black one had been standing.

Later that day, Prelate Silas Manos, perpetually wearing the black hooded robe, walked into General Ali Sanchez's central planning room. The dreaded day of reckoning had come at last to the Butcher of Barcella. He felt ill at ease; the aura of cold fear this man, who seldom revealed his face, made the General's blood chill. The voice spoke, inhuman Ali swore, as if it was devoid of any human tone and emotion. "I have come to set matters straight, Pope Amir I's wishes. While he understands that examples have to be set and does compliment you on your previous work here in Barcella, especially in quelling the open rebellion, it has come to his attention that your population elimination tactics no longer produce the desired effect. Since you have not obtained any other satisfactory results, I am here to get the peasants into compliance."

He glanced at the serving wench, who was silently filling two cups with wine. "Who is that miserable creature and what is she doing in this room?" His acidly cold voice spoke once more.

Ali found his voice trembling, suddenly out of his control. "Serving wench, she's just our serving wench. She is totally obedient, just as Bishop Turthios commands."

"She should not be here. Your name wench?" he directed his piercing voice at the meek young woman, who was barely twenty.

Since she was directly addressed, she had to reply, her voice but barely a whisper, "Jovanna, sir."

"Jovanna, I will ask this only once." He paused for effect, and then said, "For whom have you been spying?"

"No one sir. I just poured the wine for you sirs."

Turning to the General, he said, "Bring her to the Nunnery at once. I will show you how to get positive results." With that, he swung his robe in a flaring motion, pivoting on his heels, and walked out of the room. Two tiny spots of blood adorned the floor where he had stood. General Ali had no choice but to comply.

A half hour later, Ali, his arm firmly gripping the terrified woman, forced her into the basement room of the Nunnery, the confiscated ex-Sisterhood inn. There the five Adepts were waiting. Without a word, they took Jovanna and forced her onto the wooden bench. She screamed and tried to break free, but to no avail. Her legs were secured to the top with heavy belts. Next, her torso was likewise tightly tied down. At last, her arms were forced out at about a forty-five degree angle, fingers just barely still on the bench top. There her hands were secured. Only then did Prelate Silas walk into the room.

He carried a large, razor sharp knife. Slowly he walked over to the bench. Jovanna continued to scream, but he ignored her. He raised the knife and swung it down hard. The shrill scream nearly deafened General Ali, but he noticed that none of these men even showed the tiniest reaction! Blood flowed from her missing fingers on her right hand. "I ask you again, for whom have you been spying?"

Poor Jovanna, she could do nothing but scream and scream, violently twisting under the severe restraints, the pain nearly overcoming her. He asked again and again, more and more pain, unending pain. She passed out. She awoke gasping for air; the Adepts had dumped cold water over her face. Now one man passed a vile of awful smelling vapors before her nose, which woke her up to the present. "Jovanna, you are running out of fingers. I ask you again, for whom have you been spying?" Wham down came the blade once more. She screamed and passed out once more. How long did this torture continue, she did not know.

Weakened and sickened and frightened nearly to death, at long last she vaguely muttered, "Deacon Azir." A pair of final whacks resulted in complete unconsciousness, blood splattering everywhere. Two Adepts arrived with blazing hot irons and proceeded to sear the wounds, finally sealing the vessels in her stumps. Without a word, they unfastened the woman and carried her upstairs.

Sticking his knife hard into the empty bench top, Silas spoke, "That is how you get results. Spy for Deacon Azir. You said the villagers burned him, ha! She will live and be taxed, and the Church will not lose a gold coin. That is how it is done. Good day."

Half sick, half elated, the general left and returned to his office. As he walked he attempted to plan his next move. Unfortunately, he realized now that his next move would be ordered by Silas! He was now no more than a puppet! The next day, heavily bandaged, the still unconscious woman was driven to her family's home and deposited on their doorstep for everyone to see. The work of Prelate Silas was intentionally for all to see!

A week later, an old man called Genorio knocked on the solid oaken door of the Santi fortress outside the walls of Barcella. The gatekeeper slid open the viewing port. "I seek help for my only daughter." The portal slid shut with a click. He heard the latches being undone and sighed.

"This way, please." The gatekeeper led him to a bench. "Wait here." He did as he was told, clasping his hands in prayer to Tur.

A young man in his thirties, tall, lanky, wearing chain mail, and a black tunic with a large red fleur-de-lis on its front, walked up to him. "Lyle Hampton. How may we help you?"

"It's my only daughter," explained the old man. "She is deadly ill and I know not how to help her. I have heard the Santi have great healers. I came to beg you to come and save her. I do not have much, but I will pay you all that I have and work for the rest, if only you'll come."

"Where is she?"

"In our home, in Barcella. I cannot carry her, and she cannot rise from bed any more. I'm afraid you'll be able to do nothing for her. Yet, I must try. She has taken care of me for so long now. I owe it to her to at least try."

"Wait here while I fetch the Healer, Genorio. We'll come." Lyle moved quickly, thinking ah, some action today. He was quite bored with fortress life — so little that he could do. In ten minutes, he returned with three others. "This is Mary Beth Woodworth, our Healer. Anna Fellini and her friend will provide us with some protection. In these times, it is not safe for a single Santi to wander the streets of Barcella alone. Come, lead the way."

The man walked very slowly, leaning for support on a staff. His health was frail; old age had come with a vengeance. Try as she might Mary Beth could not get him to tell her what illness had befallen his daughter. As they entered the city gates, Lyle handed the gateman five coppers and they entered. It took them nearly an hour to get to the old man's simple home in the poorer part of the city.

Mary Beth, wife of the fortress commander James, was a middle aged woman, who had seen service during the Crusade, helping to heal the mutilated wounded men. She was rather portly and normally rather jovial. Anna Fellini, thirty-five now, was a battle hardened regimental commander, who had also served under the legendary Ket Bethany, for whom she had the highest respect. Indeed, it was he who had appointed her Fortress Barcella's Garrison Commander, a very high honor. She and her companion kept a very sharp eye on anyone who came too close to the two ahead of her. Her job was to ensure the safety of the Commander's wife and his second in command, Lyle.

"Here we are at last. She is inside on my bed." He opened the door, allowing the others to enter.

"Oh dear god! That smell," Mary Beth reacted immediately. She knew that odor, wishing that she had not. She rushed into the only other room in the dwelling. "Oh no! Dear god, what happened to her?"

All four stared at Jovanna lying on the bed. Her arms were wrapped in blood soaked gauze bandages, which looked rotten and soiled. Gangrene had set in, red lines streaking up both of her arms. She had no hands and lay unconscious in a pool of her own excrement. "Lyle, go fetch a wagon immediately! No time to waste or we'll lose her!"

Lyle and Anna left at once. "Now then, Genorio, sit down and tell me what happened to your daughter," Mary Beth ordered, totally disgusted. She had hoped that she would never see such wounds again as long as she lived. Horrible memories of the Crusade victims came flooding back to her; it had been ghastly.

"Don't rightly know to be honest. Jovanna worked for General Ali Sanchez. She was a serving maid. I woke up one morning and found her like this lying on our doorstep. It was a couple days ago, shortly after that strange man in black got here — from Megalos, it's said. I got her into bed but I cannot help her. Can you save her; please, can you try? I will pay all that I have and work off the rest."

"We do not want your money, Genorio, but we are going to have to take her back to the Santi Fortress if we are to do anything for her. You must come with us. Somehow, I don't think that you are going to be safe here.

While we are waiting, why not gather up some of her clothes and yours and anything that is valuable and bring it with you. You two will be staying at the fortress for some time, if we are to save her life." He obeyed and began gathering up items, placing them in a large sack.

"Here they come," called out Anna's companion. "Need some help getting her ready?"

"Yes, let's get her onto a blanket and keep her covered the whole time that we are out in the open. The fewer eyes that see what we are carrying the better." After spreading out a blanket on the floor, the two women lifted the woman down onto it. Jovanna moaned a little, but was otherwise burning up with a fever and unconscious.

The strong arms of Lyle and Anna lifted her, carried her out, and put her into the wagon. Beth Ann made sure that she was completely covered. Then, she helped Genorio into the wagon, still clutching his staff and the large sack of their meager possessions. Lyle asked, "Anything we can do for her before we get back?"

"Nothing, I'm afraid."

"Okay, I'll drive. Anna, you ride up here with me. Janine, you climb in with Mary Beth."

Twenty-five minutes later, the wagon moved through the gates of the fortress and went straight for the infirmary. Dozens of hands helped carry the woman inside. Even James came to join them, saying, "Mary Beth, you tell us what to do." All Guardians are trained at healing, but only the Healers were sufficiently specialized to handle something as serious as this. Lyle, their Judger, James, their Wid, and Elsie Hampton, their Communicator, assisted Mary Beth, who began barking out orders. A dozen other ex-Sisterhood fighters scampered to carry them out, boiling water, fetching bandages, and cutting knives. This would be a long operation, if Jovanna's life were to be saved.

Indeed, it was; ten long hours later, the four finally washed up. "Done all we can," said a weary Mary Beth. "I'd like to get my hands, or knife rather, on the bastard who did that to her. I haven't seen such a botched mess as that since the Crusade fiasco. I do miss having Ket around though."

"Will she make it?" asked her husband, James.

"Well, at least the butcher minimized her blood loss when he did it. That's the only positive thing I can say about his handiwork. We were able to keep additional loss to a minimum. I'm certain that we got all the infected areas removed. So if no further infections arise and no other unforeseen complications occur, then I will say that she probably will make it. We must watch her constantly for at least a month to be certain." Jovanna's arms were both now only about five inches long.

"Thank you, my love. You did splendidly, as always. Now it is my turn. We must find out what happened and why. I told you that I suspected something bad would come when we saw that ship from Megalos dock. It looked like the description Lilly Ann had of the Church of Jehosanity down in Megalos. Lyle, you are with me, bring Anna too. We have some planning to do. Elsie, you interrogate Genorio. Find out all that you can about him and his daughter. We must find the connections and fast, before further tragedies occur. Janine, you stand first watch over her. Come get one of us if anything happens."

"Aye sir!" she saluted the commander and went to sit beside the bed of the sleeping woman. Alone with the poor woman, Janine began to cry for her. The old days had returned for her.

Late next morning, all four having slept in, Elsie came to report. "Well, I had a good deal of trouble getting coherent answers from Genorio. His mind is not in good shape anymore. I had to use a bit of Mind Probing, but I believe I have some answers. Perhaps their last name will tell much. It's Barcella."

"Any relation to the founders of the city?" James asked, suddenly intrigued by the possibilities.

"Yes. Years ago, Genorio Barcella was the High Priest of Tur and one of the dual rulers of Barcella; the Sea Prince descendant was the other ruler. That was apparently years ago, however. Now his son, Romero Barcella, is their High Priest of Tur. He is in hiding and helping foment the rebellion against the Holy Paladins. Genorio does not have any idea where his son is now located, only that he still lives. Jovanna is his daughter. She went to work as a serving maid for General Ali Sanchez. Apparently, she has been feeding information about their plans to the underground. I believe that she saved some Deacon from his troops up in Augar. His memory is rather fuzzy about that one. Being a spy in the Butcher of Barcella's den was an awful risk to take, but as we all know, these people are taking it daily. However, he honestly does not know what happened to her."

"Well done, Elsie," James complimented his Communicator.

"I believe I can fill in some more details," Lyle spoke next. I sent out some feelers to my contacts in the city last night. Heard back just a bit ago, that's why I was a little tardy getting here. You are right about that Megalos ship. A Prelate of the Mano del Dio arrived on the Holy Yacht. He was the one who did this to her. He cut off her fingers one by one, attempting to force out of her whom she was working. From what I have heard, she held out for a long time, brave woman. In the end, she only gave up useless information; she was spying for the Deacon, who already managed to escape the clutches of Sanchez and his men."

"Mary Beth, get ready for more bloody surgery! If I am correct, we are going to be seeing quite a lot more cases like Jovanna. This man has to be stopped!" Lyle exclaimed, angrily.

"Can we get close to him?" asked James, remaining cool as he always did. He had to be level headed at all times. Lyle could afford to vent his emotions, but not the Commander, the Wid.

"Don't think so. He is secretive about his every movement and he always has five others like him around him, probably his helpers in crime. I have requested that all information about them and their activities be reported to us. However, even asking my contacts to do that is placing them in grave danger as well. These are the assassins, which killed Ket, after all, very, very dangerous men."

"They are not men; they are assassins and butchers, totally inhuman!" declared Mary Beth.

"What action can we reasonably attempt now?" asked James. The room was silent. Thus began what was afterwards called the Reign of Terror. It lasted for the better part of a year. The nobles bore the brunt of the killings, for who else stood to benefit but those with the money.

When Jovanna finally recovered enough to sit up, she was horrified at her body, at her utter helplessness. Quickly she fell into a deep apathy, even refusing to eat. She just wanted to die. Hence, Jenna ordered James to bring her to Velona, along with her father. A month after entering their infirmary, Jovanna was helped onto a caravel, which sailed at once for Velona, carrying but two passengers and one large sack.

An aide interrupted the meeting between Silas and Ali. "Sirs, we have learned that the serving maid, Jovanna has been taken into the Santi fortress. What shall we do about that?"

"Damn those meddling Santi anyway," cursed General Ali. "Always meddling."

"No problem, General, the Santi are doomed. We have eliminated their leader. The entire organization will be crumbling shortly. After all, they are mostly women. The Pope himself has spoken with me about this. He is certain that the Santi will be a problem of the past within a very few years. So forget them. No matter that they have the wench. She is of no further use to us. She, like the others, has served her purpose. Not a soul in Barcella has not heard that when I ask a question, I get my answer. You will see, General, we are beginning to crush all opposition. These underground renegades will be gone within the year, and I can get back to the Pope. I hate this dismal land."

"Have you rousted the Deacon?"

"Yes, the information you obtained was entirely accurate. We caught him trying to flee. Put his head on a pike outside the village, along with the entire family who were hiding him. One problem solved," General Ali was happy to report good news. Perhaps this Prelate's methods would rapidly solve his problems here in Barcella.

Over the course of the next few months, Prelate Silas demonstrated an uncanny ability to single out and torture just the right people. His crowning achievement came when the man whose appendages he had removed finally gave up the location of the High Priest of Tur, Romero

Barcella. General Ali Sanchez and his men rounded up the young man and summarily beheaded him. This time, they paraded his head all over the city of Barcella. Ali wanted everyone to know that he had finally eliminated the last of the two top priests who were fomenting the rebellion.

That fateful day, Prelate Silas chose to ride in his coach, behind General Ali and his men as they proudly paraded the head of Romero about the city. Long had Lyle been watching from the top of the Santi Fortress tower, looking for an opportunity. He could not help missing the crowd of people who stood and stared at the horrible sight of their High Priest of Tur. Even those who followed the Deacon and his version of Jehosanity were shocked and afraid.

Lyle spied the coach, the black coach. Anger seethed in the man, uncontrolled anger. He forced himself to calm his mind. The day was overcast; a squall was in the offing. He reached upwards to the clouds, found what he needed. He connected a line from the black coach upwards into the cloud, seething with energy. Bam! Down came the stroke of lightning, striking the coach, splintering it. A great boom of thunder echoed through the city. Bam! Down came a second bolt, striking the Prelate Silas Manos, whose body flew twenty-five feet, before smashing against the side of a nearby building, his body lifeless. Lyle smiled and went to report to James.

"You did what?" James was furious. He had not ordered the execution of the Prelate.

"Eliminated, sir!" Lyle carefully became quite formal. Whether or not James approved, he was more than satisfied with himself. He'd kept his promise that he swore over the unconscious Jovanna after Mary Beth had finished her surgery on her. Whatever else James said to him, he did not hear, for he thought only of Jovanna, wondering how she was getting along. Would Jenna Rose Weston be able to help her? She was now the last living relative of the city's founders and the rightful ruler of Barcella, if such claims would ever be allowed again.

"People get hit by lightning all the time," General Ali explained to Bishop Turthios. "It's just a freak accident. Put that in your report. Also, note on my behalf that I truly commend Prelate Silas for his Holy Works here. His good work had effectively ended the rebellion and the capture of their top leaders and many others. I will continue his Holy Work."

"Duly noted in my report. Yes, he was a devout, Holy Man. It has been an honor to have known this Prelate. Indeed nothing finer can be said of him than he truly was the Mano del Dio, the Hand of God." Bishop Turthios left to finish his report, sending it back to the Pope, along with the casket bearing Silas and one of his Adepts. It was a sad day for the Bishop.

During the time when Prelate Silas was active, a dozen men and women were brought to the Santi for Healing from their brutal tortures. Countless others had not sought out their aid, however. Mary Beth's infirmary was kept busy, busier than she wanted it to be. Needles under the fingernails, fingernails ripped off, those were the trademark beginning steps, which escalated depending upon whether the victim told the Prelate what he wanted to hear. However, she noted that the severity of the victim's wounds had greatly lessened over time. Silas was able to extract what he desired, information, without doling out massive mutilations as he had done with Jovanna. Her case had spread fear and terror throughout the land. Even mentioning the Prelate was coming was enough to scare anyone.

Now bereft of their top leadership and scattered all over the sector, the remaining priests of both religions could no longer wage any effective, organized resistance. Instead, individual cells began to spring up, each acting totally independent of each other. Without the wealthy nobles supplying the funds, commerce began slowly dwindling.

Chapter 8 The Days of Healing

For a time here in late 636, I relaxed, just letting my tiny body nurse and sleep. Yes, it felt good just to relax after the confusions and hardships I'd just endured. The Pope's Journal was safe for now, and my new baby body had a great deal of growing to do. My little body sighed as I relaxed its tense muscles. As far as I was concerned, all was well with the world. Oops, not quite, my diapers were messy, oh how icky!

Lilly Ann soothingly said as she leaned over me, "Ah what have we here, Lizzy Ann, messy pants again. Well, let's get you cleaned up or mommy's going to hold her nose." God, I wanted to reach out and hug, hold, and caress my wife! Oh — late wife, I had to remind myself! Her husband, Ket, me, had died! I wanted to say, "I'm back. It's me!" However, I dare not. Suddenly, I had a firsthand knowledge of just how Caitlyn Amir, my first wife who had been assassinated the very night she gave birth to our twins, must have felt. She wanted desperately to "get back into the game with me." She took over one of her own newborn twin's baby bodies. Like her, here I was looking up at my dear loved ones and could do so very little.

Ah, but in fact, it was worse than that. If I let everyone know that I was back, that this little body was me, then the Santi and my dear Guardian friends would be Mind Linking to me for answers, bypassing Jenna, whom I had requested to fill my shoes as the Santi leader. Her authority would be completely undermined. Thanks but no thanks! Instead, I observed my dear Lilly Ann as she changed my diapers. I was reminded of her doing the same thing with my twins, just after Caitlyn had been killed. How she dotted over the twins, spending all her free time with them. I had sometimes thought that she may have done this to get my attention, but now I saw her in a new light. She really cared for children. Around the estate, Lilly Ann was the nanny for absolutely all the children! In my eyes, she was a saint.

Since my body was nearly always around mom, I could eavesdrop on all her Santi planning and the many meetings she held. Gradually, I began to grasp what was now going on around the estate. First, John Henry Penton, Moon Circle Wid and the Commander of the Fortress of Mont Blanc, had sent my Cymry Circle to join with Jenna, who was officially their Wid now, replacing me. He also sent in his request for his Circle to be replaced; he was now seventy-six years old. All in the Moon Circle were quite old, actually, and their health was failing. Indeed, as he had forecasted to me many years ago now, the Guardians were doomed because so many were approaching old age and so few new recruits could be found. I knew that Jenna would be facing major replacement decisions in short order.

Indeed, today she was rereading John Henry's last dispatch, wondering what she ought to do. I could tell that she felt rather lost, so I placed a single thought into her mind. "Oh, yes, that is what Ket would likely have done. Lilly Ann, when you are finished with Lizzy Ann, can you tell the others to prepare a complete list of the Guardians? I need their ages, specialties, and locations. We have to find some replacements for the Moon Circle immediately and probably a lot of others as well. I know the old retirees who have been traveling the world on the caravels are probably finally going to want to settle down as well. We cannot keep on asking them to provide guard duties any longer."

"Coming up; should have them by this afternoon's briefing, Jenna. Here's your precious little one. She's hungry again." She placed me in mom's arms and then left to notify the others of the request. For a moment, I felt sorry for mom as she awkwardly got me moved into my nursing position. No hands made some simple chores quite a task and I cooperated completely. Jenna always insisted on doing things herself, as long as she was able and time was not critical. "Ah here we go Lizzy Ann, have at it; we have some time for ourselves now." She stroked my small body lovingly and kissed my forehead. I was content.

I awoke in my cradle near mom. Their meeting was just beginning. While I could not see everyone, I listened carefully, recognizing all the voices of my dear friends of the Cymry Circle. Lilly Ann was talking, "Congratulations, Paulette! You finally found the right man. Have you set your wedding date yet? When are we going to meet the lucky fellow?" Wow, Paulette is getting married! That was news to me. She and her twin brother, Paul, were married last lifetime, Simon and Sandy Donegal. Until now, they had been inseparable.

Paulette, the Communicator, was twenty-eight and a bit embarrassed with the sudden attention on her matrimonial plans. He had only told Paul last night. "Sam Donegal, our resident Master Weaponsmith. We haven't set a date yet; he just proposed at lunch yesterday. We've been dating over a year now. Can we get down to business, please?" She wanted to change the subject.

Paul Wilkens, her twin, was a Protector and still single as far as I knew. His primary action had shifted from protecting Ket to protecting Jenna. Benjamin Wilkins was their Loremaster; he was now twenty-nine, while the twins, Paul and Paulette, were a year younger. Allan Donegal was thirty-one and their Planner. His wife, Beth Ann, was a Healer and a year younger than her husband. Finally, Lilly Ann was the Judger and was now thirty as well.

Jenna began her meeting, "We have two key items on our agenda today. I've received a request to find replacements for the Moon Circle. Specifically, John Henry wants to retire. He is in his seventies and tires easily. However, that also brings up all the other retirees who have been helping to protect the caravels. I think that they ought to be allowed to finally retire as well, if they so choose. Secondly, we really ought to decide upon a subterfuge strategy for the living relatives of the Great Messiah. I know that there have been no more assassinations and some are getting restless being cooped up within Mont Blanc. We've put off reaching a decision long enough."

"I have drawn up the list you wanted," Beth Ann answered. She spread a very long scroll across the table. For quite some time, they discussed which Guardians ought to be allowed to retire and who should replace them. Additionally, I took heart that for the first time in a score of years we actually had a substantial increase in first and second year apprentices! The druwid movement might be slowly dying off, but we weren't dead yet. Perhaps it was just a fluke, but I did take heart in the figures they reported.

Time dragged on; still they could not decide on a new leader to replace John Henry. A little annoyed, I placed a thought in Jenna's mind. She exclaimed, "Oh. Perfect. I have it. Let's ask Percival Penton to take over for John Henry. That way, he can then be with some of his children and grandchildren. Pick one of the newest Protectors who have just finished their training to take over the Kingship of Southway. Oh. Better still, pick several, and have them campaign all throughout Southway, and let the people there hold an election to see who will be their next king."

"We love it!" declared Beth Ann and Lilly Ann in unison; their father would be much closer to them in Mont Blanc than in Middleton. In a few minutes, they identified two likely candidates to run for the office of King of Southway.

"Well, I suppose that I ought to visit Middleton and discuss this with Percival personally," Jenna commented. "He might have other ideas."

"I'll make the security arrangements," Paul replied, though he did not like Jenna traveling, because it made his job of protecting her more difficult.

"Good, that's settled then for the time being. Next, how are we coming on Ket's requested subterfuge?"

"Honestly, nowhere," Allan said morosely.

"Okay, then let's go over the whole thing once more from the top," Jenna suggested. "Lilly Ann or Beth Ann, will one of you outline the situation for us one more time? I would, but you two have been closer to the situation than I have been."

Lilly Ann volunteered, for this was aligned with her specialty of Judger. "The Great Messiah of Juda Arad, supposedly the Son of Jehosa, married Bethany or Ket as we now call her, I mean him. They had three children, Ahmad, Emil, and Sarah — Percival's late wife, our mother. The perverted Church of Jehosanity in Megalos, in their attempt to re-write women out of history, claim that the Son of God was pure and took no earthly wife, dictating that Bethany did not exist or was just some local prostitute that the Great Messiah had healed, certainly not his wife. However, we surmise that after re-writing history, they then discovered that

Bethany did exist and that they had had children. If the children came forward and could prove their lineage, the Megalos Church would be completely discredited and likely destroyed."

"Thus, Pope Yazi I sent out his Mano del Dio, assassins in disguise as holy men, to search for these descendants and then quietly kill them. At first, before we knew anything about this horrific project, the assassin they sent was highly successful. All but Cathleen, daughter of Emil, and Sarah, daughter of Bethany and Jes, had been killed. We also killed their killer, Kronos, or some such name. Ket send a fake letter saying that all the rest were dead, no more living relations existed. That bought us a good deal of time. However, these Mano del Dio assassins are thorough, I'll give them that point. They set back another to verify the results. They discovered that Cathleen survived and that Sarah and her children were alive, not dead as Ket's fake information suggested. We know that they then arranged a 'hunting accident' that killed Cathleen and her budding family. Shortly after that, he pushed mom, Sarah, down three flights of stone steps, killing her."

Today, the Holy Lineage, which is what it is now being called, consists of only a few of us. First, Caitlyn and Ket's twins, Tegid and Taliesin are now thirteen and the rightful rulers of both kingdoms in West Reach, Caitlyn's throne and her Uncle Emil's throne. Second are the children of Sarah and Percival: Beth Ann and myself, thirty, Arthur the blacksmith, thirty-one, and Justus, twenty-seven. The four of us have children of our own."

"Ket and I have Leslie Ann, ten, Sarah Amber, nine, Curt Thomas, six, and Linda Sarah, who is just one. Beth Ann and Allan have four but are working on five," she grinned at her sister. "Alyster is ten, Ami Lynn is eight, Ashley is seven, and Benet is five. Our older brother, Arthur and Winnie have five. Tom Benjamin is thirteen, Corey is eleven, Aura is ten, Audry is eight, and Dirk is seven. Finally, our younger brother Justus and Annie have three. Catherine is nine, Duncan is seven, and Emil is six. That makes twenty-two of us who can trace our lineage back to Jes and Bethany Amir."

Beth Ann added, "Lilly Ann and I have our children and Caitlyn's here, while Justus and Arthur have theirs safe in Mont Blanc."

"Isn't it so nice that we have fourteen youngsters running around this estate?" Jenna could not help but comment. "Raising families is what life is all about. Well, anyway, back to the problem at hand. We cannot keep them cooped up forever. What kind of a life can they have living as a virtual prisoner in their own fortress? Already Tegid has been asking me when they can go to Nuadilan and Amathon in West Reach. I keep telling them when you are a little older, but that's not going to be much longer."

"We've already demonstrated that we cannot keep them alive when they are outside our fortresses. Look at Cathleen and all the others," Paul cursed.

"Not even in their own castles; look at how they got to mom," Beth

Ann added.

"That's because everyone around the cities and towns knew their names and parents and everything about them," Ben pointed out, trying to get everyone back on the right path.

"Yes, as I interpret Ket's final message, subterfuge implies that they adopt new names and we say they are one place, while they are in another," Jenna suggested.

"But not all want to be the same thing," Beth Ann pointed out. "I mean Tegid wants to be a king for sure. Alyster is talking about one day being a king like his grandfather. Yet, Tom has told me he is an apprentice blacksmith, taking after his dad. Some, as you know, are druwid apprentices. Sarah Amber tells me she just wants to be a mother with lots of children, perhaps living on a farm away from all the strife of the world. None of us wants to be assassinated. Only a few of us really gives a hoot about bringing down the Megalos church. I think it's safe to say that we only want to live our lives as free beings."

Jenna suggested, "How about this idea? Those who want to just live a normal life, not aspiring to be rulers or part of the Santi organization — those we help them choose a town or village, have them go by a different last name. We ought to have a few Santi go with them also in disguise but unknown to the kids. Their task is to look out for their welfare sort of behind the scenes, calling upon us when needed. That way, those that want to be farmers and blacksmiths can be one. Those that want to be part of the Santi are going to be well protected anyway, so no need to worry about those. The ones who want to be rulers, now those are going to be problematical, especially Caitlyn's twins, who are already very well known here and in West Reach. We can send a Santi force to help protect them, but I don't know what else we can do for them. The assassins seem to find ways no matter what we do."

"I like that," Lilly Ann replied. "It's about the best we can do for now, short of destroying Megalos and the Mano del Dio."

"Are we all in agreement?" Jenna asked. The Circle was. "Okay, then any new business? Allan?"

"Yes, I would like to report that the new housing wings I've added on either end of this main dwelling will be ready for Lilly Ann and Beth Ann to move in later this week. The addition for the rest will be done this time next week." Cheers all around brought a smile to the Planner's face. Indeed, the make shifting and overcrowding was cumbersome at best.

"However, just as soon as these are done, I would like permission to add on two more guest wings, Jenna. I have this feeling that you may have other guests as time goes on and you can never have too many rooms, you know."

Jenna laughed, "Or is it that you, Allan, can never have built enough buildings?"

Everyone roared with laughter, even I did from my cradle. I'd never known Allan to stop building ever since I met him in his last lifetime.

A few weeks later, Percival retired to Mont Blanc, taking over the leadership of the fortress. Two young Protectors, following the pattern set down by Percival and Sarah, began going from village to village, attempting to gain supporting votes for the election in two months. The aged Moon Circle retired; John Henry moved to Velona, spending much of his daytime hours basking in the sun on the public beach there. The warmth soothed his aching joints.

One afternoon, mom, carrying me in her arms, went out to talk with Tegid, Taliesin, and Brother Jake, the monk who had come to see to their training. First, she chatted with Brother Jake about their progress. "Ma'am, I will be straight with you. The boys are very different in temperament. Tegid is very offensive in nature, fighting to win. His sole ambition is to be King of Nuadilan and be a leader of a fighting force to be reckoned with. Taliesin, on the other hand, has no offensive streak in him; he fights only defensively. He has a rare nurturing streak in him, unusual for a young lad. Both will have learned all that I can teach them when they are fifteen, as promised."

"Thanks. It is what I have already observed, Brother Jake. Continue your excellent work with my blessing." He bowed and returned to his work. She then took the twins aside for a chat, sitting under the stately oak tree, which grew just outside the front of her estate, behind which the gravel road ran to her front door.

"Boys, I've come to talk to you about your futures," Jenna began.

"Great!" Tegid exclaimed, eager to finally be allowed to become king, his promised heritage. Taliesin said nothing, fearing the worst.

"I've just talked with Brother Jake. Yes, you are both doing fine. Your training is not endless, as you might have thought. The day you turn fifteen, it is done, only a little over a year." Tegid let out a whoop of delight, while Taliesin let out a sigh of great relief!

"Let's discuss your future first, Tegid. You know all about the assassins and their insane desire to kill you?" He nodded, for it had been drilled into his head for years. They had killed his mother and recently his father. "With that in mind, do you still wish to reclaim the throne of Nuadilan?"

"Absolutely, Jenna, without any doubt," he said enthusiastically.

"Then, arrangements will be so made. On your fifteenth birthday, off you go to Nuadilan." He let out a shriek that startled even me.

"You shouldn't yell so, Tegid; you're scaring poor Lizzy Ann," Taliesin cajoled his brother.

"Now about your future, Taliesin," Jenna continued. "Do you want to do the same as your brother or do you have some other desire?"

Taliesin looked at Jenna; wonder filled his eyes. No one had asked him this before, always assuming that he would also take back his promised throne when he was of age. "Not really. Do I have to be a king? Honestly, I don't want to; Tegid can have my town to rule."

"Really? I thought. . ." Tegid's voice trailed off, and he did not finish his thought.

"That is fine, Taliesin. What is it that you would like to do? More Guardian training, perhaps like your father?"

"Well, not exactly, Jenna. I want to become the most famous bard in all the lands! I truly love music, singing, dancing, telling stories, and playing songs on my lute. I suppose I should continue my apprenticeship a little longer, but next year I am supposed to make a specialty choice. I don't want to be any of the seven choices. I get queasy around blood. I hate fighting. I could care less about other people's problems and disputes. I am not interested in animals or even plants. I have no interest in building things. Nothing at all fits, but music."

"Then music and the arts it will be for you, Taliesin. Look, I defied the seven choices myself and invented an eighth. I certainly don't see why you cannot be allowed to do the same!"

"Really, Jenna, I can! Tegid, I can be a bard after all!"

Tegid smiled at his brother. For the last few years, he knew that his brother just didn't have any heart to become a king. "What will we do about Amathon and Uncle Emil's towns?" he asked.

"Yours, Tegid. I will see that you have control of all four. That is a tall responsibility that you are taking, mind you. However, I will send a strong Santi force along with you to help back you up. We don't want anything bad to happen to you."

"That's fine by me, thanks a thousand times over, Jenna!"

"Good. Then everything's settled. Now will one of you lads help me up? I don't want to drop Lizzy Ann here." Taliesin took her arm and helped her up, while she held me tight with her other arm. Both boys were elated over the news. Actually, I was as well, because I knew that Caitlyn or Taliesin rather, loved music. This was perfect for her, er him.

The remainder of 636 was quiet and uneventful. Every evening, Jenna would take time out to play with the pile of children that now inhabited her estate, fourteen of them — her four, Lilly Ann's six, Beth Ann's four. She truly enjoyed spending two hours every day with us children. On Sundays without fail, she took everyone into Velona to the Church of the Holy Rose to hear High Priestess Elona Po deliver her ministry. Before and after the service, a dozen musicians played sacred songs derived from the melting pot of religions, Jehosanity, Blessed Holy Mother, we druwids, and Tur. During the services, her choir also sang hymns. I always left feeling tranquil and at peace with myself and the world. From a purely musician's view point — remember I was a troubadour last life time — the acoustics were fabulous in this cathedral. The echo effect was incredible to hear. I swore that one day I would play in this church.

However, in early 637, Jenna began getting communications that were particularly upsetting. Still unproven, suspicions were growing that women in the occupied sectors were again being systematically brutalized. Then came that fateful night when the mass Mind Link revealed the stark horrors of what had happened in Florintine Junction! Yes, I cleverly, discretely joined the Mind Link. After all, I did not want to be left out, even if my body was only a couple years old.

Suddenly, I realized that the Church of Jehosanity in Megalos could no longer be ignored. That journal I had stolen may well be our prime weapon against these vile men. I had to break my silence at last. How to do it remained my worry. That journal had to be retrieved somehow.

Part of my dilemma Jenna solved for me. While she lay nursing me, stroking my small body lovingly, she said softly to me, "Well Ket Bethany, I think it is finally time for us to have a talk. I know you are you. Talk with me. Things are getting very serious right now, and I really do need some guidance. Please?"

Nursing away with my mom, how could I possibly refuse her? *I'm here. How did you know it was me? I've tried to stay on the sidelines.*

A mother knows her child. Besides, I've had a few ideas here and there that weren't mine. You are a sly one.

I didn't want to usurp your control of the Santi, mom. I think you are doing a fabulous job, really I do. I knew you would, that's why I suggested you be the one to take over for me. However, can we keep this a secret a while longer?

Many others have already guessed you know. Lilly Ann has her suspicions. I think that Sally probably guessed your secret too, just a while ago.

I almost blew it with Sally. She caught me off guard for a second. I guess that you can tell Lilly Ann. She has a right to know since she has been helping you take care of this little body. Darn, if she knows, then the rest of your new Circle ought to know. There is no keeping a secret from Beth Ann, besides she would tell the others anyway. We both smiled.

But please, can you call me Bethany not Lizzy Ann?

Are you sure? If we start calling you Bethany right now, far too many are going to become suddenly curious. You can always insist we change it once you are older, you know.

Well, okay, I guess. You are right. I changed the subject. *You are really upset by the recent events in Florintine Junction, right?*

Yes, yes I am deeply troubled by them. Until now, we only had suspicions and the occasional dead body. We had no idea such butchery was going on behind closed doors. They certainly have been sneaky about it. What am I to do about it? So many women from the Junction have been so victimized.

Such trauma, we both know, will ruin not only the rest of their lives, but is highly likely to continue to plague them in their next ones too.

Are you saying I need to use my therapy on them?

Are you up to it?

Yes, without it, their futures are going to be miserable. Just think what their next lifetimes will be like with this trauma right there to be reactivated? They are likely to either live in utter terror of men or to flip around to the winning side and become brutalizers of women themselves, perverts themselves, continuing to propagate this behavior toward women. I really have not much choice. We both know that my therapy is the only thing we know of that can erase it. If I do not try and succeed, then the odds are that these victims one lifetime or another later on will become the perpetrators. I have to try for mankind's sake.

Then you have your answer, mom. Have the worst cases brought here by caravel. I'm sure glad that Allan had the foresight to add on so many more rooms to your estate. I think you are going to need them. We both laughed.

I thought he was being silly when he announced that shortly he would add an enclosed bathhouse, complete with hot water. Honestly, sometimes I think that he can see the future!

I think he just cannot stop building things. He's always been fanatically building buildings, ever since I first met him a century ago. Again, I changed the topic; this would be a very touchy one. *Mom, there is something that I desperately need done on the quiet, something that might be incredibly vital in our fight against this Megalos church and the assassins of the Mano del Dio. I had hoped that it could wait until I was much older, but after tonight's revelations, it cannot be put out off any longer, no matter the repercussions.*

What are you talking about? Have you been up to something with this small body here that I don't know about? Boy, was this ever going to be awkward and disturbing.

I don't know how to say this, mom. When they sent me off in the funeral barge off the western coast of Tewdwr, my body was somehow not completely dead. Or it was and then came to life again. A very long time later, I awoke when the boat landed on an unknown northern island. There, I regained some health, but my left side was pretty much paralyzed. When I could finally leave there, I set sail to Megalos. Back when I throttled my assassin, the Rooster was his name, I accidentally saw some of his mind. Yazi had written a journal of all the crimes that these Mano del Dio had done, storing it in a secret vault beneath their church complex. I saw the vault's precise location. I sailed there and managed to steal it right out from under their noses. However, by then the body was nearly completely paralyzed, and I was barely able to get the journal into the secret cave of Rea Helios. Lying there in that hidden place is the journal that we now critically need, along with my dead Ket body. That journal has to be recovered at once. However, only my Circle knows about that location and where we left the key to get in, but they are needed here to protect and aid you. Besides what will they think when they learn they buried their leader who was not actually dead yet?

Oh good god! Oh good god! She was speechless, ok thoughtless, for a while. The news was a double edged sword.

The fewer that know the truth, the fewer who are going to become horribly upset or worse at the mistake. I'd rather that they think of me using some kind of godlike powers than for them to know otherwise. Besides, even I thought the body was dead. Probably it floated on the sea for a month or more with me dead in it. I simply cannot explain it. If I cannot, how can I expect them to understand without massive self-recriminations?

Maybe the best thing to do is to send one of them, Paul perhaps?

Yes, I think you are right. I'll contact him and let him know that I have a top-secret mission for him. I'll tell him enough so he can deal with the mission and what he finds in the secret chamber, but nothing more. If I ever learn what really happened to me after the funeral, then I will tell the others. Until then it is all mere speculation, conjecture.

I believe that is the wisest course of action to take. Perhaps with some of my therapy, we can get to the truth of the matter. I'll get my personal caravel ready to sail at high tide.

Just then, Lilly Ann entered, "Ready for me to put her in her cradle for the night?"

"Oh that would be most welcome. I have an emergency matter to handle; something just came up. Oh, you'd better burp Ket, er Lizzy Ann." She slipped. Was it on purpose, I wondered?

Lilly Ann picked me up, looking me squarely in my little face. "Oh you little rascal you! Did you think you could keep that from me? Silly one. I knew it all along!" She patted my back.

Yes, it's me. I still love you immensely, Lilly Ann. Thank you for helping take care of my little body. She kissed my forehead.

"Can I tell the others now? They all suspect, you know?"

Sure, but you'd better put me in my cradle first; the body is very sleepy. She tucked the small body in nicely and bounced out of the room to tell the others. I gave her some time, while I tried to figure out just what to say to Paul.

Somewhat later, I touched Paul's mind. *Hi there. It's me again.*

About time! Everyone's been wondering where you've been. Sorry I couldn't stop that assassin. How did you kill him? It had to be you, but none of us could figure out how you did it.

Hey, even I don't know how I did that either. I was just very mad at him and strangled him. Paul, that may have been a key stroke of luck for us. I got to see some of his memories. Yazi knew all about the assassins. He probably hired them. Evidently, he documented everything in a secret journal. Paul, don't ask how I did it, but I managed to sneak into their secret underground maze, broke into their vault, and stole that journal!

Holy cow! That's unbelievable! How did you pull that one off anyway?

I said, don't ask! Anyway, you saw the horrible images of Florintine Junction tonight right? He had. Well, I was going to sail down there and recover it from where I left it when my body is much older. Now, it seems that we need that journal immediately. I cannot go get it, so I am depending upon you to go back to Megalos and fetch it, top secret. No one but Paulette and Jenna must know about what you are really doing. It could be exceedingly dangerous for you if anyone else finds out. We're dealing with utterly ruthless assassins who will stop at nothing to regain that journal!

But where is it at?

I stashed it just inside Rea Helios's secret passage entrance right on the beach. The key is back in the place where we left it. The journal is inside a water skin pouch just inside the secret door. There is also a dead body with it. Please ignore the dead body and don't ask any questions about it or tell anyone else about the dead body, please!

When do I sail?

I liked his enthusiasm. At the next high tide. Right now Jenna is alerting her caravel. She'll be letting you know when the captain will want to set sail. I urge you to fly at top speed. I don't know how much time we have. Maybe we will be lucky and have lots of time to deal with this journal; perhaps we will not. I just don't know. Remember this is a very deadly journey. No one must know about it. You'll be totally on your own. I cannot help you out if you run into trouble. Just get in there fast and get out.

Sir, you can depend on me. I shall not fail. With this ledger, we might be able to bring down their entire church! Just then, Jenna knocked on his door, so I broke my connection and let Jenna handle the details. Yes, I could have shadowed him all the way there, perhaps sitting in the crow's nest. I felt that Jenna may need me here more, and I was right.

The next day at our first meeting after the night of the massive Mind Link, Allan asked where Paul was. He was late. Jenna said sternly, "Paul is now on a lengthy top secret mission. Only Paulette and I know about it. She will be in daily touch with him. That is all that I dare say about it until he returns, which will likely be months. If I say more, his life could be in the gravest of danger, and worse, the mission could fail utterly to all our great sorrow. Now, let's get down to business here. We have lots of planning to do."

Weeks passed by, Jenna and her Circle were constantly busy

organizing rescue operations for the forty thousand refugees heading for Jerilum. Additional news concerning the nefarious activities of the Holy Paladins continued to come into headquarters. all the Santi fortress outposts were placed on high alert for similar activities in their sectors. While I kept an eye on the situation, well okay, listened quietly in the background, Jenna did not really need my help. She was an expert at conducting business operations.

However, August 1, we received word from Zargarb concerning Ariana Zar's incredible escape and rescue. When Jenna heard the story of this young woman, as relayed by Sally, she immediately ordered Ariana to be sent here to her estate. A little over a week later, Jenna sent her coach to the docks to meet Sally and Ariana. Jenna asked me to Mind Link her to Sally.

Jenna here, Bethany, er Ket, is helping me. I have some guidelines for you to follow when you bring Ariana here to Velona. By the way, this will teach you to forget your seasickness herbs. Well done on allowing Ariana to help you out, however.

Sally replied, *Ket? You're back! This is the best news I've had. Ok, how do we proceed?*

I need to see how observant she is. We already know that she is stuck around the age of ten, just before the trauma started. A lot depends upon how well she can see what is actually around her.

To Ariana riding in the coach, Sally explained, "Ah, here comes the estate ahead. See, they have a stone wall around it as well. Many guards. Very safe place indeed. I just know you are going to love Jenna. She's one of the finest women I know, very, very wise. Very knowledgeable. She has quite a lot of children too. She just had another one this year, Lizzy Ann, I think is her name. Be nice to see the new addition to her family. I rather miss not having many children at my feet, but then I am getting way too old for all that. Ah, here we are." The carriage came to rest outside the Weston estate house. The two climbed out and began walking up to the front door.

At once, Ariana noticed something peculiar. Jenna, via Sally's observant eyes observed Ariana's reactions. The large front doors had no doorknobs! Sally replied. "Yes, you only need to push on them to open the doors. All the doors in this estate work this way, for a reason. Ah, here she comes now."

Ariana gaped. Walking toward them came a woman, perhaps ten years older than herself, holding a baby in her arms. What shocked her was that the woman had no hands, just like herself! "Hello there. You must be Ariana. So pleased to meet you at last. I'd shake hands with you, but we'd both have a slight problem with that, but I can shake with you, Sally. Good to see you. It has been entirely too long." To Ariana's total surprise, Jenna held out her arm; Sally took it, and the two shook a welcome.

"This is our new addition to our ever growing family, Lizzy Ann." She proudly showed off me to the two women. Sally, I noticed, gave me a strange look, almost one of recognition. I purposely said nothing — well a baby should not be saying anything anyway. I was not yet ready to announce to the world that Bethany or Ket was back.

Sally took me in her arms, leaving Jenna free for the moment. She stuck her arm into the arm of Ariana and led her inside, chatting all the while. "You probably have noticed that none of these doors have any knobs. My husband designed them for me. I can go freely anywhere now and not have to fiddle with trying to get a knob turned. Rather frustrating you know, trying to turn a knob with no hands."

Ariana finally found her tongue. "You, you are the leader of all the Santi? But I don't see how you. . ." her voice trailed off.

"Yes, I am the leader of the entire Santi del Dio. We number something like ten thousand strong, if I remember right, but you probably want to know what happened to me. Well, I used to run an inn in Zargarb. The Holy Paladins cut off my hands, but I escaped and came here. The rest is history, as they say. Look Ariana, let's get one thing perfectly clear, just because we don't have hands doesn't mean we are hopeless invalids. Actually, we can do just about anything we set our minds to doing, only sometimes it is pitifully slow in the doing. Hence, no doorknobs. Come let me show you around our home."

A little later, they entered the new addition to her ever-expanding estate. "This will be your room while you are staying here with us. I hope you like it. Oh, here comes Francisca. She's originally from Barcella." Jenna introduced the two women. "Francisca will help you with anything you need. She has had much experience helping wounded people. She was a volunteer nurse in the recent Crusade. However, around here, Ariana, we expect that you will do as much as you can for yourself."

"But I cannot do anything. I can't even feed myself or go to the bathroom," wailed Ariana.

"For now, Francisca will be right here to help you. As soon as your wounds have fully healed, then I'll introduce you to some of the inventions that my husband has made for me. He has a device that I stick on my arms at mealtimes, and I can now feed myself, only someone has to cut up the meat. He's made many other little things that make life easier for us. However, that will have to wait until you are healed."

"Around here, we all eat together. I do hope you like children, because we have a flock of them running around the place; four are mine. I don't care how busy I may be, I always spend a couple hours playing with them right after supper. You are welcome to come watch and play too."

Sure enough, right after dinner, Lilly Ann brought the young ones outside under the big oak tree to watch the older kids play. Jenna with Ariana's arm in tow came outside to play. While Jenna ran off onto the green grassy playground out in front of the estate joining the pile of excited children, Lilly Ann explained, "Kick ball. Jenna and the kids love it. You can play too, if you want. I'd play, only I get to watch all the babies."

The next afternoon, with Ariana now comfortable in her new surroundings, Jenna and Ariana sat on the back patio, and I was in my baby crib beside mom. Jenna said, "Now I want you to close your eyes and return back to when your father was granting you permission to go and stay with your friend Gina. Yes, that's it. Now I want you to look at everything that happened after that, telling me all about it. What you are seeing, feeling, smelling, everything."

Ariana complied and began reliving her childhood once more. At first, she described it in vivid detail, but as the images grew worse, fewer and fewer details were related to Jenna. I paid close attention to what mom was doing, which was not much; she was just listening to Ariana with her full awareness. Soon, as Sally had explained, Ariana ran into the horribly painful times. As before, she nearly became unconscious, sitting in the deepest of apathy, totally at effect, causing absolutely nothing. I could not help but peek at Ariana's mind. What was she doing?

Blackness! I could not help but notice that Ariana's mind was full of that same kind of black mass that I experienced when I had my bouts of temporary insanity with the casting of lightning bolts. Mom had to face and confront utter insanity head on! Yet, there was mom, simply nudging Ariana on, "Yes, do continue. What happens next?" How Jenna found the patience to continue, I just did not know. Yet continue Jenna did until at last over an hour later, Ariana began to move onwards through those horrible mental images she had of what had happened to her. This first session ended after Ariana had managed to go through those hideous events but one time. It was suppertime.

The next afternoon, Jenna continued working with her, and this time Ariana managed to move through the images twice before they halted for supper. During the next few days progress improved, more and more details began emerging. Now Ariana saw that her left little finger had been cut off first, followed on down the line to her thumb. Later on, the same pattern was repeated with her right hand. However, after she had blurted out the completely out of date information about the Deacon, a massive pain in her left arm drove her into a deep unconsciousness. Even after all these days, Ariana stayed semi-comatose for nearly a half hour before she arrived at the other end and picked up with lesser painful memories. I also noticed that she was yawning more as she went through her images these last two days. Jenna took that as a hopeful sign.

Finally, Jenna had the entire lengthy incident very much reduced, except for that one period of intense pain and unconsciousness. We both speculated that it was at this point the assassin actually cut off her hands in an angry reaction to having heard about the Deacon. For two more days, Jenna worked Ariana on this portion of her trauma, but the blackness seemed impenetrable, just as my own mental blackness had been.

Jenna finally asked me, "Okay Bethany, any ideas? Have I finally found a trauma that cannot be erased or handled?" She sounded desperate.

I used to be just like her — had that black mass that seemed impervious to absolutely everything. Jes broke through with me by asking me if there was some earlier trauma behind it. There was, of course, and that was the key to erasing a lot of my own blackness. Now it is only greyish. We might try seeing if she has some earlier traumatic memories that are somehow tied into this current mess.

"Silly me! Why yes, I ought to have done that days ago! Ariana, I want you to look carefully. Is there some kind of trauma that happened to you before this time here that we have been working on? Take your time. Do you see anything else there?"

After an eternity, Ariana finally said very quietly, "I see something. I don't think it is real though."

"Well let's go through it anyway. Tell me all about it as you go through it," Jenna encouraged her.

"I see a young woman, about my age I think. She is arguing with some man. They are having a fight. He slaps her in the face. Say, my face is hurting where the man slapped that girl!"

"Thanks for telling me that. Interesting. Please continue, what happens next?" Jenna encouraged her once more.

"Well, she slapped him back. Good for her! Now the man is very angry and really slaps her hard. Ouch! That really stings my face! Oh, then she swings a frying pan at him. Darn, she misses. I rather hoped she would have hit him, you know. Oh no!"

"What is happening?"

"The man grabs the kitchen butcher knife and swings it at her. Ieeee. My right hand hurts terribly! The pain is so bad. It hurts right now! I am passing out!" Once more, Ariana fell unconscious, similar to the way she had been doing ever since Jenna began working her therapy on Ariana. A few minutes later, however, Ariana came out of the stupor, crying, "My hand's been cut off!" She sobbed for a few minutes, while we continued listening patiently to her. At last, she continued, "I awoke and had this horrible pain where my hand used to be. I am lying on our bed. It's still bleeding. I feel so weak. I cannot get up. I pee in my clothes and the bed. Now I am getting colder. I cannot move, so weak. Darkness comes over me. I hear voices. 'She's dead.' I'm thankful for that because the pain is gone. The voice says, 'Good thing for that. Otherwise she would be totally helpless for the rest of her life.' I agree. I'd be totally helpless forever after that. I was glad to die. Jenna, this cannot be real, can it? I do feel kind of relieved, though."

"Very well done, Ariana! Very well done indeed. Now let's go back through it once more and tell me every detail that's happening as you go along."

"Okay," she said, a tiny note of hopefulness in her voice, a note that we'd never heard before from Ariana. This time, very heavy yawns accompanied her viewing. When she reached the end, she exclaimed, "That was me! It happened to me! I agreed with him. I'm totally helpless for the rest of my life! I'd rather be dead! That happened to me!" And she began laughing. The more she laughed, the more she could not stop laughing. She laughed so long and hard that her sides began to hurt, but that only made her laugh all the harder. For nearly an hour Ariana laughed almost continuously, before she finally settled down.

"I feel so light now! So much better! I don't know how to say this, but I feel so alive. Sounds silly I know; I am alive anyway."

"Very well done indeed, Ariana. You have really done a super job of it. Come on. I don't know about you but Lizzy Ann here is starving and I am too. Let's get something to eat, shall we?"

"Eat?" and she began to laugh once more.

The next day, Beth Ann stopped by to examine her wounds and to change Ariana's bandages. "What's happened here!" she exclaimed, completely shocked. I couldn't see, so I looked through Jenna's eyes as she rushed to see what Beth Ann was looking at.

Ariana looked at her pinkish wounds. She didn't see anything remarkable about them, except her hands were forever gone. Neither did Jenna nor I. Beth Ann continued gawking and gasping, until at last Jenna forced her to explain. "Yesterday, when I changed the bandages, there were raw wounds here, not fully healed ones! I figured Ariana would need at least another three weeks of healing. Today I come to change the bandages and find out that at least three weeks of healing has happened over night! What in the blazes is going on here?"

Ariana said sheepishly, "You don't suppose what I looked at yesterday had anything to do with this do you"

"Well, I'll be!" Jenna exclaimed. "We ran out a whole lot of the trauma Ariana has suffered yesterday, right?"

Laughing, she replied, "We ran all of it out! Look what happened! It is a Holy Miracle!"

"This is incredible, Jenna, an incredible discovery! I have to let the other Healers know about your fabulous discovery! I wonder if it would work on other injuries?"

"Well, we could try an experiment," Jenna was feeling very ornery just now, "I'll just break your arm and then we can run the trauma of it breaking and see how fast your arm heals."

"What?" for an instant Beth Ann thought that Jenna was serious. Then she picked up on the joke, and everyone roared with laughter.

"Well, Ariana, you don't need any more bandages, that's for sure, but do be careful with your arms for a while," Beth Ann just had to say something as her official Healer, otherwise at a complete loss for words.

After she left, Ariana asked, "That wasn't real, I mean what I went through yesterday, that really didn't happen did it? I mean I could not possibly have lived before could I?"

Jenna now put on her druwid hat and began explaining that we are all immortal spiritual beings, who for a time inhabit these fleshly bodies. Her explanation lasted for several hours, during which time Ariana listened very intently, asking only a few questions.

When she finally finished her first lesson, Ariana said, "Well, they told me that you were the wisest person on Tarra. They weren't lying. That was real. I did live that life. How can I ever repay you for what you have done for me? This has been truly a miracle."

Smiling, Jenna replied, "Live a long life, Ariana, learn all that you can and help others become free. That would be the highest payment you could give me. I would like you to stay here with us for some time. There is much that we could teach you. Will you stay and learn?"

"I'd love to! But, but what can I do to help out around here. I'm not going to be awfully useful, I suppose, you know what I mean," she said holding her arms up.

"I know — been there — done that," Jenna replied in her motherly voice. "Sometimes it is awfully hard being like this. Accept help when you need it. Yet always look for what you can do and I'm sure you will find all sorts of things you can do. We still have feet, don't we?" Both chuckled.

That night around the huge supper table, the miraculous healing of Ariana was the sole topic of conversation. Everyone had to look at her arms. She did not flinch, but proudly displayed them. After dinner, Jenna as usual, headed out to play with the many children. Ben, the Loremaster, came up to Ariana. Sheepishly he said, "I brought a flower for a flower." He held a red rose in his hand and he let Ariana smell it. "Here, let me put it in your hair." He gently inserted it into her hair. Ariana did not know quite how to respond, but she was pleased.

"Care to go for a stroll outside?" he asked. "We can watch the others at play."

He offered her his arm. She hesitated a moment, rather unsure of what to do. Instinctively, she inserted her arm in his. Off they went for a stroll around the green. "I just love plants and animals. I'm a Loremaster, you know. I'd been helping Hank with the experimental gardens. He's trying to find the best way to grow the crops that he has already found grow the best here in Velona. Interesting work."

"You mean certain crops grow well in some places but not in others?" she asked. That had not occurred to her. She realized that she was almost completely ignorant of nearly everything. Her life had ceased when she was ten and before that, she had been isolated from much as a noble's daughter.

Ben, thankful for someone who at least listened to him as he talked animatedly about his passion, talked on for hours, showing her all about the large experimental plot. Only when dusk came and they could no longer see well, did they walk back to the main buildings. Ben said, "Perhaps tomorrow you could come and watch. When your arms are better, you can even help with the spring planting. Jenna used to do that for Hank when she first came here a long time ago. But then, I expect Jenna will have many other things for you to learn and do. She is our Wid after all."

"She helped plant? With no hands?"

"Yes, she came along after the seeds were dropped and covered them up."

"I see. Well, sure, if I can. I really don't know what Jenna will want me to do, so I cannot promise anything just yet."

"Sure thing. Night, Ariana. Thanks for the walk and letting me talk. No one around here listens much to me, except Hank."

Next morning, Jenna, who had observed the two last evening, said, "Well, Ariana, looks like you've already got the boys around here interested in you."

Ariana flushed, "I don't know what to do! I realized last night that I don't actually know much at all! Hardly anything worth mentioning, really. Especially boys. What do I do? Ben is very nice though, isn't he? He's not married, is he?"

"That's why I so badly wanted you to stay with us for a time. We can help you learn as much as you want to know. No, he's not married."

"Why? He seems to like girls?"

"He loves nature, plants, and animals. He has a passion for them, just like my Hank. Besides me, few around here are much interested in that. I think he is just lonely. Come; let's see what we can do about your education."

Later that afternoon, Ariana had some free time and she went in search of Ben. This was the first time that she independently and without any advice or help went off on her own. A feeling of freedom and independence swept over her, and it felt incredibly good. She found Ben and Hank hard at work in one of the carefully laid out garden plots.

"Hi there Ariana," Hank cheerily said. "Come to see our monster tomatoes?" He held up the largest tomato she'd seen, but then she had not seen that many, she reminded herself. "We grow some of the largest anywhere. We'll have to take a load of them to the farmer's market on Sunday. You want to come along with us? Jenna will probably insist that you come anyway just to hear High Priestess Elona Po deliver her sermon."

"Sure," she replied.

"Ben, why don't you take a break and show Ariana around a bit?" Ben needed no further excuse.

After showing her the expansive vegetable gardens, he explained, "When Elona Po and Hank and the others first came to Velona, people were starving everywhere. There just was not enough to eat anywhere. Hank began to try to figure out what crops grew best here. That turned everything around. Now, everyone has more than enough to eat even though the population is tremendous. Do you realize that there are over two hundred thousand folks just in Velona proper? Even more live in the outlying towns, at least another two hundred thousand. The crops that Hank developed support them all. Amazing, isn't it."

Ariana knew starvation very well. She began to see how growing the right crops could help all the starving people back in Zargarb. Of course, there wasn't any way to help them right now, not with the Holy Paladins there and all that. Still the tiniest of gem of an idea began to form in her mind.

Later that evening, Ariana had a chance to speak with Jenna lone, "Can I ask you something Jenna, something private?"

"Sure, ask away."

"Sex. Sex is ugly, right?" She only had her nightmare rapes as a measuring stick.

"Good heavens no, dear child! You've been horribly mistreated. Sex is the most holy of things. We view it as the Holy Union of man and woman. We rejoice in it, for only thorough such mating can we bring new children into the world. The entire future of mankind is totally dependent upon new generations coming into being. Sex should be the most intimate joining of two beings and their bodies. It is a thing to be cherished between husband and wife. Hank and I do it every night without fail, that is, until I become with child again."

"Oh. So it is an enjoyable thing?"

"Trust me; done right, it is so. Done as it was done with you, it becomes perhaps the most loathsome thing imaginable. First, though, you need to find the one person in the world that is right for you, that you truly love and want to share this most intimate union. Now go get some sleep." Ariana thanked her and walked away pondering and wondering what it must be like.

That night as Hank put me in my cradle beside their bed for the night, Jenna spoke softly to him. "Hank, I wonder if I could ask something of you."

He teased, "No, now haven't you asked enough of me already? We've done it nearly every night for ten years. Maybe I will wear out. Then what would you do?"

She laughed at his playfulness, which was one of the things that so attracted her to him. "No dear, not that! It's Ariana. I got word to expect a boatload of horribly wounded, traumatized women from the Junction. They will be arriving any day now and I will not have time to work with her much. Could you and Ben possibly take her on as an apprentice? Treat her as if she had the knowledge of perhaps a six year old girl? I'd let someone in the Circle apprentice her, but they are going to be awfully busy with the ever growing crises in the occupied sectors."

"Sure thing, love. I think she at least likes us. I was worried at first that she would hate all men. Probably would have if you had not worked your miracle on her. Now, I'm ready to hop in the bed, but are you?" he teased her. Playfully, she used a touch of her power to move objects to pull him into their bed.

Two days later, the caravel from Velona arrived, carrying twenty-five women who had been rescued from the Junction's Nunnery. Most all were in pathetic shape, grim indeed. However, the Healers from Zargarb had worked wonders; all were at last on the mend, physically. As before, Jenna sent a coach to fetch them to her estate. However, there were so many of them that she had to borrow some coaches from Elona. Elona also sent along her Healer, Mary Dietz, and Jenna pulled in three other Healers from other scout squads and a fortress on the border with Barcella.

Figuratively, anyway, Jenna had her hands full with all the needed therapy sessions, twenty-five in dire need. She began with those who had already recovered the most. The mornings she spent on Santi duties, the afternoons, therapy, the evenings, the children and her family. Yes, it was heartbreaking to see so many mistreated and mutilated women in one location. Yet, we saw thousands in far worse condition than these during the Crusades. Still it is one thing to see a man mutilated by a sword cut sustained in battle and another to see a woman mutilated and mistreated for no justifiable reason.

"I don't see how you can do all this therapy alone," Beth Ann told Jenna after their morning meeting was finished and they were on their way to lunch. "I was wondering if you thought that I might be able to lend a hand and do this therapy thing that you do? Is it terribly difficult to do?"

Jenna really could use help, but she knew that it took a special kind of person to do what she was doing. "Beth Ann, if you were doing therapy on me and I was describing a horse to you, yet I kept continually calling it a dog, could you hold your tongue and not correct me, telling me that it was actually a horse?"

"You mean when I really know it is a horse?"

"Yes. Can you do that?"

"I suppose, but wouldn't it be better for the patient to know the truth of a matter?" she asked.

"Patience, in time they may well change their minds and correct themselves. Other times, they might not ever, but who cares if it is a dog or a horse, if in viewing it they fully recover?"

"Well, not really I guess, if they recover," Beth Ann admitted.

"Okay, can you avoid telling a patient what to think about something that has happened to them? For example, the patient says the man then stuck something into my privates. Can you avoid then telling them that they were raped?"

"Sure, if it's important."

"It is, Beth Ann. In a therapy session, these people are reliving terribly horrible, painful traumas. For the most part, when they are right smack in the middle of the worst part, they are neither rational nor observant and can easily call a horse a dog. Telling them what to think or correcting their 'mistakes' is deadly; it will totally ruin that entire therapy session."

"Really?"

"Really. If you think you have the patience, you can observe me this afternoon and see how it's done. I already know that you are a good listener and can face the horrors they describe without flinching or you would not be a Healer." Beth Ann accepted and watched all afternoon.

When they finished, she said, "That's all there is to it? It is so simple, so easy to do!"

"Yes, as long as you don't tell them what to think or correct what appears to be their errors. Here comes the next woman. Do you want to give it a try?" Beth Ann did. It was a bit awkward for her at first, not knowing the proper way to get things started, but she managed. To her astonishment, the woman felt much better when she finished. Of course, the woman would need many more sessions to handle fully the entire trauma she had undergone.

"This is so cool!" exclaimed Beth Ann. "It's almost the rush I feel after I have just saved someone's leg or healed a deadly illness."

"You've truly helped another. I know. Good feeling," Jenna replied.

"Okay, tomorrow you can work in the next room. You can solo."

"But what do I do if I run into trouble?"

"Bethany will be monitoring you, as she does me. If you run into trouble, she'll lend you a hand."

"Lizzy Ann?"

"Yes." Beth Ann found it somewhat discomforting that a two year old baby would be monitoring her session and helping her out if she ran into trouble. It rather shattered her viewpoint of babies.

During the next few weeks, listening to all the stories the women related, I saw a distinct pattern emerging. The Arad families who tried to protest the abduction of their daughters often were killed themselves. In contrast, the Sea Prince families often turned in their own daughters! Only about a quarter of the women's families resisted and had been killed. Either way, however, these women had no place else to turn to but Velona. Either they had no families left to which to return or they would not want to return if they had families that had turned them in.

Compassionately, Elona Po would visit each woman, once their therapy had finished and their bodies healed. She offered them sanctuary in Velona. Based upon each woman's physical needs and wants, she found new homes for them, where they could continue on the path to regaining their self-respect and become productive in life once more.

Finally, the last of these women had been handled and had moved into new homes in Velona proper. "What a hectic three weeks that has been," declared Jenna. "We all could use a breather."

Unfortunately, a breather was not in our future. A caravel was bringing one Jovanna Barcella and her aged father to us, docking tomorrow! Jenna had insisted that she be brought here at once. Since it appeared that they would have one afternoon free, Beth Ann asked to speak to Jenna. "I've handled five cases totally by myself, with just a little coaching from Bethany. I've seen something that I've been wondering about, a very curious, weird thing."

"What's that?" Jenna asked.

"Always it seems that underlying everything, I mean totally buried underneath all that trauma, that pain, that unconsciousness, are simple words — like I heard the other day. The patient heard a voice standing over her saying, 'Now she'll be helpless all the time.' And that was precisely what the woman was feeling and acting when she came here, like she was helpless all the time. In fact, she told me that at least a dozen times. Then there was the rape victim, who heard a man telling her, 'Don't move or you'll die.' When I first saw the woman, she was terrified of being moved about. I had to coach her just to get her into the room, to go get some dinner. She was terrified of moving."

"It is almost like they are acting out literally what those words are saying," Beth Ann concluded.

"And what happens to your patients when they spot those words being said?" asked Jenna, using her druwid teacher skills.

"Usually, once they spot that, the whole trauma begins to evaporate, to go away, like it had not happened. No longer are they afraid to move or be totally helpless."

"Very good observation, Beth Ann. And what can you conclude from all this?"

"That words spoken to someone who is unconscious and traumatized are somehow remembered and thereafter have some kind of super control power over the victim."

"Excellent observation, Beth Ann," Jenna smiled, rewarding her pupil.

"But that means we Healers should probably say very little while we do out work on the injured. You know, not add more words which might later have control over our patients."

"Hum, I had not thought of that one. Point well taken!"

Just then, Paulette telepathically interrupted them. *Message from Paul. Object retrieved. Can't read it. Is on his way back. Expect arrival early October. Can you tell us what is going on now?*

No, not until he is docked in Velona. Until then, he is in dire peril.

Paulette had to accept this decision, though she liked it not.

The next day, the caravel docked. This time Beth Ann personally met the ship, their patient was in critical condition, in and out of consciousness, having just survived a major operation. Jovanna had suffered under the knife of the assassin Silas and her wounds had become infected. She had nearly died from blood poisoning. To save her life, the Healers had to remove the diseased portions of her arms, which now ended just above her elbows. Yet, she had survived the operation. Gently Beth Ann and her Santi guards lifted the young woman and carried her off the ship and into the waiting coach. One guard led her father, still clutching his sack holding their clothing.

The old man, Genorio Barcella, had never been to Velona. He was terribly shocked at the sheer size of the city, its apparent wealth, and vitality, stark contrast to his Barcella. He could only gape and wag his open mouth as he stared at the sights as they rode through the city and out the north gate, heading for the estate. "Will my daughter live?" he finally asked, as they left the enormous city behind.

"Looks like the Healers in Barcella have done a fine job, sir," Beth Ann sounded as hopeful as she could, although she knew that one could only say for sure perhaps a week from now. She was in critical condition.

An hour later, Beth Ann, accompanied by several other Healers, had Jovanna in her room in the estate and changed her bandages. Each Healer closely inspected the wounds to make sure that the best possible job had been done. In fact, it had been. They all agreed that Mary Beth had done a fabulous job, so Jenna sent their findings to Mary Beth later that day. Jenna always tried to validate people's good work.

For the next week, Beth Ann and three other Healers sat constantly at Jovanna's bedside. Once, she regained consciousness while Beth Ann was there. She looked confused and shocked. Talking softly, Beth Ann said, "Welcome, Jovanna. I am Beth Ann, a Healer. You and your father are now in the safest place in all Tarra. No one can harm either you or your father here. Rest now. We will look after you." Some recognition of what she said reflected upon her face before she again passed out.

Each day, her father would also come and set beside his daughter. He still held out hope that she would survive. Each day, he saw better color in her face. He wept for joy when she finally opened her eyes a week later. "Dad!" she said. He could only cry.

Beth Ann was there as well. Jovanna, now fully awake for the first time since the tragedy occurred, tried to move her arms and sit up. Of course, nothing happened; they weren't there. The shock on her face as she looked down at the heavy bandages on what remained of her arms was almost more than Beth Ann could face. Tears flowed from both women.

Beth Ann tried to find some comforting words, but could find none. What do you say to a young woman who wakes up to find that she has almost no arms left? Instead, she did the right thing, she said nothing, but cried along with Jovanna. "Oh daddy, look at me now! How will we ever survive?"

"Don't worry now baby. We'll manage somehow. We always have. These are kind folks here. They will help us. Someway we will get by. I was so terribly afraid that I would die alone, forsaken by everything I have ever loved in this world." Shakily, he leaned over and kissed her on her forehead. The loving touch works miracles; it is said.

Somehow, Jovanna found the strength to ask, "Daddy, how is your shaking? Is it growing worse?"

"Don't worry about me. You just lie there and get well. That's all that is important to me, Jovanna. You just have to live!"

Still crying, she said, "I will daddy. I will. I promise. Maybe Romero will come for us."

"Aye, perhaps he will, daughter." Then she realized that she was starving and terribly thirsty and had to go to the bathroom and was nauseous all at the same time! At last, Beth Ann was on firm ground. This she knew how to handle. In one fast motion, she got the bedpan in position, and then put her arm around Jovanna to help her up, steading her as she went. After making sure she was stable sitting on the edge of the bed, she got the pot of broth, which had been brought in periodically for just this occasion. She tested it to make sure it was not too hot and poured a measured amount into a cup. She held it to Jovanna's lips so she could drink.

"Only one cup, until we see if it stays down. Then, you can have more."

"I'd better lie down," she said. Beth Ann helped her lie back, placing a pillow behind her so she was in a somewhat more upright position. It stayed down and during the next few hours, Jovanna drank nearly all the broth. Beth Ann knew that a healthy appetite was a very, very good sign indeed.

After she felt better, Jovanna asked, "What happened to me? I remember being tortured, but then the rest is a blur. Where exactly are we and how did we get here? God, I'd be so much better off if I was dead than like this."

Her father tried his best to explain, but much was beyond his own comprehension. "I found you outside that morning. Somehow, I got you on the bed, and I watched over you, but you got sicker and sicker. Red lines began streaking up your arms. I remembered the tall tales that some of the Crusaders used to tell that the Santi were great healers. I didn't know what else to do so I went to the fortress and begged for some help. Right away, they came and took you to the fortress. They said that if I had waited another day, you would be dead. You've had a very narrow escape, daughter. After that, it is all somewhat fuzzy. I don't rightly know what was what, confusing to me. Next thing I know is they put us on one of those new, fancy ships, and we came here."

Beth Ann felt she should know a bit more and she added, "The butchers left you with infected wounds. Gangrene had set in along with blood poisoning slowly moving up your arms. Had they not operated when they did, you most definitely would be dead days ago. When Jenna Rose Weston, the leader of the entire Santi organization, heard about you, she ordered you sent here at once. You are now in the safest location anywhere on Tarra, bar none. This is Jenna's estate. I'm sure she will want to come visit with you very soon now that you are awake. Jenna is a great healer, as you will find out. Oh, yes, don't worry about any kind of payment for anything. It is all done compliments of the Santi. Helping people in need is our goal. Now you had better take a little nap. One of us Healers will be right here every minute of every day until you no longer need us." Jovanna at last relaxed and fell asleep.

The next morning, Beth Ann fed a more solid porridge to her patient. After going to the bathroom and eating, Beth Ann helped Jovanna sit up, a pillow at her back. She knew that Jenna would be coming within a few minutes and wanted Jovanna to be ready.

Just in time, Jenna strolled in. "Ah you must be Jovanna. I am your host, Jenna Rose Weston," she said with her usual cheerfulness.

Jovanna stared in disbelief at Jenna, particularly at empty ends of her arms. Jenna continued, "I'd shake hands with you, Jovanna, but as you can see, we both would have a bit of difficulty accomplishing that!"

"You, you, you are a hopeless cripple too?" Jovanna finally managed to say. "But I thought you were the leader of the Santi?"

Using a rather stern tone, Jenna answered, "One, I prefer to use the term physically challenged. Two, you and I are far, far from hopeless. In time, you will discover that you can do things, only in different ways, and it sometimes takes a whole lot longer. Three, yes I am the leader of over ten thousand Santi del Dio. Fourth, a leader leads. A leader does not necessarily need hands, but I will admit, at times it sure would be handy." That brought a slight grin to Jovanna.

"I have meetings to attend this morning. I'll check back with you this afternoon. I just wanted you to know that you and your father can stay here just as long as you desire. You are in safe hands — just not mine, get it?" Both women chuckled over the pun. Jenna thought it was a good sign that Jovanna could at least chuckle a bit, considering her situation. Jovanna would have a long road to any kind of real recovery.

Jovanna slept until noon. At lunchtime, Beth Ann put her on light solid food, bit of fish paste on bread with some cheese. It stayed down and the queasiness seemed handled. However, she again slept through most of the afternoon; her arms were throbbing unrelentingly.

However, in a few days, she was eating regularly and well, far better in fact, than she had eaten in close to ten years. Gradually, the throbbing subsided, and she felt more awake and alert, but also the reality of her handicap grew more and more real. She could not escape the fact that others had to do nearly everything for her, and she slowly began to retreat inward.

After supper, Beth Ann and the other Healers decided that was now time that Jovanna should get a bit more active. "Come on, let's get you up and outside for a bit of fresh evening air. Besides, you can watch the games." Jovanna allowed her to help her up. She was still rather weak, but had to admit that if felt good to be up. Her father, using a cane, hobbled along one side of her, while Beth Ann had her arm around her waist, just in case she became disoriented.

Outside the leaves on some trees were just beginning to turn. The air had just a slight chill to it, enough to freshen one's senses. They slowly strolled over to the big oak tree. A horde of children were running and playing on the green grass, which stretched out for a great distance. Jovanna suddenly saw Jenna out there with the kids. She watched as they played kick ball. Jenna would kick the ball trying to hit someone. If they were hit, they became it and had to kick the ball toward someone else. Meanwhile everyone else was running around trying to avoid being hit by the ball. Everyone was laughing and having a fun time. At last, Jenna spied Jovanna and waved an arm at her. Instinctively, Jovanna raised her hand to wave back, only the short bit of arm went up, and she cringed at the sight.

Half out of breath from so much running, Jenna came over to chat with Jovanna. "So good to see you up and about, Jovanna. When you get all healed up, you can play with us too. The kids will love it. These here," she pointed, "are mine. Beth Ann's and Lilly Ann's are all over the place."

"Mommy, come on I need some help," Donata complained, pulling on Jenna's shirt.

"Gotta go," Jenna replied with a laugh.

"Jenna's out there playing with the whole bunch every evening unless there is some dire emergency to handle," Beth Ann explained. "No one minds or even cares that she doesn't have any hands." She added that as a nudge to Jovanna. After a bit, she asked, "Are you married yet? Any children?"

"No to both. The evil men took over Barcella when I was quite young. I have been just trying to stay alive, help dad out, and do what little I can to help the rebellion," she answered a bit sadly.

"Boyfriend, perhaps?" Beth Ann asked hopefully.

"What man would ever want me like this? I'm better off dead!" she said as tears began moving down her face.

What could she say in reply? At last, Beth Ann answered, "Well, with someone as pretty as you are, a kind, handsome man will turn up one day. Just have faith."

Jovanna didn't believe one word of that, however. Seeing her look, Beth Ann added, "Look you are quite an attractive woman. I wish I had your hair. It's beautiful. Look at how stringy mine is. I can never do much with it and yours is so lush and wavy. Gorgeous. Just have faith, Jovanna."

At least she got a small smile in return, along with "I'm really better off dead."

Her appearance out of doors was the signal the Jenna was waiting for; now that Jovanna had regained enough strength, Jenna felt it was time to begin to erase the terrible trauma she had endured. Next afternoon, she came into Jovanna's room, along with Beth Ann, who was there to replace the Healer who had been with her all morning, while Beth Ann dealt with Santi duties.

"How are you doing today, Jovanna?" Jenna asked.

"Okay I guess, but I'd be better off dead, you know."

"I understand. Now then, Jovanna, we are going to attempt to remove the trauma that you have experienced. I want you to lay back, close your eyes, and see if you can find the first memories you have where this whole thing started." She went on to explain what she wanted Jovanna to do. This time, Beth Ann was observing firsthand a severe case.

"It starts off being a nice day," Jovanna began. Slowly she began to re-experience the events of that tragic day. She actually screamed when the man in black cut off her little finger. After that, mostly the memories were black and un-viewable. She drifted into and out of consciousness as she moved through the long memories, which included being brought to the Santi fortress and the operation there. She finally finished when she saw herself waking up and seeing clearly Beth Ann, here in this room. The incident, from her point of view, lasted for a goodly number of days.

By the time Jenna stopped for supper, Jovanna had gone through the whole tragic episode, reliving the lighter portions, twice now. However, she said, "I do feel a little better about some of it, Jenna. What's supposed to happen with this?"

"Oh whatever happens will happen. We'll do some more tomorrow afternoon. I think that you did splendidly today. Come on, let get something to eat."

For the next four days, Jenna kept doggedly at it, having Jovanna keep on going over it. Bit by bit, more of the unconsciousness lifted, and she could relate what was happening at that point. Finally, only two portions of that horror Jovanna still could not view, still going unconscious when she reached those places. One was when Silas got angry and cut her hands off, and the other was the lengthy operation to save her life in the fortress, where most of her arms had been removed. Still, Jovanna continued to say that she would be better off dead.

One morning, Beth Ann asked Jenna, "I couldn't help but notice that Jovanna keeps saying that she is better off dead. Why does she keep saying that?"

"Oh, I suppose we will find that out in due time, Beth Ann. Just have patience; she will tell us when she can at last face whatever it is all about. Say, I just heard that Paul is due to dock this afternoon. I sure will sleep easier once he is safely back in Velona!"

That afternoon, Jovanna made further progress; now she was describing in detail just how Silas in anger and revenge had cut off her hands, screaming as his helpers seared the wounds with a red-hot iron. She felt even better when the session was ended a little earlier than usual.

Paul had arrived, bubbling over with excitement, proud of his achievement. He had been successful and, per his orders, he came straight to Jenna, carrying the journal still concealed within the waterskin. "Hi everyone, I'm back. I have it Jenna. Oh, hello beautiful. I'm Paul, Paul Wilkins," he said suddenly noticing the beautiful stranger sitting on the bed.

"You must be kidding. Beautiful, like this?" she held up what remained of her arms defiantly as if proving to Paul that he was an idiot.

His face reddened, "I'm sorry miss. I did not mean to say that was beautiful, but rather you are."

She calmed down a bit. Jenna introduced her. "Paul, this is Jovanna Barcella. Jovanna, this is my Protector, Paul Wilkins. He's just back from a secret mission and is dying to tell me all about it. If you will excuse us, I'll go let him." To Beth Ann, she asked, "Will you hand me Lizzy Ann, please?" She carefully placed me in mom's arms, and we left Beth Ann to help Jovanna with some personal details.

Beth Ann said, "You really got him good, Jovanna! I've never seen him so red-faced." Jovanna managed a grin.

Once safe in the main hall with just himself, Jenna, and me, Paul spoke freely. "It went like a well-oiled machine. "Not a single problem. I snuck in there during the night and no one saw a thing. It was all just as you described, Ket. Only," here his face became more serious than I had ever seen it. I knew what was coming.

"Only what?" prodded Jenna.

"There was a mummified body still clutching the waterskin. It was dressed in clothing that I have never seen before absolutely anywhere! Yet, he had very short hair and what appeared to be a nasty wound at the base of his neck. Ket, I swear it looked like you, but you died, and we buried you, or rather gave you a funeral."

I Mind Linked to both. *Your eyes tell you the truth. I was dead or rather my body was. I am almost certain of it. I woke up a very long time later after the boat beached on an unknown island far north and west of West Reach. I met some wonderful people there who looked after me for a time. My left side was paralyzed, but I had a mission. When I strangled the assassin, Paul, I accidentally saw his memories of the secret vault and the journal. I had to steal it. I sailed in that same boat you all buried me in, believe it or not, all the way to Megalos. By then only my right arm was working; the rest of the body was near dead again. I crawled my way through the tunnels to the vault, broke in, and crawled out. I just got inside the secret tunnel where you saw me, when the body finally died a second time. I had about one minute to spare. That's how close we came to losing this prize.*

Paul gushed, "But how could you do that if you were dead when we set you adrift? Did we make a horrible mistake calling your body dead when it was only badly wounded?"

This was the line of inference that I dreaded. If I said yes, the self-recriminations would likely destroy the man and everyone else who had a hand in it, including my sister Fianna and Fergus! *No, the body was dead. I'm convinced of it. However, spiritual beings, Paul, can be powerful indeed when the need arises. I think that I tapped into some abilities that I did not even know I possessed, rather like Jenna and her ability to move things. Again, Paul, thank you for recovering what may well bring down this evil church.*

However, I want your solemn promise that, whenever you tell others about the recovery of the journal, you won't mention that you also saw the dead body there. Promise me that, please.

Paul agreed and Jenna then asked for everyone in the Circle to join her. Happily, Paul animatedly related his secret quest. Although nothing at all exciting had occurred, he made it sound like it had been a grand adventure. At last, everyone began looking over the journal. "Can any of you even read its title?" Jenna finally exclaimed in exasperation.

Not a soul present could. I had to step in. *Jenna, hold it up to your eyes, and I'll read it through them.* She obeyed and I translated into everyone's mind. *For the Pope's Eyes Only: Read Only When You Need Control Over the Mano del Dio.*

"Oh good god!" exclaimed Lilly Ann. Others had similar exclamations.

It is written in Ancient Arad. I used to read and write that when I was a young girl in Juda Arad and was copying down all the stories their prophets told to Jes Amir, part of his religious training.

"How on Tarra are we ever going to be able to read what it says?" Beth Ann whined.

"Well we cannot wait until Lizzy Ann grows up, that's for sure," Lilly Ann added. "We'll just have to find someone who can read it for us, maybe translate it. Surely, with the hundreds of thousands of people in Velona, someone must be able to read Ancient Arad. I'll get on it immediately, if someone will watch the kids."

"I'll cover for you," Beth Ann volunteered.

"I'll go with her and keep you posted," Paulette added. "Perhaps, Sam might know someone. He knows quite a lot of folks. A weapon smith makes many contacts. Besides I promised to visit him today." Having been a newlywed in the past, I knew she wanted to be closer to him.

"One final head's up for today," Jenna ended the meeting. She reported on the situation in Solamina. "Another twenty-two traumatized, mutilated women are on their way here. We have about eight days to prepare. Beth Ann, on your way out make sure that you have all the supplies you need. I suspect it is going to be a rough time again." She then had to explain to Paul about the two dozen that had come in September from the Junction.

After supper, Ben took Paul to introduce him to Hank and his new apprentice, Ariana Zar. Paul was quite surprised to see how cheerful she looked, considering what she had been through. Then, he remembered Jovanna and dropped in to see how she was doing. She had an enticing look about her. She had long brown hair, typical of those from Barcella, and the most gorgeous greenish eyes he'd seen. He meant what he had said when he first saw her; she was beautiful. He really hadn't seen her arms, because he was in such a rush to tell Jenna about the journal that he'd failed actually to look beyond her head. He decided to apologize and explain it to her.

She was sitting up in her bed when he knocked on her door, although it was wide open. "Hello Jovanna. It's me, Paul Wilkins. Got a minute?"

She wondered what he wanted. "Got a minute? Yes, I got all the minutes in the world now. I can't do much of anything. I'd be better off dead."

"Hi, I just wanted to come and apologize to you, Jovanna. I have been on a several month ocean voyage, top-secret mission and all that. I had just gotten back that very minute and was under orders to report at once to Jenna the moment I got back. I'm sorry; I was in a hurry. Okay a rush. I just looked at your face and head and said what I felt, that you are a very beautiful woman. I didn't mean to insult you. I didn't even see your arms. I'm sorry if I offended you; it was not my intention."

"Well, I might have been pretty once, but not anymore. Not like this," she wiggled what was left of her arms.

"Yes, that has got to be a horrible thing to bear. I'm a fighter. A Protector is my profession. My job is to protect Jenna with my life if need be, and then the rest of them, you know, the twins, Beth Ann and Lilly Ann and the others. I also have some Healer training; we all do, but only Beth Ann has that as her specialty. I'll be entirely honest with you, Jovanna, because I feel that I owe it to you for upsetting you earlier."

"You see, I was with Ket Bethany and the Santi Strike Force during the Crusades. At that time, my job was to protect Ket, our leader, before he was assassinated by the same folks that got to you, the evil Mano del Dio. Anyway, after we helped the Arad Raiders finally wipe out the last of the Centurions up by the Cedar Forest, I got to see and help deal with the worst tragedy I have ever heard. Thousands of Crusaders, young men and a few women, were in such a bad state that it makes what you are experiencing look like a scratch. Honestly, I never dreamed that men could so brutalize others. I saw young lads with their arms and legs cut off and the remaining portions literally rotting off. The stench of dead and decay coming from that Crusader camp was unbearable. Yet we all pitched in and began to save lives as best we could."

"One poor boy, couldn't have been over eighteen, had both legs and arms missing. He was just lying there, body rotting with gangrene, waiting for death to take him. I felt so utterly helpless. I knew there was nothing I or any of the Healers could do for him. So I just sat with him until he died. You know what he said to me? He said, 'Did we win?' He'd given everything he had, suffered horribly, and yet he was more concerned with having made a difference, helping to free people. I told him that we won and had saved Velona and New Barq. Then, he died, but his face still had a smile on it. I never even knew his name."

Paul had made an impression on Jovanna, although he did not know how. She said, "I'm like that boy, Paul. For almost ten years, I have been helping the resistance in Barcella fight back. I was the serving maid for the General, Butcher Ali Sanchez. He never even noticed me, but I listened to all his plans and orders. At night, I would relay them to other resistance fighters. Then the evil Mano del Dio men came and caught me. He did this to me and left me for dead on my father's doorstep." She wiggled her arms again.

He replied formally, "On behalf of all the free peoples of Tarra and all those oppressed in Barcella, thank you, Jovanna for all that you have done to help others survive and for your ultimate sacrifice. You are a true resistance fighter."

Until now, no one had ever really acknowledged her role and what she had done, the risks that she had taken daily for ten years. It took her completely by surprise. She accepted his thanks. "So you were with the Santi during the war? I've heard all sorts of rumors, but I've never known anyone who was there. I'd love to hear about it all, but I suppose you need to get back to your wife and family. You've only gotten back a few hours ago. They probably missed you very much."

Paul chuckled, "Married? Ha, never had time for it. My sister, Paulette, and I we are very close, but I'm not married."

"How come? Surely you have not been fighting all your life."

"No, you are right. It's just the social excuse that I tell people. Paulette has just gotten married. After all these years, she's finally fallen in love. He's a weapon smith, probably the best one around here. Me, I'll be frank with you Jovanna, I've never fallen in love, except with my sister. I love her dearly, but she's my sister. True, I know a whole lot of Sisterhood fighters that have joined the Santi. Some are dynamite women, as you can probably imagine. Yet, nothing ever, well, rather clicked with me. I guess if I am to be truthful with you, I've pretty well given up all hope of ever finding a person that I can admire, respect, and love with all my heart. Instead, I devote my energy to the Santi."

"Well in that case, since you don't have to rush off and since I cannot do anything but sit here, can you tell me all about the great Crusade? I'd love to hear it firsthand. Were you there when the Emperor was killed, near our border with Velona?"

Jovanna did seem interested, and Paul really did not have anything actually to do just now. "Yes, yes, I was there. An ex-Sisterhood fighter, Lenkova and I held off the Emperor's men, while Ket killed him. It was quite a battle."

Jovanna's eyes lit up. "Oh my! Please tell me the whole story, everything that happened!" Paul began narrating the story. Both he and Jovanna lost complete track of time.

Finally, the night Healer had to interrupt them, "Hey you two, it is very late, way past Jovanna's bed time. You can continue this tomorrow."

"Holy cow! Where did the time go?" exclaimed Paul. "I'm sorry; this has never happened to me before. I lost complete track of the time."

"Thanks, Paul. I enjoyed every minute. Please come back when you can and tell me more," Jovanna requested, although she did not know why. She decided that at least she had not been bored all evening as she had been in the past. She thought to herself, "All I can do is listen. I am better off dead than this way."

On their way to deliver the afternoon therapy session to Jovanna, Jenna commented to Beth Ann, who was holding me, "Jovanna sure is a tough one. We're making progress, but it's taking a long time. I do hope I can get her handled before this next large bunch comes."

"You're doing okay, Jenna. Each day sees more progress. It's not as if nothing beneficial is happening. Any progress is a giant step forward. Without you, no one's trauma would be cleared up. We Healers patch up bodies, but you are patching up souls, the spiritual beings. I think that may be more important in the end. Lizzy Ann and I will watch as usual. Honestly, I'm learning lots just watching you do it," Beth Ann insisted.

"Hi Jovanna," Jenna greeted her patient. "I hear Paul kept you up half the night with his war stories."

"He's entertaining, and I got to hear what really happened, you know from someone who was actually there." Then she slumped emotionally once more, "But I don't know what good it does me. I'm really better off dead, you know."

"Well, I'm glad you got to hear it firsthand. Shall we begin again?" Beth Ann and I both were taken by complete surprise. My first reaction and Beth Ann's too would have been to try to convince her that she was not better off dead! Yet, Jenna ignored that and re-enforced something positive about Jovanna's comments. Interesting. I was beginning to see why Jenna was the master. I certainly was right in my choice for the new Santi leader!

Jovanna began re-experiencing that lengthy traumatic event. Today, she flew through most of it rapidly; little new material appeared. However, with some yawns, she finally pierced that black haze of pain and unconsciousness surrounding the surgery done to save her live in the Santi Fortress of Barcella. She finished by saying, "There, I've finally seen it all, and I'm still better off dead." Beth Ann was holding me today, and I could see her face. She looked crestfallen. All this therapy and still Jovanna clung to her death wish.

"Very well done, Jovanna. Good job. Now I want you to look and see if there is another trauma that happened earlier than this one with your hands and arms. Go ahead, what do you see?" I could see by Beth Ann's facial expressions that she had forgotten all about this aspect, that if the trauma did not completely go away, there might be another one that had happened even earlier in time.

"No not really, I had a pretty normal childhood. Bumped my knees a couple time, sprained my wrist once. No, I don't think so."

"Fine, let's take a closer look there. We want something that happened earlier," Jenna insisted, prodded, and coached.

After a few minutes of Jenna's insistent request, Jovanna said, "Well this isn't real, just my imagination, but I do see some picture here of something." She yawned. Jenna thanked her and had her begin re-experiencing it. "Well, it sort of looks like Barcella, but the city is so small! Even the buildings look quite primitive even. This can't be real. It's just my imagination."

"You are doing fine, just continue going through it," Jenna insisted quietly.

"People — they look like Barcella folks — you know we have brunette hair, not blonde as the other sectors mostly have. I see people standing around looking at the ground. Doesn't seem to be anything happening, they are just staring at the ground. That's all. I am really better off dead."

"Okay, Jovanna. Let's go through it all one more time. Tell me everything that you see and feel and hear."

Jovanna let out one huge yawn and began. "God! This illusion — it's *so* real looking! The ground is so hard and warm. I can feel the dirt between my toes. I'm doing the laundry and washing a baby, my daughter, I think. It's a pretty, sunny day. I'm happy. Then, this man comes up to me, rough looking. God, I think that is my husband. He looks awful, drunk or hung over. He smells badly. 'Woman, go fix me bed now!' He says to me. 'I'm washing the baby and the clothes right now. I'll do it when I'm done here.' 'The hell you will, bitch! You do it now just as I says!' He smashes his fist into my face. It hurts. I slap him back. He goes berserk, wildly thrashing me. I put my arms up to defend myself. He grabs them and throws me on the ground. God, he is stomping on me. Pain. Oh, the pain. I hear awful noises, cracking of bones, my arms, oh, they hurt, pain is so bad. He keeps stomping on me. I pass out."

Jovanna slumped over slightly and was unconscious right before our eyes! Beth Ann nearly dropped me on the floor! She was panicking, but resisted interrupting Jenna. Jenna is one collected person! She just sat there quietly and repeated softly, "Okay. Then what happened?"

After a few minutes of repeating this, to our utter amazement, Jovanna lifted her head and said, "Crowds of people are standing around looking at the ground. They are talking. Their faces look awful worried like. Oh god! They are looking at me! I'm on the ground. My arms! What happened to my arms? Oh god, they look really, really weird. It's as if my arms now have a dozen joints instead of one. Oh god! My arms, they are broken into dozens of pieces! The pain, the pain, I cannot stand it! 'She's better off dead!' Someone says that. Oh, he's the town's physician. Someone is trying to help me, another woman. He looks down at me and says, 'She's better off dead.' God, I agreed with him! Damn right, I was better off dead than like this! I agreed with him! I did. I just floated away; the body just died there on the street. I was better off dead! Oh, there's blood coming out of my mouth. My chest is all smashed in too. I was better off dead. How about that?" Jovanna began to laugh.

"I was better off dead!" She exclaimed and then laughed so hard she choked. But that only brought on more laughter over her choking. "Better off dead! Ha, ha, ho, ho, he, he, dead. Yes, ha, ha. He's right! Ha, ha." Now she was laughing so hard I thought she might fall off the bed!

Several other Healers, who were nearby getting everything ready for the new wave of victims we were expecting shortly, came in to see what all this laughter was about. They saw Jenna smiling and Jovanna bouncing on the bed, she was laughing so hard, waving her arms about, "Dead. Better off dead!" she exclaimed and then another fit of laugher followed. After nearly a half hour of this, Jovanna's laughter finally died down enough that Jenna could say something.

"Very well done, Jovanna. Very well done indeed. Excellent. I believe that we are done with this session okay?"

"Done? Yes," and she chuckled some more. Then she said, "I agreed with them! God, I did agree. Boy did that ever do me in!" She began laughing hard once more. In fact, this time, her antics caused her bandages to loosen and threaten to unravel.

Now Beth Ann had to intervene, for fear of re-opening her wounds. As she unwrapped both arms, her mouth gaped! Healed. Yesterday, they were still quite raw, but were healing. Today, all traces of the wounds were gone; only the pinkish glow of new, healthy skin revealed itself! "Good god! Look at this!" she exclaimed, more than a little shocked.

Jovanna looked at her arms, but they just looked like the remains of her arms, perfectly usual, if missing the rest of them could somehow be considered normal. The other Healers clustered around Jovanna staring at her arms as well. "How can this be?" asked one. "Yesterday, they — they were not fully healed."

"What's the matter with them," Jovanna asked trying to become serious, but failing.

"They should not look like this for another three weeks, Jovanna," Beth Ann explained. "Bodies take quite some time to heal fully like you have." Beth Ann looked at Jenna, who merely smiled.

Finally, Jenna said very quietly, "Spiritual beings are indeed quite powerful. It never ceases to amaze me what a being can do when they so desire."

"It's a miracle, that's what it is," declared a Healer.

"Miracle or not, I now see no reason why Jovanna cannot finally have a long warm bath! How long has it been since you had a luxurious bath?" Jenna asked.

Jovanna thought for a minute before shrugging her shoulders. She said, "I cannot remember, long time. Do I have to go into Velona?"

"Oh no, dear. Allan has built us one here on the estate. It's behind this building. Beth Ann, if you will give me Lizzy Ann, you can take your ex-patient here and see that she gets as long a bath as she desires! She's earned it."

Jenna, carrying me, left the women alone. Behind us, I heard Jovanna say, "A real bath? Like the public bathhouses? Warm water?"

"You bet! Come on!" Beth Ann exclaimed. "You are going to love this. I sure do. Of course the guys don't like it so much when we dump lilac salts into the water." Both women giggled.

On their way to the bathhouse, Ariana caught up to them. "Hi, I am Araina Zar. Pleased to meet you. I heard you were going to the bath. Can I come too?"

"Hi, I'm Jovanna Barcella. Best ask Beth Ann, since she has to wash us both. Looks like they got to you too, huh?"

"Yes, but yours are so short! I heard that you were in the Barcella Resistance Movement. Golly, I bet you had all sorts of exciting times!" The two chatted all the way to the bathhouse.

Once in the warm waters, Jovanna's comment summed up everything. "This is heaven!"

Sometime later, Jenna, carrying me of course, pushed open the latch-less door of the bathhouse. I caught her using her ability to move objects again. When no one was looking, she would use her skills to move things without using her body, a skill I desperately wanted to be able to do as well. "Hi ladies. Some news, thought you should hear it from the boss, that's me. We have a boatload of injured women arriving late tomorrow from Solamina. So I am going to have Jovanna move in with you, Ariana, if that is okay with you two. That way, we only need one person always around to help you out as you need."

"Oh, that is perfect with me," Ariana genuinely meant it. She longed for company.

"Sure," Jovanna replied. "I guess we need to show my dad how to find it, though."

"Good. Now another thing, tomorrow right after lunch, how would you two like to go shopping in Velona for some new clothes? I know the perfect dressmaker. She has had a lot of experience making outfits for us with no hands."

"Oooo!" exclaimed Ariana. "But I don't have any money. How shall I pay for them?

"Me either," Jovanna added.

"While you are staying with the Santi, all your expenses are fully covered by us. You really do need some new clothes. What do you say we get you some nice outfits, eh?"

"Thank you!" the two chorused.

"Beth Ann, I've already got Lilly Ann to look after your kids, so you are nominated to take them. Ladies, one word of caution — Beth Ann is an awful flirt. She'll probably pick out some dresses that are likely to attract men's attention, perhaps just a wee bit too much, if you know what I mean. So feel free to tell her that you prefer something more modest, if she gets a bit carried away."

"Really!" Beth Ann faked disapproval. "You mean I can't get the dresses that reveal these?" She raised her breasts a bit. Jenna cracked up and began laughing, and the two joined in with her.

"Can I ask something?" Jovanna looked at Jenna. Jenna nodded.

"How often am I allowed to use this bath? I mean this bath is just unbelievable. Such luxury!"

"I'm sorry, both of you. I've been so busy that I forgot to talk with you about certain things. Glad I have you both at once. You are most welcome to stay with us here for as long as you desire. We have many things that we can teach you, many things we can help you learn. Once you have demonstrated that you can operate independent of a nursemaid, then you may come and go anywhere within the estate freely at any time. Doors will never be a problem, just push with your feet. However, once you can fend for yourselves so that someone does not have to be right there with you, you have free reign. Consider this your home for now, not a prison. Having these new clothes will go a long way for helping you become more independent when you have to go to the bathroom, for example. I can just scoot my bottoms up and sit down, for example. We just have to learn new ways to do the common, ordinary actions of life, that's all."

"Well, I'm getting there on being able to feed myself!" declared Ariana. "Hank has made me a set of strap on forks and spoons just like yours, Jenna. Is that what you mean by being more independent?"

"Yes, that's what I mean. Jovanna, you can see what we are talking about a dinner tonight. Hank has already been tinkering with some new invention that might work with your short arms so you can feed yourself. Hank has a clever mind. We'll keep our fingers crossed." All three laughed at her jest.

Later at dinnertime, Hank slid the leather harness onto Ariana's arms. Affixed to one was a fork and the other ended with a spoon. Her cup was built just like Jenna's. The top flared outward with a wide rim, allowing her to hold it with arm pressure as she brought it awkwardly up to her lips. After some experimentation, Ariana was at last able to feed herself and was especially proud of this achievement.

Genorio sat beside his daughter. His whole countenance had changed, since he saw his daughter smiling and sitting here at the table for the first time. He knew that she would live and that meant everything to him. However, Jovanna noticed that he did not eat very much at all and that he was getting even more shaky and wobbly. She was definitely getting worried about her father. On their way out, Beth Ann also warned her that her father's health was failing. "I've known it for years. Each month he gets a little worse, but now he is not eating. He was mostly playing with his food tonight."

"He hasn't been eating much all week, Jovanna. I hate to be the bearer of bad news, but be prepared. I believe that his days are numbered. I do know, Jovanna, that I've never seen him happier than he was tonight. Your recovery has really made him happy." She accompanied her father back to his room, which was not too far from the room she now shared with Ariana. Since he felt tired, she watched him crawl into bed and kissed his forehead. He smiled and held her waist for a moment before dozing off.

Just as Jovanna reached her own door, Paul came walking by. "Hi Jovanna! Care to go for a walk?" Why not, she thought. Everyone else was outside playing with the children.

The two strolled outside. It was getting darker earlier now, she noticed. Winter was not too far off. "I heard that your therapy session went extremely well today. It shows on your face," Paul commented.

"It was — well not what I expected or would have ever thought. I do feel so alive, though. Paul, can I ask you some questions about things?"

"Sure, ask away. If I don't know, I'll try to find someone who does know."

"Today, I ran through the last bits of the trauma I suffered losing these," she wiggled her arms. "But then the strangest thing happened. I ran through something strange, like I was this other woman who had her arms stomped on and broken into dozens of pieces. The place looked rather what I imagine Barcella might have looked hundreds of years ago. How can this be? Do I have someone else's memories? When I went through that though, I miraculously recovered. All traces of the pain and trauma is gone. My arms don't even hurt any more, though I sometimes still feel like I can feel my fingers. Weird."

"Well, I am not a priest mind you, but I think I can explain it. We are all immortal spiritual beings. We all have a mind. Those pictures you were looking at, those are or were part of your mind. We usually also have a fleshly body. It is the being that is the person, not their body. Many people, beings, reside smack inside their heads, while a few of us operate our bodies from outside them, usually somewhat back of our heads. Since we ourselves are immortal, we cannot die, only our bodies do. It seems that just after a body dies, the being goes and gets a new baby body and starts the game of life over again. Jenna has made a monumental discovery. If a being experiences some traumatic event full of pain and unconsciousness in one life, sometimes the same being can be adversely affected by it in another lifetime, when they have a different body."

"That makes sense to me. That would mean then that I was around Barcella in its earliest days, perhaps shortly after it was founded! But what's this soul thing that I'm supposed to have, that goes to Hell or Heaven and that these Holy Paladins are so fired up about?"

"Jovanna, there is no such thing. They have totally perverted the teachings of the Great Messiah. The immortal being is what they are now calling a soul, and they are denying that beings are immortal and live forever. There is no such place as Hell or Heaven; they invented them so they can control people — at least that's what many of us think. You probably ought to ask Elona Po about all this. I'm sure she could do a much better job of explaining it, Jovanna."

"Oh, I think you are doing just fine, Paul. I am amazed that a 'fighter' has such keen insights. But wait a minute. If they are saying that you *have* a soul, yet you are a soul, then they are denying what you really are. Instead of being spiritual, you are taught that you are a fleshly body and when you die, that's all there is. Oh my god, that is cruel, Paul, if it's true."

"Damn woman, you are a sharp one! I never thought of it that way. Golly, Jovanna, you are right! Wow." She blushed, but didn't know why.

"What's this Good Marks, Bad Marks that their priests keep hounding everyone about? Is there really such a ledger? Do women really start with their ledgers full of Bad Marks? How can anyone be watching everyone everywhere all the time?"

"Incredible, Jovanna! I never looked at it like this before," Paul replied, genuinely impressed with her great leaps of logic and reasoning.

"What's this about the Good Marks, Bad Marks thing? I couldn't help overhearing you two," said Ariana, her arm around Ben's waist pulling him with her to join the two.

Paul was about to answer her, when another older woman walked up to them. Elona Po, having heard about the results of the two therapy sessions, took time out from her busy schedule to come and meet these two women. Elona Po, now thirty-seven, had blonde hair and brown eyes; she had put on some weight after having her children. However, she still cut in imposing figure, dressed in her robes of office. High Priestess Elona Po was the sole monarch of Velona, their most benevolent monarch, widely loved and respected. It had been through her efforts with the help of the Guardians and the Santi that had so totally changed the Velona Sector.

Paul quickly introduced Elona to the two women, and they, her. "I came to chat with both of you, Jovanna Barcella and Ariana Zar. First, let me welcome you to Velona. If there is ever anything that you need, please let me know. Our land welcomes you here with open arms. Later on, if you decide you wish to remain in Velona, we would be most honored by your wishes." Both women were a bit overwhelmed by the outpouring of generosity extended by the monarch of Velona. She chatted a bit about how they were doing and such.

"When I came up, I did hear Jovanna ask some awfully interesting questions, did I not?" Elona asked.

"Well, it appears that everyone overheard my questions," giggled Jovanna. "Yes, I was asking Paul about the Good Marks, Bad Marks thing."

"Let me ask you something, Jovanna. If you had conquered a new land and wanted to somehow control the behavior of the people that land, can you think of a better way that to dictate allowable conduct?"

Jovanna leaped to a conclusion, "It's nothing more than some kind of hideous super control operation! Instead of forcing people one by one to follow your rules, you convince everyone of what right conduct is supposed to be. Anyone not following it then is prey for the Holy Paladins. But I think that they've reversed what's good and what's bad!"

Elona smiled, "Are you sure that you are not destined to be a High Priestess yourself? Seriously, you are dead on, as far as I am concerned. It's nothing more than a disguised way of controlling the people of a country, forcing them to your will. What about your other questions? Let me tell you that women are not born with a ledger full of wrongs. We have all done things of which we are not proud, just as we have done things of great value, women no more so than men. Perhaps the balance of good and bad are equal for both sexes. What intrigues me most is your last question: How can anyone be watching everyone everywhere all the time?"

"Let me explain. If you accept that you are you, let me ask you how big do you suspect that you are? Hold out your arms? What's your best guess as to how big you feel that you are? Don't be modest." Both women indicated a space of perhaps a couple feet around their heads.

"Precisely. Now look, that is space, is it not?" None could disagree; it was obvious. "Now look. If another being, God, was everywhere all the time, wouldn't he also be occupying the very same space that you are occupying?"

"Oh good god!" exclaimed Jovanna, making another leap of logic. "That would mean that we aren't!"

"Huh?" muttered Paul.

Jovanna replied, "Look Paul, it's simple really. Can two things occupy

194

the same space, I mean also at the same time? Of course not! We know that as children! So if God is everywhere all the time, then where are we? We aren't. God occupies the space so obviously we can't be there at all; God is there. If we are not there, then we aren't!"

"Yes, accepting that idea leads to the nullifying of one's own spiritual nature, one's own beingness," Elona preached. "All that is left is the earthly body, and that my fair ladies is what this fight between us and the Megalos church is really about. However, very, very few people know this. Jovanna, I am truly impressed with your observation. I can count on one hand the number of people who know what you have just concluded. Well done!" Jovanna beamed; her smile was the largest that Paul had seen.

"I would personally like to invite both of you to come to my Sunday Services. I think you would get quite a lot out of them."

"I'll bring them," Paul offered.

"Me too," Ben added.

"Excuse me, Jovanna," one of the other Healers interrupted the group. "I've some bad news for you. It's your father. Please come with me."

"Oh no. What's happened to him? I left him sleeping a while ago." Sudden worry lines creased her brow.

"I'm afraid that he has passed away in his sleep. I'm sorry," she said.

Elona quietly said, "We should perform the Blessed Holy Mother's Holy Communion. Take her to him, while I find Paulette or another Communicator, please." Tears beginning to flow, Jovanna followed the Healer. Paul ran off to find Paulette.

"I just heard," Jenna said, as Paul came running to find Paulette. "I'm sorry; she went into town this evening, Paul. Who else is around that knows the ceremony?" She found no one, except me. "Lizzy Ann, we ought to perform it, and there's no one but you available."

Okay. It's been a long time since I did one. Perhaps I can let Elona officiate. Let's go mom.

Jenna, carrying me, picked up Elona on the way, explaining that she would have to officiate as the High Priest. "Who's handing the Mind Link?" Elona inquired, not seeing Paulette with us.

"Er, a surprise for you," Jenna didn't elaborate, leaving Elona with a slight mystery to ponder.

We found Jovanna kneeling and crying beside her aged father. Elona spoke, "Jovanna, we are going to perform the Holy Communion ritual for you and your father. It works like this. One of our telepaths will link your mind with your father. You merely think thoughts and he will hear them, just as if you were talking to him. He will think his thoughts and you will hear them. This gives you both an opportunity to say a last farewell. I will officiate as High Priestess." Jovanna had no real idea of what she was saying, but did not object.

I reached out and found her father, who was slowly drifting up and away from the bed. Next, I connected to Elona and to Jenna. Finally, I gently touched Jovanna's grief-filled mind. "Oh!" I heard her exclaim as I made contact. Elona thought first. *Genorio, I am High Priestess Elona Po of Velona. I have your daughter, Jovanna here with me. Just think what you want to say and she will hear you. You can say your last farewells.*

I am so tired, but relieved it is over. Are you there, my loving daughter?

Daddy? Is this really you?

Yes. I'm afraid that I can no longer watch over you. My body just isn't working any more. Don't forget. Look in the large sack I brought from home. You and your brother are the rightful rulers of Barcella. Never forget that. I had hoped to one day see one of you on the throne. I still hold out hope, but not much. I love you, Jovanna, as much as I loved your mother. I am going to join her now, I suppose.

I love you too daddy! I will miss you very much.

Elona spoke up now. *Genorio, notice that you are a spiritual being and are floating above us. You have lived a long and productive life. We thank you for having been such a good father to your children. You have done well. Now it is time for you to go in search of a new baby body and start a new life. You are welcome to look for one here in Velona if you wish. Again, we thank you for all that you have done. Now be at peace. We will look after Jovanna now.*

Thank you. I am at peace knowing Jovanna will be cared for, now that I cannot.

Bye daddy.

Bye my beautiful Jovanna. I broke the connections.

Still crying, Jovanna said, "Thank you High Priestess. I don't know what to say. That was the kindest thing I have ever heard of. He did seem like he was at peace now didn't he?"

"Yes, yes he did. I'll make the burial arrangements. Is our cemetery in Velona acceptable?"

"Yes, thank you, thank you."

As they began filing out of the room, Elona said softly but sternly to Jenna, "I must have a private word with you immediately." A few minutes later in an empty room, she said, "I'd recognize Ket anywhere. That was Ket, wasn't it? He's back!"

"He doesn't want it broadly known just yet," mom replied, nodding her head downward toward me cradled in her arms.

Elona smiled, "Lizzy Ann, hello! Long time no see. I sure am glad you are back! We've all missed you. I'll keep quiet; don't worry. Thanks for handling that ceremony. I believe Jovanna was at a crucial turning point in her life, and the ceremony may have made the critical difference. See you all on Sunday." She left and Jenna headed off to find Hank and the other children; it was near their bedtime.

"Paul, please don't leave me just now. I feel so all alone," Jovanna begged.

"Here, lean on me; rest your head on my shoulders. I won't leave you," he said as his strong arm encircled her waist holding her tightly against his body. "Let's go for a little walk." On their way out, he grabbed a blanket and threw it over their bodies. He led her on a long, slow, ambling walk, saying nothing. He knew better than to speak. After all what meaningful words could be said to someone who has just lost a loved one? Best to let them cry and talk when they were ready.

At last, she began talking, "I knew for years that this day was coming, though I kept hoping it wouldn't. That ceremony — where did it come from?"

"Bethan Madelyn Amir, the wife of Jes Amir, the Great Messiah. When Jes Amir died, she moved herself and their children to West Reach. There she continued to preach the holy teachings of Jes. She began the Holy Communion ritual there on West Reach. It is a powerful one, is it not? After she passed away many years ago, others there on West Reach founded a church to continue her good works. Unfortunately, today, there are only a very few beings around who can perform the actual ritual, as you have experienced for yourself. Most of the ordinary priests simply say the words, but they are unable to join the deceased with those left behind, as was done with you and your father. You are awfully lucky to have had the real ceremony performed, because you two were able to share a last farewell."

"It only reaffirms the fact that we are all immortal spiritual beings. Daddy is immortal; he did not die when his body did. Words would never have convinced me as this did. It's as if I now have complete certainty that we are immortal beings, Paul. Do you think so?"

"Yes, like you, I have a complete, unshakeable certainty on it."

"Paul, I was wondering, who touched my mind like that, who did the joining of us? Was it Elona?"

"No, she does not have that ability, the ability to touch minds, telepathy we call it."

"It must have been Jenna then."

"No, Jenna is very powerful, but she does not do telepathy either."

She tried to recall who else was there. "You? The other Healer?"

"I am a Protector, a fighter. My sister would have done it, only she is in Velona with her husband tonight. Healers heal; they likewise don't know telepathy."

"Well then who did? I'd like to thank them personally. There was no one else present."

"Yes there was. There was one other person with us."

Jovanna thought for a moment, mentally checking off who she had seen with her. "Paul, you are teasing me? There was no one else there, except Lizzy Ann, Jenna's baby."

"Yes, that's right."

"The baby?" Jovanna inquired in complete disbelief.

"Yes."

"But that's impossible. Lizzy Ann isn't even old enough to talk yet! She protested. Then it dawned on her. "Oh, she's an immortal spiritual being, like us, only having just gotten a new baby body. That casts a completely new light on babies! Wait a minute, if Lizzy Ann knew how to do this ceremony, then who is she? I mean who was she? No, that doesn't make a whole lot of sense, does it? So confusing."

"Yes, you are asking it right. Let me put it to you this way, Jovanna. The being who performed the ceremony for you was the person who invented it in the first place."

"The one they call the Blessed Holy Mother?"

"Yes."

"Oh my!" She fell silent. After a time, she asked, "Paul, can we go see Lizzy Ann? I mean if she is not yet in bed?"

Paul walked her over to Jenna's building. The lights were still on, so he knocked and asked Hank. "Sure, she's nursing. Come on in." To Jovanna, he said, "I heard about your father. He was a very loving father. He will be missed. Jenna, Jovanna would like a word with Lizzy Ann, if that's okay with you?"

"Sure, hope you don't mind her nursing away," Jenna replied, rather sleepily.

Jovanna walked up to the two and leaned over me. She got over her awkwardness and just said, "Lizzy Ann, I wanted to personally thank you for giving my father and me the Holy Ceremony. It meant the world to both of us. Thank you."

You are more than welcome, Jovanna. I would appreciate it if you wouldn't go telling others that I did it. Babies are not supposed to talk when they are this young, that was a tease, by the way.

She laughed, "I won't. Thanks again. Good night, Lizzy Ann, and you too Jenna." Paul led her outside once more.

"Can we walk some more Paul?" Jovanna asked.

"Sure, I'd like nothing better." They walked slowly for a time, neither saying a word. "I'm going to go shopping for new clothes tomorrow. Beth Ann is taking me and Ariana."

"I know. I'm coming along, your Protector. No way am I letting two beautiful women loose in the city accompanied only with Beth Ann! She'll have you both lined up with several beaus in no time! She has a way of attracting men, you know." Jovanna let out a giggle and snuggled closer to Paul.

A little later, she remembered what her father had said. "Paul can you help me with something. My dad asked me to look in the large sack of old clothes that he brought along with us from Barcella. I don't know if I could possibly open it by myself."

"Sure, let's do it now while everything is quite. By this time tomorrow night I think we will all be super busy. A whole boatload of traumatized women that the Santi rescued from the Nunnery in Solamina is arriving. I know that I am going to have to use my simple healing skills to help. Now is a very good time."

A while later in her father's room, Paul found the sack. Already, Elona Po had taken his body back into Velona with her. "Well, here it is. Should I just dump the contents onto the bed? What are we looking for?"

"Honestly, I have no idea. I guess just dump it, and we can look through it all." Paul carefully emptied the contents, just old mostly worn out clothing spilled onto the bed. Something felt rather heavy. He unfolded an old shirt in which an object was wrapped. Both stared at a pendant made of gold and lined with many colored gemstones, making the shape of intertwining fish. A gold chain allowed the pendant to be worn around someone's neck. "What is it?" Paul asked, surprised.

"Oh my god! That's the Holy Seal of Tur, worn by every ruler of Barcella, ever since the founding of the sector ages ago! I had no idea dad had it! He must have secreted it away during the invasion. He never spoke of it."

"Was your dad the rightful ruler of Barcella? I'm a bit confused. I don't know the Sea Prince history too well. I'm from the Greenway, up north."

"My uncle shared power before the Barbarian Invasion sacked Barcella. After that, the High Council took over control of the sector. The Butcher killed my uncle when the Holy Paladins first entered Barcella over ten years ago. I guess dad rescued it from the hands of the invaders somehow. It now belongs to my brother. He's the High Priest of Tur, but he has been in hiding for the last ten years. We have no idea where he is at, safer that way. He should be the rightful ruler of Barcella now, not these monsters from Megalos."

"It sure is beautiful. We ought to put in Jenna's safe so that nothing can happen to it. How's that?" She agreed and let Paul wrap it back up.

"I guess I had better get some sleep myself. Can you walk me to my room?" He escorted her the short distance to the room she was now sharing with Ariana. "Good night Paul. Thank you for being with me this night. I really needed someone." He leaned over and kissed her gently on her forehead.

"Night. See you tomorrow." Paul left to deposit the pendant in Jenna's safe. However, he related its significance to Jenna. He added, "You know, if anything happens to her brother, then she is the rightful ruler of Barcella."

"I know. I have already given that serious thought, Paul," Jenna replied. Nothing escaped her observant eyes, he thought. She was always one step ahead of everyone! Amazing woman, he said to himself as he headed to his room.

The next afternoon, the women entered a dressmaker's shop, which had the unassuming placard above the shop that read: Adoncia's. Unless you knew where you were going, the shop was easily missed. Sister Adoncia owned and operated the store. She personally made many of the dresses on display, but also had six other women helping her. Having evacuated Pieta, she had resettled here in Velona, along with many other ex-Sisterhood women. While not in the Santi, she had very close ties with them. Indeed, nine out of ten customers were Santi women or their relations. "Ah Beth Ann, so good to see you again."

Beth Ann introduced the two young women and explained what they needed. "No need for explanations, dear child. I've been in this business all my life. Seen far worse cases, Jovanna. I've made dresses for three women who had lost both arms, clear up to their shoulders. I know just how to make clothes that you will be able to get in and out of by yourselves. But they need to also look womanly, if you know what I mean. Yes, I shall get you both fixed up. Married? No? Okay, no matter. How many sets, Beth Ann? Oh. At least one ought to be a fancy party dress, right? How else are these beauties ever going to attract a man, eh? Okay ladies. Colors. First, I need to determine what colors you prefer." Thus began three hours of shopping for clothes.

Meanwhile, Paul and Ben stood guard outside the shop, their carriage tethered at the hitching rail close to the shop. "I forgot how utterly boring guard duty was," Ben commented. Paul seconded it.

Sometime later, the two women came out, teasing smiles on their faces. Jovanna said, "How do we look?" She wore a blue silky dress with ruffles at the top, but was rather short. A yellow band encircled her thin waist. Ariana wore a somewhat similar yellow silky dress, which was about a foot longer. Hers had a blue waistband. Both women giggled and did a twirl before the men, their arms raised overhead like a ballet dancer. Beth Ann watched cleverly from just behind the opened door.

"Wow! Jovanna you look fabulous indeed. I had no idea you were this gorgeous!" Paul blurted out, sincerely awed.

"Ariana, you are really beautiful. Amazing!" Ben added.

Beth Ann could not miss the shock in their eyes. She teased, "Do they look sexy enough guys? These are their party dresses."

"Understatement, Beth Ann! Knock out is more like it. Jovanna, how on earth am I supposed to protect you from all the men that are going to be going after you when you look like this?" She gave a pleased giggle.

"Sexy? What man wouldn't go nuts over you, Ariana? You look very sexy," Ben replied.

Both women dashed back inside. A while later they reappeared, dressed in everyday clothes. Jovanna pointed out, "Adoncia is a genius. She knows just how to make them so I can get in and out of them! I did it. I put this one on myself. See I can easily get in and out of my own slippers now."

"Me too, though mine are easier to manage, because my arms are longer. Ben, I don't feel nearly as helpless as I used to feel. At least I can now dress myself. Strange how we take so many simple things for granted, like getting dressed by yourself. I guess Jenna is right; we just have to learn new ways to do ordinary things. Thanks for waiting for us." She gave Ben a hug, and he flushed.

Beth Ann filled the back of the coach with many packages, while the remainder would be delivered once they had been made. Then, the foursome rode back to the estate.

At suppertime, Jenna told everyone, "The boat will be docking in an hour. I'll watch the children so that the rest of you can meet the caravel at the docks. We've got twenty-two wounded to treat, so it will be a hectic night again. Let me know if there is anything you need or if I can help in any way."

Later, Jovanna and Ariana stood just outside their building, watching as a large number of carriages began arriving. Though it was now dark, they could see some women being helped out of the coach. Some were missing appendages, that much they could tell, but little else. More than half were carried on stretchers. The two knew that could only mean the women were in very bad condition. Jenna was outside playing with all the children, as usual. Since there was nothing either could do to help the injured, they decided to see if they could somehow help Jenna with all the children.

"Yes, I could use some help. These children are all ganging up on me, making me 'it' all the time. You two can be on my side! Ah ha. Now see what you've gone and done all you kids? Now I have help. Now you are all in for it! We are going to get you!" The younger kids giggled and ran helter-skelter. Jenna explained that all they needed to do was kick the ball and have the ball hit someone to make them the 'it.' Of course, then the object was to avoid being hit. Both women threw themselves into the game with a reckless abandon. Time flew by. Finally, it was too dark to continue, and Jenna ordered everyone inside to wash up and get ready for bed.

"Why don't you two come lend me an arm getting fourteen of them into bed?"

"Sure," Ariana replied.

"Not much arm to lend, but it's yours," Jovanna teased. Jenna gave a laugh, but observed that this was the first time Jovanna had teased about her situation, a very good sign.

To her amazement, Jovanna was able to find ways to pull the covers up and tuck the littler ones into their beds. Of course, Ariana simply tried to emulate the way that Jenna did it. All three women noticed how much easier it was to accomplish when they worked together. The older kids only needed a good night acknowledgment, however.

Once they were all down, Jenna check up on me, but the body was sleeping. So she took the two into the kitchen to make a cup of tea. "Tea all around?" she asked. Both nodded. Then, Jenna realized that everyone else was out in the infirmary. All three looked at each other, realizing the very same thing.

"Okay hot shot," Jovanna teased Jenna. "Now how do you suppose that we are going to strike a match and light the stove or get the hot pot of water off when it's boiling?"

Jenna laughed. "Okay you got me this time, Jovanna. As I am so fond of saying, where there is a will there is a way. I can get the fire lit, if you two can find a way to get the charcoal piled in there."

Getting the charcoal from the bin into the stove would be relatively easy; each could manage to pick up one piece at a time. Time consuming, but doable. "This I have got to see!" challenged Jovanna, and she struggled to get a piece picked up and into the stove. Ariana had a much easier time of it however. Once the two had enough ready, Jenna stuck an arm through the loop of the lighter can and managed to spread a bit of the oil over the pile. "Yes, that part we already figured out how to do," Jovanna teased. "Now let's see you light it."

Attempting to tickle the two, Jenna said playfully, "Bet you don't think I can do it?" Giggling, both agreed. "All right, watch this." Jenna fumbled around, got the flint and steel, one at a time, and placed them on the top side of the stove. Next, she sat down on the floor and raised her feet. Using her toes, she struggled a bit and got a grip on each piece. Shortly, a few sparks flew and the oil ignited. Hastily she got her feet out of the way. By the time that she got back on her feet, the fire was definitely going. Next, she carried the water pot, which had a large loop handle, over and placed it on the stove.

All three got their mugs and fumbled to get the tea grounds into the mug. "Okay, I didn't think you could do it," Jovanna finally admitted. "You win."

"I ought to be honest with you two. Yes, we can do things, but it just takes a bit of ingenuity. However, as you see, it can be painfully slow accomplishing some things. Let me warn you, getting the boiling pot off and the water poured is very dangerous. If you ever want to do something like this, I urge you to practice lots with just cold water in the pot. Normally, I will just let others handle the pouring. But tonight, I feel ornery. I don't normally do this in front of other people. You will see why shortly. Ah the water is now hot. Let me just say that we beings are far more capable than we often believe."

While the two watched, Jenna did not move. However, the boiling pot rose into the air, floated over their cups, pouring just the right amount of water into each cup. The pot then floated back over the stove, and the metal extinguisher slab floated up and over the stove, settling down on the stovetop, snuffing out the fire. At last, the pot sat down gently on top of the metal slab. "There, that is a far safer way to do it," Jenna declared. "Now let's go enjoy our well-earned tea."

Both women stood gaping, transfixed to the floor. "How did?" Jovanna could not finish her sentence.

"They moved on their own?" Ariana exclaimed, unable to find words to describe any of this.

"Come, sit and sip. Let me explain. Yes, I did all that. I can move things without using my body. I said spiritual beings can be more powerful than they often believe possible." Jenna enjoyed telling them a bit about her skills. She wanted to push them slightly, to show them that more was possible than the normal person might believe possible, that the impossible sometimes might just be possible. More importantly, she wanted to give them motivation to stay on here for some time, apprenticing with the Guardians. With both women, Jenna saw possibilities, perhaps far reaching possibilities, if only they would desire to learn.

Just then, Lizzy Ann woke up ready for her nightly feeding. Jenna asked the two lend her an arm getting her dress pulled down and the baby into the right position. While it was a bit of a struggle, the three managed to get me in position. "I'll be glad when she doesn't need to nurse anymore," Jenna said. I ignored her; this was fun for me.

The three were still sitting and chatting when Hank returned from the infirmary. His clothes were covered in blood, not a good sign at all. He looked tired, exhausted, and depressed. "God, I would like to get my hands on those butchers!"

"I know you would, love. How's it going?"

"Grim. We have them all stabilized as much as we can. It's just awful. Some have been beaten to an inch of their lives. Beth Ann thinks three or four will not make it. One is worse than you were when you came, Jovanna. She has blood poisoning lines all the way up her shoulders. The Healers still haven't decided if there is any chance at all for that poor woman. Sickening, just sickening. Sorry if I am bringing you all down in the dumps. You looked so gay when I came in."

"No need to worry on our account, Hank. It's just the way it is. We are not gods; we just do the best that we can. Do they need anything?"

"No. I came back to take a breather and maybe have a cup of tea. You know I can only take that for so long. I really bothers me to see women mistreated like that. Water still hot?"

It was hot enough, so he made himself a cup and joined the three women at the table. "What's this world coming too anyway?"

"Matter of viewpoint, Hank. You know that. When the Barbarians from the Northern Steppes invaded the sectors, the sheer number of women raped and beaten was horrific. Nearly every young woman was raped in every village. When the Centurions invaded before them, the original invasion so many years ago, they raped nearly every young woman in each sector. Their rationale was that since they had killed off so many young men, they wanted to create a new generation, hence all the babies. This time, however, the invaders have kept their raping under control. We have some twenty-two here now from Solamina. Assume three times that number did not need to come because they were not in bad shape or had died. Still what is one hundred compared to tens of thousands? Some may argue that these invaders are more humane. However, just don't ask those that they have brutalized, right ladies?"

"Well, yes, don't ask us," declared Ariana. Jovanna agreed.

Hank replied, "Okay honey, I see your point. I guess I'd better get back to work. Don't wait up for me." She gave him a kiss and left.

Having now had time to ponder what she had seen Jenna do, Jovanna asked, "Jenna, do you really think that Ariana and I could learn to do what you can do?"

"Who can say? I spent over ten years of hard study here with the Guardians, after I lost mine. Long hard study, and then some. I do not know whether or not you can, but you certainly owe it to yourselves to learn as much as you can."

The two young women looked at each other smiling. Ariana spoke for both of them, "You don't have to ask us a second time! Besides, what do have we to go back to at this time? I'm already learning tons from Hank and Ben. I haven't said anything about this, Jenna, but the other day I realized something about myself. When I was a little girl, I mostly played and lived the life of a rich little girl. I knew almost next to nothing that is useful. Then all this happened. Here I am a grown woman and I know less than a ten year old girl! I have such a long way to go."

Jenna was more than pleased to hear this. "Well done, Ariana. Knowing that you do not know something is the first step to learning about something. So many think they know and yet don't even know that they don't know!"

"Oh by the way, thank you ever so much for all the new dresses!" Jovanna remembered that she had not properly thanked her benefactor. Jenna grinned.

"Since you both want to learn from us, Ariana, you can continue your studies with Hank and Ben. I need their services the least at the moment, but that may change in time. Normally, I would prefer to place women with women tutors and males with male tutors. However, Jovanna, I really cannot spare one of the women Guardians right now, but I can let Paul begin your education, if you don't mind having a male. Just be aware that if we come under any kind of threat, I'll have to pull Paul into active duty at once. If I do, I'll find someone else for you right away. Will that be all right with you?"

"Yes, Paul is awfully nice and very considerate of me. I do like him; it will be okay." They chatted a while longer. Then, her entire Circle and Hank wandered in looking exhausted, bloody, and tired.

Beth Ann reported, "Stabilized for the night, Jenna, but I really don't believe that four will make it. Savage wounds and massive infections, beyond our skill to heal."

"Food!" declared Lilly Ann. Paulette and Lilly Ann headed for the pantry to rustle up a very late night snack for everyone.

Jenna let Hank and Ben know that they were to continue Ariana's education, while Paul was told that he should begin Jovanna's apprentice training tomorrow. "Hey, Jovanna, that's great! Love to do it!" She smiled, wondering what this training might be like.

The next morning, by the light of day, all the Healers were back with their many patients. Jenna was able to give her welcome speech to nearly half of the women who were at least awake and sentient. Unfortunately, three had not survived the night. Jenna picked out the woman who had recovered the most and scheduled her for a therapy session that afternoon.

Both Ariana and Jovanna decided to help those that were constantly working with the injured women. They carried clean blankets in, dirty ones out, and acted as general go-for's. It was their collective idea quietly to show these traumatized women that they might not be as useless and hopeless as these new arrivals might think. After all, they had been in their very beds not so long ago. More than one woman watched them.

Days turned into weeks. Only one other woman died from her wounds. Fortunately, only half of this batch of women had lost appendages, many only fingers or a hand. Only one had been blinded. Well over half, however, had been severely beaten many times. Broken bones predominated as well as massive bruising and swellings. Two had lost a foot because their crushed feet had developed gangrene.

Early November arrived along with notification to expect yet another batch of victims. This time, they came from Pieta's Nunnery. Jenna let her group know that twenty-one were en route to Velona, accompanied by the Black Avengers and a Protector. While everyone here had heard of these avengers of Pieta, until now, they had been completely anonymous. Everyone was keenly interested in meeting them, perhaps forming an alliance with them.

The afternoon that the caravel docked, Jenna sent a number of carriages to meet them and bring them to her estate. Only Beth Ann remained in the infirmary, making the rounds of the patients from Solamina. Jovanna and Ariana acted as her helpers, while the remainder of the staff worked to get everything ready for the new arrivals. For them, it promised to be another very long day.

Tino, with Benita perpetually clinging to his arm, walked off the caravel onto the docks. "It's so big!" exclaimed Benita. Tino agreed, glancing back at his sister. Johnny was escorting her off the ship. Telma was just as surprised by the sheer size of Velona as he was. A number of Santi were waiting for them as they walked toward the center of the central plaza, filled with workers loading, unloading, and moving crates, boxes, and timbers in all directions.

"Hello, Paul Wilkens. Jenna sent us to meet you. I'll send in our crew to help unload the wounded. Twenty-one of them, I believe."

"Hi, I am Tino Terzio, my girlfriend Benita. My sister, Telma and Johnny."

"Twenty, really," Benita added. "I really don't count. I'm perfectly alright, see?" She held up her arm to show him that it had healed fine.

Paul chuckled, "Okay, twenty. Welcome to Velona. While we handle the unloading, someone else wants to meet you." Elona Po stepped forward; she'd just arrived, insisting that she meet the Black Avengers that she had heard so much about over the years. She logged much of their fame to rumors, but wanted to meet them personally.

"Telma, Tino, this is the High Priestess Elona Po, monarch of Velona. Elona, these are the Black Avengers, Telma and Tino Terzio."

"Very well met indeed," Elona shook their hands. "On behalf of all the free peoples of Velona, let me welcome you to our fair city. If there is anything I can do for you during your stay, you only have to ask or send word to me." Both smiled. She moved them aside and continued chatting with them, while Paul, many other Santi, and the four Healers, who had been pulled in from their operational units, headed onto the ship to bring out the injured women.

An hour later, all the women had been safely loaded into the many carriages, and Paul climbed in with the twins and their companions. As they drove through the huge city, Paul pointed out the key sights. Everyone was in awe of the sheer size and cleanliness of the city as well as the incredible architectural sights. The Church of the Holy Rose impressed them the most, however, towering high over the city, its rounded dome touching the sky.

"Jenna must be awfully wealthy to have such a grand estate as this!" Telma pronounced as they entered the expansive ground. "So well-tended too."

"Oh, it's beautiful," Benita added. While their carriage drove up to the main entrance near the stately oak tree, now with brown leaves still clinging to it, the others stopped at the building just before the main part. As they stepped out, Jenna, carrying me, stepped out of the front door.

"Welcome everyone to our estate and headquarters of the Santi. I am Jenna Rose Weston, your host, and my youngest, Lizzy Ann."

"On my!" Benita stifled her words, putting her handless arm over her mouth. She'd noticed the obvious.

Telma grimaced, accidentally squeezing Johnny's arm. Tino just stared in disbelief.

Paul introduced Tino first, who said, "Please to meet you, Jenna. You are the leader of all the Santi?" She held her arm out to shake, and he gently, as if his touch might cause her pain, shook it.

"Absolutely, none other. And you must be Telma." She offered her hand to the astonished avenger, who also gingerly shook it. "Johnny, I've heard about you," she playfully teased the young Protector. Johnny, prepared for this moment or at least prompted by his peers, took her hand in both his and gave a firm handshake.

"I'm incredibly honored to meet you at last Supreme Commander Jenna Rose Weston," he said gallantly.

"And you must be my patient, Benita," Jenna said to the still gaping young woman.

She gingerly took Jenna's arm and shook it. "I didn't know, I mean, does it still hurt badly? How absolutely awful for you," Benita said, her voice genuinely upset and disturbed.

"No, not the slightest, unless I stick it on the hot stove by accident. You are all most welcome here. Stay as long as you desire. Paul can show you to your rooms. We can talk more at supper. I need to see that the injured want for nothing. Benita, we'll start your therapy tomorrow right after lunch."

She was still clinking tightly to Tino's arm. "Honestly, Jenna, I really don't need any. I am perfectly healed now. The others that we brought with us — they really need much help. I am fine, really I am."

"Don't worry, Benita, I only work my therapy on those whose wounds have healed enough. Let's see how it goes, shall we?" Benita couldn't say no, but just clung to Tino. Paul led them into the guest section, which lay between the infirmary and the main structure. As they passed by the two women's room, Ariana and Jovanna stepped out to meet the new guests.

"Hi, I am Ariana Zar, from Zargarb. Pleased to meet you." As Paul introduced each of the four, Ariana, having watched how Jenna managed, emulated her. She put both her arms over Tino's hand and shook it. Ditto with the others.

"Jovanna Barcella, from Barcella naturally," she said. "Mine are too short, how about I hug you instead?" She grinned and proceeded to give each a welcome hug. "You are really going to like it here! There is always so much going on, so many people being helped, and so much to learn," she tried to explain everything in one sentence, but then gave up the idea. How could she tell them everything?

"You're going to stay in the two rooms next to ours," Ariana went on, usurping Paul. "So if you need anything or get lost or whatever, just come get one of us. Maybe after supper you can tell us about what Pieta is like. We've never been there. Is it as large as Barcella?"

"Er, sorry Ariana. I've never been to Barcella," Tino admitted.

Telma added, "We've never been out of our city until now, but we sure can tell you about Pieta, though.

Paul finally retook command, "Come on you four, if you stay here,

Ariana will talk for the rest of the day."

"I do not!" Ariana faked a pout, as if he had mortally injured her. Jovanna gave her a poke with her right arm. Getting serious, she asked Jovanna, "Since we are not going to get any training this afternoon, what say we go over to the infirmary and see if we can be of any help? We can always leave if we are just in the way."

"Good idea," Jovanna replied. The two headed over to see what was happening.

They found everyone working like mad with the new patients. Only a very few were reasonably stable. They watched for a time, until Hank had one woman's bandages dressed. He was about to move on to the next one he had been asked to look after, when he spied the duo. "Jovanna, here, lend your arms. I've got her fixed up for now. Can you run the wash rag over her and clean her up a bit, please?"

Jovanna was very willing to try it, chatting with the woman who had infected knife wounds down both of her forearms. She could not tell if any fingers were missing, both hands were completely bandaged. Chatting away, Jovanna began to awkwardly clean the woman's face, which had not been washed in years, she swore.

"Ariana, can you give me an arm, please?" called out Beth Ann. She was performing major surgery on an unconscious woman whose arm was infected where her hand had been removed. She also had several other deep knife wounds on her other arm. Ariana rushed over to her side. "Here, put pressure right there; we need to keep her bleeding slowed for a minute so I can sew up these wounds. They've reopened during the sea voyage, I'm afraid." Ariana put her arm where Beth Ann indicated and pressed down hard, using her other arm for additional pressure. "That's doing it. Thanks." Deftly, using tiny stitches, the Healer began her work.

A little later, satisfied with her job, Jovanna looked around to see who else needed cleaning up. Ben smiled at her from the next bed down the line. "If you are done there, this one can stand a washing. I'm nearly done." Although it took a bit of doing and several trips, Jovanna got the washbasin, rags, and towels moved over to the next one.

At suppertime, Jenna, who was also helping as she could, ordered everyone to wash up and break for dinner. "I know that we will be working most of the night. Let's get these bodies some nourishment." While everyone broke for dinner, one Healer remained looking after all the patients, just in case. Everyone headed for Jenna's dining room. Paul had come to notify them that the cooks had supper waiting, and now he moved beside Jovanna, while Ben did the same with Ariana.

Paul commented, "Well done, Jovanna. Glad you could help. You look like one of us now, blood all over your dress." She was pleased, however, and leaned her head on his shoulder, while her left arm rested on his back.

"I hear you really helped out Beth Ann," Ben complimented Ariana.

"Yes, I used pressure to slow the bleeding while she worked her magic. I sure am glad that I could do a little something to help everyone." Ben gave her a hug.

As they filed into the large dining room, Jenna spied the four newcomers. "Sorry we all look frightful, but we are all hard at work with all those patients you brought us. Have a seat, please. We are very informal around here, especially all the children," she teased them. Soon the cooks brought in dinner and everyone ate, although the children ate the fastest, racing to get outside to play before it got dark. They knew that winter was nearly here and that restricted their outdoors playtime.

Once the chaos of the children vanished, Jenna asked, "Well, Tino, Telma, how about one of you telling us about how you all managed to rescue all these women?" True, she already knew about it, so did nearly everyone else. It was a good ice breaker. Tino began to relate all that had happened. By the time that he finished, the after dinner tea was served.

"Excellent idea to burn the Nunnery down. That will buy us some time before they can get back into business again," Jenna said. "I'm afraid that something is going to have to be done about these Holy Paladins, and soon."

Everyone agreed with that statement. Then it was back to work.

Jenna, as usual, looked after the children, assisted by one of the Santi cooks. None of the Guardians could be spared just now. Late that night, when the last stitch had been made, Jenna ordered everyone into the bath. Actually, they all could use it. Tired though they were, everyone headed to their rooms to fetch clean clothing and then the bath. Paul and Ben carried the girls' things for them, chatting all the way there. Soon some thirty men and women were relaxing in the warm waters of the bath.

"I've never felt so useful in all my life," Ariana commented to Ben, who was washing the grim out of her hair for her.

"Yes, that's the exact way to say it," Jovanna added. "Useful. I really felt like I had something that I could contribute. I never thought I'd be saying this!" she added. Paul was washing her back, and he leaned over and kissed her neck.

Just then, Jenna froze, several other Guardians also stopped what they were doing. Jovanna looked at Paul's eyes, which seemed miles away. Ariana also noticed that Ben was suddenly silent, as if peering miles way. The two girls looked around the large bath. Jenna's enture group was suddenly occupied somehow. Jenna finally nodded and they all instantly animated.

In reaction, eight sets of eyes turned to look at Jovanna. Unsettled to say the least, she asked, "What?"

"I'll tell her," Ben spoke up quickly. "Jovanna, we just got the latest news from our fortress in Barcella, both good news and bad news. The bad news first, I guess. There is no easy way to say this, Jovanna. Your brother has just been caught." He paused to allow a little time to pass for her sake. Just as she was about to reply, he added. "The evil Mano del Dio fellow, Silas, who did this to you, beheaded him, and paraded his head about the streets of the city."

"Oh no! Not him too!" She began to cry. Everyone stayed silent for a while, allowing her to grief. After some time she asked, "What could possibly the good news?"

"You remember Lyle, the one who helped out, the second in command of the Santi Fortress?" She nodded. "While he was parading your brother's head around the city, Lyle killed him, the Mano del Dio fellow called Silas. You have your revenge. The man who maimed you and killed your brother is now very dead, rather dramatically too, I might add. Lyle struck him down with a pair of lightning bolts from the sky. He was atop the fortress tower, spied him, and blasted him but good. Reports say that his body flew twenty-five feet through the air before being smashed to bits against a wall. Very dead is that evil man."

"Now that is good news! I've only wished a few men dead in my life. He was at the top of the list along with the general I used to work for; too bad he didn't get it too. Good riddance. My poor brother. At least he didn't suffer, not as I have. That's something. I'm like this for the rest of my life. I wish we could have cut off his arms and seen how he liked it, though maybe his feet too so he couldn't kick us either. Maybe even his tongue so he couldn't berate us. Maybe even pulled out his teeth so he couldn't bite us. Maybe even his eyes so he couldn't see us when we poke ice picks into his sides to see if he makes any noise." She was angry now, and everyone just stayed silent and allowed her to come to grips with her feelings and emotions. She had moved from grief all the way to anger, Jenna knew she still had a ways to go.

"Damn Mano del Dio. I don't think there is a more hateful group anywhere on Tarra. They are much worse than the Unholy Paladins," she said very antagonistically. She sighed, "Now I wonder when those Unholy Paladins are going to get it, probably not soon enough," she rattled on becoming bored with it all. "Well, at least my city no longer has to worry about the Mano del Dio anymore. That is something. The paladins are bad enough." Now that she was rather conservative and her tears gone, Jenna spoke, a signal for which the others were waiting.

"I'm sorry about your brother. Jovanna, I've instructed Lyle to attempt to sneak in, recover your brother's remains, and see that they are properly buried. Is there any special rites he should have or location where he ought to be buried?"

"No, he was the last priest of Tur. So there is no one to perform it. In the city cemetery, there is a Barcella family plot. It's well marked. If he could, would you have him buried there, please?"

"You got it! I'll let him know," Jenna said and glanced at Paulette, who relaxed and seemed to drift off.

Jovanna said, "Thanks. I haven't seen him in nearly ten years now, not since he had to go underground. I always feared this day would come, you know. Actually, I guess I am surprised that he lived for ten years."

Now the subdued group gradually began talking discussing the latest news. Jovanna nudged Paul with her right arm. "Paul, how did you all get that news? You all stopped and looked like well you were staring off into space or something."

Tino and Telma also pricked up their ears, as did Ariana. "A select few of we Guardians are able to use telepathy to communicate across any distance, to connect one mind to another. Elise in Barcella contacted Paulette here, and Paulette joined us all with Elise. Elise then told us all about it. It seems Lyle acted without orders and got in a bit of trouble with the Commander for killing Silas, but it seems smoothed over now. Honestly, Jovanna, if I had been standing on the tower and saw that Silas fellow, I'd of done the very same thing!"

"No wonder the Santi always seem to know everything! Finally, it all makes sense," Jovanna declared. "Wait a minute, no it doesn't! Lightning bolts? How can he do that?"

Jenna answered her, "Nearly all us Guardians learn how to bring down lightning bolts and sheets of fire and ice in our tenth year of study. Of course, some of us are much better at it than others. Lyle is darn good with lightning."

The girls and the avengers just stared in awe. Their respect for the Santi rose enormously.

"No kidding!" Tino finally spoke, "what an incredible advantage you all have over your opponents, instant communications! Incredible. I just now realized how useful this actually is!"

Jenna replied for everyone else, "Yes, yes it certainly is a distinct advantage. Now if everyone is cleaned up, while we women dry our hair, how about you guys making us some hot tea? A bit of cheese would be nice too. We ought to get to bed fairly soon. We've another long day ahead of us tomorrow."

Later, Paul walked Jovanna back to her room. At the door, Jovanna put her arms around him and whispered, "Thanks for everything. I hope you don't mind me leaning on you for support. Now I am so alone in the world. I've only got you folks here."

"Lean all you need and want to, Jovanna," he replied and kissed her on her forehead.

The next afternoon, Benita showed up for her therapy session, her good arm holding tightly onto Tino. Jenna noticed that she was almost never without her arm securely holding on to him. Curious, she thought. Once settled into a comfortable chair, Jenna explained what she wanted

Benita to do, re-experience the traumatic incident with her hand.

"Oh, there is really nothing much to tell, he just cut it off," she lightly explained.

"That's fine. What are you seeing there as it is being cut off?" Jenna prodded.

"Oh he has knife." Suddenly she screamed; she had contacted the actual pain and unconsciousness that had been hidden from view. Jenna thought, now that's better. Several hours and many re-countings later, much of the trauma had been seen, only the moment of intense pain remained.

"Okay, let's go through it once more, Benita. Tell me what you are seeing and feeling and hearing."

Part way through it, she described, "I feel a sharp cutting pain in my wrist. It just keeps getting worse. He's moving it back and forth, sawing it. Oh, I heard someone saying something, but I can't make it out."

The next time through this portion, she yawned heavily and said, "I hear the man who is doing the cutting. He is saying to the one how is assisting, 'Hold on to her. Hold on tightly. Don't let go. You've got to hold on.' Then, the pain crescendoed. I think that's when he finally cut my hand off." She opened her eyes and looked at Jenna.

"Hold on, got to hold on! That's what I have been doing with Tino! Hold on, I've got to hold on!" She burst out laughing, repeating, "Hold on!" Each time she said the words, she laughed all the harder. Jenna continued to smile and allow her to talk and laugh. When the laughter finally subsided, Jenna ended the session and Benita thanked her profusely and ran off to find Tino.

"Oh Tino! I don't have to hold on to you. I love you and I want to hold on to you, incredible difference!" she laughed. Poor Tino had no idea what she meant, but held her tightly anyway.

At last, she explained what had happened. "I feel so free, Tino, so clean and free now. I had no idea all that pain was still there locked away in my mind." The two hugged for a long time. He now knew that the trip was more than worth it, no matter what else might happen!

By late-December, the last of the recovering women had left the infirmary. True to her word, Elona found new homes and families for all the women. Only one wanted to return to her home sector. More importantly for their recovery, she made sure that each woman now had a job for which she was both suited and liked to do. Elona was a master of matching skills, capabilities, and likes and dislikes. She was a master organizer.

No more boatloads of victims were expected and things finally quieted down around the estate. The first significant snowfall came, dusting the world with a thin white coating. Velona was sufficiently far south that the snow was rarely very significant, just pretty. Now was the time for decisions, Jenna concluded.

Chapter 9 What Is Justice?

Just after the winter solstice celebrations, Jenna called everyone into her meeting room for an extended conference. Besides her Circle, she also insisted that Hank, and the two apprentices, Jovanna and Ariana also attend, along with Tino and Telma. Yes, she had my crib at her side, my insistence.

Jenna opened the planning session. "I think that we have sat on the sidelines for far too long. I've had just about enough of maimed women coming through our doors. It is time that the Santi do something about the situation. The meeting, which I expect will go on for days, has as its goal deciding what action or actions we should take. I've instructed the staff to bring us our meals in here and to look after the children, except Lizzy Ann here."

"The comment I've heard mentioned a lot is 'No Justice.' I think that everyone here fully believes that it is high time that these people are brought to justice." She received an enthusiastic response from everyone.

"I believe that the place to begin is to discuss exactly what we mean by justice. What is justice?" Anyone care to share their ideas?"

"Well that evil Mano del Dio man was killed. That is justice," Jovanna volunteered.

Telma added, "The Holy Paladin who was brutally raping that woman, I gave her justice, I ran him through with my sword."

Paul threw in his ideas, "In Zargarb, the mistreated women of the Junction got justice. They poisoned all the Holy Paladins and priests who were responsible and also all the locals who either turned in women to be brutalized or actively supported the suppression of women. Some five thousand were killed; that's big time justice, if you ask me."

"We've publically hung quite a few Holy Paladins who were in the act of sodomizing small boys," Tino volunteered. "That's justice."

"Yes, and when we find out that the Holy Paladins have robbed someone, we break into their house and steal the money back, returning it to the victims. That's also getting justice," Telma added.

Beth Ann put in her ideas as well. "We Santi get some justice by making those from Megalos pay steeply for our services to safeguard their shipments. We use the collected fees to pay for helping those whom they have harmed. In short, your stays here and your expenses and those of all the victims who have been here this last year have been actually paid for by the Holy Paladins, though they do not know it. That's justice too."

Allan added another dimension, "We also know that some who have been forced to build new constructions for the Holy Paladins purposely sabotaged them. Buildings fell down; ships sank, and so on. Isn't that also justice?"

Paul said, "Yes, and don't forget the banditos of Solamina. They have been outright killing the vile men and robbing them blind, giving back the townsfolk the taxes the Holy Paladins took and even food and supplies they desperately need to live. That's justice."

Jenna asked Jovanna, "Some time ago in the bath when you found out that the Mano del Dio who maimed you had been killed by a lightning bolt, you had something else in mind for justice."

"Oh yes I did! Look, if a man cuts off your hands, isn't a sudden, quick death letting him off far too easily? He tortured me, one finger at a time! I wanted him to suffer as I had suffered, feel the pain I endured. Only I wanted his pain to go on and on and on! I feel slightly cheated that he did not suffer the pain that he inflicted on me. Besides, I now have to face the rest of my life like this!" She raised what remained of her arms. "Sometimes I feel that he got off entirely too easy for what he did to me and to others."

"Yes, they should pay for their crimes," Ariana spoke up. "Maybe take all of their money and possessions away and give them to their victims. Look, Jovanna and I are two of the incredibly lucky victims. We have you to help us, but what of all the other victims that we don't yet know about, those that did not come here? It might not be the best justice, but they ought to be made to pay and support all their victims somehow. After all, for most like this," she raised her arms, "life becomes horribly more difficult, perhaps impossible without the support of the Santi or the Sisterhood when it was around."

"Hey, another method of justice that I like goes along with that, sort of," Paulette interjected. "The sea captains have been doling out justice to these evil paladins. They shanghai them, put them in chains, and put them to work as slave labor for the rest of their lives, doing something productive for us all, cutting down trees, making the timbers everyone needs to build new ships. Now that's what I call justice!"

For quite some time, the ideas flew unrestrained. We took a break for lunch and then resumed. This time Jenna spoke her mind.

"This afternoon, I want us to focus on the larger picture. We are all immortal spiritual beings who for a brief time inhabit a fleshly body. When the body dies, we do not die, do we? Instead, we merely go off, find a new baby body, and begin to play the game of life once more, though most usually forget completely the life they just lived. Bethany or Ket has some theories about why it is that we usually forget the live just lived. She wants me to share these with you. Mind you, they are merely her speculations at this time."

"Imagine for a moment that your body has just died. You lose all of your possessions. Most all cannot any longer talk with their loved ones who still live. In short, all the meaningful objects in your life are now gone, lost. You cannot communicate to your family or friends. Usually no one living can even see you. Apparently, the only thing you can do is to look at your memories of all these things, which are now gone or denied to you. Next, you pick up a new baby body, which is often in a new location, with new parents and strange people around you. Your attention is on the objects and people nearby. These are now what are important to you, not the lost past. Perhaps this is why people forget their past lives."

"Another reason to forget the past may come about from your having done some very wicked things, which you wish you could undo, but cannot. Naturally, one would very much like to forget about that life and what you have done. Bethany suspects there may be even more reasons why we tend to forget the past."

"However, I know that some of you have seen portions of some lives you've lived before, right?" Quite a few agreed fully with that statement. "Some of you have directly experienced what I am about to say while others here have witnessed such in others who received my therapy sessions. And that is simply this: severe trauma suffered in one lifetime can directly and very negatively affect the person, the being, in another lifetime later on in time. This is a vital point that I am making, critical I believe."

"Hey, I am case in point!" exclaimed Jovanna. "You all probably remember that when I first came here, I kept saying that I was better off dead. I had a strong suicide wish, little will to live life. Of course, everyone probably thought it came from this," she raised her short arms up for visual effect, noticing that it did not bother her anymore for others to stare at her. "But that was completely, entirely wrong, very wrong. What really happened is that I lived before; I think it was shortly after the founding of Barcella, or certainly not long after that. The city was very small and the houses were very crude adobe. The bay still looks like it does today, however. Anyway, my husband and I got into an argument and he knocked me down and jumped up and down on my arms, even stamping on them. They were both broken in so many places it was hard to count all the pieces! My arms looked very weird, bending in all directions and bits of bone sticking out here and there. Then one man who had come to tend to me said that I was better off dead! When he said that I was right there unconscious in the middle of the most intense pain I had ever felt! Somehow, those words deeply affected me, although I could never on my own remember it! I could never have recalled those memories outside of Jenna's therapy sessions, ever, I am certain of that. Heck, I could barely recall them in her sessions. Took a very long time. I had to get through all that pain and unconsciousness even to hear them. Yet, here I was in the here and now, different lifetime unknowingly saying those very words, that I was better off dead! Jenna has a very important point here. Trauma does affect our future lives. I hate to think what my next life might have been like if Jenna had not helped me get rid of this current trauma! Oops, I seem to have monopolized the conversation." She flushed.

"I'm glad that you did," Jenna smiled. "We all have benefitted from your observations."

"Hey that happened to me too," Ariana was eager to share her experiences. "When I came here I just knew that I was now absolutely completely useless. That's what I kept saying and feeling, I was useless for the rest of my life. I ignored everything I saw with Jenna and how she does nearly everything. I just knew as a total fact that I was now useless for the rest of my life. Nothing would ever change that! Then in her therapy session, once I got through the trauma of getting this done to me," she also held up her arms for emphasis, "I found out that I had also lived before. I got into an argument with my husband and after I hit him in the head with a frying pan, he cut off my hand with his knife. While I was in great pain, lying there slowly bleeding to death and mostly unconscious, one man said 'Well, she is better off dead. Otherwise she would be useless the rest of her life.' Boy did that ever stick with me! I really was convinced utterly when I came here that I was completely, totally useless for the rest of my life and nothing could ever change that. Jovanna and I are living proof that trauma suffered in a previous life can horribly effect you in this life!"

Jenna could have yelled for joy. These two women had just dramatically made the critical point that Jenna just had to get the others to see and grasp. This was fundamental to the entire discussion of what was to be done. "Excellent you two. Precisely the most vital point we must take into account when we dole out justice. People are beings, no question. That trauma undergone today comes back with terrible repercussions lifetimes later must play a vitally key role in whatever solution we devise."

"Now then as Guardians we realize that to talk about a person's actions in terms of good or bad is useless. At the fundamental level, these terms are simply a matter of viewpoint, something that we as Guardians know theoretically, but often find hard to view that was in real life. That's because we are living it. For the benefit of those who are not Guardians, I should elaborate what we mean by this, because I am sure you all are convinced otherwise about the terms good and bad."

"Suppose that you see a man watching his house burn down. It is starting to burn, but the man simply shrugs his shoulders and runs away. That is all that you see. Has he done good or has he done bad, assuming nothing living is inside the burning house?"

"That's obviously bad, assuming that he could have easily taken the time to put the fire out," Telma volunteered. It seemed plain to her. Several more agreed with her.

"Now another person also witnesses the man fleeing the burning house, but this person also sees that the man is running up to a person who has been robbed and stabbed. He stops the bleeding and keeps the person alive until others arrive and the person is thus saved. Now, is the man's action of failing to put out the fire good or bad?"

"I see what you mean," Telma replied, realizing that she had been had.

"There are always at least two points of view surrounding an action that involves people. I'll give you another case in point. A century ago, when the Centurions first invaded and captured the Sea Prince sectors, each sector fielded an army composed mostly of all the younger, fit men. The Centurions butchered all them on the battlefield. Afterwards when they took control of the towns and cities, they raped vast numbers of women. Good act or bad?"

"Bad," several chorused.

"Yes, from the viewpoint of the women, very bad indeed. Now here is the other side. The Centurion leader, seeing that all the able bodied men of all the sectors had been laid to waste saw that long term the entire population would suffer enormously if a new generation of people was not quickly created. By raping vast numbers of women, in fifteen years, there should be a great increase in the number of young men to begin to rebuild the society. Without the influx of the new younger generation, the society was doomed. Now can you see how from that point of view this was a good action to take?"

"Even on a more mundane level, Paul here thinks olives are really bad, but Jovanna thinks olives are really good. You see, we cannot get very far in analyzing situations if we use the labels good and bad. We need another method, one that is not subject to the vagaries of good and bad. Bethany had long ago pointed this out to us. Measure the action against the Seven Aspects of Life. You do not need to believe what we believe; this does not affect any known religion. It is a statement of all life. The First Aspect is our own personal life. Each of us wants to do well, to succeed, and to live life fully, in short to survive and survive well."

"The Second Aspect is our families. We are born into a family, which we usually want to have do well too. Later on, many join with a partner, beginning their own families. Again, everyone wants their families to survive and do well, plenty to eat, have fun times together, the list is nearly endless."

"The Third Aspect is our social groups. The Santi is one such group. Velona is another. The Axemen, a third. We all want the groups to which we belong to succeed and do well, to survive."

"The Fourth Aspect of Life is all mankind. We all want our species to continue to thrive and multiply. Think about that one for a minute. What if a vast plague wiped out all human bodies in one generation's time? What kind of bodies would there be for you to use in your next lifetime? A dog's?"

"The Fifth Aspect contains all the plants and animals on Tarra. Most of these we definitely desire to survive and do well. For where would we be if all the sheep died? Or all the fish in the sea left us? Life would become drastically more difficult. I cannot imagine life without any trees anywhere. No caravels."

"The Sixth Aspect is the material, solid universe around us. We want our houses to last. We need the air to breath, water to drink, nature to bring rains, sun to grow our crops. Without the physical universe, there would be no place for us."

"Finally, the Seventh Aspect of Life is that of us Spiritual Beings. I know that we are immortal and cannot die. Yet, we have just seen visible proof that a being can be so traumatized that their lives become horrible to live. Perhaps all suicides are merely the command acting on the person from some past trauma. Interesting idea, at least."

"Bethany has demonstrated a foolproof method of judging actions, based upon these Seven Aspects of Life. Everyone knows what the word harmful means. It is harmful to stick one's hand in a blazing fire. It is harmful to swallow poison. It is harmful to cut off someone's hand if it is not infected or diseased. It is harmful to burn down an entire forest. It is harmful to kill all the sheep in a healthy flock on which a town's livelihood depends. You get the idea." Everyone nodded, Jenna made sure that the non-druwids did before she continued.

"The method is simple. Examine the action taken measuring it against the Seven Aspects. Does it help an Aspect or does it harm that Aspect? Then, tally the numbers. You can never end up with the slate balanced because there are seven of them. If that action harms more broadly than it helps, that action is an incorrect action. If it helps more broadly, it is an action that is beneficial to do."

"In the example I gave with the man allowing his home to burn down while he saved the life of the other person, true, it chalks up an incorrect mark on both the First and Sixth Aspects, for he now has no home and his house is gone. However, it helps on many others, even his First, because a human life is more valuable than an object. You can rebuild a house, but can you rebuild a body? I know that several of us here would most certainly like to do just that!"

Jovanna and Ariana giggled, the rest smiled. "More than likely, the others in the town would pitch in and help him rebuild his home, resupply him with the necessities of life for having saved the person's life. People are generally good, only a few are wicked."

"So what I am proposing is that each proposed solution we come up with to the problem at hand be measured up against this yardstick. That way, we can rest assured that we are making the best possible decision on what action to take. Bear constantly in mind that trauma experienced today definitely can adversely impact life years and lifetimes later."

"I'm sorry that I may have sounded like I was preaching, but Bethany wanted you all to have the same viewpoint in this that she and I share. Okay, ideas?"

Jovanna spoke first, "This fits right in with what I was feeling all along, that the Mano del Dio fellow got off way too easy. Yes, he's dead and that ends the reign of terror he has been causing, though I personally am not sure how many others he harmed, only that I was the first. We are all glad that he has been stopped; otherwise, so many more people would have been harmed or killed. However, me personally, I really feel like I was denied my justice, personally that is. That he is dead is very important and all that, but what about me? Here I am like this for the rest of my life. I wish he could have been made to pay the piper somehow."

Lilly Ann stared at Jovanna, barely a first year apprentice! Yet, the wisdom and insight she just displayed many tenth year Judgers would not have shown. "Incredible insight, Jovanna! You've impressed me. You are completely right. What is missing is the step of making amends for what they have done or caused. Bingo. That's what we somehow have to insert into our grand plan. The perpetrators must make amends for what they have done."

Now everyone began talking at once, adding more examples, and fully backing the two women. Paul, on the other hand, just stared at Jovanna, seeing her in a completely new light!

Jenna finally regained control of the meeting by saying, "Lilly Ann, write that one down. The guilty must make amends to the victims."

"Wait a minute," Tino interrupted. "Don't we have it out of order? Shouldn't the very first thing be somehow to force the guilty party to stop committing the harmful actions? That's what Telma and I have always been doing, stopping them from committing more. They surely are not going to make amends while continuing to commit more harmful actions."

"Excellent point, Tino," Jenna acknowledged him. "Lilly write that one down at the top of the list: prevent the guilty from continuing to do the harmful actions. We are now really getting somewhere."

"Wait a minute," Ariana spoke up. Everyone turned to look at her. She flushed for a brief moment. "Something is missing. I just feel that something else, something important is missing between these two. It doesn't feel quite right. I think that we are overlooking something terribly important, but I am not sure what it is. He cuts off my hands and rapes me. Then he is somehow prevented from doing it to others. Then he sends me living money every week so I can afford to continue to live. It doesn't feel quite right to me."

"It doesn't to me either," Jenna said.

Lilly Ann was about to speak up, when Jovanna beat her to it. "Of course it is not right. The man must make a public statement in front of all your friends, relations, the whole town, declaring that he was very wrong in harming you so!" Lilly Ann's jaw dropped.

She recovered, and added, "Precisely, Jovanna. "The guilty must make an honestly given public statement that they now realize their actions were harmful and should not have been done! Bingo once more, Jovanna! I'm going to add that one in between the other two, if no one has any objections?"

"Hey," Paul said while she was writing away, "when they say that their actions were harmful and should not have been done, the Protector in me says that they also should explain to the best of their ability just why they did it. What was their motivation? Who ordered it? And why. You see, then we can backtrack and find the ones behind the scenes who are instigating the harmful actions in the first place. We all know what any of the Holy Paladins will say, 'I was just following orders.' Well, whose orders, you see what I am driving at? I want to know the motivation behind it so I can go after others who have been ordering these men to commit harmful actions!"

"Bingo," Lilly Ann, hastily adding his request to what she already had written down for the second point.

Finally, she looked up and asked, "Are we missing anything else?" Dead silence.

Paulette, who up to this time had said very little, but agreeing with all the points, said softly, "Yes, I think that we are." Now all heads turned to her, many wondering what could possibly have been overlooked. This seemed so straightforward.

"Well, you've somehow gotten the perpetrator to publically renounce his harmful actions and then you have gotten him to make amends. Then what? How does he ever return to a normal life? If he has no way to rejoin society, he will eventually protest and start in all over again, lashing out at us."

"You are very right, Paulette. I missed that. I was so focused on punishing the fellow that I forgot about that," Lilly Ann replied. "Folks, we should add a last step that after doing the above, he can rejoin society once more, otherwise, there is not motivation for him to even finish making amends. What's the use if he is imprisoned for life? None."

"Well now wait a minute here," Tino protested slightly. "Are you saying that we just let him make amends and then is allowed to become a free man in our society again?"

"Yes, I see what he is driving at," Jovanna spoke up for him, seeing that he could not quite say what he felt was wrong. "Suppose that the Holy Paladin cuts off a peasant's hand. He admits that his priest ordered it and that he now sees that it was a harmful action to have done and says so. Now he goes to the poor woman, who has only seen a copper coin during her life, and gives her ten gold pieces. She is ecstatic with her newfound wealth. Since she feels he has made amends to her, the man is free from all further restrictions? I think not! I might change my opinion if he agreed to give her ten gold pieces every few months. Isn't this that viewpoint thing that Jenna began with?"

"Right you are, Jovanna," Paul came to her defense. "I'd want a say in whether or not he has met his obligations! After all, I am responsible for protection of people."

Lilly Ann, the Judger in her coming to the fore, suggested, "Why don't we add a fourth step, petition the group, town, village, or whatever, for permission to rejoin them? That way everyone else could look over what he has done to make amends and catch the sly tricks they might try to pull, such as Jovanna suggested. If the majority agrees, he's allowed to be free; if not, he is asked to honestly do what he had tried to pass off and repeat it."

"Excellent, add it," Jenna declared, most impressed with the way the meeting was going.

"Of course, everyone, this whole thing depends utterly upon catching the perpetrator and somehow preventing him from doing more harmful actions. How are we going to do that? Lock him up in some room somewhere?" Paul declared. He still felt that we had not handled the situation and that we were leaving out the vital initial action.

Allan finally had something to contribute, "Hey, I can build a secure facility, call it say a prison or a dungeon. We capture the guilty and lock them up. Once behind iron bars, then you can work with them to get these steps done to rehabilitate them. Of course, you have to feed them and such. Perhaps the city could afford to pay for their food and few necessities."

Everyone thought that this was a good idea, a way to keep them out of society until they were rehabilitated and had done the steps. Allan then ignored the rest of the meeting and began making sketches of potential prisons or dungeons, they would have to be secure and not allow any potential of clandestine escape.

Jovanna rubbed her head with her arms; something was still bothering her. "There is still something missing here. I cannot quite put my finger on it." Suddenly she burst out laughing, a roaring laugh. "Put my finger on it?" she repeated mid-laugh, waving her arms in the air. Now everyone roared with laughter. Jenna was very pleased with Jovanna's action, very much so. She now could make jokes about herself.

A few minutes later when the laugher died down, Lilly Ann asked her to explain if she could. "Well what if we get the wrong person locked up?"

"Wow, you are right," Lilly Ann interrupted her. "Look, suppose someone has a grudge against you. As it stands, all they have to do is say you did a harmful action, and you find yourself locked up. Somehow someone has to get at the truth of the matter before any of this starts!"

Jenna said, "Yes, add a new first action. A fact-finding tribunal is convened whenever any charges are made. Their task is to unbiasedly find out the truth of the charges, find the facts. If the facts cannot be found or the charges are found to be untrue, the entire process stops right here. Only if proven without any doubts that the person is guilty, only then do we carry on with the remainder of the steps. Golly, this sounds positively fantastic!"

"Yes, Jenna, but," Paul added stressing the word "but," "do you realize that you've made the job of the Protectors drastically more difficult? Now, we do not want to kill them, but rather capture them alive. This is going to make our job much harder and more dangerous for us."

"Yes, for us too," Tino added. "When we come across a Holy Paladin committing a crime, we might be able to stop him before he completes it, but we stand little chance of capturing him alive."

"I see your point. Well taken. If you come across someone committing a violent, life threatening or highly damaging crime and it is not feasible to take them into custody, then do what you have to do to protect society. The first requisite must be to prevent them from further harming society. What we are suggesting is that if it is at all possible, feasible, practical, and doesn't place your own lives in greater jeopardy, then try to capture before killing. The first action has to be to get these men and possibly women out of circulation, so that more are not harmed by their actions. Does this appease you?"

"Well, that's better," Paul replied. "That we can do."

The next day, discussions began on just how to go about removing those who were causing the harmful actions. That is, how do we retake control of the occupied sectors back? Tino asked, "If as you say, there are some ten thousand Santi members, why can't you just march into a sector and take it over by force of arms?"

"I can explain that one, Tino, my specialty," Paul explained. "First, only two-thirds of the Santi are fighters, a little over sixty-five hundred. The rest are supporting personnel, such as cooks, planners, and so on. Of the fighters, two thirds of those are strictly defensive fighters. That means they are very able defenders, but are just not offensive attackers, like yourselves, Tino, Telma. You are more likely to defend yourselves than to go for an all-out frontal attack, face to face, right?" He agreed; they avoided that always! "That means the actual attack strike force numbers a little over two thousand."

"Now if we were to march that force into a sector, it would be easily seen and the Holy Paladins would begin to take strong defensive measures, holing up in the easily defended walled cities. Two thousand would not be enough troops to conduct a lengthy siege action. Secondly, if we did march our troops over the border, that would be a declaration of war with Megalos. While right now we are stronger than their presence in the Sea Princes, they would ship or march their vast legions up from Megalos, and we would be hard pressed to do anything but retreat. Thirdly, a large percentage of our forces are scattered across the lands protecting the various fortresses and on the many caravels providing security for them. Another bunch handle security on the overland shipments, which we make them pay dearly for our services. Thus, collecting them all together for a siege would drastically weaken every other place we defend and our other services. This is why we did not press on into Barcella after we defeated the Centurion army on the borders here. We just did not have enough forces to deal with a lengthy siege. Finally, if we do an all-out attack on a neighboring sector, then we are indirectly placing all the other citizens there in grave peril. Would not the Holy Paladins demand military service from all able-bodied men? We'd end up fighting the very people that we so greatly desire to help. No, I am afraid that another war is the absolute wrong action to take."

"Well said, Paul," Jenna validated him. "Yes, an all-out war is most definitely out. What we need are alternatives. That is what we need to explore today."

"Large scale goal is the destruction of the entire Megalos Church of Jehosanity," Lilly Ann suggested. "Is this the time the Great Messiah's descendants come forward and decry the falsehoods they are passing off as the truth? The translation unit at Mont Blanc has only gotten one of the ten disciple's texts translated. I wish they were all done."

"How about Yazi's journal? How's the translation of that going?" Beth Ann asked.

"Well, slowly. It has pretty incriminating information in it," Paulette reported. "Unfortunately, as far as the Church goes, it only proves that they used assassins to provide their security. Yazi made it very clear that the Church did not order the Rooster to go assassinate some senators, only suggested it would be in the best interests of the Church if they were no longer a problem. If the journal is widely distributed, it can only embarrass the Church, not bring it down. Yet, it might force them to rein in their assassins, but I don't think it would have any effect upon the conduct of the Holy Paladins up here."

Paul spoke up, "I don't think now is the time for Amir's decedents to make an appearance. The assassins are on the loose. If we can get the assassins out of the picture somehow, then it would be safer for you to expose yourselves to the world. Even then, there are likely to be some religious fanatics who will make attempts on your lives. I think we should concentrate on getting the Mano del Dio destroyed first, somehow."

"We like that idea," both twins grinned. Neither relished becoming a walking target for the nuts of the world.

"Well, we at least have some sectors under our watch now," Jenna added. "Perhaps with the agreements worked out by our fortress commanders there, they will stop mutilating women and start paying for their whores. That is a step in the right direction on that front. So it seems to me that we are facing two challenges here. One, the elimination of the Mano del Dio, and two, the restraining of the Holy Paladin's brutality toward women. If those were handled, things might just calm down a while, so that further change for the better could occur."

Ideas were tossed out and rejected. Hours went by, but no real headway was made in finding any solution that was doable. Finally, Jenna suggested, "Well, there is one thing that we could try. Suppose that I paid a visit to their senate. I tell them just what has been occurring up here. If I hold up my hands, it is hard to dispute it. I give them a choice, rein in the savagery against women or we will do it for them. I also would meet with the new Pope and tell him we have the journal. I threaten to publish it and broadly distribute it across Megalos, unless he gets his assassins under control — again he does or we do it for him."

Hank nearly fell out of his seat! "Dear woman no! I love you! I don't want you killed! Surely, this would be a death trip! You cannot go, please; think of the children if nothing else."

Paul backed him up completely, "How could I possibly protect you, Jenna. You are dooming me to failure! I could not protect Ket from one assassin. You are going into the lion's den with all the assassins at hand! Dear god, don't do this!"

Quietly, she said, "Then give me some other alternative that will satisfactorily begin the resolution of our situation here."

Now the group talked in earnest! No one wanted to allow Jenna to go to Megalos! However, the ideas became wilder and wilder. I think that Jenna allowed them enough time for them to see that there was no other viable alternative. Either that or she did hope to spur some better solution from their minds. Hours flew by with no reasonable alternative. I sensed that everyone was now becoming quite frantic and emotionally upset. They would now be able to think rationally any longer. I had to step in.

Already relaxed, I gently touched all the minds present. *Bethany here. I've been listening to everything during these meetings. I compliment you all on your brilliant handling of the handling of the guilty parties. However, this time I side with Jenna. There is no other way that we can deal with the assassins and the Holy Paladins except to get their masters to rein them in. The only way to get the Pope to cease is to directly confront him and use their Senate to apply additional pressure. I know that you all believe that she would be going on a suicide mission. If I felt that this was the case, I would not back her plan. She is my mother now, after all. I will go with her. I believe that I can also bring several other unseen helpers with us to guarantee her safety. On this, I ask you to trust me.*

In addition, I must go because I speak their language. I have been to the Senate. I know intimate details of the Pope's new city. Paul must also go as her Protector. Paulette, I give you your choice to go as the Communicator or stay here as the Communicator. I can easily handle the mental communications needed. However, Lilly Ann and Beth Ann must not go. You are all very correct in deciding that now is not the time for them to reveal themselves, not until the Mano del Dio is under control. I would prefer that the rest of you remain here. The fewer physical bodies that we have to protect from assassination the easier our job will be.

Jovanna, you represent what has been done in Barcella. Jenna represents what has been done in Zargarb. It is an awful lot to ask of you, Jovanna, but I would like you to come along for that reason, but only if you desire. No one will force you to go, and no one will think less of you if you choose to remain here. You have endured so much that I even hesitated to ask this of you. It will be your choice.

Based on her performance during these past several days, I was almost certain of her answer. She replied, *I want to go. I want to represent Barcella. They beheaded my brother. This is the very least I can do for my land and my brother. I will go.* She also had another thought, but I did not relay that one; it was a private thought, personal.

Paul, create a full squad of the best Santi defensive fighters you can find and bring along at least two Healers. Make sure that your fighters are also equipped with longbows and plenty of arrows. We will travel in two caravels, just in case one of the ships runs into trouble.

Finally, Hank, once again, I am taking your wife away for a time, only this time the mission is a dangerous one. You may come along if you choose. I will let you and Jenna discuss this between yourselves. Whatever you decide, I will fully support your decision.

I would like to set sail as soon as everything can be arranged. Beth Ann, make a copy of the title page and the first two pages of Yazi's journal. Just duplicate the writing. We may need to show the Pope physical proof that we have it. Find someone who can teach us to speak Megalos and bring them along. Thank you all. Mom, I'm getting hungry again. I added that last as a hint that I was finished. It worked. Jenna flushed and everyone left to get the wheels in motion, all except Hank.

"I'd feel better, Hank, if you stayed behind for the children's sake. Although we do not believe anything bad will happen to me, if it does, I would rest easier knowing that you are here to raise our children, but I also know how much you care for me and how badly you want to be by my side."

Hank had calmed down now, having accepted the fact that there really was no other way. "I suppose that I ought to practice what we have been preaching about how to make helpful or harmful decisions and actions. It would potentially harm more aspects than it would help if I went along and something bad happened to both of us. As usual, my love, you are right. I will stay behind and look after everything here and the children, but please don't take any unnecessary risks."

After a pause and while staring at me, he asked, "Why Lizzy Ann? How is a baby going to be able to stop assassins? I am having a very hard time grasping that point."

"Hank, I didn't want to mention this in front of all the others, but of all the Guardians, only Bethany, Lizzy Ann here, can move out of her body at will and operate, bringing down fire, ice, and bolts. The rest of us need our bodies nearby. She doesn't and I am depending upon that."

Hank looked at me hard and smiled, "Well, I'll be." He did not finish his sentence, only leaned over, and gave me a loving kiss on the side of my face.

That night while everyone else was sleeping, I moved out of my baby body and took off heading southeast. I knew just where I wanted to go and what I wanted to accomplish. I was back before dawn.

At breakfast, the decision was made to leave on January 7 at high tide. It was finally time for the Santi del Dio to make itself more broadly known in Megalos. The ball, as they say, was now in our court. We must not fumble, for too much was at stake. By my reckoning, this was our only chance to reign in the Mano del Dio. We just had to succeed. If not, all out-war was the only other option.

Chapter 10 Into the Mouth of the Lion

I relayed instructions to the captain of the Sleepy Hollow via Jenna. Jenna gave the sailing instructions as our ship finally cleared the harbor of Velona on a cold January morning, 638. "Sail southeast until you come within sight of the Red Desert. Then, weigh anchor and await my orders, please."

"Aye, Aye, ma'am," Captain Alano Romeriz replied, and issued the orders to his crew. Behind us, the Golden Streak, with Captain Goyo Mar in command, followed our moves, bringing the coach and a quantity of horses with them. We were heading to the island of our enemy. However, the direction to sail ought to have been southwest. Everyone looked at each other, wondering whatever was going on; this heading took us far into the Med Sea and likely somewhere south of Solamina!

Paul wanted to say, "Jenna, this is the wrong direction," but bit his lip instead. As Protector, he needed to know what she planned, so he discretely got her attention and whispered, "Wrong way?"

Jenna smiled and answered, "Slight detour. We will not dock, just anchor for a very brief time. Nothing to worry about, totally secure." She would say no more, my insistence. Besides, I couldn't resist giving them all some mystery to ponder.

Onboard was a small strike force. Besides Paul, Jenna, Jovanna, and me was the Fortress d'Grange Santi Strike Force, consisting of their first two squads and their regimental Commander Adriana Socorro, a veteran field commander, whom I had known for a long time. She began her long career as a Fighter Group Leader for the Sisterhood and now was the Regimental Commander. She and her forces had played a major role in our final attack on the Centurion army on the border of Barcella. All were seasoned veterans. Her top scout was Felice Bugattti, Fel for short, and I knew both her and her mother quite well. Adriana brought along her Regimental Communicator, Eve Stockbrook. In addition, she brought only the first two squads, due to the limitation of only a couple dozen that I requested. Diego Tog led the first squad while Fabio Paca led the second group of ten fighters. Their fighters were about equally divided between ex-Sisterhood fighters and men from d'Grange. Additionally, both bought along their wives who were Guardian Healers for the regiment. Marcia Tog and Novia Paca were two battle-seasoned healers, having seen battle on the line at the border of Barcella.

Each caravel had a crew of seven, including the captain. However, Santi policy dictated that each ship also have a Security Force traveling with it. Sam and Jean Wade were the retired Guardians, who headed the security team on our ship. He was a Protector, and she was a Communicator; both were in their late sixties and really enjoyed sailing the high seas. Neither desired officially to retire to land. Berta Al Meer led the ex-Sisterhood fighters, a group of six who manned the giant crossbows and longbows in defense of the ship. Lief Sven, an Axeman from the far north who now lived out of Velona, fired the enormous catapult that launched flaming oil balls. He had discovered that he loved sea travels and had not yet wanted to move onto the mainland.

I felt that with the Strike Force surrounding us, we should not have any problems while en route to and from the capital, Galantas. I intended to dock in the small port city near Constanza City, where the Pope lived.

The first three days at sea, everyone had to re-acquire their sea legs. Jovanna had the most difficulty maintaining her balance when the ship pitched; it was difficult for her to grab hold of some support. Jenna had similar difficulties, though not as severe. Me, I slept a lot and tried to get used to eating from a spoon stuck into my mouth.

"Land Ho!" the lookout perched high in the crow's nest called out. We were now just off the coast of the Red Desert. While everyone looked inland at the vast panorama of red dunes before us, I kept looking at the crow's nest. I had to move some distance from my little body to do so, however. Soon I spied them and sent mom, *Okay. Now set sail for Megalos. Top speed.*

Jenna gave the order to the captain. However, nearly everyone now looked at each other completely baffled. What was going on? We'd sailed three days in the wrong direction to no place in particular and then turned around and headed off where should have in the first place. Paul pestered her for an explanation. She finally gave in and told him in confidence, "We have more allies than you think."

Naturally, this did not satisfy Paul in the slightest. So he climbed up into the crow's nest to have a look around. He saw no other ships, though he was expecting to see one, given Jenna's hint. However, he began noticing the magnificent view from this height, truly awe inspiring. When he climbed down, he said to Jovanna, "You have just got to see the world from the crow's nest! There isn't anything like it in the world!" So excited was he, that Jovanna could not help but decide to try.

"I'm not so sure I can do this without any hands and so little arms." Looking at the narrow rope ladder reaching up so terribly high to that tiny little crow's nest, she faltered. "Paul, I really would like to see up there, but I am afraid I can't make the climb."

"Don't worry, I will be climbing over you, using my body to hold you to the ladder," he tried to quell her fears.

Jenna overhead the two. Looking up herself, she smiled. "Jovanna, I will use my special skills on your body. I will not let you fall. Actually, I could just lift you all the way up there and plop you in the nest, but why don't you see what you can actually do. There is no way that I will let any harm come to you. Trust me."

228

She grinned; that Jenna would catch her made all the difference. "Okay, let's do it!" she exclaimed enthusiastically. Slowly, the two made their way up the long, slanting rope ladder. For her it seemed an eternity of climbing, since each step had to be very carefully taken. Ten minutes later, she stepped into the nest with Paul beside her, steading her.

"Oh, it was worth the climb!" she exclaimed, bubbling with enthusiasm. The view was indescribable, as she later told her friend Ariana. The two watched the world go by for nearly an hour, enjoying every minute of it.

Just then, Jovanna felt a strange sensation, as if someone were watching her. "Paul, is someone else here? I feel like I have eyes staring at me, but there is no one else up here."

Paul tried to quell her fears, unsuccessfully. "Paul, there most definitely is someone else up here with us! I can feel it." Jovanna strained her senses, trying to locate where her fear was coming from or where this other person was. "Someone is all around and over me!" She declared at last. Paul looked all around but saw nothing. He was about ready to get his apprentice down; this was starting to spook him.

Ah. You have seen me. Very good. I am Julie, a good friend of Ket Bethany. He asked us to come with her and lend aid if needed. My body is now a long way back there in the Red Desert. What is your name? Just think it and I will hear it.

Jovanna, Jovanna Barcella. Are you a god?

Jovanna felt that Julie was somehow laughing. *No. No, I am just me, a being, much like yourself, inhabiting a body, well that is not so true any longer. I have a body down there, but others are looking after it while I am aiding Bethany.*

I joined their conversation. *Hi Julie. Glad that you and Karmanski are with us. We may need your help to keep all these bodies alive. I see Jovanna has already spotted you. She is observant, isn't she? Jovanna, I told Julie that you would very likely be the first to spot her, outside of Jenna and me, of course. Julie has been training for a very long time under the Guardian of the Anuir in the Red Desert. It was he who helped Jenna learn how to move objects.*

Wow! Very pleased to meet you, Julie. I've seen Jenna lifting a pot of boiling water and pouring our teacups with hot water. That sure can be useful. I wish I could learn how to do that.

Jovanna, I'd like nothing better than to work with you and see what we two can do. However, for now, don't tell the others about Karmanski and me. He's my husband and he's on the other ship's crow's nest. We are here incognito. Our presence on this voyage must not be known to others. Can you promise me this?

Ten minutes later, Jovanna had climbed down and was sitting on the main deck, her back to the poop deck. Here she could be out of the way and yet watch others as they did their jobs on deck or milled around, looking at the coastline or out into the blue Med Sea. Paul had left her to go inspect the strike force weapons at Adriana's suggestion.

Now then, let's see what you are the most likely to be able to recover knowing how to do.

What do you mean?

Normally, when we train someone, we have all the time in the world to do it. In your case, we only have the slight duration of this voyage, which is a few months at most. It is best if we tackle something that you can master in that amount of time. You do not have to do anything. I am just going to observe you for a time.

Jovanna did not see anything happening. She did continue to have the sense of someone looking at her, her mind, and memories, though. Time passed. Evidently satisfied, Julie placed in her mind, *See that crew man coiling the rope there? Okay now I want you to have him stop and scratch his nose.*

How do I do that, call out to him?

Well that is one way to do it, but when you were a little girl, did you have dreams of doing something like that an entirely different way?

Yes, I thought I ought to be able to just think a thought and have it do it. You know — my toy dolls. It seemed like I should be able somehow to command them to do little things. Is that what you mean?

Precisely. Now have the seaman scratch his nose.

It didn't work.

I didn't think you would be successful on your first try. After all, if you were, you wouldn't need my help learning how to do it again. This time, imagine that you are sitting right on top of his head. Pick up his hand and scratch his nose with it. Still nothing happened.

Now imagine you have this enormous crane, as they have here on the ship. Let's get the crane ten times larger with much stronger ropes. Hook one end of the rope to his hand and now crank the crane and make his hand scratch his nose.

To Jovanna's astonishment, the man scratched his nose. Jenna, holding onto me, sat down beside Jovanna. "We'll make sure that you are not interrupted during your training. Julie's good, isn't she?"

"Did you see what I just caused?" Jovanna exclaimed.

"We did. Good going. Now listen to what Julie is saying; pretend we aren't here."

Thus began the training of Jovanna. During a long ocean voyage, unless you were a crew member, there is little to do. Unless you are interested in the coastlines or the sea and its creatures, it is mostly just one long period of complete relaxation and idle time. Hence, Jovanna could spend most of the daylight hours sitting here on the deck apparently watching the world go by without anyone paying any particular attention to her. Many of us did nearly the same thing.

With these sleek, fast caravels, our journey would take around six weeks, given good sailing weather and no typhoons, that is. Paul found himself being the unofficial tour guide, pointing out the various sights along the way to all the others. He'd made this same journey last year, when I sent him to retrieve Yazi's journal. Hence, with everyone nicely occupied, Jovanna could concentrate on learning from Julie.

Me, I eavesdropped on her training. Okay, what she was apparently learning how to do I thought could be very useful. It appeared to be somewhat similar to the Judger's specialized training. I listened in and experimented on my own. To me, it seemed more of a drill than anything else. However, the entrance point had to be that skill level at which the person could actually do what was being asked. By having Jovanna imagine or create the idea of huge cranes lifting the hand, she actually got the other person's hand to move. Now, Julie had her doing little things using only one small crane. Finally, Julie simply had her imaging that she was standing above the person and causing his hand to rise without the use of machinery.

Julie then said something I found keenly interesting. *It is simply a matter of intention, Jovanna. You get the intention firmly created and hold it solid and steady until it is carried out. Often what will happen is that while you are projecting your intention outward, an intention that is counter to or opposite of yours will try to come in on you. For example, if I said make the man trip, you are going to likely have a counter intention yourself, as he might get hurt, or that isn't such a good idea. These counter intentions are what cause the original intention to fail. You are trying to light a fire with wet wood.*

But how do you handle these counter intentions? Jovanna asked, very perplexed. She had been experiencing many of them, many along the lines of "You are not supposed to be able to make other people's bodies obey you. That isn't normal."

I listened carefully for Julie's answer. This was precisely my problem too. *Just remake your original intention once more and hold it firm until it occurs.* It seems so simple until you actually try it! Jovanna kept doggedly at it.

One day while she was trying like mad to carry out Julie's request, she suddenly cried out, *Oh no! I will never ever do this again, ever!* I sensed she was in very heavy grief! A large greyish mass had appeared over her entire being.

Okay. I want you to go through what is happening, starting at the beginning and tell me what is happening, what you see and hear, as you go through it. She was using Jenna's therapy methods! I concluded that sometime in her past she had used this ability and perhaps used it wrongly. I watched and listened.

I didn't know he couldn't swim! Jovanna wailed. With more

coaching, Jovanna finally began to run through what had happened to her in the past. *This man and I were madly in love with each other. We loved to tease each other, playing all sorts of games with each other, fun things. I really loved that man! Then one day we are standing beside some cliffs. The sea is below us, roaring on the rocks. He is teasing me about some bird doo in my hair. I fell for it and felt around for it. He laughed. I had his body jump off the cliff, intending he go take a bath and wash off the horse dung. His body all on its own follows my command, jumping off the cliff. He hit the water. I look over and see him flailing in the water. I didn't know he couldn't swim, honest I didn't know. I got scared and am running back to our village to get help. When we all get back there, he is dead, drowned. I said he fell off the cliff, but really, I made his body jump off.* Jovanna was now crying about it.

Julie had her go back through the incident several more time, each time more and more details appeared. All of a sudden, Jovanna began laughing. *I should have just gone down to the seashore and pulled him out. Instead, I felt guilty about causing his body to jump and went for help, knowing that he would drown. Oh good grief. How utterly stupid of me!*

Well done, Jovanna. Now how about making that crewman over there pick his nose? The man picked his nose.

By the time that we neared the island of Megalos, Jovanna spied Paul on deck and had his body dance a jig. When he stopped, he looked at her with a silly grin, and said, "Sorry, I guess I just felt like doing a jig just then. Many people on this voyage found their bodies doing many silly, little things.

The cry from the crow's nest ended all that, "Island ho!" Everyone rushed to the bow to take their first look at the land of our enemy, Megalos, home to the Centurion fighters. We arrived in mid-February; still the weather was uncommonly warm, from our point of view. The daytime temperatures were in the eighties. The huge island with its rocky mountains going down its center loomed large on the horizon. As we passed by the Shallow Firth, the huge sprawling city of Sud on the mainland of the Southlands caught everyone's attention. Hundreds of boats of all sizes were plying these waters. Some were small fishing boats, while a few were the large, slow ocean vessels typical of Megalos construction.

As we sailed around the southern coast of the island, towns, villages, and cities were clearly visible, particularly because so much white marble had been used in their construction. We could see numerous people moving about in the streets of the port towns, as well as ships docked, unloading and loading. Indeed Megalos was a thriving land. For two days, we sailed the length of the island, before rounding the eastern edge and then heading back west toward the middle and the port called Athos with Constanza City, cradled next to it, just to the west.

Our destination, Galantas, seat of the Senate and capital, lay some twenty-five miles inland and upwards. A paved roadway led from Athos to Galantas over which daily fresh water wagons carried much needed water to the city. A century ago, a unique dam and aqueduct provided clean, fresh water from the mountains. However, my Lightning Circle destroyed it to save ourselves from being killed by our pursuers. It still had not been repaired. We would have to travel up this road to get to the Senate. There was no other easier or shorter route to Galantas from the ocean. That meant that our ships would be docked dangerously close to the Church of Jehosanity's main headquarters, but a few miles from the docks.

While the crews docked, Jenna briefed everyone on our plan. Tomorrow, with the carriage and horses unloaded, we would leave after breakfast. Late morning, we would speak at the Senate, whether they liked it or not. By mid to late afternoon, we should be back here. We would send word for the new Pope to meet us here near suppertime. That should give everyone time enough to get the carriage and horses reloaded. If all went well, we would sail just after the meeting with the Pope, which should not take very long. That was the initial plan, anyway.

We watched as the crew worked the cranes that lifted the coach and horses up out of the cargo hold and onto the dock. At the same time, our captain took a bag of gold coins to the harbormaster to pay for our docking stay. It was fascinating to see just how these heavy horses and coach could be raised so easily with the pulleys and cranes. Still, several hours passed. Dark came before the last horse was on land, though. We posted guards and had our supper on board the caravels. While it might have been fun and exciting to try local foods and inns, such actions by the Santi would just be asking for trouble. Chain mail and black tunics with our red crosses drew much interest and many prying eyes from the local people near the docks.

The bright sun broke on the day of our big gamble. Marcia and Novia, the Healers, rode in our carriage. Marcia was in charge of carrying me. Novia carried the copy of the first few pages of the journal. Of course, Jenna and Jovanna were in the carriage as well as Eve, who would act as Communicator, maintaining a Mind Link to those back at the estate. There, Paulette would link into other Guardians. The objective was to have as many people as possible witness the event. If we failed to notice some crucial detail, perhaps another would.

Fel drove the carriage with Paul at her side, ever on the alert. On either side, the two squads rode, Adriana taking point herself. We all hoped that the language lessons we had received on the trip would be sufficient. Just in case they were not, our translator rode along, bringing up the rear.

As the small party rode through the streets of the port town, everyone stared out the windows. "It's so similar to some of the buildings at Mont Blanc," was often repeated. Raphael, the Lightning Circle Planner who came here with me a century ago and who was now Allan, had emulated some of these designs. Tall marble columns were perhaps the most prominent architectural feature, that and many structures with few or no walls. This was a land of high heat nearly all year round. No wonder they attempted to take advantage of cooler sea breezes whenever possible.

Around us, the rocky hillside looked quite barren. Ever upwards the road ran, climbing into the beginnings of the mountains. The white domed buildings of Galantas were visible from nearly ten miles distant. We passed several water wagons lumbering up toward the city and quite a few other travelers. Everyone stared at us as we passed. That the Santi were paying Megalos a visit was obvious even to the normal folks.

The streets of Galantas were crowded with people, horses, wagons, and even push carts. Open-air markets, shops of all kinds catered to every taste and desire. The going was slow, as I directed our route through the city to the large Senate amphitheater. Several times, Paul and I conferred, trying to remember the route we had taken when we were here before as Lightning Circle members. Only once did we need to ask directions. Around ten in the morning, we pulled up beside the Senate. Even from this distance, we could see that they were in session. Their robes or togas dotted the rows of marble seats.

The speaker stood in the center. Each row of stone seats rose higher than the last. Even if one was unlucky enough to have to sit in the top row with the speaker appearing very small below you, the acoustics were such that you could hear clearly every word that was said. Four city guards were on duty at the entrance. We pulled up and climbed out of the carriage, while the fighters dismounted. The Healers made some last minute adjustments on Jenna and Jovanna, pulling their tunics just so. Now no one could see either of their hands, it looked like they were merely folded beneath their tunics. Surrounded by the Santi force, we marched toward the entrance.

"Halt. You cannot enter. Senate is in session," one guard said, as he stepped slightly ahead of the other three, who moved to block the entrance.

Paul, in the lead said quietly, "We have not traveled a thousand miles to have you stop us. Either you can step aside or we will go through you, leaving you quite dead. Your choice." Seeing thirty chain mail clad fighters armed to the teeth with various weapons, they chose to step aside. Diego and his squad of ten stayed behind to ensure the safety of our horses and carriage. Paul led the way, followed by Jenna and Jovanna, who were flanked by Adriana and the entire other squad. The two healers followed right behind Jenna, one holding me so that I could see, although she need not have. No way was I going to miss this.

The President was conducting a vote on some bill as we marched onto the center platform where he was standing. "What is the meaning of this? You are interrupting an Official Senate Meeting. Please leave before I have you thrown out."

With Paul somewhat in front of her, eyes peeled for any sign of trouble, Jenna walked up to the man. "Excuse us please, senators, the Santi del Dio have come to address the full Senate. You will, Mr. President, please stand aside." Several chain mail clad ex-Sisterhood fighters moved toward him, hands on the hilts of their swords. He quickly said, "The Santi wish a word with us," and quickly stepped back a good distance.

"Good day to you esteemed senators, one and all. I am Jenna Rose Weston, Supreme Commander of the Santi del Dio. I have heard that Megalos is a cultured civilization, well educated. Thus, men of your stature are not barbarians or barbaric or inhumane in nature. I wish to address a most serious problem that has been going on in what we call the Occupied Sea Prince Sectors or which you may call your Conquered Sea Prince Sectors. This heinous, barbaric practice has been going on now for over ten years, unabated with time. The perpetrators are the Holy Paladins, the priests of your Church of Jehosanity, and their Mano del Dio."

From several rows back, a senator leaped to his feet and began shouting her down. "Don't listen to these foul words from this heathen bitch, this destroyer of men, this natural born sinner who —." He never finished his diatribe. Suddenly his body began floating up in the air, high over the amphitheater. Jenna had pulled her left arm out from under her tunic, revealing her missing hand. More to the point, she was pointing it at the levitating man, who continued to rise even high into the sky. She moved her arm, and he went flying off into the city; she lowered her arm, and he came down several miles away from the amphitheater.

"Where I come from, that is considered extremely rude, brash, and uncalled for behavior. I will tolerate none of that. We Santi are a civilized people. As I was saying, the Holy Paladins and their priests have been committing unspeakable horrors, wanton, baseless mutilations of women. Look, this is what they did to me some dozen years ago." She raised both arms up. Gasps of shock and disbelief echoed throughout the Senate. She paused for dramatic effect.

"Yes, my crime is to have been born a woman and to have been running my own inn in Zargarb. Nothing more. Without a trial or even being accused, they cut off my hands and forced me to stay in their Nunnery against my wishes. They have blinded women, cut out their tongues, and pulled out their teeth. Ah, senators, that is not the half of it. If this was not enough, they then raped these women, not once, but continually until their battered and diseased bodies at last died. Some women they beat and raped, and sometimes they died from the severe beatings. Tied arms and legs across a bench, gagged to muffle their screams, they had their way with these women, always in the basements of the so called Holy Nunneries."

"Now you are seeing only me, and I am from Zargarb. You think it is isolated to just that sector. I'm afraid it is not. Behold a maiden from Barcella, Jovanna is her name." She stepped a foot forward and pulled her very short arms out from under her tunic, raising them towards the sky. Visibly shaken, upset, and annoyed — these were the emotions I could sense from the crowd. Jenna continued, "Her mutilations were done by the Mano del Dio. First, he began by cutting of a finger. Once all fingers were gone, he removed each hand. Leaving her to die on her aged father's doorstep, he showed her no mercy whatsoever! Had we not intervened she would have died of gangrene and blood poisoning in another twenty-four hours!"

In the past half year, we have rescued and aided over a hundred of these mutilated, beaten, raped, and brutalized women from nearly all the Occupied Sectors. All were kept as prisoners in the Nunneries there. All were brutalized by the Holy Paladins, their priests, and the Mano del Dio. In Pieta, young boys, not yet in their teens have been sodomized and then killed so that they cannot identify their abuser. I have come before you today to tell you that the Santi del Dio will not tolerate any more of this abuse of women in the Occupied Sectors."

"I assume that you did not know of this savagery being committed against women there, all under the disguise of religion. I certainly hope that you did not and have not condoned such evil behavior."

"One other detail I will share with you. The yearly progress reports that you have been getting along with your gold taxes are an outright lie, a complete falsehood. Under this barbaric rule of the Holy Paladins there, Zargarb's population has fallen to below one hundred fifty thousand counting everyone who is still there. Zargarb has not had this few people in over two centuries! Where did they all go you ask? They fled the barbarism being foisted off and forced upon them by the Holy Paladins, priests, and the Mano del Dio. You probably heard that in Florintine Junction a massive plague struck last year, killing nearly five thousand people. That is a total fabrication. In fact, the women of the Junction decided that they had finally had enough of this oppression, this suppression, this barbaric treatment. They rebelled and poisoned every man and woman who in anyway contributed to their mistreatment during the last ten years. Then, they burned the Junction, the entire city, which used to hold one hundred fifty thousand people, to the ground. No building remained standing. Such was the outrage of these brutalized women. They did it all on their own. Hell hath no fury like a woman mistreated. Then, forty thousand of them fled the Junction to begin to live as a free people elsewhere."

You, esteemed senators, have been lied to continually by the men your Church has put in charge to govern. The purpose of this visit is to put you on notice. The Santi del Dio will tolerate no more of this savagery of the women in the Sea Princes. We will give you until spring to put a complete and total end to the mistreatment of women there. If you do not act by then, we will! This mutilation and raping and beating of innocent women will stop, one way or another. Either you see to it by spring or we will do it for you. Thank you for listening to me. Good day, senators."

She turned around sharply and quickly; the fighters escorted her off the platform. Behind her, she heard several men begin to clap! However, other men quickly silenced them. Jenna knew then that the Santi would most likely have to put an end to it come spring.

A few minutes later, the group was once again making its way through the crowded streets of Galantas. Now the fighters were on keen alert. Message or threat delivered. Repercussions were sure to follow. Inside the coach, everyone was complimenting Jenna on having delivered a most powerful speech. However, Jovanna asked, "That man, how did he go flying up and away?"

"I lifted him and plopped him several miles away," Jenna said quietly. "Ill-mannered man. I had no more patience with him."

He was a Mano del Dio senator, elected to represent Constanza City, I sent her and she relayed that to the others. She did not ask how I knew that fact, however.

Jovanna laughed, "Never cross Jenna!" Everyone laughed. Yes, it had been a most impressive display, one that would give these people something to discuss and ponder. Jenna's idea was to strike a bit of fear that the Santi were indeed the knights of god, with godlike power. I had argued against such a display of her powers, however. The demonstration could go either way. Either they would so greatly fear us that they would never cause us any harm or they would become quite fanatical in their attempts to eliminate us out of fear of what we could do to them. Only time would tell whether Jenna's gamble paid off.

The ride back down to the port city was completely uneventful. No one attempted to hinder us. Actually, I did not expect that they could react swiftly enough anyway. It was a group, and a group takes time to decide anything. That's one difference between one person running the country and a group. Had we just seen the Emperor, you could bet that he would have emptied his cavalry garrisons on our trail. No, the real threat lay before us. We had sent the message to the Pope early that morning. In the message, we told him what we were going to do at the Senate along with a requested meeting at dinnertime at the docks. He would have the entire day for his assassins and fighters to make their preparations. No, ahead lay the real threat!

It began about five miles from the port city. Suddenly, around fifty men jumped up from their roadside hiding placed. They had placed huge rocks on the road, blocking our passage. While everyone prepared for combat, our two unseen companions began doing that for which I had asked them to come. As we watched, huge sand and dust clouds formed, like miniature tornadoes just ahead of us. Two funnel clouds swept over the ambushers, picking them up like leaves in the wind, throwing them great distances, smashing bodies hard onto the rocky hillside. By the time that the carriage arrived at the blockage, the tornadoes had vanished as well as those who intended to ambush us!

"What was that? Who did that?" everyone yelled at nearly the same time. It was the most incredible display of power that any of us had ever seen. Even Jenna was appalled, still gaping at the horizon where the clouds had finally vanished as suddenly as they had come. I Mind Linked to everyone rapidly.

Bethany here. Our two unseen guests did that for us, Julie and her husband Karmanski. They have been with us from the beginning. At my request, they have been watching over us and will continue to do so. I said that we were not without friends.

"Are they gods?" someone asked aloud.

No, they, like Jenna and myself, can operate without the need of a fleshly body.

Julie and Karmanski decided to make their location visible to us. Briefly they each radiated their favorite color. "I see them. There they are!" many called out. Yes, both were floating above us and ahead of us. Each glow appeared to be perhaps fifty feet in diameter. *Impressive, Julie, Karmanski. You have gained more abilities since I last saw you. Thanks for adding to our reality a bit there,* I sent to them privately.

Jenna now levitated the rocks, lifting them as if they were but grains of sand, pitching them far away. Thus, everyone got a second display of the power Jenna had. Still talking about what we had just witnessed, our small party moved forward once more toward the port.

When we were about a mile from our destination, Julie came back to me. *Bethany, the docks have been cleared of people. Well over a hundred lie in wait for your return. We detect many poisoned weapons in their possession. They literally surround the entire docks. Karmanski is there protecting the boats and their crews. What course of action do you wish to follow?*

I called a halt and relayed the news. Jenna volunteered, "Look, if I sit on top of the coach, I can see in all directions at the same time. If our party is bunched up close and tight, I can keep any projectiles from hitting everyone. The rest of you take offensive action, but do stay close together or I will not be able to protect everyone."

Paul added, "They probably will not reveal themselves and attack until we are in the center of the dock, where we have no escape route available."

"Makes sense," Jenna replied. "Julie, can you keep those at our rear occupied? If so, then each squad can fire at those on their respective sides. There is not a cloud in the sky today, so no lightning bolts. So flames it is, Guardians. They believe in the Eternal Flames of Hell, so let's show them what that means! Healers, you two protect my body, Lizzy Ann's, and Jovanna's. Okay everyone, battle stations!"

Paul yelled out our old battle cry, "One for all and all for one; ride Santi!" We were off; dozens of bows were out and at the ready. I moved up and joined Jenna, sitting on top of the carriage. It was a beautiful, sunny afternoon, refreshingly warm, considering it was cold back in Velona.

A few minutes later, we entered the port. What a difference the few hours had made. Not a soul was on the streets. Everyone was inside their homes. Those with open walls had fled to safer locations. The town looked utterly deserted, except I occasionally spotted curious eyes peering out of windows as we rode past them. We maintained our trotting pace, unwilling to be a slow moving target. Ahead, we spied the docks and our two ships still moored to the docks, one on either side of the walkway.

No sooner had we reached the center of the large open area than the assassination attempt began. Hundreds of Holy Paladins wearing their sky blue tunics with white crosses on the front and back began running out of the nearby warehouses and buildings. Interspersed were a number of men wearing black tunics, the Mano del Dio. We were greatly outnumbered, nearly ten to one. The only positive detail was the fact that they all could not get out into position at the same time. They could only swarm us in smaller waves.

Uniformly, as each Holy Paladin rushed to the attack, he would fire his heavy crossbow at a member in our group. Dropping the device, which took considerable time to reload, each drew his sword and charged us. The air between us and the enemy, some two hundred feet on either side, became filled with flying quarrels. To their utter dismay, the flight path of each projectile was most peculiar. Every one of these potentially lethal quarrels curved downward, striking the cobblestones around twenty feet from our mounted perimeter! Jenna was going full blast, pushing each one downward in its flight. The intense concentration she needed for this rapid firing I found truly amazing!

Our fighters reacted with their longbows, firing at the blue coats as fast as they could. No time to coordinate targets, some men were hit multiple times. Within two minutes, their quivers were empty. Now they drew their swords prepared to go hand-to-hand, while mounted. However, Paul urged them to restrain from moving out of the tight formation surrounding the carriage. His steadfast orders were critically needed.

From the rear, at least a hundred formed ranks, blocking any possible retreat back the way we had come. Just why we would want to go back towards Galantas escaped me at the time. However, Julie was protecting our rear. Annoyed with the absence of sand to form into a swirling cloud, she began to improvise. A nearby chimney of a blacksmith inexplicably disintegrated, its bricks formed into a swirling cyclone. Wham, the high speed bricks smashed into the forming lines of men. As her mini-tornado swirled here and there, more and more debris was swept into the swirling mass. Men dodged this way and that to avoid the cyclone, however, the cyclone had a mind of its own and followed them until it struck and then veered on to the next man.

Near the front by the boats, Karmanski was very busy. Unlike his wife, he just picked up the blue tunic bodies and threw them. Bodies arced high through the sky, landing against the upper walls of the warehouses and then falling to the ground. Onboard the ships, the Protection Squads were firing arrows like mad; they had a nearly inexhaustible supply of them. The two massive crossbows fired giant spears, which, when they hit a man, went clear through his body, often pinning the body against the warehouse walls. The tips of the spears penetrated into the stone walls, sticking hard. The shipboard Guardians, as did I, brought down sheets of flames, roasting a man here, setting another on fire there. Fire was not as effective as it might have been because the Holy Paladins were not bunched up in a line.

Quickly, the enemy stopped all attempts to shoot our forces with their crossbows. Far too many of their own men now blocked the line of fire of the new forces just coming out of the buildings. Many from the first wave had nearly closed the distance to our two mounted squads. Now, the real melee began — armored mounted riders versus a human wave. The clank of steel upon steel drowned out all attempts at speech.

From inside the carriage, Jenna's body sat motionless, a mere form. The two Healers, one protecting my small body with her own, looked out one window, her spells at the ready in case someone got through. The other Healer did likewise at the other window. Jovanna watched wondering how she could help. Then, she realized what she could do. She spied a blue tunic just coming out of the warehouse, drawing his sword. She issued her command, and the man raised his arm and cut his own throat. It was slow going for her, because it took her considerable time to locate the right person and to take over control of that body with total certainty.

Now many of our riders had been pulled off their mounts. As soon as one fell, those riders closest to the fallen would close the gap, giving the fighter time to regain his or her feet and prepare for foot combat. Soon, with most of our fighters on foot, they pushed into the waves of Holy Paladins, driving them back enough for the rest to dismount. Adriana was attacking three men simultaneously, while the two squad leaders took on two at once. Still the Holy Paladins continued to arrive. I sensed Jenna getting rather annoyed.

About a quarter mile uphill from the docks, a temple like structure glowed brilliant white in the late afternoon sun. As I watched, its roof rose slightly and one of the huge supporting marble columns broke free and floated over to the combat zone. What happened next was frightening to behold. Imagine someone swinging a baseball bat in a circle around their body. Now translate that into a swinging marble column sweeping in a wide circle around our position. Literally, Jenna began wiping out all bodies that were beyond about ten feet from our forces! Bodies either smashed into the marble bat and stuck there or they went sprawling lifelessly in all directions.

Unfortunately, by now over half of our protecting force was down with one or more wounds. The enemy was slowly, by attrition, achieving their objective, before the arrival of the swinging column. At last, our fighters eliminated the remaining ones that were close to them, bodies lay everywhere. During this temporary lull, our unwounded began dragging the wounded back and under the carriage for protection. Jenna's swinging column continued to fly around our position. All the Holy Paladins now backed off. Perhaps we were winning, I thought.

Just then, the Mano del Dio, who until now had pretty much stayed out of the actual attack, began to move forward. Watching the moving column, they timed their advance to either duck under it or sprint forward just after it had passed by their position. One of our Healers called out, "Poisoned blades!" Indeed a black sticky substance dripped from their swords.

The nearest one was hit in his back by an arrow from one of our shipboard fighters. His body jerked from the impact, but his steely countenance did not waver. He continued his slow march towards our very thin line of fighters. Thud. Another arrow hit him. Still as if in no pain at all, the man stared at Adriana and continued straight for her, his eyes steeled on her. I noticed that Adriana now held her sword in her left hand. That could only mean she had been wounded in her sword arm! Thud. Thud. Two more hit him, yet still he approached her, his transfixed eyes penetrating her soul. Just as he was about to swing a sharp down stroke on her, his other hand pulled out his dagger and he cut his own throat. Adriana, barely three feet from the assassin, saw a look of utter shock in the dying man's eyes.

Now more of these vile, evil assassins circumvented Jenna's swinging column, closing upon our position. We Guardians immediately began attacking them with sheets of flames. Obviously, these assassins would not stop if hit with arrows. With their poisoned blades, we just could not let them get close enough for our fighters to strike with their swords, entirely too dangerous. At last, with many going up in flames, the remainder slowly backed away.

I detected that someone was ordering them to retreat. The orders seemed to be coming from inside one particular warehouse. Perhaps, we had won the day? Now both protection squads ran off the two caravels and headed to support us. Within a minute, the battlefield emptied. Our enemies, who were uninjured or still could move on their own, vanished as rapidly as they had come. Only the moaning of many wounded broke the stillness, along with several sea birds flying overhead.

Jenna returned to her body and stepped out of the coach. "Get the wounded on board immediately. Move the carriage and horses down into loading position. Now where is that Pope? He is late."

While everyone began following the orders, a half dozen ex-Sisterhood fighters began a systematic sweep of the immediate battlefield around us. Each body was stabbed through its heart before they kicked and shoved it out of our path. This was one aspect of their former training that we Santi had been unable to undo. Make certain each is dead was their motto.

I told mom where I thought the Pope may be hiding. Just as soon as our party was beside the boats, the crews began the loading process, Jenna ordered, "Now let's have a word or two with the Pope. Paul, pick five and join me. Julie, Karmanski, stay alert for treachery. Get Lilly Ann and Jovanna on board and then begin tending wounds. Now it's time to find that rat."

Paul, though bleeding from several wounds, grabbed both caravel Protectors and three other uninjured Santi, all women. They formed up a defensive line surrounding Jenna. I was hovering over her head. No way was I going to let anything happen to mom! However, behind us, Jovanna protested and wrestled her way free, "I can help, honestly I can!"

Before anyone could catch her, she came up behind Jenna. "Where is he? I can get him out of there, if I can see him."

Jenna relented, "Okay, as soon as he comes out, I want you back on the caravel as fast as you can run, you hear me?" She used her stern voice, so that Jovanna would not think of disobeying her this time. "Bethany thinks he is in that warehouse window, looking out." She pointed with her arm toward where I had seen someone giving the retreat orders.

Jovanna concentrated. It was funny actually, looking back on the sight. The rather portly Pope Amir I, Silas, came walking out, but not of his own free will. His body looked rather like a child's puppet — the child pulling the strings to make the puppet appear to be walking! The terrorized look on his face told us that he was not coming by his own choice. Immediately, four black robed Mano del Dio slipped out and surrounded their leader. If death were demanded of them, they would go gladly. We could all sense their intense dedication to the Pope and this religion. "Ah, there you are at last, Pope. You are a bit late for our meeting. Glad you could make it."

"Now then, I will come directly to the point. We know what your Holy Paladins have been doing to the women of the Occupied Sectors. We know what goes on within the basements of the Nunneries. As my letter stated, we have already spoken of this to the Senate this morning."

"Paul, hand him the copied pages please." Paul had retrieved the pages from the Healer as he was rounding up the fighters. Paul did as he asked, handing them to the assassin standing in front of the Pope. The man took them. "This is proof that we do have the journal. As we speak, it is being translated into many languages. What happens to it next depends upon you and your assassin squads."

"I will be exceptionally blunt. The Santi del Dio gives you until spring to cease all of this wanton molestation, mutilation, raping, and beating of women in the Occupied Sectors. If you do so, we will take no action. If you do not, then we will do it for you. Do I make myself perfectly clear, Pope?"

Pope Amir I, trembling beneath his robes, having just witnessed a slaughter that only the gods could dole out, and in terror for his life, said, "Yes. It shall be done."

"Good. That is all; you may leave. Perhaps next time we can meet under friendlier terms." Jenna turned and walked slowly back to the ship. One of the assassins attempted to throw a dagger into her back. Suddenly the man went flying through the air, landing far out at sea. To the Pope, it looked like the Hand of God had reached down and picked him up and thrown him away. The Protectors fell in line behind her, blocking any further sneak attacks.

Hastily, the Pope and over a dozen other Mano del Dio maneuvered across the body-strewn cobblestones, leaving by the same road that we had entered. Paul ordered Jenna to go below deck, but she ordered him to accompany her. The two did as instructed, leaving the crews and the uninjured to handle the loading of our horses and carriage. Once below deck, Jenna took Paul to the healing station, which was now the center of the main cargo hold. Already the Healers and several other Guardians had lain the wounded out and were prioritizing their patients.

Just as soon as Jovanna saw Paul, she rushed over to him. "Come on. You are wounded. We have to get them to look at you right away. You are all bloody. Does it hurt much?" Using her short arms, she tried to push him over to the healing station. He allowed her to do so.

The adrenaline rush gone, now his body did hurt. Try as she might, Jovanna was unable to help him remove his chain mail. However, Jean Wade stepped in to lend a hand. Paul was badly bruised on both arms and legs. He had several cuts on each arm as well and on one leg. None was serious though, a prime benefit of the chain mail.

Marcia and Novia, having finished their cursory examination, came to look over Paul's wounds. "Are they really bad?" asked Jovanna, very concerned about Paul.

"No, dear child. We'll have him fixed up in a while. Paul, you sit here, in the middle of the line." He knew that meant others were in much worse shape than he was. He lay down before he fell down. Jovanna sat beside him and refused to budge until he was patched up.

Marcia reported to Jenna, "We have twenty casualties, two serious ones that we will handle immediately. I am putting Sam and Jean on the lighter ones. None are critical, mercy's sake I don't know how that was avoided!"

At once, the two Healers went to work, one taking Adriana and the other Diego. Sam and Jean began with the next two in line after those. Soon other Santi fighters climbed down into the hold to lend a hand, playing go-fors. Jenna and Jovanna made themselves useful by bringing mugs of ale to the wounded that had been patched up, though Jovanna could hardly bear to be away from Paul's side. When Jean arrived to patch him up, Jovanna sat with him through the whole procedure.

By the time that all the horses and carriages had been loaded, it was full dark, and the two Healers finally finished up with Adriana and Diego. Sam and Jean had also finished with the other eighteen who were not in critical shape. The captain's request to set sail was relayed to Jenna who Okayed it. We felt the ship move free of the dock, bobbing on the waves. I think that at that point everyone felt a huge relief. Now we were safe, soon out of the reach of any further treachery on their part.

Next, all the wounded were washed, put into clean clothes, and helped into their hammocks. By this time, the cook had a late supper ready for us all. First served were the wounded. Undaunted, Jovanna managed to get a plate for Paul over to his hammock. Another woman volunteered to help feed him, but she insisted on doing it herself. "Honestly, Jovanna, I am not helpless. Ouch!" Paul had tried to move his arms to reach for the plate.

"See, we know best. Now I am going to feed you, tonight at least. You must be a bit patient with me. I have to figure out how to do this the easiest way. In the end, she put the fork or spoon in her mouth, bent down for a scoopful, and then wiggled over to put it into Paul's mouth. She declared, "After all I am his apprentice and apprentices are supposed to look after their mentors." However, inwardly, she knew that this was not the only motivation behind her actions tonight. There was something else compelling her to help Paul, but she did not want to admit it even to herself.

Once the patients were fed, the others ate themselves. Jenna then ordered everyone to bed. It had been a long day, and she, for one, was exceedingly tired. Although Jovanna wanted to sleep on the floor beside Paul, just in case he might need something during the night, she allowed herself to be helped into her own hammock. A Healer insisted that they would be up all night and that she would be needed in the morning, while in turn they slept.

The next morning broke bright and sunny, typical of the weather around Megalos. The two ships had rounded the eastern edge of the island and were heading along its long southern coast. Jenna gathered everyone near the injured's hammocks. "I want to thank you all personally for all that you did yesterday. We were successful in our mission, completely successful. However, I know that many of you have many unanswered questions about what miraculous things you saw happen. First, let me say that we could not have done it without the help of our unseen guests. Very well done, Julie, Karmanski. They were responsible for all of those cyclones and such. Yes, I knocked down all the quarrels mid-flight. I got very angry with them closing for battle, so I borrowed a marble column to use as a bat. So that was me swinging the column around."

"Boss, can I ask a question?" Adriana asked, a note of pain in her voice. She and Diego had taken the most wounds, although they had doled out drastically far more than they had received. Jenna nodded.

"When I was down, that black Mano del Dio fellow kept coming at me. I know he was hit with a bunch of arrows from the folks on the ship here. Why did he not stop? Do they not feel pain? And why did he, when he clearly could have stabbed me with his poisoned sword, why did he cut his own throat? I don't understand that. His eyes, they were so cold! As if he was some kind of inhuman monster."

I spoke a few words to Jenna. She then relayed, "Bethany suggests that they have trained long and hard to carry out their mission in spite of physical pain inflicted upon them. Yes, these are our most dangerous enemies."

"I can see that," she replied. "Why then did his slit his throat?" Several others also reported seeing other men cutting their own throats with their own blades.

Jenna chuckled, "Ah that, well that was all Jovanna's doing. She is developing a new specialty, similar to the way that I did years ago. It appears that now we may yet have a ninth area of specialization. It's too early in her training to tell. As I understand it, she took command of their bodies and made their bodies do it. She was the one that made the Pope walk out of the warehouse. You noticed how funny he was walking?" Everyone laughed, but then all eyes turned to Jovanna. She blushed, rather embarrassed with the sudden attention.

Adriana exclaimed, "Well, I owe you my life, Miss Short Arms! I am forever in your debt! Just don't go making me do something silly! Watch out guys, Miss Short Arms here will be having you remove your pants before you know it."

Jovanna beamed and then roared with laughter. "I like that, Miss Short Arms." Everyone joined in laughing. She realized that she now had an amazing power, unlike any other, one that could make a person kill his own body. With that awesome power came a great responsibility to use it wisely. In her distant past, she had failed to do so and had lost her ability to use it. She would not make that same mistake twice.

Privately, Jenna and I discussed what had happened. She said, *Well, I've certainly let the cat out of the bag, as they say. That was one incredible display of force.*

Yes, a very, very terrifying display. As I said, it could go either way. Either they will be so terrified of the Santi del Dio that they will fall in line and treat us with respect or they will be so terrified of us that they will try to hunt us down and kill us. Time will tell.

Six weeks later on the last day of March, our caravels sailed into the harbor of Velona. Quite a crowd was there to meet us. Many of them, particularly Elona Po, had witnessed the confrontations via Santi Mind Links. Everyone wanted to cheer us and thank us.

By this time, all the minor wounds had healed nicely. Only Diego and Adriana still wore bandages. As we were preparing to dock, Adriana took

Jovanna aside. "I just wanted to thank you again for saving my life, Jovanna. I am getting too old for these battles. I hope I never see one again. Of course, now I have a few more battle scars to show the others, especially the new recruits," she jested.

"Honestly, Adriana, until that battle I did not know that I could have done what I did. Before that, all I was doing was making people scratch their noses and silly things like that. I learned a lot too, but I don't want to see any more battles either!"

After the cheering subsided, Elona Po announced that a large dancing party would be held on Saturday night to celebrate our victory and the returning heroes. Rapidly, everyone at the estate began talking about the fancy dance.

As soon as the coach arrived at the estate, Paul escorted Jovanna to her room. He found that Ben was there with Ariana, who gaily announced, "Ben is taking me to the dance!"

"That's great!" Paul said. He looked at Jovanna and asked, "Jovanna, would you like to go to the dance with me? I mean not as my apprentice or anything like that, just with me."

"I was hoping you would ask me! You bet I would," both girls giggled. Paul could not see what was so funny or why they were giggling. Neither could Ben, for that matter. The men left with the girls still giggling.

"What's that all about?" Paul asked.

"Dunno, it's just girls," Ben replied. "But we'd better bring them some flowers to pin on their dresses. I think that's the way it's done, though I haven't actually done it before."

"Flowers? Oh yes. Right. Wonder what kind?" The two went to see where they could find flowers here at the end of the winter.

"Wow! Do you ever look good!" exclaimed Paul, noticing just how beautiful Jovanna looked in her blue party dress. Saturday had come at last. Someone had fixed her hair as well. Although she had shown him her new dress when he and Ben had escorted the girls to get their new clothes, he didn't remember her looking half this good. She blushed and offered him her arm.

"Thanks. Beth Ann fixed my hair. Do you like it?" she explained.

"Yes, you look, well, ravishing! I'm going to have to fend off all the guys tonight."

He helped her into the waiting coach. Ben had already met Ariana and they were waiting on Paul. Since many others were also going tonight, including Jenna, Hank, and many of the older children, several Santi were acting as drivers and protectors. "You look great too, Ariana, Paul said as he climbed in to the coach and shut the door.

Ariana fairly bubbled with excitement. "I've never been to a dance before. My folks always said I was too young to go. And then all this happened," she raised her arms. "What's it like?"

Ben tried to explain, but found it somewhat hard to do. "I have learned how to dance. It was part of our training, dexterity and all that. I have to admit, Ariana, I've never been to one. Oh yes, I'm sorry that I couldn't get you any flowers to wear. Nothing has bloomed yet, way too early."

"Yes, me too," Paul hastily added. "I've been to a few dances. I always took my sister, so I guess that means I know mostly what to expect. There's lots of music and dancing and eating. It really might be a lot of fun."

"I'll bet Paulette loved to go. I'm glad that you took her," Jovanna replied. "It's my first time at a big dance as well.

"I guess I really ought to just come out and say this before we get there and all, Jovanna. Actually, this is, er, ah, well, I've never been on a real date before. It's my first time, so if I make major blunders, please excuse me." There he had said it, so if he committed a major goof, perhaps she would not hold it against him.

"Me too," Ben hastily added, taking advantage of Paul's admission. He'd not been brave enough to just come out and tell Ariana.

Both girls giggled, making both men feel slightly ill at ease. "We haven't either," Ariana finally admitted. It's our first dates too. So I guess that makes us all pretty much in the same boat, you know, not knowing how things should go and all that."

The dance was being held in the Friendship Hall, a giant room that was part of Elona's enormous Cathedral complex. Usually, parishioners would eat in this room, but tonight it had been turned into a dance hall. When the carriages rolled up, already many had arrived. The men, escorting the women inside, saw that hundreds were already there. They spied the musicians getting setup on a raised stage.

"Look, there's Taliesin. He has his lute. Looks like he is going to be playing with the musicians," Ben pointed out. They waved at him, and he waved back, slightly embarrassed by the currently unwanted attention. This was his first public performance, and he was very nervous.

Then, the dance began. Fast dances, ballads, and many slow dances echoed thorough the huge hall. By the fourth song, the place was packed, but the two couples barely noticed. None of the four ever had so much fun before in their lives.

Near the end of the evening, Jovanna was getting a bit tired and Paul took her for a walk around the giant complex of buildings. In a dark corner, Jovanna stopped. It's now or never, she told herself. He's too shy to do it. She faced him, put her arms on his shoulders, and gave him a loving kiss. At first, Paul was startled. Then he returned her advance, passionately.

Emotionally, Paul wanted to jump and scream! The most beautiful woman in the whole world just passionately kissed him. He restrained himself from doing so. He put his arms around her and held her tightly, and she rested her head upon his shoulders. After a time, she whispered in his ear, "I love you, Paul. I didn't mean to fall in love with you, because you are supposed to be my mentor. But I did. I hope you don't mind and it won't wreck my apprenticeship."

"So that's what this feeling in my stomach and nerves is all about. God, Jovanna, I'm madly in love with you. I think I fell for you the very first time I saw you! I'm in heaven!" He held her waist and together danced in small circles — he was so utterly happy with the revelation that she could possibly love him.

"What are you two doing out here dancing in a circle?" asked Ben. He and Ariana had just walked in and saw them. They were out looking for the two.

Paul announced, "Jovanna and I are in love! Can you believe it? I'm mad about her, and she is actually in love with me too! Isn't that just incredible luck?" Then the two noticed Ariana's face. She had a grin that went from ear to ear. Her cheeks were quite pink.

Ben replied, "Ah, that's nothing! Ariana's just agreed to marry me! We came to tell you."

"I thought he would never ask someone like me! I'm so happy I could just fly!" Ariana radiated.

"Oh Ariana!" Jovanna exclaimed, and rushed to give her a huge hug.

"Congratulations!" Paul attempted a bit more dignity, shaking Ben's hand vigorously.

"We wanted you to be the first to know about it and to witness that we are now pledged to each other!" Ben explained.

"Thanks!" Paul looked at the radiant Jovanna and hesitated no longer. He moved to her and got down on one knee. "Jovanna Barcella, I humbly ask for your arm in marriage. Will you marry me?"

Jovanna nearly tackled him, holding him as tightly as she could. "Oh yes, yes, yes, a thousand times yes!"

"Now we can witness for their pledge!" exclaimed Ariana. All four hugged each other en mass.

The four rode home a thousand times happier than when they came to the dance. They decided upon a dual spring time wedding.

Later that night, the four visited Jenna to tell her about their decisions and to ask her blessings. She was, after all, the men's commander in chief. "I'm delighted for all four of you. However, gentlemen are you sure that you know what you are getting into with these women? After all, look at how much trouble I have been for Hank!"

He walked in and heard that remark. "What trouble have you been to me, Jenna, my love? Yes, you have been loads of trouble. You keep going off on all these secret journeys leaving me here all by my lonesome self!"

Jenna grinned, that was plainly not what she meant at all. "Dear, these four want to get married. They are apparently madly in love with each other. Now tell them just how much trouble I've made for you." She used her stern voice on him.

"Yes, dear," he said politely. "Guys, you realize that in time you are going to have lots of children running around, getting into everything, with messy diapers to change. Oh and wait until they get to the ornery threes, then they start throwing food at you when they don't like it. Yes, guys, you are getting into a whole lot of trouble by getting married." He was teasing of course. Jenna gave him a cold stare.

"Okay, okay. Seriously, Jenna dear, I love you and nothing you have ever done has caused me the slightest trouble, except when you go off and leave me behind. When you love someone, it doesn't matter what inconveniences their body presents. I would not trade a minute of our life together, not for a million gold coins. That's how I feel, Jenna. You are *not* going to get me to say I hated that I had to make all sorts of allowances for your missing hands. No way. If you want to make up how miserable they might feel having to wash their wife's privates, then it's your problem, not mine. I never ever felt that way. Who cares if you need a little more attention than someone else does? I love being with you and doing things with you, period."

"Oh Hank!" She gave him a long hug and kiss. Then, she faced us once more. "Okay so you get the idea that you will have to do more things than you would have to otherwise do." Both men nodded. "All right then, you have my blessing, but I insist that Elona Po perform the ceremony here at the estate. In the springtime, it's just gorgeous around here. Hank has planted so many flowers that it's like heaven!"

"Yes!" the four young folks cried.

Jenna then got that serious look back on her face. I could tell that all four were thinking, "What now?"

"Gentlemen, you both realize that your fiancés, due to their long years of imprisonment, are lacking in knowledge in a certain area. So, ladies, beginning tomorrow, we three will hold some very private lessons." From the looks on both women's faces, I knew that this was probably the single biggest worry that they had. Ariana knew nothing about being with a man; her experiences were nothing but brutalized rapes. Jovanna, on the other hand, had never had any education or experience either.

Jenna shooed them all out and began to give me my last feeding for the night. I sent her, *I told you that pairing those women up with those men would likely lead to this.*

Jenna coyly whispered into my ear, "Well, maybe that's what my intention actually was."

Chapter 11 Counter Moves

Pope Amir I sat at the head of his meeting table, a crushed man. Gone, everything gone within a day. How could he have failed so utterly? Any moment he expected the dead Pope Yazi I to walk through the door and chastise him or perhaps the Hand of God would simply puck him up from his chair and cast him into Lucifer's Realm. However, it wasn't either that walked through the door into the gathered meeting of the Cardinals and Pope, it was Supreme Prelate Thondakas.

"Cax is dead. We lost two hundred thirty-one Holy Paladins and a dozen Mano del Dio. Another hundred will survive their wounds. All bodies have been removed from the dock and the street cleaners are washing away the blood. However, that enormous marble column will have to wait for the engineers to handle. I received word that the fifty sent to ambush them are also dead, smashed into the rocks around the site. Gruesome sight." He took his seat at the rear of the assembly, just as had his mentor, the late R. Thraxton.

"I have failed you all," a deeply grieving Silas began. "I have led Pope Yazi, you, and the entire Mother Church to our doom. I cannot express the sorrow that I feel. I cannot even bring myself to pray to Jehosa for forgiveness, I am utterly unworthy of such. If there was any way that I could resign as your Pope, I would do so at once. Unfortunately, there is no such provision in the Holy Rules. I have failed you all so utterly. Leave me now to grieve for our lost ones. I beg, though I no longer have the right to do so, that each of you will pray to Jehosa tonight for guidance. Whatever should we do I have no idea. Perhaps one of you will achieve Divine Guidance and can enlighten us on the morrow. That is all. I am sorrier than words can express."

Solemnly the Holy Cardinals filed out of the room, muttering to themselves. A calamity of monumental proportions had just struck their Holy Church. They depended upon their Pope for Holy Guidance. Yet, he was wallowing in self-pity and could not even offer them consolation. Small groups began whispering behind closed doors that night.

Supreme Prelate Thondakas paced his room, deep in thought. Unlike his predecessor, the Rooster, who had undying loyalty to the Pope, Thondakas did not. He was a pragmatist, a realist in outlook. If the Holy Church went down, he went down, along with a highly profitable and powerful career. He'd come to enjoy his work for the Church immensely. "I cannot let a foolish old man ruin everything!" He paced around his austere quarters once more.

Senator Dax knocked on his door, and the Prelate let him in, "What news, Dax?"

"Horrible, I am afraid to say. I tried to stop Lucifer's Bitch from spreading her vile lies in the Senate, but failed, due to no fault of my own. We are indeed dealing with Lucifer's Spawn!" He then related how he had been ejected from the Senate by the accursed woman. Hundreds had witnessed it, so his flight through the air could not be denied. Later, when he had gotten back to the Senate, he found out about the details of what Lucifer's Spawn has told the Senate. "Supreme Prelate, the Senate will be demanding an explanation and very likely a complete, independent investigation of the entire matter. I could not stop them from passing said legislation. However, I can attempt to stall and delay the implementation of said resolution. What are your orders?"

"You are unharmed?" He was. "Well, then let me sleep on the entire matter, Dax. I will speak with you in the morning before you leave for the Senate." Senator Dax quietly left, heading for his private quarters.

He had a hunch that part of the witch spawn's words may have been true. His Mano del Dio representatives in the Controlled Sectors had alerted him to numerous taxation and census discrepancies. That may well be true. Certainly, the poisoning of five thousand Holy Souls in the Junction was true. His field men had already ascertained the truth of that detail, though he could not fault the General for disguising it from the Church. Women truly were and are the downfall of men! There could be only one answer that might save the Church and his position. "We need a scapegoat, someone to take the fall. We can place the entire blame for this fiasco upon his head. That handles the Senate and gives us time to deal with this hideous calamity. I know just who it should be — he cannot even lead any more, the idiot. After all the needs of the Church are greater than the needs of one man," he justified. He found a vial of blackish liquid and poured a measured amount into a cup, then added some wine. He then carried the cup to another room and knocked on the door.

A loud knocking woke Thondakas from a sound sleep. "Come in," he said sitting up in bed, wiping his eyes.

A priest entered looking forlorn. "Sir, I bring grave news. Pope Amir I has passed away in his sleep. You must come at once."

"Thank you." Hastily, he dressed and headed to the Pope's bedroom. Many of the Cardinals were standing outside his room. It was the Supreme Prelate who must enter and determine the cause of death, security reasons. He bowed to them and entered the room. He pretended to examine the dead Pope for appearance's sake, before he spoke the words that the Cardinals were anxiously awaiting. "Died in his sleep as reported. Nothing serious or sinister. The shock of yesterday must have been too hard on his heart. Your Holiness's — we should assemble in the meeting room at once. Send for Senator Dax as well. Have someone carry Silas down to the crypts for now."

Thondakas took charge now. Per the Holy Rules, the Cardinals should now elect someone to be their new Pope. In the meantime, many actions had to be taken, if the Church were to be preserved and all not lost. Who knows how long the Cardinals would take to elect their new leader? Once everyone was seated, Thondakas spoke, "Our very Church is in dire peril, unlike any crisis that has come before. You must meet and elect our new holy leader, the new Pope. However, we cannot wait for that. Actions must be taken today. With your approval, I am sending Dax back to the Senate with the news of the death of Silas. He will explain to the Senators that we suspect that he alone was responsible for the misdeeds in the Controlled Sea Prince Sectors and are investigating it. He will tell them that the mistreatment of women there was not nor ever will be a Church approved action, that we believe that Pope Amir I authorized such on his own motivations, that the many Cardinals had no knowledge of it. In the meantime, we must draft orders to all the generals there to cease and desist the mistreatment of women, at least until clarifying orders are sent. Spring is nearly at hand. We cannot afford to have the Santi attacking our sectors. We must convince them that the situation is being handled, until we have time to determine a proper course of action, whatever that might be."

"Have no doubts, brethren, we are dealing with Lucifer's Spawn, for who else could cause the destruction we've witnessed? Indeed, we have all grossly underestimated the Santi del Dio, who have now shown us that they are definitely in league with Lucifer. Who knows what bargain these vile women have made with the Devil? Yet, we must exercise the greatest of care when dealing with the Santi. I will draft up the orders to send to the Sea Princes today and bring them for the Conclave of Cardinals to sign. Finally, I would urge all of you and the Holy Fathers beneath you to distance yourselves from our late Pope. Stress always that Silas often acted on his own, without your actual approval."

"But we did go along with his plans?" one Cardinal objected, feeling just as guilty for the horrible aftereffects.

"Did you really? Can you honestly sit there and say that you could not have protested to Silas and not done as the Pope ordered? Nay, the Pope's word is law; we both know that. You could have done nothing to prevent this hideous calamity from befalling us. Be at peace with yourself, Cardinal. This seemed to appease the man. The Cardinals gave their approval, and Thondakas and Dax left them to begin their task of electing a new Pope.

When the two men were alone, Thondakas whispered to Dax, "Go to the Senate and explain things. I give you complete authority to do whatever you have to do to place the entire blame upon Pope Amir. I will have some supporting documents 'discovered' by the end of the day and will send them to you at once." Dax grinned and left for Galantas.

Thondakas set to work. First, he drafted two letters to be delivered to the generals, the many priests, and his Mano del Dio operatives in the Sea Princes. The Holy Conclave would signed the first letter. The second they would not see; it was a private letter to only the generals and to his operatives, not to the priests. This took him several hours to compose; wording was everything in these documents. Satisfied at last, he then tackled a third document. When he had finished it, he copied the signature of Silas and put the wax mark of the Pope's official seal on the document. Then, he rolled it up and secretly placed the document in Silas's room. Satisfied, he ordered his men to make a thorough search of the Pope's living and working quarters, looking for any incriminating evidence.

Late in the afternoon, he visited the Cardinals. Their meeting was not going all that well. Thus far, they had not yet agreed upon just how they would elect the new Pope. Did they need a simple majority vote, a two-thirds majority, a three-quarters majority, or a unanimous vote? Thondakas said, "I have drawn up the necessary orders. Would you be so kind as to read them and let me know if you deem any changes are needed? With spring so close, I would like to get these posted yet today if at all possible."

One Cardinal read the letter aloud to the others. He skipped the salutations.

The Santi del Dio leader, Jenna Rose Weston, paid both the Senate and Pope

Amir I an unexpected visit here on Megalos yesterday. She issued an ultimatum to both. The mutilation, beating, and raping of women in the Controlled Sea Prince Sectors must stop by spring. If you do not, they will attack you and destroy you, showing no mercy. Yes, they displayed to the Senate two women whose hands had been removed, though they did not tell them of what crimes these women had been convicted.

As they left Megalos, the Santi have proven beyond any shadow of doubt that they are indeed Lucifer's Spawn! At the Senate, our duly elected representative, Senator Dax, was lifted from his seat at least a mile into the sky and placed safely on the ground over three miles away. This was witnessed by all the senators! On their way back to Athos, they mutilated fifty of our Holy Paladins, smashing their bodies upon the rocks. Only Jehosa knows what forces of evil they could command to have done that. At the docks, they proceeded to murder nearly three hundred of our men. Here, only Lucifer himself could have carried out what our men witnessed. Hundreds of quarrels were cast away from their targets, bodies burned beyond recognition by the Fires of Hell. Even wilder, one of the marble columns supporting the theater was uprooted and used as a bashing ram, flying through the air as one would swing a bat. Only the hand of Lucifer could have done this.

Alas, all this has been too much for Pope Amir's heart to handle. It is with great sadness that I must report that Pope Amir I is now dead. The Cardinals are now meeting to elect a new Pope to lead us.

You now have new orders until the next Pope is elected and a new strategy is formulated. The orders are quite clear. Abduct no more women against their will. No more mutilations, beatings, and raping must occur. After spring comes, if the Santi discover more of this has occurred, they have given us their word that they will attack and butcher you and everyone connected with our church. We beg you to be overly careful of actions taken by your subordinates. Do not give these Lucifer's Spawns any reason to destroy you and our Holy Church.

More orders will be forth coming.

Quickly, the individual Cardinals added their signature to the bottom of each copy. One thanked Thondakas profusely for handling this for them. He left to get them posted. The secret letter read as follows.

The official letter you have received with this one is essentially true and to be followed. However, we both know that without some means of persuasion, so many women, who insist upon earning Bad Marks, cannot easily be convinced to begin to earn Good Marks. Here are my suggestions.

First, dispose of any women who have been mutilated, raped, or mistreated. Perhaps you might give them over to the Santi, where those in league with the Devil and be cared for by Lucifer's Spawn.

Second, if you do need to convince women and feel the necessity of continuing what has been done for the last dozen years, then do it is secret and away from the Nunneries, which the Santi are closely watching.

Third, I would recommend using an alternative method. Have a blacksmith create an iron, lockable harness which binds their arms across their back, or locks their hands inside a metal ball, or locks a ring in their mouths forcing it to be always open, or locks a blindfold around their heads. Use creative imagination. The goal is to force them to begin earning Good Marks by removing any possibility of earning more Bad Marks, yet done in a way that leaves no permanent, physical marks upon their bodies with which the Santi can use as an excuse to attack you and your sector.

If the Santi attacks you, the Church is powerless to aid you at this time. Expect that they will use the evil forces of Lucifer, which they now command against you.

Fourth, I would recommend that you begin looking at the local men who would make good candidates to join our Holy Paladins. I will be proposing this to the new Pope. One major mistake we've made is not recruiting many local men into our forces. As it is now, the locals feel that all the Holy Paladins come from Megalos. If they can see that the Holy Paladins are their own people, then that may go a very long way to creating some stability. For now, begin making a list of possibilities. I hope that the next dispatch will contain the Pope's request to recruit locally.

Finally, as soon as you have read this letter, you are ordered to burn it at once. No record shall remain of this dispatch.

Sincerely,

Supreme Prelate Thondakas

Sometime later, one of his men came running to fetch him, "Supreme Prelate, we have just found the most incriminating of documents in the Pope's bedroom."

"Go ask the Cardinals to meet me there, please. Tell them what this is all about." Thondakas walked slowly to the Pope's bedroom. He saw three of him men guarding the entrance. Soon the hallway filled with Cardinals, all talking at once. "One of my men has just told me that in searching the Pope's quarters, a revealing document was found. I have not yet seen it. I want you to bear witness; I am only now entering the room. Sir, where is said document?"

"We found it here, tucked under his mattress. We have not disturbed it, just quickly read it, and replaced it where it was found, sir."

Thondakas removed the rolled up document and opened it. "Will one of you please verify that this is the signature of Silas and the official seal of the Pope?" Several Cardinals did just that, many more were muttering among themselves. Thondakas gave it to one of them to read aloud for the others.

Generals,

Concerning the vast problem of so many women continuing to desire to earn Bad Marks instead of your pleadings for Good Marks, I hereby give you the authority to make it utterly impossible for them to continue to earn the Bad Marks. Specifically, I order you to remove that with which they continue to use to earn Bad Marks. If they fight back with hands, remove them. If they continue to speak ill and profanity, remove their tongues that they may not continue to do so. If they will not consent to a Holy Union with our Holy Paladins, then tied them down and mate with them forcibly. Do not let them continue to earn more Bad Marks, for we would then be aiding and abetting Lucifer. Do what is necessary that they cannot physically continue in their evil ways. I so order it.

However, I cannot let the Conclave of Cardinals know of this order. I am sure that some of them will find this unacceptable. Yet who else but we can ensure that their souls will in the end go to Heaven? No one but us. Please, let's keep this between us.

Pope Amir I

The letter was written in the language of Megalos. No one wondered why it was not written in Arad, the nationality of Silas. Instead, to the last Cardinal, they gasped and all realized the vast importance of this document. One Cardinal spoke, "Supreme Prelate, you must get this document to the Senate. It explains so much! They deserve to read this!" Others agreed wholeheartedly.

"If this is your collective wish, so be it. I will send by secure courier at once!" Unanimously, they insisted. Thondakas bowed and left to get it delivered, while the Cardinals returned to their meeting, more relieved than they had been all day.

What a difference between the aftermath of the death of the two Popes, Yazi and Amir! Thousands lined the streets and even camped alongside of the road between Galantas and the Port of Athos just to get a glimpse of Yazi's funeral caravan. This time, no one came to pay their respects to the deceased Pope Amir. Part was the massive campaign that Thondakas and Senator Dax instigated. Within days, every person on the island had heard of the declaration made by the Santi del Dio leader at the Senate. Dax wasted no time making the recently discovered secret document, presumably written by Pope Amir and discovered under his bed, widely known. In fact, Thondakas had the document officially published and circulated to all churches, to be posted prominently on the entrance doors. Within a week, the commonly held conviction was that Pope Amir alone had ordered this brutality upon the women of the Controlled Sectors of the Sea Princes.

The only people who did not fully believe this were the women of Megalos and the die-hard supporters of Sol, their original god. The women had seen their rights and respect in society plummet to new lows, though many blamed themselves for having gone the route of open promiscuity back in the days of Emperor Titus. Still, they did not fully trust the Church, which was increasingly controlling their lives.

By the end of the week, the Senate seemed appeased that Pope Amir had acted alone. Dax was successful in getting the investigation ended. However, the Senate did want to follow up on the mysterious plague, which the Santi said was really the women of the Junction poisoning five thousand people. Also the reported census anomalies had to be investigated. Thondakas accepted this investigation, because anything found could be easily linked to the generals following the Pope's orders. Even though the Senate planned to send an investigator of their own to the Controlled Sectors to check on the figures, he knew that one investigator would be unable to conduct any accurate head count. It took the official tax collectors months to do that. In the end, he guessed that the investigator would report that there were many people living in the sectors.

What became the topic of the next week was who would become their new Pope. The Holy Conclave had yet to reach an agreement. Thondakas steered clear of the intense political battles going on inside their sealed meeting chamber. He could care less who became the next Pope. He concentrated on working out what steps the new Pope must take quickly and what long range planning needed to be done.

Finally, after three weeks of intense deliberations, the new Pope was announced, Pope Anaxagoras was elected. He was an older man, wise in political dealings. Thondakas later learned though several younger men were seen by the Cardinals as far more qualified than Anaxagoras, choosing a younger man meant that he would hold the position for far longer than anyone currently desired. At sixty-one, Anaxagoras might lead them for ten or so years, certainly no more than twenty. As soon as the Cardinal had chosen the new Pope, word was sent to all Churches and broadly promoted.

After settling in for a few days, Pope Anaxagoras finally met privately with Supreme Prelate Thondakas. "I must thank you for your most efficient and timely handling of Church affairs while the new Pope was chosen. You have performed more than brilliantly. You have my undying thanks, Thondakas. Now then, I have been going over both Senator Dax and your reports for the past few weeks. Is the Senate investigation of our Church really ended?"

"Yes, Your Holiness, expect no further inquiries in that matter. The Senate has officially placed all blame upon Pope Amir I, whose name will go down in infamy, I'm sad to say."

"That is most excellent news. We do not need to undergo an investigation at this most troubled time. I read that the Senate will be sending someone to the Sea Princes?"

"Yes, to check up on the supposed irregularities. Be advised that they will discover that the women of the Junction did indeed poison five thousand and burned the city to the ground. It has not been rebuilt yet. The general will have some explaining to do, I'm afraid. I took the liberty of sending him a dispatch suggesting how he might defend himself against the charge of lying about the cause of the deaths."

Pope Anaxagoras chucked, "And how can he do that?"

"Simple, if he made it widely known that the deaths of so many was at the hands of women, the general population of Zargarb would have wreaked massive revenge and retribution on all the other women of the sector. He reported as he did to defuse vast retribution upon the innocent women of the sector. To date, there have been no reported cases of vigilante acts against their women, so his action has proved the correct one to have taken."

"You are an absolute political genius, Supreme Prelate! Well done indeed. So then there is nothing to overly concern ourselves with about this Senate investigator visiting the sectors?"

"None at all."

"Excellent. Next, I read your suggestion about recruiting local Sea Prince young men who are worthy into the Holy Paladins. I believe your idea has great merit. Besides, if enough are recruited, then we can bring our men home and put them to better use. That is another advantage that you did not mention in your suggestion and one that I can use to help convince the Cardinals to back this decision. Consider the request approved. I'll have the official documents drawn up most likely by tomorrow night."

Pope Anaxagoras continued, "When I first saw the disaster occurring,

I thought that I was looking at the total destruction of our entire Church. Now, with the extreme efforts of yourself and Senator Dax, the repercussions seem altogether minor. I would never have believed it possible. Privately, I did and still do support taking any means necessary to coerce recalcitrant women from gaining only Bad Marks. However, I now see how our best intentions can be viewed as barbaric by the ignorant and the lay. I suppose that we have no choice but to accept a major setback in attempting to get such women onto the proper righteous path."

"Well, Your Holiness," Thondakas ventured to reveal his thoughts on the matter, "There is another way. Suppose that a woman was using her hands and arms to resist all efforts to earn Good Marks. If we had a metal device, which would lock her arms across her back, fitted with a lock so that it could not be removed, that would serve nearly as well. Or perhaps a metal ball that encloses her hands, locked on tightly. Or for those that constantly speak wickedness from their mouths, a metal ring could be wedged in her mouth forcing it open, locked on tightly so that it could not be removed. No more blasphemy could issue forth. The great benefit is that all these devices could be removed should the Santi desire an inspection. They would see no mutilation of the recalcitrant women."

"Thondakas, you are a living genius! Positively brilliant indeed! That would solve all our problems. Make it so, but let's not widely broadcast it this time. I'll let the Cardinals know and they can in turn speak to their priests about it — all very low key this time. Actually, in our Nunneries here on Megalos, we could use those devices on the women who simply will not behave and work toward earning Good Marks! Excellent thinking, Supreme Prelate, excellent. Make it so."

"I'll have the documents drawn up at once," he replied, a satisfied smile on his face. He now knew that he could work very well with this new Pope!

"Next, we have the matter of what to do about Lucifer's Spawn. Also if memory also serves me, your people were conducting some undisclosed missions in West Reach and the Greenway."

"Ah that secret business is for the Pope's eyes only. A grave matter, though now I don't know which is the graver, that or the Lucifer's Spawn. Come, let me show you the documents to read that are stored in the Pope's Private Vault." He led the very curious man into the secret maze below the complex. Only the Pope had a key. After opening it, Thondakas pointed to a red covered journal. "That one, Your Holiness. Read it down here. I will return to your quarters after supper and the evening Mass. We can discuss it then." He left the Pope alone, knowing just how shocked the Pope would be, come the evening meeting.

That evening Thondakas entered the Pope's quarters. All traces of its former occupant had been removed. As expected, he found a very upset and distraught Pope anxiously awaiting him. "Do you realize the gravity of this situation?" the Pope began. "If word of this ever got out, think of the repercussions! Worse, what if just one of the Great Messiah's lineage publically made all this known? It would ruin the Church, destroy us utterly!"

"It is wise that you, too, see this threat as the most serious one ever to our Church. Well, at least it was until Lucifer's Spawn appeared upon the scene."

"According to the documents, the Mano del Dio has already done an unbelievable amount of fantastic work in the removal of these Unholy Children of the Prostitute. Your predecessor, R. Thraxton apparently lost his life while attempting to eliminate more?"

"That is a complex situation, Your Holiness. As far as we can tell, all remaining Unholy Children have been secreted away in either the Santi Fortress at Mont Blanc or at their many fortresses in Velona. We have been unable to penetrate those fortresses. However, R. Thraxton was able to kill the Santi leader, the man responsible for killing the Emperor during that horrific battle. At first, we rejoiced in this Ket Bethany's death. Then, we cheered when we heard that a woman with no hands became their Supreme Commander."

"This was the greatest mistake that your predecessor made, in my humble opinion. He believed utterly that the Santi would disintegrate in short order because of this woman being their leader. However, as we both now know fully, she is no mortal; she is Lucifer Spawn wielding evil Wicked Spells that could only have been given unto her by Lucifer himself. There is no other possible explanation."

Pope Anaxagoras agreed, "Yes, my son, there is indeed no other earthly explanation for what we have witnessed. Lucifer's Spawn. Correct me if I am wrong, but now are not our two most serious problems interlinked one within the other?"

"Yes, Your Holiness. That they are indeed. We cannot reach the Unholy Children because they are under the direct care of Lucifer's Spawn. After what we have seen here in Athos, we cannot touch Lucifer's Spawn. It is perhaps the greatest challenge that we shall ever face."

Pope Anaxagoras once more agreed fully, "Yes, that is most certainly is. I suspect that Lucifer himself has seen all the fantastic progress that our Church has made and cannot stand it that so many souls are now going to Heaven instead of into his service. Thus, he has personally chosen to intervene. Lord Jehosa now has his eyes upon us. Can we rise to meet this devil threat or will we succumb to Lucifer? I say we fight back. How, remains the key question. I don't suppose that you have an answer for that one too?"

"No Your Holiness. I had hoped that the Pope might, however." Fighting inhuman demons from Hell, Lucifer's Spawn, was far beyond the assassin's reach. How could mortal man fight with the Devil? This was in the realm of Jehosa to handle.

"I have always believed that man must take charge of his own destiny, if only to prove himself worthy of entering Jehosa's Realm," Pope Anaxagoras preached. "You and I must find ways of forestalling disaster. It is our responsibility to do so. While we cannot hope to defeat Lucifer's Spawn in direct combat, there may be other ways that we can be effective. I point out to you that thus far, the Santi have not made the slightest move to retake our Controlled Sectors. After they defeated utterly Emperor Justinian and his mighty army, I fully expected that they would begin the retaking of the cities, beginning with Barcella, which borders with Velona, where their entire forces were located after the battle. Yet, they did not. Neither have they moved from New Barq up into Zargarb. No action for a dozen years. No buildup of armies that might signal such an attempt."

"So I have asked myself why this could be? With the Unholy Power given unto Lucifer's Spawn, why have they hesitated? The only answer must be that something in or about these cities is or would be utterly deadly to them. Perhaps their Devil Spells are not powerful enough to reach that far from Velona. Yet, something has kept Lucifer's Spawn from even making the slightest move in that direction. Thondakas, send some of your best men to study these cities. We must find that gift that Lord Jehosa has bestowed upon us of which we remain completely ignorant! We must find out what is keeping them at bay. Perhaps then we can use it to our advantage."

"I see what you are implying. I don't know why I didn't think of that before now. It seems more than plainly obvious now that you have spoken of it. I will see to it at once!"

"I grow tired, Thondakas. Yet there is one more matter on which I wish to obtain your views yet tonight. I have been considering writing a friendly letter to this Devil Woman outlining our findings regarding Pope Amir I. It would be an attempt to appease her and possibly help prevent her from taking the drastic actions she swore she would do. What do you think? Ought I attempt to write Lucifer's Spawn directly?"

Thondakas thought for a moment, "Yes, I believe that anything that we can do to prevent the Santi from taking violent actions against us at this time should be attempted. If they should begin to retake one of the sectors, you can be sure that we would have the entire Senate on our backs and we cannot afford that at this time. We have far more important matters with which to deal. I believe you have an excellent idea here."

"Thank you, Supreme Prelate, for being so utterly honest with me. After all, I am a new Pope. I believe that we can work well together. Good night, may the blessings of Jehosa be on you as you partake of Holy Rest." Thondakas bowed and departed to his room. He had much to do now. From his point of view, things had taken a turn for the better.

Several weeks later, Thondakas again met with Pope Anaxagoras alone. "Your Holiness, because of the utter folly of your predecessor, I have undertaken a study to learn all that I can about our enemy, the Lucifer's Spawn, the Santi del Dio. Amir, the fool, merely thought that they would fold up and go away, once their leader, Ket Bethany, as eliminated. We both know that was only wishful thinking."

"Here's my analysis of the situation. At present, no one knows their true numbers. Best estimates range upwards from six or seven thousand, possibly more. We also know that when the Emperor was able to destroy the old Sisterhood organizations in the Sea Princes, most of those abominations joined the Santi. My guess is that well over two thirds of their fighting force is made up of these ex-Sisterhood bitches. History has shown us that these amazons are not to be taken lightly, Your Holiness. Remember they used to be the very best fighters in the world, save our Centurions. Yet their weakness is that they are defensive fighters only, which suited their purposes."

"As long as they existed, this Sisterhood organization was responsible for security during shipment of valuable cargos. They must have earned a fortune doing that, because they were the only ones who could guarantee the safe arrival of goods. Thus, we have always had a symbiotic relationship with them. We could not transport our valuable shipments without their protection."

"With the abolishment of the Sisterhood, the Santi del Dio has stepped in to fill the void which Justinian created. Indeed, Your Holiness, we would be in a precarious position today if we did not use their services to guard our key shipments. You see, we have no choice but to use their protection services, yet they are our greatest enemy."

"At first, I believed that maybe the Santi were supporting and aiding all the bandits that attack our shipments. However, I can find no evidence of that, indeed, they seem to be against these renegade bandits as much as we are. The Santi do not supply the bandit with either weapons or material support. That is at least a positive aspect of this mess."

"I interviewed a number of survivors from Justinian's last stand. I believe I had identified three key reasons why Justinian lost the battle. First was their use of the new type of bows invented in West Reach. They call them longbows. I have sent in a request for our consulate in West Reach to purchase a number of these. We should make plans to see if our fletchers can duplicate them here, so that we may field legions of these archers."

"Second was their use of chain mail armor. Nearly every soldier was so equipped. As you know, our Centurions only wear bits of armor on key body locations. It is far, far too hot to wear such heavy armor here in Megalos. That has been the major blunder made by every Centurion General to date. Our Centurions were not fighting in Megalos; they were fighting way up north. Hence, we should begin a massive campaign to provide chain mail armor to every one of our Holy Paladins. While this is my speculation only, had Justinian's Centurions been wearing chain mail, they might not have lost that battle!"

"Third was their use of mounted troops. Reports indicate that every Santi fighter was mounted. Apparently, not all were what I would term cavalry, in that many did not fight from horseback. However, this aspect gave them a tremendous mobility, which the Centurion foot soldiers lacked. We normally do provide mounts for our Holy Paladins. Still, we should redouble our efforts to have every one of our fighters mounted."

Pope Anaxagoras exclaimed, "Most well done, Supreme Prelate. You have explained it so that I, ignorant of such matters, can completely understand your analysis! I completely agree with every point that you've made. See to it that all are done as you have suggested. However, what of the Lucifer's Spawn? How can they be attack when they wield powers given unto them by Lucifer himself? Have you any news of what in the Controlled Sectors is keeping the Santi from attacking and taking them from us?"

Thondakas looked downward before he spoke, "Alas Your Holiness, I am not knowledgeable in such matters as spells bequeathed by Lucifer. Men, they I can deal with, but not the devil and his kind. I regret that I must beg you to find ways that these vile Devil Spawn can be slain. However, from the field reports that I have studied, perhaps the actual numbers of these Lucifer Spawns is not that large. While I cannot be sure of their numbers, it appears that only about one in twenty or one in fifty of the Santi are Devil Spawn. The rest are amazons and men, with which we can deal. Does that help in any way?"

"Oh indeed, indeed it does. Let's see that would make the number of Lucifer's Spawns somewhere around a few hundred all total. That is far better than having to deal with thousands of them. Good news indeed, Thondakas. Good indeed."

"As to the other matter, Your Holiness, what in our sectors is preventing the Santi from attacking us, I believe I may have stumbled upon that by accident, while preparing this report. As you recall, most of the Santi fighters are defensive only. To assault a walled city, one would have to lay down a lengthy siege, requiring a large number of attacking men. From the survivors of Justinian's campaign, his plan was to avoid besieging any of the walled cities. Even with the mighty army he fielded, he did not have enough men to fight such a lengthy battle; the loss of men would be horrific. That's why the cities have defensive walls. In short, if the Santi really only do possess a few thousand attack fighters, their numbers alone would be insufficient to besiege even one walled city. I believe that is the secret weapon that we possess."

"Why, I do believe you are right, Thondakas. It is so clear now, so simple. I ought to have determined that one! You are truly gifted with keen insight, Supreme Prelate! Perhaps then, Lucifer's Bitch was making a threat that she cannot back up. Nevertheless, I do not wish to provoke the Devil's Spawn just yet."

"Wise, Your Holiness. Not until we have some means of countering their Devil Spells," the prelate added.

"I will pray for guidance on that issue, Supreme Prelate. Now, I must brief the Cardinals. Thank you so very much!" He gave the prelate a warm hug and left for his meeting.

However, Thondakas had other secret plans whose details had yet to be finalized. His clandestine operation had come to him in a dream. He knew if great care were used, his plan would work. He needed to find just the right men for the job. That would be the most difficult aspect to handle. Ordinarily, he would always do this personally. Yet, just now, he could not easily get away to West Reach or the Occupied Sea Prince sectors. Worse, this plan would only work until it was discovered. One error committed and it could never be implemented again. He would have to trust this critical task to someone he could trust with his life. Only one man fit that bill and he was due to arrive within the hour. Thondakas made his preparations.

A knock on the Supreme Prelate's door was expected. "Come in."

His aide announced, "Erebos is here to see you. He says that you sent for him, Sir."

"Send him in, and see that we are not disturbed." The tall, bronzed skinned man walked into the Supreme Prelate's room. "Welcome, Erebos, I'm so glad to see you. It has been far too long. Come share some wine with me. How went your trip to Pieta?"

The two friends held some small talk for a brief time. Finally, Thondakas said, "Erebos, I have a super top secret mission for you. If you are successful, upon your return, you will be called Prelate Erebos!" The man grinned, that meant a triple promotion. Prelates were second only to the Supreme Prelate and often a Prelate became the next Supreme Prelate. Erebos was keenly interested in what his boss had to say.

"You are to go to the Occupied Sectors and even West Reach. Search out someone who has reasonable prowess as a fighter, one who is completely loyal to us, the Church of Jehosanity. Then, here's what you are to do." He talked in a low voice, unwilling to have any errant ears overhear these orders. Nothing was written down for that matter.

"Oh, I love it! Diabolical to say the very least! Thondakas, you old fox! You can count on me. I shall not fail!"

"Excellent. In any communications back to me, the code word is 'fox.' I will be anxiously awaiting news that the fox is in the hen house!" Both men roared with laughter, and then Erebos departed, taking the next ship north.

Chapter 12 Reactions

Spring burst forth in 638 with a multitude of new growth. Indeed, flowers blossomed all over the estate. Hank was a master with arrangements of the perennials. Nearly every color of the rainbow was to be found somewhere along the outer walls of the estate and along all the walls of the many buildings of this Santi estate. By mutual consent, the two weddings were delayed until Jenna knew whether the Pope would officially end the brutal treatment of women in the neighboring sectors. Nearly every Santi daily expected to hear the orders to prepare for an assault. Anxiety snuck into nearly everyone, whether they were conscious of it or not. No one really wanted to go to war, but to the person, they wanted the atrocities to end.

At last, a courier arrived carrying a dispatch from Megalos, laying it in the outstretched arms of Jenna. "I hope this brings good news," he said and then left.

"Lilly Ann, if you would be so kind," Jenna said. Just as soon as word came that a courier was bringing a dispatch from Megalos, everyone else had gathered around her in the meeting room. Jenna looked at Jovanna and Ariana, and said, "This is one of those really awkward times that you and I have. Not much we can really do about it." Letters and hands went together. Once more, the two women were reminded that life was going to be much more difficult for them, even though they were about to be married.

Lilly Ann opened the pouch. "Ah, it bears the Pope's official seal. Keep your fingers crossed everyone, and you two keep your arms crossed, and you keep your legs crossed," she winked playfully at Jovanna, whose arms were too short to cross. Lilly Ann opened the official document and read it aloud to everyone.

Commander of the Santi del Dio,

Let me begin by saying that to the best of my knowledge all of your demands have been made at this time. Quite a lot has transpired since your visit earlier this year. Let me fully brief you.

Everyone let out a cheer, interrupting Lilly Ann. "Best news I've heard in a long time," Paul declared. "Looks like we don't have to go to war! Yes!" It took a minute for everyone to calm down enough for the Judger to continue reading.

Pope Amir I died the night that you left. His heart gave out our experts say. A thorough search of his quarters revealed a secret document whose contents condemn him utterly. I have attached a copy of said document with this dispatch. The document bore his signature and his official seal. We do not doubt its authenticity. In it he revealed that he and he alone, and in secret, ordered the brutal mistreatment of recalcitrant women in the Occupied Sectors. It was he alone who suggested that mutilations be done from a misguided notion that by doing so the women would have no choice but to earn Good Marks.

None of the other Cardinals knew of these secret orders to the priests in the field, the generals, and the Mano del Dio. Had we known, we might have been able to stop it, then again, we might not have had the authority to stop it, since the Pope's decrees must be followed. His word is law. The generals had no choice of their own in this matter.

With the Pope's death, the Cardinals have elected me, Anaxagoras, as the new head of our church. My first action was to issue direct and in no uncertain language that the mutilation of women must end immediately. I have also attacked a copy of that Papal Decree #42.

Additionally, I have sent representatives of the Church to each of the sectors to confirm that this decree is now being followed to the letter. Thus, it is with a clean heart that I can now request that you send your own representatives to verify to your own satisfaction that the situation is fully handled. Each general has been put on notice to expect your representatives and to cooperate fully with them and any requests that they might deem appropriate for full verification.

Let me personally say that I found this entire situation highly disgusting and revolting. My intention and that of the Church of Jehosanity is to help each person's soul gain entrance into Jehosa's Realm of Heaven, when their earthly body passed away.

In closing, I hope that this marks a new era of trust and cooperation between our two organizations.

Yours in Deepest Faith,

Pope Anaxagoras

Everyone yelled and cheered for several minutes, before Jenna could add, "Looks like we may have been successful after all. Well done, everyone."

Lilly Ann then read the two attached documents for everyone. When she finished, everyone felt elated and very relieved. The crisis was over. Only two among us did not share that opinion, Lilly Ann, the Judger, and me. While everyone talked about how great everything had turned out, Lilly Ann stared at the confession document. Something didn't quite add up, from her point of view.

"Hey gang, I know that this is an official copy. The standards for an official copy are for the duplicator to reproduce the exact writing, by laying this transparent sheet over the original and then tracing the writing. Look at this document, everyone; look at the handwriting carefully." She placed it on the table, and everyone crowed around to have a look.

"So what are we supposed to be seeing," asked Paul, baffled.

"The signature is different somehow," Jovanna replied. "Look Paul at how the tails of the signature do not match those in the body of the letter."

"Precisely, Jovanna. Good observation. Conclusion?" she allowed

Jovanna to make the call for her.

"If the signature is indeed the Pope's," she said, "then he did not write the letter. If the signature is not the Pope's, then he may have written it, but we cannot say yes or no definitively without seeing other copies of his writing."

"Exactly. Now since the new Pope has said that they verified his signature, we can probably safely conclude that it is Amir's. Thus, someone else wrote the letter and forged his signature on the document! In short, the proof is a complete fake!"

Many curses flew around the room. The heady elation evaporated into a very serious mien once more. Lilly Ann continued. "Knowing that this supposed confession is a forgery, then we must examine what the new Pope has said and his tone in the dispatch. He is just too propitiative for my liking. If we believe him, the entire church is totally against the mutilations. Yet we know that is not likely the case. Priests, generals, and the Mano del Dio were very busily engaged in these harmful acts. My opinion, Jenna, is that he is telling you want you want to hear, enough to appease you so that you do not take the drastic actions that you threatened to take."

Jenna replied, "Well, that does make sense, Lilly Ann. If you totally trap someone in a corner, they are likely to say what you want them to say so that they can get out of the trap. However, he has invited us to conduct our own observations. Certainly, he fully expects us to find no further traces of women being victimized as they were before."

Jovanna piped up, "Well, it's still a victory. If we have stopped them from doing this," she waved her arms around, "to another woman anywhere in the sectors, then I'm more than satisfied that we have stopped them, but how can we get any justice for the ones that they did mutilate or kill?"

"Remember, the first step must be to get the perpetrators to stop committing their crimes. It would appear that we have at least accomplished the first step," Lilly Ann answered her.

Jenna took command, "Okay. Let's notify the entire fortress garrisons in the Occupied Sectors, have them contact the generals, and arrange the inspection. I want them to be completely thorough, visit every known habitation of these men. Leave no stone unturned."

"You got it!" Paulette declared and set about making the many Mind Links.

During the next couple of days, everyone waited anxiously for each fortress to report on their findings. One by one, they came in. The Nunneries were carefully searched. All traces of the bloody messy areas in the basements were gone, scrubbed clean. Not a single mutilated woman resided at any of the Nunneries or in any of the other church dwellings.

In the Nunnery in Zargarb, the Head Nun, unlocked all the metal devices from the six women, devices which had bound their arms, forced mouths to stay open, and hands to be useless. "Now remember," she spoke sternly to the six women who were being dressed by other nuns, "if you are asked any questions, you answer that you are not being mutilated. Your arms have not been cut off; you have not had your vile tongues cut out. You have been very fortunate indeed. If during the visit of the Santi, you attempt to earn more Bad Marks, then I promise you that you will be forced to wear all the devices at the same time for the next month! Further, I swear to you all, if you get this Nunnery in trouble by your bad conduct, I will have these devices put on you, and have liquid metal poured into the locks so that they can never be removed, and I will send you to live the rest of your lives in the northern caves! You are to act like civilized women, religious women, and not some gutter trash whores. Do I make myself perfectly clear?"

The frightened women, so glad to be free of the diabolical devices, even if only for a short time, nodded their agreement. None wanted to be forced to wear all these hideous devices; just being forced into one was horrible enough. Soon, all six looked like the other fledgling nuns. Just in time too.

The general knocked, and a nun opened the door, "Good afternoon, sir," she said and bowed, her eyes staring at the floor out of respect for him.

"This is the Santi representative, Art Longton. We are here for an inspection. Fetch the Head Nun, please," General Helas Taxos said calmly. He had long ago gotten the secret dispatch from Thondakas and had acted precisely according to the orders. Well, all but one. He kept the letter, not burned it as ordered. One day, he felt that he might just need that document.

"This way, Art. Be just a moment." The two stood in the entrance hall. Soon the bustling Head Nun appeared, and the tour began. Art looked into every room and closet in the entire huge ex-Sisterhood inn, but found nothing amiss. All the nuns and those in training were politely lined up along one hall wall. As he passed them, he looked each over, but all seemed healthy and not missing body parts.

One very shy nun he addressed, "Are they treating you well here?"

"Yes, yes, sir," her voice faltered slightly. "We are not mutilated, if that's what you mean," she said meekly. Art moved on to the next nun. He saw no signs of traumatized women as had been in the Junction Nunnery. Satisfied, he and General Helas met with the Head Nun in the entrance hall a half hour later.

"Ma'am, my compliments," Art said. "I have found no traces of mutilated women. I suspect that your job here is now vastly improved. It must have been awfully hard on you and your staff to have to handle all of those seriously injured women."

"Yes, sir. In fact, it was most trying and upsetting. Yet, we did our best and still do our very best to help other women gain Good Marks that their souls may enter Heaven, Jehosa's Realm." Art saw that she fell back onto the party line, but she had answered honestly.

"I'm happy things have improved for the better," Art replied.

The Head Nun asked, "I understand that you wish to inspect our nuns weekly?"

"Yes, that would be prudent, at least for a few months."

"Sir, could I ask that you make your visits on Sunday afternoons? You see, at that time, all of us are in our small chapel here. The High Priest comes and delivers a High Mass for us nuns at that time. If you came then, you could see all of us together in one place. It would not be so disruptive of our daily activities. You see we bake bread for the poor, make quilts for the needy, and such. Having to stop everything for an inspection is disruptive of our daily pious life. If you just need to see our nuns, then Sunday afternoons would be ideal. You could also see then that all the other rooms are indeed empty since we are all at High Mass."

"I can accept that, having found nothing amiss on this visit. I will come by on Sunday afternoons for a time. It has been a pleasure meeting you and your nuns." He bowed and the two men left. Inspections of all the other structures yielded only the Holy Paladins and priests. He sent in his official report, which he found highly encouraging. He did not state that he had suspicions that something was still occurring; they were only suspicions.

When all the reports were in, Jenna held another all hands conference in the morning. "Okay, it is official. All fortress commanders have reported on their first investigation and not a single injured, mutilated, or beaten woman was found. Either they have at least complied with the order and are no longer torturing women as they used to or they have taken such mutilations deep underground. It would appear that we have successfully achieved the first step."

"Or they have invented some other less horrific way to torture these women," Lilly Ann cautioned. "There can be other possibilities. Yet, on the surface, the Judgers have given their opinion that the mutilations and severe beatings have stopped."

"Ah Judgers," Jenna jested, "just try to get a definitive statement from a Judger!" Everyone laughed, including Lilly Ann.

Smiling and coming to the defense of Lilly Ann, Jovanna added, "I think it is safe to conclude that we have gotten the fox inside the chicken coop to stop eating the chickens. Yet, my view is that the fox is still in the chicken coop, and he still has teeth, and he is still hungry."

Lilly Ann recognized the insight she showed, and replied. "She's right. I would not trust these people."

"All right," Jenna consented to allow her meeting to diverge from her plans, "are you saying that we ought to take some other action?"

"Yes, most definitely. We ought to put ourselves in their position, their shoes, and make some educated guesses about possible actions that they might take. Based on those, we can then work out what we may do to be able to spot such happening before it is too late for us to respond."

"Makes sense. Let's try it, everyone. Pretend that you are this new Pope fellow and have just inherited this situation. What would you do? Someone take notes, please."

Paul spoke at once, "Well, from my point of view, it has been demonstrated several times that wearing chain mail drastically reduces combat injuries. I'd start making my Holy Paladins wear chain mail armor. Oh yes, I'd make double sure that all my forces were mounted, though I think most of the Holy Paladins have been. They continue to use heavy crossbows. During the last battle, our fighters shot entire quivers at them while they got only one shot at us. Maybe I would try to rearm them with bows instead of heavy crossbows. It's a tough call, since a heavy quarrel can be far more damaging, but in battle situations it takes forever to reload them."

Jovanna began just the instant Paul finished, "Look, even in the Pope's letter, he is still obsessed with this stupid Good Marks/Bad Marks idea. Obviously, not all women in the sectors are going to be willing victims to whatever whim these men try to foist off on them. Some are bound to protest one way or another. They are always going to be dealing with quote recalcitrant unquote women. So now, they cannot get away with cutting off my hands. Still they must find a way to force me into following their orders. I conclude that they must find some other way to do it without leaving behind physical evidence, like missing eyes, teeth, and hands. It must be something that leaves no trace, yet is effective. Maybe they tie their arms up or gag them or blindfold them. I would suspect that they have just altered their means of delivery in some as yet unknown manner."

Jenna added her opinions, "Well, they certainly do need to recruit more men. The attrition of Holy Paladins has been rather severe in the last couple of years, not to mention our own contribution a while ago. Yet, perhaps in a different way. I was thinking, uniformly all the Holy Paladins are natives of Megalos. During their occupation, probably several thousand have been lost, a bunch here, a few there. It all adds up to quite a manpower drain on Megalos. Eventually, that has to be felt among the general population down there. So, if I were this new Pope, I might consider recruiting local men, men from the very sectors in which they will see service. Besides, if they could find men that they could trust to become Holy Paladins, then that would be a big show of support in those sectors, besides lowering the steady drain of Megalos men."

"Our visit took them completely by surprise," Lilly Ann spoke up next. "None saw it coming. If I were running the show, heads would roll because I had no advance notice that something like this was even possible let alone a probable occurrence. Hence, I would devote a good deal of resources to spy on the Santi, gain far more information about them than I already had. I would want to know if they were vehemently against something else that I was doing and might react against it. I'd do anything I could to find out their advance plans."

Beth Ann, who was taking the notes, piped up, "Hey, we did step one, stop them from committing further crimes. We should now somehow get the truth about their religion disseminated among the citizens of the occupied sectors. You know, show them the truth of the situation. How else will they ever possibly come to know that they have been committing harmful actions?"

"Most of them can't read," Ariana spoke up. "It would have to be spread by word of mouth, I am afraid. That might not be so easy to do, what with the Holy Paladins there. They would surely stomp hard on anyone preaching against their Church."

"I agree, Beth Ann, somehow the truth ought to be disseminated. Jot that down as an avenue that we need to explore," Jenna concurred.

Ben, who often had little to offer at such meetings, decided to mention something that seemed a bit perplexing to him, as he sat there trying to imagine being the Pope, their enemy. "You know it is a bit weird. If I was the Pope, then the Santi are our worst enemy. Yet, we have to depend upon them utterly to get our vital supplies delivered to just about anywhere in the Occupied Sectors. If I was him, this would be an incredible touchy point: being forced to do business with the enemy, because without their protection service, I'd be out of business. Kind of weird, don't you think?"

"Absolutely," Paul agreed. "So I would begin to recruit lots more men so that eventually I could safeguard my own shipments."

Now Ariana decided to speak up, since no one appeared to address what she had thought about. "You know that the next step is to educate those who have been committing the crimes, by showing them the actual truth of the situation. Why don't we send a copy of the ten disciple's Holy Writings to the Pope and tell him here is the actual truth, which contradicts so many of the lies that Yazi has convinced them is the truth?"

"You are very right!" Lizzy Ann complimented her. "We are forgetting our own steps. Yes, I think we should at least give him an opportunity to avail himself of the truth. After all, probably all that he believes in has been what he heard from Yazi and others that Yazi preached to, he's heard only one side. We ought to at least make the attempt to educate him."

"I completely agree. If we are promoting our Justice System, then we must present him with the actual facts. Then, it becomes his choice," Jenna concurred. "I suppose that I ought to reply to his dispatch, now that we have verified the sectors. After all, he was at least civil and polite in his message to us."

Based upon the ideas discussed, plans were made to deal with these eventualities. Notices were sent everywhere of certain things that we wanted every Santi to be alert for and to report if they were observed. Beth Ann had drawn up a large chart on which we could jot down specific observations in each of the various potential categories. Jenna also composed a letter to Pope Anaxagoras, which Beth Ann wrote for her, though Jenna did spend a good deal of time signing it, using the strap-on quill that Hank had devised for her. She could at least scratch out her name.

Then, she had to deal with my twins. They were now of age and ready to spread their wings. Brother Jake pronounced their training complete and had left Velona. All that remained was to organize Tegid's return to West Reach and his assumption of his mother's throne.

Paul advised her, "At this time, Jenna, Tegid just isn't willing to put in the necessary time to study and concentrate. His attention and energies are totally spent on becoming a king in West Reach. You really cannot blame him; he's been in double training really, what with that given by the monk as well as the various Protectors. We will have to be satisfied that he made ninth year Protector status. Perhaps one day he will return and finish up and learn the power spells."

"I guess you are right; we can't force him to stay another year. Have we got support personnel lined up? You know that we are sending him off most likely to his doom? He will become assassin's bait! West Reach is wide open to the Mano del Dio; their so called consulate is little more than a safe haven for those men."

"Yes, we've rounded up a Healer and her husband, a Judger, to be his advisors. It took some doing, but we found a Communicator to go as well. Finding the cavalry was the easy part; one regiment of Santi cavalry volunteered for duty there. Tina Fairwell, Communicator, and her husband, Jake, an armorer, have agreed to move there with him. Rosamund Blackwater, Healer, and her husband, Henry, Judger, although in their forties, are willing to act as advisors to Tegid. Henry is on his way here as you asked, Jenna."

"Thanks Paul for finding them or persuading them. I suspect you twisted a few arms," Jenna teased. Indeed, he had. Tina had an avid interest in music. Paul had used that as a selling point, "Go to West Reach and hear and learn the local songs. Remember, that's where Ket Bethany got his start. Look up Fergus and Fianna. They were part of his troubadours." She took the bait and convinced her husband to move.

A short while later, Henry entered Jenna's meeting room. "Hi Jenna. It is a pleasure to see you once more. You are looking as beautiful as ever." He was forty-six and well-liked by everyone in Velona. He still cut a handsome figure. She gave him a hug and the two sat down.

"You realize the gravity of the situation that the impetuous Tegid is getting himself into, right?" she began.

"Foolish kids. Ah, but then, dear Jenna, we were not foolish when we were fourteen, now were we? Oh no. Well, grounded were we, feet flat on solid terra." They both chuckled. "Seriously, though, what special instructions do you have for me? Otherwise, you would not have sent for me."

"Shrewd are we? Reading my mind?" she teased back. He was a typical Judger; it was difficult to put anything over on these folks. "You know your job, Henry. Tegid is opening the door to all manner of plots by the Megalos folks. I was thinking last night about it. This would be an excellent opportunity for them to get a spy into his confidence. Rather than killing him outright, they could infiltrate his court and glean valuable secrets about the Santi and our plans and so on."

"Absolutely, Jenna. What I fear most is that one of them will become a close friend of Tegid's, and then he brings him along when he comes back here for a visit. Now the assassin has free reign of your complex! In one night, the damage an assassin could cause around here is terrible to contemplate! You want me to be alert for all manner of disguises and treachery, right?"

"Yes, keep your eyes and senses pealed. I know this sounds harsh, but I'd rather see Tegid assassinated than to have him innocently bring an assassin into Mont Blanc or Velona or here. I just do not trust these people."

"I will do my very best, Jenna. Tina will keep you informed. Besides, Jenna, you know I love subterfuge! Give me a good plot, heh, heh. That's one of the reasons I took this assignment — been rather boring around here."

"Should have taken you with us in January; you might be singing a different tune," she teased back.

He grinned broadly, "Say that reminds me. I've heard that you have something of a Judger protegee on your hands with this Jovanna Barcella. Is it true?"

"Yes, she is rather unique. She often displays tenth year and beyond Judger skills, although she is only in her first year of official training. Paul has been stepping up the pace, however. So really, she is the equivalent of a fourth year trainee. Still, it is uncanny. Several times, she has out done Lilly Ann at our meetings."

"Good for her. We Judgers are a unique breed, eh? I hear she is getting married?"

"Yes, May Day is the date, she and Paul."

"Ah, I do detect your arms in this one, dear Jenna?" he double teased.

"Sly old man, now would I do that? I don't even have the hands for it," she bantered back.

"Seriously, though, I've heard that she has somehow extended our special skills to being able to actually make another's body carry out some desired action. Is this true?"

"Yes, she had some Holy Paladins and even a Mano del Dio fellow cut their own throats."

"Wow. When she becomes officially a Judger, many of us would like to train under her to see if we can also learn this extended skill. It would dovetail nicely with our current repertoire."

"I rather guessed it might. I will discuss this with her when she graduates, Henry." With that, they shook and he left to continue packing. The caravel was to sail in two days' time.

Later that day, Taliesin dropped by as she had requested. He gave her a welcoming hug. "Hi Aunt Jenna. You wanted to see me? Tegid is ecstatic, you know. He leaves day after tomorrow."

"I know, been arranging things for him. Now it's your turn. By the way, you played very well at the big dance a while back. You've got a great voice; you are going to make all the ladies fall in love with you, you rascal."

He smiled. She went on, "Okay, have you decided upon a traveling, stage name. It is not prudent or safe to continue to go by Amir."

"Yes, I am going to be known only as Bard Tal. Most musicians just use their first names. One day I will be so famous that everyone will know that name," he declared proudly and confidently. "I'm going to follow in my father and mother's footsteps."

"Excellent, Bard Tal. Have you given any thought to how we can help protect you without drawing attention to it?" she asked seriously.

"Well, I cannot go around with a Santi escort now can it? That'd be a dead giveaway. I was hoping that maybe you would just send one who somehow could fit in, you know."

Jenna smiled; she was already way ahead of him. "What would you say if I found you a gig manager, who was also a Judger and also a musician himself and even related to you?"

Taliesin frowned, "That would be unbelievably great, but who could that possibly be, Aunt Jenna?"

"He arrives tomorrow on the caravel that your brother will be leaving on the next day. He's even your age. Okay, I see you have completely given up. It's your cousin Angus, Angus d'Aine, Fergus and Fianna's eldest."

"Angus? Wow! Oh, wow! They were with mom and dad the whole time, part of the Cymry Minstrels! Wow! He's a Judger and a musician too? Amazing. I didn't know that! Oh Aunt Jenna, how can I ever thank you?"

"Just be cautious and don't get yourself killed, my boy," she replied, and Taliesin gave her and enthusiastic hug.

"You have enough traveling money?" she asked.

"Yes, dad's left us a nice treasury I can draw upon. But I, we, will be planning to make our own way, as much as possible."

"Still planning to spend some time in d'Grange first with Jolina and Edgar?"

"Yes, that's still my plan, unless Angus has any better ideas. They are the most famous musicians around. We can learn tons of songs from them, before we begin traveling the Greenway and beyond. Thanks for everything,

Aunt Jenna!"

"Go knock'em dead, Bard Tal," she teased, as he bounced out the door, his long held dreams were finally about to become reality!

At lunch, Hank asked her, "How come you are so bubbly and excited? You look more sparkling than ever."

She raised her eyebrows twice, saying, "I'll tell you in bed tonight. You had better be ready!" She teased him.

He grinned back, "Oh I am always ready for that!" Both laughed. She thought, "Men are always ready for that!"

May Day came filled with lush flowers all over the edges of the estate. The air was filled with a wide variety of fragrances. Warm temperatures and a sunny sky, all made for a picture perfect wedding day. The two brides wore their new white gowns, which Lilly Ann and Beth Ann helped them get into as well as doing their hair, complete with a garland of flowers. Still both women were exceptionally nervous. Over a hundred guests arrived to join the festivities and wish the two couples well; many were top-level Santi personnel. Jenna even had a small band of musicians come to provide entertainment.

Elona Po personally conducted the ceremony. I'll relate part of her words here, because it will help you understand the reverence that we Santi hold for the institution of marriage. "Ladies and gentlemen, boys and girls," she nodded to the many children here as well, especially the girls who attempted to stifle their giggles, "we are all gathered here on this beautiful day in spring to celebrate Renewal of Life. Just as the world around us is reborn fresh and new, so too are these two couples being reborn fresh and new into a Holy Union of two. These two brothers, which by the way many of us thought would never find love, have indeed found and earned the love of these two beautiful women. Likewise, these two women have overcome monumental obstacles in their lives only to find true love, earning the love and respect of these two brothers."

"Today, we rejoice in their Holy Union. Before this day, each of the four were traveling life's path, the First Aspect. Yet, to be complete, one must be all Seven Aspects. True, the brothers have led a powerful Third Aspect here with us and the Santi. Yet, the Second Aspect, the Holy Union, was missing in their lives. Today, these two couples are joining together as one, creating the Second Aspect, completing their path of the Seven Aspects."

"This Second Aspect, this Holy Union of man and woman, is a sacred union. From this union come our future generations and that of all mankind. Without this Holy Union, there would be no future for any of us. Thus, this of all unions becomes the Sacred Union."

"I speak to you four now," she said focusing her attention onto the two couples, "before today, you acted upon your own council, your own desires, and your own wishes. After today, while that remains true, you four have chosen to create a Holy Union. Now, you must act together of one mind, forging out that path that best strengthens and supports the union. A new dimension is being added. No longer can you make decisions based upon only what you want and desire. Now you must factor in the long-term survival and goals of your Holy Union. True, sometimes a man and wife have disagreements. I say unto you, never let these disagreements weaken your Union. Always act in ways that strengthen your bonds and you will flourish beyond your wildest dreams."

"As your High Priestess, at this time, I must impart some guidance to the new couples. Undoubtedly, you believe that your Union is based upon the love each of you feels toward the other. While that may be true, I ask you what is love? How can it be strengthened? Unless you know what this thing you call love actually is, you can only guess at what might strengthen it. Fundamentally, love is the combination of admiration and respect. You admire your partner and you have the highest respect for them. This then tells you how each day you can strengthen the bonds of your Holy Union. Each day, I invite you to find something about your spouse to admire and do admire it. Find something that day to respect about him or her. If you do this conscientiously every day, you will find your love soaring to new heights."

"Ah, what about life's bumps, the disagreements or arguments that married couples may have?" She glanced aside at the audience and added, "Of course none of we married couples here today have ever had a disagreement with our spouse or an argument, now have we?" More than one chuckled over her tease. "Yes, disagreements are part of life. As your High Priestess, it is my duty to impart some wisdom on how to handle these when they occur. Today, you may swear to me that you two will never have a disagreement let alone an argument. Yet we all know that eventually they occur. In the past, when you were in disagreement with someone, notice that you also were more distant from them, you did not like them as much as before the disagreement, and that you tend to stop talking with them and stop listening to them. Often when one detects the other has stopped even listening to him or her, they get very angry, intent upon making the other one listen. This is the wrong way to deal with a disagreement."

"The right way is to begin to really listen to the other person and continue to communicate with them, perhaps saying it in different words and different ways. As you communicate more fully, slowly the reality of what you are discussing grows, and you tend to like the other person better. Your goal is understanding, and understanding requires good communication to establish a better and more complete reality with each other, and in its path comes an increased liking of the other person. That is the path, the road out of a disagreement or argument."

"I would also like to share something from my own life and Holy

Union with Alton. I urge all four of you to never, ever let your spouse go to sleep when they are in the middle of an upset with you. Always take the time to communicate more fully and completely to bring about a shared reality and build the love between you back up. Then, go to bed. He and I have practiced this religiously in our Holy Union and it has paid us back handsomely."

"Now, I've preached long enough. It's time that I officially join these couples into their Holy Unions." She then began the usual marriage vows. When the two couples took their official marriage kiss, everyone stood, clapped, and cheered, further embarrassing the two couples. That rapidly faded. The musicians began playing dance tunes, and the party began in earnest and did not end until dark.

Allan had already fixed up two adjoining rooms off the main complex in which the other couples lived. Quietly both new couples quickly disappeared into these new quarters just as soon as night fell. This had been one of the happiest days anyone could remember around Jenna and Hank's estate in a very long time.

Chapter 13 What Is the Truth?

Mid-summer, a large parcel arrived in Constanza City, addressed to Pope Anaxagoras. After a close inspection by Thondakas, who pronounced it safe to open, he did so, finding a letter and a large number of hand-copied books. The letter was from Jenna Rose Weston, whose signature was crudely written at the bottom of the letter. He raised his eyebrows, wondering how she could ever have signed her name. He took the items to his private room and began reading her letter.

Dear Pope Anaxagoras,

Rest assured that our inspections of the sectors found nothing amiss. Thank you for halting the mutilation, beatings, and raping of the women in those sections.

I would also like to extend a courtesy to you and your church. As you undoubtedly know, the Great Messiah had ten disciples who ministered with him and upon his death were asked to write down his teachings as each saw them. The Santi have come into possession of all these very same original manuscripts, as well as all the voluminous scrolls that were written during the childhood of Jes Amir. During that time, all the Arad prophets dictated all of their teachings that had been handed down verbally during the long history of these people.

All documents are, of course, written in Ancient Arad. However, the Santi have hired a very knowledgeable linguist who is fluent in Ancient Arad to translate these ten works into both modern Arad and into several other languages, such as the Sea Prince dialect.

As a courtesy to you and your Church, I am sending along a copy of these ten works, translated into modern Arad. Unfortunately, our translator does not know your dialect.

I admit up front that I am not a theologian or even a priestess. However, I have read these ten volumes, believing them to be as close as one can come to knowing actually what the Great Messiah preached and how he lived his life. If you read these, you will see what I, a lay person, saw at once. Nine of the ten disciples told similar stories, while one of the ten wrote a much different version. The one, which was so very different from the other nine, was the late Pope Yazi I.

From what little I know of your Church and beliefs, they seem to be based upon the teachings of disciple Yazi. My opinion is that nine of ten cannot be that far adrift from what the Great Messiah preached and accomplished. I would suggest that you read these for yourself and draw your own conclusions. I hope that you find this enlightening, not only for yourself but also for all of those who believe in your religion.

I would be interested in knowing your opinion of these.

Sincerely,
Jenna Rose Weston
Supreme Commander Santi del Dio

Pope Anaxagoras reread the letter five times! "All ten? Even we do not have all ten! And the entire written teachings of all the prophets? That is a priceless find indeed! And in the possession of our most evil enemies! Lord, what has this world come to!"

After calming down, he could not resist examining the ten copies. The copies that were stored in the Pope's private vault were indeed written in Ancient Arad. Unfortunately, none here could read this ancient writing, certainly not Anaxagoras. "Of course when they were translated, the translator could have subtly altered everything to fit the Santi view of things. I ought to send someone whom I trust to check on the validity of the translations. I wonder what wisdom these may hold?"

He began to read them, beginning with Pope Yazi's writing. "Some of this is not quite right," he muttered on more than one occasion. "Perhaps as he grew older, he became wiser and realized that he had mis-interpreted the Great Messiah's words at the time he wrote this. After all he was in his youth then."

Next, he read the other nine books. As she had suggested, they pretty much agreed on the basic facts, differing only in emphasis as would be expected when a fisherman wrote one and a blacksmith another, for example. When he finished, he sat back and pondered what he had read and its significance upon his religion as he had been taught all these years.

Everything hinged upon whether or not this was an accurate translation or not. Yet, if it were not in serious error, these books would have a far-reaching impact upon the very foundations of their belief! Jes was an ordinary man born of ordinary men, who married as any man would and had his own children. Accepting this as the truth would crack the very foundations of their faith!

Poor Pope Anaxagoras. If these translations were true, he faced the greatest moral challenge in the history of his church, and he knew it. Thus, he sent his Cardinals in search of a translator whom they could trust, one who knew Ancient Arad. A week later, they brought Amin al Waddi, a sixty year old apothecary, who had fled New Barq when the Santi had taken control of that Megalos port city on the far eastern edge of the Med Sea, south of Zargarb. He was one of the Arads who chose to go New Barq when life in the Arad had become so utterly futile. Now he ran a small apothecary shop in Athos.

"You sent for me, Your Holiness?" Amin was hesitant. "It was an unexpected honor to be seen with the Pope, let alone be summoned before him. Imagine as he might, he could find no earthly reason for why the Pope would want to see him, of all people!

"I am told that you are fluent in Ancient Arad. Is that correct?" Amin nodded. "Then, I have a top secret mission for you to perform. I will pay you well for your services. The task will take many weeks."

Amin could scarcely believe his good fortune. Everyone knew that the Church of Jehosanity paid well for services rendered. Many artists were currently becoming wealthy painting frescoes and paintings, sculptors, likewise with many marble statues being created to adorn the many churches scattered throughout Megalos. Yet, what did Ancient Arad have to do with all the art? He agreed to accept the mission without even knowing what it was.

The Pope led him to a well-lighted, private room. "Here you will work undisturbed until you have completed the assigned task. You will not be allowed out of this room until you finish, and you will talk to no one about this, except to me personally. An adept will bring you plenty of food and drink, and empty the chamber pot as needed. This is a top secret work you are embarking upon, very top secret."

Poor Amin still had no idea of what he was to do. "Your Holiness, what am I to do? Locked in this room for months?"

"Translating. Rather verifying a translation of six books. Here, these are the originals written in Ancient Arad, and these are some copies that I have acquired which have been translated into Modern Arad. Your task is to go through each of these six books and verify that the translations have been done properly. You may freely mark up any needed changes in this translated copy, but under no circumstances whatsoever are you to make the slightest mark upon these originals. Is this clear?"

"Yes, Your Holiness."

"When you have finished, I will give you one hundred gold coins for each book, that's six hundred all total. Will that be sufficient?"

Six hundred gold coins! That represented his profits for nearly twenty years of work! "Oh yes, Your Holiness, more than sufficient. Most generous indeed. I will start today, if that is acceptable?"

"Yes, I will leave you to the task. If there is anything that you need, let the adept know, and I will see that you get it. I will drop by at least once a day to see how it is going. Thank you for accepting this mission for the Church." He left the translator to do his work.

That night after conducting the evening mass, he paid Amin a visit. Pope Anaxagoras was more than a little curious to see what, if anything, Amin had found thus far.

"Your Holiness, thus far, it seems to be a reasonable translation. I have marked a few small changes that I would have used. A plural here and there. A few places I would have used of instead of in."

"Nothing of substance is mis-translated?"

"No, Your Holiness. It appears on the whole, thus far anyway, to be a good translation."

"Thank you. Please continue." Pope Anaxagoras left, feeling more and more worried.

As the days stretched into weeks, Pope Anaxagoras grew steadily more and more ill at ease. Thus far, each book had checked out as an accurate translation; still Amin only found minor alterations from what he would have used had he been doing the original translation. None of the changes made any substantive difference in the result. Slowly, the Pope began to realize that the translations were indeed authentic; the words he had read were what the original disciples of the Great Messiah, the Son of Jehosa, had preached. Yazi's work did indeed look very different from the other nine!

Six weeks later, Amin finished and, as promised, the Pope paid him six hundred gold coins. However, he told Amin, "You are never to speak of this to anyone. If I ever find out that you have told another person what you have read here, I will send the Mano del Dio to find you and imprison you here for the rest of your life. Do I make myself perfectly clear?"

"Yes, Your Holiness. I will say nothing to anyone." Amin, like many others, greatly feared the Mano del Dio. Even though he knew what he had read was utterly priceless, he valued his remaining years highly!

That night alone in his private room, Pope Anaxagoras began crying, sobbing endlessly. "Whatever am I to do? So much is so utterly false! Yet do I dare to change it? How do I tell the world that we have been so wrong? Would they even believe me? Woe is me." He began to pray to Jehosa for guidance. To his great sorrow, he received no reply. It began to consume him. Daily he prayed; daily no answer came.

Then a horrid idea floated into his mind. What if the Santi actually published these ten works, made them broadly available throughout the world? What if people read them? What if their own followers read them? The consequences of that were too horrible to contemplate, utter ruination of his Holy Church!

Even the news that Tegid Amir had returned to West Reach and taken the throne over two kingdoms did little to cheer him up. The existence of some distant relative of Jes Amir now seemed of vastly less importance to his current situation. He became more and more reclusive, spending long hours alone in his room, debating with himself, winning none. Others took his scheduled masses. Many inquired about his health.

"Whatever can I do about this? I feel like I am trapped with a lion in my church. I cannot ignore the lion and go about my business. I cannot just leave the building and flee. I cannot attack the lion. I cannot try to find a way around the lion. I cannot just lie down and let the lion find me. Woe is me. I can do none of these things! If I ignore these writings and they become widely known, our church is eaten. I could flee Megalos, give my position to another, and let them be eaten, but I cannot in all honesty do that. I have no way to attack the lion, the Santi caretakers are Demon Spawn. I can see no way to go around the lion; it speaks the truth, and I am not a good liar.

Whatever would Jehosa think should I stoop to outright lies about him? I can do nothing and wait until the catastrophe occurs, but then it is too late; we are all eaten. Yet perhaps it will not happen until another is Pope. There is just no solution to this lion!" He began to cry in hopelessness once more.

He had not noticed it, but he had lost thirty pounds during this span of time. His skin tone turned ghastly pale. Finally, Thondakas forced himself to intervene. Late one night, he merely entered the Pope's private room. Normally, he would never dare to enter unannounced or unbidden. However, his failing health had become the talk of the Cardinals and Thondakas just had to do something. He found the Pope on the floor crying silently to himself. He helped the old man up onto his bed.

"Pope Anaxagoras, something is very wrong, very, very wrong. Within the Mano del Dio, I take the Holy Confessions of those in our security group. I could take your Holy Confession. It would benefit you greatly to confess what has troubled you so for all these weeks. You know that what is said in Holy Confession is held strictly private between us. No word would I ever speak beyond these doors."

"Oh was it that easy, dear, dear Thondakas. If it were this easy." He looked up at the Supreme Prelate and added, "If I speak of this to you, then I have only doubled those who would be as afflicted as I am."

"Take comfort in that, Your Holiness. That is the purpose of Holy Confession, to give your burden unto the bosom of our Lord and Savior."

"But will he accept it? I fear not; it is so utterly horrible."

"You will never know the Mercy of Lord Jehosa unless you bare it all unto him and ask him for forgiveness. I will listen and pray on your behalf. Come, let's give it a try." Pope Anaxagoras yielded at last. For the next hour, he outlined everything, sparing no detail. When he finished, he did feel better.

"I have been carrying this horrible burden upon my shoulders alone for months. It does feel so much better that another now knows. It is the worst crisis our Church has ever faced."

Thondakas smiled slyly; now he knew for sure that the whole Church of Jehosanity was the complete fabrication of Yazi. However, he was pragmatic, if nothing else. His position was one of incredible power, to say nothing of the fortune he was slowly amassing. Give this all up saying it was an elaborate hoax? The thought never entered his consciousness! "I wish that you had come to me with this when you first found out, dear Anaxagoras. Many solutions present themselves to those who are willing. We cannot let our Holy Church come to ruin, that is a given."

"Yes, I know, but how can it not be avoided? I can see no way to survive," he wailed.

"Look, we can do many small things, which, in the end, may win us the battle. First, I assume that there are some details that could be included in your Jehosanity Theology, some facts that do not so totally alter your beliefs, am I right?"

"Well, yes, the major ones completely undermine us though."

"Forget those for now, completely. Perhaps you can prepare an addition to the Holy Gospel that Yazi wrote. Insert in there the many smaller pieces that you believe true and that do not pose a major threat to the Holy Body of Worship. Meanwhile, we stall. Write the Devil's Spawn back saying that you found much of value in them and are working on incorporating them into the theology. Ask if the Church could purchase the originals. Of course, they will refuse, unless they are utter fools. Ask if you could send a scholastic scholar to verify the authenticity of said originals. Ask if the Church could purchase the library of early works. Again, they will refuse. So ask if you could send a scholastic scholar to study them for a time. See how much time gets wasted?"

"During this valuable time period, we do everything that we can to infiltrate their organization, build up our forces here, and in the sectors, prepare to find ways and means of defeating them. If all else fails and they publically release the incriminating books, the Church can take the official position that they are elaborate forgeries. We can make up any number of 'facts' that support this claim that they are a complete and utter falsehood. We can launch a huge public campaign denigrating the Santi for pushing such an elaborate hoax upon the common man. We can wave the originals that you have around in public demonstrating that we have the true originals. No one can read them anyway, so it will not hurt us. It will be our word against theirs, in the final analysis. After all, none that wrote them are alive nor is anyone who may have lived with them and might know the actual truth of the matter. Scholars can be tied up for centuries debating whether these are the originals or elaborate fakes. You see, all is not lost."

Hope rekindled in the old man. "Yes, yes, I see. So simple! Thondakas, I don't know what we would do without your brilliant abilities! Yes, this is the path that we must follow. Let us together make it so! I should write the Demon Spawn immediately!"

Thondakas left his Pope and returned to his quarters; now he had many plans to make. He found it interesting that his next monthly stipend had an additional five hundred gold pieces in it. He smiled as he counted the coins.

Late that night, Pope Anaxagoras wrote in his private journal. "Holy Father, I am sinning. I know that these teachings are the truth. However, if I allow them to be known widely, your Church and everything we've built totally in your honor, Lord Jehosa, will be destroyed. Thus, I knowingly commit these sins for the good of your Church and all the good that it does. Forgive me Holy Father, if you can. Your Humble Servant, Anaxagoras."

Footnote: there are times when one man has the power to change history. The question becomes do they possess the personal integrity necessary to do so.

Chapter 14 An Unusual Happening at the Market

It was first Friday of June 640, a warm, sunny, cheerful day. It was market day for the estate, Fridays always had been. As usual, Jovanna and Ariana accompanied the small crew who went into Velona proper to shop for the weeks groceries. Two Santi women fighters always accompanied the shoppers, which also included four of the cooks who prepared all the meals at Jenna's estate. Often Jovanna or Ariana would request a little something extra be acquired to please their husband's tastes, though it was sometimes theirs that they pleased. On occasional trips, the two would also shop for other needed items among the multitudes of small shops that dotted the ever sprawling, thriving city of Velona.

Jovanna had set a new record for speed of training. She had just finished her last year and was now officially a Judger. However, she simply could not learn the three power spells, bringing down lightning, sheets of fire, or of ice. It seemed that she had some kind of barrier to casting these spells. In the end, she was allowed to graduate, if she agreed to continue to try to learn them. On the other hand, her Judger skills were first rate, far exceeding the norm for her specialty. What other Judgers considered their masterpieces, the ability to create illusions so that a person would see what they expected to see, Jovanna found nearly trivial to do. After all, she could take control of anyone's body and make it do what she desired.

Ariana was in her eighth year of study as a Loremaster, taking after her husband. She had a love of Nature, which he nurtured until it blossomed. Further, totally enthralled with Hank's many agricultural experiments to determine the best crops for a given climate and soil along with the best methods of raising said plants, she continually drilled him on his methods and the how and why of them. I think even now she had some distant thought that one day she may be able to use this knowledge for her people back in Zargarb.

Jovanna and a cook were busily picking out ripe tomatoes for the various dishes they were planning for the week. Early afternoons were the best time for both women to get a way for a few hours. Both now had year old babies. Marta Paca Barcella Wilkins was the name that Jovanna and Paul finally settled upon when she came into the world a year ago. Everyone said she had Jovanna's eyes and Paul's brownish hair. Nicolina Sue Zar Wilkins was named after Ariana's mother and Ben's mother, a nice compromise. While the two new mothers took a welcome break, Lilly Ann, as usual, looked after the babies.

Jovanna was bent over the pile of tomatoes, picking up a large one in her short arms, discussing just how many the cook thought would be needed when a male voice from somewhere behind her called out, an urgent sound in his voice. "Jovanna Barcella? I'm looking for Jovanna Barcella? Does anyone here know Jovanna Barcella, please?"

She turned around, tomato lodged between her short arms, "I'm Jovanna Barcella. What do you want of me?"

"Oh all praise be to Tur! Thank the gods that I have found you at long last!" he gushed out; the relief he felt she could already sense. He closed the distance to her, as the alert Santi guard swiftly moved to intercept him, if he attempted any harm to her charge. He saw her face and then her arms and gasped, "Oh my god! Not you too. Oh no! Now all is surely lost! Doom has finally come unto us all. I am so terribly sorry for you Lady Jovanna Barcella; I did not know." The young man was near tears. He sank down to his knees before her, crushed beyond all hope.

The Santi fighter loosened her grip on her sword. The man was evidently not a threat to Jovanna. His clothes were leather, probably costly when new, but now they were dirty, stained, and had many holes crudely patched in their knees. His hair had not been trimmed in a long time, probably not washed for that matter. His skin was tanned, perhaps an outdoors man. Jovanna recognized his slight accent at once, he was from Barcella, no doubt of that. She handed the tomato to the cook and bent towards the man. Perhaps he is twenty-five, she thought. "Please sir, we have not been introduced. Pray what is your name? You have me at a disadvantage."

"Roberto Peña, Lady Jovanna," he said, remembering his long forgotten manners, offering her his hand, before he realized she had no hand and very little arm. His face reddened as he realized his awful gaffe. To his dismay and surprise, she lifted her arm outward towards him.

"Shake please? I know it is very short, but I can still be civilized. Come on, Roberto," she said, attempting to put him at ease. She found that more often than not, it was she who had to put others at ease with her arms, which she thought rather funny since it was she that had the short arms. Gingerly he took her arm in his hands and they shook. "Peña? Any relation to Antonio Peña, head of the House of Peña in Barcella?" Long had it been now that she had any contact with her homeland of Barcella. Antonio had been killed when the Butcher had taken control of her sector so many years ago now.

"Yes, he was my father. Alas, I was on a hunting trip in the far north when the Butcher came. I could do nothing to save Antonio. For years I have been an outlaw in my own country."

"I knew Antonio a long time ago it seems. So much has happened since then. I'm sorry for your loss."

"Nay, my Lady, it is I who am so terribly sorry for your losses, which so greatly exceed mine. Do you know that your brother was butchered several years ago? And look what they have done to you? May Tur curse them all into the watery depths of the sea!"

"Yes, word reached me here of his death. Pray, Roberto, what did you want to see me about? Perhaps I can help in some way."

Before he could answer, one of our Santi guards interrupted, "Time to go, Jovanna." Ariana had stopped her shopping and was watching them as well.

"Okay, I know, Marta is waiting and will be starving if we are late. I'm married, Roberto, and have a beautiful daughter back at the estate. Why don't you come with us, and then you can tell me everything. I long for news of Barcella."

"It would not be an imposition, My Lady Jovanna? I have traveled long to get here, and I must apologize for the way that I appear." He realized that his appearance was hardly worthy of a noble, let alone a Lady.

"Not at all. Besides, while I am nursing Marta, you can take a bath and clean up. I'm sure that Paul has some spare clothes you can wear while we get yours attended to. Come on, it's this coach here."

Roberto rushed to open the coach door for Jovanna. As she stepped inside, Ariana came up beside him. "Hi, I'm Ariana Zar Wilkins, her best friend. We married brothers." She offered him her arm.

"Oh, I am so terribly sorry for you as well, My Lady Ariana," yet he took her arm exceedingly gently, but she shook it so firmly that he nearly let go.

"Pleased to meet you too, Roberto." She climbed inside and the cooks joined them along with one of their Santi guards. Roberto got in last and shut the door, while the other Santi drove the carriage back to the estate.

Surrounded with sacks of produce and the cooks, there was no time for any serious talk. Roberto did ask, "Ariana Zar. If I know my history, didn't the Zar family found Zargarb? Perhaps you are from that sector, originally, I mean?"

"Oh yes, my distant relatives founded Zargarb hundreds of years ago. Now I guess I am the last of that line; everyone else was killed long ago when the so called Holy Paladins took over. I managed to escape quite some time ago. I couldn't help overhearing that you are from Jovanna's sector. Have you just come from there?"

"Yes, My Lady Ariana, only just arrived yesterday in Velona. I was on what I thought was the greatest mission of my life. We'd just received news in the rural village in Barcella, where I was hiding, that Jovanna Barcella was still alive, had been married, and was now living in Velona. At the time, I thought that this was the greatest news I'd heard in a dozen years. But now, all that is dashed; I am truly so sorry that they took your arms, Lady Jovanna."

"Nothing to be sorry about, Roberto. I was caught spying and paid the price. I've recovered; it's mostly just a darn nuisance now."

"Major darn nuisance," Ariana could not help adding. "But we still do most everything, just in very different ways."

"Still, I do feel greatly saddened by it, for both of you beautiful Ladies. Say, we have left the city gates. Where are we going, if I may be so brash to ask?"

"Oh, I'm sorry. I assumed everyone knows us. We are going to the Santi estate just north of the city. We are all Santi members now. We call it Jenna and Hank's estate; it's the main Santi headquarters in Velona, a very big complex. Hank and Jenna have some of the most incredible flowers, but I suppose that you are not so interested in that," Jovanna teased, lightening the conversation."

"Oh my! Santi? Oh that is news indeed. This Jenna, I've heard that the Santi commander is called Jenna Rose Weston. Probably many women bear the name Jenna though."

"Oh no, you are precisely correct. She is the Supreme Commander of the Santi del Dio. I'm sure she will love to meet you, Roberto," Jovanna added, seeing his surprise and then his discomfort at his ragged appearance.

Ariana added, "You bet she will be interested in meeting you, though she'll probably want you to fully brief her on everything that has been going on in Barcella. It's difficult getting accurate information on what's going on in the Occupied Sectors, you know, I mean what is really going on, not what the Unholy Paladins want us to know. Hey, here we are, isn't this the grandest place that you've ever seen?" Ariana took immense pride in the appearance of the estate, flowers in full bloom, many she had helped Ben and Hank plant.

When the coach had rounded the entrance cobblestones by the stately oak tree in front of the main entrance of the central building, Lilly Ann came walking out holding a baby in each hand. "Hi all, about time. I am afraid the two young ones need their moms. Antie Lilly Ann just won't do. Oh," she said in surprise, seeing Roberto climb out of the coach first. He nodded and immediately began offering his hand to each woman as they exited. After the cooks climbed out laden with all the sacks of produce, Ariana began to climb out, and he gallantly held her arm to steady her, likewise with Jovanna.

"Hi and thanks Lilly Ann for watching Marta. This is Roberto Peña, son of Barcella's nobleman Antonio. He has traveled a very long way and wants to talk with me. Probably Jenna will want to talk with him as well. However, while we are nursing the babies, can you show him to the bath so he can wash the trail off himself. Maybe find him some clean clothes too, please?"

She carefully handed Nicolina into the waiting arms of Ariana, then even more carefully placed Marta into Jovanna's arms. Jovanna could just barely carry Marta, though she knew in another year, her daughter would likely be too heavy for her short arms to carry. Hence, she relished every minute while she still could. The two mothers headed inside. "If you will follow me, Roberto, I'll show you to the bath. I'm sure that we can find suitable fresh clothes. I hope you like a warm bath."

"You have a bath here? I am most impressed, Lady Lilly Ann, most. Yes, I would deeply appreciate fresh clothes, if it is not a bother. I have not had the luxury of a bath, let alone clean clothes for far too long. Thank you very much, My Lady."

Lilly Ann wondered if all the nobles talked this way. She did feel rather pleased with his politeness and calling her Lady. She left him in the bathhouse and went in search of some clean clothes. Shortly, she returned with clothes and with some shaving gear, along with scissors and a mirror, guessing he might like to alter his gruff appearance. "Oh bless you, My Lady, such kindness, such thoughtfulness! Yes, these will work wonders for my rough appearance. Thank you ever so much." She smiled and told him to take as long as he desired to clean up. Smiling and humming a little tune, she went to check on the two mothers and all the other children.

Much later, Hank joined Roberto in the bath. "Hello, you must be Roberto. I'm Hank, your host. Jenna says I must wash the dirt off before supper. Ah what's a little dirt anyway," he'd been planting all afternoon.

"Most pleased to meet you, Hank," he shook his host's hand. "Thank you so very much for such fine hospitality to a stranger a long way from home."

"Well, my wife will probably grill you to find out all she can about what's going on in your sector. So be prepared," he joked with him. "Say we should hurry up; I think they are about ready to serve dinner."

"I do feel so much more presentable now. What should I do with these?" he asked pointing to his pile of dirty clothes.

"Leave them for now. We'll take care of them later on. Come on; I'll show you the way. We've got quite a large number of people dining at one time, lots of kids around these days."

Paul had helped Jovanna into one of her fancier dresses and even put a yellow flower in her hair for her. Now she looked more like a charming host to her visitor from her homeland. Yes, dinnertime was quite a gathering of Santi and their children. Jovanna saw Hank bringing in Roberto, and she moved over to him quickly so she could do the introductions. "I see the bath did wonders for you," she teased.

"Yes, my Lady, but you look positively beautiful this evening."

"First you must meet the other half of your hosts," she said, guiding him over to Jenna. "Jenna, this is a fellow countryman of mine, Roberto Peña, son of the late nobleman Antonio. Roberto, this is Jenna Rose Weston, Supreme Santi Commander."

"Very pleased to meet you," Jenna said, extending her arm. Again, he was momentarily shocked by the sight, but recovered quickly and shook her arm.

"I am deeply honored to be in the presence of such a great Lady," he said. "Your fame precedes you. In Barcella, we have heard many tales of about your achievements, but I did not believe them when they said you had no hands. Such a tragic loss."

"Yes, lost them a long time ago in Zargarb, but that's in the past. What matters is the present. Come do sit down here between the twins, Lilly Ann and her sister Beth Ann. Ah, introductions all around while we wait for the cooks to bring out our dinner." Quickly, Jenna began introducing all the adults gathered around the large table. all the children were at a separate table close by, the older ones helping the younger ones. Several cribs were at the side with the babies.

Once the meal was finished, Jenna explained, "Roberto, traditionally, after dinner, I spend some time with all the children here. Once they've burned off some energy, then we can all meet and discuss things without many interruptions. I know that Jovanna and Ariana need some time now to feed their young ones, so why don't you come out and chat with the others. If you want, you can even join us with a round of kick ball, but I warn you, the older ones go for blood these days," she jested.

"We do not, mom!" declared her eldest son, Alaric, who was nearly thirteen, as he dashed outside the door.

Jenna chased after him. Many of the others came outside to enjoy the beautiful early evening, with mild temperatures and the heady aroma of so many different flowers in full bloom. Scads of children from early teens down to small fry were already running all over the grassy play area just beyond the oak tree, which grew beyond the cobblestone driveway in front of the main building of the complex. As soon as Jenna got onto the grass, the game began. It was utter chaos in motion. Roberto just watched the action, laughing at such a sight — happy, carefree children having fun. He longed for those days to return to his homeland, Barcella.

A while later as darkness grew, the game ended and the children ran off to start getting ready for bed. The adults all filed back into the dining room. The cooks had already cleaned up and had hot tea ready for the adults. While everyone took their seats, Roberto noticed that the cups of Jenna, Ariana, and Jovanna were of quite a different shape than the other normal tea mugs. These had wooden flairs surrounding three-fourths of the lip. He soon saw that this enabled these women easily to lift their mugs to drink. Clever, he thought.

"Okay, Roberto. Now you have my undivided attention at least until morning," Jovanna began. "I don't know what you wished to discuss with me or whether you wish to speak to me in private or not. I know that everyone here is anxious to hear about Barcella. However, if you want a private chat first, we can use the next room."

"I came to meet with you, Jovanna, expecting to find you all by yourself or perhaps, well I didn't quite know what to expect, just that you were alive. What I wanted to ask I now see is folly, you know because of, well, your tragic loss. Nevertheless, if I speak to all, then I will not have to repeat myself so often, my Lady."

"Well, let's not be so hasty in concluding that it's folly just yet. Why don't you begin at the beginning and let me be the judge of whether or not it is folly," Jovanna answered.

"Very well, my Lady," he took a sip of tea and began his lengthy explanation. "Ever since the Holy Paladins and the Butcher took over our country, I have been working with the underground resistance movement. For many years, we were well coordinated, due in part to your brother, the Tur Priest, and the Jehosanity deacon. However, with the deaths of both men, everything fell apart. They were the only two men who knew everyone in the movement, you see. With them gone, those in one pocket didn't know how to contact others or even who or where."

"At that time, I was hiding out in the far northern villages, along with my sister, whom I had managed to secret out of our home just before the Holy Paladins planned on capturing her. Her husband refused to leave, however, and he paid the price. She and I plus our local band continued harassing these wicked men as often as we could, but without the overall knowledge of their plans like we used to have, I am sad to report that our efforts were not often very profitable."

"Two years ago, I began traveling the length and breadth of Barcella intent on locating the other resistance group members. In the back of my mind, I had visions of perhaps replacing the role that your brother had had. Someone had to lead us, to coordinate our actions. It was about a year ago now that I finally had covered all the outlying towns and villages and was about to enter Barcella, which was the very tricky part, finding what was left of the resistance movement right there under the Butcher's very nose."

"Can you imagine my shock when I spied a group of the Holy Paladins riding into the city carrying my sister tied up on a horse? I had gotten off the road when I heard them coming and spied on them as they rode by me. She saw me and winked her eyes helplessly; she was tied and gaged. You bet I followed them into the city. They went straight to the Nunnery with her. I saw nothing of her after that. For days, I kept watch on that vile place, but only saw a few other women being taken in there, likewise tied and gagged. None came out. I could do nothing by myself, so I began to track down others who might have been in our movement. I did meet several hundred, before I made an error in judgment. However, I am quick to act and managed to escape the city. I just had to rescue her, but I could find no way, not with so many of their fighters constantly in the vicinity. I decided to wait and watch from outside the city. Actually, I admit, I had no other ideas except to wait and see. I know, pathetic. I am not particularly good at devising plans and such."

"However, in hindsight, this was exceedingly fortuitous for me. About a month after she had been captured, late at night, I saw a group of the Holy Paladins come riding out of the city. This time they drove a wagon. I got a glimpse inside and was tremendously shocked at what I saw. There were a dozen women in the wagon; one was my sister. It was dark so I could not see clearly then, but they all appeared chained up somehow. I followed them and waited for daylight."

"When dawn came, they pulled off the road and into the cover of some trees, hidden out of sight. Later I concluded that they were moving these women from the Nunnery in secret, they wanted no one to see them. I crept up to their camp on my belly so I could spy on them and try to figure out a way to get to my sister. That's when I saw the horror my sister and these poor women had to endure. While their torture is nothing, absolutely nothing at all to you three, still I was horrified. My sister had some kind of metal contraption that forced her arms to be locked across her back. At first, I thought that she too had lost her hands; they were invisible, encased in the metal. If this was not enough, they had a metal contraption encasing their heads. One portion forced a round ring between their teeth, so that their mouths were always wide open. Another portion covered their eyes so that they could not see. All were chained about their ankles to each other. I overheard one man telling them that they would wear these devices now for the rest of their lives. No one could remove them because liquid metal had been poured into the locks. They could not be removed even if someone wanted to free them. It was awful."

"I continued to follow them northward. They took them into some of the limestone caverns there in the isolated far north of our sector. Guards are constantly there; no way for me to free them. I tried to get others to help me, but everyone is now worried about what the Butcher would do to their village when he finds out that they have been freed. I learned from some others that I promised not to name that these women officially no longer exist and that anyone who has even seen them is subject to instant execution! Apparently, five travelers saw them and were found beheaded. Innocent travelers, they were. Everyone is now extremely scared of this."

"I couldn't give up, so I kept trying to recruit some others to help me. No luck. Then, I began to ask about those who fled to the safety of Velona. A contact put me in touch with a resistance cell in Velona, so I came to meet with him. There are over a thousand men who would fight to take back our sector! A thousand, it seemed like a miracle. However, they refuse to take action, not unless they can be united by someone with authority, someone they could trust to lead them. That's when I heard that you existed, that you were still alive, Jovanna. My heart nearly burst when I heard that news! I thought, 'You are the one, Jovanna!' You are the only one left who can trace their lineage back to our city's founders. You are the rightful ruler of Barcella — the only living person who can make that claim, the only one who could rally all our forces to take back our homeland. I thought if I came to you and pleaded our country's case, you could not refuse. Then, I when I saw you, I realized it was all just a silly dream of mine; you have suffered most horribly at the hands of the Butcher. So you see, I cannot ask that of you. You have already given far, far too much. I am so sorry that I acted in such haste, that I did not make further inquiries about how you were. Please forgive my brashness, my foolishness, my Lady."

For a moment, Jovanna sat stunned by his tale. What words could she say? "You are forgiven, Roberto. However, do not think that because I am called Miss Short Arms by my close friends that I am utterly helpless. Jenna, I believe that this has become a matter for your attention, not just mine."

"Right, Jovanna. Beth Ann, take notes. Roberto, I want you to go back over some of the details. Try to be as specific as you can about just where they are holding these women and your sister," Jenna said, suppressing her outrage and anger. I think we all felt the betrayal of the Megalos Church, which had apparently switched one form of torture for another. True, this was not mutilation or beating of women. Yet, it was just as sick.

I heard it all. I was now five and often quietly crept into the room. No one thought anything about it, since I was always around. I knew when to keep quiet and not be a little girl. Jenna grilled him for over an hour, flushing out as many details as he could remember. She did not press him to reveal any confidences, however. I could see that he noticed that and was appreciative of that.

Finally, Jenna suggested that Beth Ann show him to one of the many guest room. I knew that Jenna would conduct a late night meeting, just as soon as Beth Ann returned. The mothers quickly tucked their older children in for the night, while others nursed the babies. Perhaps an hour later, I had my jammies on and was curled up on a blanket in one corner. Everyone else gathered around the table. Jenna said, "Well, at last we have some hard evidence on their activities. The question before us is now what do we do about it?"

Jovanna answered first, "I know that it is my homeland that we are talking about, but I cannot ask the Santi to attack them. Look that would only tend to breed open warfare with Megalos."

"She's got a good point, Jenna," Lilly Ann said. "I think with this sector, we have an opportunity to try something a little different. It's common knowledge that this sector has been in rebellion against their overlords ever since the Holy Paladins first set foot there. True, over time, the impact of their resistance has varied, but it is still present, if uncoordinated. We could use this to our advantage. If Roberto is correct in his estimation of the numbers of willing rebels, then with disguised aid from us, and rallied under the banner of the rightful ruler of Barcella, they just may well retake the sector. That is, if Jovanna is willing to be accept that position. You would have little choice but to rule Barcella if the rebellion is successful. That is an awful lot to ask of you, Jovanna. We all would completely understand if you didn't desire it."

She looked at Paul. "I don't want to be the ruler of Barcella and never have. Nevertheless, the good for many so utterly outweighs my own desires. Yet I totally and completely refuse not to be Santi! I am Santi first and always. To free our people and finally take back a sector is awesome, but then having to rule it? Oh no, I cannot even imagine doing it alone! How can I dare ask Paul to come with me? He is the sworn protector of Jenna and your Circle. This whole problem is just too overwhelming."

Jenna answered her, "Jovanna, we all know that you are one of us and always will be so. Nothing will ever change that. Paul is a Protector. If he did not go with you, I would order him to go! A Protector is replaceable. A birthright ruler is not. However, Jovanna, none of us will force you to make any decision. It must be yours to make. I will say this, that if you choose to do this and become the ruler of Barcella, I and the entire Santi del Dio will back you, support you, and assist you completely! You will want for nothing. Besides, you would only be a few days ride from here, certainly less than a week. Look, Elona is Santi and she manages just fine. I know that she is a High Priestess and a superb organizer and that you are not of a religious mind. So you run Barcella your way, not hers."

Paul added, "Darling, I knew when I married you that this day might possibly come, when Barcella might make further demands upon you. If you want to try to help Barcella, then I'm with you all the way. If you don't want to do it, again I'm with you. No matter what you decide to do, there is one thing you can totally depend upon: I'll be at your side."

Tears began trickling down her cheeks; her emotions got the better of her for a moment. "If I believe in anything that I have learned, then I have to try it. To do nothing is always the wrong action to take."

Lilly Ann added, "Okay then, but let's not get hasty. We need to first see just how strong these rebels actually are, how loyal they might be to Jovanna, and work out just how Megalos can see a Barcella rebellion retaking the sector and not the Santi."

"Allan has the holding building ready to go, you know when we have captured some of the enemy and need to keep them locked up until they can work through our official rehabilitation steps," Beth Ann spoke up. "I suspect that we can capture a bunch of these Holy Paladins and put them through our official steps." He had a month ago officially pronounced the holding cells ready for operation. Just south of Velona lay a small uninhabited island known as Isla Roca, the rock island. Here he had built a secure facility in which humanely to house prisoners that had to be forcibly removed from society to prevent them from committing further harmful actions. Here, they would be given the opportunity to go through the official steps, which would lead to their recovery as valuable citizens once more, assuming their plan actually worked.

"Well, I don't want another big war going on," Jovanna said. "They have already suffered enormously. Putting them through another bloody war is not the way to go, if we can avoid it."

"I see your point," Lilly Ann answered, an idea forming in her head. "Jenna, just how many Judgers can we get together at one time these days? The Santi must not be seen leading the rebellion or fighting it. After they have retaken Barcella, then we can straightforwardly come to their assistance in all manner of ways. Megalos can have no quarrel with that, only with the Santi being seen doing the actual takeover. Me thinks this may be the hour we Judgers shine," she winked at Jovanna. "The Judgers are going to war, a very, very different kind of war. Jovanna, in the morning we need to talk this out. Meantime, let's get some sleep."

The next morning, Jovanna went to speak to Roberto before breakfast. She knocked on his door and opened it. "My Lady," he said, fussing with his appearance, while tying up his pants.

She smiled, "Roberto Peña you have just got your rebellion leader. I will make the attempt to retake back our country and lead us all to freedom once more."

"My Lady, but how can you — I mean you have — I mean as you are now — I cannot allow you to suffer any further," he blurted out, quite unsure just how to say what his conflicting mind thought.

"Obviously, Roberto, I will have to make use of many others' hands. A leader leads, whether or not they have hands or even much in the way of arms, for that matter. I have agreed to retake Barcella. I believe the retaking will be the least of our problems. The recovery of our prosperity — now that will take some doing. Are you willing to have me as your sole ruler? Will the majority of our people be willing to have me as their sole ruler? No more High Councils, no more dual rule between Prince and Priest. Just me."

"Oh yes, my Lady, though I know you not. I am willing to place my trust in you who have given so much and still are willing to give more. I have been all over our land, everywhere our people are suffering. Yet they continue to pray that someone will come forth to free them and lead. Hardly anyone would dare to dispute your sole right to lead. It is your birthright, one for which every living Barcella man would fight!"

"Thank you for your vote of confidence, Roberto. Now here's what I want you to do. We need to hold an assemblage of all those who are willing to help retake our country. Make us a pile of our country's flags, large ones, sky blue with a large yellow moon in its center. Let's hold this large rally at noon on Monday in the large Central Park, where lots can gather. I can use the musician's stand there to speak to everyone."

"Oh my Lady, this shall be done! I will get onto it immediately!"

"Thanks, be sure to come back here when you are done. For now, you are staying here with me."

"My Lady! You are most kind indeed. Thank you. I am off!" She returned to the meeting room, where the others were beginning to gather for the morning briefing. Today, the Santi had much to plan.

As the group walked into the meeting room, there waiting for them with their arms crossed and looking awfully stern were three of their children. Alaric, Jenna's eldest, Leslie Ann, Lilly's eldest with Ket, and Alyster, Beth Ann's oldest, standing like immovable statues. Alaric spoke for the group, "Mom, we are absolutely not moving until you give us your okay," the fourteen year old lad stated. The other two nodded their complete agreement.

"What this? A conspiracy? Agree to what?" Jenna finally asked, slightly exasperated. She had no idea what they were planning, though she ought to have, they were all full-fledged Guardians now, though her son only just recently.

"We're going to go with Paul and Jovanna and be their Circle. Leslie's good friend, Aura Penton, she's going too, as the Healer. We won't take no for an answer. We are of age, and we now have earned the right to do this," he declared. The other two again nodded. Though Alyster was three years older than Alaric was and Leslie Ann was one year older, evidently they thought that he had a better chance dealing with Jenna, and nominated Alaric to be their spokesman.

"What? But your not —" she didn't get to finish her protest. He knew exactly what she was going to say.

"I am too old enough. I'm fourteen and they are even older. After all mom, Ket took off on his grand adventure when he was only fourteen."

Recovering from the surprise, Lilly Ann added, "Leslie Ann! You know that this could be very dangerous indeed! There are assassins out there just looking to get you because you are an Amir."

"Mom, we've already worked it out. I'll go by Donegal; Alyster is going to pretend that I am his younger sister. No one will know!" Leslie Ann countered. She'd already figured out that was what her mom would say.

"Alyster, did you put them up to this so you could get away?" Beth Ann asked sternly.

"Mom, would I ever do that?" She couldn't tell if he was teasing her or serious. "Honestly mom, we four have been planning how we could get away on some assignment for nearly a year now. We are ready, really we are mom, Jenna," Alyster defended himself.

Finally, Jenna got in a word, "But what about Jovanna's wishes? Maybe she wants some older, more experienced Guardians with her. Paul cannot be looking out for you four when he is watching over Jovanna and their daughter." This, the trio had not expected. Alaric's face reddened slightly. He'd never considered that Jovanna would not want them because they were beginners without field experience.

Jovanna decided it was time that she said something. "Well, I am a beginner too, Jenna. In some ways, it is best if most of us are beginners; we can bond tightly together. Paul has had much experience and can keep us on the right path, but I can understand if you don't want to let them go to Barcella; they are your eldest. I know that I would be fretting all the time if Marta goes off on her own."

Hank added, "Children do grow up, honey. We knew this day was coming. We cannot stand in their way. Besides we all know that to bring in other Guardians will mean breaking up other working installations. Let's give the children a chance, shall we?" He looked at Jenna, Lilly Ann, Beth Ann, and finally Allan.

Alyster saw an opening and took it. "Dad, I am a Planner just like you. After Jovanna retakes Barcella, there is going to be an enormous amount of new construction that must be done and done right. This is my chance to really make a difference."

Leslie Ann added, "Aura's been listening in to us and she says that her dad will give his consent if you okay it, Jenna."

Jenna sighed; she knew they were right. It's just that she was not yet ready to let Alaric leave her home, her care, her protection. "Well, you do have a point, using others will only make other groups weaker at the moment, and you are right about the construction. Okay, if Jovanna is satisfied, then I will give my agreement." All eyes turned to Paul and Jovanna, she nodded, and the three let out a yell of joy and jumped up and down. They had finally succeeded.

"Well, then you three need to begin meeting with us. We have many plans to make. Go fetch Aura, please," Jenna replied, scarcely keeping from laughing at the exuberance the children were making. Children, she reminded herself, they were no longer children.

Later on during the meeting, Lilly Ann outlined Jovanna's and her idea. "We know that attrition has lowered severely the numbers of Holy Paladins in the sector. Our idea is to capture as many of them without a fight as possible. We will be using all the illusions we Judgers possess along with Jovanna's special skills. The first action must be to rescue the women from the northern caves. From there we will systematically move southward, liberating the outlying towns, villages, and hamlets as we go. Jovanna suggests that after we have taken a town and are ready to move on to the next one, we will leave a force behind to intercept any Holy Paladins that might come riding to that location."

"Per the estimates of Roberto, by the time that we get to Barcella proper, we ought to have dealt with over half of them. If we are to capture them, we need plenty of wagons following us to bring the captured men back here to be sent to Isla Roca."

Jovanna added, "The key to this whole operation will be to confront only a few of the Holy Paladins at one time. We will use all manner of deception to avoid an outright battle. We believe that it is possible to do it.

The only challenge we think will be the city itself. We must be able to get enough of us in there as 'innocents' as possible before we make our move."

"This should be the most interesting rebellion in history," Jenna replied, rather excited about the unorthodox tactics the two women had worked out. We should send along some blacksmiths to work on freeing the women. Until we actually see these vile devices, we really cannot estimate properly what must be done to remove them. If it looks like it cannot be done locally or if the women are in poor shape, you are ordered to have them sent here at once."

"Agreed," Jovanna said. "I do hope that they are not permanently harmed as we have been. If they seem to be suffering from the ordeal, emotionally I mean, I may I send them here as well?"

"You bet!" Jenna exclaimed, rather eager to have some new people for her therapy sessions. Now they all began to work out the specific details of how many wagons, men, supplies, and such should be positioned where and when. In addition, Jenna planned to send along an entire Santi Strike Force Regiment, particularly those who hailed from Barcella. They would know the land.

Later, Lilly Ann and Jovanna set to work on the speech that she would deliver on Monday noon. She would need all her Judger training to handle these crucial men. If they did not support her move, all their plans would have to be hastily altered.

Five carriages pulled up at the edge of Central Park. All the Guardians at Jenna's estate came with her. Some, like her new Circle, were there to protect and aid Jovanna; others wanted to hear this historic speech in person. Jenna needed to judge the crowd's reaction, adjusting her plans accordingly. Roberto was already there, putting the finishing touches on the Musician's Stand, a raised platform in the center. He had erected an enormous flag of Barcella, sky blue with a yellow moon in its center. "Well done, Roberto!" Jovanna praised him as she walked up, her Circle in tow.

"Ah my Lady, it's the best I could do on such short notice. Oh, you look lovely today, my Lady. Oh!" he spied the official pendant of the founders of the sector around her neck.

"Yes, my dad rescued it from the Holy Paladins. Will many remember it do you think?"

"Many will, my Lady, yes, it will bring back memories of happier times."

"Roberto, I want you to meet my close associates who will always be at my side." She introduced each one to her countryman. Of course, they were all wearing their Santi del Dio cloaks over their chain mail. He was very impressed.

"Then it really is true? The Santi del Dio will be backing us?"

"Yes, most importantly they will be helping us with our economic recovery, which will be much more difficult than merely retaking Barcella," she explained. Just then, a hundred other Santi arrived from with Velona and took up guard positions surrounding the perimeter of the huge park. Soon others began arriving, mostly on foot. Men predominated, but many brought along their whole families. These had fled the occupation and largely now were living a profitable life here in Velona. Jovanna was quite surprised to see Elona Po and her Circle of Guardians arrive, taking up a position within the crowd. Even Elona did not want to miss this speech. She knew just how much depended upon it.

By the time that the huge cathedral bells chimed the noon hour, Central Park was packed! Thousands of people stood watching the stage. Paul made a last minute adjustment to Jovanna's wardrobe and said, "Knock them dead, honey," and kissed her forehead. Jovanna took a deep breath and stepped upon the platform.

A tall brunette, whose hair dropped to her waist, with piercing eyes and radiant complexion stood before them. Her black tunic with the red fleur-de-lis cross emblazoned prominently across her front and back highlighted the gem encrusted pendant that hung from her neck. She raised her short arms out before her. As she expected, the crowd gasped and whispered among themselves. One thing she intended to make very clear was her physical limitations — none of this "but we didn't know" excuses later delivered so one could back out of agreements.

Once the shock and noise level diminished, using the loudest voice she could project, she began. "Welcome fellow countrymen. I am the great-great-great granddaughter of Ruggiero Barcella, the HighPriest of Tur who founded our country. To my knowledge, I am the sole living descendant of Ruggiero. I here today lay my claim to my birthright heritage, the Rule of Barcella." The crowd clapped and cheered; it was a good start, many believed, bringing up her claim to rule the sector.

"As many of you can see and recognize, I wear the official pendant of office, first worn by Ruggiero himself, hundreds of years ago. Who am I? I know that is perhaps your most important question to have answered first. When the invaders took over our land, I was just a young teenager. Yet, as many of you have done, I immediately joined the resistance movement, along with my late brother. I took a position with none other than the Butcher, Ali Sanchez, acting as his housemaid for nearly a dozen years. During those years, I constantly fed key information of their plans to the underground, saving many lives and in my own way helping to thwart many of their carefully laid plans. However, when the Mano del Dio came to Barcella, although I had done nothing but pour their wine, he did this to me." She raised her arms once more.

After the cursing and crying had died down, she continued. "Yes, he began by cutting off my fingers, one by one, demanding me to tell him the secrets of the underground. When I had none left, at last I yielded years' out of date information, which they would find useless. He thanked me by cutting the rest off, dumping me on my aged father's doorstep, there to slowly bleed to death or die from the infections of my wounds."

The crowd really cursed and swore for over a minute. She went on, "My father took me to the Santi del Dio. The rest is history. Their skilled Healers saved my life, and their commander's therapy healed my emotional scars as well. They allowed me to study and learn from them. Today, I stand here before you not only a Santi del Dio, but also a full Guardian among them!"

Now they roared, cheered, and yelled for nearly five minutes. Everyone held the Santi in the highest respect, but a Guardian — they were more like gods among men. That the new ruler of Barcella was both was an incredible stroke of good fortune!

"Today, I am here to put you all on notice, that I am claiming the throne of Barcella. Within days, I lead the fight to retake our country and rebuild it to a level of prosperity never before seen in our land!" Again, she had to pause to let the crowd quiet down.

"With me is my husband, Paul, so I am officially known as Jovanna Barcella Wilkins. We have a young daughter, Marta. So yes, the line will not die with me. Paul is also a Guardian." Once more, the crowd drowned her out.

"I am blessed with four other Guardians who will be my advisors and constant companions." She motioned toward the four teens, who stood proudly erect.

"Now I have but one question for you all. Will you accept me, Jovanna Barcella, as your lawful ruler, swearing allegiance to me?" The roar was deafening; clapping did not die down for five minutes.

"Within days, I will be launching my campaign to take back our country from the barbarians from the south. It must be we of Barcella that do this, not the Santi. It is our own respect that we must buy back. Yet, know this, the Santi will ever guard our backs and support us in every way, but it is and must be *our* fight, not theirs. It is our country! I ask for your help. Will you help me in whatever way you can best contribute?" This was her key question. Everything hinged upon their reaction.

She had her answer immediately. The noise and yelling was almost deafening. "We need all types of assistance. Some of you are trained in the fighting arts, and certainly, we need your services, but we need so much more. Many of you have come here leaving behind friends and relatives, and you know the horrid conditions that we will find upon reentering our country. Food, blankets, clothing, you know what they will need. This is what I mean by contribute as you can. As we begin to liberate the towns one by one, those there will be in dire need of supplies. Wagons will be needed to bring your donations to them. Drivers are needed. The Santi will graciously coordinate all the massive relief efforts for us, while we are liberating more towns. Now is the time to step forward and lend me your hands, for you see

I have no hands." It was meant as a joke. First, a few chuckled. Others seeing her broad grin realized it was well. Their leader had a sense of humor and could even joke about herself. Now laughter spread widely.

"Right from this very beginning, I want each and every one of you to know that as your ruler, I am always there to meet with you personally. After I am done speaking here shortly, feel free to come and meet me personally. If you wish to make arrangements for donations, please see one of my friends here; look for the Santi tunics. My door is always open to you, my people. In fact, you will soon see that none of the doors in my estate will have any doorknobs." The crowd didn't get the significance of that remark, so she jested with a big grin and raised her short arms up, "No hands?" Laughter once again sprang up. She heard many comments along the line of, "I like this spunky woman!"

She stepped down off the platform; the crowd yelled, clapped, whistled, and in general made quite a racket. She waved and waved, until the noise subsided. Roberto came up and said, "Fabulous, you did fabulous, my Lady!" She startled him by leaning over and giving him a hug.

"I can hug better than I can shake," she jested. "Seriously, Roberto, you did a magnificent job of rounding them all up today. I would like to give you a high position in my court. So don't take any other jobs just yet."

"My Lady! Thank you. Thank you."

"Just so you know, Roberto, our first action is to free your sister and help those other women. You will ride up front with us always. I'd make you a General but I think you'd rather have another position."

"Thank you from the bottom of my heart, my Lady, and for my poor sister too. Yes, I am not much of a general. I know shipping and very little else."

"Roberto, very soon now I am going to need all your experience and wisdom in that area, if Barcella is going to survive, let alone thrive. Ah, people are coming up; we'd better meet them."

Long lines stood to meet Jovanna in person, once they saw that she did meet with those who attempted to greet her. Uniformly, she would offer her arm to the men, performing a handshake as best she could. It was the custom to do so in Barcella. To the women, she gave a hug instead. Often the women would comment, "Oh you poor thing, I feel so sorry for you." To which she replied, "Oh you have it all wrong. I am so lucky; I get out of having to sew, cook, and weave!" It generally brought about a grin or chuckle from the woman.

Her companions and the others were kept busy until late afternoon, taking down pledged donations and informing people how and where and when to deliver them. Paul and Alaric had a list of over five hundred men who volunteered to help with the actual fighting. This was the key, they needed a strong show of Barcella fighters so that the world, and Megalos in particular, would not see this as a Santi invasion, but a rebellion of the countrymen of Barcella.

Of course, right in the middle of the flurry of activity, Jovanna and Ariana had to take a brief time out to nurse their babies. Both sat on the steps and nursed, while trying to continue meeting people. When the last had left, Elona came up to Jovanna. "Well done, compatriot! It will be fabulous to have you as my neighbor. Once you have regained your country, you can count on Velona to support you fully. If you need any advice or guidance, just let me know. I'll help you any way that I can." Jovanna just gave her a loving hug.

On the ride home, Paul told her the good news, "Love, five hundred twenty-one volunteered to fight for you. They are to report in one week to the North Border Fortress." This was the last in the chain of fortresses that Elona had built on the border of Velona and Barcella. Just beyond this fortress lay the Paese di Dio, God's Land, the grassy high plateau that stretched across all the Sea Princes and from which the high mountains of the Appian Way rose. It was largely uninhabited, save for a very, very few shepherds. From this point, it was only two day's ride to the first of the many limestone caverns, their first target.

The next five days were incredibly busy. Between packing, buying of supplies and equipment, and getting ready to live out of a wagon for the next month or so, no one had time to ponder what would happen next. It was a two-day ride to the northern fortress. Hence, in five days everything had to be ready. At last, the day came. Jovanna hugged and held Jenna tightly for quite some time before she could bear to part with her. With everyone in the estate cheering her on, Jovanna and her group of five wagons rolled out of the estate heading north.

Just outside the estate, they were joined by an entire regiment of Santi, over four hundred well-armed, seasoned veteran fighters. Additionally, two Scout Squads were temporarily assigned to the regiment and over a hundred support personnel, mostly in wagons as well. Among them were four blacksmiths, who had been briefed on what they were expected to be able to do. None of them had any idea of what lay ahead, however. Jovanna heard periodical reports of many Barcella fighters catching up with their group. Each night when they stopped for the evening, she would go to their section of camp and personally thanked each one of these brave volunteers. Her actions made a long lasting impression on these men. Never had any of their previous leaders given them so much personal attention as did Jovanna.

Once at the fortress, they regrouped. Now she had Paul organize her fledgling fighter group. Though she followed him everywhere observing, she always let him do what he thought best. He made the most skilled men the leader of a squad of twenty-five others. This gave them twenty squads. Next, he found a number of the volunteers who had had previous leadership positions and put one man in charge of each group of four squads. In these times, such groupings were common, for one could easily tally up the total number of men this way. These he then called the brigade commanders. Finally, he picked what he hoped was the best leader among them to be the regimental commander and assigned five others to be his liaison men for the brigades. All this took the entire day.

That evening, Jovanna briefed all of these new leaders. "Tomorrow we begin the liberation of Barcella. We are going to do it my way, which, if it works out as planned, you may not have much actual fighting to do, meaning I don't want you all killed or wounded if I can help it. Now here's what we are going to do." She outlined her plan. However, she knew that nearly none of these men would believe that it had even the remotest chance of working. No, she knew that they would just have to witness it themselves, Judger Power, as she later referred to it.

The next morning she donned her new tunic, sky blue with a yellow moon on its front. Indeed, all of her companions had similar, hastily made tunics. A group of six Judgers arrived, one of which was indeed Lilly Ann. Likewise, they wore similar tunics. Then, she sent her Circle out to hand out identical tunics to the various leaders. There was not time enough to have tunics made for all her fighters. She promised herself that they would have them one day.

Fel Bugatti, perhaps one of the very best scouts, came up and reported in to Paul, "Sir, our scouts are out. No activity to the east. I know every inch of this sector, so if you need any directions or have questions, let me know. Our Communicator will stay in touch with Leslie Ann. Sir, let me say that it is an honor to have been chosen for this liberation strike force. I speak for all of us, we will not fail!"

"I know, Ket always said you were the best. Thanks, I guess it's time to move out." He gave the order, and the wagons and riders began moving eastward into the Barcella sector. They traveled along the edge of the Paese di Dio, because the wagons could easily roll along as if on a road. Just to their right, steep sided gullies cut their way through the land, making east-west travel very awkward for wagons, let alone horses. This was the first time that many had ever been up here in this mile-high country. Absolute quiet, sea of green grass, and very low undulating landscape made this a serene land; one felt close to god up here, it is said.

Mid-afternoon of the second day, they took a ninety degree turn and headed down the beginnings of a gully. Already the scouts had the limestone caves under observation, reporting seeing a number of the blue coats there. That term stuck ever after. These men were anything but Holy Paladins; blue coats seemed more appropriate. Since they could not reach the caves before dark, they made camp some seven miles north of the caverns, posting a heavy guard, just in case. The scouts took turns keeping the caves under observation all night long. Indeed, they spotted several more blue coats arriving, while two left, heading south.

Around ten the next morning, Jovanna and her group crouched behind a rock barrier that separated their position from the wide-open entrance area some twenty feet below them. Two blue coats paced around before the entrance, guards, she supposed. These would be the first that she would have to deal with today. She took a deep breath and calmed her nerves and mind. Lilly Ann whispered, we're ready whenever you are. "Now, let's do it." Six Judgers began chanting softly. Then to the shocked surprise of her five hundred men who lay further back hiding behind whatever cover they could find, the seven began walking slowly down toward the two blue coat guards.

"Good day to you," Lilly Ann said, but the guards heard a man's bass voice and saw seven Holy Paladins walking towards them. They answered in kind. She then said, "We brought a whole case load of hearty ale with us, why don't you take a break while we watch the entrance for you. We left the wagon just back there."

One guard repeated, "Why don't we take a break and have some ale?" His companion agreed. Now the seven were right in front of the two men.

Lilly Ann said, "Here, we'll hold your weapons for you."

Both men repeated her, "Here, hold our weapons for us."

She then said, "Don't get too drunk, will ya?"

Both laughed and walked quickly to where the case of ale was supposed to be on the wagon. They found the wagon, but as they began looking for the case of ale, one hundred men, swords drawn, stepped out from behind the rocks. Several wore the traditional colors of Barcella. "You are under arrest for high treason," said the newly appointed brigade commander. Take them away men and get ready for more."

Meanwhile, as soon as the brigade commander waved to Jovanna, they began the next step. How many were still inside the cave and how to get them out — that was the problem. Another Judger spoke out, "Hey fellows inside, can you lend us a hand? Got a huge case of ale here. We need a hand carrying it inside."

Shortly, three more men came out. They saw seven Holy Paladins standing there. "Where's the case? Boy, ale's mighty welcome around here. A whole case you say?"

Before they could react, the Barcella fighters swarmed from seemingly nowhere, surrounding them, and capturing the three who just stood gaping. Actually, the Barcella fighters had been standing off to either side of the entrance, but the Judger's illusions forced the blue coats to see what they expected to see, nothing.

While this was going on, two more plus their lieutenant came out to see what was going on. Seeing all these enemy soldiers tying up their men, they quickly drew their swords. Jovanna was faster. While her fighters were hastily attempting to meet this unexpected trio, drawing their own swords, preparing to fight them, she acted. One by one, each man dropped his sword and began walking awkwardly toward her fighters, as if they were a child's puppet with someone was pulling their strings. Quickly, her men overpowered and tied these three up. More than one stared at Jovanna and her companions. Never had they witnessed anything quite like this!

Paul signaled for Leslie Ann, who came dashing up to them. "Find out if there are any more Holy Paladins inside, please. He's their leader." He pointed to the man struggling in vain as he was being tied up. She concentrated and then broke her connection. "Only their cook."

"Okay, Judgers, let's go inside," Jovanna ordered.

"Not without me, you don't!" Paul jumped to her side and moved out slightly ahead of her. Just inside, they found a passageway that led to the left and right. The sounds of someone humming a tune came from the left, along with horse noises. They veered left. Ten feet ahead, the encountered a section of the cavern, which held a dozen horses, tethered and munching on flakes of hay. The noise was louder and deeper inside the cavern. Quietly, they followed the noise and came upon the cook in the combination kitchen and pantry. "What the devil?" he exclaimed.

Paul put his sword blade to the man's throat. He offered no resistance. One of the Judgers led him out to join the other captives. Meanwhile, seeing that this was a dead end, they retraced their steps and headed down the right tunnel. After about fifteen feet, they came upon a gruesome sight; they'd found what they had been looking for. One Judger ran off to fetch Roberto, the blacksmiths, and the Healers. A locked iron fence had been affixed to the stone, creating a prison area some twenty-five feet square. Inside were a dozen women, wearing nothing but the poorest rags imaginable. Each had some kind of iron contraption that partially encased their heads, with a ring permanently inside their mouths, forcing them wide open and a leather blindfold tied on so that they could not see. Each also had another iron contraption around their upper chest, which somehow held their arms permanently crossed across their upper backs. Only their legs were free to move. Into the floor in the middle a long groove had been cut, forming a latrine of sorts. Their jailers only had to toss dishwater down it occasionally to wash the filth away. Near the iron fence, long metal cans only an inch high lay attached to the fence. Some held water; some held the remains of some kind of liquefied food, porridge perhaps? These women could not even eat like a dog!

Roberto came running in and stopped, staring in disbelief at the sight before him. Even the blacksmiths froze. No one had ever seen a sight such as this! He called out, "Nicolina! Nicolina! It's Roberto. We've come to free you all. You are going to be safe now!" The dozen were lying in various positions against the back wall, lying in beds of hay or straw, trying somehow to stay warm in the chilly cavern. One woman, very weak, struggled valiantly to rise, so awkward was her movements to do so. All were powerless to aid her; the gate was locked. She made some gurgling noises and just stood there.

Jovanna ordered, "Get this gate open at once!" Quickly, the men set to work, and the gate sprang open in less than a minute. Meanwhile, Jovanna spoke to the women, who could at least hear her. "I am Jovanna Barcella. I am now retaking control back from the Holy Paladins, eliminating every one of them. You are now safe. I have many Santi Healers with me. We will get you out of these horrid contraptions just as soon as we possibly can. Hang on for just a little while yet." They all stirred and made strange noises and tried to find ways to sit up.

Just as soon as the gate was opened, Roberto rushed to his sister and held on to her for dear life, "I'm here, Nicolina. It's me. We'll get you free just as soon as we can." Quickly, the blacksmiths began inspecting the diabolical devices. Their comments, I will not repeat here; they were curse-filled.

Meanwhile, all the blindfolds were easily removed. At least the women could see their rescuers. "Hi, I'm Jovanna Barcella," she repeated, now that they could see her. Uniformly all made gasping noises when they saw her. "I lost them many years ago to the Mano del Dio folks, but that hasn't stopped me. I'm retaking our country back town by town. You are my top priority. We've got food and clean clothes and Healers standing by, just as soon as we can get you free." She tried to sound as encouraging as possible. Many women just began crying.

Finally, one blacksmith told Jovanna what she greatly feared. "I'm sorry Jovanna; they've poured metal into the locks. They are fused. We don't know how we are going to get them off. Can we take them outside where we have better light and all our tools? I think this may take us days!" The women cried even harder.

"Okay, here's what we do. Healers, let's get some warm water going and give them a hot bath, they've been forced to lie in their own excrements. Then, let's get some fresh clothing on them and feed them something hot and nourishing. As you are doing that, check them over for injuries as best you can. No woman wants to go outside looking like this. Let's at least give them back some of their dignity. While they are doing that, blacksmiths, you put your heads together and figure out a way to get these things off them. I have to go nurse Marta. Action everyone."

Two hours later, the Healers began leading the women out to the wagons, where the cooks had made up a healthy soup, having mashed everything so that the women could swallow it without chewing. Aura gave Jovanna the official report. "They all have various female infections, probably from many rapes. All have numerous bruises, scrapes, and infections on their bodies, probably from the way that they were forced to live. We cannot tell about their arms. No one knows what damage has been done to them. We won't know until they are freed. Otherwise, these women are remarkably healthy, given their horrendous imprisonment and treatment. We expected much, much worse. I'm going to go help feed them."

From the way that they devoured spoonful after spoonful, I concluded that they were also half starved. The blacksmith report was dismal. "Ma'am, we are going to somehow have to cut them out of these devices, without harming them. This could take us days."

"Which would be easier to do, their head devices or their arm devices?" Jovanna asked. She needed to make a decision quickly.

"Oh, their head ones, we think we can cut through the side piece and then bend it out of their mouths. Getting the rest off will take much longer, but at least they could talk and eat properly."

"Okay, I agree with you. See if you can get those rings out first. I'll give you until tomorrow morning. Then, I'll have to make my decision."

By morning, the rings had been finally removed from each woman. They ate solid food for the first time in a very long time. Jovanna talked with each, explaining that she was sending them back to Velona, where the blacksmiths could work their magic and free them. In addition, their wounds and infections would be cared for there as well. She also insisted that Roberto accompany his sister. At ten, three wagons headed back the way that they had come. She knew that in three or four days at most they would be in very capable hands. She hoped and prayed that someone would figure how to remove those metal entrapments!

As they were about to leave, a scout reported that two blue coats were heading this way. The Judgers made short work of their capture, allowing them to ride up to the cave entrance and dismount before they were swarmed by the Barcella freedom fighters. All the captured men were then sent back to Velona in another wagon under a heavy guard.

Chapter 15 Barcella Resurrection

Jovanna watched the wagons carrying the helpless women leave. She knew that they would get the very best help there was to be had at Jenna's estate. Now she had the rest of her country to seize from these vile men. Paul told her to expect a battle conference before they left, so she patiently waited. She left these details to her husband.

Within a few minutes, all the Barcella Freedom Fighters commanders, that's the name they had adopted, along with a fair number of the Santi group leaders met outside the cave complex. All expected the real fighting to begin now. Paul began, "Okay, well done everyone. We took them all without even so much as one sword fight. Questions?"

"Yes, I have some — heck, we all do. Why did they just walked out like that? Why didn't they see us standing there until we jumped them? And why were they walking so funny like out of the cave? My men are confused."

Paul looked at Jovanna and Lilly Ann. "Our doing," Jovanna stood up to speak. "This group here is a very special type of Guardian. Paul is a fighter and protector, few know more about such than he. Yet, we are another type of Guardian; we can make people think they are seeing what they believe they should be seeing. Put yourselves in their position — come on all of you do this. Imagine you are one of the blue coat guards out here in the middle of nowhere at this secret women's prison. You hear conversation outside. Would you expect to see more of your fellow blue coats outside or would you expect to see an invading army?" Many answered our fellows, as she knew they would. "Right, we can touch their minds so they continue to believe they are seeing what they expect to be seeing, until it's too late."

"Say, that's mighty effective," one man replied. "Could be useful in all sorts of ways." Many chuckled at his inferences.

"Now as for the others that were doing strange things, I'm afraid that's my doing. Your ruler can make bodies do what she wants them to do. I just had the guards let go of their swords. Next, I made their bodies walk, kind of like a puppet. Honestly, when I take control of their bodies, they can't do a thing about it."

"Good god! You mean you could make a man walk off of a cliff to his death?" Fel asked. She'd heard rumors to this effect in her Santi quarters.

"Yes, Fel. I could. A Mano del Dio assassin was about to kill Adriana, who was lying helpless on the ground. As he was about to cut her head off, I made his arm draw his dagger and slit his own throat." The murmurs that ran through her commanders told her she had made an impression. "Don't worry guys. I am not often that bloodthirsty. I may be Miss Short Arms, but you don't want to mess with me." That did it, the juxtaposition of the concepts, a nearly helpless woman with almost no arms and god like powers to make men kill themselves, combined with joviality, was just too much for them. They began to laugh good-naturedly.

"Ma'am," her new regimental commander Bartolo Dovino, exclaimed, "I speak for all of us. We thought perhaps that we had a nearly helpless woman as our leader, at first when we saw you in Central Park, but then we saw all the Santi and that they were totally backing you. We figured that would guarantee our success, and they'd end up really running the show for you. Honestly, we had no idea that we were getting the most powerful leader that any sector ever had in history! We'll fight to the death for you, 'All hail to Jovanna Barcella!'" The other commanders followed his lead and chanted as well. When they settled down he added, "I've only got one request, ma'am. Please don't go having me or my men go taking off their clothes and parading around here naked."

Jovanna couldn't help laughing; the image he'd created was just so funny. Others joined in laughing too. "Glad you have a sense of humor too, Bartolo. I so promise, I only want to see one man running around naked," she pointed to Paul, whose face reddened slightly. "Seriously though, I will say this. We are going about this retaking of our country in this unusual way for a very good reason. There are only five hundred or so of you loyal men. True, I hope to add more volunteers with each town that we free, but think ahead; there is the walled city to take. If we attempt to take that by force, we cannot hope to succeed. Only a massive army can lay siege to these walled cities. They would take a huge number of casualties in doing so. Even the Emperor of Megalos did not even try to lay siege, but found other ways to take them. I don't want to lose even one of you, my brave men. We have already lost far too many of our country men and women to these vile blue coats."

"Ma'am, one more question, if I may. Since we are taking them alive, where are they going? We see them being carried away, but where? Are they going to be executed later in Velona?"

"They are being taken to the new Santi prison on Isla Roca. There the Santi will attempt to rehabilitate them and get them to make amends to us for what they have done. If they do not, they will spend their lives on the rock."

"Serves them right!" another replied.

"So you see, I'm not trying to stop you from fighting. I'm trying to retake our country back with just you handful of volunteers. Now, Paul is going to brief us on what's next."

Paul rose, but he couldn't resist a playful tease; after all, she had just gotten him. "Fellows, I wouldn't go messing around little Miss Short Arms, if I were you. I speak from experience!" The men roared, and she gave him a playful poke with her arms. "Okay, down to business. Here's what we do next. The plan is going to be exceedingly simple until we get to Barcella. We enter a town, and these folks here systematically get all the blue coats and their priests to surrender to your men. We tied them up and put them on a wagon to Velona. However, we all know that these men are often riding between towns. So after we liberate a town, we will have to leave enough around to be able to catch these others who come riding along. The one thing that we must prevent at all costs is having one of the blue coats discovering that we are here retaking the sector and running back to Barcella with the news. If that happens, you can be sure that the Butcher Ali Sanchez will send out everything he has and even force our own citizens to fight against us. We cannot let that happen. Thus, whenever a blue coat appears in areas that we control, he must be apprehended, dead or alive."

"We understand," Bartolo replied. "You are right; the Butcher would do that — force our own people to fight against us. Probably hold their wives and children hostage to make them do it. You have our word. None will escape our net."

"Good, now let's ride. Allyende is the nearest town, right?" Everyone acknowledged that it was. Allyende was the last northern town on the north-south spoke road out of Barcella. It lay at the intersection of the last east-west rim road. The small army mounted up and began moving south. Allyende was one day's ride south. Paul sent the scout squads many miles out in a fan-shaped cone ahead of them. He wanted all the intelligence of the area he could get. They could not afford the slightest mistake.

The next day, the Judgers walked into Allyende alone, only Paul was with them. Just out of sight behind them lay all the others, who were in the process of encircling the town. This northernmost town was home to around five hundred, including their children. One Church of Jehosanity stood prominently dominating the town, its steeple rising twenty feet above other buildings. As they walked down the dusty main street, they kept their eyes peeled for the blue coats. People were going about their daily business; some twenty children were playing ball in the street.

Paul stopped an older man who was carrying a load of firewood. "Excuse me, sir. Can you tell me how many of the Holy Paladins are in Allyende and where they are currently located?'

The man looked at these strangers for a moment, "Ten, they took over Arsinio's place, over there." He pointed toward a large home, which once had been owned by one of Allyende's wealthier families. He continued down the street, but kept an eye on the strangers. As they walked closer to the building, he noticed a large number of soldiers sneaking into town, evidently following these strangers. He grinned and hastily moved across the street where he would have a clear view of the action. Clearly, something was about to happen to their vile overlords, and he wasn't going to miss it!

They waited until hundreds of their fighters were in place. By now, all the children had stopped their games, watching the excitement. Other parents came out to usher their children a safe distance away. "Of course the real problem is how to get them to come out," Lilly Ann said.

Shrugging her shoulders, she knocked loudly on the door. Another Judger said, "Hey come on out here and lend us a hand with these supplies." Lilly Ann banged even harder on the door.

Shortly, the door opened, revealing several blue coats. Jovanna wasted no time and had the three marching marionette style on outside and into the waiting arms of her troops. Feigning an angry tone, the Judger yelled in the open door, "Hey come on fellows, will you please lend us a hand? These boxes are heavy!" Soon three more men joined their tied up mates.

"It's too dangerous to just walk in there," Paul objected, as Lilly Ann started to enter the building.

"I wish I didn't have to actually see them to control them," Jovanna added.

"How else are we going to get them out of there?"

"Well, let me go right in front of you all then," Paul consented, "but Jovanna, you stay at the rear." She did as instructed. They began searching the house, room by room. The original three had been playing a card game when Lilly Ann had first knocked. Soon they surprised several others and quickly captured them, but not before one managed to sound the alarm.

As they wrestled the three other men out into the waiting arms of Bartolo's men, their leader, sword drawn charged into the room. Paul and the other men were struggling with the other three. The man rushed to stab Paul in the back. Just as he was about to strike Paul, his legs froze and his hand lost its grip on his sword, which clanked onto the floor. Suddenly he could not move a muscle, frozen in place. Jovanna glared at the man. "Thanks honey," Paul smiled at her.

"You are going to have to carry their leader out," Jovanna said to Bartolo. "He was trying to stab Paul in the back, and I am teaching him a lesson in manners!" He saw his ruler was quite angry. He went inside to see for himself. There stood the man, arms still raised as if to strike a killing blow; he was frozen as if he were a marble statue!

"Impressive, ma'am," Bartolo said. "But ah, are you really going to make us carry him out?"

"Oh well, I guess not," she declared, relenting at last, "holler when you want him released."

Five minutes later, they were all securely tied up and had been searched. Now, they walked down to the church. As they approached the church, Jovanna could not help notice that everyone in the entire town was now out on the street watching the action. Someone yelled, "Get the dirty bastard!" Another yelled, "Only the priest's inside along with Mandy, his cook."

The Judgers saw an open second story window and the figure of a man peering down at them. "Vile Demon's Spawn Santi!" he spat down at them. "You cannot get me in here. This is a Holy House of the Lord. Sacred

310

Ground."

"Come out here this very minute!" Jovanna declared loudly and flatly. "If you don't come out here at once, I will make you!" The priest cursed at her and the others around her.

To everyone's surprise, the figure of an elderly woman appeared beside him. She held a large butcher's knife in her hand. She yelled at him, "Move or I'll cut you into beef steak!" Their last glimpse of them showed him with his arms raised, walking away from the window.

After a few minutes, the door opened. However, the sight was not what Jovanna and the others expected. Evidently, the priest had somehow overcome the cook, and now he held her body in front of him, the knife at her throat. "Make one move, and I'll cut her throat. I am going to walk out of here and to the stables. Someone will have my horse saddled when I get there or she's dead. I'm going to leave her or she dies before your eyes, you vile Lucifer's Spawn!"

Jovanna spoke loudly, leaving no misunderstanding about who was in charge of this mission. "You sir are correct; you are leaving Allyende forever!" She raised her arms and pointed them at him.

"You hopeless cripple! Haven't you wised up yet? We'll have to cut your tongue out next!"

At that instant, the man froze. Slowly his arm holding the knife moved carefully away from the cook's neck. Then, his other arm that held her tightly to him relaxed, and she was free. As soon as she felt him let go, she dashed for freedom, leaving the priest standing there like a statue. Jovanna spoke sternly, "Beast, if you move a muscle, I'll cut your throat! Bartolo, go get him and tie that bastard up." Quickly, several men rushed up to the frozen-in-place priest, removing the butcher's knife first. Then, Jovanna let go of the man's muscles. He began a diatribe of curses, so she forced his mouth shut tightly and didn't release it until he had been tied and gagged.

Since she now had the entire town's attention, she decided this was the prime time for her speech. She stood on the porch step of what had been the blue coat's home. "Greetings fellow countrymen. I am Jovanna Barcella Wilkins, by birthright, your new leader. This is my husband Paul. Today, Allyende has been freed from the tyranny of the Megalos barbarians. In the ensuing days, we will be working our way through out Barcella, driving out all the vile Holy Paladins. Then, I will take over rulership of our country. My goal is to turn Barcella into a thriving country of unparalleled prosperity for all our citizens. You have undoubtedly noticed my short arms and have doubts. Yes, I too have sacrificed much for our land at the hands of the Mano del Dio. Yet, I'm here and driving them out! I will be making all the laws and decisions, and my husband will be my hands to carry them out."

"I'm also a member of the Santi del Dio, a Guardian in fact. The Santi have pledged their full support for me and our country. Thus, I don't stand alone nor do you. We now have very powerful allies who will fully back us up and help in our economic recovery."

"What do I need from you at this time? If any of you have fighter experience and wish to lend a hand, see Paul. Next, do you still have your alcalde?" Someone yelled out no. "All right then, you all get together and elect yourselves a new alcalde. Your first order of business is to draw up a list of what you and your town most desperately need, whatever that may be. Once I have Barcella in my possession, I will send for your list and get your needs met as fast as possible."

"Finally, on a personal note, I intend to run our country vastly differently than it has ever been run before. I have an open door policy." Again, she began her tease, raising her short arms, "I have a wee bit of trouble with closed doors, you see." Several chuckled, and the others seeing her grinning, joined in. "Anyone who wants to see me about anything only has to drop by. Well, hold off until I get a place to which you can drop by. Further, I will personally come by to visit every town and village at least twice a year just to see how you are all doing. If you cannot easily get down to Barcella, you can meet with me then. While my men are searching the enemy's home, I would like to take this opportunity to visit with as many of you as I can."

As she stepped down, the town yelled and cheered her. Paul ordered the two premises carefully searched and the prisoners loaded into a wagon. Several townsfolk spat on the prisoners, and one older woman dumped a bucket of pigswill over them. Such was their outrage. Meanwhile, Jovanna began going up to the people who were crowded in the wide main street and saying hello. Paul was ever at her side, just in case. Following the precedent set by Jenna, she endeavored to take each person's hand between her arms and give them a welcoming shake. She observed that doing so brought the person closer to her. They began to like their new leader. "She's certainly got a lot of spunk; I'll give her that!" one old man commented.

Late that afternoon she climbed back into the coach with Lilly Ann and the other Judgers. Her forces moved on out of the town. However, several mounted riders took up positions about a mile south, west, and east of the town. Their job was to cut off any other Holy Paladins that might come riding this way. She left fifty more blocking the rim road to the east, while her main forces went west. Paul's idea was to clear this outer rim road over to near the Velona border so they would have a clear and easy path into Velona, should they need supplies or reinforcements. They made camp about half way to the next village.

Late afternoon that same day, Fel had her scout squad out on patrol, fanning out far to the west, and miles ahead of Jovanna's main force. She was now riding about a half mile from the road, cutting across the hilly, forested countryside. "This is what I live for," she said to herself. Indeed, riding along across the open countryside, free as a bird, this had always been what she enjoyed the most. It was why she had always been a scout, just for times like this. Had she not been on assignment, Fel would have been humming a tune. Her keen eyes and ears picked up something unusual.

"The birds are silent. Caution, Fel." She continued her slow pace, now more vigilant than ever. She heard a noise ahead of her and gentle reigned in her horse, intending to take whoever this was by surprise. "Running," she concluded from the sounds. Shortly a middle-aged man appeared running up the little hill in front of her. Then he saw her and stopped short, breathing hard from his run. With his hands on his knees and looking at her, he breathlessly asked, "Santi? Are you Santi?"

She had her sword in her left hand, and slowly she slid it back into its sheath. "Aye, sir. I am Santi."

"I thought so from your colors. Don't see many Santi around these parts. Never mind. You must come with me now. It's a matter of life and death. Come, follow me, it's not too far." He turned around and began running back the way he had come. Fel had no choice but to follow him, but from a safe distance. Shortly, they left the forest and entered a cleared section of farmland. Grape vines grew in long rows across several hills. Far ahead, she saw a homestead; the man was heading for it. She continued to follow him, growing ever more curious.

He looked back several times to make sure she was following, always saying, "Hurry!" At last, near the many homestead buildings; he made straight for his barn. Fel continued to follow him. He got to the door and knocked on it, saying, "It's okay. I'm back. Brought Santi with me." The man's wife cautiously opened the door and saw Fel still mounted on her horse.

"Glory be. She's Santi all right. Miss, come inside quick so we can close the door! Hurry up!"

Now Fel was curious. This did not feel like a trap, so she rode into large barn. Quickly, the woman shut the door and placed the heavy locking timbers into place.

Fel dismounted, and the man said, "This way. Over here. Please help us." Fel followed him into a side stall. There on the soft hay was a woman encased in the same iron devices, as were the women that they'd just rescued from the caverns. "I can't free her. I've tried everything, but failed. You must help her." The young woman looked scared to death and made unintelligible noises from her mouth.

"I've got her cleaned up and tried to feed her something warm and nourishing," his wife explained. "We just can't free her from these metal devices. Please, you must help her."

"I will. We have just freed a dozen women trapped just as she is. Are there more like her? Where did she come from?" Fel asked, examining her for other injuries.

"Early this morning, I spied two of the vile paladins camping out on the edge of my vineyard. I snuck up on them to see what they were up to, expecting to find them stealing my vines. I was shocked to find they had her with them. I listened for a time. They were taunting her about having to live the rest of her life with these evil devices locked on her body. They said they were taking her to join others like her who wouldn't behave. One went off to spy on the road, so I decided to act. I crept up on the one and ran him through with my pitchfork. I waited for a while until the other came back and then ran him through as well. I helped her into the wagon, put the dead men in there too, and brought it here. Wagon's over there. I buried the bodies; now they can feed my grapes. I tried everything I could to free her, but they have melted these devices onto her body. At last, I decided to go for help in Allyende; that's when I ran into you, Miss Santi."

"Fel, name's Fel. You have done well sir. Your new ruler, Jovanna Barcella, has already taken Allyende from the enemy and is riding west on the rim road for the next town. You two ought to visit Allyende and find out the latest news. Meanwhile, I will take her with me at once, get her to safety, and to those that can free her. The land's too rough here to take the wagon, and I can't chance running into the evil ones by myself. So miss, you will need to ride double with me on my horse. Think you can do it?"

The young woman nodded; she would do anything to be free of these horrible devices. "Are you still hungry?" She nodded, so Fel asked the older woman to feed her some more. Next, she helped the woman go to the bathroom. Finally, everyone pitched in to the help the nearly helpless woman up into the saddle. Once that was accomplished, Fel climbed up behind her. The man cautiously opened the door; seeing no one, he opened it wide for Fel to ride out. "Thank you both!" Fel called out and headed back the way that she had come.

While they rode, Fel began chatting to the woman, figuring some semblance of normalcy would help keep the terrified woman calmer. "We rescued twelve who were in far worse shape that you are. We brought along some blacksmiths who were at least able to get the rings out of their mouths. However, they didn't have the right equipment, so I'm told, with which to get their arms free or the devices off their heads. So Jovanna had all the women taken back to safety in Velona, to the main Santi headquarters. There, I'm sure that they will be able to get these horrendous things off the women and heal them. I am positive that Jovanna will want to do the very same thing with you, just as soon as we get back to her camp. That means you will get a safe trip to Velona and be looked after by the best Healers on Tarra." Fel felt the woman begin to relax, and Fel did likewise.

A few hours later, near dusk, Fel rejoined the rim road and shortly rode into the main camp. She made straight for Jovanna's carriage and her group. "Hey guys, little help here please?" she called out.

"Oh no! Not another one!" exclaimed Jovanna, who was nursing her daughter. While Paul and several others helped the woman down off the horse, Aura rushed to get her healing kit. Lilly Ann took Marta from Jovanna, who went to greet the woman.

"Hi, I am Jovanna Barcella. You are now completely safe! Guys, do you think you can get that ring out of her mouth the way the blacksmiths did?" She put her arm around the woman's waist and moved her close to the warm fire. Aura arrived and took charge of her new patient, helped her sit down, and examined her for any obvious signs of injury. Finding nothing major, she then draped several blankets over her so she would stay warm.

Later, after two hours of trying, the men failed to get the abominable ring out of her mouth. Care had to be used so as not to break her teeth. "Okay, it looks like you are going to have to endure this torture a little longer," Jovanna explained, watching the tears flowing down the poor woman's face. She wiped them with her arms. "There, there, it is for just a little while longer. In the morning, I will send you to Velona and the Santi headquarters. There they will be able to free you properly without harming you. A month from now, you will be looking back on all this as just a nightmare. Mine never ends, you see." The woman tried to say something, but it was not intelligible. "Mano del Dio got my hands, but in a little while, you will be just fine. So be brave. I know you can do it." She gave the woman a hug.

Later, Fel gave her a full report. Jovanna said, "I should have expected that we would run across some more imprisoned women, but I didn't. Well done Fel." The next day, the woman seemed to take her rescue in a braver manner, especially the way that everyone looked after her every need and fed her well. She had been half-starved before. Jovanna waved farewell as another wagon took her back eastward to the north spoke road. They would follow the path that the others had taken.

Days passed into weeks. On the average, each day Jovanna's Freedom Fighters retook another town. After reaching close to the border of Velona, they returned to Allyende and went all the way east along this outer rim road. At its end down by the Med Sea, they rode down the coast spoke road to the next rim road and town. From there, they followed that rim road all the way around Barcella to the Med Sea far west of Barcella. Then it was back down that coast road to the next rim road and then along it to the sea on the eastern side of Barcella.

In each town, they captured the blue coats and the priests, usually without a fight. However, those that were left behind to guard against other Holy Paladins riding out into captured territory did indeed see brief combats. Per her orders, none of these blue coats was allowed to escape to warn the Butcher Ali Sanchez safely inside Barcella's walls.

In his meeting room, Ali paced small circles around his table. For nearly a month now, he had no word from his men who were in the outlying towns and villages. True, he had sent messengers from time to time, but they had not returned either. Yet, there were no signs of any open rebellion in the streets of Barcella. Indeed things were calmer than normal, the condition he attributed to the actions of the Mano del Dio, who had been utterly ruthless, before that freak lightning storm had killed several of them.

Still, Bastillo was only a day's ride north. Why hadn't his men returned? He'd given them explicit orders that no matter what they found, they were to return immediately and report in. Three days had passed. They were now overdue. "I'm rapidly running out of men," he calculated. Fewer than five hundred remained within Barcella. Yet, with the calm that had followed the Mano del Dio's trip here several years ago, he had not needed as many men. This he had used to his advantage."

In the early years of his occupation, he lost many men and was forced to ask the Church for as many replacements as he could acquire. After doing that for so many years, the Pope had finally sent the Mano del Dio to find out what was going on here in Barcella and deal with permanently. While Ai found the Mano's methods vastly more brutal than his own, which he though were brutal enough, he had been wrong. They had just needed the utter ruthlessness shown by the Mano to put them into their proper place. The calm had lasted for several years now. Thus, even though he had still lost men, mostly in the outlying areas, though a few had simply disappeared from Barcella itself, he did not feel any need to report those losses.

He reached no conclusion. That afternoon, he took a walk around the city. True, it had far fewer people than when he first arrived, but then so many had moved back out to the outlying towns once they were not needed to defend the walls or to seek their safety. Satisfied that all was utterly quiet within the city, he returned to his mansion headquarters. The next day, he called his staff together, but still the men had not returned. They were two days late now.

"Okay, enough is enough. There must be something going on out there that we are not aware of, not even the citizens of Barcella know what. So I am ordering out five patrols of twenty-five men each. They are to ride to the nearest five towns, see what is going on, and by god they will return here by this time tomorrow night or heads will roll!" He used enough anger to instill some fear into his aides. That way, he knew, they would instill it in these hundred men. He was determined to find answers and find them quickly. His aides rushed to get his orders obeyed. He watched as the five columns rode rapidly out of their garrison and out of the three main city gates. He climbed to his roof top observation post and watched their dust trails settle down, confident that tomorrow night he would know what was going on out there.

The next evening, the Butcher of Barcella was beyond furious. None of the hundred had returned. Now he knew that something had to be out there gobbling up his men. Ali did not tell anyone about the nightmares he had been having for some time now. Only last night is dreams had been particularly gruesome and vivid. He swore that a giant green dragon was out there just waiting, a huge green monster. There were his men riding towards a village. Swish, out of the sky the monster swooped, down upon his men. One man it crushed between its teeth, while two other men were ripped out of their saddles by its enormous claws. Repeatedly, it swooped down until nothing but horses remained and Ali awoke sweating profusely.

Down to his last four hundred men. What could he do? His aides trembled when they got the summons to his office. All knew that the hundred were late, overdue. Each knew that they had drilled into the leaders that they absolutely had to be back before this evening or there would be hell to pay. All had sworn they would not fail, but that was typical of these Holy Paladins. Nervously, the five aides joined and entered the General's office. "Well, they did not return, did they? There is something out there. Now do you believe me?" Ali held back his anger. He wanted to say it's big and green, but dared not.

One aide suggested, "Sir, we cannot afford to send more men out, only four hundred remain within the city. That's way below your specifications. If any disturbance should arise. . ." he did not get to finish his thought. Ali's fist hit the table hard.

"Damn! Don't you think I know that? Listen; here's what we do. You know that we have been under orders to recruit and train local fighters to become Holy Paladins like us. You know my utter contempt for that order, a Sea Prince man will never, ever be a Holy Paladin, a fighter wearing a blue tunic, yes, but not one of us!"

"Yes, we all agreed on that point," another aide volunteered.

"Here's where we demonstrate once and forever that they are worthless swine, disgracing the very tunics that we wear. Call all of them together. Tomorrow, I want all of them to ride forth at dawn. They are to go up the north spoke road to Aldovino, just that far. Check on the town, and then they are to return here. In fact, arm them with the great lances. It'll be good training for them."

Very surprised with this bold move, the aides quickly left to deliver his orders. "Lances, lances for the green monster. This time, you beast, I will have a large surprise for you," he said to himself.

He slept fitfully once more, the green monster ever in his dreams. Yet, he rose in time to see all five hundred Barcella Holy Paladins, lances held high, issuing forth from the northern gate — a proud, gay sight, his men going off to fight the dragon of his dreams. "Let's see you eat all these men, dragon," he said to himself as he watched from his rooftop.

From another tower observation post a mile to the east, Lyle used his far seeing eye to watch this next batch of riders leave. He spoke hastily to his wife, Elsie, who then relayed the communication to Leslie Ann who notified Paul. "Damn, five hundred this time. Well, looks like a real fight," Paul commented. He called a hasty meeting, outlining this bold move of General Ali Sanchez.

"We've got about six hundred volunteers blocking that road, but that is bad odds. We are here on the connecting Rim Road #1, if we ride all day and night, we can come at their rear, assuming that the volunteers can hold them off until we get there."

"What about pulling in the two groups guarding the adjacent spoke roads?" suggested Alyster. "They could get there yet today and reinforce them. Look, by the time that we get there, the battle will be over. Besides we have finished with all the outlying towns yesterday and ought to be making our move on the city today."

"You are right. I was trying so hard to avoid any major battles with Jovanna's volunteers. I guess it's really your choice dear," he looked to Jovanna for guidance.

"Well, we all knew that one day they would have to fight for their freedom. I guess it is today. Really, if we can get into position somehow today, then maybe tomorrow the whole thing will be over."

"Okay, Leslie Ann, get a hold of the captain whose guarding the north spoke road. Let him know the situation and that I suggest laying an ambush. Let him know he will have two other groups of five hundred men joining him later today. He is to delay and hold them off until the others get there. Then, contact the other two captains and have them abandon their positions and ride with all possible haste to meet these five hundred Holy Paladins. Once everything is arranged with that battle, get a hold of the other four groups and let them know to move into position, but not make themselves visible. Tell them to expect the signal just before dawn, assuming we get our forces into position by then. Finally, let James, the Barcella Fortress commander know that we will be arriving by late afternoon as planned."

By late afternoon, Jovanna's main force came in sight of the Santi fortress and the walled city. They had followed along the ancient Centurion paved roadway that paralleled the coastline. They halted just out of sight of the city. It was imperative that those within the city did not know of their existence. Here they waited until darkness hid them. Then, in single file and as quietly as possible, they rode into the Santi main gates.

During the day, the fortress cooks worked overtime, preparing an evening meal not only for their garrison but also for the nearly seven hundred that were expected to arrive just after dark. Once inside and after the many introductions, James took Jovanna and her group to his Great Hall. Meanwhile the troops ate in the mess hall, sharing stories with the Santi fighters, who were keen on hearing all about the last month's adventures.

"Well, we meet again, Jovanna," Mary Beth, the Healer who had saved her life when Lyle and her father had brought her here so many years ago. "You look good!"

"I owe you my life, Mary Beth. Thank you!" she hugged the old Healer. "All of you, I cannot thank you enough for helping me and my father."

"Who would have thought that the poor injured and near death woman that I'd rescued would have ended up becoming a Judger herself and now about to retake Barcella from the butchers of Megalos?" Lyle exclaimed. "So good to see you, Jovanna." He gave her a good hug.

Then he asked the question that he had been waiting a long time to ask her, "Say, Jovanna, is it really true that you have extended the Judger skills to actually control other bodies, physically, I mean? I've heard a lot of talk, but is it so?"

"You want me to demonstrate?" she rolled her eyes playfully, as if she were about to make Lyle's body do something unexpected.

"Whoa, not on me please?" he jovially protested.

"Yes, that is the best way to explain it. I've rather taken our illusions to the next step. However, during this past month, I wish I had the skills of Leslie Ann or Elsie, here. I have to see their bodies. If I could only sense their presence within a building, I believe I could take control that way. So far no luck; I'm just not telepathically inclined."

Jovanna really enjoyed this reunion with those who had risked their lives to save her and her father. However, once the meal was finished, it was time to review their plans. She whispered to Paul, "I'm a bit scared that I am not going to be able to climb that vertical ladder in the dark. How will I ever hold on?"

"Don't worry. I will be supporting your body with mine. If I have to, I will just throw you over my shoulder like a sack and carry you up," he teased her.

"Don't you dare! How undignified," she feigned annoyance. "Seriously, you think that I can do it?"

"Sure, love. Just take your time, no rush. The others will go first and secure the area." She snuggled her head against his shoulders. Now they all rested up for a few hours. At midnight, the action was scheduled to begin.

Lyle went out the main gate of the Santi fortress first. He snuck over to the eastern gate where two men stood guard. He spoke softly and the two men dozed off asleep. Using his lantern, he gave the all clear signal. One by one, with the fortress Santi leading the way, Jovanna's Freedom Fighters and Santi crept along the seashore toward the sleeping city. When they reached the barrier wall, they stepped out into the Med Sea, moved around its edge, and then back onto the shoreline, only now they were within the walls of Barcella. After crossing the public beach, they ducked under the docks. Here was the garbage dump, rotting fish heads and entrails stank horribly, but the Santi whispered orders that they were to breathe through their mouths to avoid the awful smell.

Paul and Jovanna brought up the rear, because she would have to take it very slowly, so as not to lose her balance. Paul's arm was always around her waist, supporting her. Finally, Jovanna had to face that which she feared the most about this whole rebellion: trying to climb the vertical ladder some twenty-five feet straight up in near total darkness. Bravely, she steadied herself with her arms locked on one step and managed to get both her feet on the first rung. That was the easy part. Paul then joined her, with his arms around her body grasping the sides of the ladder. Now she could not fall and could actually lean on him for some balance and support. One step she took and then another. Then, she saw the stars and several strong arms reached down and lifted her up onto the docks. "Thanks!" she whispered.

Once Paul was up, he closed the trap door. Already the Santi were leading her forces in groups of twenty-five to their designated areas within the city. Regimental commander Bartolo Dovino whispered, "I'm ready to raise our flag. With your permission, my Lady?"

"Do it!" she whispered back. When the dawn came, the entire town would wake up to see the enormous flag of Barcella flying at the docks, not the brown one of Megalos! That would give her people some clue as to what was about to happen. Her Circle and attached Guardians plus the Santi Guardians and another twenty-five Santi fighters began to move out through the deserted streets to take up their position. An hour later, after putting six wandering city guards to sleep with their spells, the group ducked into an alleyway not far from the northern wall and gates. Now they waited until dawn came.

Out there in the darkness, she knew that her forces were already on the move. Nearly two thousand volunteers, who had joined up as she retook each town, were riding hard. Their task was critical. By dawn's first light, they had to be visible from the walls of the city and riding toward the city, with their huge sky blue flags with the yellow moons prominently displayed. They had to make General Ali Sanchez believe that they were about to assault the city. In turn, they counted upon his then ordering all available Holy Paladins to man the walls at once. So they waited in the darkness. True, an occasional person, waking on the new morning would come out into the alley and discover their presence. A simple caution was all that was needed to have the person dash back inside quickly, though of course, they would know that something major was brewing!

A lone cock began to crow as dawn's twilight began appearing. "It won't be long now," Jovanna thought to herself, and she took a deep breath. Today was the day that Barcella would be liberated! Soon other cocks took up the call and around the alley; she could hear people begin stirring.

Then a new sound vied for her attention, a most welcome sound indeed. Oh how she wished she could be seeing the view from the walls. She distinctly heard the sound of four trumpets coming from four directions! Louder they grew; now she could hear distant hoof beats. Her volunteers were precisely on time! The late night guards upon the walls began banging the huge gongs, a signal that there was serious trouble brewing. Shortly, she heard bugles sounding from other quarters of the city. That would be the Holy Paladins reacting to the alarm. She hoped that the General would be looking at what was coming and issue his last order to these vile blue coats. Still they waited, crouched in the dark alleyway.

After an eternity of waiting, they finally saw Holy Paladins rushing past the entrance of the alley heading to man the walls beside the northern gate. So far so good. Patience, patience, she kept telling herself. Finally, she heard the shouting of her men outside the walls, riding back and forth, but just out of bow range. Finally, Paul whispered to Leslie Ann and Elsie, "Are you ready?" Both nodded. They concentrated and made the mental connections to four other commanders. Once they finished, Paul gave the signal and their force moved quietly out of the alley and formed ranks facing the northern gates and the walls. The Holy Paladin's backs were to them.

Making sure that all bows were drawn, Jovanna spoke, timing her words with the soft chants of the other Judgers. "You are completely surrounded. Throw down your weapons and surrender, and you will not be harmed." The startled fighters whirled around only to see hundreds upon hundreds of rebels pointing bows and arrows directly at them. In truth, there were less than fifty in Jovanna's immediate area. All the rest she had sent to make sure the other groups could greatly outnumber the blue coats on the walls. While the Holy Paladins had the distinct advantage of height, the arrows eliminated it. Jovanna kept her eyes on the men who ought to be the leaders, their tunic markings were slightly different.

One man called out, "Attack these rebels!" He made a lunge for the steps. Jovanna concentrated on him. He suddenly dropped his sword. To the dismay of his men who were attempting to follow him, he then raised his arms, as if surrendering. He tried to say something, but his mouth would not open. Then, like a puppet, his legs began stepping down toward her fighters. On their far flanks, two groups of twenty-five men began to rush down the steps to fight the rebels. Instantly, two walls of flames blocked their descent, terrifying the men who halted and then ran back up to their original positions completely confused about what action to take.

Still not a single projectile had been fired. In front of her, this first leader was grabbed and quickly tied up. She repeated her words, and finally one by one, the Holy Paladins dropped their swords and stepped down off the walls. As soon as they were close enough, the Santi and her volunteers tied these men up. In ten minutes, it was over here at the northern gates. Paul opened the gates wide, the signal for the two thousand outside to charge triumphantly into the city, guaranteeing that all additional resistance, should any materialize, would be swiftly handled.

Jovanna and her group climbed up onto the walls, hoping to catch a glimpse of what was happening elsewhere along the walls. She was most concerned with the safety of her volunteers. Unfortunately, little could be seen. Elsie, however, was in contact with James, who was on the roof of his tower, watching everything with the far seeing eye. Elsie reported to Jovanna, "James says that all have surrendered. A slight battle took place at the western gate. Only a few of your men were hurt."

"Okay, let's march these into the central plaza to await the wagons. Now we must find the General and his staff, and then the nasty priests must be flushed out," Jovanna ordered. By the time they marched their group of prisoners to the plaza, several other groups had already brought theirs and were standing guard over them. As soon as they saw Jovanna and her group, they began wildly shouting and cheering! Jovanna waved her short arms their way, and they yelled even louder.

"Follow me," Jovanna said, "I'll lead you by the shortest way to the mansion that the General has been using." Her group then marched through the streets toward said mansion. However, now the local inhabitants began coming outside to see what was going on; slowly they began to grasp that Barcella had just been liberated. Many began rushing to the plaza to see if it was true; the rumors began flying rampantly.

"Here we are at last," Lyle said as they stopped before the largest mansion in Barcella, a huge estate that used to belong to the wealthiest noble family in the city. They were long dead, of course. Already several hundred of her freedom fighters had arrived, encircling the estate, staying well outside the wrought iron fence that surrounded the mansion grounds. Lyle explained, "The main building there, the one with the tallest building, that's where he stays. I've often seen him up on the roof watching his men leave the city."

Leslie Ann and Elsie conferred, and Elsie said, "We believe that there are six people inside the mansion."

"Okay, let's go get them," Paul ordered. Slowly, on the lookout for crossbows being fired out the windows, they advanced, Paul in front of Jovanna. They reached the front door. Paul tried to open it, while several pointed bows at the door in case someone tried a quick shot. "Locked," he said. "Break it down!"

Several of the larger men smashed their shoulders into the door until it gave way and they fell inside. Five men raised their hands, "We give up. Don't shoot."

"Those are his aides," Lyle recognized them from his frequent spying on the General. So did Jovanna.

It was rather like deja vu for Jovanna. "I know this place like my own home. I spent ten years being a maid here. He is likely in the upper planning room. Come on." She marched in even before Paul could stop her. He was forced to follow her as she walked down the hall and up the stairs. She stopped by one door. "Okay, General Ali Sanchez, I will take your surrender now. Open up. Don't make this harder than it needs to be."

Paul reached her back, sword drawn, but he couldn't get in front of her. Lyle and the rest of her group were right behind him. The door opened,

Ali Sanchez stood before her, sword in his hand, glaring at whoever was addressing him. He gasped, "You!"

"Yes, me. I am now the sole ruler of Barcella, and you, sir, are under arrest for crimes too numerous to mention against the citizens of my country. Surrender your weapon immediately."

"Bitch!" and he began to swing the sword towards her neck. Paul was powerless to stop it.

Half way through his swing, his arm stopped of its own volition. He stared at his motionless arm and watched his fingers loosen their grip, and the sword drop harmlessly onto the floor. "Much better, General. Now you will follow me outside," Jovanna ordered.

Try as he might, he could not get his legs to do otherwise than ordered. "Impressive!" Lyle whispered to Lilly Ann, unsure whether voices would disturb Jovanna. Lilly Ann grinned.

Jovanna marched the Butcher of Barcella out of the mansion and made him stand before the hundreds of her freedom fighters. As soon as they saw the two of them, they began wildly yelling and cheering her, while jeering this most feared man. "Tie him up and take him to the plaza, please," she ordered. "Now we have to go flush out all their evil priests. How many churches are there to cleanse?"

"Ma'am, we've already rounded them up, pulled them out of their beds in most cases. One hundred or there abouts. All nicely tied up with the blue coats," regimental commander Bartolo Dovino advised her.

"Then it's officially done?" Jovanna asked. "Nothing else to conquer yet?" She began to feel a let down from the month long excitement of the chase.

"No ma'am, the city is secure, though everyone is wondering what has just happened. Our lads have been spreading the word, but it's still a bit chaotic in the streets."

"Well, then, I'll let you get the wagons rounded up. Load the prisoners as quickly as possible."

Lyle interrupted her, "I have a better idea. Let's put them in the hold of our caravel docked at our fortress pier. We can send them to Isla Roca faster that way and without using so many men and any possibility of mass escape."

"Well that does sound an awful lot better. Do it. Oh, we forgot the Nunnery and any women trapped in there," Jovanna suddenly remembered.

"Already taken care of by our fortress women. As soon as the walls fell, they headed there to free any that were trapped. The nuns have been taken as well. I believe that they are with the others in the plaza," Lyle explained. "The Scholastic University was also visited and the teachers rounded up. Most likely, Jenna will send the nuns and the teachers back to Megalos."

"Okay, then is there anything left to secure?" she asked.

"Nope. Impressive, casualty figures are just now coming in from the skirmishes along the western gate walls. Ten of your men took relatively minor wounds. Mary Beth will be looking after them. One sector conquered without losing a single freedom fighter, well, I guess we don't yet know about those five hundred blue coats that rode north yesterday. I may be speaking too soon. Still, it is an impressive feat, Jovanna!"

She smiled, "Thanks, Lyle. I never thought I would be doing this, but we all did it. Amazing. Now comes the really hard part, trying to get this country back on its feet."

"I expect you should address everyone soon," Lilly Ann reminded her, "before too many rumors take a life of their own."

"I guess this porch here is as good a place as any. Quite a lot of folks can stand out there on the lawn," Jovanna decided.

Bartolo issued an order, and soon a huge flag of Barcella draped from the second story windows, covering a large section of the front wall. "Well done, I love it!" she admired his idea. "Send forth the word to all sections of the city. I will address them about a thousand at a time here on the lawn. I'll repeat the speech every half hour for the rest of the day; that way hopefully everyone can get a chance to hear me firsthand. I can quell the rumor lines before they get out of control."

Just then, one of the Santi women brought Marta to Jovanna, "She's hungry if you can take the time."

"Great, Julini, thanks for watching her. Yes, now is a perfect time. Let me sit down and lean back against this column, and then give her to me." Paul steadied her as she sat down and leaned back; he also loosened her dress so Marta could nurse easily. Julini carefully placed the little girl onto Jovanna's chest, as Jovanna's arms cradled her babe.

"I'll wait on her and take her when you are done. I expect that you are going to be awfully busy this afternoon." The two chatted about how well Marta had behaved herself.

While everyone was carrying out other related actions, including rustling up some food and drink, Anna Fellini, the ex-Sisterhood group leader, now the Garrison Commander, led a group of fifteen ill clothed women up to Jovanna. "Ma'am," Anna saluted her, "these are the women that were imprisoned in the Nunnery. All had been forced to wear those diabolical devices. We've freed them. However, they all wanted to come and thank you personally. Honestly, Jovanna, they were brutally mistreated, if you want my opinion. Ladies, this is your benefactor and the new ruler of Barcella, Jovanna Barcella Wilkins."

"One young woman rushed closer to Jovanna and began, "Words cannot describe how utterly grateful we all are for your rescuing us! Oh!" she gave a startled cry as Jovanna pivoted around so she could better see this young victim. The woman saw the short arms for the first time. All fifteen gasped and some began crying.

Jovanna merely said, "Mano del Dio did it to me a number of years ago. Hasn't stopped me yet. Pray finish what you wanted to tell me."

"It, it, I mean, it pales compared to what you have endured and must endure every day," she said completely unable to express her thoughts. "I was going to say that we were forced to wear those horrid metal constraints. We were completely, utterly helpless. It was so horrible. Yet we knew that if we didn't obey, they would pour metal into the locks and force us to be like that for the rest of our lives. We know of several who had that happen to them, and they were taken away to some place in the far north. We all wanted to say, but now it seems foolish of us," she looked at her companions who had endured this torture with her. "I guess I'll say it anyway. We thought you wouldn't know just how horrible it was to be so helpless, confined in those devices, so humiliating, so awful. We wanted you to know how much we had suffered. But now what we endured is like nothing compared to you, Jovanna. I don't know what to say except that we all feel so deeply sorry for you. At least we fifteen know what it's like to be so, well so like you are now every day."

"Thanks for going out of your way to come to me and tell me. Rest assured that those women you spoke of, they were the very first ones we rescued, over a month ago now. I sent them all back to the main Santi headquarters in Velona. We couldn't get those foul devices off them, so I'm sure they can back in the big city where they have all the proper tools to do the job. Plus, I wanted them to have the very best healing on Tarra. All were alive and as well as could be expected. Yes, I can relate easily to what you fifteen have been through. At times, it can be a darn nuisance. I can barely hold my own baby. But it could have been worse; I might not have even had these little arms. I'm told that some poor women in Zargarb lost both their arms completely. Now that has got to be even worse." Jovanna figured that about wrapped up what these women wished to say.

She was wrong. The woman looked at the others whispering something and most nodded their agreement. "My Lady, we all suffered horribly together, and we formed a bond between ourselves. When we were alone in our rooms and able to speak, we all swore that if we could ever get free of those devices and get out of that horrible place, we would band together and help other women who have been mistreated. I, we, well, we wonder, are you really going to be the ruler of Barcella?"

"Yes, it is my birthright, and with tons of help from my friends, I have at last liberated our country from the southern barbarians. So yes, I'm your new ruler. I will be giving everyone a speech here on the lawn every half hour starting pretty soon."

The women looked at each other and nodded, "We would like to offer our services to you, Jovanna. You could certainly use the help, and we kind of figured that you would know if there are other mistreated women around the country that we could help. Please, it is all that we really have left that we can contribute."

As far as Jovanna was concerned, she had said the magic word, the one word that meant everything to Jovanna, contribute. "Ladies, I would welcome you as my staff. While I am able now to make a bed, it just takes me so darn long it's not funny. Plus no way can I cook anything. I am not sure where Paul and I will take up residence, but we would love to have you as our domestic staff."

"Honey," Paul interrupted, "I've decided that we are going to take this here estate as our place. We need the space for all your many visitors, and besides, it is now vacant, and its prior owners were long ago slain by the men we've arrested today. That is, if it meets with your approval, and you don't have nightmares about living in the house that you used to work in, bad memories and all that. We can also protect you better here."

"Well, then ladies, you heard him. I guess this will be our new residence. It's fine with me, Paul. Really, the memories I have are actually good ones. Remember, I eavesdropped on all his plans and relayed them to the underground. Really it's okay with me. I rather like the open spaces here. Marta will have many places to play when she is older. Aura, can you take our new staff here inside?" To the women she added, "Aura is our Guardian Healer. Make sure that none needs any medical attention after their ordeal. See if you can find some decent clothing and get them a bath. It's the third door on the right as you enter. Thank you all for your kindness." Fifteen women held their heads high as they walked inside, following Aura.

Julini took Marta and went inside as well. Since people were beginning to arrive, men, women, and their children, Paul issued orders for the freedom fighters to welcome everyone and help get them ordered so as many could hear Jovanna at one time as possible. Paul whispered to Jovanna, "You know, they are going to want to know how to address you and also me. Are you going to be called Queen Jovanna or what?"

You are right, Paul, as usual. I certainly don't want us to be called king and queen, not unless you want to be called King Paul," she teased him, knowing perfectly well that he hated it.

"No way!" he feigned alarm.

"You know, I've thought a lot about that, and I think I will take my cue from Roberto of all people. Ah, look at the crowd now. I guess I'd better get going; this is going to be a very long afternoon."

She stood up, with Paul's help, and walked to the edge of the porch. She raised her short arms in the air. Immediately, her freedom fighters began wildly yelling and cheering her, and the crowd of people joined in with them. After she lowered them and the noise settled down, she began her first speech of the afternoon.

"Ladies, gentleman, children of Barcella, this day, July 16, is our independence day, the day that I, with the help of my friends, the volunteer freedom fighters, and the Santi, have at last driven the barbarians of the south out of our land forever." More cheers followed. "Long have I fought for this day. While I know some of you, most I do not. I am Jovanna Barcella Wilkins, recently married, and have a year old daughter. I'm the last of the line of our founder, Ruggiero Barcella. It is a proud day that I take over the sole rule of our country. My father, Genorio, rescued the official pendant of office that I now wear proudly. I wish he were alive to witness this day, so too my brother who was the last priest of Tur. Long had we been leading the resistance against our overlords. He paid with his head; I, with my arms. Most of you have also suffered greatly, lost loved ones, been tortured and brutalized by the foul, evil men from Megalos."

"Today, that has all ended. Yes, losing one's arms as I have can throw one into the depths of depression and total helplessness, total uselessness. Yet, I refused to be cast out of the game of life! I fought back as I could. I learned from the Santi del Dio. Now, I am both an honored member of the Santi del Dio, but also one of their highly trained Guardians. I will always be Santi, but now I am also your ruler. As your ruler, I want you to know that my goal is to help our country and every one of you achieve undreamed prosperity. Know this, the Santi del Dio will back me up and will lend us any aid that we need to survive and grow. We do not stand alone, we stand with the Santi del Dio and Velona and Fortress d'Grange totally behind us, ready to back us up in any way possible."

"Right here at the very beginning, I want you all to know that I make the rules, decisions, and laws that govern our country, not the Santi. We are and always will be Barcellans!" Again, the crowd cheered loudly.

"I want you all to know that I will rule totally unlike anything you have seen or experienced in the past. I have a completely open door policy; anyone can come and talk to me about anything and I promise that I will listen and take what action I deem appropriate. Already, I have told this to all the people in our outlying towns and villages, for I have spent the past month liberating every one of them. I took the time to meet with each one who wanted to meet with me personally, and I will visit each town at least twice a year just to find out how they are doing. Here, however, there are thousands of you, so if you want to meet with me, realize that it may take me many days to get to everyone. I will get to you, I promise."

"Just so we are clear, I alone will make the decisions. Yet, I always will have an open door policy so that you can let me know your opinions, feelings, and ideas. It will have to literally be an open door policy — no hands!" she said with her usual broad grin, raising her short arms. A few chuckled and then, the others seeing her continue to grin joined the laughter. "It will fall to my husband, Paul here, to see that the decisions are enforced. He is my hands, along with my dear friends, whom I cannot do without. Come up here so I can introduce you all properly." Paul, Leslie Ann, Aura, Alaric, and Alyster stood beside her and were presented to the crowd.

"In closing, I have to keep this first speech short because the entire city wants to hear it. First, how are you to address Paul and me? I wish to be called Lady Jovanna. One of our few remaining young noblemen fought in the resistance movement until his sister was taken and permanently encased in those devilish metal devices and sent to live a life worse than a dog up in the northern caves. Unable to rescue her on his own, he came to Velona and found me. It was his encouragement plus his skill that allow me to raise enough of our people living in exile in Velona to begin our battles to retake Barcella. It is in his honor that I wish to be known only as Lady Jovanna. Paul wishes to be addressed merely as Sir or Sire."

"Second, when you return to your homes today, I want you to meet with others who live in your block. Elect one to be your representative to me. Have your representative come here two days from now armed with two things. One, how many people live in your block? Two, what do you need most? I do not know the actual situation here in our city. Are we short of food? Blankets? In two days, I will begin to meet regularly with your representatives to figure out what we most desperately need and see that those needs are met. Will you do this?" As expected, the crowd yelled that they would and clapped for some time. Jovanna signaled Bartolo to have his men escort this bunch out, while letting the next group onto the grounds. He had cleverly arranged for the side gate to be used as the exit. Jovanna was pleased with his initiative and its execution.

She gave roughly the same speech twenty more times that day, though not everyone in the city actually was able to hear it. Now the real work would begin.

Just after sundown, Jovanna and her group finally headed inside. Every lantern in the huge mansion was lit. Aura and the fifteen women had not been idle. While the women's arms were very weak from their long ordeal encased in the metal restraints, still they were determined. Aura found only minor health problems and quickly attended to them. Thus, when the rest of the group entered at dusk, the aroma of dinner greeted their noses. The dining room was huge and could seat fifty. However, the women had set places for Jovanna's group, not themselves.

"Thank you all for fixing supper. Say, where are your places?" she asked.

"Oh, we figured you would want us to eat in the servant's area," the woman who had spoken for the group replied timidly.

"I hate that word, servant. You are not subservient or second-class people. You are our domestic staff. Go get all the others; bring your plates out here. Around here, we all eat together and share stories. You are going to be part of my group, and I won't have you treated any differently." Quite surprised at this unexpected idea, she hastened to fetch the others, who rather timidly entered with their plates and cups.

While Paul fed the two of them, Marta was awake and sitting on her mother's lap, watching everybody. Jovanna asked, "So do you have families? Married? Children of your own?" She was addressing the fifteen volunteers.

"My name is Alessandra, my Lady. I used to have a seamstress shop. I used to make the finest dresses for the noble women. I learned from my mother, but that all ended when I was fifteen and the barbarians came. If I may be so bold, we've all rather have our own skills. I would like to be your personal assistant, dress you, comb your hair, look after your personal needs, along with making you some fabulous dresses. You have such a fine figure, you know."

"Normally, I wear these so I can get into and out of them, but I admit, it would be really nice to be able to wear fine looking clothes, that is, if you don't mind helping me that much. I hate to put such a burden on you for so vain a thing as a dress."

"My Lady, we, all of us, we do know what it's like to be as you are. Please, it is no burden," Alessandra replied sincerely.

"Francesca here, she is the best cook. We think she ought to be in charge of the kitchen. Vanna used to work at an inn and knows where to find most anything from food to cloths to needles. We don't know if her husband still lives. If he does, she would like to return home at night, but she will come each day and be our purser, rather like the head steward on one of our ships. Carmina, Bella, and Celeste, they used to be maids at some inns. They want to look after your beds, linens, and such. Donatella used to be a gardener, growing vegetables and flowers to sell in the markets. She believes that with so much space around here, you could have a large garden. The rest will scrub and clean, and do anything else you might ask of them. We promise to always be your hands."

"Excellent, well done all of you. Alessandra, you will be my Chief of Staff in addition to your other duties. Can I ask you all something? I can't help but notice that you are having some trouble with the silverware."

Aura spoke up, "It's their arms, Jovanna; they are very weak after being so constrained for so long. If we were back at Jenna's estate, I would recommend taking long, warm baths and having someone massage their arms several times a day. That coupled with a gradient of exercise ought to heal them up fine."

"I'm sorry, ladies. I forgot that you have only just been freed. Say, there ought to be a large bath just behind this building. The general never used it much. After dinner, Alyster, go check it out and see if it can be made operational. We need to get our staff following Aura's suggestions."

"You bet. Alyster and I already planned to survey the whole complex by lantern light right after dinner. This sure is a huge estate. It's got lots of possibilities."

"Thanks. Tomorrow morning first thing after breakfast, I will send an escort with each of you so you can go back to your homes and see what remains. Getting your lives back into some semblance of order comes first."

Just then, Anna Fellini entered. "Lady Jovanna, Anna reporting in. I have two hundred Santi fighters now camped around your estate for the night. We don't expect any trouble, but we are pledged to make sure that you are safe here, until you all get organized. Will there be anything else my Lady?"

"Yes, Anna, you don't have to be so formal around me. Just Jovanna will do. And thanks for watching our backs, though I too don't think that there will be any trouble, unless we missed some of the Mano del Dio assassins."

"Yes ma'am, that's what James is worried about, assassins. Give a holler, Jovanna if you want something." She left with a smile.

At eight that night, Alyster came inside to find Jovanna, who was just finishing putting Marta to bed. "Great news, I got the bath going, water's fairly warm. What say we all indulge ourselves? We've not had a bath for a month now."

"Yahoo!" exclaimed Leslie Ann. "I'll go fetch all the towels and wash rags from the wagon. Aura, you get all the staff. Jovanna, you get everyone else. Hit the hot tub everybody. Way to go Alyster!"

Ten minutes later, we all entered the large bathhouse. Leslie Ann brought piles of towels, and everyone peeled off their soiled clothing. Paul helped Jovanna and the two stepped into the warm waters. The fifteen staff needed a bit of help with their clothes; Jovanna could now see just how stiff and painful it was for them to move their arms. "Gang, I'm not going to be much use giving these women their massages, so I leave it to you." Quickly, everyone chose one of our new staff to assist. Aura demonstrated the proper technique that she wanted followed.

They quickly discovered just how much these victimized women needed the physical therapy. Jovanna began to wonder just how the others who were sent to Velona were faring. She promised herself to make very sure that these were well healed before asking them to do any heavy work.

The next morning, Anna and her group of fighters, all ex-Sisterhood, accompanied the fifteen to their homes. Meanwhile, Jovanna and her group toured their new home. The main house was three stories tall with over twenty rooms. The bathhouse lay behind the main house. Off to the side was the cook and pantry building, complete with several baking ovens. On the south side, two guest cottages stood, which could sleep ten each. To the north lay a large barn with hay mow and an adjoining stable, capable of holding a carriage and at least thirty horses. All told, the overall shape of the estate was about four city blocks on each side, huge.

Lyle showed up midmorning along with a large work crew and ten wagons loaded with supplies and equipment. Jovanna was kept busy just answering questions of what she wanted where. His plan was by nightfall, the place would be made comfortable and livable. He knew that she would have her hands full with the upcoming meetings.

Shortly before noon, a small group of young boys wandered up her long cobblestone drive. The taller boy walked up to Jovanna and timidly asked, "Yesterday, did you mean that we can some see you whenever we want, Lady Jovanna?"

She moved closer to him and said, "You bet. What's up?"

"Well, we, I mean all us boys, some didn't think we would be allowed in here, we would really like our park back so we can play ball again."

"What happened to your park?" she asked wondering where and what.

"The new soldiers, the ones that left here a few days ago going north, they took away our park and put up shanty buildings to live in. Since they are gone, can we have our park back?"

"You bet you can have it back. Let me see if I can send some workers to get rid of those shanty buildings this afternoon. Would that be all right with you fellows?"

"Oh yes!" he exclaimed, and ran off to tell the others.

"What was that all about?" asked Lyle, who had seen her chatting with the boy. Jovanna explained and Lyle sent word for some more Santi workers to deal with removing the hastily built housing.

"I wish all our problems were that easy to solve," she teased Lyle. He grinned; he did not envy her, come tomorrow.

Early that afternoon Alessandra returned; she had been crying. Jovanna took her inside to a quiet corner. Putting her arm on the young woman's shoulder, she asked, "What happened?"

"My husband is dead; my shop was looted. I have nothing to go back to anymore." She leaned over had hugged Jovanna, crying on her shoulder. For a time, Jovanna just patted her with her arm and said nothing.

When she stopped crying, Jovanna said, "Alessandra, you now have a new home here to come back to. We can support each other."

"Thank you," she whimpered sincerely, "you who have lost so much and yet you have so much to give. Thank you, I will work hard to repay such kindness to others."

"That would be a fabulous repayment. Now why don't you go upstairs and fix up your room next to ours? Paul and I are in the last one on the left. Why don't you take the one opposite us? That way, if I need anything at night, you're close at hand." Alessandra gave her a loving hug, wiped her eyes, and went to find the room.

Sometime later, Alessandra came down stairs looking for Jovanna. "Jovanna, you must come with me. I have found something in my closet that I no longer have the strength in my arms to open. Perhaps you can bring Paul?"

Shortly, the three entered the bedroom, which was going to be Alessandra's. "I found the chest in the closet. I'm afraid my arms are still too weak to open it or move it." It was a very large chest, over four feet long, three feet wide, and three feet deep. It had a heavy latch on it, but was not locked. Paul attempted to move the chest out into the room so they could see better, but was unable to budge it.

"Weird, this thing is heavy! Maybe it's fastened to the floor." He struggled with the heavy latch, which finally yielded. He lifted the lid. "Wow! Will you look at this?"

Both women peered over his shoulder into the chest. Neatly stacked were thousands of gold coins, heavy sacks filled with gemstones, various pieces of jewelry lay strewn over the top of the loot. "I'll give you two guesses where this all came from," Paul said. "Roberto said that they killed all the nobles; guess they also took all of their wealth."

"Well, the nobles got it off the backs of the working men and women of Barcella, so it rightfully belongs to us to use to help everyone get back on their feet economically once more. This is the best news I have had in a long time. I was so worried about how we could possibly finance everything that must be done here so quickly. Now I have the means of exchange," Jovanna explained.

"You will use it to help all of our people and not keep it for yourselves?" Alessandra asked, in disbelief. "I am so used to people taking, never giving. Are you not gods?"

"No, not gods, we just try to do what is right and just. Using this to help everyone get back going again, I could not think of any better use for it. Can you?"

"No, my Lady, no." Alessandra gave her another hug, whispering, "Thank you," in her ear.

"I'd better get some help and get this out of your closet, Alessandra, or you won't have any room for your clothes," Paul teased.

At the evening meal, the staff situation report was discussed. Donatella and Vanna both had no other living family members left. Thus, Jovanna gave them permanent homes at her estate, joining Alessandra. Further, all were ordered to continue getting daily massages and only to do light work, until their strength returned.

The next day proved illuminating for Jovanna. Indeed, during the first week, information continued to arrive, particularly from the alcalde of the outlying towns and villages. She followed the Judger's advice and only collected data the first week. The statistics were grim indeed.

Before the Centurion invasion, Barcella's population was a little over two hundred thousand. Today, twenty-five thousand lived in the outlying towns, but only thirty thousand lived in the city itself, a drastic reduction. Many had fled to Velona and Jovanna held out hope that some of those might choose to return to their homeland once she had the situation under control.

The noble houses were gone, compliments of the Mano del Dio and their reign of terror. Still, Jovanna held out some hope that there were others scattered around like Roberto Peña. The shipping industry, the lifeblood of the Sea Princes, was in a complete shambles. Only twelve old style boats remained, and the only contracts they could get were hauling ore and coal for Megalos far down in the Southlands. The city depended upon shipments of goods from other sectors now. Life in Barcella was at the barest subsistence level.

Saturday night, with the last of the data in, she could do nothing but cry on Paul's shoulders. "Everything is gone! Destroyed. No ships, no industry, no nothing. This is utterly hopeless," she sobbed. Paul could handle a good fight, but he could not handle the mess in which he now found himself. Two thirds of all the city buildings lay empty. The euphoria of finally becoming free of the hated overlords had dissipated, leaning stark reality facing everyone.

Alessandra heard Jovanna crying and came to see what was wrong. "My Lady, is everything all right?" She sounded very worried.

"Oh Alessandra, I don't know what I can do. It is so hopeless, everything is gone, nobles, ships, industry, all gone. We have a quarter of the people we used to have. It is so hopeless," Jovanna confided in her. Just then, Marta insisted on being fed. After Alessandra changed the diapers and Paul aided Jovanna to get ready, Alessandra set the little girl down onto Jovanna's chest.

"Oh do my arms ever ache tonight," she said as she stood back up. "I thought everything would be back to normal once I got freed from the devices. Now I ache all the time, a constant reminder."

"Let me see what I can do about it," Paul offered, having nothing else to do for his wife right now. He began massaging her arms, relieving the pain a good deal.

"I don't know how you could ever have recovered from your ordeal, Jovanna. It's just horrible what they did to you. I mean we were so utterly, completely helpless. We just can't do anything for ourselves without our arms. I am so grateful to be free of that horrid thing, even if my arms hurt so. But you, you are in prison all the time; it seems to me, Jovanna, there is no escaping it ever for you. I cannot even imagine how horrid it must be for you," Alessandra attempted to console her.

Feeding Marta and hearing Alessandra's outpouring of emotions, Jovanna calmed down. She sighed, "I did feel helpless and hopeless at first. Where there is a will, there is a way. I have just had to find new ways to do the simple things of life, that's all there is to it. True, I now must depend upon others for some things that would take me an impossibly long time to do now, like cooking and sewing. I spent my efforts at learning to do things with which I can in return help others. I think I learned that one must be able to both accept help and to give help. Once I accepted that and really set to work on finding ways that I could help others, receiving help no longer bothered me."

"Say, that's the answer for Barcella! We are all in the same boat. We all feel helpless and darn useless at this point. No economy, no food, no nothing, we are all scraping the bottom of the barrel. Help is the answer. Alessandra you did it, you showed me the way out of this mess our country is in! I could just hug you!"

Paul didn't follow her exactly, but welcomed her dramatic mood change. Neither did Alessandra, for that matter. "Look, you are just now recovering from your ordeal; your arms are stiff and sore and you cannot do much heavy work and are getting some help from Paul, the massage, which is helping, right?" She nodded, very much enjoying the massage. "That's you receiving the help you need right now. At the same time you gave me the help that I needed, because you helped me see the way I can get our country out of this mess."

"But really I did nothing, except talk to you. Paul is doing something with my arms," she looked confused.

"You are getting the actual help that you need, and you gave me the kind of help that I needed. Who cares what the details of that help might be, only that it was what I needed and what you needed."

"I am beginning to see," she replied,

"Me to," Paul added.

"I have to go find Leslie Ann right now. No, I can manage Marta still. You keep on getting her arms back in shape." Jovanna carefully got up, holding Marta securely and headed for the door, kicking it open. "Sure glad Lyle got the doorknobs removed." She returned looking very pleased. Leslie Ann carried Marta, tucking her into the crib.

The next day, just after breakfast, Jovanna outlined her grand plan to everyone and drilled them on what she needed them to do. "Also, see if you can find thirty people who would like to become message delivers to the outlying towns and villages. I need a Ruler's Messenger Service. I can drill them on what message I want delivered, and they can ride to their town and deliver it, get the responses and such written down, and bring them back here. They need to enjoy riding a lot, can read and write, and enjoy talking with people."

That day, she sent out fifty groups to cover the city, armed with pen and ink. Paul, Leslie Ann, and Paul went together as one of the groups, heading for the main shipping district, or rather what was left of it.

When she got to the largest shipping company, she asked them to go fetch all the others in the city who also handled shipping, four other smaller ones. A half hour later, Jovanna and her group sat at their largest meeting table, facing twenty men who now handled the scheduling, control, and planning for all the meager shipping of Barcella. "Gentlemen, glad that you all could spare me some time today. First, let me explain what I am doing throughout the entire sector." She spent a good five minutes describing her help system.

"Now, if any of you wish to help in some other way than you currently are, such a opening up a blacksmith shop or whatever, let me know before I get started on shipping." None wanted to switch occupations. "Okay, then gentlemen, here we go. I have arranged for ten brand new caravels to be delivered to us later on this year."

She had to pause for all the excited cheers, yes's, and "it's about times" that flew around the room. One then asked, "Who's making them? How are we to pay for them? What strings are attacked?" Many others nodded, agreeing with these vital questions.

"Velona is making them. The strings are we must send them ten crews of seven men or women to get hands on training with their ships so the crews are ready to man the new caravels after they come off the assembly line in Velona. I paid for them personally; they belong now to the city as a group. The harbor master and shippers of Velona will be contacting you shortly to begin to line up jobs for the caravels to handle just as soon as the new ships are operational. Your job is to continue to coordinate the activities, find us the crews, and carry on a profitable shipping trade."

"This is just incredible news! You bought ten of them! That must have cost you a fortune. Gentlemen, Barcella is at long last back into the shipping industry!" exclaimed Alfio Visa, who ran the currently largest shipping company.

"It's a miracle," added another man.

"And you are relinquishing ownership of them?" asked a third.

"Yes, as long as you ship other cargo that will be requested of you by many others in our sector. As we speak and over the next few weeks, many people will want to get their current businesses going full speed or will want to get some new enterprise started. They will be asking for various supplies to be sent or received. It will be your top priority to get our people's needs serviced first, before accepting other land's requests. As long as you do that, the ships are yours to command. Until they are on-line, Velona will help you coordinate getting what our people need shipped in and their products delivered."

"Well, that is certainly fair. Our people ought to come first," Alfio declared. "However, this is going to create one large, massive coordination problem," he cautioned. "If I understand what you are doing, Lady Jovanna, then we can expect to see thousands of small orders and requests coming in within the next few weeks."

Jovanna grinned, thinking to herself, "Observant, wise old man." She explained, "Yes, maybe even tens of thousands of small requests. So how do we best handle that? This is the main reason for this meeting. Let me be the first to admit that I know nothing at all about your jobs and how to accomplish this, so I need your help. Here is where the turn-about in help begins. I've just helped you, now you have to help others. How are we to handle this expected in rush of requests and deal with them in a cost effective and timely manner?"

Now the discussion began in earnest. Ideas flew. Rapidly it became apparent that this task of coordinating so many small requests would be more than a full time job. Slowly, they all agreed upon what this new job would have to do for them, combine the smaller requests into a large package that these men could then schedule and get handled, since they usually dealt with large shipments. Many smaller orders would have to be combined into a larger one. It became apparent that warehouses would be needed in which to store up similar shipping requests, bundling them into a larger package. In reverse, when the larger shipment arrived, it would then need to be broken down into smaller packages and those delivered.

Near lunchtime, Benigo Venuto, a smaller shipper, declared, "You know, this new job appeals to me. I've always wanted my own business, and I think that I would really like to handle this coordination project. Lady Jovanna, is it too late for me to switch?"

"Not at all, great!" she replied. "You'll need some warehouses, and we've got plenty that are empty and idle now. So pick some close to the docks that will serve your needs best, hire the staff you need. I will begin letting the others know to send their shipping requests to you, Benigo Venuto. I suspect that by the end of the week you will have lots to do. As soon as you have enough, route the combined request up to these here, and they will coordinate with Velona to get it handled quickly. Elona Po has graciously told her shippers to expedite all our requests, until we get our own ships."

"Wow! I am excited about this," Benigo replied. "I'd shake your hand in thanks, but er," he faltered. A handshake was the customary sign of a closed deal.

"I have no hands to shake," she teased and finished his sentence. "That does not mean we cannot shake though." She got up, walked over to him, and offered him her arm. He clasped it between his hands and they shook. Not to be left out, the others also shook, respectfully closing all that had been agreed upon at the meeting.

"I see what you mean by reciprocal help," Alfio commented as the others began filing out, heading off for lunch. "If everyone is honest with this, we cannot fail. In fact, I must talk to my wife about this, say even my sons. If everyone gives what they can and gets what they need, how can we fail? Thank you Lady Jovanna!"

The trio rode their coach back to their estate for lunch and Marta. That afternoon, she met with her volunteer soldiers and their many leaders, including Bartolo Dovino. Once more, she outlined her reciprocal help plans, before launching into the more significant aspects.

"Gentlemen, Barcella needs a security defensive force to protect our borders with Vito. I propose that we follow Velona's lead and build a line of interconnected stone fortresses along our border with Vito. I have the necessary funds to begin their construction at once. We will need a defensive force to man them and patrol our borders. I want every soldier to be mounted. Further, the job of soldiering should pay well and be a respected occupation here in Barcella. We all know how the enforced soldiering of the walls in the past has failed utterly. Hastily called up men are ill-trained and have no idea what is needed and wanted from them. They are merely cavalry fodder. No, this time we want skilled men who know what they are doing and why. They must be competent and able to think what's best for the good of us all."

"However, you were, after all, a volunteer force. Now that we have our land back, you are free to return to your homes, families, and businesses. If any of you are stonemasons or construction workers, obviously we need quite a lot of workers to build all the fortresses. Those that wish to stay on can form the start of our Civil Defense Force, and we will need leaders for those soldiers. Hence, I come to you first, you who led our troops, if you wish to return to your life elsewhere, that's fine, do so now. If you wish to remain in our new army, then stay and we can work out your positions."

The volunteer force had swelled to nearly twenty-five hundred freedom fighters. Now that they had accomplished their goal, more than half were glad to be so quickly allowed to return to their lives. Bartolo asked a key question, "Lady Jovanna, I was wondering with so many men still desirous of forming up our defense force, could not we also use them to help with the fortress constructions?"

Paul answered for her, "Yes, indeed. While some will constantly need to patrol our border with Vito to guard against any retaliation from the Holy Paladins there, having them lend a hand will certainly allow the fortresses to be finished faster. Once we get this series of border fortresses built and manned, it will be very difficult for an invading army to attack us without besieging each fort in turn. Otherwise, the cavalry there could easily cut off their supply lines."

He continued, "I would still like the basic unit to be twenty-five men per squad with a squad leader. Group four squads into a battalion with a battalion leader. Group four battalions into a regiment with a regimental commander. A fortress garrison would consist of a complete regiment. Unless our terrain is vastly different from the border with Velona, seven such fortresses along the Vito border would be sufficient. Ultimately, that would field twenty-eight hundred soldiers on the border. We should have one general to oversee all of these."

"Then, we have the city defense to consider. Two regiments would be enough to have stationed in Barcella proper. While the cavalry at the border fortresses would have something to do, active patrols and such, those here in the city would be far idler. Hence, we could periodically rotate the regiments, making the tour of duty in Barcella more of a rest and relaxation thing."

"City Guards is another aspect to consider. While none of us would like to admit it, there are still thieves and troublemakers around. There ought to be some City Guards on the streets to handle such things as they occur. At night, we need to have some on patrol to protect all the many shops. I would like to see the City Guards number no more than two thousand, split into the three shifts. Until we get our city security up and running, the nearby Santi will help with street patrols. Some of you might prefer being in the City Guards."

"Take a few minutes to discuss what you wish to do. Once you know what you wish to do, see me if it's the defense force, see Alyster here if it's the City Guards that interests you." The men chatted among themselves and then began lining up in the two lines. By suppertime, the totals were in and Jovanna and Paul knew where they were at in terms of immediate full time support troops. Eight hundred wanted to remain in the Defense Force. Another five hundred preferred the City Guards.

Bartolo Dovino was appointed to the position of General of the Barcella Defense Force and allowed to choose his own staff and appoint the lower commanders. His first task that Paul gave him was to organize the first two full regiments. His second task was to have one regiment on patrol on the Vito border, while the second accompanied Alyster on a survey for likely locations for the series of defensive fortresses.

Enrico Zo was appointed the leader of the City Guards, which numbered three hundred volunteers. His first task was to organize his men to handle the daytime city patrols. Paul insisted on only one detail. Always, the guards had to patrol in pairs, never alone. Both leaders were promised more manpower in the next few weeks as manpower issues resolved themselves and the positions were advertised.

By the end of the week, everyone in the sector had heard about the reciprocal help plan of Jovanna's. Nearly all endorsed the idea. Many people actually took advantage of this opportunity to begin doing what they most desired to do for work, something until now they dared not do.

The only detail that Jovanna wanted to handle that she could not was to let the few remaining old ships which were on the ore runs in the far Southlands know about all these changes. Some ought to be given the opportunity to crew the new caravels. She finally asked Elona Po about how she might accomplish this. To her surprise, Elona asked her caravel captains, who were about to make runs down to the Spice Islands, to spend a few days tracking down these older ships and notify them. Per Jovanna's orders, these captains and their crews could at once sail back to Barcella, if they chose.

She knew that a full recovery would take time and that problems would develop along the way that she would have to settle. Still, she and her

Circle thought that they had made a good start. Indeed, the Santi Fortress folks began spending a good deal of time within the city, often spending time with Jovanna and her group.

One final footnote. All city gate entrance fees were abolished. Anyone could enter and leave through the gates freely, as long as the gates were opened. Since the construction of the walls and the gates so many years ago, this free passage had never been allowed. It did wonders to boost the morale of those who needed to travel frequently between the city and the outlying areas.

In mid-August, she and her Circle spent three weeks traveling to each of the outlying towns and villages to meet the people again and see how they were fairing. Of course, although she had promised to visit each town at least twice a year, until she actually did visit, many did not truly believe that she would. Slowly, the citizens' respect for their new ruler grew.

Chapter 16 The Fallout from the Devices

The wagons carrying the dozen women who had been imprisoned in the metal devices for so long finally arrived at Jenna's estate on July 1, 640. Two days later another came with the final victim. By the time that the women got here, they had been receiving a steady diet of nutrition and their half-starved bodies were beginning to respond.

Of course, all were shocked to see Jenna's missing hands and knew that they shared some common ground. That went a long way with these victims. "Just be patient a little longer while we work out a safe way to remove these devices," Jenna told each woman personally. She had them all placed in the infirmary, where the Healers could not only keep a sharp eye on their health but also help them with their daily needs.

During the long ride back, the blacksmiths had been formulating ways and means to remove these devices. The iron bands around the women's heads had been easy to remove, just requiring a good deal of sawing. Quickly, all the head contraptions were gone. Two women had to have four teeth removed each, where the long-term metal ring had actually begun to rot these four teeth. Still, this was not anyone's real concern. It was the metal devices, which locked their arms across their upper backs, which made them so utterly helpless.

These proved far more difficult to remove. Still, Roberto Peña insisted in sitting beside his sister, Nicolina, helping her in every possible way. Soon, he began helping many of the other women as well. He even chose to sleep on a spare bed alongside her, just in case she might need something during the night, which she didn't. Every day, he continued to ask about any progress that was being made, and he never failed to offer his thanks and encouragement to the victims and the Healers and anyone else who would listen to him.

For a week, various methods were attempted, all meeting with failure. Either they would cause more damage to the women or they did not open the devices up. The biggest problem, the blacksmiths decided, was that they did not know how the devices were made and how the locking mechanism worked. Once one could be removed, it could be studied and more effective ways to remove them invented. Getting that first one off proved most difficult indeed.

At last, Allan came up with a method. His reasoning went as follows. The devices were hinged at the front chest center. The locking mechanism was in the center portion of the back. However, the construction was flawed in that unlike sword blades, the metal had not been tempered. He positioned the woman lying on her chest, metal joint hard against the stone floor. Using a pointed rod, positioned on the metal filled key hole, and a heavy hammer, he directed a solid blow. The metal instantly gave way! Cautiously, the Healers and Allan began to open the device, freeing the woman from her imprisonment.

It was quite by accident that the woman he freed was the most recent arrival, the woman that Fel had found. She had not been incased in the metal torture device for very long. Her arms were stiff and muscles weak, but she was free at last. Everyone cheered and the enthusiasm soared. Rapidly, the other twelve were placed into the same position and rapidly the six men, Allan plus blacksmiths, delivered twelve crushing blows, cracking all dozen metal cases.

Now the real horrors began. While four women were able to move their arms sufficiently to have the devices removed, the other eight had immediate problems. The Healers were being very gentle, uncertain of what they would find. In hindsight, this was perhaps the most crucial detail. The other eight, including Nicolina, could not move their arms enough to allow the devices to open. Hence, Allan improvised again. This time, a sledgehammer was held securely to the bottom of the front hinge. Allan then used the pointed rod and heavy hammer to crack the hinge, which likewise gave way easily. Now the casing could be removed without moving the women's arms.

Beth Ann carefully removed the metal from Nicolina, revealing her arms, which went across her back. "Oh my god!" she exclaimed in horror. Everyone dashed over to see.

"Are my arms free yet?" Nicolina asked pitifully, her voice full of fear. She had no idea what Beth Ann was seeing back there. The others stared at the sight, unsure of what they were witnessing!

Quickly, the other remaining women were freed, while Beth Ann and the other Healers continued to stare at Nicolina's arms. Finally, Beth Ann reacted. "Can you feel my touch on your arms?" she asked and gently touched one.

"No, please hurry up," Nicolina began crying.

"Nicolina, do not move. Continue lying there on your chest," Beth Ann ordered and made Roberto, who was speechless, see that she did as ordered. Quickly, the Healers examined the other seven. Two of these at least had some feeling in their arms, however. That was the only encouraging thing.

Nothing in Healer experience compared to what they were seeing. However, Beth Ann reached an immediate conclusion: the immobilizing of joints for long periods is deleterious for the person. Muscles atrophied, joints stiffened, skin tightened. Two of the women had been encased a year longer than Nicolina had been. Their arms were in the worst condition. All soft tissue beneath the skin was gone. Even the bones had become very thin and brittle. The skin had turned into the texture of thin leather and had tightened up against the bone. In short, their arms were not only frozen in this position, but they looked like the arms of a corpse that had been dead a long time!

Beth Ann asked one woman if she could feel her finger, while she touched the withered arm. Although the woman replied that she could not, all heard a sickening popping sound. Beth Ann's touch had actually broken one of the long bones in her arm — they were that brittle. Now the woman's hand dangled at a crazy angle. "Do you feel anything now?" Beth Ann asked half-frightened of what she had done.

"No, nothing. Well maybe a tiny tingle of something. What is going on?" the very frightened woman asked.

Jenna, sensing something awful was happening in the infirmary, led me in there with her. She did not speak but just stared at the arms of these prone women. While everyone was staring, tremendously shocked, Nicolina, unable to stand the suspense any longer, tried to roll over to see what the others arms looked like. As she rolled over, the sound of someone crushing many crackers echoed in the silent infirmary. She felt nothing, but was able to see the woman next to her. She shrieked in terror at the sight, which caused the other women to panic and try to see each other. More crackers crushing echoed in the room. Sheiks of sheer panic echoed were followed by the stunned silence of the observers. Uniformly, the women fainted from the sudden shock.

Beth Ann finally recovered. "There is only one thing that we can do and we must do it fast, remove them before what little blood is in there moves the particles into the rest of their bodies. I've never seen or heard of anything like this. Let's get these eight on the operating tables at once."

Jenna spoke sternly. "Save the remains of their arms. I am going to send some to the Pope!"

The five whose arms still functioned were taken into other rooms. No one had any ideas how to help them just now; all haste had to be taken with these eight or they might not survive at all. The five Healers began at once, while Allan had the blacksmiths get water boiling. Soon many other helpers arrived, compliments of Jenna's fast actions. I stood alone in a corner watching them work.

Distant memories of the seemingly endless surgeries we all had to perform during the Crusades slaughter nearly a decade ago came back into my mind. However, this time, the surgeries went very rapidly indeed. However, each Healer took special care in their final stitching so that their shoulders would show only tiny scars. It was the best that they could offer their unconscious patients. Roberto turned a sickly green, ran hastily out of the infirmary, and vomited for some time. One of the helpers found him and helped him recover.

Two hours later, the surgeries were completed. All were alive, though it was too soon to tell if any additional damage had been done by the sudden crushing of all their bones. Roberto came back in and sat quietly beside his unconscious sister. "You can help her and the others by wiping their forehead with these wash cloths. If any wake up, get one of us immediately."

He whispered, "My Lady, I will not fail them."

Now, the Healers went to examine the other five. They tested their arm's movements, their sensitivity to touch, and did as many actions as they could think of, trying to understand what the damage actually was. All five were in a panic, fearing that they too would lose their arms. At last, after conferring on all their observations, Beth Ann, spoke to all five.

"Time will tell, but we Healers believe that you five will recover in time. We do not need to amputate your arms at this time. Possibly physical therapy will help your arms recover. So first, we want you five to take plenty of warm baths. Others will come with you and gently massage your arms. Expect them to be exceedingly stiff and quite painful to movement. We five think that it is critical that you endure the pain and continue to move and exercise the arms. However, do not overdo it. Your bones are also somewhat brittle and might break if you do too much just yet. Possibly a diet may help, we are not sure, but we are going to try having you eat more cheese and goat's milk. We have our children eating that and they grow strong bones. Maybe that will work with you five."

The relief she saw on the five faces was gratifying to say the very least. Others led the five off to the heated bath. The Healers then cleaned up the infirmary and took up their positions beside the eight women. They would remain under constant observation for the immediate future. None of the Healers had any idea how the women would fare, physically. This whole mess was beyond their knowledge or skill.

Me? I had sat quietly in a corner of the room observing everything. I took the liberty of Mind Joining the other Communicators in all our towers. However, I asked that Elsie in Barcella not relay this to Jovanna just yet. I knew that mom, Jenna, was visibly upset by this horrid discovery, and was probably meeting with others working out what the Santi could do next. She had forgotten about me for once. Just as good, because the Healers, particularly Beth Ann, needed me.

Now that there was nothing to do but sit and wait, Beth Ann began to cry silently to herself. Of all of us, the Healers had the worst of it. They always had to "clean up" the messes that others created. Only this time, I knew it was far worse, for they had no idea about this situation or how to handle it. I walked my body up to Beth Ann and snuggled up to her legs.

"Oh, Lizzy Ann, you shouldn't be here," she started to say, rubbing my head with her hands.

"It's okay, Aunt Beth Ann. I know none of you has ever seen such atrocities. There was nothing that you could have done besides what you did. Their arms were just dead, that's all. Please don't cry Auntie. You have saved their lives and that's what counts." Those who did not know me often called me a very precocious five year old girl.

She pulled me tightly to her, "But what kind of lives will they have now, Lizzy? They might rather be dead than like this. I know I would."

"Yes, Auntie, but we know that we are not these bodies, and we know we can go get new ones when these aren't any good any more. They don't remember that any more. This life is precious to them. It's the only one they believe that they have. We can discard one at will because we know we can just go get a new one and continue life. We mustn't allow them to succumb and wish to die and so die, because we are only adding to their own personal spiritual dooms. That'd be letting them go into the deepest depths of apathy. They would leave and get a new body by going the wrong way, the unknowing, total failure, total effect of everything route. They will have let everything else in the world dictate their own fates, not themselves even the tiniest bit. You've got to keep them alive long enough for mom to use her therapy on them so that she can bring them back up to some cause over their lives. Then, if they want to go get a new body, they can do it knowingly. Big difference, Auntie Beth Ann."

Stroking my hair, she kissed my forehead, "For such a little girl, you speak the wisdom of Ket. I still have trouble with that you know, seeing you as my brother in law. I see a five year old little girl, but I love you anyway. How about going and getting us all some tea and biscuits?"

"Okay, Auntie," I scampered off to be useful. "I had to make three trips to the kitchen to bring back the six cups, teapot, and the tray with biscuits, but I had fun. Mom was so preoccupied that she didn't pay me any notice, although it was way past my bedtime. I fell asleep in Auntie Beth's arms that night.

I awoke to the screaming and crying of the women. They finally awakened and saw the stark reality of their missing arms. Poor Roberto was trying to console Nicolina. She wailed, "I wish I were dead! Why didn't you just let us die? We cannot live like this. Please, I beg of you, let us die, just die!" She wailed, sobbed uncontrollably.

Actually, five others completely echoed her, though with slightly different words. Three others just lay there and cried, oblivious to everything around them. Beth Ann sent one to fetch Jenna. One woman, she might have been able to handle, to calm down a bit, not eight. She and the other Healers felt utter sympathy for their patients; it was horrible to be in their situation.

Roberto was sobbing just as much as the women were, hurling self-reproaches wildly, "I should have charged in there and tried to kill all the evil bastards. It would have been better to die there than have you like this, dear Nicolina. I should have died trying to save you. Then. . ." He was interrupted.

The stern voice of Jenna broke his diatribe, "Then what? Roberto, then what? You would have left your sister to suffer further humiliation, raping, slowly starving to death? Left her to die a most horrible death

344

without anyone to comfort her, to love her, left alone to be tortured endlessly perhaps for years to come? You would have wanted Nicolina to endure such slavery, such brutality, such wickedness, with no one left in the world to have the slightest care for her, abandoned by the entire world?"

Mom had a way of slapping one in the face, even though she had no hands with which to do so. In that minute, all nine felt like they had just had a cold, hard whack across their faces. She had thrown the stark reality of their torture right at their minds. It reached the beings, uniformly, the uncontrolled wailing and sobbing died down.

Roberto muttered, "Well, no," and said no more, feeling ashamed of what he had been saying.

Jenna switched to the tone of a loving mother, "I can only imagine the horrible degradation that you have all endured. I, too, have seen my share. I am speculating here, but I believe that each of you managed to stay alive and fought to live while imprisoned in that cavern because you always held out some hope that you would somehow be rescued from those horrible devices and set free at long last. Hope for freedom kept you all alive, am I not correct?"

Nicolina answered, "Yes, yes, we all kept hoping that one day we would be somehow rescued, that what they kept saying would not be true, that we would be imprisoned like that for the rest of our lives. We saw three of us just give up all hope. They stopped even trying to eat, just lay there and did nothing until they died. The guards laughed at us when they dragged the corpses out, saying, 'We said you will be like this for the rest of your lives, hurry up and die and make our lives easier.' I wasn't going to give up and let them win, not without a fight." The others echoed her sentiments, adding, "We refused to let them have their satisfaction. We made them care for us."

"To you women, I say very well done indeed! You didn't succumb yet still fought back as best you could. I know from personal experience that right now things look awfully bad to you, horrible beyond imagination, but you remember the woman who rescued you don't you, Lady Jovanna Barcella? Did you see her situation? True, she still has a bit of arms left, but she underwent a brutal, most painful torture as the Mano del Dio used a knife to cut off her fingers one by one and then even her hands. At least, you have not undergone such a massive pain as she did. Yet, look at Jovanna. Has she let that stop her? No! She studied here with us Santi, learned much, and has now led the revolution, which has driven out the Holy Paladins and freed Barcella from the invaders. Barcella is once more a free country. Lady Jovanna, who likes to be called Miss Short Arms by her dear friends, is now the sole ruler of Barcella."

"Your own leader has never given up, neither should you, ladies. I know that for a while, you are in for an awful, humiliating time of it, but here we can help you to learn new ways of doing things. You still have your feet, haven't you? Well, let's let your feet become your new hands. Follow the model set by your ruler, don't give up, and keep on trying. If you try, you will find many, many helping hands here. If you give up, I'll personally smack you!" She waved her handless arm as if she were paddling a child. It was so out of place, so funny, that the eight women could not help but crack a small smile.

"Now then, that is much better. What our Healers need to know right now is are any of you in any pain from the surgeries?"

Unlike normal surgeries, none felt any significant pain at all. All their nerves had long ago atrophied, and they'd lost all sensation in their arms. All they felt now as the itching sensation where the stitches were holding the skin tight so it could mend.

"And you Roberto," Jenna finally turned her attention to him, "you stop belittling yourself. If you had not done what you did, neither the Santi nor Jovanna would have known about all these women and would not have been able to rescue them. Then, the Holy Paladins would have won, as they would most certainly have eventually died most horribly."

"Now then ladies, the Healers are going to inspect your shoulders. Meanwhile, I want each of you to give us your full names, what town you are from, what relatives, husbands, children, and so on may still be alive. We want to contact them and let them know that you are still alive. Finally, each of you may stay here at my estate for as long as you desire. I do not want any monetary pay for your stay. However, when you are healed and able, I would like you to contribute in ways that you are able to help around here. Who knows now just what that might be, but when you are ready, you and I will figure it out. Santi, please write down their names and their information. I want to get on with notifying their relatives that they are alive and recovering here."

During the course of the next week, via Elsie and the Santi at the Barcella fortress, the home situations for these eight women were discovered. Besides Nicolina Peña, they included Zita Seppina, twenty-one years old, with no family remaining. She used to be a dancer before she was abducted by the paladins. Velia Dette had a husband and young daughter in Allyende who were elated that she was alive and most anxious to have her come home. Tonia Agosta was twenty-two. Alas, her husband had been killed. She had twin six year olds, Gianna and Gianni Agosta, who were found living in an abandoned building, half starved. They were brought to Jovanna's estate to live until their mother returned. Sandra Ziella's husband and son jumped and cheered when they received the news that she was alive. It was all the Santi could do to prevent their traveling at once to Velona to see her. Orabella Dovica, the oldest of the women at thirty-three, still had her husband, although her two sons had perished fighting the paladins some years ago. Pina Landa now only had her daughter, Gina, age seven. Fortunately, her neighbors had taken Gina into their home when Pina had been abducted. She was fine and very anxious be reunited with her mother. Finally, Lia Ines Giulino was twenty-one, but had no one left in her family. She had been a singer before being abducted.

What I found fascinating indeed was that these women were in the arts. Besides the singer and dancer, the other six had been painters, sculptors, and ceramic designers. The artists had held out the longest against this kind of suppression. Their current condition made their loves, hopes, and dreams totally dashed. I wondered if anything could be done about that aspect.

During the week, Roberto insisted that he remain beside his sister at all times, helping her with everything. In fact, he just went ahead and assisted all seven others. He continued to address each one as My Lady, as was his custom. This small courtesy did brighten the women up with a tiny spark of life. One day, Lia Ines asked, "Roberto, why do you keep calling me Lady Lia Ines? I am hardly a noblewoman, and certainly I am now not much of a woman either."

"Oh my Lady Lia Ines, don't say such things. I was taught that all women are to be considered Ladies. It is a term of honor and respect, for it is you who bring new life into the world. Normally, when addressing a Lady, I would bow and kiss her hand in honor of her. Now I must change my custom," he leaned over and kissed her forehead.

"Ah, charming the ladies again, I see," Jenna teased as she walked in bearing the news she had received from Elsie. "Well, ladies, I have just gotten the news from the Santi Fortress in Barcella. Some of you, it is bad news; others, great news. First, the bad news. Zita, Lia Ines, I'm very sorry to say that all your family members have perished at the hands of the vile Megalos barbarians. I'm very sorry for your losses."

"Tonia, while you already knew that your husband had been killed some time ago, we have located your twins, Gianna and Gianni. They are now safe and living at Jovanna's estate, anxious for your return. Pina, your daughter has also been found. Gina is living at Jovanna's as well. Velia, Sandra, and Orabella, your husbands and children have been found, and it was all the Santi could do to prevent them from rushing here to Velona to see you."

"I also have a message for all of you from Lady Jovanna herself. When you have all recovered and are ready to return home, your first stop will be her estate. She wants not only to meet you in person again, but wishes to extend an offer for those of you who wish to come and live with her on her estate. You can relax; you will always have a home, either here or in Barcella. Now I understand that today the bandages come off. If the Healers find all is well, then I would like to have you all come and join me in our warm bath. Yes, we do have a heated bath here. I think you all will appreciate that nicety!"

"God, hurry up!" exclaimed Lia Ines, as Beth Ann was removing the last of her bandages. "A bath! God how I want a real bath! I cannot remember when I last had one. Years ago!"

Roberto followed the group, bringing piles of towels with him. Once there, he helped each one safely into the warm waters, while Jenna went to retrieve her special surprise. Roberto had been in on it as well. During this past week, she had the seamstress make eight dresses specially designed for these women. Although Roberto knew his sister's favorite colors, he cleverly got that information from the others and passed it on to Jenna.

"Jenna, this is absolutely heaven!" exclaimed Lia Ines. The others echoed her sentiments. Beth Ann and several other women arrived, intending to hop in and wash the women. However, Roberto had the situation well in hand, going from woman to woman, gently washing them. Jenna winked at Beth Ann, who got the signal. They merely sat back and allowed Roberto to contribute his assistance. He felt more useful than he had ever felt in a long time.

For three hours, the women indulged themselves in the relaxing, warm waters. Finally, as Roberto helped each one climb out, steadying them, Lia Ines asked Jenna, "How often can we take a bath? This is so nice. I feel like all those years of utter filth are washing off of me."

"Dear, since your bodies are healing nicely, after today you have complete freedom to go any place around here you desire. Just don't overdo the time spent in this bath. And please have someone, like Roberto, with you. I don't want you slipping and falling down. After you are dried off and dressed, you are welcome to go for a stroll outside. You must see all the flowers Hank and I have planted around the estate. Just magnificent."

Beth Ann and the others lent a hand drying the women off. "I've a little surprise for you all." Jenna pointed to their new clothes. "They are especially made for you. You ought to be able to wiggle into and out of them yourselves, though with a bit of difficulty, I expect. Roberto and I conspired to find out what your favorite colors were."

Nicolina's was yellow with sky blue stripes. He helped her slip it on and adjusted it. "There, sis, now you look quite beautiful once more. It's been so long since I saw you looking this good!" She beamed. The other women also were very pleased and showed off their new look to each other. Then, the Healers brushed out each woman's hair. Here, Roberto paid careful attention to how the women did this. He had never brushed a woman's hair before, but knew he would be doing his sisters' soon, maybe the others as well.

When the grooming was finished, Roberto looked at the eight and pronounced, "Ah, now you all do look like the Ladies that you really are. Eight beautiful women. My Ladies, would you care to go for a stroll and view this magnificent estate?" Nicolina snuggled up to her brother and he put his arm around her waist. He offered his other arm to Lia Ines, who smiled and moved in close to him. "This way, my Ladies." Roberto led them all down the hall and outside the estate.

As they walked around admiring the multitudes of flowers and watched the many children playing on the grassy zone, Lia Ines commented, "Now I feel finally alive. I know it sounds weird, but I do feel alive."

"Me too, before I was just numb to the world," Nicolina added. "I'm so, I don't know what I am, really, rejuvenated or something. Gosh, she has the most beautiful estate I have ever seen! Did she really help plant all these? No hands? How?"

"Dunno," Roberto answered, "but everyone claims that she did. Notice that none of the doors anywhere on the estate has any doorknobs. You just have to push them open with your feet. I looked at them, and they have unique hinges that can swing open in both directions. Clever, so you see, here Jenna is really right; you can wander around everywhere, but I think I should accompany my Ladies, just in case something unexpected happens."

Nicolina looked concerned, "Roberto, we are being such a heavy burden on you, being like this."

"Sis, you would only be a burden if I had to carry you. No, I'd do that too, if I had to; you are my only sister!"

"Well, I'm not your sister, yet you dote on me and the others too," Lia Ines teased.

"Well, you are all Ladies in need, and I am in a position to help. How could I not, fair Lia Ines? Surely you would do the same for me, if I were in trouble," he replied.

Later Jenna introduced all the many children to the women, and shortly after that, the other five who still had their arms came out of the bath after their daily therapy sessions. Most were still having a painful time moving their arms, but the color had returned to their limbs, which was taken as an encouraging aspect. All the women hugged and chatted and talked about how they were progressing.

Around suppertime, a carriage pulled up. Lilly Ann and the others from here had finally returned. Her children ran up to her and gave her giant hugs. In truth, Lilly Ann was very glad to be back home. She was more than a little shocked by the condition of the women, however. Later that night, Beth Ann filled her in on all the details.

The next afternoon, Jenna began her special therapy sessions. Beth Ann also helped with these. Jenna took on the eight worst cases, while Beth Ann worked with the other five. Both women knew that these were likely going to be long sessions. All these women had undergone the torture for several years. Much trauma had accumulated, and it was slow going indeed.

That night, with little else to do and feeling so much more alive, Lia Inez began to sing once more. Before her abduction, she had been a singer of folk songs. The women were now staying in three adjacent rooms instead of the infirmary. Roberto constantly hovered between all three assisting whenever anyone needed anything. Now, he stood fascinated by the beautiful melodies coming from Lia Inez.

Zita who shared the same room with Lia Ines and Nicolina, stood up and began her undulating dance movements. Like Lia, she had not danced since her abduction so many years ago. Now, however, she had no arms, which crimped her usual movements. Undaunted, she simply invented new motions that she could do. Roberto just stared at the two women, awed. When they finished, he said, "My Ladies, that was just magnificiento! Bravo! Bravo! Never have I heard finer music nor seen such dance!"

"Well that's because you probably never seen an armless woman dance," Zita countered. "Really, that was just awful. God, how I missed dancing! You feel the same way with singing, Lia?"

"Absolutely! I used to sing to myself all day long."

"Well, I say sing away, all you want to; it's just incredibly beautiful, Lia, such a voice! And your dancing, Zita, so enticing, so provocative, such feeling!" Both women blushed slightly. "Really, you two should work up a little routine and perform it after dinner for our hosts! I'm sure that Hank and Jenna would love the entertainment." Inspired, both women continued to practice together part of each day. As soon as Jenna overheard them, due in part to Roberto's suggestion, she insisted that they perform for everyone after dinner and before she went out to play with the children.

By mid-August, most of the women's therapy sessions had ended, trauma gone. Each felt like they were somehow reborn with renewed life or vitality. Singing and dancing began the norm right after dinner, with many of the children joining in with Zita dancing around the dining room with her. One night, while everyone was enjoying the song and dance, the door opened and two men stepped in the room. At once, Zita and Lia stopped, everyone turned to look at the unexpected visitors.

"Hi mom, heard you were back; thought we'd drop by and see you. But will you look at this? I'm barely gone and here you have already replaced me with a fabulous singer and dancer!" he feigned being upset.

"Taliesin!" a number of children squealed delight, and his brother and two remaining sisters mobbed him. Even though she was now a teenager, Sarah Amber hugged her big brother anyway. Curt held onto his leg, while Linda Sarah, now five, clung to his other leg. Lilly Ann came over and gave him a big hug.

"Hi Angus, good to see you too. How have you boys been?" she asked.

"Just fine, mom. Learned all Jolina and Edgar's songs. So are you going to introduce me to these fine artists or do I have to introduce myself?" he asked, adding, "Hi Aunt Jenna, Uncle Hank, Aunt Beth Ann, and the rest of you all."

The thirteen women looked at the dashing young men, while Lilly Ann explained, "This is one of my older twins, Bard Tal, and his friend, Angus d'Aine from West Reach. They've just gotten back from spending several years with Velona's most famous musicians, Jolina and Edgar Elms.

Bard Tal, Angus, these women were rescued from Barcella by Lady Jovanna. Your singer is Lia Ines Giulino and her partner is Zita Seppina." One by one, she introduced the others to the pair.

"Most pleased to meet you Lady Lia and Lady Zita," he bowed; Angus, likewise. "Now pray, please, please continue with your song and dance!"

Sarah Amber insisted, "Tal, why don't you join them? I'm missed your music so much! Please, Tal?" she fluttered her eyebrows teasingly at him.

In a flash, Tal got out his lute from its case, while Angus fetched his bag pipes. "Oh, oops. I'm sorry everyone, I forgot to introduce you to our new musician, everyone, this is Sam Elms, their son. He plays flute with us now." The boy was barely thirteen, but he smiled and bashfully said hello to everyone.

"All right then, one-two-three-four," and he began to play a bit of a pick up to the last song that Lia Ines had been singing. As soon as she began to sing, then Angus added a bagpipe drone sound, while Sam flittered away with running notes over the top of the others. Zita began her dance once more, unable to resist the fabulous sounds. All the children began dancing too, trying hard to emulate the moves of Zita.

When that song ended, Bard Tal asked, "Know Leomund's Lament?" She did and Angus played a long lead in to the melancholy song, one by one the voice, lute, and flute entered. Everyone loved the slow moving dance. Song after song brightened up the evening. Bard Tal kept noticing how Zita danced. He had an idea.

"Mom, Aunt Beth Ann, will you two show Zita here how to do the Greenway Hop Dance? She is just perfect for it. That style of dance would be the most perfect fit for her, please mom, please?"

"I haven't danced in years, not since your father," she did not finish her sentence. "Well, all right. Beth Ann, Allan, Ben — you two up here; you got to join us." While they all protested that it had been a long time, Bard Tal ignored them.

"Zita watch how they do this. I think you are going to like the Greenway style of dance. It is unique. Okay, Angus, Sam, let's do it." Angus began thumping a log against the floor, making a unique percussion sound. Sam, feeling the beat, began stamping another one in between Angus's beats; the result sounded fast. Tal began strumming and singing his mother's favorite song from the Greenway. At last, the four began to demonstrate the Greenway dance. Holding their arms perfectly tightly against their bodies, they began jumping up and down, and tapping out rhythms with their feet. It was indeed an energetic dance; they would bow to their partners and twirl around, even move about the room. Zita began to grin. Indeed, these dancers looked an awful lot as she did, completely avoiding all use of their arms, as if they too had none. Soon she began mimicking their steps. Now the others began clapping in time to the music and Tal had to sing very loudly to be heard.

Me, I was right in there dancing for all I was worth. Before we realized it, hours had passed. Before Jenna could call a halt, Bard Tal, spoke up, after flashing a sign to Sam. "Finally, here comes the last song for the evening. We play it in honor of my father; this was his favorite. Sam?"

Lilly Ann saw the enormous bass flute in the boy's hand. Tears began flowing even before he played the first note. The haunting lament stirred fond, long ago memories both for her and for me. Lyneth's Lament brought back memories I had forgotten, of the Cymry Minstrels when we toured the Sea Princes so many years ago. I think that I had as many tears streaming down my little cheeks as Lilly Ann had. Mom understood.

When it was done, I ran up to Caityln, I mean Taliesin, and hugged his leg. He bent down and kissed my head. He whispered in my ear, "He's pretty darn good isn't he?" Lilly Ann came up and lifted me up to I was head high with him.

"Thanks, Tal. We both enjoyed that. I am so proud of you, son. You are well on your way to being the most famous bard in Velona."

After the others had gone to bed and Angus and Sam had been given rooms, Tal and Lilly Ann met in the kitchen to catch up on news about each other. Tal wanted to know all about how his sister, Leslie Ann, was doing down in Barcella. They talked until the wee hours.

The next morning, just after breakfast, Bard Tal knocked on their door. Nicolina said, "Come in." It was rare that someone came to actually visit them, knocking on the door. Roberto was in the process of brushing out his sister's hair. Zita and Lia were patiently waiting their turn. Both women flushed slightly when Bard Tal entered.

"My Ladies, please excuse this interruption, but may I have a word with you two?" he asked of Lia and Zita. Both nodded, so he continued. "Are either of you under contract to play or dance with some group?"

"Oh don't be silly," Lia Ines answered. "Well, I guess it's not all that silly. I used to sing a lot before I was, well abducted. Zita was a dancer before. No, contracts? Us? Like this?" She shrugged her shoulders.

"What a relief!" Bard Tal exclaimed with enthusiasm. "I have a group, Bard Tal's Traveling Minstrels. We travel from town to town, entertaining folks with song and dance. I would be most honored if you both would consent to joining up with the three of us. You two are a perfect match for our music. Your voice and mine fit together beautifully, and your dancing, well, I'll need my sword to keep all the gents from coming after you when the show is done, Lady Zita. I know that you probably already have other plans, but please think over my offer. It is so utterly rewarding to play for ordinary townsfolk and watch them become so enthralled with music and dance. Really, there is no better feeling in the world, except perhaps love. Please think it over, Lady Lia, Lady Zita. Just consider it. However, just ask mom, I mean Lilly Ann. I can be very persistent and patient. Please? Oh, I am forgetting my manners. Allow me to assist you Lady Lia."

He found another hairbrush and began gently brushing her hair. Lia was impressed. It was if it were her own hands doing the brushing. He somehow had just the right touch, the right motions, as if he had been doing it all his life. He even found a yellow ribbon to tie it up slightly, with a pretty bow sitting right on top of her head. While she looked in the mirror to see how it really looked, Tal began doing Zita's hair as well, putting a red ribbon in hers.

Nicolina commented, "Roberto, you had better take lessons from Bard Tal here. Golly, he does a fabulous job! Did you use to do your mother's hair or perhaps Aunt Jenna's?" she asked Tal.

He blushed slightly. "No, mom always does hers and my sisters and Hank always does Jenna's. Perhaps one day I may tell you. Just please consider my offer, my Ladies. I am a hard man to say no to, but come; let's go for a walk before it gets too hot. Isn't Jenna's estate here incredibly beautiful?" While Roberto put his arm around the waist of his sister, escorting her out, Tal put one around each of the other two, gently guiding them out of the room and to the fresh out of doors.

"Tell us about yourself, Tal," Lia Ines asked while they were walking.

"Yes, do, we know so little about everyone here," Zita added.

"Not much to tell really. I have lived here most of my childhood, but I was always in to music. Only when I came of age was I able to convince Aunt Jenna and mom to let me become what I wanted to be, a bard. Spent the last three years with Jolina and Edgar learning their entire repertoire. Now we are ready to travel and play music, song, and dance."

"Are you Santi or one of the Guardians like your mother?" asked Lia Ines.

"Insightful are we," he teased. "Yes, Lady Lia, yes to both, but I am a bard first. If you are worried about our security, I am well trained in fighting techniques, though I hate it. Besides, mom always sends along a number of Santi guards with us."

Later that evening, the two asked Lilly Ann about her son. "Lilly Ann, Bard Tal has asked us to join his traveling minstrels as a singer and dancer," Lia Ines said. "Do you think this is a good idea for us to even consider? I mean traveling around as we are? We are so helpless still."

"First, you should finish your therapy sessions, and then Lady Jovanna wants you to come visit her. After that, it is your life to do with as you wish. Singing and dancing are certainly something that comes easily to you. I'll talk to my son and get back to you, all right?" They agreed.

Lilly Ann marched straight to Tal's room. He was sorting out his dirty clothes, "Hi mom."

"Taliesin! What are you doing asking those poor women to go gallivanting who knows where with you fellows?" She was slightly angry and slightly annoyed and slightly worried, all in one package.

"Mom. Do you know just how talented both women are? Lia has a fantastic voice and a natural feeling for music. Zita, mom, did you see how she flows, making herself one with the music? I swear that she has had formal dance training. Such talent must be nurtured and brought forth so the whole world can have more beauty in it. I can't help what has happened to their arms, but to make music and art fit for the gods, they don't need arms."

"Yes, but do you realize how much they will be utterly dependent upon you for so many things that the rest of us take for granted?" she countered.

"Mom, how often have you and dad drilled into us that we are spiritual beings, not our bodies? I see two phenomenal, creative artists there, not bodies."

"Yes, that's all well and good, son, but their bodies will make demands upon you. Are you really ready to take on that additional responsibility?"

"Mom, if I wasn't, I would never have approached them with my offer."

"Well, all right then. I wish you would have spoken with me first, but it's so hard thinking of you as all grown up, Tal. I remember when I first picked you and your brothers up and held one in each arm. Come here," she gave him a loving hug. He returned her love as well.

A short while later, Lilly Ann knocked on the women's door and entered. Roberto and Nicolina were out for a walk, watching the children play. She said, "I talked with Tal. It seems that he has considered everything. I must say that your artistry has definitely made an impact on him. If you decide you wish to go traveling and become troubadours, you will have the support of everyone. However, if you discover that it is not working out as you believe it may, do not hesitate to let one of the Santi know; they will be traveling with you. They will see you are quickly and safely returned to Barcella and Lady Jovanna's estate."

Both women smiled. Zita asked, "He really sees us as artists?"

"Oh yes, according to Tal, you two are gifted. You've made quite an impression on him. However, I ought to tell you a bit about him. I'm his stepmother. The twin's birth mother died the very night she gave birth to the twins. I looked after them from that time onwards, and their father and I married a while later. All the others are his and mine. He might not talk about it, but his mother was assassinated by a Mano del Dio fellow the very night she gave birth to the twins. Many years later, his father, my husband, was also assassinated by another Mano del Dio. All of us here are worried that the Mano del Dio may want to kill him too, that's why we always send a group of body guards around with him."

"I, we had no idea," exclaimed Lia Ines. "So he has suffered twice at their vile hands."

"We actually have something in common with him," Zita added. "I wish, though, that it was something far happier."

The next day, the buzz around the estate was the fact that these two women were becoming troubadours in Bard Tal's Traveling Minstrels. The five met all morning long in animated discussions about music, song, and dance. Jenna had to break them up just to get in their therapy sessions. Jenna knew that both women were about done erasing the hideous trauma that they had endured for several years. Still, Jenna was thorough, if anything. Before she would sign off on their completion, she insisted that no trace of that horror still affected them negatively.

Around mid-afternoon, Jenna knew that Lia Ines was now finished. Her laughter was contagious. Buried underneath all of that humiliation, torture, rape, and imprisonment lay her decision: "I'm not alive anymore." Once she spotted just how silly her decision had been at the time that she had made it, all vestiges of the traumatic events evaporated.

She came running into her room where the others were still discussing the arts, laughing. "I'm actually alive," she said while laughing. If she had arms, she would have rushed up to Tal and given him a great big hug. She was that excited and cheerful about her discovery. Instead still repeating, "I'm actually alive," she bumped her body into his and moved it up and down his body. He got the idea and gave her a solid hug. "I feel so completely, totally alive! This is so incredible. I never thought I could feel this happy ever again. Thank you Jenna!" She had just caught up to her ex-patient, and entered the room to fetch Zita. Lia Ines rushed over to her and rubbed her body against Jenna's, who put her arms around her and gave her a return hug.

"I'm so happy for you, Lia. Very well done indeed. Now, Zita, it's your turn." Zita followed Jenna out, smiling at Lia. Lia continued bobbing up and down for some time afterwards.

"You look so alive, so radiant! I guess you had a good session with Jenna," Tal gave her another hug.

"Yes, yes, yes. I was holding myself back. I won't do that anymore, I promise."

"Well, let's finish up cataloging the songs you know and the ones we know that you don't. I'm thinking that we ought to head up to the Greenway, around Mont Blanc and Calgary, so we can learn many more of their songs, and give Zita the opportunity to learn their style of dancing. How does that sound to you?"

Just before supper, Zita returned from her last therapy session. Wearing the largest grin imaginable, and she undulated her body into the room, like a master dancer. Lia could not contain her enthusiasm. "Wow! What a move, Zita. Your face looks so bright! What happened?"

"You know how I told you that dancing always came easy to me?" Lia nodded. "Well, I just found out why."

"Why?" exclaimed Lia. The others stopped everything they were doing and listened intently for her explanation.

"I'm not my body! I'm an immortal spiritual being. I cannot die. I lived before! I was a master dancer! But one day, I slipped in the muddy street and fell beneath a wagon which crushed my arms and then my head. It was so similar to the way we were being treated in the caverns, you know. Even as a little girl, I still remembered all my dancing skills! Now, I can only get better at it!" She did a graceful undulation move across the room to express herself.

"Come here and get a hug!" declared Tal, and he gave her a loving hug. "Well done, Master Dancer!"

"Hey, don't forget us," declared Angus and Sam. Both men gave Zita a loving hug as well, and then hugged Lia too.

At supper, Jenna told everyone that on September 1, the women would be ready to head to Barcella and meet with Lady Jovanna and be reunited with their families. She explained that they would go by coach along the beautiful Med Sea coast, taking around four days travel.

With that date only a couple weeks away, Tal asked Jenna for permission to take the women into town. He had to get costumes made, not only for the two new additions, but also for the three men. She agreed as long as three Santi guards accompanied them. That afternoon, two coaches rolled down the streets into the heart of Velona, stopping at one very specific shop. The sign above the storefront said simply, "Suzana's."

Just as soon as the five entered the store, both women knew that they had just entered a very, very expensive and exclusive clothing store. Suzanna was middle aged, but impeccably dressed. Her reputation for the finest in clothing was well known throughout Velona. "Bard Tal, I was wondering when I would see you. We heard that you were back from d'Grange."

"Lady Suzana, I would like you to meet two new additions to our minstrels, Lady Lia Ines and Lady Zita. Ladies, this is Lady Suzana, the finest dress maker in Velona." Suzana curtsied, while the two bowed, realizing that they would have a bit of trouble following suit.

"I have your costumes ready. I take it you need some matching ones for your ladies?"

"Absolutely."

"Follow me, please. I would like you fellows to try yours on, just in case any last minute adjustments need be made. I always deliver the finest quality, you know." As if she had been expecting them, she led them into a private room. The floor was done in plush red carpeting. The walls were mahogany with various oils on the walls, a bronze statue of Tur sat on a teakwood end table. They sat on a plush velvet couch. Quickly, several other equally well-dressed women came into the room carrying the finished costumes that Tal had ordered some time ago.

The bottoms were black, the tops, red. A bright green sash went around their waist. The material was the finest silk. "Here feel this," Tal said as he rubbed the red fabric across Lia's face, and then Zita's.

"Oh my, that is so soft! It must be very expensive!" Lia replied, very impressed.

"Who cares, certainly not me. The idea is to have an impressive costume, and I think this will impress everyone."

"Well go on, you fellows try them on, while we measure your Ladies here." They did as asked. Suzana tested the fit on each man, before pronouncing the clothing a finished product. "Three sets of these for each of you three, correct?" Lia gasped, three sets?

"Yes, we may want more later on, but three to start with. Thank you very much, Lady Suzana," Tal replied.

To Lia, she said, "Seldom do we find a gentleman with such excellent tastes. Now then, Tal, about their dresses. Two aspects are in complete opposition here. I must know at once which way to go."

"What do you mean?" he asked.

"Well, the clothes they have on are more like sacks, so I suspect that they are designed so that they could wiggle into them and out of them on their own. I could make matching dresses similar to these. However, for elegance and style, such pretty women ought to have a proper fitting dress, but that would mean they could not possible dress themselves. Do you see what I mean?"

"Yes, we want elegance and proper fitting, if you please. Zita is a dancer, she ought to have a bottom that has many folds so she can spin and flair it outwards. Probably, she also ought to have a sleek style so that her undulating form can be seen. Two different styles."

"Ladies, I am so glad that Tal has the good sense to dress you as elegant women. Now, about your missing arms. Some who have lost a limb wish me to leave an empty sleeve there. I find that annoying. If I may suggest, let's make your dresses unique. Let's display your actual beautiful forms, as they are, not suggesting you are missing limbs, but that you are celebrating the body you have. Do you find that too unpalatable?"

"No, we don't have arms, so why have constant reminders of what we don't have?" Lia Ines replied, intently curious as to what she actually had in mind.

"Oh yes, Suzana, both should have proper undergarments as well," Tal added, nearly having forgotten. Currently, they wore nothing so that they could more easily use the chamber pot without help.

"But of course! Silly boy, I would not dream of sending elegantly dressed women out of here without the proper attire. Why don't you three take a walk for an hour and give us some time here to work my magic. When you come back, you can examine the proposed final design." Tal took the hint, and the three went for a walk. However, he sent one Santi woman up to be with the two women, just in case. The other two Santi followed the three around town.

When they returned and walked in, Suzana said, "Now how about this?" All three men gaped at the two women. Sleek, tight bodices presented their bosoms in sharp relief. Their necks were open revealing their necks. They could wear a necklace to good advantage, if they chose. The top was a matching red, while a green sash outlined their small waists. The bottoms were black and followed their curves, with a deep walking slash at the bottom.

"Real stockings," squealed Lia. She'd never owned such a pair in her life.

"Now then, let me switch the bottoms on Zita. Quickly, she undid the black sleek bottoms and slipped another around her waist, holding it in place temporarily with the sash.

"Isn't this fabulous," exclaimed Zita. "I can twirl and the dress flairs way out. Incredible!"

"Stunning, ladies, stunning! Suzana, you work miracles! I want four for Lia Ines and two of each style for Zita. We are to leave on the first. Is that enough time?"

"For you Bard Tal, I'll make the time. Are you staying at Jenna's?" she asked. He said so. "I'll have them delivered before the first then."

Tal gave her a hug. Then, he handed her a heavy money pouch. A few minutes later and with the women chatting gaily about these fabulous new clothes, Tal took them to another shop. Here, both women were outfitted with warm, winter leathers and a set of everyday clothes. Finally, he visited the shop, which Jenna used, and had three more of these easy to slip into dresses ordered.

On their way back, Lia asked, "Tal you spent a fortune on us today. All those clothes. How do we repay you for this?"

"As owner of this troupe, it is my responsibility to acquire the costumes we need. Who knows how often we will be able to wash them, so we need several sets. Besides, in those dresses, you two are going to drive the crowds silly! That will bring us in more money. Anyway, I have all the money I could possibly use. I'd like to spend it on my friends."

The last day of August, a large covered wagon was delivered to the estate. It was painted in the same style as the costumes. The bottom was black, the top, red. A green band went around the middle. Inside the spacious wagon were five beds, three on one side, two on the other. The front portion held many cabinets where food supplies had already been stored, along with cooking and eating utensils. Another section would hold all their instruments securely and another large set of cedar-lined drawers were to hold their clothing. A small stove sat beside the rear door, which could provide either heat or cooking facilities in inclement weather.

An easy to climb stairs with wide steps led up to the door. Lia noticed at once that it was double hinged, just like Jenna's. Tal explained that this way, both women could easily go in or out. However, at night, when they wanted security, there was a low sliding latch that could be easily moved with one's foot, securing the door. Tal insisted that both women try it. Actually, it was very easy for them to slid into place and unlock as well.

"Tal, you've thought of everything!" declared Angus. Tal smiled. He had had years to plan this. While his brother was studying the combat arts, Tal had been planning his wagon.

Just then, Jenna came marching up to the five, five chain mail Santi del Dio fighters marched behind her. "Ah here you are, magnificent wagon, Tal. Impressive. So this is what you spent your study time on instead of fighter training?"

Tal's face reddened. "Auntie, how did you?" he didn't finish his sentence.

Jenna grinned, "Lad, nothing escapes the eagle eyes of Jenna Rose Weston. Don't you ever forget that." Both laughed.

"Seriously, Tal, now that you are finally ready to travel about, I want to introduce you to your constant companions, your security guards. This is Captain Vanna del Illaños, she is in charge of the Santi group. Vanna is a veteran fighter and was on the line with your father when he killed Emperor Justinian. She knows her business; listen to her, and follow her advice." Vanna was forty and well-muscled. "This is her husband, Thomasio del Illaños. Rosetta Salada and her husband, Gregorio. Both are superb long bowmen. And miss shorty here is Paolina Turelli; what she lacks in size, she makes up in power. I've seen her throw a two hundred pound man! So boys, do not mess with Paolina!" The young woman grinned, knowing that she was the youngest of the Santi party at twenty-one.

"Very pleased to meet you, Bard Tal," Vanna gave him a hearty handshake. "I fought alongside your father. Fantastic man, that Ket. I am indeed most honored to provide security for his son." She bowed. The Santi began shaking each of the musician's hands. When Vanna got to Lia and Zita, she was unsure of the proper greeting. Lia leaned toward her, and she got the idea; a hug would work well. The others followed suit.

Vanna said, "Tal, I must inspect your wagon, so that I can know its capabilities. Do you wish us to also travel in a wagon or may we ride our familiar horses?"

"Sure, check it out. Travel whichever way you most prefer. I will bring along five spare horses. The girls would have a hard time riding, so they would be for emergencies only. Plus, in bad weather, there should be enough room for you all to camp out beneath the wagon for shelter."

"Well, let's use your spares to carry our gear," Vanna suggested and began inspecting the wagon. Her husband went to check on the harness and horses; of these, he was the master.

While they were off inspecting, Paolina asked the women, "Say do you like pasta? I make mean pasta dishes. I'm playing cook on our trips. If there is anything special you enjoy, let me know, and I'll see if I can make it."

"Did you really throw a two hundred pound man?" asked Zita.

"Yes, he might have weighed a bit more, but he wasn't that good a fighter, however. You can count on us for protection. Those two are some of the best archers in the Santi. Vanna was on the battle line with Ket Bethany. She was part of that massive cavalry charge that went straight through their entire defense lines right for the Emperor. She knows her business. I don't think you could be in safer hands. Say, do you two really have silk dresses like they have been saying?" The women soon discovered that Paolina was quite talkative and very friendly and would quickly become their close friend.

On September 1, many carriages lined up in front of the main doors. It took over ten minutes for everyone to say goodbye to everyone else! The minstrels would travel in a coach so that they could see the scenery. Slowly the large group, escorted by an entire Santi squad, rolled out of the estate, with many hands waving farewell.

Four days later, the group rolled into Barcella. What a stark difference in cities, from a thriving city into one that had only begun to recover from years of suppressive, destructive occupation. However, Lady Jovanna's estate was still impressive, having once belonged to a wealthy nobleman.

As the group rolled up the long cobblestone driveway, many people came out to meet them. Jovanna had brought all the other women's relatives here to the estate so that they could finally meet their loved ones. Besides, she had something special in the works. For five families, there would be the shock of seeing their loved one with no arms. Jovanna had already instructed the family members of these five. Hugs, the women ought to be simply hugged.

Aura and Leslie Ann were watching over Gina, Gianna, and Gianni, the children of Tonia and Pina. Both women would now be living here with Jovanna, since their husbands were deceased. This way they would have all the help needed to raise the twins and Pina's daughter, Gina. "Here they come," Aura said to the very excited kids.

Once the carriages halted, everyone disembarked. Many just ran to their loved ones. Just as soon as these three children saw their mothers, they squealed and broke away from Aura and Leslie Ann, running toward them. The two women chased after the exuberant children. All three just grabbed their mothers and held on for dear life. Both women were crying tears of joy. They squatted down so they were at the same height; now the children could really hug their mothers. Gina asked, "Does it hurt mommy?" Gianna proclaimed, "We will help you with everything, mom, honest, won't we Gianni?"

Jovanna gave them all plenty of time to hug and chat. Meanwhile, she went to Tal and his group. As soon as Lia saw Jovanna coming toward her, she exclaimed, "It was you who rescued us!" She rushed to Jovanna and leaned in so that Jovanna could give her a hug. "Thank you, thank you, thank you!" she exclaimed.

Zita joined in, not wanting to be left out. Jovanna gave her a warm hug as well. "You two look like you have recovered from your ordeal. You have good color in your faces and high spirits. What's this I hear that you are going to go traveling about with Bard Tal here?"

"Yes, Lady Jovanna. I dance and Lia Ines sings," Zita proudly announced.

"Oops, I had better get these festivities going, follow me will you. Tal, get all the women you brought together up on my porch." Then she signaled Paul.

Paul called out loudly, "Places everyone. It's time for the ceremony." Evidently, the large group already knew where they were to stand. They congregated in front of the porch. Tal, Angus, and Sam led the women up to the porch and steadied them as they went up and stood in a line facing the large crowd.

"Ladies, gentlemen, children. Today we welcome back home the true heroes of Barcella. These brave women who stand before you represent the true spirit of Barcella, never giving in to suppression and oppression! They never gave in and have sacrificed everything. In a large way, their supreme sacrifice led to the successful freeing of Barcella from the overlords. Only when I learned of their plight was I able to obtain the forces require to invade, rescue them, and drive the barbarians from our land. These are the true freedom fighters, our true heroes. Today, ladies, I renew my pledge to you. All of you are welcome to come and live here in my house at any time, now or in the future. My house is now and forever more also your house." The crowd clapped and cheered.

"However, at this time, I wanted to do something to really honor you heroes. I wanted something that you could wear with the utmost pride, something that anyone in our land could see and recognize the wearer as being one of our most honored freedom fighters. Since I do not have the hands necessary to make the presentations, at this time, Aura and Leslie Ann will do the honors for me. Ladies, I present each of you with a very special medallion necklace, made of gold with emeralds. The inscription reads, 'Hero and Freedom Fighter of Barcella.'" The small crowd yelled, clapped, whistled, and cheered. Meanwhile, the two women began placing the medallions around each woman's neck. As they finished, Jovanna stepped up and gave each a hug as best she could. Uniformly, the women gasped at the gorgeous medallion, each worth at least a thousand gold coins; tears of emotion trickled down everyone's faces, including those watching the ceremony. To each woman, Jovanna said only, "Wear it with well-deserved pride."

The ceremony being done, the women stepped back down on the grass, and their relatives rushed to them. "Mommy, mommy, can I see it?" Gina, the seven year old daughter of Pina exclaimed. Pina, still teary, knelt down so she could see it. "Mommy, I've never seen anything so beautiful!"

"I know, honey, I haven't either! Hug me, hug me." Gina didn't need to be asked again. She threw her arms around her mother and hung on for dear life.

Roberto was hugging his sister, but Lia and Zita felt a bit distant. All of their families were dead. They had no one. Tal and Angus immediately remedied that. "Come here you hero," Tal said to Lia. "How come you never told me that you were a hero freedom fighter?" He hugged her tightly and let her cry for happiness on his shoulder. Beside them, Angus did the same for Zita. Jovanna saw the four and had to wipe tears from her eyes. She was now satisfied that all the women she'd help rescue were going to be all right. That meant everything to her.

Later, Jovanna held a banquet in their honor. After Tal and his group had finished eating, he whispered to his companions who agreed. He then spoke to Jovanna and the five left quickly. Meanwhile, the large gathering enjoyed their desert. Outside in their wagon, the men dressed Lia and Zita and themselves. Finally, helping the two down the wagon steps, they grabbed their instruments. One arm around Lia and the other carrying his lute, Tal proudly escorted her back to the dining room. Angus did the same for Zita. When they entered the dining room, they instantly had everyone's attention. The two women, so elegantly dressed, drew many whispered comments.

"Ladies, gentlemen, children, Bard Tal proudly presents the Traveling Minstrels. However, I must let you know up front that we five had not yet had time to do much practicing, so this may be a bit inelegant. For your evening's enjoyment, the Traveling Minstrels." Clapping broke out at once, and they moved to a spot in the large dining hall where everyone could see. Tal said, "One-two-three-four," and the music, song, and dance began.

They played for an hour. After they were done and the overwhelming round of applause died down, all the women surrounded Lia and Zita. Those with no arms had to brush up against the exquisite silk. Tal overheard several women commenting, "You both look so sexy — it is incredible!" Tal flushed, because they were supposed to comment about how fabulous they sang and danced.

Leslie Ann ran over to her brother and leaped into his arms. "Tal, you were great! What you did for those two makes me just want to hug you forever! Thank you!" Tal noticed that all the women were heading for a hallway. She whispered, "They need to use the pots. Besides, we all want to feel their dresses. Wherever did you find them?"

"Suzana made them," he replied.

"You old rascal, that cost a fortune!"

"They are worth it. Did you see how she danced? Hear that voice from heaven? True artists!"

Now Alyster, Lyle, and Alaric came over to shake Tal's hand. Leslie Ann hastily ran off after the women. "You call that an improvisation?" Lyle teased. "Bard Tal, you are well on your way to famous-hood!"

James came to shake his hand. "Well done on both accounts, Tal," he said in his usual reserved manner.

"Sir?" Tal queried, not sure of his meaning.

"Magnificent music and dance. And what you have done for those two women who have lost everything," he explained.

"They did it themselves, sir," Tal replied. "They are masters of their art forms. I am the one that is honored that they would consent to play with our troupe."

The next day, Bard Tal and his group said farewell and hit the road. They traveled the coast road back to Velona, then north to d'Grange, and into Mont Blanc. Each night, they practiced and rehearsed. However, Paolina and the two Santi men were commandeered into playing the logs for the heavy percussion sound so common in the Greenway. Tal definitely decided he needed a percussionist and soon. His plan was to learn as many Greenway songs and particularly the intricate dances as they could. This would really help Zita expand her routines. For these five and their Santi guardians, life had suddenly blossomed into full bloom with joy and happiness in abundance.

Not so elsewhere in Tarra, however.

Chapter 17 The Megalos Response

Pope Anaxagoras opened the package from Velona. It was addressed to him and came from the Lucifer's Spawn, Jenna Rose Weston. Inside, he found a letter addressed to him, but packaging hid the majority of the box's contents. Putting the letter aside, he remove the packaging, revealing several dried, corpses! He nearly dropped the box in shock and disgust. "Revolting woman!" he cursed angrily. "How dare she send me corpses!"

A while later, he cautiously opened the letter, wondering why this vile woman would send him dead bodies. He read.

15 August 640

Pope Anaxagoras,

What part of stopping the mutilation, savagery, and mistreatment of the young women of the Sea Princes do you not understand? Stop means ceasing, ending, doing it no more.

I agree that you and your cohorts in crime have apparently stopped cutting off women's appendages. That I commend.

However, your new methods are equally abominable! Encasing women's arms across their backs in those metal entrapment devices and then pouring hot metal into the locks so that they cannot be removed caused what you will find in the box. These belonged to several women that were rescued from your devices in the caves in northern Barcella. These women had their arms locked this way for many years, along with similar head devices that lock a metal ring in their mouths forcing them always to be wide open, so that they cannot speak and only eat like licking dogs. The result of such long-term mistreatment is what you have in the box — arms that have become the arms of corpses. One touch and the arm crumbles! Eight women no longer have any arms at all, thanks to your new tortures.

This evil mistreatment has caused a wild reaction among the people of Barcella. In fact, this last straw broke the donkey's back, as the saying goes. Under the leadership of the last living heir to the throne of Barcella, Lady Jovanna Barcella, Barcella Freedom Fighters have retaken control of that sector. Every one of your Holy Paladins and your priests has been eliminated. The nuns have been sent to Vito, as were the Scholastic University teachers.

The new ruler of Barcella Sector has asked for assistance and support from the free peoples of Tarra. I have pledged Barcella with the full and complete support of the entire Santi del Dio. High Priestess Elona Po has likewise pledged the full support of Velona. Count d'Grange, the Commander of Mont Blanc, and the King of Calgary have done likewise. If you attempt in any way to interfere or retaliate against the Barcella Sector, the Free People of Tarra will take this as an act of war and call for another Crusade to drive you and your people out of every Sea Prince Sector.

Already, I have instructed the Santi Fortresses in your Occupied Sectors to begin a thorough search of those sectors to see if you and your people have so brutalize women in those sectors. If we find such is occurring there, you may expect further repercussions. I hope and pray that this was an isolated occurrence, perhaps committed by overly zealous religious fanatics and is not your Church's current policy toward women.

Sincerely,

Supreme Commander Jenna Rose Weston

"Oh dear god, what has been going on? We've lost Barcella?" He immediately sent for Supreme Prelate Thondakas.

"Look at what the Devil's Spawn has sent me. Oh, this is very bad, very bad. How are we ever going to deal with the repercussions from this?"

Thondakas smiled, his Pope had sent for him at once, not delaying for months as he had done before. Good sign, he thought. He looked at the disgusting box contents and then read the letter twice, before saying anything. All the while, the Pope was studying his face, attempting to glean some sign from him. Thondakas maintained his cold outlook.

"As far as I am aware, you have issued no such orders to have women encased in metal. You could safely reply to that effect. I will launch a full investigation and see to it that these things do not become known."

"Yes, yes, that seems to be a proper course of action to take, Thondakas, but what about the loss of Barcella? How are we going to explain that?"

"General Ali Sanches failed to put down the rebellion. He completely hid the true situation there from us. By the time that we found about his treasonous actions, it was too late. However, the loss is very small. There are hardly any people in that sector; it's largely uninhabited anyway. It is not an important development."

"Well, when you say it that way, it doesn't seem like much of a problem after all. I guess I was just overreacting, as usual. Forgive me, Supreme Prelate for bothering you over such small matters. However, I do fully appreciate your viewpoint. One day I will have a more complete picture of our situation. Thank you very much."

"Anytime, Your Holiness. I am here to protect and serve you. I will see that the Sectors are properly notified."

"Excellent. I will dispatch our enemy at once and then compose a document for the Senate. Again, thank you so very much, Thondakas. I don't know what I would do without you."

He smiled and left. Back in his private room, Thondakas spat on the wall and swore a curse at Sanches and the Demon Spawn. He'd lied; this was a powerful blow to the Church! How had his scheme gone awry? He'd never issued orders to seal the women permanently in these restraints. Curious, though how diabolically effective they had been. He pulled on his pointed beard lasciviously, wishing he had been there to witness the outcome. This he found a most useful fact and wrote it down in his private journal. One day, this ought to be very useful data.

"Brilliant, positively brilliant!" He grabbed his quill and paper, writing furiously.

General,

Bishop,

The Santi are on to the use of the metal encasements. Do not, I repeat do not leave them on permanently. There is a much better procedure to be followed from now on.

Any recalcitrant, unrepentant women whom you feel cannot be convinced to earn their Good Marks and for whom you have given up hope, lock them in the devices and send them here to the Mano del Dio. Do not inform the Pope of this action, for he has much greater concerns and worries than recalcitrant women.

Also, instead of hanging, crucifying, or beheading men who will not obey, place them into similar restraints and send them in secret to the Mano del Dio.

As soon as you have received this letter, under pain of the Holy Fires, burn it!

Supreme Prelate Thondakas

After making the necessary copies, he addressed the outer casings and sealed them with wax, placing his ring firmly on the molten blob. "There, step one done." He handed them to a messenger to be sent by the next boat. Now, he went in search of the Holy Constructor, the man in charge of building design and construction.

"Good afternoon, Supreme Prelate, how may I be of service?"

"I need a special set of underground chambers built in secret. There must be a concealed entrance just off the main tunnel by our dock. Here is a sketch of what I want the chambers to look like and the rough dimensions. How soon can this be completed?"

"It's priority, my son?"

"Top."

"Two months, maybe three at the longest."

"Good, sufficient time. Not a word of this to the Pope; he has far more critical items with which to deal. This is a security construction and is to be only between the Mano del Dio and you, highest security level."

He grinned, "As you order, Supreme Prelate. It shall be done. When finished, do the workers meet an accident?"

"No, not this time, just keep it secret." He shook the man's hand and left. All was falling into place. Sufficient time was always a consideration. The hidden chamber would be finished long before any possible occupant

366

could be brought here by ship. He wondered why it had taken him so long to realize this was precisely what was needed for the Sea Princes and any place else for that matter. He whistled a cheery tune as he walked back to his room, for this was a great day indeed.

He felt so good in fact that he decided to send a Mano del Dio to each of the sectors to deliver the messages personally!

Chapter 18 Jenna's Reaction

Aghast at what she had just witnessed, withered corpse arms resulting from the women's long imprisonment in these horrid devices, Jenna left the infirmary as the Healers prepared for the emergency surgery. She hoped that these poor women would survive the operation. They had suffered so much and had not given up hope; they just had to make it.

She found Paulette and ordered her to begin making the many Mind Links with the other Santi Communicators in the fortresses of the Occupied Sectors. Meanwhile, she rounded up the others in her Circle and brought everyone into her meeting room. She was furious, of that Hank was utterly certain.

"Jenna, you have got to calm down. I cannot make the Mind Link with you," Paulette urged.

"Okay, okay, okay! Oh, okay," she said at last, realizing that she was indeed quite angry. She sat down, took a deep breath, and calmed her emotions. She felt the tug of Paulette's gentle touch on her mind. Soon she recognized the presence of all the others as well.

Jenna here. I have the most horrific news to relate. Jovanna has indeed rescued the imprisoned women, but it is far, far worse than any of us expected. Let me replay what I just witnessed in our infirmary.

She forced herself to relive the last hour, beginning with the final attempts to remove the metal encasements. The shock, horror, surprise, and revolting disgust that she received from the others backlash hit her strongly, but she was expecting it and dealt with the violent mental reactions of the others.

God, like corpses? A slight touch and the bones crumbled? These and similar comments flooded uncontrolled back into her mind from the others. *Yes, yes, yes,* she sent back.

One by one, each of the Occupied Sector Fortresses reported to her that thus far no one had seen anything amiss, no secret prisons, and no torture devices. Every inspection had turned up nothing unusual at the various Nunneries. James Woodworth, Commander of Fortress Barcella sent, *We had no indication that this was going on in our sector either. Yet, this torture has been nevertheless going on for years, right under our very noses!*

Jenna asked each of the commanders to double check everything. Perhaps we had all missed a vital clue. Paulette broke of the many connections. "Well, that was ghastly," she commented. "Right under our very noses. Not so observant are we?"

Jenna thought for a moment and then said, "Go fetch me maps of all the occupied sectors, as detailed ones as we have. Let's clear off the table.

We must be missing something."

Allan, Ben, and Hank returned shortly with their arms full of maps. Everyone helped spread them out; even Janna and Ariana helped hold down their curling edges. "Hank, place a cup on where Jovanna found the secret prison. Put a biscuit where Fel came across the other one." He did so. "It's obvious that they were taking her north to the prison and in secret. Let's assume that the entire operation is a secret one, from the prison to the transportation of victims there. Now where would you place such a prison?"

Allan answered, "Someplace where it is not likely to be discovered. Ah, like in the far north, beyond the last rim road. The limestone caverns of northern Barcella would be perfect. No one goes there; no one lives anywhere around there."

"Then we should concentrate our efforts only in the far northern portions of each sector. Let's see if anything pops out on the maps as likely locations in the other sectors," Jenna suggested.

"Good god! North Point," exclaimed Allan. "It was the Sisterhood's secret base where they kept secure for their mothers and children, their safe house. What irony if it is now being used as a torture chamber for the very women it used to be protecting. We ought to have the Zargarb Circle check it out."

"Excellent, but what about these other sectors?" she asked.

No one had any real ideas. "Okay, then we need to get all the ex-Sisterhood folks in here who are totally familiar with the far north of each sector. Send out messages to all the scout squads and regiments. Have them contact Paulette if they have someone who has such knowledge," Jenna ordered.

After another two days, they had all the information collected. Solamina had many caves in the far north, however, these were now being used by the banditos, hardly a place for a secret prison. Only a few other sectors had caverns in the far north, unfortunately. Armed with the most information she could acquire in such short a time, Jenna began contacting the individual sector leaders, via Paulette.

Jenna here. Andre, you and Lenkova take your Circle and check out North Point. Be careful, we suspect that it would be an idea location for their secret prison.

If it is, what are our orders? Andre asked.

Spy on them; find out as much as you safely can. Report back. Do not attempt to rescue them at this time. If there are other prisons, I want to hit them all at the same time, so that one sector cannot alert another and quickly move their prisoners.

An hour later, Jenna relaxed a bit; she had all the Occupied Sectors now out checking the far northern areas. All except Solamina. This sector was far more difficult, because the banditos controlled nearly all the outlying areas. Instead, she asked the commander there to get into communication with the banditos and see if they might have seen anything unusual or had other ideas where such a prison might be, if indeed there was one in Solamina.

Now there was nothing more she could do, but wait. It would take days before anything concrete could be found and relayed to her. Instead, she went to check on the well-being of the women and see about therapy sessions for those whose arms were still intact.

Andre was the first to report back. He was angry, but Lenkova was positively livid! Indeed, the Holy Paladins had found their abandoned complex at North Point. Six men were stationed there. Despite Jenna's orders, he and Lenkova had snuck into the complex in the middle of the night. Both were very familiar with the complex's layout, having lived there quite some time many years ago. Andre reported seeing twelve women prisoners all encased in metal contraptions. They could not see their condition, however, because it was very dark in that room. Andre literally had to drag Lenkova out of there to keep her from attacking on the spot. The rest of his Circle nearly had to restrain her physically from trying to go back, kill the bastards, and rescue the women on the spot. Jenna reiterated her orders not to do anything until all actions could be coordinated.

Vito reported in next. They had found what appeared to be a recently used complex of crudely built buildings, but they were currently empty. Based on the descriptions of the living conditions that Jovanna had discovered in the caverns, this place may have held similarly imprisoned women. A close study of the nearly grounds yielded a cemetery with relatively fresh graves. On a hunch, they dug up two of the graves and found two dead women, whose bodies were encased in similar metal devices. Although now empty, the group was going to stay there and keep watch, perhaps more prisoners would arrive in time.

Bonilla reported that one cavern complex was in use by the Holy Paladins. However, they could not tell if there were any prisoners being kept inside. Awaiting further instructions, the small group would keep it under close observation.

Pieta reported in a day later with a similar finding to that of Bonilla. Indeed a cave complex was in use by the Holy Paladins. Purpose: unknown as yet.

Solamina was very problematical. Since all the other sectors apparently were mistreating women in the same way, assuming the caves in Bonilla and Pieta did indeed house such prisoners, Solamina shouldn't be different. Only the actual location was a complete secret, because the far north was controlled by the banditos, who swore there was no such prison anywhere around the north.

"We can hardly just go in and attack the complexes in Bonilla and Pieta," Allan complained. "We have no proof that anything is amiss there."

"If they are holding prisoners there, and we attack North Point in

Zargarb, surely they will hear about it and take preventative measures in Bonilla and Pieta," Ben reasoned.

"We really need to have a look inside those places," Jenna concluded. "We cannot presume they are guilty."

"Well, we could have them watch the place for a long time. Eventually, they may see them bringing in another victim. Then, we would know for sure," Hank said.

"Yes, but then those in North Point would have to suffer even longer; some may die. Besides, how long can we hold Lenkova back?" Allan replied.

"Well, they've kept her constrained for several days now; a few more won't hurt," Jenna said.

Paulette interrupted, "Saxon Bye of Solamina wants a word with you." She finished the Mind Link between the two, going via his Communicator, Matilda Brighton.

Saxon here. I am on my way back to the city. I just had an idea, Jenna. I think we can discount any possibility of a secret prison up here in the north. The banditos control every inch of it and know every movement they make outside the city walls. If there is such a prison, it must be within the city walls. However, I got to thinking, Jenna. The prisoners are likely to make noise. Instead of gags, their mouths are forced open. Hence, any such prison within the city cannot be above ground; the noise would surely attract someone's attention. My bright idea is to see if there has been any new underground construction that has taken place within the last few years. I've put Emil Brighton on it until I can get back to the city. Can you give us a few more days to see if this pans out?

Jenna validated him on his excellent analysis and theory. He would have his few days; besides, she still hadn't worked out what to do about the other two sectors. Waiting, we all hated the infernal waiting, but we had to be sure, and we had to give them time to find Solamina's secret location.

The next day, both Pieta and Bonilla reported in. The Judgers had snuck in late at night by using their spells to put the guards to sleep. Both sites reported women prisoners, though the count was not accurate. That was clinching news, at least. Now we made plans for their rescue, while waiting on Solamina.

Beth Ann stood firm, "Absolutely under no circumstances are they to make any attempt to remove the arm encasements! If they have been locked up for years, their arms are likely to have completely atrophied, just like those in Barcella, requiring immediate surgery! You can't do that out there in the field; it's too risky. And we all saw the difficulty of removing the head locking devices. No, they must all be brought back here where we can deal with them properly. After all, they deserve the very best care that we can possibly give them!"

"Well, they can't travel by horseback," Jenna ruled that out. "Although that could be fast, how would they stay on the horse, especially if they are severely starved? Caravels would be the fastest, yet getting them transported in secret from the far north all the way down to our fortresses would be nearly impossible without being seen. So caravels are out. That only leaves one possibility, wagons traveling across the very high country, the Paese di Dio. We should send along plenty of wagons, Healers, and a fighter escort force, sufficient to defend them, if the Holy Paladins make any attempt to come after them."

"Are they to kill the paladins running the prisons?" Allan asked, thinking ahead.

"Good question," Jenna replied. I sent her the answer. "The one thing that is utterly imperative is to let no one escape to tell what we have done. Either they are killed or they are captured and brought back here. Further, any corpses are to be buried and the burial site disguised. The facility is to be torched, burned. If it is buildings, burn them down. If caves, burn out what is inside. We do not want these facilities to be back up and running quickly."

"Coordinated attacks are the key. We must have wagons at the ready when they are to attack. I'll estimate that we need ten wagons, plus one for supplies. Pull in five scout squads to accompany each pair of wagons into a sector. Let's use the Strike Regiment for security. It can divide up to provide support against counter attacks in any given sector."

"Finally, after the wagons and people move out heading north, I want their tracks wiped clean until they reach the high country. I don't want trackers easily figuring out where we went. Okay, got all that written down?"

"Yes, got it," declared Beth Ann.

"Paulette, let's contact the forces who are right now watching the prisons and get their reactions to this plan. The major delay is waiting for a pair of wagons to get all the way across to Zargarb. Maybe they will have some alternatives."

First, she made contact with Andre and the Zargarb group. After she explained Jenna's plan, Andre sent back, *Lenkova and I already figured that you'd want them sent overland and that wagons are needed. We've already snuck three wagons up here; they are parked just off the high country waiting for our move. Tell Jenna not to send them here; that will shorten the time needed to get this going by at least ten days.*

Things improved with each contact. The Pieta, Bonilla, and Vito groups had also brought up a supply wagon for their own use. They needed food and water, hence the wagon. Since they did not know the number of prisoners, they suggested that we gamble on all fitting into one wagon. Then, if one sector had too many, they could off load some on another wagon when it caught up to it. Of course, that did not make sense. If the attacks occurred simultaneously, each set of wagons would be leaving at the same time, but from vastly separated locations.

In the end, Jenna bowed to the consensus of those in the field: let them use their own wagons. Have her Santi forces ride as fast as possible to get to their locations. That would delay the starting date the least. Another Protector pointed out that sending an entire regiment would be far more likely to attract attention because of its size. She settled for sending out the five scout squads, each of which had a Healer and Communicator with them. She also got the agreement from those in the field to remain near the high country until the last wagons pass their location. If trouble developed, the Guardians would be able to aid the scout squads. That meant the Vito group would be out there on guard duty for quite some time until the Zargarb group traveled all the way to their location.

With everyone in agreement, at last, Jenna sent the five scout squads out. The designated date of the simultaneous rescues would be August 20. Once more Jenna spent her time on therapy sessions, anxiously awaiting the 20th. When the day arrived, she was more jittery than normal. So much would happen, so much would be revealed. Now they would know how bad things really had been, how much the Church had hidden from them.

However, Solamina reported in first. Saxon had indeed found their secret prison, well hidden with the city proper. It lay below an inn. An underground prison had been dug, and at least one woman was brought in late at night. Two paladins led her inside the inn, draped in a blanket so no one could see her or her encasement device. Later the paladins left the inn. Saxon decided to coordinate his raid on the inn with the rest of our raids. The women would be sent to Velona on their caravel this very night, if any were found in there. Saxon launched his raid at midnight as well.

"Finally!" Lenkova declared, as the three wagons rolled up to their position just north of North Point. The scout squad dismounted, tied up their horses, and fanned out surrounding the cave complex.

"Remember, let me put the two guards to sleep before you sneak down," Art reminded Lenkova in particular. He waved his hand as the signal that he was heading down to the complex. Art stole up as close as he dared to the two guards, who were standing near the main cave entrance. He chanted briefly and watched as the guards slowly slipped to the ground fast asleep. He waved his hand, and many dark forms swarmed over the outer grounds heading for the entrance. When the rest of his Circle joined him, he conjured his blue light, which provided just enough illumination for them to see their way around inside the very black caverns.

They headed to where they suspected the others were sleeping. Quietly, the seven moved up to the four sleeping forms. "Now," Art whispered. Strong hands clamped down on mouths, while swords touched the necks of the sleeping men. Startled awake, they were instantly subdued. Without a word, all four were tied and gagged. Art then led them outside into the arms of ten of the scouts, who led them north away from the complex.

Next, all seven cast their blue lights and thoroughly searched the rest of the cave complex for other men. Satisfied that they had all of them captured, methodically, all the many oil lamps were lit, and Lenkova went to the fenced area containing the imprisoned women. "Santi are here to rescue all of you. It will be just a minute." She heard moaning and other unintelligible sounds from some of the dark forms lying on their hay piles. Other forms stirred awake. Art arrived proudly displaying the key to unlock the gate.

All seven went inside to the women. First action, remove their blindfolds. Second action, Le Ann, their Wid, explained slowly and carefully what had happened and what was about to occur. "The Santi have at long last learned of your imprisonment and torture. We have captured all the Holy Paladins here in the caves. You are now finally safe. However, we do not have the tools necessary to remove these horrible devices from your bodies. Thus, we are sending you all to Velona and the Santi main headquarters, where they can remove these nasty metal things. They have already freed over a dozen Barcella women from these devices. So yes, you will be freed from them just as soon as we can get you there."

"We will take you there by wagon and make all haste to get there as fast as possible. We leave shortly. First, our Healers wish to examine each of you to see if there is anything that we need to do for you first. Second, our cooks have prepared good, healthy, nourishing food, fixed so that you can swallow it. As soon as the wagons roll, someone will feed each of you. In fact, we hope to fatten you all up by the time you get to Velona. Third, when you need to go to the bathroom, just rock back and forth; someone will help you at once. Fourth, we will all ask questions that you can answer yes or no by shaking your heads. Now does everyone understand this? Shake your heads if you do."

All eyes watched the fifteen women. All heads answered yes. At once, the two Healers began making their observations. Just as soon as the Healers passed one, a Guardian helped the woman walk out of the complex and into a wagon. There, she was covered by blankets. "None have injuries that require immediate attention," Ann reported to Le Ann. "The Scout Healer can take care of the minor cuts and scrapes from groveling on the stone floor while en route. Let's get them on their way."

Nine women occupied two of the wagons, while the six captured men rode in the third. Part of the scout squad led the wagons northward, while the remaining ones followed, using brush to scratch out signs of their passing.

Meanwhile the Zargarb Circle thoroughly searched North Point. They found little of value. Next, they gathered all the oil kegs and doused everything, emptying it all. Finally, beginning with the back panty room, they brought conjured fires down upon the oil soaked items. At once, fires began to rage and crackle. As they backed out, they set that room on fire. Finally, using a rope attached to several horses, they pulled down the iron fence. That was Lenkova's touch.

Fred, their Loremaster, went to examine how well the trail of the wagons had been covered, adding his expertise to the cover up. Satisfied, he returned to find the others now mounted and ready to depart for Zargarb. He put the final additions on hiding their tracks, while the others watched the flames that were coming out of the mouth of North Point. Nothing outside was in danger of catching fire, however. Quietly, the seven left, heading east and south. They would arrive at their fortress beside Zargarb from the east as if they had come from New Barq.

As they rode, Mary, their Communicator, made contact with Sally back at their fortress and with Paulette, relaying the results. Jenna sent back her thanks for a job well done.

In Solamina, Saxon led a party of twenty-five Santi fighters in the back way. That is, they walked along the beach until they reached the wall. Here, they stepped out into the Med Sea and moved around its edge and walked ashore inside the city. Next, they hiked along the deserted public beach and ducked under the docks. Here they waded through piles of garbage until they got to a trap door in the deck. Quickly they scrambled up the vertical ladder twenty-five feet to the planked surface of the docks, near the moored ships. Once everyone was up, the door was closed, and Saxon led his party along the deserted streets of the city. They made their way eastward until they were fairly close to the eastern gates. Here lay the pub called Ale Alley, beneath which lay the secret prison.

Saxon fiddled with the lock and soon had the door opened. Once everyone was inside, he shut and locked the door, but left a master key in its lock, in case they needed a quick escape. Now using his blue light, he began searching for a way into the underground chambers. He found a trap door in the floor of the storage room. Next, he carefully raised the door. A faint light from an oil lamp desperately in need of a cleaning shown back at him. They are making it too easy, he said to himself. Cleverly, a ramp led downward, not steps or a ladder. It would be too difficult to get a helpless victim down stairs or ladders.

Silently he headed downward. He was in a long hall, narrow and crudely dug. A few feet further on down, two rooms opened on either side. Both were dark. Using his blue light, he peered into the one on his left. It held a crude kitchen with food supplies. He turned to the one on his right. Ah, it had a table, two chairs, and two beds. Two men were sleeping on the bed. He signaled the Santi behind him, holding up two fingers and making an X sign, meaning they were to take them out. He walked on down the tunnel hall. Another ten feet ahead, the tunnel opened into a large room, a metal fence blocked further passage. He looked beyond the fence and counted sixteen women lying on beds of straw on the floor. All were encased within strange metal devices, a leather blindfold over their eyes. At least they were consistent in their methods of torture, he thought to himself.

Behind him, he heard the guards being captured.

Once the men were tied and gagged, oil lamps were lighted, and everyone searched for the key to the fence gate. One woman found it and Saxon opened the gate. "Here's where I take over for a spell, Saxon," Elaina, the fortress healer said. "Ladies, the Santi have arrived to free you. We are going to remove your blindfolds first." Quickly, the many Santi moved over to the women and untied the leather blindfolds. The women gazed somewhat fearfully from person to person.

Elaina now said, "We have captured your guards and are going to get you to freedom as fast as we can. Unfortunately, we do not have the necessary tools to remove your metal devices. However, at the Santi headquarters in Velona, they do. There, they have successfully removed a dozen from freed Barcella women, just as you are. So have hope, you will be free of these horrible things just as soon as we can get you there. We will be sending you there by fast caravel tonight. Only a few more days, ladies, and you will be forever free of these restraints."

"First, I am a Healer, and I want to examine each of you to see if you need any attention before we leave here. When we leave, we will walk out of the eastern gate over to our fortress. If any of you are too weak to walk that far, someone here will carry you. We will not leave any of you behind; have no fear of that. Now let me quickly examine each of you, please."

Again, she found them to be in remarkable good health, considering they had been living worse than dogs. Mostly cuts, scrapes, and bruises from the hard stone floor were found. A half hour later, Elaina told Saxon they could be moved. One Santi per woman was the plan. Each Santi put their arm securely around a woman and helped her along the hall and up the ramp into the inn. When all were in a line there, Saxon opened the door and like a pied piper, led his band along the deserted streets until they drew close to the gates.

Here, the two night guards were on duty as they were every night. A simple chant from Saxon and both dozed off. Quietly, he opened the door within the big gates, which allowed a single person to step through. One by one, the women were led through the door. Saxon watched as another Santi took over leading the long string of people toward their fortress gates. After the last ones went through, he shut the door and secured it. He and three other Santi headed back to the inn. They had left one other man back at the inn, and when they arrived, he had everything ready. All the oil that he could find had been spread liberally all over the insides of the wooden structure. Saxon brought down a sheet of fire and the blaze began. Quietly, they all stepped outside, and he re-locked the door. They all slipped quietly through the streets back to the docks, down the trap door, across the beach, around the wall, across more beach, and finally entering the fortress gates, which they closed behind them. Mission accomplished; it had been too easy!

As soon as Saxon reported in, Matilda, their Communicator, made contact with Paulette, outlining the results. Even as she talked with Paulette, the Santi caravel was tacking out of their small port, carrying the sixteen women and Elaina to Velona, along with the two captured guards.

It was a long night for Jenna and Paulette. Slowly, the various Communicators began reporting in to Paulette, who wrote down the key details and relayed the reports to Jenna. It was nearly dawn when the last report came in to them. The final tally was this.

Zargarb	18 women (14 in the arts),	6 prisoners
Solamina	16 women (12 in the arts),	2 prisoners
Pieta	20 women (15 in the arts),	4 prisoners
Bonilla	10 women (7 in the arts),	2 prisoners
Vito	15 women (13 in the arts),	4 prisoners

"Oh my god, seventy-nine women!" Jenna exclaimed, overwhelmed by the numbers.

"The good thing is that they won't all arrive at the same time," Paulette sleepily replied. "Solamina's will be here first, probably within ten days or so. Vito's will probably take at least a dozen days to get here, the others after that four to five days apart."

"Yes, but once they are here, we'll have seventy-nine to care for and for quite some time! Seventy-nine armless women — that is going to tax us all!"

"Perhaps some will not lose them," Paulette tried to sound hopeful. "Not all the Barcella women lost theirs."

"True, but still, this is not good. I will have to call in all available healers within a hundred miles! And cooks, and nurses, dear me. We will be busy here." She yawned and the two finally went to bed. Hank rose shortly afterwards and carefully pulled the blankets over his sleeping wife. Today, he would manage all the children; she needed sleep. On the table, he found Paulette's tally sheet. He cursed and set about his morning chores. He knew that his wife was going to need lots of support in the weeks and months ahead of her.

In the early evening of September 1, just after the Barcella women left along with Bard Tal for Barcella, another large number of coaches pulled into the estate, accompanied by a large number of Santi Healers and their helpers. The caravel from Solamina arrived that afternoon. For the sake of the women, they did not disembark until full dark, whisking them off the caravel and into the waiting coaches. Almost no one saw them; besides, each woman was covered with a blanket.

They were ushered into the infirmary, which was now well lit. Jenna introduced herself and gave them her pep talk. She explained that tonight, they were going to get the rings out of their mouths and tomorrow morning, they would work on freeing their arms. At once, eight strong arms began the sawing operations, cutting through the headpiece at its critical point. It took several hours per person, but each finally had the ring removed. They could speak at last. In the meantime, the others were bathed and more properly clothed. A Healer did a close inspection to make very sure that nothing had been missed. Finally, all thanking everyone for everything, the women were made as comfortable as possible on the beds. Four women stayed up with them all night to help with any needs they might have.

The next day would tell all, and Jenna feared the worst. Beth Ann, now experienced with these devices, had catalogued the Barcella women's final condition along with the duration of their imprisonment. All those who had been encased for a year or less did not lose their arms. After that amount of time, most had. Hence, she did not want a repeat of the near disaster with the Barcella women, where they removed all the devices at once, only to have them accidentally crush their limbs prompting emergency surgery on a whole bunch of women at the same time.

Beth Ann decided upon the truth. Besides, they would find out the truth anyway very shortly. "May I have everyone's attention? We are now going to begin removing these horrible devices. However, before we begin, I want to sort you out a bit. Will all of you who have been encased like this for a year or less please step over by Jenna?" She watched the women move there, four had.

"Thank you. Next, will those of you who have been encased two years or less as best you can guess move over to Elaina?" Eight moved over to her. Four remained.

"Now why have I sorted you like this? I will be very frank and honest with you all. You deserve it, and we are going to give you the very best medical care on Tarra. As you probably have heard, we have finished rescuing a large number of Barcella women who were encased just as you are. In fact, the traps are identical to theirs. When we opened the cases, what we found was horrifying to behold. Trapped like your arms have been for so long a time, your muscles atrophied, bones lost their strength, and skin shriveled up."

"Uniformly, although I cannot guarantee this, those Barcella women who had been encased for less than a year still had their arms. It was a slow, painful recovery, but they all regained the full use of their arms. Those that had been like this for over two years were not so lucky. Their arms had died and were so thin and brittle that the slightest touch crushed the arms completely and to save their lives, these ghastly remains had to be amputated quickly. I'm so sorry to have to tell this to you four, but I do not expect that your arms are still alive."

"Those of you in the middle, I just don't know. We will do everything in our power to save your arms if it is at all possible. I just want you to be prepared for the worst." Naturally, the women began crying and sobbing.

"Now while I know this is the worst possible news that you could have right now, let me tell you a bit about the Barcella women who lost their arms. First, everyone here recognizes that all of you are true heroes. None of you ever compromised your principles and gave in to the vicious demands of your tormentors; you did not believe their lies, for this whole mess of Good Marks/Bad Marks thing is an outright lie, a total falsehood. I am so glad that you did not give in to their demands. You are true heroes and will be treated as such."

"Even if the worst comes true for you today, it is not the end of the world or your lives. Let me tell you a bit about two of the Barcella women who lost their arms. They continued in their determination to live and recover. One has become a singer and another is a dancer; both are now doing well and are out on a tour with a traveling minstrel band, having the time of their lives! Thus, I say, this is not the end of the world. Further, Jenna here has told you that you are welcome to stay here with us for as long as you desire. We will help you with everything. Cry if you like; it is worth crying over. Just do not despair. Wait and see just how all this works out for you, please. Now we will begin with the ones whose arms are likely to be saved. The rest of you may watch and see how it goes. Just be brave. We all here completely respect you and grasp what you have been through."

Jenna beamed. Beth Ann had done a fabulous job of communication with her patients, perhaps better than she could have done. Me, I sat quietly in the back of the room; mom had once more completely forgotten about me. Beth Ann, however, had not and winked at me. I smiled back.

Crack! The sound of a heavy hammer upon a steel rod pointed at the precise location on the metal casing echoed in the infirmary. The case cracked open. Another blow on the opposite side on the chest hinge and the whole device was opened. Very gently, Beth Ann began removing the contraption. She saw two arms that did not look too bad appear. "Can you feel my finger?" she asked. The woman could. Only with great effort and grimacing from pain was she able to undo her crossed arms, bringing them around to her front. They looked thin and very pale, but they worked.

The next three were about the same, somewhat atrophied, sore, but definitely, their arms would recover. Hank was taking notes, logging the results with the total time the woman estimated she had been restrained. She gave these four the option of being escorted to the bath and begin their therapy or they could stay and watch. All four declared that all sixteen women were in this together one way or another. They had formed a close bond with each other through their nightmare ordeal. Jenna took this as a very positive response indeed.

Now came the iffy ones. Of the eight, two had arms that were salvageable. However, everyone noticed how thin and gaunt their arms were. Their full recovery would take a much longer time. The other six women's arms looked much like those on a desiccated corpse! Uniformly all the others gasped at the sight. "Dead?" asked several women. Beth Ann replied they were. Very gently, these women were lifted up and placed in a sitting position.

"Whatever you do, do not bump those arms. They will crush into a thousand pieces, and we will have to do surgery immediately if we are to save your life!" They sat still as a board.

Now crying, the final four laid down on the floor to have theirs removed, knowing that their arms would look worse than the ones they had just seen. However, now they only wanted out of the abominable devices. True to form, their arms looked completely dead, which was Beth Ann's clever way of describing the atrophied arms in a way that the women could understand.

"You women are incredibly brave. I commend you," Beth Ann encouraged them. "Now the Healers will perform the surgery needed to save your lives. There is a very positive thing going for you however. Most of us were involved in the Crusades, attempting to heal those badly wounded in the battles. When we had to remove a man's arm, such as we will be doing here, they underwent intense, horrible pain. However, your arms are dead. You have no feeling in them. The surgery will be mostly pain free. The worst you are likely to feel is the needle pricks as we sew up your shoulders, and you have all probably felt needle pricks a lot, right?" Many forced a grin, what woman had not? "Here's how it works." She explained what she wanted the women to do and the eight Healers began to work on the ten women.

By lunchtime, the whole process was finished. The six with arms were now getting their first bath in years and their first massage. The ten were now resting comfortably in the infirmary, though many complained that they were still hungry.

I sent Beth Ann, *You did a super job! Thank you.*

Jenna just thanked her and gave her an enormous hug.

A week later, the Vito group arrived on September 8. The other ten were now able to get their first bath in years and were afterwards moved into the dormitory rooms. Interestingly enough, the other six insisted on helping tend to the other ten.

Beth Ann handled the Vito group of fifteen women in the same way. Once more, the results went as she had hoped. They took it bravely, though not without a lot of deep grief, which was to be expected. Six women still had their arms, while nine lost theirs.

On September 13, the Bonilla women arrived. Five lost their arms; five did not. On September 18, the Pieta wagons rolled in bringing twenty women, of which thirteen needed the surgery. On September 30, the Zargarb wagons pulled up at the estate entrance carrying eighteen women, of which ten were doomed to have the operation. All told, we had forty-seven women who were badly traumatized and needed heavy therapy.

Beth Ann took charge of handling the therapy for the eight recovering women from Solamina. However, Jenna wanted to give the worst cases the best possible therapy, but I knew that she was very much overwhelmed by the sheer numbers. Here on September 2, she would have nine bad cases. I knew that unless these women could actually remove and erase these horrible years of humiliation, trauma, and degradation, the loss of arms would prove too much for them to recover and have any kind of life. I walked up to mom that night as she sat at the table staring at her teacup, arms holding her head.

"Mommy, let me help you handle some of these worst cases. You know I can do it."

"But you are only five, Lizzy Ann." She suddenly looked very stupid, "Doh, as if that has anything to do with it! I must be tired. Lizzy Ann, are you sure that you want to take on this kind of responsibility? These women have been horribly brutalized."

"Mommy, what I had to deal with in the Crusades makes this look like almost nothing. We both know their fates if they do not get the trauma erased. They deserve the best we can deliver, and while you are the best, I think I am a close second."

"True, true, but what will they think when a little five year old girl sits down beside them to run their therapy sessions?"

"I know that might be initially a problem, but at least let me try, please mommy?"

"You should be out playing and enjoying your childhood, having fun. You've more than earned it you know."

"How can I play knowing the suffering they have endured and what their lives will be like if I didn't lend a hand?" She hugged me for quite some time, caressing my hair with her arms.

The next afternoon, Jenna spoke to the ten women who were in the infirmary; their stitches were nearly ready to be removed. "Today, I will begin your therapy sessions. I cannot promise you anything specific, but if you will just follow my commands, when we are finally done days from now, I believe you will love the results we get. However, there are so many of you that need it. We've told you that we have also rescued seventy-nine women all told from the Occupied Sectors. The others will be arriving during the next three weeks. I cannot handle all of you by myself, and yet I want you to receive the very best possible therapy. There is only one other person who is as good at this as I am. She has begged me to let her help, and I could not refuse. Some of you will be treated by her, my five year old daughter, Lizzy Ann."

The little girl who they had always seen standing around in the back ground, occasionally helping anyone who needed some assistance, stepped forward beside her mom, me. I smiled. Jenna continued, "If you will just follow her orders and do what she asks, you are very likely to find out for yourself that she knows what she is doing. I ask you to trust her. I know that she is only five, but you trust me, and I ask you to just give her a chance, please."

Mom picked out two women, those who had been encased for the longest times. Both followed us into side rooms off the infirmary. While mom pushed open the door with her foot, a sight not missed by her patient, I led mine into our room. "You can lay down on the bed if you like or you can sit, which ever you find the most comfortable. This will likely take us quite some time," I said as politely as I could. She chose to lie down, but I was not strong enough to help her down without a slight bump of her head.

I explained what we were about to do and had her close her eyes. "Now I want you to go back to the very first moment when you knew that something awful was about to happen to you, just before they took you away." She did so easily. "Now I want you to go through all that happened to you, step by step, telling me all about it, what you are seeing, what you are touching, what you are tasting, all about it."

She protested, "But this isn't fit for a child to hear. I would never tell any child these awful things; it's not right."

"If you want to have any chance of recovery, you must tell me absolutely everything, holding back nothing, and I do mean nothing! I am old for my age. I know all about rapes and tortures. Nothing you can say to me will ever offend me. I truly do understand what you have been through. Now what is it that you are seeing right there at the beginning?" She continued to have social reservations, so I peeked and said, "What is it that you are seeing there at the beginning, is that your husband that you are having sex with?"

"Well, yes, it is night. Someone knocks on our door. He answers it. "We've come for Julianna. She has been earning too many Bad Marks and must be taken to the Nunnery for retraining. We will return her when she has learned only to earn Good Marks. Now hand her over to us. He fights back. They tie me up. I scream as loudly as I can. They put a rag in my mouth and carry me out. I see my husband bleeding to death on the floor."

Thus, it began. Once I had her solidly back in the years long incident, she cooperated fully, not even realizing that she was talking to a five year old little girl. Her images were so strong, so vivid, so emotionally charged, so painful, that she could do nothing else but relive them. Every so often, she would repeat, "I'm so dead now. I have no life anymore." I worked her most of the afternoon until she grew tired, when I ended the session for today.

"I do feel somewhat relieved," she said to me afterwards. "But how can I live like this? I can have no life anymore."

"I understand, Julianna. Come on, let's get you to the chamber pot, and then let's get us some supper. I'm starving."

After dinner, I asked mom if I could also run a morning session and an evening one too. That way, I could triple the time and get three women working toward the removal of their traumas. We compromised. As long as I went outside and played after supper, I could do another session during the morning, while she conducted Santi business.

I ran Julianna the next morning, and finally we had gone through her entire ordeal one time. It had taken us over eight hours for this first pass. However, while she was running through it, I noticed that in fact there were two different aspects to her trauma. The obvious trauma came from her arms situation and all that that entailed. However, at various times she had also been raped, supposedly to earn Good Marks. These were two separate lines of emotional upset and pain, not one! I pointed this out to mom, who debated its significance.

That afternoon, I concentrated only upon one of the two. Julianna found moving through the rapes far easier to do, so I worked her through all those quite a few times. Each time she found more details, and the images became very vivid in her memory, but they were not discharging. Late afternoon, I asked her if she could spot an earlier time when she was raped. At first, she denied any such thing, but I gently kept her looking. All of a sudden, she spotted something, "This cannot be real. I'm imagining this." I coaxed her to run through it anyway.

Now we were off and really running! The lifetime before this one, she had also been beaten severely and raped! Although she felt some relief after going through this one several times, she found another earlier one, and then another earlier one. It was getting close to suppertime, but she then insisted that she had found yet another one! I had her go through it.

"I am a young woman in Zargarb. My father, oh god not him! My father rapes me and beats me. He breaks my jaw. I am in pain and feel such hatred for him. I take a butcher knife from the kitchen. He's snoring now. I cut his throat and watch his blood flow all over his chest, the bed, the floor, and even on me. The dirty bastard."

I had her go through it again, now for the first time, heavy yawning began. She could hardly talk because of the yawns. All of a sudden, she sat straight up as if a bolt of lightning had hit her. "Oh my god! Oh my god! I joined the Sisterhood, became a good fighter." She had her eyes open wide staring at me. "I was there! I was there! I was with Sister Isabel on the hill defending the city from the invading Centurions! I fought at her side! Lightning, she was pulling down lightning bolts everywhere. Thousands of Centurions, I killed many!" Suddenly, she screamed in pain.

"What happened?" I asked, although I was now also watching her pictures as they flashed by in her mind. Sorry, I was keenly interested.

"So few of us left now. A Centurion swings his sword, and my arm got cut clean off! The intense pain was horrible. I shrieked. He stabbed me in the throat; I gurgle and choke on my own blood and died beside Sister Isabel. Gods, I was there! I fought in the most famous battle Zargarb has ever known! I helped stop the Centurions when no one else could. We women did that, not the men. Wow! Incredible. Amazing. I knew I was powerful. No wonder I've never taken any crap from men! Wow!"

I ended off and took the still chatting Julianna off to dinner. While we all were eating, Julianna couldn't help but tell all the other women about what she had done. However, when she finished, she still insisted, "Well, that was then. Now I don't have any life anymore, not this way. Life is finished for me, you know. Can't live this way." I knew that I still had more to do, but I pointed out to mom the key finding: having no use of her arms in the present had somehow latched on to this earlier trauma of having her arm severely cut in a battle.

"So it is like grouping two or more sets of trauma together," she mused. "I can see how that can occur. Very well done, Lizzy Ann!"

The next morning, I found Julianna far easier to run through her basic trauma. She ran like a gazelle through all of it, yawning, and adding new details here and there. However, after another three passes, nothing more was happening, so I asked her if there might be something like this earlier. Immediately, she found something.

"Golly, this is a long time ago. It's Zargarb — looks like the city, but it is so small, not too many people like today. Oh, I was a thief!" she suddenly exclaimed. "My husband dies, and I have two small children to feed. No one is giving me a job. I am pilfering money pouches off the noblemen who are parading around the streets. Damn! I am caught. He's sentencing me. Oh god no! No! No! I cannot live that way! They didn't listen to me. Intense pain. Pass out. Woke up. Hands are gone. I scream and scream. I cannot live this way. I cannot take care of my children! I just cannot live this way. No. No. No. Now I am dead somehow."

I had her go back and run through it once more. She found more details, the colors of the noblemen's clothes, how heavy their money pouches were, and similar facts. Again, she went through the trauma of her punishment for thievery. "I cannot live this way," she repeated over and over and over again. Then, she brightened up, "Oh, I pulled my bandages off with my teeth and bit hard into the stumps. I let myself bleed to death. My two young children are crouching in the corner watching me. Oh no! Whatever possessed me to do that? Right after I died, I felt horrible. My poor kids! I totally betrayed them. Now they had no one. They will starve to death or worse. I want to take it all back, but as I was sort of floating upwards, and I knew I couldn't. I had really, really screwed things up this time."

"Yes," I encouraged her to continue talking. There just had to be more, I felt.

"Oh!" she said quite startled. "Oh, I was only thinking of myself! I was wallowing in self-pity and not being responsible for my children. Damn. I know better, honestly, I do. I really messed that one up. I should never have turned to thievery. I knew what would happen to me. God, it was all just self-pity, all about me and not what it should have been, about raising my children. Stupid me!" She began laughing. Occasionally, she would say again, "Stupid me." Immediately she laughed even harder. She was still carrying on at the supper table! She would look at one of the others who was now like her, and say, "Stupid me," and then laugh so hard that she nearly choked.

After dinner, she asked Jenna, "Excuse me, but do you have any ideas how I can do things with no arms? How can I do anything to help others?" That was music to Jenna's ears!

"It is not a problem, Julianna; we just have to learn new and inventive ways to do things, that's all. If you are willing, we can begin tomorrow."

"Thanks. I'd like that. I was being selfish and stupid once. I won't make that mistake this time!" She then walked over to me. "You wonderful little lady! I don't know how to thank you. If I had arms, I'd hug you forever! How about a kiss instead?"

She squatted down and gave me a kiss on my forehead. In turn, I threw my arms around her and gave her a long hug, saying, "Thank you, you did very well. Want to come outside and play kick ball with me a little while?" She didn't hesitate, throwing herself into the game as if she were my age, laughing all the while.

That evening, I overheard her talking to the other women who were waiting their turn at this therapy thing. "You just have to get that little girl, Lizzy Ann. You wouldn't believe what she can do! I am so alive! I've never felt this great ever!"

Beth Ann whispered to me, "You've made a fan out of your patient!" I grinned.

The next day, Jenna didn't have to ask twice to get me a new patient. They all wanted me. Okay, I won't bore you with more of these women's stories. Everyone was different. Everyone had horrible things happen, but they were never quite the same happenings. Still, they all had the common thread of imprisonment, loss of limbs, pain, humiliation, and/or rape, accompanied by massive degradation. Some patients took three or four days to remove the trauma, others more than a week. It seemed that we would never run out of patients. More and more kept arriving every few days, it seemed to me.

Mom and I worked on these cases every day for well over one hundred straight days! Finally, we finished the last of these women on February 1, 641. It had been a long ordeal for us, but one that we would not have traded for all the gold on Tarra. Seventy-nine women now had a real new lease on life. I had a whole lot of people to play kick ball with in the evenings, though we had to play indoors during the wintertime.

It was one thing to remove these women's trauma and another thing entirely to have them useful, helpful, productive members of society, not utterly dependent upon someone waiting on them hand and foot. Worse still, many had been artists or in the arts; I still had no answer for that problem. On the other hand, one afternoon after Julianna's great wins in therapy, Ariana and Hank found both Julianna and Rachele, who was

Jenna's first finished patient. Hank said, "Hey you two. I understand that you are not busy this afternoon. Can you come and lend Ariana and me a helping foot in the garden, please?"

"Okay, you asked for it," teased Julianna, who had now found her sense of humor. "A foot we can lend you, but I'm not so sure it's going to do any good. Besides we were painters, not gardeners." They headed out to the huge garden at the far end of the estate.

It was a warm early fall afternoon. Hank explained, "Ladies, we need to pick three baskets of tomatoes and a bag of beans for the cooks to use for supper tonight. Now don't ruffle your feathers, I know you don't have arms, but you have feet. You can sit on the ground and pick the best ones with your feet. I have made these baskets especially for you. See, this long leather carrying strap. You pick it up with your teeth and raise it up so, then quickly duck your head underneath the loop. Now the basket loop is over your head and shoulder one this side while the basket part is on your other side. It cannot be dropped or fall off. When you want to get rid of the basket, you merely squat down and duck your head out of the loop."

"This will take us hours to do," Julianna complained slightly.

Hank replied, "Julianna, Rachele, we have all the time in the world. I don't care if you take all afternoon to do this. All that matters is that you somehow manage to do it. That's what is important. You are learning new ways to do the simple things of life, that's all. And yes, it is awkward, downright clumsy at times. Just keep in mind the goal and keep at it until you achieve it. That's the key to success."

"He's right you know," Ariana added. "I get to pick the peas. While I am in a much better situation than you because I still have arms, I cannot pick peas with them. I use my toes. Rather get one between my toes and twist. Just try it and keep at it. You'll soon get the hang of it. I certainly did."

"Well, Ariana, if you are going to get any peas picked, I'm going to have to take Nicolina Sue from you and set her over there so she can watch you." She was holding her thirteen month old daughter in her arms. Ariana never went anywhere without her little girl.

"I can do it, Hank," she insisted and proceeded very carefully to place Nicolina Sue on the ground so she could watch everyone with her big blue eyes. Hank smiled.

"Which should we do first?" asked Julianna.

"Try the tomatoes; they are the easiest to pick. Mind you no green ones."

"Silly man, we're women, if you hadn't noticed," she jested and walked to the start of a long row of plants. Rachele joined her. First, they got themselves out of their baskets and then got down on the soft ground. Next, they began experimenting on how to use their feet to get a tomato off the vine. "Hey, I got one!" exclaimed Julianna. "I actually did it."

"Way to go!" Ariana complimented her. "I told you that you could do it. Takes time, but we have lots of that."

An hour later they each had a basket full of large, red tomatoes. Ariana also had enough peas in her basket, so she suggested that they take this first round up to the cooks. She put her loop over her head and then very carefully picked up her daughter, while the two women managed to get their loops over their heads without much trouble.

"She's cute," Julianna said to Ariana. "You sure do that well, I mean with no hands and all."

"Yes, but I cannot easily change her diapers, which need changing now. Honestly, by the time I get them changed, she has them dirty again, so I am willing to let someone else do that. I take her with me everywhere."

The three strolled up to the complex and through to the back where the kitchen was located, not far from the bath. The sense of pride and accomplishment shone on the two women's faces when they dropped off their baskets before the cooks. One said, "Well done you two, you have a good eye for the best tomatoes." Another cook took time out to change Nicolina Sue's diapers. Then, the three headed back to the garden, chatting all the way back.

"You are married?" asked Rachele.

"You bet. I met him here, where they brought me with my arms like this. You have to meet Ben! He's like the absolute nicest man, well Hank is too, and Allan. Oh heck, there are a whole lot of great men around here, really there are. But no one's quite like Ben. You just have to meet him." She chatted gaily away while they walked. "He's kind of shy, you know, took him forever to ask me to marry him. I had to kiss him first to get him started." All three laughed.

Just then Ben came around the other side of the garden, "Get who started?" he asked playfully as if he didn't know.

"You silly. Hey, this is Julianna and Rachele. They've just picked their first baskets of tomatoes for supper. Isn't that great?"

"Hi. I've seen you all at dinner, pleased to actually meet you in person." Since handshakes were out, he gave them each a solid hug, which brought a bit of a flush to their cheeks. "That is just terrific on the tomatoes. There is always so much to do around here, and no matter how hard we work, there always seems to be so much more that needs doings. I do hope you two will continue to help Hank, Ariana, and me here around the garden and fields. So few are actually interested in plants and gardens, I've found. Ariana here is a gem among gems! She loves this stuff as much as I do. See all those magnificent marigolds over there along the edge of the garden? All her work. She planted them all by herself. Helps keep the insects off the vegetables, you know."

"You did all that by yourself?" Rachele asked in wonderment.

"It took ages, but I kept at it until it was done. Now I am so glad that I did. Aren't they beautiful still? They last long into the fall so he and I can have fresh flowers in our room," Ariana gaily replied. "I'll give you a big tip, use your feet! I kept trying to use these and that slowed me down. Do you know that the legs are the strongest muscles in our bodies? Once I just let go of trying to make do with these and used my feet, why, things just went a whole lot better and faster. But if you keep at it, you will see for yourself."

Hank walked up, "She's right you know. You are only as helpless as you decide that you are. Where there is a will, somehow you will find a way, that's what I always say. It's served me well all these years. Now kids, we still have lots to do before supper." Ben gave Ariana a kiss and then Nicolina Sue. He and Hank went off to do some heavy plowing where the maize plants had been.

While the three women again set about their tasks, Ariana continued to chat away. "As I was saying, we just find new ways to do things. Like eating. You've seen the clever fork and spoon attachments that Hank made for Jenna. They slip over her wrists and then she can pick up and maneuver her food. He made some for me too. However, sometimes no one is around to put them on or take them off my wrists, so I just learned to use my feet. Good thing that I did, because very soon now I will have to start her in on solid foods. I'm going to have to feed her and I can't be asking everyone to put those bands on me and take them off so frequently. I've already practiced a lot. I'm sure I can do it all with my feet and toes when the time comes. It's my first child, you know, so I am not so sure when that time is supposed to be, but I'm sure that Ben or Jenna or Beth Ann or Lilly Ann will tell me."

She would have chatted on had Julianna not interrupted her, "Say, this isn't all that difficult. I think I have the hang of picking beans! Two weeks ago, I would never in a million years believe that I would be out here actually picking beans! It feels so good, you know!"

"Yes, me too," Rachele added.

"I know," Ariana replied.

During the course of the next week, they learned to pull up dying plants, pile them on the compost pile, and even loosen the soil. When she had finished loosening the soil where the row of plants that she had pulled out a few days before, Julianna said, "You know, Ariana, I rather like doing this, this gardening work. It's rather fun, don't you think?" Of course, that was the wrong thing to ask of Ariana, now a Loremaster herself, well, she had everything learned except learning to survive in the wilderness and finding paths. Those she would learn next year.

Although Jenna and I were constantly busy with therapy sessions, others lent a hand and took those that were ready into Velona to get new clothes. At last, the seamstress decided to make bi-weekly trips to the estate, because there were so many women who required new dresses. Yes, to borrow the mariner's favorite phrase, it took an all hands to keep everything running smoothly during this time.

Both Jenna and Elona Po were also looking ahead. Eventually, the women would need to find more permanent homes somewhere in Velona. They could not return to their homelands, that was a given, at least while their countries were being controlled by the Holy Paladins. Elona, ever the practical administrator viewed it this way. Some women may prefer to find a new husband and become a homemaker. Others might want to live independently, working in some career. Some, Jenna pointed out, were now sitting outside of their heads as a result of the therapy, and these were prime Guardian candidates, if only they were younger. Thus, there was always the possibility that they might like to become apprentices, much as Jovanna and Ariana had done. In any case, the women would inevitably need to become part of the Velona society.

What better way to do that than to hold a number of public dances, especially during the colder winter months. Maybe love might spring forth, maybe not, but Elona wanted to give these women an opportunity. Besides these late winter dances had become sort of a tradition in Velona, breaking the monotony of the long winter nights for the younger set.

Jenna also wanted the women to look and feel like real women, not as an armless cripple at the dances. Therefore, she ordered the seamstress to make each of the seventy-nine women a new fancy party dress based upon the designs the Bard Tal had bought for Lia Ines and Zita, sleek lines that did not try to disguise their lack of arms but celebrated their body's current form. She had seen how the women's opinion of their bodies had soared because of those dresses. Perhaps Tal was wiser than she had given him credit for, maybe anyway.

As to be expected, the women were a bit hesitant about going out to a formal dance. However, as soon as they saw themselves in these elegant dresses that showed off their womanly aspects, all agreed to participate. Many had doubts about how they would be accepted. If they were to be integrated back into society and not live as hermits, this they would have to face and conquer.

The afternoon of the first dance, the entire staff was kept busy helping the women into these dresses. There was no possibility that they could do this for themselves, not with this dress design. Then, hair had to be brushed and done up and so on. For transport, Jenna had hired nearly all available carriages in Velona that had not yet been hired, and after supper, nearly everyone at the estate piled into the many coaches for the short ride into town to the huge room of the Church of the Holy Rose, which served as the dance hall for nearly one thousand younger people.

I say younger people, but that really means thirty and under made up the majority. However, some Santi were obviously older, and some, like me, were quite young. As expected, the women made quite a splash in their party dresses. Other women took them under their wings and chatted, asked numerous questions, and introduced them to anyone they knew. Men flocked around them, begging for a chance for a dance or two. In short, these women found that they blended in with the local younger folks very easily. Many new friends were made that night; many received invitations to other parties, for visits to their homes and shops, and even some were asked for dates later in the week.

After this first experience, Jenna only had to mention the word dance, and everyone was eager and ready to go again. Thankfully, Elona had six more scheduled through the end of March. Two women were asked to join a couple amateur music ensembles that played for weddings and other celebrations. Three were asked to join the Expressive Dance Club, where the dancers worked on making their dances communicate entire stories. Nearly half already had official dates lined up as soon as the weather warmed up.

Ten women greatly desired to study and learn as apprentices. Julianna and Rachele were among those then. Thirty others asked about the possibility of joining the Santi del Dio, but only if they could find something that they could contribute. However, before Jenna would allow any to commit to such decision, she wanted to ascertain the situation with any possible family members who might still be alive back in their homelands.

If any still had a husband who had not deserted them or who had not actually turned them in to be tortured, those had to be contacted, assuming the woman desired it. Some women had children when they were abducted. Those had to be located as well. Where appropriate, the children who so desired to move to Velona to be with their mothers were brought here. Ten women were finally reunited with their fatherless children, which I thought was excellent. Four husbands also came to Velona. While these numbers were small, it meant the world to those women. In short, what could have been a complete disaster turned completely around into renewed lives for these badly mistreated women.

Chapter 19 A Blow for Justice

Aghast at what she had just witnessed, eighteen women horribly tortured with the damnable metal devices forced to live worse that a pig, Lenkova was positively furious. She and the Zargarb Circle had returned to the Santi Fortress Zargarb, just east of the city. All were in Thomas Whiteheath's large planning room, along with the other fortress leaders. "I am not going to stand for this brutal treatment of women here any longer. We must take decisive action!"

While no one in the room disagreed with her, Le Ann, the Wid, and Tom, the Fortress Commander and Protector, attempted to calm this emotional fighter, perhaps the best fighter in the land. "Lenkova, we all feel as you do, total outrage over this situation. I feel just horrible knowing that ten of our women lost their arms due to our missing the fact that this was even going on!" Le Ann agreed, in her usual subdued tone. "However, what remains is simply what is it that we can do here? One factor that we have in our favor is that we have the one remaining person who can rightfully claim the throne of rulership, Ariana Zar. However, she is a Loremaster and not interested in claiming her birthright."

Art Weatherby, the Circle's Judger, and Art Longton, the Fortress's Judger, had been chatting together for some time now. Longton decided to interject a thought, after nodding at Weatherby. "There are other factors we might leverage: the steady attrition of the numbers of Holy Paladins, the local thugs, led by Rodrigo Decasas, the low morale of the citizens who are eating at bare subsistence level still, and the near failure of Helas's attempt to recruit local men into their paladin organization."

"Hold on a minute," Le Ann cautioned. "Before we go making grandiose plans, we all should realize that we cannot count on any substantive assistance from headquarters. Seventy-nine women are en route, and she and her total staff are going to be totally tied up for months dealing with that mess. I insist that we do not bother her with our problems. She's got plenty of her own, do I make myself clear?" Everyone nodded affirmatively.

"Good. Now then, let's do this properly. Leave absolutely nothing to chance. First, we need a precisely accurate analysis of the current fighting strength of the Holy Paladin organization in the sector. We need to know just how far this thug Rodrigo is willing to go. We know our fighting strength already. Finally, we must consider the aftermath. Who will lead the sector? Who will run it? We cannot just kill all the paladins and then expect the sector somehow to get better. If we take out these evil men, it is our responsibility to replace them with a government that will rapidly improve conditions here. As far as our taking such an action, I believe that we are within the guidelines stated by Jenna in her ultimatum to the Senate of Megalos and the Pope. I would so argue anyway; these latest tortures will provide all the ammunition I would need to so argue. However, let's keep this conspiracy just between us for the time being. The rest of the fortress and staff do not need to be involved just yet. If we can devise answers to the complete situation, then we can fully brief them. Agreed?" Everyone one did.

General Helas Taxos sat quite drunk in his easy chair. It was only midmorning; perhaps the day would pass him bye he thought. "Everything is falling down around me! Incompetence lies everywhere! I'll drink to that!" and he took another long gulp from the half-empty wine bottle. He'd received more bad news this morning. "Damn dispatches anyway. Maybe I should just burn them without opening them! I'll drink to that," and he took another long drink and burped. The room was slightly spinning, but so was everything else in his life here in this god-forsaken land. Whatever did the priests think was so valuable here anyway?

One dispatch contained the latest census estimates, preparatory to the official tax collection time, which would begin next month. "Down yet again! Where are all the people going? Surely we have not killed that many, not that I can recall anyway, but maybe I'm not recalling so well anymore. I'll drink to that," and he did so. The population figures indicated the city only had some thirty-five thousand left and barely twenty thousand in the outlying towns. Fifty-five thousand! When he had taken control of Zargarb, the first census listed well over two hundred fifty thousand people here in the sector. He dare not report fifty-five thousand. No, for years now, he continued to report two hundred thousand people in Zargarb. That meant that he had to pay the required taxes on the missing people, costing him personally two hundred thousand gold coins this year alone.

For many years, he had the funds to do so. His first brilliant action upon taking over Zargarb was to eliminate all the nobles and their families, confiscating their massive wealth. Gold, gems, jewelry by the crates lined one room here in his mansion, which had belonged to some nobleman whose name he had long ago forgotten. Yesterday, he had gone into the treasure room to estimate the funds needed to cover this year's taxes. Barely ten thousand coins remained, no gems, no more jewelry, he'd sold them off to cover last year's shortfall.

He suddenly either reported losing two hundred thousand people or failed to send in the required gold. He was doomed. His head would be placed on a pike either way. His career was officially over, but the second dispatch had sent shivers up his spine. A Mano del Dio representative was coming here to speak with him personally. These ruthless, cold men in black frightened him. Not even battlefield combats so affected him as the mere presence of these men. Although he had no clue about what the security forces might want of him, in no conceivable way could it be either good or beneficial to him. He drank once more.

The High Priest, Rolan Dax, was of no use either. The silly priest continued to preach, and the people continued not to listen to him. He knew, he sat in on some services and watched the locals doze off or nod their heads as if listening, all the while playing cards with each other in secret. "Stupid old man thinks he is actually doing something here! Idiot! I'll drink to that," and he did once more.

Maybe the Mano del Dio wanted an accounting of the number of his Holy Paladins. He'd stopped reporting their losses right after the Junction affair years ago. He continued to report that his forces were at full strength, nearly two thousand strong. In reality, the third morning dispatch from his aide worried about possible security problems because there were only four hundred give or take a few. All attempts to recruit local men into their organization resulted in total failure. "These people here are complete idiots!" He'd watched as a new recruit drew his sword from its sheath and managed somehow to cut the cinch of his saddle, sending the saddle and rider tumbling to the ground. "Idiots, all of them are idiots! I'll drink to that!" Unfortunately, the bottle was empty. He had drunk the entire half gallon of wine this morning. He stood up to go fetch another bottle, but was so drunk he could not keep his balance; his head was swimming in circles. "Gotta lay down!" He saw a nice rug on the floor and more or less fell onto it and went to sleep.

Sleep, sleep, I cannot even sleep anymore, he thought to himself, though he found it funny that he was talking to himself in his sleep. As soon as he closed his eyes, the same haunting images reappeared! That girl, that young innocent girl. So many, many years ago. Down in the basement of the Nunnery. They'd dressed her up nice and pretty for him. He was kind to her. Yet she scratched his face. But those were not the images that haunted him, no, those were always the images he saw before the haunting ones came. He could do nothing about these images; they just came of their own. He'd tried, oh how he'd tried to extinguish them from his mind, but nothing worked, not even so much wine. Now they just came in a more jumbled fashion, but they came anyway. Drunk, he didn't hurt so badly, so he drank a lot these many years.

There was the basement. There she was tied helpless on the bench. Was that his hands on the axe? Perhaps not, perhaps they were; he could no longer tell. Blood squirting everywhere, on his face, chest, and arms. He saw blood everywhere. Now his imagination went wild as it always did. Like two fire hoses, her stumps shot blood all over him, covering him, drowning him. He was panicking, couldn't breathe. He felt like he was drowning in her blood, which continued to drench him endlessly, as if she would never run out of blood! He tried to scream, but could only gurgle. He twisted to escape, but no matter which direction he turned, there were the two stumps pumping away straight into his face. In total desperation, he began using his hands to swat the streams away from him, faster and faster he thrashed. Then, it stopped as suddenly as it began. It always did, he'd thrash so hard and then nothing. No, not nothing. It became utterly spooky, un-worldy, ghastly.

Now his eyes saw the two disembodied hands, pretty hands, nice nails lying on the floor, lifeless; he'd cut them off her. They would never scratch him again. He showed her all right! As usual, the general peed his pants involuntarily at this point in his nightmare. The hands began to move! Slowly the fingers stretched out, touched the ground, and contracted, bringing the hand an inch closer to him! Petrified, he watched the pair continue relentlessly inching their way towards his body. Now he was running, running for his life. When he was at last totally out of breath, his heart pounding, he stopped and looked behind him. As always, there was the pair of hands inching their way towards him still, only now they were mere inches from his foot!

Now panic really took hold of the general. He stood frozen to the ground. His feet refused to move. He felt the touch of each hand, a cold touch, not the warm touch he had felt from her before. Both hands inched their way up his pants, slowly but relentlessly. He tried to shake them off but could not move his legs. The hands sucked all warmth from his legs. Ice, his legs felt like two icicles. One tap from the hands and his legs would shatter into a thousand tiny pieces. He dare not move now! Upwards ever upwards the hands moved. Now he knew what the hands wanted. No. No. No. No. He cried out. I'm sorry. I'm sorry. I'm sorry. I didn't mean to do it. He knew that was a lie. He'd meant it all right. It didn't matter what he said. He'd experimented with saying everything he could think of, nothing had the slightest effect on these Hands from Hell. They merely continued inching their way up his body. Now they both began crawling up the front of his chest!

He knew their final destination. He'd lived this nightmare a thousand times now. He felt his chest turning cold, bitterly cold, but he dared not touch these hands. He'd tried grabbing them and throwing them off his body. Tried that many times when these nightmares first began, shortly after he'd discovered that the young woman had mysteriously vanished from the basement of the Nunnery that night, vanished without the slightest trace! That's when these hideous nightmares first began. He'd grabbed the pair of hands intending to cast them far from him, but the instant he touched them, his own hands froze. Cold, oh the deep penetrating cold, instant freeze. His hands went solid as ice in the dead of winter. Worse still, that deep penetrating freeze slowly seeped up his arms. Now it reached his elbows, then his shoulders. At last, it reached his neck at the same time as the pair of hands reached it. The hands began to choke the very life out of him, with that seeping cold flowing directly to his heart. A minute, was it but a minute? He could never tell. Yet, he knew what happened when that cold reached his heart. It froze. His neck ached in eternal pain from the strangling, yet his entire body was totally frozen, colder than ice. He lost consciousness. No, he could not touch those hands.

All he could do was wait. Yet the pair of hands always moved up to his neck and choked him anyway, that horrible, penetrating, icy cold froze his body, beginning with his neck and seeping its way down to his heart. Always the choking sensation, always the pain remained as his very heart froze and stopped beating. It stopped. He awoke drenched in sweat and urine.

"God, am I ever thirsty." He got up, noticed it was the afternoon — same day, he presumed. He walked over to the water pitcher on the dresser. He calmly poured himself a tall glass of water. No sooner had he drunk the water than the drunken swoon flooded over his body. He could not stand up and promptly fell to the floor once more. Again, he had to close his eyes to keep the room from spinning wildly out of control. Once more, he saw that beautiful, innocent young woman. He moved towards her as she lay on the bed in the Nunnery, dressed in her finery, waiting for him. Again, the nightmare sequence of images overwhelmed him.

Twice more he awoke, feeling perfectly fine, but dying of thirst. Twice more he drank a large glass of water. Twice more he collapsed into a drunken stupor. Twice more the horrible haunting images came to him. The third time he awoke, his head hurt badly, but the water stayed down. It was daylight again. He wondered what day it was now. He was finally sober once more.

He changed his soiled clothing. Grabbed a few coins and headed out onto the streets of Zargarb. As he walked, his mind began to clear. The day was warm and sunny. Fine day, if only he did not close his eyes, all would be fine. He found himself near the Lion's Den, an establishment relatively new in Zargarb. Strangers came to town several years ago and opened up this den. Some of his men had used it and swore by it. Their claims for the pure pleasure the sweet smoke gave them gnawed at the edges of his mind. He knew better than to use such stuff, but now perhaps a bit of pleasure was justified after enduring so much horror the last few days, was it really days? He did not know. On impulse, he entered the establishment.

An Arad looking man sat at the simple front desk. "Good afternoon, General. How can I help you? A smoke perhaps? Pure pleasure?" The General handed over several gold coins. "Ah, a very big pleasure you desire. This way, please. Here we are," he opened a room with no windows. Plush velvet covered the walls. Soft cushions lined the floor. In the center stood a large metal smoking device. The man placed a large amount of some power into the bowl. "You sit, make yourself comfortable. Here, inhale deeply." He handed the General the tubing end of the pipe and lit the powers. "Inhale deeply. That's right. Deeply and slowly. In and out. Ah, I shall leave you to your most beautiful dreams. Sensuous dreams." He slowly backed out of the room.

Time and space twisted; he felt so vastly different, a bit disconnected, but so much pleasure. Oh, so sensuous. His fingers, ah the merest touch sent waves of pleasure through his entire body. He felt his lips, oh so gently. He relaxed deeply for the first time in years; he thought to himself that he should have come here years ago. Images, sensuous images flowed through his mind, more real than the room he was in. Was he even in a room? No, no longer. The sweet undulating movements of the Megalos woman he had known in his youth caused him to drool, although he saw that not. Pleasure, pure pleasure.

Oh no! There was that beautiful, innocent, young woman! Oh how sensuous she had seemed to him. He wanted to wrap himself in her silky soft dress, caress her wonderful smooth body, and press his lips gently to hers. Wham! In came the horrible, hideous nightmare images once more. Only this time the images were a thousand times more real, with a thousand times more emotion and pain. If before he was frightened, this time he was almost scared to death, so real, so vivid, and so powerful were all the hugely magnified sensations and feelings! No, no, no, he could not escape this. No, no, no, he screamed and screamed and screamed. Yet the sequence played out completely yet one more time, the worst it had ever been, so magnified by the opium he had consumed.

At the end of the long sequence, he lost complete consciousness. All was total blackness. Then, someone was slapping him in his face. It hurt; it woke him up. He was in some back alleyway somewhere in Zargarb, with no idea where he was or how he had gotten here. Someone was standing over him, that someone had slapped his cheek. He felt the slight burn of his skin.

His eyes took a long time to focus, was this even real? His face felt like it was, but then what was real? Only that haunting image of the young, innocent woman — that was really real, the only real thing in his life any more. "You look the worst for the wear. Let's get you some coffee," a disembodied voice spoke. Was someone speaking to him? Maybe so, an arm was lifting him up. Was the arm connected to the voice? His eyes cleared. He saw the head of Art, the friendly Santi fortress man whom he'd often seen wandering the streets of Zargarb.

This was his enemy. "No, my enemy is that demon woman, that innocent young woman," he muttered. *Was that my voice? It sounds so disembodied.* "Am I dead?" he heard his voice say aloud.

Now Art was walking his body. "No you are very much alive, bad shape though."

"Thanks. What's that awful smell?" Helas said.

"You, I'm afraid. Seems you've had a bad night. Ah, here we are. Two coffees and bread loaf with fish paste please," Art said to the market vendor. He'd helped the man from the back alley walk to the nearest open market, which served light food. He maneuvered the man into a seat at one of the three tables here in the sunlight. Beyond them, the noise of the street provided a nice backdrop, Art thought. He enjoyed these open-air markets. The vender brought the steaming cups, the loaf, and a crock. Art passed him some coins and began fixing a couple light sandwiches, handing them to the general. He said nothing until the general had the entire cup in his system along with several sandwiches. Instead, he studied the general closely.

It was obvious that the general had lost his bowels in his clothes. From the filth on his shirt and the tear in the sleeve, the general had probably been tossed out of some place and dumped in the alleyway. The sweet smell of opium still lingered, so he knew that he'd probably been thrown out of the new opium den that had opened up a few years back. What confused him was that opium users were usually hooked on the pleasure sensations, the sensuous nature of the addiction. Yet, the man before him showed just the opposite, bad reaction to the drug perhaps?

The coffee and food brought the general finally into the present. "God, I am not dead."

"No, you are very much alive," Art replied.

"Well, I am as good as dead then. All is lost utterly," the general muttered, wondering if this establishment served wine. He could use a good drink about now.

"I don't understand," Art cleverly replied, cleverly attempting to pump him for more information. That's what he was doing in the city, searching for information.

"I'm broke. Can't pay the taxes this year on two hundred thousand people, only fifty thousand here. I make up the difference. Mano del Dio is coming to investigate me in a few days. Only got four hundred men left, but my boss still thinks I've got two thousand. Pick one. I'm a dead man."

"I see, that's quite a mess you have. Is that what's bothering you so?"

"No," his voice fell strangely silent. After a long pause, the general looked up at Art, "You are supposed to be Healers, right?"

"We are, but that's not my specialty. I can handle smaller matters, not major surgeries and such. Why?"

"What the hell! I don't give a blasted coin for those other things. Maybe being dead will end this horror of mine. I just cannot go on any longer like this, really I can't!" The general began crying like a child. Art's mouth dropped. He was most interested in the apparent lies that the general had probably been reporting up the line to the Church of Jehosanity in Megalos. His lies all these years were finally catching up to him. Yet, that wasn't what was bothering the general!

"Tell me about it," Art said trying to remember how Ket Bethany used to handle major upsets.

"I'm haunted by ghosts and a demon woman," the general began, oblivious to how all this may sound. For five minutes, he described the horrid nightmare dreams that he had every time he closed his eyes. "Been like this for so many years I've lost count. I can't tell what's real and what isn't any more. I just want them to stop. I just want to go to sleep. Can you help me?"

"General, I just don't know, such is beyond my feeble knowledge to heal. I will ask our Healers in the fortress. I would not like to make promises, sir, but there is a good chance that something positive can be done for you. There might be a way to end the nightmares, but I will have to research it. However, General, there is one thing that I can state with utter certainty."

"What's that?"

"If your body is killed, these nightmares will continue, only they will be much, much worse, because you will not have a physical body to help bring you to the present time. It's like right now, your body is feeling better because of the coffee and food; you are awake and seeing me and your surroundings, thinking clearly. If the body is gone, all you will have left are the nightmare images; nothing else will be real to you. We have got to keep your body alive somehow."

"You mean if I die, this all won't stop, go away, be gone and done with?" he looked utterly forlorn, as if his last line of defense was shattered.

"We are all spiritual beings who cannot die. Your religion calls it a soul, but you don't have a soul, you are the soul. I'm afraid, General, that your priests have been feeding you a crock of lies, so that they can control everyone without swords. You, sir, are in more peril than you can possibly imagine. If we do not get this cured and your body dies, god, I hate to think of what it will be like for you after that."

"The opium den," he suddenly remembered yesterday. "Oh my god! I — I — I — I can't take that! No! No! No! No! You've got to help me, please, I beg you!"

"Well, the first thing we must do is get you into our fortress where our Healer has her infirmary. Then we let her see if she can work her magic on you. If you had an infected arm, I know that she could fix you up. Your malady is not physical in nature, so she may not be able to do much. However, we do have special Healers back at the Santi del Dio headquarters in Velona. Your malady is their specialty. If Ann is unable to treat you, it may be that those in Velona can."

"Can we at least try?" the General pleaded.

"Yes, yes we must at least try, sir. However, we will need a cover story for why you are spending some time at our fortress. How about this, we are making a deal for the importing of a large quantity of food for the winter?"

"Yes, yes, that is actually going to be needed. How soon can we go?"

"As soon as you wish, General. How can you go about letting your staff know about the food deal?"

"We can drop by my office on the way. I've really go to change these clothes. I smell worse than a chamber pot left standing for a week!" The two men rose and began the long walk back to the mansion the General called home and office. Once there, he barked his orders in the usual way. One aide insisted that he read the latest dispatch from Megalos. Begrudgingly, he read it. For once, it was good news; the ship bringing the Mano del Dio had been delayed, and he wasn't to expect the visit for another month. Twenty minutes later, the two men walked out of the gates of Zargarb, across the short distance to the fortress, and entered the gate of Fortress Zargarb. Art led him to the infirmary.

This was a first! Everyone who saw them stopped and stared! Art had just brought the enemy General into the infirmary. Art had one Santi keep an eye on the General, while he went to find Ann and notify the others of this fantastic opportunity that had fallen onto their plate. How incredibly opportune!

It was full dark. Ann and Mary had just returned from the infirmary. Both women were ghastly white. Ann had convinced the General that he needed to sleep so that she could see precisely from what he was suffering. Since it was primarily mental in nature, Ann had found nothing physically wrong with the General's body except bad nutrition and over drinking, so she had called in Mary to Mind Link them to the General's. Both women had witnessed part of the horrible nightmares which so haunted the General. However, before the worst parts began to re-live themselves in his mind, Ann had given him some powdered herbs that dulled them down considerably, and now the General was actually sleeping soundly for the first time in years.

"God! That's the man who cut off Ariana's hands and raped her so!" Mary finally found her voice. all the others were sitting in the meeting room, her Circle and the Fortress Guardians and regiment commanders. "He's got some sort of hideous illusions of her drowning him from gushers of blood flowing from her arms, and then her disembodied hands are strangling him. In short, the man is now nearly completely insane. He is way, way beyond anything I can do for him. Besides, I have no desire to do anything for this butcher! He's done so many evil actions here that I won't touch him," declared Mary. "Neither will Ann."

"I could only make him comfortable, ease the effect of the nightmares," Ann added. "Beyond that, it is not a Healer related situation. Mary's right. I am loathed to do a damn thing for that hideous butcher. Looks like Ariana has gotten some sort of revenge on him for maiming her for life! The only possible, outside chance, he has of a cure is with Jenna Rose Weston and her therapy. But gods, this might be the man who cut off her hands or at least ordered it!"

"We don't dare put this on Jenna's plate right now. Lord knows she has more than she can handle with the seventy-nine mutilated women heading her way as we speak!" Le Ann added more animated than normal for this matronly older woman. "Is there anyone else that we know of anywhere that might be able to help his insanity?" she asked looking from face to face around the table.

Art Longton, scratched his chin before replying, "Well, there is one other who might have some idea." He paused.

"Well, who?" impatiently demanded Le Ann. Art loved to tease this Wid. She always had that uptight, stuck up aura about her. He loved it when she lost her composure as she was doing now. "Out with it, man!"

"Ket Bethany, he has had some experience with insanity. I guess he'd be what, Lizzy Ann now? She might know. At least, we wouldn't be bothering Jenna with this."

"She's what about five years old now? A mere child able to barely walk and talk? You want us to put this hideous mess onto a five year old girl?" Le Ann replied a bit peeved that Art would even say such a thing.

After another half hour of bantering around ideas, they still had no other ideas than Lizzy Ann. Le Ann had no other alternatives but her. "Mary, make the connection. Art, if this causes any wild repercussions with this child or with Jenna, I am placing the full responsibility for it on your head!" She knew that this was nonsense; as Wid, it would fall on her head; but she felt better having said it. If only Art Longton was in her Circle and not the Fortress, she'd put him in his place. Why couldn't he be more laid back and mellow as Art Weatherby, her Circle's Judger?

Hi Lizzy Ann. Mary Bridgeport from Zargarb here. Can we talk for a while now or are you busy?

Hi Mary. No I am in bed, but not sleeping yet. Mommy's tucked me in for the night.

Okay. We have a terrible situation here in Zargarb but we know how very busy your mommy is now with all those poor women. We don't want to bother mommy with this problem. Can we keep it just between you and us for a while, dear?

Oh sure. I'm helping mommy with therapy now. I cured Julianna yesterday. She's now so happy and alive, but yes, mommy is very stressed out now. So many more are coming. That's why I volunteered to help her with the really awful cases.

Honey, this stuff we are about to share with you is pretty awful. If you get too scared of it, just tell me to stop, all right?

Sure. What is happening?

It's the General of Zargarb, Helas Taxos. He's gone insane. Whenever he closes his eyes, he gets these horrible nightmares. I captured some of his images this early evening while our Healer Ann was working with him. I'll replay them for you so you can see what our problem is. Remember, if they scare you or are too awful for you to watch, you just interrupt me, okay?

Sure. I'm ready to watch.

Mary replayed the beginning sequences of the General's nightmares.

Is there more?

Mary reluctantly continued through the rest of the awful, hideous sequence of images.

That is Ariana, isn't it? He's the one who cut off her hands!

I'm afraid so.

Looks like his actions have finally caught up to him. They always do, you know, sooner or later. Sooner for him.

What can we do for him? He's asked us to help him.

Jenna's group came up with a five step Plan for Justice. First, all the facts are gathered and a decision is made whether or not the person is guilty of harmful acts, it protects the innocent. Second, if guilty, he must be made to cease committing more harmful actions. Third, he must be educated so that he can clearly see how what he has done is harmful. He must make a public announcement that he has done these things and what his motivation was when he committed them. Fourth, he must make amends to those he has harmed. Fifth, he must petition the community for re-admittance into society and the majority must approve his request.

I think in this case we can safely say he is guilty of numerous harmful acts against the people of Zargarb. What do you do? I suggest that you first make it clear to him that we know that he has or had done by his orders many harmful actions against the people of Zargarb. Second, make it clear to him that before any real help can be had, he must see that all harmful actions done by him or those under his control cease and desist committing any further harmful actions. Third, if he is still cooperating, tell him that he needs to be educated so that he knows the truth of what is or is not a harmful action. To do that, he must report to our facility on Isla Roca; there he will be well treated and schooled in the truth of life. Forth, once educated in the truth, if he is willing to identify those that he has harmed and willing to begin finding ways to make amends, then I promise that I will attempt to treat him and cure him of his nightmares. If he will not do these things, then he will get no help from me. Knowing mommy, she would insist that these same requirements be met before she would even consider using her therapy on him, but even then, she might not do it until amends was made and accepted.

One more thing, you can tell him that I believe that if he does not get the therapy, these nightmares will only get worse and cause him far worse problems later on.

Thank you, Lizzy Ann. These are so simple to do. I will relay them to the others and get back to you when we know more. Thanks again.

The next morning, Art, armed with Lizzy Ann's suggestions, went to the infirmary to check on the General, who was eating his breakfast. The Santi fighter at the outside door of the infirmary, ask, "Do we kill him today?"

"I think not," Art replied as he entered. "How are you feeling today?"

"Ah, Art. Well, yes actually, much better. I actually slept last night. Still had part of the nightmares but it was very mild. Those herbs really took the edge off it. Thanks."

"Well, I have news for you. There is one person on Tarra who might be able to fully cure you of these nightmares forever."

"Really? Gone, no more nightmares?" Then, his face lost its excitement. "Only one person?"

"Yes, one. Let's be completely honest with each other, General," Art said, sliding his chair to the bedside of the General. "The Healer has laid out three conditions which you must meet before she will even attempt to cure you. However, before I lay those conditions before you, I must ask you about that young woman in your nightmares. The woman in your images with the missing hands, she did indeed exist, did she not? She is not some imaginary person you have never met?"

Helas's face felt like it was on fire, but he managed to say, "Yes, yes she was."

"Thank you. Further, you did actually cut off her hands, did you not?"

Now Helas felt like his face would melt from the heat, "Well, ah, yes, but. . ."

Art cut him off, "Yes or no will do, Helas. I am not after justifications for what you did. You did indeed force her to have intercourse with you against her will, did you not?"

Was steam rising from his forehead? Helas muttered, "Yes."

"Do you realize that raping her and cutting off her arms was a most harmful act to commit?"

"Damn it, yes. I meant to do it! But yes, yes, it was harmful. Is that why I am having these awful dreams about her?"

"It is not for me to answer that question, Helas. I have no way of knowing that. Since you have answered me truthfully, I can now proceed to tell you the conditions set forth by the Healer."

"Wait a minute, how do you know that I am telling you the truth? Maybe I am just saying so, so that you will have the Healer help me."

Art looked Helas straight in his eyes, speaking slowly and distinctly, he said, "I know the woman in question. For your information, she is alive, happily married, has a daughter, and is doing as well as may be expected for someone who has had their hands cut off. So, yes, I know whether you were being honest with me."

If his face had been hot, now it felt completely ablaze! Myriad of emotions and thoughts flew through his mind. She still lived! She had vanished without a trace. None knew her fate. Now he knew she had not died. Part of him wanted to scream for joy; the other part wanted to find some hole in the ground in which to hide. Yet, he did not even know her name! Something wet was on his face; however, he did not recognize what. "Thank you. In some small way, I am so utterly glad that she did not die because of what I did to her. What must I do?"

"The Healer said that I must make it very clear to you that we, the Santi know that either directly by your hand or by your orders to your men, that many very harmful actions have been committed against the people of Zargarb. That the population is now barely a fifth of what it was when you came here ought to be a good indication that many crimes have been committed. Two hundred thousand people gone! That is not a coincidence."

"Second, the Healer asked me to make it clear to you that before any real help can be had, you must see to it that all harmful actions against the people here are stopped and are no longer being committed either by yourself or by those under your control. As long as harmful actions continue, the Healer said that you cannot possibly get well, even if the Healer tried."

"Third, the Healer insists that you become educated so that you know the truth of what is or is not a harmful action. The Healer told me that the Santi will help you with this, if you voluntarily come to our facility on Isla Roca. There in quiet and without distractions, you will be well treated and schooled in the truths of life. Finally, the Healer said that once you know the truth, if you are then willing to identify those people that you have harmed and are willing to begin to try to find ways and means to make amends to them, the Healer will at that time come to you and attempt to cure you of your nightmares so that they will always be a thing of the past and will not ever bother you again."

Art looked at him and added his own threat, "Know this, Helos Taxos, you, like me and all the rest of us, are an immortal spiritual being; you cannot die. Nor will the deeds you have done die of their own accord. They will continue to haunt you forever. You are being given this one single, golden opportunity to have someone assist you in removing them so that you can at last be free from your past actions."

"If it were up to me, I'd sooner kill you in combat and let you rot in your own nightmares forever, but then, I am not the Healer. They are currently helping hundreds of women so badly mistreated that their arms have died off. Armless women caused by your Priest's actions. Why one of our Healers who is working with so many of your victims would ever consent to curing the very person responsible for this maiming I cannot say. I'd rather just kill you outright. All I can say, General, is don't blow it. You will not ever get a second chance at redemption."

Helas sat there stunned for a moment. Art was being honest with him. When it came to combat, that he knew completely. Art was not lying; he would just as soon slit his throat on the spot as help him. Yet, Art had not, though he could have easily done so, while he was unconscious in the alleyway. He'd helped him recover, even bought him food. God, one good night of sleep he'd been given! Sleep, he not had that for so many years now. He made up his mind.

Helas said softly, but with full intention, "As one old soldier to another, we understand each other. Actions speak louder than words. I accept the Healer's terms. You will be hearing from me soon. I assume that I will be allowed to leave?"

"Absolutely, General. You are not yet our prisoner. We have not yet declared war upon you. You are and have been since you came here, free to leave when you desire," Art replied.

The General got up to leave and then turned to Art, "Between us, there are things that we do in life that, after we have done them, we wish to god that we could undo them. She was like that for me — just wanted you to know." He left at once, ignoring the glare from the Santi soldier who still stood guard at the door he passed through.

Art thought to himself, "There is still some tiny ounce of humanity in the General. Perhaps he will make it, though I would not care to be either Jenna or Bethany and have to deal with him."

The General walked outside the Santi fortress. It seemed to him to be an exceptionally beautiful day. Clear skies, warm sea breeze, a perfect day. He decided to walk instead of heading directly back to his home. Slowly he walked the outside circumference of the great walls. He had been here for close to two decades now and four-fifths of the people were gone, dead or fled. Now that he thought about it, the figure seemed very alarming indeed. Helas was not a religious man, never had been. That was the province of the priests and the Church, not his. Yet, it seemed to him as he walked the very deserted streets that, if their religion was all that it was supposed to be, then four-fifths of all the people should not have left. To his military way of thinking, that made perfect sense.

In a large measure, the priests had brought much of this doom upon them, not the military. Sure he had slain all the nobles, but once that was done, he'd done very little else, except rape women at the Nunnery. Yet if the priests had not forced the women into the Nunnery and forced them to have sex with him and his men, the rapes might not have happened. More and more, he began to see the Church as the ultimate ones responsible for his downfall and his crimes. He had no control or authority over the priests and their nuns, none at all. Yet, if he were to follow Art's instructions, the priests would have to be stopped. His men, these he could control.

"You seem to be in good spirits today, General," his top aide commented as he entered his office, whistling a little Megalos tune from his childhood.

"Ah yes, pretty day indeed. Any dispatches today?"

"No sir, all quiet."

"Good, that I like. That will be all then. Take the rest of the day off. There's nothing much happening around here today. You might as well enjoy it."

"Thank you sir!" the aide saluted and left.

404

Helas made himself some coffee and sat back pondering how he could meet the conditions.

A week later, he decided upon a course of action. He had been sleeping fairly well, as long as he took those powders given to him by the Santi Healer. Helas decided that the very first thing he needed to do was to see for himself if what Art had hinted at was true. That evening after supper, he walked in unannounced into the Nunnery.

"Oh it's you, General Taxos," said the surprised Head Nun. "We were not expecting you. You should have given us some notice. I'm afraid that we have not got a woman ready for you. They are all in bed for the night, so it will be a while."

The General walked past her, completely ignoring the Head Nun. He walked down the hallway and began opening doors and looking inside. At first, he awoke several nuns and merely shut those doors. Then, he began seeing what he had hoped he would not see.

As he gazed into this room, two women struggled to rise up to see. They had some kind of metal contraptions on their heads holding a ring in their mouths, forcing it to stay wide open. Worse still, another device was strapped around their chests, holding both of their arms across their backs. Hence, they had to wiggle and squirm just to sit up to see what was going on.

He left that door open and rapidly flung other doors open; more women were caged like animals. Now all the nuns were out in the hallway, holding their robes to their chests with their hands, looking completely bewildered. "What are you doing?" implored the Head Nun. "That's all the women we have here. The other rooms are empty."

"Why, woman, are they in those metal constraints?" he spat toward the Head Nun.

"We've got to teach them to behave and stop earning Bad Marks," she attempted to explain as if he was a dope. She did not get to continue her explanation. In one sweeping motion, now long unused, he whipped out his sword and beheaded her on the spot, blood flying everywhere.

The other nuns in training began screaming. Helas yelled louder and domineeringly, "Unlock those women now or join her!" Frantically, they ran to the dead body and found the key chain. As fast as they could, the four raced into each room unlocked each woman. In about five minutes, all the frightened women were standing in a line against the hallway, staring at the beheaded corpse. "Ladies, you are now totally free. Go home to your families; go anywhere you want; just get out of here now! You four, clean up this mess; then go home; say nothing about this for a day or you can join her." They jumped, but the General was already heading out the door after the fleeing women.

He walked over to the main Priest Rectory, where most of the priests slept. He walked in and began going systematically through each room in the building. He'd never been inside this rectory, so he just tried each door. Whenever he came upon a person, he killed them without a saying a word. Most never knew what had happened to them. Near the end of the hallway, he opened a door and found the High Priest Rolan Dax, who was still reading the Holy Gospels as written by Pope Yazi I. "What's the meaning of this?" he asked as he looked up to see a very bloody Helas standing at the doorway.

"Bloody pervert!" Helas said vehemently, raced over to the chair, and severed the priest's head. He spat on the corpse and continued his room by room examination. Satisfied at last that all the priests were now dead, he stopped by the Holy Water Basin near their private altar and washed himself off somewhat.

Next, he headed to the barracks of his Holy Paladins, stopping first at the fancier building where his aides stayed. "Rise and shine, gentlemen. Today is a great day. I have fabulous news for everyone. Join me in the barracks ASAP!" A chorus of yes sir's echoed from the several bedrooms. It was only four in the morning., however.

In the barracks, he first woke up the trumpeter. "What's up, sir?" the sleepy soldier asked as he tried to get to his feet proper like.

"Sound reveille. Need a total muster immediately. I have great news for everyone! Hurry up man!" Hastily, pulling on his pants, the soldier fetched his trumpet and blasted out the notes. At once, the General heard his men jumping out of bed, donning their pants, a sudden adrenalin rush going through their veins. However, this time there was not a big battle to face.

Shortly, his aides arrived, mostly dressed. "Summon all the men, every one of them, into the mess hall."

"Yes, sir!" The aide dashed about ordering men left and right. Helas strolled into the large mess hall, which had once been some nobleman's dining room. Five minutes later, the place was packed with men, half dressed, standing rigidly at attention.

"My great most worthy Holy Paladins," he began. "Today, I have just received the best news that I have had in a score of years! We go home, home to Megalos!" The men cheered, yelled, and whooped it up for several minutes. All had lost all hope of ever going home, alive that is. Two thousand of their comrades had been killed here already.

"Yes, I received the official orders just a short while ago. All hush hush, you know how these things go. It seems that we have been sent a complete replacement force. We all get to go home and have some much needed rest and relaxation time before our next assignment. I would like to take this opportunity to say that it has been a real pleasure working with all of you. You have been the best troops any general could desire. I, General Helas Taxos, salute you, my honored soldiers." The cheering and noise was a bit deafening, but was precisely what Helas desired.

"Now the only annoying detail is that we must have these premises vacated by nightfall! I have been ordered to go to Vito, don't ask me why because I don't know. Probably the General there needs my advice before I leave for Megalos. In my place, I leave you in the hands of my highly competent aides. You ride south at noon today and then on down the long road through the Southlands to home! I will see you all when you and I both get there. Noon, I say, now get packing. No guard duties, no nothing but pack and get your gear together. Leave everything else that may come up to the arriving replacements that will arrive later this afternoon. Heck, you can even leave this place a mess for them," he laughed. The men roared and laughed as well. "That is all; now get your sorry asses moving. If you are late, you can join the replacements for the next twenty years!"

The men danced and cheered, and began packing everything in sight. They were going home alive! One aide asked, "Sir, what happened to you, you are bloody. Are you injured?"

"Oh it's nothing, minor brawl on the way from the docks and the messenger. He'll never pick on this general again," he laughed. His aide joined in as well. "Now you aides have a big responsibility here. I need you to get every one of my men and those new local recruits galloping out of here by noon today. Otherwise, there'll be hell to pay if the replacements get here, and we are in their way! I'm depending on you five, don't let me down." He shook each aide's hand.

"We will not fail you, Sir!" the five echoed each other.

"I know you won't. I have to let the Santi folks know of your passing. We don't want them meddling in our troop movements. I'll try to be here to see you off, if I can. Not sure when my boat sails for Vito. I'll come wave if I haven't set sail yet. Good luck and see you all in Megalos!"

He then walked to the western gates of the city. He found the gate men arriving early as usual. "Good morning gentlemen."

"General!" they said shocked to see the General here at the gate at this hour. None could ever recall seeing him here this early. "I have new standing orders that you and everyone else will love. From now on, there will be no charge whatsoever for entrance through the gates. That fee has been officially cancelled. Anyone can come and go as they please!"

They let out a whoop of joy. "You are right. This will please everyone, sir. It is a great day indeed."

He strolled up to the north gate and repeated his orders with the same effect. Then, he walked all the way down to the eastern gate and repeated the orders a third time. At last, he said, "Got to deliver a message to the Santi. Back shortly."

He knocked on the gate of the tall Santi fortress. When the gatekeeper slid open the viewing hole, he called out, "General Helas Taxos to see Art Longton, please."

A few minutes later, Art opened the gate, but he was fully dressed, as if he expected some action. He said, "Come in General. We heard the premature reveille call — kind of woke me up. Is something wrong?" He saw the blood on the man's shirt. "Are you wounded?"

"No, I'm fine. Never felt better. I came to report that at noon today, the entire Holy Paladin force garrisoned here in Zargarb will be riding south down to Megalos. If all goes as I have planned, by noon today, there will not be a single Holy Paladin anywhere in the sector. At that time, I will return here and present you with the city and sector. The priests have been handled; you will find them eliminated. I took the liberty of freeing ten women who were forced to sleep in those horrible devices, which you mentioned. By now, they are back at their homes. Oh yes, one more thing. I have issued orders that eliminated all gate fees. Anyone can leave and enter the city at no charge at all. See you just after noon." He saluted Art and left, heading for his home. He intended to bathe and dress properly before seeing his troops off on their long journey.

Meanwhile, Art raced through the fortress waking everyone up, calling for an emergency meeting at once. Half-sleepy eyed Santi stumbled into the meeting hall wondering what terrible calamity had just occurred now. As soon as they all were present, Art explained.

"We have a real situation on our hands. General Helas Taxos has just informed me that at noon today, all the Holy Paladins in this entire sector will be leaving by the south road, going back to Megalos! Apparently, his orders. He said that the priests have all been eliminated. He was pretty much covered in blood, so I suspect he killed them. He went to the Nunnery and found ten women who were being forced to sleep in those horrid devices, and he freed them and sent them home to their families. I believe he killed the Head Nun who had ordered their imprisonment. Oh, yes, he also eliminated the gate fees permanently. He said he will return at noon to officially hand the city and sector over to us."

"Oh good grief!" declared Le Ann sitting down. "Now what will we have on our hands? A city ruled by thugs?"

"I think that Helas is attempting to do what Art asked of him, stopping and preventing any further harm," Ann commented. "Honestly, I didn't think that he would do that."

"I never thought that I would live to see the day Zargarb would be free once more, but what's left is just a bunch of thugs!" Lenkova added.

After an hour's lengthy discussion, Art decided to have a chat with the head thug, Rodrigo Decasas. Daylight had arrived and people were going about their usual early morning routines, save those who were leaving the gates. Those had a most welcome surprise. It took Art an hour to arrange a meeting with Rodrigo.

Inside a concealed room in a warehouse, plush with every conceivable amenity, Rodrigo welcomed his friend. "Good morning, Art. Been a long time. All must not be going well. You only come see me when trouble is brewing. So what is it this time? Have some tea?"

"Tea would be fine. Trouble. Ha, different kind of trouble, Rodrigo. Actually, I come bearing news almost too good to be true."

"Now that, my friend, I find impossible to believe. Come sit; tell me what your old wharf rat can do for you today."

"I'll come right to the point, old buddy. Keep this a total secret until noon. Promise me." He did, only now his curiosity was heightened considerably. He lowered his voice, in case there were other ears listening in on their conversation. "At noon today, or shortly thereafter, General Taxos is surrendering the city and the sector to the Santi. All the Holy Paladins will be riding out of here at noon, heading back to Megalos. All the priests have been eliminated; the Nunnery freed. He has even eliminated all city gate entrance fees! In short, at noon today, Zargarb will be a free sector once again."

"Surely you are teasing me," Rodrigo stared at Art.

"Nope, check out the gates for yourself. Keep an eye on the eastern gates around noon."

"I will do so. Mind you, I don't believe you, but just say that I do for a moment. Once they leave, who is going to run the city and sector? He's handing it over to the Santi. You are going to run the city?"

"No, no, heavens no. What would we want to run the sector for? No, we will attempt to keep the sector in some kind of semblance of order. You've hit on the exact problem, however. To whom does the Santi hand the rulership of the city over to?"

He chuckled, "For a second there, I thought that you folks would now be our new overlords. So you do mean to give us back our freedom?"

"Most definitely, but to who is the real question."

"Damn, I see your point. My hands are long, but not that long. We do have a problem, don't we? None of the old High Council is left. The founder's line is gone, and all the ruling nobles and their families are gone too. Who is left to lead?"

"There is one who yet lives and who had the bloodline right to rulership. The Zar line is not yet gone, my friend."

Rodrigo frowned, "Nay, they are all dead. I saw their bodies myself. Who could it be?"

"Ariana Zar, his young daughter. She escaped the slaughter and is living now in Velona."

"No, she lives? If so, the rulership rightly belongs to her, no question of that."

"Yes, but will the people here accept her as their ruler? Besides, if she becomes the ruler, she's certainly going to want you out of business, you know."

"I've kept an awful lot of people alive, though I admit that I've made my share of profit in doing so. It's no secret, if we get our freedom and a ruler who can lead us out of this starvation existence, then I'll gladly give up this business. I think that is what most will think. Does she offer us any real hope for things getting better? Hardly anyone's left in the sector, you know."

"Okay, then I will ask Ariana if she wants to return to Zargarb and take over its leadership. We still have a security problem once the townsfolk realize the Overlords have abandoned the city."

"Art, you work on getting Zar to take the leadership role. Leave the city in my hands, at least for the next week or so. Some of us have old scores to settle. If you or the Santi are in our way, you might be forced to take the brunt of the released hostilities."

"Rodrigo, that's what we're afraid of. Haven't you all seen enough violence to last a lifetime? Four-fifths of your population is gone. You want to reduce it further?"

"Art, you have to understand something. Many here have been under this yoke and suffered dearly. However, a few have cow-towed to the Overlords and actively joined in with them. No matter what you and I may think or even do, they are going to get their justice, one way or another."

"But couldn't we just arrest the traitors and make them make amends to the rest of you?"

"Nice words, Art. Won't mount to bean pile with folks that are still here. Might have with some that's left a long time ago, but not with those that are still here. That's just the way it is. I don't want any of your folks getting hurt. The Santi have been our only hope all these years. I owe it to you to convince you to keep out of the city for perhaps a week. Meantime, I'll spread the word everywhere that a Zar still lives. I can test out their support for her and let you know."

Rodrigo then changed the subject, "So what's to keep the Paladins in Solamina or elsewhere from charging in here once they find out that Taxos left?"

"I can see no choice but for the Santi to step in and claim that we are supporting your freedom, that any attack on our protected sector will be considered a declaration of total war with the Santi. Meantime, I will try to persuade Tom to send out a large force to the Solamina border, just in case. Perhaps some forces can be also pulled in quickly from New Barq."

"Ah, if you can do that and if Ariana would have the full support of the Santi, I know I can persuade everyone to let her have a chance here."

Art chuckled, "Rodrigo, Ariana is Santi. She is fully one of us already and a Guardian as well. You can count on the Santi backing her every move here."

"Why didn't you say so in the first place? Damn, that makes all the difference in the world."

"Think about it Rodrigo. I wanted her to be accepted as a Zar first, not as a Santi. Otherwise, everyone will just believe that she is merely a Santi puppet head. She has suffered most horribly at the hands of the Holy

Paladins; she deserves Zargarb's highest respect."

"Yes, Art, you are once more right; she should be Zar first, Santi second. Heck, all of us who still live here have suffered horribly at the hands of the bastard Overlords. Well, most all, I, er, seem to have escaped that part. Er, so have a large number of my close associates."

Art stared hard at Rodrigo, before saying, "When she was barely in her teens, they cut off both of her hands."

His smile faded, "Damn bastards! Well, she will be useless then, is that what you are saying? I thought when you said she as Santi, you meant like yourself, good fighter and all that, good leader. Not a hopeless cripple, gods, what can she do?"

"Oh just about everything you can do, only slower and in very different ways. She hates fighting, but if you provoke her, look out. Besides, we both know that a leader leads. Still, she will need others to help maintain order and such. You will find that she is a very able person, but yes, she does need looking after. She's married and has a daughter too."

"Well, if you vouch for her, then I can accept that. Actually, it might play to her advantage when folks see that she has suffered so horribly at the hands of the Overlords. Will you keep the Santi out of the city for a while, assuming that they do indeed leave at noon as you say?"

"I will argue for your request. Since we have to consider Solamina's reaction, our forces will likely need to be positioned near the border. In case I need to see you again quickly, how can I find you? It took me an hour to get to you today."

"I'll be here. I'll let the others know to send you directly here." Both men shook hands, and Art returned to the fortress.

After relating his conversation with Rodrigo to the full group, Le Ann commented, "Well, now we have no choice but to contact Jenna. We don't dare bypass her and go directly to Ariana; she's officially under her care, but let's not be hasty. Let's see if all this comes to pass at noon. A few hours will not make any difference. Lenkova, see exactly how many fighters we could possibly send to the border with Solamina. Sally, contact New Barq and ask them how many fighter they could possibly spare us, should we need it. Keep the details at a minimum until we know for sure. I hate civil unrest, but given the choice of keeping the next door Holy Paladins from retaking Zargarb or protecting a few traitors within the city, I have no choice but to go after the paladins."

Tom said, "I'm going to the roof and keep an eye on things. This may well be liberation day for Zargarb." The brief meeting ended. Now they could only wait and see.

Sure enough, shortly before noon, hundreds of sky blue tunics with their plain white crosses proudly rode out of the city heading south and east to New Barq and then the great north-south road. These men were finally going home. Not long after, General Helas Taxos walked through the gates of the Santi fortress and handed his sword to Art. Not long after, a caravel left the Santi dock, carrying the Helas off to the prison on Isla Roca. Haste was needed, because surely the assassins of the Mano del Dio would be after him as soon as they learned what he had done.

Hi Paulette. Sally here. We have an emergency here in Zargarb that needs fast action. Is Jenna available?

No, she is in the middle of a therapy session.

Is Lizzy Ann available?

No, she is too.

I rather figured they might be. Can you get them a message to contact me just as soon as they have a minute? This is critical. We now have total control over Zargarb. The General has surrendered the sector to Art Longton.

What? Wow! You got it. I'll slip them a message. Back at you as soon as they take a break.

An hour later, Sally, Paulette, Jenna, and Lizzy Ann joined in a Mind Link. *Sally sent the details. Jenna, Lizzy Ann told us what to do about the situation that arose here last week. Please don't be angry with us; you were tied up with the therapy sessions, and it was rather of an emergency on which only you or Lizzy Ann could advise us.*

Out with it! Jenna was slightly impatient. She wanted to say, "Lizzy Ann, what have you been up to?" but thought better of it.

The General here, Helas Taxos — Art found him in an opium daze lying in an alleyway. She described fully what had happened, so Jenna would know all the facts. *Honestly, we didn't think that your new procedure for handling those who are or have committed so many harmful actions against people and society would actually work. Well, it appears that it has, Lizzy Ann. Just as you outlined for us, it did work. Helas actually did it! An hour ago, the General handed over Zargarb to us by. He surrendered his sword to Art Longton and is now on our caravel bound for Isla Roca, where he wishes to be educated so that he can take the next step towards getting the Healer to help him with his nightmares of insanity.*

Lizzy Ann! I am not going to let you anywhere near that vile, butcher of a man! Look at all the women he has ruined or killed or had mutilated! No way!

Mommy, it is your Circle's actual plan for their spiritual rehabilitation. Only you or I can do it; there's no one else, and he has so far done what your plan actually requires of him.

Well, yes, but, he's a murder and butcher.

And if we don't help him now, next lifetime he will only continue hurting more women, mommy. You said we need to look beyond one lifetime.

Well, yes, but. Well, it seems that I have been caught in my own plan. All right, Lizzy, one of us has to do it. It might be better if you do it.

Who knows, it might have been him who did it to me. If I suddenly find out in a therapy session that he was the one who cut off my hands, I might, well, lose my cool and do something I'd regret. But I insist that you are not with him alone!

Okay, Sally, you can continue.

In short, he has killed all the Jehosanity priests. He went to the Nunnery and found that they had ten women in bed, locked in those horrible metal devices. He beheaded the Head Nun who had ordered her adepts to put the women in them. He freed the women and sent them home to their families. Since the priests were behind this whole thing and since he had no control over the priests, he killed them all to ensure they stopped doing it. There's some logic behind it after all. Then, he ordered every one of his Holy Paladins and all their new local recruits to ride back to Megalos. They all left around noon, an hour ago. Not a single Holy Paladin is in the sector. He also ordered the city gate entrance fees permanently cancelled, and everyone has free access to and from the city. That's when he came to Art and surrendered his sword.

We put him on the caravel at once. As soon as they find out what he has done, you can bet every assassin will be gunning for him. He should be safe at Isla Roca; besides, no one but us knows where he has gone; he's just disappeared.

As you know, the city is really controlled by the thugs. Art visited their leader, Rodrigo Decasas earlier today and outlined the situation. I am afraid that there will be more bloodletting happening here shortly. Many of those who have suffered under these years of oppression are very likely to go after those they deem traitors, who went along with the Overlords. Tom and Art don't believe that there is much we can do about that mess. Worse, just as soon as the other sectors hear about this, they are likely to send in their Holy Paladins to retake the sector. Tom has mobilized all the Santi here and awaits your orders to deploy them along the border with Solamina. New Barq is standing by to send as many fighters as they can to back us up here. We just cannot let them retake Zargarb now that it has been freed.

Yes, Tom is right. Get to the border. I'll send official notice to the other Occupied Sectors that Zargarb is now free and has asked for our support. I hope that no one will dare risk a counterattack.

Good. There is also one additional problem. Who will take over the rulership of Zargarb? Art has discussed this with Decasas, who is the one person with the most power at this time. He's told him that Ariana Zar is alive and with us. Rodrigo has stated for the record that he and the others will both honor and back Ariana's birthright to rule. I guess she must be informed and see what she wants to do. Oh, by the way, Helas was the one who cut off her hands, tortured, and repeatedly raped her. We've seen his insane nightmares. Lizzy Ann can fill you in, but there is no doubt about it.

I know that she is a Loremaster and probably has no interest in becoming the ruler of Zargarb. However, we need to put a ruler in charge fairly soon or things could get out of control here.

Jenna agreed to speak with Ariana at once, and they broke their Mind Link. "Damn inopportune time for all this," she declared to Lizzy Ann.

"I know mommy. Want me to cover for you this afternoon? I can work your patient and mine, switching back and forth every hour or so."

"Would you do that for a bit? I don't think I will be tied up all afternoon, maybe for just an hour or so." Jenna ran off in search of Ariana and Ben. She found them in the garden along with Hank, Julianna, and Rachele. "Ariana, Ben, Hank, I need to speak with you immediately and in private."

"Whoa, something's up?" whispered Julianna to Rachele, as they watched the three walk out across the lawn, Ben carrying their little girl.

When they were far from any possible listening ears, Jenna began to tell them what had happened in Zargarb. "Ariana, we now know who the identity of the man who did this to you. It is the man who was in charge in Zargarb, General Helas Taxos."

She looked down at her missing hands and asked, "How do you know it was him?"

Good question, Jenna thought to herself. She began to explain all that had gone on with him and what had just happened in Zargarb. Ariana could not help but comment, "Well, it serves him right, having such nightmares! But can he really be rehabilitated? How can he possibly make amends for all that he has done?"

"That's why we have a petition as the last step. If you don't think he has made enough amends, you can veto his petition, assuming it ever gets that far. I guess time will tell on that one."

"Well, at least the Plan for Rehabilitation seems to be working. I am sure glad that he found those other poor women and freed them. That's just awful," Ariana declared.

"Well, dear, there is just one really big problem. Who is going to rule and lead Zargarb back out of this mess? By birthright, the rule of Zargarb is yours, Ariana."

"But I really don't want to be a ruler. I am a Loremaster and Santi," she protested. "Isn't there someone else who wants to be their ruler?"

"Four-fifths of the original population of Zargarb is gone, dead or fled. The only remaining heir, as far as anyone knows is you, Ariana. We all will understand if you do not want to go back there and become their ruler. Lord knows it's one grand mess; people are starving; crops don't grow properly, and the port's not even cleared of all the boats that were sunk there twenty plus years ago by the Emperor."

"Crops don't grow?" Ariana inquired. Jenna had purposely dropped the only thing she could think of that might prick the interest of a

Loremaster. "I wonder why that is?"

"Maybe they don't get enough water. Maybe they are using the wrong seed. Perhaps even the wrong crops," Ben suggested.

"Maybe we should go and see if we cannot at least get their crops producing. Then, they would at least have enough food and wouldn't starve. I bet they are awfully tired of eating fish!" Ariana declared.

"If you decide to accept the rulership for now, perhaps relinquishing it later on, the Santi and Velona will be behind you all the way. Anything you need, just ask. Of course, I will send as many Guardians and Santi forces as you desire to help get things going there. What do you say, will you at least give it a try? You can always get someone else to take over later on, if you really don't want to rule," Jenna said, certain that she had Araina's willingness to make the attempt.

"I can't ask Ben to leave here and move to Zargarb. All his friends and family are here. This place is so wonderful, and Zargarb is now the pits. I can't ask him to leave all this," Ariana pleaded.

"Hey there Miss Cutie Pie," Ben teased, "don't go laying this on me. Remember when I first kissed you there at the dance?" She smiled; she certainly did remember.

"Before I kissed you I had already made my decision about just such a day as this. I knew you were a Zar and what that meant. One day, however unlikely, you might be called upon to return to Zargarb. Would I be willing to follow you there? If I had not decided that I would, I would not have ever kissed you. I just couldn't start something only to later let you horribly down. I'm ready to go. Besides, in Zargarb, I have a lot I can learn, so do you. We still have your trail mastering to pick up, and there is a lot of open land there in which to practice not getting lost and finding your way in the wilderness. When do we leave, dear?"

Jenna said, "Thank you Ariana. Remember if you really don't like it, you can always find a replacement, perhaps hold an election, and let the people choose their leader. How about leaving a week from now? That will give you time to pack and get anything you might need, and I'll have time to arrange others who can go with you."

Jenna headed back to resume her therapy session, while the others headed back to the garden. "What was it? Something top secret?" asked Julianna. Rachele was just as keenly curious.

"Zargarb has just been freed! The General there gave us our country back! The Holy Paladins and their awful priests are all gone!"

"Wow! No one had to fight them?" asked Rachele incredulously.

"No. I guess he finally realized just how much they had harmed us, and he gave up. Only now, they want me to become the sole ruler of Zargarb. I guess I am the only Zar still living. I really don't want to be a ruler, but there is no one else to take over and turn the country around. I hear that people are starving, and for some reason cannot get their crops to grow at all well. Ben and I shall have to fix that at once. I don't know much about being a ruler, though. I may make a complete flop of it all."

"Nah, you will do just fine, love," Ben insisted.

Julianna looked at Rachele, as if by some telepathic sign, both said in unison, "Please, can we go with you? We want to help too. Besides, we are Ben and Hank's apprentice Loremasters. Aren't we supposed to go where he goes? You will need court helpers, we volunteer. Please let us come. Besides, Rachele has a grandfather who lives in Zargarb, well he used to live there. She doesn't know if he is still alive or not, but we can find out. Please, Ariana?"

"Well, you two are my dear friends now," Ariana began to relent. "But then who is going to help you with things? I have Ben, and I can't really ask him also to look after you two's needs. I'm enough of a burden on him as it is."

"Just one darn minute, little Miss Cutie Pie!" Ben interrupted her. "Just when have you been a burden, huh? Name one time when I got upset because I had to wipe your dirty behind? Ha, you can't, can you! See," he picked her up and swung her around in a circle, sat her down, kissed her forehead, and said, "a lover isn't a burden! Neither are my friends. You two are my friends!" He looked at Julianna and Rachele and then dashed for them. Julianna managed to dodge him, laughing wildly, but Rachele was not fast enough. He grabbed her, picked her up, and swung her around in a circle, before sitting her down, and kissing her forehead. Then, he chased after Julianna, causing her to laugh even harder, before he caught her and did the same with her.

"You are my friends; you are not a burden, never will be. As far as I'm concerned, they've half a right to come with us. Hank's got the other half of the say; he's also their teacher as well."

"Oh no you don't!" said Hank, although he had been listening in on the conversation, he stopped to watch the youthful antics, grinning all the time. It brought back fond memories of chasing Jenna around the grassy knoll. "You don't make me the bad guy who has to say no to these beauties. If I say no to them, they'll be forever bombarding me with rotten tomatoes! Then, Jenna won't let me near her!" Now everyone roared with laughter.

"What's so darn funny?" Jenna asked; she just walked up. "Lizzy Ann still has my patient, so I have to wait for their next break. So what's so darn funny?" She had seen Ben spinning the girls around while she was walking down here from the house, but had not heard their words.

"Oh, she doesn't know?" teased Hank. "Jenna dear, come here, let me show you." Before she knew what was happening, Hank had grabbed her and swung her around as Ben had the others. However, when he sat her back down, they embraced lovingly. "Love you dear," he whispered in her ear.

Straightening her clothes and hair, to regain her composure, she asked again, "So what's this all about? A conspiracy among Loremasters?"

"Ah yes, a deep, dark conspiracy, Jenna dear," Hank teased. "Your Loremasters are rebelling."

She chuckled. Hank decided he'd speak for them, "The girls here heard about Ariana and Ben going to Zargarb, and they are insisting that they be allowed to accompany them. Jenna dear, you must let them go; otherwise they will be pounding me with rotten tomatoes all the time."

"Really, we do; we do want to go with her and with Ben," Julianna began to plead.

"He is our teacher, after all," Rachele decided to play her trump card.

Jenna smiled, "So it's Loremaster blackmail is it? Either I let you two go with them or you clobber my Hank with smelly awful tomatoes and not let him into my bed at night, is that it? Seriously, of course you can go with them. Remember, I said when you first got here that you could leave anytime you desired. I think it is terrific that you both want to continue your studies. I will make more arrangements for you both to go as well. Now how about getting the gardening done or the cooks will serve you only fish paste for supper?"

"Thank you Jenna!" both women exclaimed. Everyone went back to work except Hank and Jenna, who stood passionately embracing for another minute.

This late in the season, not much remained in the garden to pick for meals. While the three women carried the baskets of produce to the cooks, Hank and Ben worked on pulling the dead and adding to the compose pile. "You will need several fancy dresses," Julianna gaily chatted, "a ruler should look as good as she can, you know. Everyone will be looking up to you. Do you suppose that we should ask Jenna if we can get some fancy court dresses made for us?"

"You are right; we will need to look presentable. I can't go meeting people as their ruler wearing old working clothes like these, though they are comfortable. No we mustn't bother Jenna. We'll just get Ben to take us into town. Besides, I'll have to get something made for him too. I can see that I am going to need lots of advice. You two will have to be my extra set of eyes. Keep me advised, and all that."

"Oh absolutely, we three will have to help each other out as much as possible," Rachele added. "That way we won't have to bother others so much. I hate having to bother someone to wipe my rear. From now on, we will help each other with that, Julianna and I have been practicing; we are getting more and more independent."

Indeed the next day, Ben took the three on an all-day shopping spree. He explained that they should get everything they might need. Money was not a problem and explained that the funds came from the Holy Paladins themselves. How? The Santi charged them a steep rate to safely escort or transport their cargos around the Sea Princes. Besides, he wanted to obtain a carriage as well, since he did not expect that they would be riding horses.

That morning, Jenna's daughter, Donatta, and Lilly Ann's daughter, Sarah Amber, stood in the meeting room waiting for Jenna to appear. She took one look at the two with such determined looks upon their faces, and she knew what they wanted. Lilly Ann was right behind her and saw them too. "Oh no, not you too," Lilly Ann exclaimed.

"Mom," said Sarah Amber in exasperation with a hint of pleading mixed in with it.

"It seems that our daughters are ready to fly the coup as well. Soon there will be no one left here but us, Lilly Ann," Jenna teased.

"Oh you have the other seventy-nine, well make that seventy-seven now," Donata retorted, as if she ever expected her mother to have no one else around her. "Really we will be fourteen in a few months! We want to go with Ben and Ariana, and that's that. Oh, Cory's going too." Cory Amir was Arthur and Winnie's son.

"Let me get this straight," Jenna began in her stern voice. "Sarah Amber, you are to be Ariana's Healer; Donata, you are to be her Communicator; and Cory, I presume, her Protector?"

Donata smiled, "Yes, mom. That's right. If you don't say yes, then we will both throw all the rotten tomatoes we can find anywhere in Velona all over Hank!"

All four laughed. They'd heard about the Loremaster's Conspiracy of yesterday afternoon. If it worked for Julianna and Rachele, what the heck, Donata was ready to try anything!

"If we give our consent, then you must accept who else we send along for your Circle."

"We will mom, really we will," Donata could not believe her luck. She remembered how the others had to beg and plead to be allowed to go with Jovanna.

"Good, then you won't mind Sedwick Alyster being your official Judger."

"That old stuck up man?" Donata questioned as if the world were ending. Sedwick was forty, dressed impeccable in clothing that went out of style several decades ago. He lacked a sense of humor and always appeared boorish to the girls.

"It's him or you both stay. I won't have underage girls gallivanting across the Sea Princes without an escort of an older, wiser man," Jenna said stoically. "Now go get Cory and start getting your things together."

"Thank you mom," Donata gave her a big hug, and Sarah Amber did likewise.

A while later when everyone had assembled for the morning briefing, Jenna introduced Ariana and Ben to the rest of their Circle team. "In addition, I am sending along your personal bodyguards, four handpicked Santi, who were originally from Zargarb and Juda Arad. Use them wisely.

Ah, here come the four now. Come on in; let me introduce you formally. This is Captain Alessa Zia and her husband, Adriano." She was twenty-nine and he, thirty. "This is Celeste al Mardi and her husband, Mahdi. He is from the Arad originally." She was twenty-eight and he, thirty-one. "All four began their careers as longbowmen fighting on the Barcella Battle Line against Justinian. You have good archers, expert fighters, and one who knows the Arad. These four are the very best I can offer you." Everyone chatted for quite a while, before the four left to begin packing their belongings. Then the meeting began with a summary of what was happening in Zargarb, naturally.

Chapter 20 Double, Double, Double Trouble

October 6, 640, Emil Brighton, Commander of Fortress Solamina, finally determined how to respond to the mutilation of the sixteen women whom had been rescued from the underground torture chamber beneath the inn. For some time now, he knew that Lenkova and her forces were stationed on the eastern border with Zargarb. Saxon Bye had kept a close ear on the news in the city, waiting for the word that Zargarb had been freed, given back to the Santi by General Taxos. The news had come; what would be General Hecate Lox's reaction? Would he send his men to cross the border to attempt to retake the sector? That had been Emil's greatest concern.

This morning, he called his staff together. "Still no reaction from Hecate. Thus, I wish to implement my move. Saxon, will you see if you can bring him here to me? If not, we will go to him in force."

Saxon smiled, for finally Emil was going to do something in retaliation for the poor women he'd rescued. "About time," he muttered and left. Emil, a Wid, ignored the intended criticism.

"You think he will come?" asked his wife, Matilda.

"Yes, probably. We gave him the thirty thousand coins he was short a while back. I don't think that he will forget that. Come, we should see that we are civilized and offer him some refreshments, though I doubt he will desire any at this hour."

A little over an hour later, Saxon led General Hecate Lox into the meeting room. "Ah good day to you General," Emil was being cordial to the man, before he dropped his hammer on his head.

"Yes, fine day. Things are going well here. With the shocking treason of my counterpart in Zargarb, I was wondering if you might be wishing to see me."

"Well, there is the small matter of whether you would send your men across the border into Zargarb hoping to retake the sector."

"Just between two old soldiers, Emil, the thought did cross my mind more than once when I heard the news. However, you know my situation here as well as I do, I suspect. I've got around five hundred Holy Paladins and another two hundred Local Paladins in training. We both know that with those numbers, I can barely retain control of this city, abandoning entirely the outlying towns and villages. Even though I would really like to retake Zargarb — it would be a grand feather in my career — I would not get very far and lose Solamina as well. It would be utter folly to make such an attempt just now. If some other sector would send me a thousand men, why, then I would not have the time for this friendly chat."

"Excellent, General, we are in agreement on this point. However, this is not the reason that I requested this visit. If you will recall when we last met here some years ago and I lent you the funds to make up your shortfall, I stipulated three conditions."

"Oh indeed I do. We have religiously lived up to those conditions. We have established the Red Light Inn for that purpose. They are well paid, and, I might add, it has worked out extremely well for my men and for the women. It was a brilliant idea. I am ashamed that I had not thought of it first. I did document the arrangement in my yearly reports to the Mother Church in Megalos, though they have not yet commented upon it. I suspect the Church as more important matters with which to deal."

All the while, a blind woman was sitting in the shadows in the back of the room. Lorissa Moeti now spoke quietly, "Emil, he is telling you the truth." General Hecate turned to look at who spoke; the others were around the table. He saw a blind woman sitting on a chair in the dark corner of the room. He'd not noticed her before she spoke.

"She is blind as you can see, compliments of the priests of Zargarb many years ago. However, she has the uncanny ability to tell when a person is lying. She has never failed us yet. I had her brought her from Velona for just this conversation that we are having, General. I must know the actual truth of the matters at hand."

"Well, I don't see how a blind woman can see anything," he replied, more than a little flustered. He decided to test her.

"You are aware of the fire at the Ale Alley?" Emil asked.

"No, what fire?"

"He is lying."

"You are aware of the underground prison that lay beneath the Ale Alley, accessed through the storage room of the inn?"

"Well, yes, yes I am aware of it," he replied shifting his voice around, trying to sound like he had been caught in a trap.

"He is lying." His face twinged and reddened slightly. Maybe there was something about this blind woman after all, but what was this all about, he wondered.

"I know that a few of my men have had to run errands there for the High Priest. I assume it was to fetch His Holiness more wine. What's all this about a prison? It was just a cruddy inn, poor one at best."

"Then you do not know what we found locked away in that prison before we burned it down?"

"You, you burned it down? How dare you? No, what did you find? I have absolutely no idea of what you are talking about."

"He speaks the truth."

"Right I am. What is this all about anyway? I've lived up to our agreement."

"No sir, you most definitely have not. Your men were the prison guards. We rescued sixteen women prisoners who were locked permanently in metal bindings. One was wrapped around their heads, forcing a ring into their mouths so that they could not close them nor speak. They were forced to lick their slop called food with their tongues, like dogs. The worst part was the devices, which locked their arms tightly across their backs, making them immobile. These devices had locks upon them, which could be undone to release them. However, these sixteen had molten metal poured into the locks so that these devices could never be removed. Some had been caged like this for many, many years. Their arms literally withered and died upon their bodies! Ten women now have no arms at all, while six are slowly recovering, their arms, I'm told, look like match sticks."

"This cannot be! I ordered my men to stop. I ordered the priests to stop. Everyone gave me their word that there would be no more mutilations of women. I, you, you inspected the Nunneries. You didn't see any of this now did you?"

"He is telling the truth."

Saxon spoke with a catch in his voice, "Yes, I inspected, but I failed. They made the devices removable. Thus, when I made my inspections, the women were free of their bondage, yet they were probably placed back in them the minute I left. I could kick myself in my butt for having been made such a fool. It has cost ten women their arms!"

"Damn those priests anyway. It must have all been their doing!" Hecate exclaimed, becoming livid. He calmed down. "Are these women going to live? God, I hope so."

"Yes, they are alive, but what kind of life can one have without arms, eh General?" Emil replied, purposely punching in the despair most people would conceive that these women would be enduring for life.

The General looked most upset and troubled, as he got a vivid imagining of such. Emil chose this precise moment to add, "Which brings us back to the original bargain. As you will recall, I said at that time that I would double the fees that we charge you for our transportation and security runs on your behalf to the outlying towns and villages as well as between sectors. More to the point, I said I would double it for each woman we found harmed. In this case, it is sixteen women. I am a man of my word. I ought to double it sixteen time. However, if I did, even I cannot easily count that large a number. Hence, I have decided that I will only charge you twice the total value of the cargo the Santi are delivering. That is, if we are hired to deliver one thousand gold coins, then our fee will not be a hundred as before, but will now be two thousand gold coins. At least I can easily calculate the fees this way."

The General gaped; he could find no words. "But that will ruin us totally!"

"Ten women from Solamina are already ruined, so these fees will help support them. They will need someone to be with them constantly to help them eat, cook their meals, clean them, and even wipe their butts. Someone has to pay for what you've done. Since you folks from Megalos did this, it is only fair that you pay for their keep. What would you have a helpless woman do, General?"

"Well, perhaps they would be better off dead than forced to live such a horrible existence. I know many a wounded soldier that would have wished he'd been left to die than exist as he is. Sometimes, perhaps, a death is a release. Nevertheless, I agree, since they live, they must be supported and made as comfortable as possible. You won't get an argument on that point from me. Perhaps I could get the Church to fund their support. If I could get the Church to fully fund your relief effort, would that be sufficient?"

"I'm afraid that we cannot any longer believe anything that your Church says it will do. You understand. We had written word from your Pope that this sort of thing would be halted. Instead, they continued in other ways and hid their torture of women from sight. No, my decision stands. A Santi always keeps a promise, though I have compromised a good deal on the doubling."

"At least, I always know where I stand with the Santi del Dio. I wish I could say the same for my organization. May I get back to you on this matter?"

"Certainly. Anytime, General Hecate Lox." The two men shook hands, and Saxon escorted him out of the fortress.

"Thank you very much, Lorissa," Emil took her hand. "I thought that the General might be involved in this plot. Now I see that he knew nothing about their subterfuge."

"You have loosened a wild card into the mix, Emil, you realize that?" she said, warning him.

"I know that I have. They may well attempt to handle their own protection in the future by sending along half his army with each shipment to the outlying towns or even cross country. It could mean more trouble for the banditos or a loss of revenues for the Santi."

"Or it could be far more serious, Emil. Time will tell," she said softly.

"Thank you again, Lorissa. Let me escort you back to your ship. I know that you are eager to return to Velona."

"Aye, that I am. Perhaps the next time you could make this in the summer. I was hoping for a nice, balmy, warm time at sea, but it is the stormy season, they tell me. I just felt chilly all the time. It's been a pleasure aiding you, Emil. Until we meet again?" she held out her hand, and Emil bent over and kissed it. He walked her out and to the ship, escorting her up the long gangplank, handing her over to another Santi woman fighter. Both nodded at each other. He waited and watched her caravel slip slowly back out to sea. What a woman, he thought as he walked slowly back into the tower.

General Hecate Lox walked into Solamina. He was fuming. This whole operation had been nothing but a fiasco right from the start. Now the lying, deceiving priests had just sacrificed everything, the entire sector was lost! All because they continued to harm women with their idiotic notions of Good Marks. Hecate was too angry to return to his office. He began walking the streets of Solamina alone, talking to himself. "This is not what I signed on for. Gone are the good old days of riding off on holy quests to retrieve lost Holy Relics. Ah, now that was what appealed to me. That's why I signed on. Haven't done any of that in a score of years, probably never be able to do it again. Stuck in this hellhole of a place. Won't give me enough men to do the job right. Banditos control everything but the city. Yet, in my darkest need, the Santi did loan me the thirty thousand coins which saved my butt."

"They didn't have to do that, but I see now that they wanted to help the women who were being mistreated. Well, my hands are clean. I didn't ever authorize chopping off body parts. Damn priests anyway. I wonder if the Pope knows all about what they used to do and have been doing recently. I just cannot believe it, the Pope said no more, even promised it. Hell, I even went with Saxon to inspect the Nunnery. Well, small consolation; he didn't find out about it until recently either. I shouldn't blame myself too harshly on that account. Yet, these priests used my men for their nefarious actions and without my permission! That violates every military principle of command! I might have needed the men to defend the walls, but no, they were off chopping off poor women's body parts. Idiots, I am surrounded by idiots and liars."

He walked some more, "Hecate, you should commend yourself. After that horrible year when you had to borrow coins to pay the taxes, you handled the ensuing tax years just fine on your own. That should count for something." He'd made up the deficit long ahead of tax season by using his own pay, skimming on the pay of his men, and charging a higher shipping cost. He'd kept at it dutifully all year long, and by tax time, he had the funds to cover the shortfall. No one could collect taxes from the outlying lands; the banditos always seemed to end up stealing the collected funds.

"Charging double for our shipments! That about ends everything here. I cannot afford to use their services for anything now. I might as well just hand over all the supplies destined for an outlying town to the banditos! Heck, my only recourse is to pretend there aren't any outer towns! Even if I did that, three-fourths of our supplies comes in overland from the other sectors. By January, even I'll be starving! All because of those damnable priests!"

He walked on down the street. Dusk was falling, so he stopped at the nearest pub and had dinner, a very long dinner. "I must see if this is true for myself," he declared and then burped. He'd had a little too much ale. It was full dark when he hit the streets once again.

Ah hour later, he found himself standing outside the Nunnery. "Everyone seems to be in bed. If they are up to something, now is a good time for a bed check. He knocked on the door and waited. A few minutes later the Head Nun poked her head out the door a crack. "General Hecate. I'm here for a bed check."

"But it is nighttime. Everyone's in bed. Do come back in the morning," she said sternly and softly.

"Out of the way woman," and he pushed inside past her, she could smell the ale on his breath.

"I'll have to report this to the High Priest!" she declared shutting the door and following him inside. He was now going door to door, opening them and peering inside at the sleeping women. The first two contained other nuns whom he had seen around the town on various occasions, one was a cook as he recalled. However, when he opened the third door, he saw what he had been dreading all along. Emil had not lied. Three women were encased in some strange metal devices. In all, he counted fifteen women being terrorized. How they could possibly sleep this way, he did not know. Now he was very furious indeed.

"Woman, fetch me one set of those diabolical devices and make it snappy." He was seething, the nun did as he asked, fetching another set from a storeroom, although she had no idea what he wanted it for. "Now get those two up, and you three go release those women right now! Move woman!" he yelled, frightening all the women.

Five minutes later, while he watched, all the women were freed. Now, his mind formed a twisted idea. "Here put these on her," he ordered the Head Nun to put the devices onto the cook. She protested but did as he asked, terrified that the drunken general might draw his sword. She would bide her time and let the High Priest know of this affront in the morning. "Now her," he ordered. Again, she locked her other assistant into the devices. "Now you, Head Nun. It's your turn." She tried to fight him off, so he slugged her, knocking her out. It took him several minutes to get the Head Nun snug into the devices.

The freed women stood staring at the spectacle. Most wanted to cheer him, but remained dutifully silent, for fear he might put them back into the torture devices. "Now then, ladies, are there more keys to these devices than the ones I took from the Head Hun?"

One meekly replied, "No sir." He looked at all the other women, who nodded this was true.

"Good. I will take the key with me. You put them to bed and get a good night's sleep for once. Good evening ladies," he could not keep from smiling. He grabbed a one complete set of devices and the keys and left, heading for his office and quarters. "That felt good," he said to himself as he walked briskly home.

First thing in the morning at reveille time, he mustered all his men in the dining hall. He dismissed the priest after the morning unison prayers. Once the priest had left, he called everyone to attention. "Today men, I and the Santi Commander have just uncovered a diabolical, treasonous plot. Our so-called priests have violated a Papal Order and by doing so have destroyed our military governorship of this sector. No wonder we have been fighting banditos ever since we came here. You recall that several years ago, we uncovered the fact that the priests were brutalizing, raping, and cutting off women's body parts. I know that some of you were involved with that treason. Yet, when the Papal Orders came, I chose not to press any charges against you, my trusted Holy Paladins. However, I have just last night discovered that the priests did not stop as our Holy Pope decreed. Instead they made these metal devices in which to lock a ring in their mouths that they may not speak or eat. Worse, the other device locks their arms tightly across their upper backs, making the women completely helpless."

"If this were not bad enough, I have finally found out what was going on at the inn that just burned down. A secret prison was built underneath the inn. There, the priests sent some women encased in these devices. Only they poured hot metal into the key holes so that they could never be removed. These women slowly lost their arms! Ten armless women was the result at the time of the fire. I know that some of you here were and are working for the priests and not me. My aides are conducting a full investigation. When I find out which ones of you were betraying me and working for the priests, my justice will be swift. I will have both your arms cut off so you can become like those you imprisoned! Do I make myself perfectly clear? I will not tolerate high treason against our Pope!"

"Today's orders: after you eat, each one of you is to come up here and closely inspect these devices. We will divide evenly up into seven groups, with six riding up a spoke road. You are to stop at each town and village that has a Church of Jehosanity. There, you are to search thoroughly every nook and cranny in the Nunnery and the church itself. If you find any women encaged, free them. If you find so much as one of these devices here, you are to put the Head Nun into the device and bring me the key. Also you are to arrest every priest in that village. The charge is high treason against the Pope! The seventh group is with me, we are going to search this city, and we will be arresting the Nuns and the High Priest immediately. Do I make myself perfectly clear on this matter? High treason will not be tolerated!" He was now screaming; he suddenly realized how passionate he had become.

"Sir, what if they resist?"

"Resistance is nothing but a sign of guilt. Kill them on the spot!" Simply handled, he thought. "Now eat fast men. We have high treason with which to deal today!" He walked out to get his meal, which was waiting for him in his office as always. He never ate with his men; it was unseemly to do so.

He watched some six hundred men in groups of one hundred each riding off northward up the six spoke roads. Many of these men were the Local Holy Paladins, as he called them, but for this operation, he needed every available man. He had some hundred of his most trusted men with him. They rode through the streets, while a wagon followed along behind them. First stop, Nunnery. Sure enough, the three women were just as he had left them, only now they made awful noises, probably trying to beg to be released. Hecate had no such idea, however. He had his men place them into the wagon, while he moved across the block to the priest's rectory building. His men stormed in and interrupted their morning breakfast.

"All of you are under arrest," General Hecate spoke loudly and distinctly. "The charge is High Treason against our beloved Pope! Arrest them all!" His men fanned out to begin tying up their hands.

"What's the meaning of this? What are you talking about?" the High Priest demanded.

"You will see in the wagon. You have violated the Papal Order not to harm women. When you poured hot metal into the locks so they could never be removed, the effect created after many years is the same as cutting off their arms, armless women. Ten women now have no arms; ten of those you kept like animals in your underground prison in the inn that recently burned down. You have violated the Papal Order, and as a result, the Santi have every right to attack us and kill every one of us. I am hoping to preempt that assault on us by arresting those involved in this High Treason against our Pope. If I fail, then you, High Priest, have doomed us all! Now get him out of my sight!"

There were some twenty churches to search in Solamina alone. It took the better part of the day. In ten of these, more of these devices were found, though no other women were discovered. All the priests at those locations were also arrested. Late afternoon, General Hecate had finished searching all the Churches of Jehosanity in Solamina. Satisfied that he had them all, he ordered them all to be taken onboard one of the ships that was now docked awaiting a load of cargo, which, thanks to Emil's pledge of fee increases, would never be coming. He ordered all the men to be chained and stowed below. He paid the captain well, ordering him to take the prisoners back to Megalos. However, they would not be ready to sail until all of his six other groups returned. There could be more of them.

Next, after dinner, he sat down and composed a long letter to the Pope, outlining the charges, and spelling out all the details of their crimes, as best he knew them. He then explained what the actual situation was here in Solamina, that failure to send him an additional thousand Holy Paladins all these years had caused the current crisis, total manpower failure. He outlined what he was about to do and tore off his braids and enclosed them with the letter. He sealed it with his official seal. Now all he could do was wait.

After a week, all six of the groups had finally returned, bringing another two dozen priests with them. Even more of a conversation piece as the wagons rolled through the city to the docks was the dozen women encased in the metal devices. The general smiled at the sight. He walked up to each wagon and smirked, "Enjoying the taste of your own medicines are we?" The terrified nuns could only make strange pleading noises, which he ignored. "Take them onto the boat and see that they are all properly chained. Tell the captain that he can sail as soon as I present him with his sailing instructions. Well done, men. Get some supper, and then I will meet with all of you for your next set of orders."

A short while later, he presented the captain with the sealed package and told him to hand deliver the package to the Pope. Under no circumstances was he to unchain these men until the Pope so ordered. A handshake shake later, the captain barked his orders, while the General watched the ship slowly navigate out to sea. He smiled when he remembered he had forgotten to give the captain the keys to the women's metal devices.

After dinner, he once more addressed his entire force. This time, he noticed that a number of men were missing. He smiled; they had likely fled for their lives, given his warning. "Men, thank you for a job well done. I have sent the charges and proofs to the Pope. May he find the mercy to forgive what they have done. However, we now face an even greater problem, the consequences of their treason. As you know, they violated the Papal Order, which was also used to appease the Santi del Dio, which first brought to light these atrocities against women. True to their word, the Santi have taken action against us. They are now charging us double the value of the merchandise that we ship via their secure, guaranteed delivery. If we use them to obtain a thousand gold coin shipment of grain, then we must pay them two thousand coins, said funds are to go to supporting the women that these treasonous priests have mutilated."

As expected, there was furor over this information. When they calmed down, he continued, "Of course we have only a few choices. One, we can refuse to pay and be starved to death before the winter is over. Two, we can go to war with the Santi del Dio, we few against the thousands of them. Or three, we can quietly leave Solamina and head to Pieta and there await further orders from the Pope. Gentlemen, as your leader, I cannot accept the first two. So it is with a sad heart that I say, tomorrow morning, pack up all your gear and ride the coastal road to Pieta. In time, our new orders will come. In the meantime, perhaps we can lend them a helping hand."

The cheering was deafening. Given that the first two choices meant certain death, the men wanted him to know that they were behind him all the way. "Finally, Holy Paladins, I will stay behind a day or two to see to the proper transfer of governorship. I will catch up with you as soon as I have the affairs handled here. See you all in Pieta. Open all ale taps tonight, men!" They needed no further excuse to party!

While his men were partying, the General loaded one of the wagons with a number of heavy sacks. Then, he drove the wagon out of the eastern gate over to the Santi fortress. He knocked and asked for Emil. Shortly, the

428

gates opened, and he drove the wagon inside. Emil was standing watching, along with many others. "Emil," the General acknowledged. "I wanted you to know firsthand that I found what you said to be true. I found the devices being used on women in the Nunnery. I freed them and put them onto the nuns who were in charge. I arrested all the priests who were likely involved. My men visited every town and village and arrested all those who also had these devices in their buildings. Their nuns were put into these devices. I just sent them all back to Megalos in chains. The charge is High Treason against the Papal Orders, of which I believe your organization was sent a copy as well." He then chuckled, "I intentionally forgot to send the keys to the devices along with the encased nuns. I guess they will get a firsthand look at what it was like for the women that they tortured."

"Two final things. In the wagon is my donation to assist those women who are now in need because of their high treason. With your new fees, I cannot continue to run this sector. Thus, I have instructed all my men, who are right now drinking all the remaining barrack's ale, to leave Solamina in the morning. They will be going to Pieta, there to await new orders from the Pope. Although I have already officially resigned my commission, the Pope will not get it for several months yet. I present you with a set of the keys to the city gates as my last act as General. Also, here are the keys that I forgot to send. My men have left a number of the confiscated metal devices in my office. Perhaps you will see to their destruction?"

Emil replied, "I commend you on all that you have done, General Hecate Lox. At first, I believed that you were conspiring with the priests. Now I see that you most definitely were not. What you have done will long be remembered by the free peoples of Tarra. You have done the right and just actions. I will see that your donation gets to those women who will have such a great need for it. Thank you sir. However, may I ask will you be joining your men in Pieta?"

He grinned, "I have told them that I would, but that I must stay behind a few days to see to the orderly transition of power. In truth, I have resigned and will depart the Sea Princes to destinations unspecified. It is perhaps better if you do not know where I will go. You have indeed been a fair and honorable opponent, Emil." The two men shook hands, and General Hecate walked proudly out of the gate and back to Solamina, his head, finally, held high. Whether the Pope concurred, whether the Mano del Dio was behind all this, he did not care. He was a soldier, not a religious fanatic. He did what was militarily correct and proper. His integrity remained intact. As he walked, he had a flash of insight. He recognized that this day was coming when he had been ordered to kill all the nobles and their families. That was the turning point, which had led inevitably to this day, of that he was convinced.

The next day, he waved farewell to his hung over men as every Holy Paladin rode ceremonially past him on their way out of the eastern gate.

They circled around the city and headed west down the Med Sea coastal road. Meanwhile, once they had left, the general, now wearing old clothes instead of his usual sky blue clothes and carrying a large sack walked on board another ship at the dock. Later that afternoon, the ship, already loaded with a modest cargo, set sail for the Southlands.

October 18, 640, Solamina regained its freedom. Messages flew back fast and furious. The banditos were notified, and Emil asked that they come out of hiding in force and take control of their city until proper leaders could be found. Additionally, he sent half of his Santi troops off to the border with Pieta, just in case the Holy Paladins there should try to retake Solamina. He asked that Lenkova and her large group come into Solamina for a few days until the banditos arrived.

As in Zargarb, once the folks realized that their oppressive overlords had fled the sector, many vigilantes sought revenge on the few who had collaborated with the Holy Paladins or priests. In the outlying towns, the few remaining priests who had not been arrested were lynched by angry mobs, while their supporters were driven out of town, exiting toward Pieta with nothing but the clothes on their backs. In Solamina, five hundred people were slain in the first two days of chaos, before Lenkova and her forces arrived.

From our viewpoint, the first action had to be putting some kind of government in place. Unlike Barcella and Zargarb, we knew of no living descendent of the sector's founders, who had a birthright to rule. The nobles were long dead and likewise the Sisterhood. For a week, Emil held out hope that someone who had been in hiding all these years and who had a birthright to rule would step forward. None appeared. At the end of the month, Praedo Garcia and his wagon rolled into the city, accompanied by Silvas Armato and Benito Fuella, the two "generals" of the banditos. Five hundred bandito men escorted them into the city. The three received a hero's welcome.

As planned, Emil met them officially at the largest open space in the city, the docks. There he formally presented the keys to the city to Praedo. In a formal speech before the thousands gathered, Emil pledged the full support and assistance of the Santi del Dio. Privately, he asked Praedo to take stock of the true situation and then meet with him to figure out ways and means of solving the many problems facing the sector in its long road to recovery.

Chapter 21 Ariana Takes Charge

October 21, 640, the sleek caravel called Dingo's Rat, left Velona bound for Zargarb. Ariana and her large group were all onboard, their large cargo of personal items, including a carriage, stowed securely in the cargo hold. Knowing that food for the winter was going to be a problem, Jenna had filled up the remainder of the large hold with dried rations, making this a dual run. Yes, the ship was loaded to capacity and would take several weeks to travel the length of the Med Sea.

"Captain Dingo, why is your ship called Dingo's Rat?" asked Ariana. She and her two close advisors had puzzled over this ever since they had heard its name. Rachele had no idea why someone would name a ship a rat.

"Ah, my fair Ladies, t'is this way. When I first came aboard 'er, something did not smell right. Me crew held their noses. As Captain, twas me duty to see to the ship-shape of me lady 'er, so I went looking, using me nose. Ah ha, I says, look laddies, I found yer rat. It'd gotten aboard jest after she was made, see, and no food were there to be found. Poor thing starved to death. I pitched the rat overboard. But the name stuck, Dingo's Rat. Don't smell anymore, my Ladies." All three chuckled at the story, but wondered if it were really what happened.

For Julianna and Rachele, this trip was enjoyable. Memories of their previous trip in a similar caravel were nightmarish, trapped within the metal cases, rings in their mouths, hopelessly helpless, half starved, and scared to death. Now, going back, so much had changed for them. Perhaps the biggest change was their cheerful attitude toward life. Both women were enthusiastic and content with life, a renewed vigor toward living, especially since they had just learned that Solamina had been freed as well. However, neither woman had any real desire to return there.

For the first twelve days, the group just relaxed and enjoyed the trip, using the time to get to know one another. However, late October was the beginning of the winter stormy season. The next day, Captain Dingo tacked to the southeast to avoid a nasty looking, large squall line. That afternoon, they sailed very near the island Venutua, which at one time used to be the vacation spot for many noblemen and their families. The island lay far to the south of Solamina and Zargarb. "Ahoy, there be Venutua, the noblemen's retreat."

All eyes watched the island grow in size as they neared it. Suddenly, Ariana's childhood memories stirred. "My dad brought me here when I was a little girl, around five! I remember this place! Captain, can we dock and have a look around? I wonder if anything is still here. It looks so deserted."

"Aye, aye," Dingo called out. "Make for yonder cove; there be docks there."

After twelve days at sea, everyone could use a short land break, if only to really stretch their legs. An hour later, the mooring lines were cast and the gangplank secured. Ariana was very excited, distant memories of her family returned. Happy times. It was about this time of year that her father had brought her and her mother here for a vacation. Gaily, she began pointing out the sights that she remembered. Her group followed her around, observing the buildings. Many were open aired buildings, designed for hot summer days. A few had regular walls. All were made from stone. Vines and underbrush grew everywhere, in a valiant attempt to retake the land usurped by men ages ago. Not a soul was around; it was deserted. Ben pointed out signs that indicated the Centurions had searched the island quite some time ago. He took the opportunity to train his three apprentices in looking for such signs.

"Hey, I remember this building. This was dad's house," Ariana exclaimed. "Let's go inside. Darn, the door is shut."

"Allow me, my pretty," Ben said gallantly, while holding Nicolina Sue, so that Ariana was free to explore. He gave a hard push, and the stuck door opened. Inside, the place looked like it had been thoroughly sacked and looted. However, much of the heavy stonework remained. Stone tables, chairs, and such were covered with dust.

"I remember, we used to dine on that table. A man with a lute stood over there playing the most soothing music. Wow, I remember this place." She wandered about, while the others did likewise.

"Hey Ben come here," Ariana called out. She was standing before a huge throne made of grey stone. A stone throne rested upon a two-foot block of stone. "I remember something my dad told me several times. I used to climb up there and sit on that very throne. Dad would say to me, 'Ariana, what's below will be yours one day.' I remember getting down on my knees and looking under the throne, but as you can see its just empty space with four stone legs. I wonder what he meant by that remark?"

"Ooh, a mystery!" exclaimed Julianna. "I love mysteries. What exactly did he say, Ariana?"

"What's below will be yours one day; those were his exact words. Whatever could he have meant, do you suppose?"

Rachele squatted down and peered under the throne. "Nothing written underneath the seat. Nothing is here below it either, except empty space. What a strange thing to say, 'What's below will be yours one day.' Makes no real sense. Normally, noblemen give their daughters a large dowry when they get married, you know. It would have made more sense if he had said: when you get married one day, I'll give you a big dowry."

"You are right," Ariana said getting into the mystery herself. "That would make much more sense than what's below. There isn't anything below. I remember telling dad that very thing, but there's nothing below. She closed her eyes to look at her memory of that time. "You know, he never answered me. He did have a sort of teasing twinkle in his eye, and he smiled. I liked it when he smiled."

"Well, Loremasters, I say it's time that you solved the mystery," Ben said. "Let's see you use your powers of observation and see if the three of you can figure it out. It'll be a good exercise."

"Yes, right, solve a twenty year old mystery without any clues," Ariana teased, but knew that she had been challenged. "Come on, you two. Let's show him we are not dummies."

"Yes, let's," echoed Julianna, tossing her hair.

The three began examining the throne area carefully, looking for clues. "There really is nothing at all directly beneath the stone chair and this slab," Rachele concluded. "I wonder just how far beneath the throne we were to look?"

"Maybe it's hollow or there is a secret room directly beneath the throne," Julianna wondered aloud.

"I'll bet that is it," Ariana exclaimed. "That would make what dad said make sense. There just has to be some secret room directly below the throne. Now how do we find it? If I had hands, I could take a spear or something and tap around here and see if it's hollow or anything."

"We don't have arms, so we'll have to figure another way to do it," declared Rachele, more determined than ever to solve this mystery.

"Hey those old torch holders over there on the wall, they'd make nice tappers," Ariana said looking for something with which to tap around the floor. "Would one of you be so kind as to fetch us three of those please?" Sarah, Donata, and Cory immediately went and brought them to the three, holding them out for the women.

"Can you just put it on the floor there," Julianna explained, "we have to use our feet. Rachele, I'll tap around here and you try over there."

"I'll go over here directly behind the throne," Ariana said, grasping the torch holder between her arms. Everyone else watched the three women. Seven of their companions looked pleadingly at Ben; they wanted to rush to help the women tap. It seemed so cruel to see them awkwardly trying to work this out. Only Sedwick did not, for he remained as ever, straight-faced.

Ben whispered, "Allow them their self-respect. If they want your help, they will ask for it, as they did in fetching the torch holders. Allow them their dignity to work it out first. I know, it takes a good deal of getting used to, but you have to let them try on their own first."

Rachele had sat down on her butt and picked up the torch holder with her feet. Now she began tapping the stone around one side of the throne. Opposite her, Julianna was now doing the same thing. "Darn, this is just too awkward," Ariana declared. She glanced at her two companions to see how they were managing and promptly sat down on her butt and used her feet, emulating the other two. She could more readily pivot to another spot because she still had arms.

Soon all three women concurred; they looked up at the others and exclaimed, "Hollow!" Ariana said, "Listen." She tapped in one spot close to the throne and then further away. There was a distinct difference in sound. Then, Rachele did the same, followed by Julianna. "Hey, I have an idea. Ben, you come stand here and mark the outer edge of the hollow spot. The rest of you, join them, and let's see just what the dimensions of this hollow spot are."

Five awkward minutes later, the three finally got up, and looked at their friends who were now marking out the dimensions. "Looks like it is a square, fifteen feet on a side," stated Ariana flatly. "Now the real question becomes where's the entrance? Probably nothing down there now but cobwebs, but I would sure like to see the chamber that my dad teased me about when I was five."

"But we don't know anything about secret chambers," Julianna protested. "Ben, are we supposed to know this?"

"While this is not directly related to plants and animals, it is well within your abilities to work out. The key is observation. Give it a try. I understand that this one might well be beyond your current abilities to work out. If so, I will lend a hand. If I cannot work it out, then Sedwick can lend us all a hand. I'm afraid that Cory's method we will try last. A Protector would just smash the stone covering the room." Cory laughed, he was right. Why waste all this time?

"Well, when I escaped from the Nunnery, I found a level hidden behind a tapestry. When I pulled it down, the secret door slid open," Ariana explained to her companions. "I don't see any tapestries, but let's see if we can find anything that looks out of place or like a lever." The three began walking around the huge room, examining the walls and the few fixtures that remained.

"I think that we must be missing something. How could a lever be this far away from the entrance?" Julianna asked. The others concurred, twenty-five feet was an awful long way from the secret chamber.

"Well there's nothing here but the throne," Ariana said after looking it over once more.

"Maybe it's the throne," suggested Rachele. All three squatted down and began closely inspecting the four legs. "Look, there are scratch marks here on the floor going from the leg about a foot towards the other front leg."

Sitting on the floor and looking up, Ariana said, "Yes, there are scratch marks on top too, just like on the bottom. None on the other three. This leg must somehow move, but how?"

"Hey, I'll just push it," decided Rachele, who awkwardly scooted over to get behind it and to get her legs in position to push against the stone leg. Using her leg muscles, she gave it a good push. To her surprise, it pushed easily. A grating sound echoed as the stone slid over the stone throne bottom and floor. However, that was lost in the noise of Ben's startled yell as a section of the floor beneath him tilted down, causing him and Nicolina, who was in his arms, to go sliding down into the dark room below the chamber.

"Are you all right? Is Nicolina okay?" yelled a frantic Ariana.

"Yes, bit bruised is all. Say Nicolina likes it. I think she wants me to slide down with her again. It's pitch black down here. How about some light?"

Ariana asked, "Will some of you light a lantern or two please?"

Soon four lanterns shone down on Ben, who still held the eighteen month old infant. He was standing before a door. "Come on down; slide on your butts," he called out.

First, two went down with lanterns, Cory and Sarah. Then, Ariana and her two associates slid down joining them, but there was no room for more in the small space. "Naturally, there would have to be a door," declared Ariana. "Okay, will one of you try to open it please?"

Cory did the honors. The door swung inward revealing the hidden room. However, nothing prepared them for the sight the lanterns illuminated! "Oh my," Ariana's words floated off into stunned silence. Rachele and Julianna just stared open mouthed.

"I think, my dear, that you have just found your dowry," Ben commented, trying to restrain his excitement. Piles of gold coins lined the walls; brilliant sparking gems lay neatly on shelves; golden plates, candleholders, serving trays and similar items were neatly stacked, but quite dusty now. On the top shelf was jewelry, broaches, pins, hairpieces, and even crowns.

From top side, the steady voice of Sedwick offered an explanation, "Long have we known that the Sea Prince noblemen would secret their wealth out of cities about to be besieged. You father probably secreted this away many years ago, from the amount of dust on some of the pieces. Others show less of an accumulation. I would guess that over the years, he merely continued to add more items here. With your permission, ma'am, I shall go arrange for many sacks to be delivered and more bodies with which to carry them."

"Yes, sure," Ariana finally managed to speak. "This is unbelievable! Someone pinch me; this cannot be real!"

"Try biting into one of those gold coins," suggested Julianna. "If it's gold, you should be able to leave teeth marks."

Ben handed one to Ariana, "It probably is gold, cause this one is heavy for its size." She bit into the coin and left marks. "Honey, you are richer than rich. You are wealthier than wealthy. Would you consider buying me a new suit?" he was teasing of course.

"This is amazing!" Ariana finally grasped the magnitude of the find. She began jumping for joy, and Julianna and Rachele joined her; it was an outlet for their exuberance. Later, when Sedwick returned with his arms full of sacks and half the crew and all the Protection Squad, everyone climbed up the ramp. However, as soon as Ariana tried to walk up, she had a hard time keeping her balance. Cory put his arms around her and helped her up. He then aided the other two women who had a much more difficult time going up the rather steep ramp. He took Nicolina Sue from Ben and lifted her up into waiting hands,and the rest scrambled up.

"By the way, Ariana, Julianna, Rachele, you all pass the test. Very well done on solving the mystery," Ben acknowledged their good detective work. The three beamed.

The rest of that day, everyone got a good work out. It was no small task to move that quantity of gold and items! Another day was spent carrying it to and securing it in the caravel. They arrived in Zargarb two days later than expected, landing on November 5, 640.

As they neared the docks, the three women fussed with their clothing, each wearing the new style fancy court dresses they had recently had made for them. Ariana's gown was emerald green velvet, flared open with many pleats below her waist. Among the many pieces of jewelry, she had found a nice tiara, which she though looked proper for the ruler to wear. Her assistants, Julianna and Rachele both wore matching pink silk gowns, which fit tightly around their upper torsos, highlighting their assets well, but also calling dramatic notice to their missing arms. The material had smooth, sleek lines where sleeves would otherwise be located. Similar to Ariana's dress, theirs was flared open with many pleats. Ariana had also insisted that each of them wear a nice tiara, although theirs were smaller than hers was. Ben, Sarah, and Donata spent the better part of an hour getting the three dressed and ready for their first appearance before the welcoming crowd that would surely be waiting for them as they docked. Even Nicolina Sue wore a cute dress, though she was too little to appreciate all the fuss.

Once they walked off the ship onto the docks, they confronted the huge crowd at last. "Oh my," exclaimed Ariana, very much surprised to see the entire dock area packed with people. All the Santi at the fortress were present in their dress tunics, including Lenkova and her group, which had just arrived back from Solamina. Rodrigo Decasas stood beside Art Longton, and the many men in his employ were behind these two. As many townsfolk as could squeezed in, filling up all the remaining available space. More leaned out of upper story windows of nearby warehouses.

As soon as they approached, the crowd began clapping louder and louder until the noise was rather deafening. Ben, holding their daughter, stood at her side, just behind her. Her assistants were on either side, while her Circle stood behind them, her Santi guards, behind them. She waved her arms, and the noise grew even louder. Finally, they settled down so she could speak to them.

"Hi, I am Ariana Zar Wilkins. I'm so honored by your welcome. I do hope that I can live up to your expectations. I'm sorry that I don't know most of you. I was only ten when I was taken by the paladins; after that, I saw no one, except those at the Nunnery. This is my husband, Ben, and our daughter, Nicolina Sue. These two are my assistants from Solamina, Julianna Rosso and Rachele Tinelli. As you can see we three have been victimized by the Unholy Paladins, but then so many of you have suffered even more than we, lost loved ones and all that. As I see it, we are all in this together, for the better now, I do hope."

"Just so that you all know, I am a Santi del Dio member, and thus I can guarantee that we will be very much supported by the Santi from now on. Behind me are my Santi advisors. She introduced each member of her Circle, and then her personal guards were presented.

The formalities out of the way, she then began to give them some substance. "Right here from the start, I want everyone to know that I am not an experienced ruler and may make many mistakes along the way. My goal for us all here in Zargarb is one of abundant prosperity and happiness for every person in our country. We do not need another collection of nobles siphoning off profits. Any excess funds that my government makes I will somehow funnel back into better facilities for all of you or directly into your pockets."

"Now I obviously do not know what dire problems you are facing, what things need handling or fixing. Therefore, I plan to meet personally with as many of you as I can during the days and months ahead. I want to be a ruler to whom any citizen of Zargarb can come and discuss what they like when they desire. You will find that I wish to have a very open, forthright administration. We face many bad situations here, and I will definitely need all your helping hands, for I seem to have lost mine." She again waved her arms, all the while smiling broadly. A few chuckled at her pun.

"I know that many owe your very lives to the ceaseless efforts of Rodrigo Decasas to keep the food supplies going, admittedly at a high price. Those of you who are in debt to him, as of today, your debit is paid in full. Rodrigo," she looked at him, "bring me a final tally of what is owed to you so that I may pay it completely." Now, she got another loud round of applause.

"While we are finding a place to live and getting moved in, I have some things that I want each and every one of you to do. We have lost four-fifths of our population. I'm told that many skilled tradesmen have been forced to move out of the city and take up other skills for which they have never been trained or desired to do. I would like all of you who are skilled tradesmen, whether you still have your tools or not, to contact each other. Let's get an accurate count of just what skilled craftsmen are still with us. As you work out what skilled craftsmen we have available, please get the information to Rodrigo. I am appointing him as my official coordinator, since he knows many of you and I don't yet. Rodrigo, select one from each skill to be their representative to me."

"The other thing that I wish everyone to do for me is to hold a meeting of all those people who are living in your city block. Elect one person to be your representative. Then, work with your representative to draw up a list of all the problems and situations that need handling. Please prioritize them so that I know which ones need to be handled as fast as possible. Once I get settled in, I would like to meet with all the representatives, probably each day for a while, until we get the most critical things handled."

"Finally, I and my staff would like to meet each one of you personally, so in a few days, we will be spending a part of each day visiting. It will take us some time to get to meet every one of you, not to mention all those living outside the city, but I'm determined to meet each of you somehow. I want Zargarb to be a city where my new daughter can wander where she will and be safe. I do not want her to suffer as I, my assistants, or many of you have suffered. Together, with all your hands, we will do it! Oh yes, ships, I nearly forgot the ships. In the very near future, we will have new caravels! I just don't know how many we need, though, and don't say as many as possible, that's a joke by the way," she teased.

Ben, his arm around her, nudged her forward and the crowd saw that the meeting was over. Once more, they clapped and yelled her name. She smiled and waved her arms. At last, they were able to get into a coach that Le Ann had acquired until theirs was unloaded. Ariana continued to wave out the window as the coach, followed by everyone else in her party, passed through the crowd.

Finally passed the crowd, Le Ann could talk, "You ladies look quite elegant indeed. I believe you three have made quite an impression on the people." All three smiled. "Now, per our discussions via Donata, your Communicator, we have taken the liberty of arranging housing for you. As I pointed out days ago, the absolute best location would actually be the Nunnery, the old Sisterhood inn. However, Ariana, I know that place must hold such ill memories for you that you might not be comfortable there. Yet, it would be perfect for your base of operations. I know that you said via Donata that it would be fine, but I still want you to know if you find yourself too uncomfortable with it, we can easily find some other location."

"Oh it will be fine. My trauma has been long gone. I just wish the place could be cleaned up somehow."

"We have been very busy doing just that. You will soon see. Hank gave us many instructions, and I do hope that we duplicated them properly. Oh yes, Jenna was very surprised to hear about your dowry, and she is most pleased that you will be paying something for the new caravels, though she insists that you only pay the actual cost of construction. No one wants to make a copper in profit, you see, because everyone wants to help you and Zargarb as much as possible. Oh, by the way, Cory and Sarah, I do like your choice of a disguised last name. Rima works well. No one outside of us must know your true last name; it's for your own protection, and besides, Lilly Ann and Jenna would have my hide if I let anything happen to you two."

They rolled up to the main entrance of the ex-Sisterhood inn, where all traces of its previous use as the Nunnery had been removed. "Now there are one hundred fifty bedrooms in there, most sleep at least two. The heated bath is on the first floor opposite the large dining room, which we figure can double as a mass meeting room for all the representatives. Guests that you may have staying with you ought to be housed on the first floor as well. We have all debated for some time now whether you would be safer on the second or third floors. While we figured you would be safer on the third floor, we have gone ahead with your decision to use the second floor. All those rooms have been thoroughly cleaned and most of the doors are now double hinged. Please, ladies, do not venture to the third floor; it has not been cleaned, and you could become trapped inside should the doors close. There has not been enough time to deal with so many doorknobs."

"Finally, as we head inside, please ladies, notice how Hank's idea for a sliding lock that you three can manage has been implemented. At night and when you desire privacy, you slide the bars across, keeping the doors from being opened. Now, have I forgotten anything? I'm sure that I have. Mary, help me out?"

"Oh Le Ann, just let them get out and see for themselves," Mary answered her.

Everyone climbed out, just as Lenkova rode up and dismounted. "Hi there," she said and reached for Ariana's arm. Ariana put her other arm over Lenkova's grip, and they shook, while Le Ann formally introduced them.

"You are the most famous Sisterhood fighter I've ever heard about! So very pleased to meet you at last!" Ariana said, thrilled to meet this long-standing hero of Zargarh legends.

"Well, you do look smashing!" Lenkova replied, "not at all what I thought a Loremaster would look like."

"What? All covered in dirt?" she teased. Lenkova had images of just that with Fred Waterton, her husband's Loremaster. "My two assistants from Solamina." She introduced her two friends.

"Come here," Lenkova gave each woman a strong hug. "I must say you two look, well, positively beautiful, so radiant. I guess Jenna took very good care of you. Your dresses, wow. You are going to be driving the guys around here positively mad, seriously," she bragged. She knew men, and with these dresses and their looks, Lenkova though their prospects for attracting men were quite good. "Come on, let me show you around. I've lived in this inn for many years before the evil ones took it over. I wonder how badly they have trashed the place? It was once the finest establishment in Zargarb, you know." She put one arm around Julianna's waist and her other around Rachele's and led them all up to the entrance. One thing that Lenkova had learned from her many years in the Sisterhood, and that was just how to make women who had suffered horribly feel comfortable and not ill at ease around others. She was determined to make these two most welcome and comfortable. Both women enjoyed the attention of this legendary woman fighter.

As they entered, Lenkova commented over her shoulder to Ariana, "I heard what you said about traveling to all the other towns and villages to meet everyone. I will be honored to take you around myself. Who else knows this land better than Andre and me?" Ariana answered that would be terrific.

(While a few readers might find it interesting to hear how Ariana went about the challenging task of Zargarb reconstruction, I am only going to present a few key examples. From these, I hope you will be able to get a feel for how it went.)

Ariana met with Rodrigo Decasas the next day. Dwarfed in the large dining hall, the small party discussed the situation. Sitting beside her were her two assistants, Ben, and her four Circle members. "There, Rodrigo, you have been paid in full. Now we must discuss some things. First, we know that you are now the richest man in Zargarb, that your secret warehouses are stuffed full of every imaginable item. I know that you have ruled by blackjack, forcing others to go along with your orders. Further, it is obvious to me how you came to have all the original stocks in the first place. Correct me if I am missing the mark here, but when they first got here and began their wild killing spree, did you not wisely begin secreting away much of the stock that was being held to supply the city during the siege?"

"Well, yes, if I hadn't," he replied.

She cut him off, "If you had not had that foresight, thousands more would have starved to death. With the nobles gone, who is left to rule? Certainly, the Holy Paladins did not rule; they just ordered people around, forcing them to do whatever, but that's not ruling. Some may say that your tactics were a bit heavy handed," she paused and added, "that's a pun, heavy handed, blackjacks." Now he got the joke and chuckled.

"However, you got the job done and for that I thank you. The question is now what are we going to do? The time for such heavy handedness is over. People need much of the hoarded supplies right now, if they are to begin to get things going quickly. Yes, I brought in many food supplies to help see us through the winter. The real question is what about you? What do you do now? What are your plans for all that wealth you've accumulated? You must know that so far, you and your men have made any number of enemies with all your strong-armed tactics over the years. However, right now, what you and your men do is pivotal. You can become the heroes of Zargarb or just another black memory of the occupied days."

"You see much for such a young, pretty woman," Rodrigo chose his words carefully. "At first, I just wanted to stay alive and keep my men alive. I saw the theft as a way to thwart the Holy Paladins, right under their very noses. Yes, I and my men did become quite wealthy. I've been thinking about what happens next ever since Art came to tell me that the Overlords had fled the city. I admit that I have come to enjoy being the top dog, the boss of it all. Yet, if I do nothing, two years down the road with Zargarb thriving, I and my men will have become a dark thing of the past. I do not want that, Ariana, but I am afraid I don't know what to do about it. Giving you back all the money and all the supplies isn't going to help me or my men."

"No it isn't. Perhaps we can help. Have you thought about what it is that you would like to have in life, to own or possess?"

"I own damn near everything, pardon my language, Ladies. I got just about every imaginable thing."

"But you are not happy are you," Julianna asked astutely.

"No, I am not happy."

"Having a bunch of objects seldom makes anyone truly happy," Julianna replied. "Are you married, got a family?"

"No, I've never been married. I never found one who wanted just me; they all wanted my money and power. I will say one thing though, but I'm not too good with words. While I was running things, I really enjoyed the respect that others gave me, though I know it was because I held the power strings over them. I got a taste of what it would be like, you know, having the respect of everyone. I'd like to honestly have that."

Ariana agreed, "Yes, I think that's a very worthwhile thing to have. Now, Rodrigo, what would you need to do in order to have that kind of respect from others?"

"Well, certainly not using my strong arm tactics," he blurted out with a smile. "I don't really know what I would have to do. You seem to have it, Ariana, and you've only just arrived. Even you two, from the little I've seen of you, you have it, and it isn't just sympathy for you, though I've seen some of that among many people. How do you command the respect of people?"

Ariana thought this was a good test for the apprentices. "Why don't you answer that one?" she said to Julianna.

"Oh that's easy. You have to earn it by demonstrating that you sincerely want to help others and then really do help them. When we first got like this, we felt so awful. I mean everyone had to do absolutely everything for us. We felt like we just wanted to die," Julianna explained.

"But then, slowly but surely, Jenna, Hank, Ben, Ariana, all showed us that we could do things to help out. Terribly slow, incredibly awkward, I might add," Rachele added. "At first, I thought that this was really dumb. They could do these things so fast and efficient, while we were taking forever. Yet, they allowed us the time to do it. I will never forget the pride I felt when I carried my first basket of fresh tomatoes that I picked myself up to the cook so she could use them for everyone's supper. It felt so good that at long last I could indeed do something useful to help."

"Yes, that's the key, Rodrigo; you look around and see what needs doing and then just do it. It will be noticed, I assure you. Before you know it, you will have the respect you want," Julianna finished up.

"You picked tomatoes, carried them from the garden to the cook?" Rodrigo asked dumbfounded. "But how? You have no arms, let alone hands."

"We have feet, silly," Julianna explained. "We have had to learn different ways to do things, that's all. Honestly, we are nearly full-fledged Loremasters, just like Ariana and Ben and Hank. Well, we are nearly there, few more years of study and work yet."

"I guess this I need to see. Okay, I am probably the most knowledgeable about what really needs to be done around here. I could get things done, like getting the sunken ships out of our harbor so the new caravels will be able to dock."

"Precisely, and the final question is what would you have to be in order to be able to do all those things to help out around here?" Ariana asked.

"Well, I would need to be someone with the authority to get things done. Oh, like the official coordinator." He paused as he realized that she had already thought of this whole thing. "You, you already figured this all out, didn't you?"

Ariana grinned, "Our situations, mine, Julianna's, and Rachele's, rather gave us keen insight. Yes, you are hereby the Zargarb Sector Coordinator, answerable only to me and my staff here. You have the authority to put into action what you think is most needed and wanted. Of course, we will also be adding to your list. However, it is your new job, congratulations, Rodrigo."

"Sly ones aren't we," he winked at the three. "You know I just had an idea what I can do with all this money. So many things and people need funds to get their businesses going again, that I can loan them the money at no interest and pay back only when they are recovered and can afford to do so."

"Wow, now that is going to make you an extremely popular man about Zargarb!" Ariana declared, very pleased with his new attitude and goals. She also extended an offer for him to dine with them each evening and to stay with them at the inn, if he so desired. A few weeks later, he moved into one of the guest rooms on the first floor, because it was more conducive to conducting the business meetings, which were held in the large dining hall.

Another example illustrates the approach Ariana took to land grants. A week after arriving, she took a tour of the Ternio estates, just north and west of the city. Here, sprawling across many acres of country side were the sprawling estates once owned by the late Ternio noblemen and their families, all of whom had been slain when Justinian conquered the city many years ago. She found that many of the staff had stayed on, attempting to run the vast enterprise, famous for its quality wines. She summoned everyone who still lived and worked here to a brief meeting.

Ariana explained, "Now here's what we are going to do with this vast estate. As of this minute, it is owned by all of you as a co-op venture. Decide among yourselves what jobs need to be done, from kitchen duties, to maid service, to gardening, to harvesting, to wine production, to marketing and sales, financial record keeper, and so on. Then, decide who is best qualified for these jobs and appoint them to that position. As the profits come in, divide them up equally between yourselves. This way, each one of you is doing his or her part to make the company grow and prosper."

The thirty folks could not believe their phenomenal luck. They had gone from mere workers to wealthy landowners and business people in one minute!

In a similar manner, she handled the other six noblemen's estates and properties. Slowly, the inhabitants became responsible for their own industries. Between her funding of projects and Rodrigo's loans, by spring, all who wanted work was back in business. Production of goods and services had begun in earnest.

Next, Ariana and her group traveled to the other towns and villages, paying close attention to the crop situation. The four Loremasters discovered quickly that many different problems existed, which combined to yield the dismal crop production figures of the past. Most of the "new" farmers were not farmers and had no training or knowledge in the growing of crops. More than half of these took Ariana's offer to return to their old skilled jobs and/or restart their shops. At each farm, they examined the soil and asked about the yearly rainfall and temperatures throughout the year.

Rachele pointed out a crucial detail. They were trying to grow many kinds of melons here, but those plants required a lot of periodic water. Zargarb was rather dry during the summer months, being so close to the semi-arid Juda Arad, which was nearly a desert region. In more than half the instances of failed crops, the root cause lay in attempting to grow a crop that could not do well here. Rachele suggested that almond nut trees would likely do well. Other suggestions included the carob tree, sorghum, legumes, lentils, and various types of peas. In addition, cover crops for fodder were added to the growing list.

Armed with some beginning observations, Ariana had the Santi searching everywhere to find sufficient quantity of starter seeds for the spring planting season. Although insufficient quantities were acquired, the crops began thriving, and within a few years, they had a large excess at harvest time and could begin exporting produce and nuts.

Rodrigo took another action which turned out to be extremely beneficial to nearly everyone at some point in time. He had amassed vast quantities of nearly everything imaginable, which people had traded for food rations during the occupied years. Couple that with the alarming fact that the city itself now had lost nearly three-quarters of its population and that translated to nearly three in four buildings now being empty within the city walls. He picked out one whole city block worth of buildings and moved all his accumulated items into these buildings, sorted into general categories. He hired some shopkeepers to run the new General Stores. All goods were priced well below market value, and anyone could obtain items that they needed on credit if they were unable to pay for them outright and with no-interest accounts.

So convenient was this one-stop shopping, that as items of one type were sold, he began acquiring replacements. Two years later on, everyone went to the General Stores first when they needed something.

Some abandoned buildings were in poor shape. These, Ariana had torn down, salvaging any construction materials worth saving. In the process, she expanded Central Park five-fold, adding a musician's band stand as well. A year later, on summer nights, public band concerts and dances were held weekly, enjoyed by both young and old. It became the thing to do on Saturday nights.

Six weeks after they moved in, Rachele's grandfather was located in a northern town and was more than happy to move down to the inn to live with his granddaughter. Ruffo Tinelli was seventy and had no other living relatives in Zargarb, but now he had a granddaughter to dote upon. Though he cried long and hard when he saw her armless body, she soon had him cheered up. She was so full of life, he could not remain sad, especially when she demonstrated that she just had different ways of doing things now. Further, he had been eating poorly ever since his wife had passed away. Good meals did much for his overall health as well.

Another singular event occurred in early March 641. A young man rode up to the Zargarb Palace as the inn had now become known. He had long brown hair and bits of dried oil paints covered his clothes. He smelled of linseed oil. After tying his old mare to the hitching rail, he entered the inn hesitatingly, not knowing what to expect. "May I help you?" said the Receptionist, an elderly Santi member who was on the domestic side of the organization as opposed to the fighter side.

"Well, yes. I have heard that a lady may be staying here in Zargarb. I'm told that I might find her here, though the sign says Zargarb Palace."

"Her name, please?"

"Julianna Rosso. I knew her by that name, though she may be married now. I don't know," he said hesitatingly.

"And whom should I say is calling?"

"Benigno Furri, ma'am."

"Wait here, please. I shall fetch her. I believe that she is out back tending the garden at the moment, before she has to go to the Daily Meeting."

A few minutes later, Julianna, dressed in her leathers and rather dirty, having dug and planted a row of flowers, walked in along with the receptionist.

"Hello, I'm Julianna Rosso. Have we met, sir?" she said politely. All the way here, she kept trying to place his name, but decided that she must not know him, even though he apparently knew her.

"Oh dear god! What happened to you? Oh, such a calamity should befall such a brilliant artist as yourself! I had no idea." He looked utterly crestfallen, as if his entire world had just collapsed upon him.

"I take it you mean my lack of arms. Holy Paladins got to me, but really, I am now doing really well, actually. I am a Santi and have greatly expanded my love and knowledge of nature, but yes, I used to be a painter in Solamina, if that is what you mean, sir."

"Benigno, my Lady," inadvertently lifting his hand to shake hers.

"Can't shake, but I'll take a hug," she grinned. Others often found initial meetings awkward, and she had learned simply to defuse them. A hug usually did the trick. He gingerly gave her a hug, as if he feared he might cause her pain. "Oh harder than that, Benigno; I can barely feel you. Ah, much better. Good to meet you. I have a little time before I need to change for the meeting. I'm the ruler's advisor you know. Come on; follow me. Let's get some tea and chat. You've obviously ridden a very long way to see me, and you are a painter, so that must be somehow related to your visit."

He followed her into the huge dining room. "Two teas, please," she said to the cook. "You hungry? We've got biscuits and cheese if you want something to eat."

"Could I really? I am rather hungry, been on the trail for days now."

"Add a tray of biscuits and cheese too, please." When the cook brought the tray, she said diplomatically, "Will you be so kind as to carry it to a table? While I could do it, it is so much more convenient if you don't mind. Let's sit over there by the flowers I picked early this morning; freshens up this room, you see." He followed her. "Mine's the cup with the flared top. I can grab it better that way." He helped her with her chair and then sat across from her. He watched in awe as she picked up the cup with her foot and took a sip.

"What brings you all the way from Solamina to Zargarb, Benigno?"

"I, I, well, I, I didn't know about your arms. I feel just awful, Julianna." He looked incredibly uncomfortable.

"Well, why don't you just start at the beginning; that's the best way you know," she suggested, helpfully.

"Okay, you are probably right, otherwise this is going to make even less sense to you. I am an oil painter, and two years ago, I had the greatest fortune to have had a private viewing of one of the portraits that you did for a nobleman, who must remain anonymous for now. When the Overlords came into the city and began killing the nobles and their family, one butler had the greatest wisdom imaginable. He secretly removed many of the paintings his employer had around the estate. He hid them in a location, which must still remain a secret. Two years ago, I had the opportunity to assist him in the restoration of a couple paintings, which had been attacked by fungus. That's when I first saw your work, my Lady."

"Your artistry made an indelible impression on me. I resolved to see as many of your other works as possible. I spent nearly two years tracking down well over a dozen, and each one seemed more brilliant than the last! Your paintings are so dramatically better than mine that I resolved to find you and beg you to allow me to study under you. However, I learned that you had been taken by the Overlords and had not been seen for several years. I presumed that you were dead, as so many have been killed by those evil men. Much to my surprise, I learned from friends that the Santi had been making discrete inquiries about any of your surviving family members. My heart nearly stopped, for that could only mean that you were still alive and had most likely been rescued! I saved some funds and went to the Santi Fortress to learn what I could of your whereabouts."

"They did not know at first, but promised to find out. A few days later, they told me that you were now in Zargarb and to try the Palace. I sold everything I had and rode my old mare here. My plan now seems the height of folly, but I was intending to beg you to take me on as your apprentice. I was prepared to do anything just to learn from the master. Now, I'm so terribly sorry, Lady Julianna. I didn't know, honestly I didn't know. The world has lost the best portrait artist it has ever had." He was near tears just contemplating the loss to the world of art.

Just then, Rachele came in to grab a bite before the meeting. "Oh, hello. Am I interrupting anything?" She noticed that this strange looking young man, who must be a painter, was fighting to hold back tears, and her dear friend was near breaking down. She had not seen Julianna in grief for such a long time, and she was more than a little concerned. "What's going on? Has something dreadful happened?"

Fighting to keep from crying, Julianna explained, "This is Benigno Furri, a painter from Solamina. He sold everything he owned just to come and study painting under me. Only he didn't know about us. I thought that I had put the life of a painter behind me, but it's back. I didn't think I'd miss it, Rachele, but I still do. It is a part of me, though I've kept it well hidden all this time." Now she couldn't fight back her tears any longer.

"I'm so sorry, Julianna. I didn't know. I should just leave. I've caused you such grief. I'm sorrier than you will ever know. Please, please forgive me for upsetting you so," he was now crying almost as much as Julianna. Worse still, this pungent reminder of her past also brought Rachelle's keen loss into her consciousness from where it had lay dormant. She too began to feel grief over her own situation as a painter and tears began to trickle down her cheeks.

However, Rachele recovered more quickly, "We have a meeting in a little while. Why don't we put Benigno up in a guest room and then we can all discuss this at lunchtime? He's given everything to get here, so the least we can do is to put him up for a while, Julianna."

"Yes, Benigno, you must stay here with us a while. Come on. I need to change, and I'll get you a room. You can use the bath while we are at our meeting," Julianna said, sniffling her running nose.

"But I have so little funds left," he protested, also sniffling, wiping his face on his shirtsleeves.

"As long as you are here with us, all expenses are on us, Benigno. Don't worry about needing any funds." She told the receptionist to get him a nice room on the first floor and to show him where the bath was located. "I'll come fetch you at lunchtime." She dashed off to change.

Benigno was thinking that perhaps he should just get back on his horse and leave. He had caused the opposite effect than what he had desired. For so long now he had planned how to beg to allow her to accept him as her apprentice. Instead, he'd upset both women. However, he didn't get any chance to flee. As he was standing beside his horse, presumably to get his gear, he saw quite a lot of local men and women arriving, pushing past him to enter. He was literally swept up by the surge of people entering, and he found himself, sack in hand, pressed up against the reception desk.

"What's that all about?" he asked her, after the last person had gone down the long hallway to the dining room he had been in earlier.

"Daily town meeting. Lady Ariana and her group meet with these folks every late morning, planning what needs to be done." Just then, Julianna came dashing down the stairs. "Hurry up, Julianna. They've just got here," she hastily said to her. "Lady Ariana Zar Wilkins is the ruler of Zargarb, you know, and Julianna and Rachele are her close personal assistants. That's why she was rushing." He was impressed and followed her to his room.

As he entered, he noticed that there were no doorknobs. The receptionist noticed and explained, "The three women can come and go as they please without the barrier of unopenable doors. Just push on it. If you want privacy, push the slider into place. If you need anything else, just ask." He entered and was immediately stunned. Here was the nicest room he'd ever seen! Indeed the sign outside claiming this to be a palace was not in error. He unpacked his belongings and his dozen paintings, which he'd brought along to use as leverage to convince Julianna that he would be a worthy student to accept. These, he merely stowed, now knowing they would not be needed.

Bathed and dressed in cleaner clothes, he was ready when the two women came to fetch him to take him to lunch. He was more than surprised to find the entire group dining together. Quite a few minutes were needed for all the many introductions. He was once more shocked to discover that

Ariana Zar had also been harmed so horribly by the Overlords, plus there were so many Santi here as well; he'd only seen a few in his life.

Ariana, always the gracious host, said, "Benigno, Julianna tells me that you are a painter."

"Yes, but not too good of one, I am afraid. I had hoped to come and learn from the master portrait painter of Solamina, Julianna." Again, he had put his foot in his mouth and wanted to take back his words.

"I didn't know that Julianna was that famous. You never told me that, Julianna. Portraits?"

"Yes, before I was abducted, I did quite a lot of portraits. If you do a good job of it, it pays well. Rachele was even better than I was, I'm afraid. I saw a lot of her work; she painted still life scenes, mostly nature scenes, from the ones that I saw."

"Yes, mostly nature scenes," Rachele added, "Nowhere near the pay that one gets from doing portraits. I did a few portraits when I really needed the money, but I always tried to paint what I desired, not what others wanted. Hence, I never had many funds. Those were the days! Golly, that was so much fun and so rewarding to see my final product. Ah, well, that's past now." She sighed.

While they all ate, he could not help noticing that all three women used their feet and toes to eat, manipulating the forks and spoons rather cleverly. However, Ariana was able to use her arms to hold her drinking cup. No one else paid any attention to this, so he kept a discrete eye on the three, watching fascinated by the agility they displayed.

After lunch was done, Julianna apologized, "I'm sorry for becoming so emotional on you this morning. I had forgotten all about that part of my life. Rachele and I both realized that after we were abducted and were being tortured so, what had kept us alive and fighting was our determination to get free somehow and go back to painting what we wanted to paint. Obviously, that idea got crushed some time ago. We had no choice but to move on with life and were doing really well, until you took us off guard and reminded us of what we had both lost. It certainly wasn't your fault; we had mostly put that part of us out of our minds."

Rachele asked, "So what we both were wondering, Benigno, did you bring along some of your paintings to show her? If so, we both would really love to see them."

"Well, yes," he tried to squirm out of this request. "Mine are so inferior to the masters that I am almost embarrassed to show them. Yes, I brought some that I was going to use to plead my case."

"Well, then, let's have a look at them! Good or bad, we all start out with much to learn. I know I painted some so badly that I covered them over and started again," Julianna confessed.

A few minutes later, Benigno had his dozen samples spread out over the second bed in his room. Both women studied them closely, commenting to themselves. At last, Julianna gave her analysis. "Benigno, you definitely have an eye for portrait painting. With a little coaching, I think that you could become as good as I used to be, really I do. Rachele and I both agree that two things need work. Your colors are slightly off, especially on the faces. That one thing makes them look slightly wrong to the observer. The other thing is your shapes are also not quite right; perspective is somewhat distorted, which makes them look a bit unnatural. Both of these things are easily correctable if you can train your eyes to see what is there and not what you imagine is there."

"Think we should try?" she asked Rachele.

"Yes indeed, he shows promise. I've seen many that are far worse," she replied.

"Okay, Benigno, you have your wish. We will take you on as apprentices and see if we can't get you doing a much better job at it. In return, once you meet our standards, we would like you to paint portraits of all our dear friends here. We both can envision tons of paintings adorning the bare walls of this inn, but we can't make them. Of course, your expenses will be covered as long as you are here. We can set up a studio on the third floor, because nothing is being used up there and probably will not be for a long time. Is this satisfactory to you, Benigno?"

"You are teasing me, my Lady?" he asked dumbfounded.

"No, while we can't paint any longer, we think that together we can talk you though the points that need correcting, that is if you will listen and try," she explained.

"Oh I will, I will. This is beyond my wildest expectations. I will work hard. How can I ever thank you, Lady Julianna?"

"Get good enough so that we are satisfied with your portraits. Then, paint lots of them for us so we can hang them on all the walls around here. That will be more than enough payment for us. Now do you prefer morning or afternoon lighting? Afternoons work better for us."

"Afternoons it is! Alas, I only have my brushes. I could not bring any other supplies with me. I assumed that you would already have a fully equipped studio, forgive my ignorance."

Rachele replied, "Well, the canvas won't be a problem. I assume that you can make the wooden easels and such. Pigments for the paint will be a problem. No painters seem to be in Zargarb anymore. Nevertheless, not to fret; we are nearly Loremasters, and we ought to be able to scour the countryside for the proper pigments. Next week, we are scheduled to travel all over the sector to assist and advise on the spring crop planting. We can search for the pigments then."

"Right," Julianna added, "so let's go see about a room for the studio. Actually, Benigno, I'm excited about this project. While I greatly miss being able to paint, if we can get you up to the level that we were at, then once more we can have fine paintings around us. Come on." She led the way up to the third floor. "We're supposed to be very careful up here, because the doors have not been fixed for us, and we could become trapped inside or so we have been told. Let's try the ones on the far western end of the hall."

During the week, Benigno spent his hours working on getting the studio ready for work. First, it needed a thorough cleaning and most of the furniture had to be moved into another room. He had to make various easels and a storage cabinet with a nice top on which to mix his paints. All three tested the lighting, adjusting and readjusting the position of the sitting chair until all three were satisfied.

While this was going on, Donata contacted me about this new project that Julianna and Rachele were tackling. She knew that I was very interested in salvaging all the many artists who we were treating back in Velona. I thought this sounded quite promising and had Donata keep an eye on how it was working, keeping me discretely informed.

The big spring survey of the Zargarb sector was now only days away. Lenkova, true to her word, would be leading the party. She, Andre, and their children were coming along, accompanied by Ariana's Circle, protectors, and an additional twenty-five Santi fighters. While the stated purpose of the six-week long trip was to assist and advise on the spring crop planting, Ben had two other purposes in mind. Ariana still had several skills to master. The learning of the spells of power, such as bringing down lightning, would not be attempted until next year. What she still lacked was tracking and navigation in the wilderness. A Loremaster, more so than any other of the specialties, was never lost in the wilderness, could always find his way, could always find even the faintest of tracks, and could always follow a trail left by animal or man. These, he intended upon teaching Ariana this spring. Also, Julianna and Rachele needed to learn these same things, although they might not be fully up to these just yet. Normal training patterns, year by year, had been drastically altered because of their special circumstances.

All her life, Lenkova dealt with Sisterhood members who had lost hands and limbs for various reasons, combat not the least. She was determined to find a way for the three to be able to ride a horse again. Repeatedly, she saw the swelling of independence appear in a woman who could once more ride, instead of having to be ferried around in a wagon or carriage. She already had found three of the gentlest mares around and which responded very well to gentle neck reining. Ariana would be the easiest to adapt.

This morning, she brought Ariana outside into the large courtyard, where she already had the mare waiting. "Notice how I have the reins in a loop. You only need to insert your arm in it and lock it in your elbow. To go left, lean that way, and pull the reins to the left, she will respond easily. Got the idea?"

"I think so, if only I can climb up. Oh, she isn't that tall, I can just barely hook my elbow around the horn. Catch me if I fall," she said. A minute later, Ariana was sitting in a saddle for the first time in her life. "Oh, you sit so high up!" she exclaimed. Lenkova had a lead rope attached to the bridle, so she had ultimate control. Slowly, she began to put Ariana through her paces. An hour later, she unfastened the lead line, and Ariana soloed, proudly riding around the large enclosed patio and garden area. Ben watched from a window, holding up Nicolina Sue so she could watch mommy riding the big horse.

Next, during the afternoon, Lenkova brought out the other two mares for Julianna and Rachele, who were most hesitant about the whole prospect. "I've rigged up these two bridles especially for you. Each has a wooden fastener here at the end of the reins. You can put this in your mouth. When you lean to turn, you move your head so, and it puts a slight pressure on their neck and the horses will get your message, especially if you also lean that way some. Lean back and this tells the horse to slow down and stop."

"Yes, but how do we hold on with no arms?" Rachele complained very worried about falling. This was both women's greatest fear since losing them; they had to be especially careful about always maintaining their balance.

"Use your legs, silly, like the rest of us do. How do you suppose that we fighters can fight from horseback? Actually, a good horse person does not even need reins to control a well-trained horse. You do it all with leg pressure and leaning. The only real problem that I foresee is mounting and dismounting. Come let's try it. I will not let you fall."

Julianna tried it first. "It's scary," she called out to Rachele, "getting up is tricky." Nevertheless, by suppertime, both women were doing quite well. Indeed, Ben decided that they would not bother bringing along the coach as backup. The supply wagon would do if they ran into troubles.

Six weeks later, when they returned, all three women were more than comfortable riding. All three had passed their latest round of training, and all the crops had been planted properly. Ariana had met many of the local inhabitants personally, bringing honest smiles and respect from these who chose to live far from the city itself.

During this time, Benigno had quite a lot of time to observe how Julianna and Rachele now accomplished their tasks. Sitting on their butts, they would use their feet to dig holes, plant seed, and pack the ground. Further, they seemed amazingly able to find all the right ingredients from which he would be able to make all the oil paint colors he would need. If left on his own to find them, by now he estimated that he would only have found perhaps a third of the needed pigments.

At one village, a little girl had fallen, bruised her face, and was crying. Julianna had sat down and using her toes, wiped the dirt off the girl's face. She even wiped away her tears. Seeing that scene, an idea formed in the back of his mind. During the next three months, it finally germinated, but of that later.

When they returned, the painting lessons began in earnest. He paid close attention to their comments and instructions. By the end of summer, Julianna was finally satisfied that he had remedied all the deficiencies in his style. "To graduate, I need you to make a portrait of Lady Ariana," she instructed. For a week after that, Ariana had to sit on the chair for an hour or two each day. Per Julianna's instructions, she was not allowed to see his work, not until she had given him his final pass and verified the quality of the portrait. During this week, she kept her mouth closed, offering her pupil no advice whatsoever.

Finally, when he decided it was finished, Julianna and Rachele both observed the portrait, comparing it to the impatient Ariana, who was still sitting in the chair, wondering what the painting actually looked like. "Hold still, Ariana, we are comparing details," Julianna declared, as she continued her careful examination. Benigno held his breath. Had he forgotten some detail? Had he overlooked something? He fidgeted with his shirt, more than a little worried.

At last, Julianna broke the tense quiet, "Congratulations, Benigno, you get a pass. We can find no flaw in your work. You have now reached the skill that we once possessed. Very well done. Okay, Ariana, you may have a look at your portrait now."

She needed no further encouragement, rushing over to have a look. "Oh my! It's me! It's like I am looking at myself in a mirror!"

"Yes, that is the point of a really good portrait artist," Julianna explained. "We strive to make the image on the canvass be an exact duplicate of the person, at least as exact as we can make it. Do you like it?"

"Like it? I love it! Wait until everyone else sees this! It's just incredibly beautiful."

"Well, there you have it, Benigno. Now you can get started on doing the portraits of everyone else here," Julianna teased. "That should keep you busy for many months. And then there are all the Santi fortress members who need theirs done, and then. . ."

"Whoa, one person at a time! I've only just graduated," he chuckled, very proud to have finally succeeded in achieving his lifelong goal of becoming a quality portrait painter.

"Okay, do Ben and Nicolina Sue next, please," Ariana suggested. "When should I send one of them up?"

Julianna expected Benigno to say tomorrow afternoon. However, to her surprise, he said, "I need about a week for another project. Then, I'll get started on all the many portraits. Thank you all, and thank you Julianna and Rachele!"

The next day, Julianna heard hammering and sawing going on in his studio, but he had a sign on the door that said, "Do not disturb." She honored it, but her curiosity rose daily as the sign continued to be displayed. Even Rachele became intensely curious, but Benigno would say nothing about what he was doing in the studio. They noticed rather large pieces of lumber being carried up there. What was he doing?

Finally, he finished and led both women up to the studio, whose double-hinged door was closed. "My Ladies, I believe that I have something to offer you both. Mind you, this might not work out as I had hoped, but there is a chance that it might."

"Whatever are you talking about?" declared Julianna rather impatiently. She felt rather like their roles had reversed, and he now was the master.

"Come inside and have a peek." He pushed the door open and let them inside.

They saw two very strange looking chairs, if that was the proper word for them. Taller than most chairs, their backs were tall and slanted back at a forty-five degree angle. The seats were well padded. Both were positioned close to the cabinet top on which he had his various paint pots arranged. In front of each chair stood an easel with a new canvass already prepared for a fresh painting. Brushes lined the cabinet top within easy reach of the chairs.

"My Ladies, I've been watching how you do things for many weeks now. It occurred to me one day that with an arrangement such as this, you both might be able to paint once again. It will probably take a lot of experimentation to work out the best way for this to work, but maybe, just maybe, you two can do it. I just had to try. Come have a seat and see how it feels."

"Well, I don't know," Julianna hesitated.

"Oh, heck, look at all the trouble he's gone to. Let's at least see if we can paint a crude line, Julianna," Rachele declared and sat down on one of the chairs. "Come on; it is at a really good height, and we can just lie back and let our feet do the work." Julianna sat down as well. Before long, both women were excitedly experimenting on the canvasses. Benigno just watched, pleased to see their faces smiling.

"Look, it's pretty easy to pivot to get to things," Rachele noted. Before long both women were experimenting in earnest.

"I feel like a little girl learning how to paint," declared Julianna. "Benigno, this might actually work out."

"Well, it's going to take us a long time to develop the proper skills and even longer to make a painting," Rachele added, "but at least I can paint again! I may never be as good as I once was, but I can paint!"

"Me too, I can paint. God, I really can paint! Oh Benigno, I could just hug you!" She suddenly realized that she couldn't. "How about a kiss instead?" She offered and she did so. Not to be left out, Rachele also gave him a kiss. He lost his shyness, put an arm around both, and hugged them together.

After that, both women spent several hours each day up in the studio. At the end of the year, a new painting of the refurbished docks of Zargarb hung in the hallway, compliments of Rachele. Similar to all of her earlier works dating from before her abduction, this one was nearly a mirror image of the actual docks, very realistically done. It had taken her nearly six months of work to accomplish, but it was a masterpiece. Around the same time, a new portrait appeared in the hallway. This one depicted Ariana, Ben, and Nicolina Sue, in a family pose compliments of Julianna. Like Benigno's paintings, it was extremely realistic looking, so much so that one could hardly tell any differences between the models and the painting images.

Donita send me all the details and the results. I had her obtain exact specifications of his special chairs and other equipment and began experiments of my own back here at the estate in Velona. If I could somehow help salvage even half of these artists, that would be something of great importance, to me at least. An artist was someone to be highly valued, not suppressed and mutilated. Quickly, I had Hank construct several of these and began my own experiments.

When the group returned from their mid-April six-week trip, the public Saturday night music and dance concerts were already going strong. Ben, of course, took Ariana and their daughter; everyone else at the inn went too. After this first trip, Ariana insisted that she wear her fanciest dress. Of course, both Julianna and Rachele also wanted to go as well, and they, too, wished to wear their fanciest dresses.

Three days before the next dance night, Rodrigo, who now also lived in the inn, cornered Rachele. "My Lady, there is a dance in the park on Saturday night. Would you do me the highest honor and accompany me to the dance?" She readily accepted; now she would have a real excuse to wear her finest dress!

Two days before the Saturday night dance, Benigno formally asked Julianna if she would consent to going to the dance with him. She readily agreed.

Neither man was quite prepared for the stunning looks the two women had when they appeared coming down the steps to meet them near the reception desk. Each wore their little tiaras, silky dresses, complete with hose and well-made shoes that were tied with bows. Their faces were as radiant as their sparking tiaras.

Benigno stammers, "Julianna, you look absolutely stunning!"

She smiled, "Thank you. Glad you like this outfit, because in it and with these shoes, we cannot do the normal things that we do. You are going to have to look after me all night long, whether you like it or not."

Rodrigo brought a lily for Rachele. He'd seen her in her fancy dress when she had arrived. She had made an indelible impression on him that day. Now that he had all the many urgent pressures of life under control, he found that he continually dreamed about her and finally got up the nerve to ask her out. Gently, he fastened the lily in her long hair, just over her ear.

"Thanks, I can smell it all night this way. Oh yes, and the same goes for you too, Rodrigo. In this get up, we don't have the free use of our feet. And as tight as these dresses are, form-fitting they are called, we can't bend very much. That means you are going to have to wait on us hand and foot."

"My Lady Rachele, I can think of nothing finer to do. Such an honor you do me to accompany me to the dance."

Ariana whispered to Ben, "I hope we are seeing love finally blossom here. Do you suppose so?"

"Who can say? Each is suited for the other, but then that is just my opinion. I have the prettiest two women in all of Zargarb with me, however." She gave him a loving kiss.

By the end of the year, both couples were married in a double wedding ceremony.

Chapter 22 General Thadeus Tassos Makes His Move

"Fools! Idiots! All three of them! Not one of them has the brains of a donkey's ass!" General Thadeus lectured his aides in his briefing room. I still cannot believe that they let three sectors slip from their grasp. Not one, but three!"

"Well the good news is that they at least sent their men here to us. We've added eleven hundred men to our forces. We now have thirty-six hundred men, that's thirty-six legions sir. Surely with this much force we can take some action," his second in command, Roxy, suggested hopefully.

"Aye, that we can, that we can. Come spring, we are going to earn glory and fame for Pieta's Holy Paladins. We will show the world that we are invincible. We will retake Solamina first and then Zargarb. New Barq shall follow and we, Pieta's Holy Paladins, will go down in history as those that reopened the land bridge to Megalos. No more of this forever shipping. It's not right for a horse or man to travel that distance over water. It should be on our own power."

"But don't we need the Pope's permission?" asked another aide somewhat concerned about the overly grandiose plan.

"Leave that to me, son. I am the general. You will not find me surrendering the sector. Cowards, every one of them. Now get to work with the supply officers and begin working out the logistics. We must make sure that ample supplies follow our swiftly invading army. The strike date will be March 21, 642, the first day of spring. Let's get all the squad leaders fully informed so they can sharpen up training schedules. I want every man ready when the time comes."

"Aye, sir. We will get the dispatches drawn up tonight. Are you planning on celebrating the new year with us later on tonight, general?"

"No, I have other plans. Now send in Arkadios. Leave us." They saluted and left. The general grinned to himself; tonight was the night he would get revenge, and prove these Santi were merely weak women. A little while later, Captain Arkadios entered and saluted.

"Greetings Captain, are the hundred handpicked men ready?" he twirled his moustache in anticipation of a great victory tonight, one that would speed his spring offensive along nicely.

"Yes, sir. Armed and ready. Is it still a go for midnight?"

"Yes, last message confirms it. I'll be watching and taking notes on you and your men's actions. This ought to be a very easy mission. Promotions for everyone and pay increases, naturally."

"Thank you sir." The two men shook hands and the captain left.

Tino and Telma were throwing a New Year's Eve party at their little teashop to celebrate the coming of 642. Johnny Blackwater, a Protector, and Telma were recently married, as were Tino and Benita. Their close Santi friend and Judger, Sam Stone, was celebrating with them. Tino had splurged and hired a lute player to play for his customers and themselves. Many local regulars crowded the small shop, gossiping as usual, sipping tea, and sampling the many different pastries that the twins baked specially for tonight. All had a good time. When the hour got late, they closed up shop. The last one to leave, Sam thanked them for a delightful evening and left to return to the fortress.

As usual, Sam walked to the docks, climbed down the trap door in the floor into the garbage dump. From there, he hiked along the shore until he got to the city wall. Here, he stepped out into the Med Sea and went around the wall. He was half way to the Santi Fortress when he spied a large number of fighters sneaking up towards the gate! He crouched down and observed. Damned if someone did not open the gates! He heard the steel scraping sound of swords being drawn.

High on top of the tower, his wife Willomena was intently observing the stars. He shot her a blue light spell, causing her to look down at him. Then she saw the large number of men rushing in through the opened gate. She acted at once, dashing down the stairs. He knew that she would shortly rouse the alarm. However, most of their Santi fighters were in bed, probably sleeping. They would be murdered in their sleep. He drew his short sword and crept toward the gate. Off in the far distance standing by the eastern gates of the city, General Tassos stood watching. Damn him, a sneak attack in the night, he thought. Cautiously he crept around the corner and peered at the open gates. He saw no signs that the gates had been forced open. No one was around. He heard yelling and screaming coming from the barracks. He slipped inside and closed the gates. Further, he locked them shut and took the key with him, nearly tripping over the dead body of the night gatekeeper!

Just then, the heavy door of the tower burst open, out came Alice Auguato, the Santi Strike Force Commander and twenty-five of her troops. Behind them were the rest of the Guardians. Moans, cries, and screams came from the barracks. In her alto voice, Alice cried, "Attack the bastards. Show no mercy!" Sam charged along side of her, running into the front door of the barracks.

Inside, a hundred Holy Paladins were trying to go room to room, murdering the sleeping occupants. However, by now, those at the far end of the long hall had arisen and stepped out into the hall to fight them off. Sam and Alice flew into the rear of the men, stabbing left and right. As they stepped over the fallen, her troops behind them made doubly sure these were dead. Boxed in, what ensued was a compact, mass melee.

Adding to the chaos, Willomena and Jasmine dropped sheets of flames onto the tops of the paladins in the center of the fighting, where the flames would not hit their own forces. Now attacked at both ends of the hall and from the center, the paladins quickly panicked, but there was nowhere to go. Those trying to escape the flames pushed into those trying to battle the Santi and were knocked off balance. Blades quickly found their marks and the noose tightened.

Several attempted to surrender, but Alice merely swung her blade into their necks, efficiently eliminating them. Battle lust, vengeance for her murdered troops filled her eyes. She did not even notice the many cuts on her arms and legs, so intense was her concentration on butchering these vile men. After a half hour of intense combat, the two ends of the Santi line met in the scorched, smoldering center of the hallway, standing on top of the smoldering carcasses of what had minutes before been men.

Efficiently, the Santi women backtracked, stabbing each body through its heart, even the headless ones. Meanwhile, Sam, Willomena, and Alice dashed into the side rooms. "Oh dear god!" exclaimed Willomena. "Alice, get your fighters to search each room. Take the wounded to the infirmary immediately. Have someone get lots of water boiling. We must try to save those that we can!"

Sam lifted one bleeding woman and carried her out, stepping over the many bodies littering the hallway. After placing the woman on a bed in the infirmary, he tried to stem her blood flow, working as rapidly as he could. Soon more women and men were brought in and placed on beds. "Here, get a tourniquet on her arm and leg," Sam ordered a fighter who had just deposited another man on a bed nearby. He obeyed. As soon as Sam dared let go, he did and joined Willomena and Jasmine as they rapidly tried to prioritize their patients. There were so many seriously wounded Santi that they could not afford to spend more than a few seconds with each.

Where possible, they ordered those standing by to apply pressure to stop the bleeding or a tourniquet, until they could get to them. Seven had severe chest wounds; these they had to work on at once, but there were only three of them. Five of the seven died quickly. All told, there were now thirty-five who needed fast action. Leaving the two worst cases to the women, hastily, Sam began to work on the remaining thirty-three, hoping the helpers could slow or stop their blood loss until he could get to them.

Once all the rooms had been searched, Alice had her remaining forces cart the dead enemy bodies and their body parts outside, piling them against the stone wall. One hundred and one bodies she counted. "Oil them and torch them!" she ordered.

"Commander, you are bleeding. We've got it under control; you'd better head to the infirmary yourself." She looked at her arms and felt pain for the first time. After glancing around one last time, she too headed into the infirmary. Quickly, one of the helpers began applying temporary bandages to her arms and legs.

Meanwhile, just as the twins and their spouses were getting into bed, Johnny received the Mind Link message from Jasmine. *We are under attack. Surprise attack. Many dead. Help quick.* That was all and she broke the link. He jumped up and told the others, dressed quickly, strapped on his weapons, and dashed out of the shop, heading for the fortress.

"The Avengers ought to be on patrol," Tino told his sister. "Benita, you watch the shop. We'll be back later." Quickly, the twins donned their black outfits and slipped outside. Slowly, they worked their way towards the eastern section of town. Soon from the rooftops, they could see some kind of fire near the distant wall of the Santi fortress, but the fire was on the inside. Both were fearful that something dreadful had occurred and moved a few blocks closer, now on top of the paladin's barracks.

Shortly, two night guards walked outside, taking a break and smoking their pipes. The duo overheard their conversation. One voice said, "What's ya think of this spring offensive? You think we'll be able to sweep through Solamina, Zargarb, and on down to New Barq?"

The other voice answered, "Dunno, but they ain't got no army to stop us. Don't ferget we's got eleven legions more with us now."

The first voice added, "I hears there ain't many Santi there anyhow. Maybe it'll be an easy sweep, but New Barq? Dunno 'bout that one. Hear there's all them Crusaders still there."

"We can siege them an' starve'm out."

"Probably that's what Tassos has in mind."

"We'll know fur sure if'en we don't get no orders ta build siege towers. Probably lose too many men if'n we's ta straight out attack them fortresses."

"Ya, donna think he's a gonna do that."

"Hope's so. Hey, look at the light comin' from their fortress. Wonder what that is?"

Just then, Tassos came walking up. He had a very angry look on his face. Both men jumped to attention, but the general ignored them, continuing he walk to his home. The two immediately went back inside.

Johnny snuck in the back way into his fortress. Soon he came upon the others carrying the dead bodies out, stacking them in a pile against the outer wall. Being a Guardian with some healing abilities, he headed for the infirmary. "God, what happened?" he asked one of the many who were frantically attempting to bandage wounds temporarily. He began attending to the nearest wounded man, while the other explained that they had been attacked while they slept.

When dawn's first light arrived, accompanied by crowing cocks, the Guardians had finally finished up with the last of the wounded. Inside the infirmary, seven more had died of their wounds, but the other thirty would likely recover, the Guardians decided. At last, Sam finished sewing up Alice's six wounds, and then Johnny sewed up the one wound that Sam had been ignoring until the others had been helped. Alice's second in command,

Elmer, came in with the final report. All told, twenty-one Santi had died during this nighttime raid. One hundred-one enemy soldiers had paid dearly for that tally.

The Guardians covered in the blood of their many patients, exhausted after working all night long, stretched, and went outside. The funeral fire was now merely smoldering. "How in heaven's name did they get inside?" asked Johnny.

"I saw them entering the gate when I was coming back," Sam explained. "Someone obviously opened the gates. I know the gate man. He would never do that."

Elmer, the second in command, answered, "The gate man was stabbed in the back, sir. Someone on the inside obviously killed him and opened the gates."

"Then either someone climbed the walls or we have a traitor in our midst!" declared Willomena.

Alice ordered, "Elmer, take a bunch and cover every inch of the walls. See if you can find any trace of someone having climbed them. Likely they would have used a grappling hook and rope. The action happened so fast, and Sam shut the gates after he entered, so the rope ought to still be around here somewhere."

"Aye, aye, Commander." He took off to conduct the investigation.

"A traitor, this is serious business," Johnny exclaimed. "I'm going with them, lend my powers of observation. We need to be very sure of this. I cannot believe that we have a traitor here. God, that's all we need!" He ran after Elmer. The others washed up and ate a little breakfast, which the cooks had prepared for everyone.

An hour later, Elmer and Johnny, faces looking very distraught, came to report. "No signs of anyone going over the walls," Johnny said. "All we found were the still damp footprints that I left when I came in the back way late last night."

"Donkey's ass!" exclaimed Willomena, who rarely got angry. "We have a traitor in our midst. Now what in the blazes do we do? Council meeting at once. Get everyone together."

"Oh, Jasmine, can you contact Tino and Telma for me? Let them know what's happened and that I will be here for some time helping with the wounded." She agreed and did so while the others were entering.

Once everyone was present, Willomena outlined the observations and conclusions. "Thank heavens that you two were up late," pronounced Alice. "I'll never tease you about that again!"

"I hate to think how awful this could have been," Willomena replied. "I think we were incredibly lucky last night. Now to business. Any ideas about how to ferret out the traitor in our midst?" She threw open the discussion. Sam wanted to know if the door to the tower was still locked from the inside when Alice first came out. She said that it was. Hence, the traitor had to be among the several hundred Santi forces that slept in the large barracks. Many expressed their views, but no satisfactory method could be found. A while later, she concluded, "Okay, since no one has any better ideas, I will contact headquarters and see if we can get Lorissa Moeti to come here. She will be able to find our traitor, that's for sure."

Jasmine spoke up now, "There is one other detail that has just emerged. It seems the Black Avengers were out last night, spying on the Holy Paladins. They overheard two of them discussing plans." She outlined what Tino and Telma had heard. "With your permission, I will relay this to Jenna as well. We need to begin preparations at once; we have less than three months to get counter-forces in place."

"This place has become a keg of action," Sam declared. "So what will be our official reaction to last night? Are we going to confront the general?"

"We are too few and they, too many, Sam. No, we will use mystery to our advantage. He sent in one hundred of his men and none returned. Let him stew about what happened. We will say nothing. If anyone asks about the fire, say we held a New Year's Celebration and had a cookout. Just don't say what we cooked," Willomena grinned.

Ten days later, a caravel from Velona arrived. Lorissa Moeti, the Blind Rose from Velona, was led carefully off the ship by her Santi attendants. Willomena welcomed her with open arms. Within a few minutes, they had her sitting in the back of the meeting room with numerous guards around her. One by one, the various Santi members who had been outside of the actual tower that night were led into the room. Willomena asked but one question, "Did you open the gates and let the enemy inside?"

Quietly, Lorissa continued to say, "Truthful."

After an hour of this, Fingall Breckenstaff was led in and seated. Willomena asked him the same question. "Why do you want to know? Don't you trust us?"

"Just answer the question, Fingall, yes or no," she replied slightly annoyed with his response.

"No. So what?"

"He lies."

"What? Are you going to take the word of that stupid blind woman who cannot see any damn thing?" he raged.

Jasmine, who was also sitting beside Lorissa, touched his mind. She added, "He has the memories of stabbing the gate man and opening the gates."

"Bitches, all of you are bitches!" he raged, but Alice and Sam held their swords at his throat.

"I ought to run you through!" Alice spat on him, barely able to keep herself from doing just that.

"Search him and throw him in chains," Willomena cursed at him.

While Alice rough handled him to search him, hoping that he would do something so that she could run him through, Sam noticed a curious mark on his left forearm. "Hey, look at this. Tattoo, no, more like a brand." Willomena drew up a sketch and asked him what it meant. He, of course, refused to answer. They sent the sketch back with Lorissa.

Willomena walked with Lorissa back to the caravel. "I don't know how to thank you, Lorissa. Without your aid, we would still have this murderous traitor in our midst."

She smiled, "There may be more in other fortresses. We shall see won't we?" She gave the Commander a hug and was assisted in boarding the caravel. Soon it was tacking slowly out of the small harbor, heading for Velona and her home. In the hold, secure in chains lay the traitor, on his way to Isla Roca.

Based on the treachery at Fortress Pieta, all the other fortresses established a dozen nighttime guards, hoping to prevent similar treacheries at their fortresses. Meanwhile, word of the impending attack by General Tassos was spread to everyone. Here at Jenna's estate, the Protectors began to work out how to counter this bold move. If this was not enough for us to worry about, a dispatch came from Ariana in Zargarb. While searching and cleaning up the mess left by the outgoing Holy Paladins, they had discovered a letter from the Mano del Dio to the General, outlining their alternative strategy with the nasty metal devices. The General had been ordered to burn it upon reading it. For whatever reason, he had not. Now, it seems they were secretly going to ship both men and women encased in these torture devices to Megalos! Clever, then they would be forever out of our reach. Jenna fumed over this one, even more than the sneak nighttime raid upon Pieta's fortress.

Our planners decided upon a new overall strategy. Since the enemy had now begun infiltrating our own organization, only the direct commanders would know the precise plans. That way, if we did have one or more traitors here in Velona, they would not be able to warn the enemy of our counter moves.

Jenna had made two personnel changes in her Circle. Hank replaced Ben as Loremaster and Adam Smythe replaced Paul as her Protector. Adam came from Mont Blanc along with his family. He was thirty-three and a veteran of the Line as well. On Adam, Jenna placed the burden of constructing and executing the counter move in Pieta. Adam was one of these fellows who loved and excelled in subterfuge; the more devious the method to achieve the result, the better. During the next three months, he nearly wore Paulette out with all the secret, highest priority communications.

I took a liking to Adam, and not because he often brought me a piece of rock candy after one of his many trips into Velona proper. He was exceedingly efficient and took the advice of those who knew the most about a particular detail. As I listened in on his many planning sessions, I also figured out before anyone else did, just why he was arranging the positions of our forces the way he was. He had an ulterior motive that he did not relay to others until the very last minute. I think it rather startled him when I, now a six year old girl, said to him, "You're going to try to take back Pieta this way, aren't you?" He was staring at his large map layout on which he had placed counters representing all the forces about to come into play. I was quietly watching him. If you are little and are very quiet, why, you can go just about anywhere you want, and the adults often don't notice you.

He grinned, "Observant little Lizzy are we? Well, yes, I just believe we might accomplish that as well. Can you keep a secret?" I nodded, still sucking on the latest rock candy he'd brought me. "Good girl. Let's keep this between you and me for a while yet. Otherwise, the bad men might find out about it and ruin everything."

"Okay, you mean the potential spies we might have around, like in Pieta," I replied.

"Yes, you don't miss a thing." We both smiled at each other.

Adam had to coordinate the activation and deployment of the entire Santi Strike Force, which for years now had been broken into its smaller units and scattered throughout the territories that we controlled. Further, this all had to be done in secret, both because of the new threat of traitors in our midst but also to keep from alerting the usual spies.

Alice Augato, who was the Longbow Regimental Commander in the last war with the Centurions, was currently on assignment as the Santi Pieta Garrison Commander. She led four squads of garrison fighters. However, she was notified that her commission had been reactivated and to expect eight more squads to arrive in secret, docking only at night.

In the old days, there were ten regiments of short bow archers, not counting the five longbow regiments in the actual strike force proper. Now, however, all ten were equipped with longbows, making them even more deadly than before. Further, two more regiments had been added, bringing the total to twelve longbow regiments. In our current organization, three regiments were formed into a brigade, led by a brigade commander. In Adam's grand plan, these dozen regiments would play the most crucial role, and he insisted on each of the dozen commanders come to Jenna's estate for a personal briefing. He'd been in nearly constant contact with Praedo Garcia of Solamina, the planner for the banditos, now one of Solamina's new rulers. No one knew the terrain of that sector better than he did.

The third week of January, the dozen commanders and four brigade commanders arrived. The four brigade commanders were Jason Bart, Sam Weston, Eli Helms, and Thomas Wolf. Adam had the maps all arranged and a copy prepared for each. Additionally, he had placed counters on the map outlining in detail his devious plan.

"As you probably know, Praedo Garcia led the banditos for years, and he knows every inch of the land there, from a combat point of view. Now the army will undoubtedly take one of two possible approaches in their assault. I am allowing for either, though we will position first for the most likely choice. As I see it, either he can bring his entire force down along the paved roadway paralleling the coast or he can break them up into smaller groups and attempt to sweep broadly across all the rim roads. I believe that is less likely, because Praedo has not positioned any forces there at all, just long the border here by the seacoast. There is nothing to be gained by splitting his forces and sweeping through towns and villages, which would offer no resistance."

"I've numbered each of these counters with your regimental id number to show you your initial position. Each of your regiments will send out a scout squad who will fan out far in front of your position to alert you of the approach of the enemy forces. Those of you who are to be positioned up north don't fret; if the enemy does not split up and are all together down south, then you will be ordered to change your battle plan. I'll get to that in a moment."

"Notice how only one regiment will appear to be directly in the path of the invaders. Your attack plan is this. When the scouts notify you of their precise location and disposition, you are to move from these secluded locations to the correspondingly marked positions that bear your id number. From there, you will have the element of total surprise. Praedo has selected these spots carefully. You will be at the edge of some kind of cover, often light trees. They will be out in the open, so you will have a clear line of sight. You are to empty your quivers, but as soon as they get too close, you are to abandon the position, galloping to the rear, and take up your next position, also marked with your regimental id number plus the letter B. Meanwhile, as the enemy approaches the next regiment's position, the same thing happens."

"We've laid out positions for three such ambushes each. If the battle gets that far, you are to retreat into the city, and man the walls. From there, you will be able to keep them from closing upon the city."

Jason asked, "What do you mean by gets that far? Where will the main Strike Force be located?"

"Ah, here, up here. They will sneak down from the Paese di Dio and come at them from behind after you have softened them up sufficiently. They will be attritioned first and then attacked from the rear. The objective is the total elimination of the Pieta Holy Paladin army, every one of these men."

Jason chuckled along with all the other commanders; he liked Adam's intentions. He replied, "Well, good old Alice Augato, she's going to like this aspect. I bet she is chomping at the bit locked away in her Pieta fortress."

"Ah, she will see her own action, for I intend to take over Pieta sector as a direct result of this war. Now, remember use extreme caution. I do not expect that you will take any casualties. I will not be sending the Healing Squads with you on this assignment. Think of it as extra certainty that you follow my plan and retreat well before they can get to your positions."

"Now as to deployment. You all have heard that the Mano del Dio has infiltrated at least the Pieta Fortress. It is highly likely that they have hidden members elsewhere within our ranks. Thus, speak not a word of the plan to your subordinates, not until you take to the field. You will receive your supplies from Solamina itself, caravels will unload them, and wagons will bring them to your positions. How do you get there? Ah, again we must move you in secret and by sea. It is well known that both Zargarb and Solamina are in dire need of supplies. Hence, we are going to slip your forces in along with the humanitarian aid shipments."

"Brigades 1, 2, and 3, you will be taken to Zargarb and travel overland from there to your assigned initial locations. As spring gets closer, Brigade 4 will be sent directly to Solamina, arriving close to the time of the planned attack. Two squads will be ferried by each caravel. The orders you are to give your men is first that you have been ordered to attend a spring training exercise to be held at Mont Blanc. This you can tell your fighters today. If word of this should find its way to the enemy, all the better, for they will believe our forces are going to be far, far from their army. As you ride toward Mont Blanc, you will stop at Point Bleak and board the waiting caravels. Once loaded, you can them tell them what they have been ordered to Zargarb to help bring order there. That will be rather believable. Only when you are on the trail to your initial positions are you to notify them of the actual plans we've discussed here today. After that point, I want a very sharp eye kept for anyone attempting to desert and head to Pieta to notify the enemy. Anyone who does is to be at once chased down and eliminated rapidly. Is this understood?"

It was and he gave them each a set of maps and a paper denoting the date at which they were to be at North Point.

The next day, the brigade commanders and regimental commanders of the main Santi Strike Force arrived for their briefing. This strike force had changed appreciably over the years since I had first formed them. Many had been pulled off to fortify the many fortresses we had built. Five long bow regiments were completely tied up on garrison duties. Now the force had only one brigade of four long bow regiments of a hundred each, led by Gualtiero Timorelli.

Adriana Socorro, promoted from regimental commander, led the ex-Sisterhood cavalry brigade of four regiments. The regimental commanders were Leda Furstio, Ana Fellini, and Ali Bastia. Romero Sachs took over for Alice Augato.

The Greenway Brigade had been expanded to four regiments, led by Mark Hamilton. One of Elona Po's Circle members, Protector Thomas

Algrove, led the Velona Brigade. Jason d'Grange, who was third in line to the throne there, led the d'Grange Brigade. Finally, the Hodge-podge Regiment of Mont Blanc, as its members jokingly like to call themselves, consisted of thirty Guardians who could be spared, mostly Protectors and Judgers. Lem Thin was now their leader, a Protector who was only twenty-one. Lem was also in charge of the other brigade commanders, taking up my old position as leader.

Thus, the strike force as fielded this time had, in round numbers, four hundred longbows, four hundred defensive cavalry, eight hundred offensive cavalry, and thirty Guardians. Along with this force, went four complete Healing Squads with their six Healers each, and four Scout Squads. All told, our main attacking force was barely one third that of our enemy! Adam was totally depending upon the archery brigades to reduce the number of the enemy.

First, Adam showed them the maps and detailed what the longbow brigades were to be doing. Finally, he showed them the counter that represented this main force. It was located way up north in the Paese di Dio area.

"What the heck are we doing way the heck up there?" Adriana protested. She wanted action!

"Waiting to see the enemy's chosen deployment. If they bring their entire force along the coast road as I anticipate the most likely move on their part, you will sweep down rapidly like so, and slaughter them from their rear!"

"Oh I do like that, such a deadly move!" Adriana commented, the other commanders agreed.

"If they split into smaller groups, then you too will do so in a similar manner, which I leave up to Lem to decide based upon the reports from the scouts. Again, you will be attacking them from their rear. The bottom line, I want none of the enemy to leave the battlefield. I want this to be a total, complete loss of every one of their men. No prisoners, no survivors to run off to some other sector to fight us another day. I wish to send this Church a profound message: do not mess with the Santi del Dio. Is this understood?" Everyone cheered.

Adam then went through the deployment issues, especially concerning security. It was at least a month's easy riding to get to the Pieta-Solamina border from Velona. To avoid sending such huge numbers at one time, the deployment would be staggered, with the scout squads and the Hodge-podge regiment would be leaving fairly soon. The Healers and the supply wagons would bring up the rear. Over a two-month period then, the other five brigades would be staggered at two-week intervals, with the archers arriving just in time to move out south to battle. The cover story to be told to the individual members was that Jenna had requested battlefield exercises in the north of Velona this spring to hone their skills. Only when they hit the Paese di Dio were the fighters to be told the true nature of their plan. After this point, many guards would be posted in the event a traitor was among these soldiers. If anyone tried to desert, they were to be hunted down and eliminated as a traitor.

During the next three months, numerous Santi fighters used our estate as a rendezvous point, before riding off toward the northernmost fortress on the Velona-Barcella border and the gateway to the Paese di Dio. When I wasn't tied up with therapy sessions, I'd watch them. Shiny chain mail armor, clean black tunics with the red fleur-de-lis crosses, smiling faces, all gave no hint of the horrors of war that I knew they were about to face. I hated war then, and I still do now. Yet, this General Tassos had to be stopped before he harmed even more people than he already had there in Pieta. This time, I was very glad that I did not have to lead them into battle or even witness it, though I suspected I would have to deal with its aftermath.

I was especially concerned when I heard one intelligence report that indicated some of the Holy Paladins were now wearing their own chain mail armor. I knew just how valuable such armor was to our forces in earlier conflicts. However, this twist meant two things. One, these new enemies were going to be much more difficult to slay, and two, the men from Megalos were finally learning from their mistakes.

General Thadous Tassos smiled as Bishop Theophilus moved down the long lines of his large army of men, giving them the Holy Blessing before riding off to battle. The Bishop had more than once argued with him not to launch this attack, even threatening to send a letter to the Pope. General Thadous knew that even if this priest did so, it would be six months before he received the Pope's reply. Who knows, the Pope might have even gone along with his plan. It made perfect sense. Nothing could go wrong. All reports had the Santi off on some kind of training exercises in their northern lands.

To his field commanders, he had made it very plain: swiftness was the key. They would sweep down the main road between the two cities, wiping out any token resistance they might encounter. Swift like the hawk, his men would swoop down and pluck Solamina back into their control. Just as swiftly, Zargarb would also be back in their hands. This was especially true because the fools had chosen or allowed a helpless crippled woman become their leader. It was said she had no hands, which could only mean that she had been abducted by the Church and had resisted all attempts to earn Good Marks. He expected even less resistance in Zargarb.

No, the only real resistance would come from the Santi fortresses, which he intended to leave alone. While he might enjoy and even relish taking them down, first he needed to accomplish his objective: retaking of New Barq, thus opening up a land route to the conquered lands. Why the

Pope had not attempted this before he could not fathom, but then, he never did understand the wimpy priests.

He observed the lines upon lines of his Holy Paladins, all mounted ready for action, their sky blue tunics with the simple white crosses. He knew that nothing could stop him from swiftly achieving his complete, total victory. His men, he knew, greatly valued their Bishop's Holy Blessing, and had insisted the Bishop deliver it or else he wouldn't leave a single soldier in Pieta. Theophilus gave in at that point. Ah, the shining chain mail! This was his latest addition. True, only three hundred of his best fighters wore it; yet it was a good start. Chain mail was both expensive to make and required significant time to construct. Still, three hundred suits was a good beginning.

The Bishop finally finished and the General, with his aides at his side, rode to the front. He drew his sword, pointed it high in the air, and then brought it down in a slashing motion. He kicked his horse, and the army began to move out from the staging area just outside the eastern walls of the city and just in front of the Santi fortress. Yes, he picked this spot on purpose — to show the Santi just how strong his army actually was. He'd pulled all Holy Paladins out from the outlying towns and villages. Only one hundred, one legion, remained to keep the city secure. Nothing much ever happened in Pieta, so this, he felt, was more than enough to guarantee the safety of the Bishop and his many priests. It was a sunny, spring day. Green shoots had already pushed their way towards the warm sunlight. Life was returning to Pieta. He felt totally alive, totally ready for conquest, for fame.

When he reached the main road, he paused and let his first legion move on out ahead of him. These would act as his scouts, while his group fell in line behind them. General Tassos was not stupid or cowardly as the late Emperor Justinian, who always was found at the very rear of his army. Tassos was a leader, though it was prudent to send out an advance scouting legion ahead of his main force. After all, there might be a few Santi guarding the border with Solamina, perhaps a hundred at most.

As he crested a hill, he turned in the saddle to look back upon his mighty army, strung out over several miles behind him. In the far distance, he could barely make out the hundreds of supply wagons rolling along behind them. Each man carried two day's rations in their saddlebags. Thus, every two days, they would resupply.

When the army began moving out, Jasmine began the many Mind Links, communicating the information to all the others in the field and to Paulette and Adam back at headquarters. Adam was particularly interested in their deployments. As requested, ten Santi scouts left the Pieta fortress several hours later, following behind the army.

For five days, the army moved relentlessly down the road. Up hills and down, always the Med Sea lay on their right. Occasional stands of trees passed by. A few coastal towns offered the General a brief respite for a hot cup of tea. The army trampled many small farmsteads as it moved on towards the border. On the fifth afternoon, they halted for the day at the border with Solamina. Ahead of them lay the River Sola, which though not more than a stream, did mark the official boundary between the two sectors.

They camped a safe distance from the grove of trees on the Solamina side, however. General Tassos half expected to meet some Santi fighters in those woods, in a vain and futile attempt to halt his mighty army. However, because of the lateness of the day, he did not send the scout legion on ahead. He did not want a battle with darkness so near. It still got dark by six pm.

The next morning, he reviewed his plans with his aides, who then circulated among the various legion commanders. When all was ready to move out around nine the next morning, three legions spread out all along the River Sola. On his command, the three hundred men began crossing the stream together. They would ride ahead of his main army flushing out any possible defenders in a wide path. He and his crack three legions followed a safe distance behind, followed by the remainder of his mighty army. If the scouts ran into trouble, legions of his cavalry would charge forward and totally annihilate any opposition.

The General heard no sudden alarms and began moving forward along the Centurion made paved roadway. Evidently, the Santi were not hiding in these woods. Shame, he thought this would have been his choice. Good concealment. Ah well, they must be more cowardly or stupid than he had thought. Now about a half mile ahead of the General, the long, spread out line of the three legions of cavalry came out of the woods onto open grasslands. One small farmstead lay near the seacoast. They rode on across the rolling lands. About two miles ahead lay another small patch of forest. They continued their slow plodding along. This was going to be an easy trip.

"Steady, hold until they reach the marks. Steady," Jason Bart called out to his regimental commanders, who had their hundred longbow fighters at the ready, concealed here at the edge of this small cluster of trees. The sun was at their back, which meant their enemies would be at the disadvantage. Further, Jason had another trick up his sleeve. Having been here for some time, he had placed rocks in a line that indicated the maximum range of the longbows. A second line was the kill line. He wanted to allow them to reach the kill line before opening fire. That way, if any attempted to retreat, then another wave of arrows would still reach them. "Fire!" he yelled. Instantly, four hundred longbows twanged, nearly in unison. Steel tipped arrows arced high into the blue sky before beginning their curved descent.

The bright sun prevented the Holy Paladins from seeing the wave until it was almost upon them. Wham! Wham! Wham! Arrows thudded into heads, horses, chests, arms, legs, and the ground. The well-trained archers emptied their quivers in less than two minutes. Their objective was simple; fire all the arrows rapid-fire as a group. Six thousand arrows peppered the nearly mile long line of Holy Paladins in less than two minutes. Mass pandemonium, total chaos ensued for that brief time, and riders fell from horses; horses collapsed; others spun around and attempted to gallop out of the kill zone. Others trampled both horse and man. Some fell on top of others. At the end of the volley, a lone horse trotted to the rear.

"Retreat full speed!" Jason ordered, and he kicked his horse into an all-out gallop. Riding beside him was the Communicator for the forward scout squad. He yelled, "Send the report when you get a chance." They raced across the country at top speed, formed back into a long line, and cantered down the paved roadway, past fields, open lands, and the occasional farmstead. When they entered a tiny fishing village, they at last slowed down, they were now past Brigade 2's position. Now they walked their horses to cool them down. They could relax, for it was a good day's travel to their B position.

General Tassos heard the noise of combat and ordered an all-out charge. However, when they broke out of the woods and reached the beginnings of the rolling grasslands, the devastation lay in a long, wide rectangle, nearly a mile long before him. Dead horses, men, wounded horses, men lay everywhere. A few men had managed to get to their feet and were walking towards him. Instantly angry, Tassos yelled, "Where's the enemy? Who did this?" The few men, who could, pointed to the distant woods.

"That's impossible. No arrow can travel this distance! It is completely beyond bow range!" Check it out!" he ordered his three crack legions, which cantered across the carnage heading toward the woods. "Clean up this mess. See to the wounded." He barked orders.

A while later, the report came back. "Ambush. Estimates are about four hundred archers were in the woods near its edge. From the tracks, they lit out toward Solamina like the Fires of Hell were on their tail. No chance of catching them, sir." The General glared at the soldier making the report.

He decided to make camp here; too many wounded needed immediate attention. Around the campsite, he called his commanders together. "What I want to know is how their arrows could cover that distance? See if you can find me that answer." Several went off to measure and examine the battlefield.

Later the casualty lists were complete. One hundred fifty were dead. Another one hundred were badly wounded and could not safely be moved for some days. Another fifty had been bandaged and could ride. Two hundred horses were dead or had to be killed. Fifty would need time to recover, while another fifty could be pressed into light use. Grim, they had not even seen the enemy archers!

That evening he issued new orders to the next four legions who would take point tomorrow. "If you come under fire again, I want everyone to charge full speed toward the archers! You've seen the folly of standing around doing nothing. You have to charge them. That will force them to break off their attack. Then, you can deal with them, with the rest of us right behind you." He went over the new strategy, drawing out how he wanted the lines to appear. This time, the line would only be two hundred in length, with the second two hundred following closely behind. Thus, if the front line was attacked, the rear line was ordered to do an all-out charge of the enemy position. He convinced them that this would break up an archery assault. "You have to hit them quick and fast!"

"Quick and fast." The words were repeated to the four hundred men who were taking the point the next morning. Tassos decided to leave the wounded here, along with one supply wagon. They would pick them up on their return trip. This far from the front lines, they would be safe enough.

He watched as his men moved out, joining them after they were a half mile ahead. "Keep a sharp eye out. We charge as soon as we see any ambush happening," he bellowed his orders. "Going to get you evil cowards this time," he said to himself. Once more, the gentle rolling countryside passed by uneventfully. When they passed a farmstead, he halted and interrogated the residents who reported seeing a large column of fleeing Santi, if the black tunics were the Santi. By afternoon, he was beginning to think that he would see them next behind the walls of Solamina.

However, Praedo had taken likely reactions of the enemy into account. The next ambush happened slightly differently. Ahead, the roadway snaked along a little bluff above the seacoast some twenty feet below. A nice sandy beach was clearly visible. However, just a quarter mile north of the road lay a stand of trees. A vineyard lay in between the two; its nearly manicured rows paralleling the road. Suddenly a wave of arrows appeared from the stand of trees. Sam Weston had called for the fire at the precise time. The entire left half of the two rows of Holy Paladins were hit with a rain of deadly arrows. This time, however, only three thousand arrows were shot, because the remainder of the advance line pivoted and began to charge toward the archers. Worse still, seeing this, the General immediately ordered his three crack legions to also charge towards the archers.

Sam allowed ten fast volleys before ordering a galloping retreat. Instead of heading on east toward Solamina, he rode nearly due north, leaving the stand of woods at his rear. His four hundred raced over the rolling grassland, bypassing the farmed lands as much as possible. A half mile behind them cantered the remainder of the advanced legions and just behind them came the General with his three hundred. Much farther behind came the majority of his army, though one legion halted to assist the many wounded.

The sun was getting low in the west when the General realized two things: that this chase was futile, and that his forces were being deliberately pulled away from their objective, Solamina. He ordered a halt, and they returned to the ambush site and made camp. He had lost another hundred and fifty or so men and was forced to leave another fifty men behind to heal their wounds sufficiently before they could rejoin him.

"Yesterday, we drove the Santi far north of us. It will take them days to angle around and get in front of us again, if ever. We may have seen the last of these ambushes." He tried to sound positive, though he had to admit that the vain attempt to pull his whole army far to the north was a clever idea. However, he had been too smart to fall for such a deceit.

The next day, he reminded his men that they were but another three days from their objective, the walls of Solamina. Again, he sent out four legions, two abreast. That tactic had proven effective yesterday, though he doubted he would meet any further resistance. Intelligence reported that at most, there were only perhaps three hundred Santi in the entire garrison force, and many of those were non-combatants. He wondered if the cooks had been forced into firing arrows.

At noon, the advance legions came over a rise and out of a small patch of woods. Before them lay a nice grassy valley. A ridge line obstructed their view across the mile width of the valley. As the front line moved out onto the grassy patch, and reached the bottom of the valley, another rain of arrows suddenly appeared coming from the ridge line ahead. Men and horses began falling once more. As ordered, the second line charged the distant ridge, and the General ordered two of his legions to follow, while he led the third sweeping far to the left. His plan was to out flank them and cut off the retreat of these cowards. Galloping at full speed, he entered a narrow valley just north of the location from which the rain of death had appeared compliments of Battalion Commander Thomas Wolf. His group was only able to get off six volleys before dashing off at top speed to the east.

From the north side of this valley, another rain of arrows came at the left flank of the General and his troops! Battalion Commander Eli Helms ordered his men to open fire on the long line of Holy Paladins sweeping east through the valley that were attempting to outflank Thomas's men. Tassos held up his chain mail clad arm to protect his face as he veered hard to the right. Once more men and horses went down. However, the backup legions came thundering following the General's route, and the hail of arrows quickly ceased, as Eli ordered the retreat.

"Damn those bloody cowards!" screamed General Tassos. His horse was dead. "Get me a fresh mount!" he bellowed, surveying the damage. Thank heavens he had the foresight to begin to supply his men with chain mail. His legion had only lost one man; an arrow had pierced his forehead. Another fifty had minor wounds. At this extreme distance, the arrows only infrequently pierced the armor. He himself had a couple small puncture wounds, minor, for his armor had stopped the arrows. However, he realized that with the power that these arrows had at this range, they most certainly would penetrate their chain mail had they been at close range!

This time, he lost roughly another hundred fifty men dead. Around fifty men were patched up as best they could be and were asked to lead the wounded horses back to the camp of the earlier injured men. The loss of so many horses was now becoming a serious problem. He was forced to send another fifty on foot, helping the injured and the wounded horses get back to the other camp. He requested that as soon as they thought the wounded there could be moved, take all of them and walk back to the first camp, where the first had been left behind. The fifty men whose horses had been confiscated by his chain mail clad men could help guard and aid all the wounded.

Around the campfires, the General laid out his next tactic. "It is plainly obvious that these cowards will never stand and do battle; we are just too powerful for the measly rats. I cannot afford any more losses like these past few days. So here's what we do next. Five scouts out of each front line legion will ride out in front about a half mile. Their task is to make sure that our main forces are not going to be ambushed again. They will be able to spot those waiting under the cover of the woods and such. If they are shot, then we have advanced knowledge of the ambush, and we will ride to the flanks and hit them right straight down the edges of their lines, annihilating every last coward archer!"

"Further, the outriders need some protection. Hence, they are all going to get chain mail. After today, we all see the tremendous advantage the armor gives us. I only wish we had more suits. Take a note," he said aside to an aide, "order a chain mail suit for every Holy Paladin."

The next day all went well. They passed through several seacoast hamlets and one sizeable village, where they confiscated several more horses. Early afternoon, the road veered inland a ways, bypassing a tall rocky bluff. A nice vineyard lined both sides of the roadway, smoke curled from the main manor house in the far distance. Far to the left a stand of trees lay. The two groups of five outriders paused and looked at the scene before them. Nothing caught their eyes, so they headed on down either side of the roadway. They passed by the manor house, which had a small side road leading the half mile up to its entrance. Behind them, the main force had now entered the valley and all looked perfectly normal.

Without warning, two large swarms of deadly arrows arced high through the pale blue sky before they continued their deadly path to the ground amidst the main lines of the General's legions. One swarm came from the stand of trees, while the other came arcing up and over the rocky bluff near the seacoast. For a confused minute, the arrows rained death down upon the men. Tassos yelled for men to charge in both directions. However, as soon as the lead riders reached the rocky ridge overlooking the sea, they frantically reined in. They stood dangerously close to a hundred foot drop off to the shoreline below them. Arrows now came flying directly at them, forcing them to pivot and retreat back into the others coming up behind them, perfect targets for the next two rains of projectiles. They heard the thundering hooves of horses as their enemy galloped on down the seacoast, but there was little they could do except search for a way down to the coast. By the time that they found a way down, Jason's group had entirely disappeared in the distance. The legions charging the stand of olive trees fared little better, taking another two volleys of arrows before all firing ceased as suddenly as it had begun.

This time the General insisted on pushing forward as quickly as possible. He was again forced to leave another fifty men behind to care for the seventy or so wounded and to bury the two hundred men who did not survive this deadly ambush. They were given orders to join up with the other wounded when they were at last able to move again. Relentlessly, Tassos pushed on toward his first objective, ending the day only another eight hours from the walls of Solamina. They made camp at a larger town, commandeering all the available inn space and consuming all the town's stock of ale. However, none in the town could provide any useful information, even when beaten unto death. Three locals perished that evening.

The next morning, he gave his men a briefing. "By tonight, we will be at the very walls of Solamina. At last, these incredible cowards will be forced to stand and do battle. If the Santi are indeed manning the walls, we will show them what you can do, my fine men. We'll give them a taste of what thousands of arrows can do. We will decimate those manning the walls. You have my order to use flaming arrows, every one in five. Burn them out if need be! Tonight we camp before the walls and tomorrow Solamina shall be ours!" The men cheered and yelled their support, anxious for an actual battle. They were quite demoralized by having taken so many casualties and not even once having an enemy that they could strike.

"Okay commanders, Pieta reports they have left and are following the coast road. Time to move out!" The Santi Strike Force, having been holed up here in the extreme northern valleys along the border of Pieta and Solamina, were more than ready for a change. All this hiding was not to their liking. According to the plan, they were to head nearly due south, completely across country. No spoke road was near here, and there was not much chance that they would be spotted. They rode hard and fast, however, and finally reached the coastal road on the fifth day.

The five scout squads had days before fanned out all along the border and were tailing the advancing army from approximately three miles back. The Communicators in these scout squads made daily reports on the combat attrition losses that the ambushes had taken. Thus, Lem Thin knew precisely where each wounded campsite was located. The next day, they came upon the first of these sites.

The shock and surprise was total. None of the Holy Paladins expected to see an entire cavalry army charging at them from Pieta! Although wounded, a few tried vainly to establish a hasty defensive line, but Lem's lead group merely galloped on through them, the Greenway Brigade just behind him did attack them, while Adriana Socorro dispatched one squad to stop and finish off any that may still be alive. With their usual Sisterhood efficiency, they guaranteed that none of these men lived before they remounted and galloped after the main force. The Healer Squads and the supply wagons rolled into the site some six hours later and paused to bury the dead, before pushing on far into the night before stopping.

With continuing intelligence, Lem maintained his position at approximately one day behind the advancing army. However, each day he shortened the separating distance by a fifth. Timing was critical. He had to be able to bring his full force to bear on the Holy Paladins just as they were going to close upon the walls. If he were late, the Archery Brigades might suffer greatly as they manned the walls.

Lem had already received the news that Gualtiero Timorelli and his longbow brigade was in position north and east of the walls, camped out in a dense patch of forest. Thus far, Adam's grand plan was working to perfection. Another couple of days and it would be over. The Santi Strike Force continued its head long charge in the wake of General Tassos's army.

Cresting the last ridge line before Solamina, the General paused to view his long sought target. Two miles of cultivated fields lay before him and the prize. Smoke clouds curled from the many chimneys within the city. Even from this distance, he thought that he could see ants moving upon the walls that faced him. He'd encountered no further ambushes and was now satisfied all the cowards had finally given up and were awaiting their certain death within the walls of Solamina. A couple of ship's main masts stuck up over the city like match sticks. All seemed quiet. He gave the orders to move down onto the fields, staying however out of bow range from the walls. Here he boldly made his camp, lighting large bonfires to cast fear into the hearts and minds of the defenders. Tomorrow would be the greatest victory of his career. Tomorrow his name would go down in history. In fact, his name did go down in history.

The day dawned sunny, a perfect spring morning. The General waited until ten to launch his attack, giving the sun time to move from being directly in their eyes. His men lined up as if on parade. As ordered, they all prepared their short bows. Yelling to be heard, Tassos infused his men, "Holy Paladins, one and all. Today we at last face the dirty cowards that have been ambushing our companions. No longer can they run from us. There is no place else to run to! Upon yonder walls they cower, terrified of our might. Let lose all of your arrows. Give them what they have been giving us this past week. I want no survivors. I repeat. Show them no mercy of any kind. Our fallen comrades in arms demand vengeance. Justice is mine, saith the Lord Jehosa. Today, you are the long arm of our Lord Above. Wreak out his justice upon the vile Santi on yonder walls."

He started chanting, "Kill the Santi! Kill the Santi! Kill the Santi!" Soon the entire army was shouting the chant along with him. Now was the time; he signaled the trumpeters. Loud attack notes pierced the chanting. Amid wild yelling, the entire army charged toward the walls of Solamina. Just as soon as the lead riders were within extreme long bow range, the four battalions opened fire and continued to fire. Each man had several full quivers at his side there on the walls. Men and horses dropped under the falling shafts, but soon the Holy Paladins were close enough to launch a rain of death of their own. Now the dark shafts flew high into the defenders on the walls. More than one man fell down, struck by a shaft.

No sounds did Lem's mighty Strike Force make as they galloped over the ridge, heading down into the valley before the city. That was the signal for Gualtiero Timorelli to open fire from his position to the northeast of the city. His battalion had less than two minutes to deliver a second crushing blow before the Santi cavalry clobbered the enemy from their rear. After that, the only shots they could take were carefully aimed shots of opportunity fire.

The rain of arrows coming from the northeast took the Holy Paladins by surprise, temporarily halting their counter-fire. Hundreds of shafts landed in their midst, casualties began littering the ground. Tassos turned to face this new enemy, but then heard the thunder of thousands of horses. He turned completely around to see the five charging battalions of Santi rushing down the hill towards the rear of his men. He yelled orders to reform lines to face the enemy, but it was too late. The confusion of the battle was now too much. Arrows coming from two directions, riders from a third, his men spun around helplessly in small circles, unsure what to do. Then the arrows stopped and the galloping cavalry smashed into the Holy Paladin army, ripping their way through the ill formed lines.

Sword upon sword sounds were deafening as thousands of men and women fought for their very lives. Without the benefit of chain mail, his men took devastating losses quickly. While one of the paladins might land a blow upon a Santi, the chain mail often turned it into a mere bruise. Yet the strike of a Santi blow met flesh and bone. Soon the field became one of a complete hack and slash between riders, whose horses often trampled the fallen.

Within a half hour, the mighty Holy Paladin army had been reduced to around two hundred fifty of the chain mail clad fighters, who had formed a circle around their General. Out around them the battlefield was strewn with thousands of wounded, dead or dying men and horses. The Santi battalions had now completely encircled them, and both sides had finally paused, gasping for breath from the tremendous exertion. When he left Pieta two weeks ago, his mighty army outnumbered the Santi force by nearly three to one. Now at the end, his remaining few soldiers faced over a thousand Santi. All combatants now wore chain mail. Even though outnumbered, man for man, many things were at least equal.

Lem looked at the General and spoke loudly, "Will you yield, General Tassos?"

He was a cornered rat in a maze. Still, he fought to survive. He did not become a general because of birth or political favors. His mind calculated the odds. Man for man, equals. Ah, but the Santi were spread out encircling him. He decided that his best option would be to attempt to bust through the encirclement, heading back toward Pieta. He estimated that his small force ought to be able to bust through the encirclement lines and be able to gallop off to safety, out of archery range. He felt something cold touch his mind, something that he had never before experienced.

"Will you yield?" Lem called out one last time. Lem was also sizing up the situation. He now faced the most powerful of the enemy forces, primarily because of their equal armor. To fight man to man now would result in a good deal of casualties on the Santi side. Already he could see many Santi tunics lying on the ground. If there was some way he could minimize further losses, he would try.

He is deciding to break through towards Pieta. His Communicator placed into Lem's mind. Lem replied, *Use Push Spells.* The dozen Protectors received his order and began their chants. Suddenly, the General barked his orders, kicking his horse into a gallop as best it could do trampling over the many obstacles that lay in his path. His men obeyed, nearly three hundred pushing forward against the line of Santi that lay to the west of them.

They had just barely closed the distance separating the two sides when the Protector's spells detonated. It was if some mighty hand of god swept down and knocked the men completely off their horses. The General and three quarters of his men fell to the ground, tumbling over the wounded and dead beneath them. Now the Santi closed to battle once more. Steel upon steel sounded once more as the deadly parry and thrust continued. For thirty minutes more, sweat poured, mixed with blood. Hack, slash.

Adriana Socorro delivered the final blow. Seeing an opportunity, she swung her sword backwards, catching the General off guard. Her blade pierced his forehead; the last image his mind recorded was that of the icy, hate-filled glare of this Santi fighter. The General down, the remaining fifty threw down their arms. Lem could not give the order to kill them anyway, but accepted their surrender. Adriana's remaining women fighters began their usual systematic battlefield examination, ensuring no Holy Paladin lived, excepting only those few that were being escorted off the battlefield.

The Healing wagons rolled up over the ridge line and continued to move down toward the carnage. They would be busy cleaning up the mess that men did here this day. One hour of fighting made such carnage. Nearly at the same time, Gualtiero brought his archers down to the field to lend a hand, while the gates opened, and the other battalions rode out to help as well. Many of their comrades were wounded or dead. Now the grim, stark reality of war had to be faced. No, it is not the glory of combat, but the horrid aftermath that is so utterly sickening. What had been the point of the deaths of three thousand men from Megalos? Nothing, nothing at all.

The Strike Force had lost fifty-three men and women during that hour, with another two hundred ten wounded. Most of the wounds were either head wounds or broken limbs, fortunately. Once again, the armor had saved the Santi from devastating losses. Yet, Lem realized that the enemy had taken a key step toward neutralizing the effects of the Santi fighters. Their own use of chain mail nearly cost them the battle. He vowed to find a better form of armor.

"Shall I send the signal to Pieta?" asked Matilda, the Solamina Communicator, who had come to lend a hand with the healing, as had all the other Guardians in Solamina.

"Yes, send them the signal and the news. Victory at the walls of Solamina is ours, but at a steep price," Lem replied.

Around the campfires this night and for many thereafter, indeed even into the history books, all the talk centered around Adriana Socorro's clever backhanded swing that had killed the General. Her fame grew near legendary after this day, just as had mine, as Ket Bethany, the man who had killed Emperor Justinian years ago.

"Thank goodness it's time!" declared a very impatient Alice Augato in her mellow alto voice. For days, she had been waiting for the order to come for her to lead her bolstered forces into the city and retake Pieta, finally freeing it from the hands of the Megalos Overlords. She now had a full battalion under her command, and Johnny and Sam would come with her. Willomena and Jasmine would be watching from the tower roof.

"Everyone ready?" Alice asked, looking at her small force of Santi fighters. Satisfied that everyone was, she led the way out of their fortress and walked the short distance over to the eastern gates of Pieta. It was nearly noon on April 1, 642.

"You should not be coming in here with so many," the gatekeeper made a hesitant attempt to stop her advance. He winked at Alice so that she would realize that he was only putting on a front for the Holy Paladins, who would have his hide if he had not made the attempt.

"You going to stop four hundred of us?" she asked. "I think not. Shortly, Pieta will be once more a free sector. The General and all his men have been eliminated." She marched on down the street, her battalion marching in step, chain mail sparkling in the sunlight where it could be seen outside the edges of the black tunics with red crosses. She headed toward their main barracks where Sam believed the remaining men were probably having lunch.

Two guards saw them approaching, along with a huge crowd of locals who just had to see what was going to happen. Some real excitement was about to occur — Santi marching in force into Pieta. Some hoped against all hope that the Santi would put an end to the terrors of their Overlords. The guards dashed inside and soon returned with the remainder of the garrison who came rushing out, hastily forming a battle line. While Alice dearly wanted a good fight, this one would hardly be a fair one.

In her mellow alto voice, she barked, "Tassos is dead; so is his army. You are all that remain. I, Alice Augato of Fortress Pieta, will accept your unconditional surrender at this time. That is, unless you wish to make my day and do battle. What will it be, boys?" she said, a part of her wishing that her taunts would cause them to attack. She felt as if she had missed the whole battle thing by being forced to stay here in Pieta, just to take out these pitiful men, well and free the sector too.

Sam whispered, "Ah, trying to provoke them I see, eh, Alice? Tisk, tisk." She smiled; Sam always saw through her.

Outnumbered four to one, one would expect that they would have surrendered. However, most of her battalion was women, ex-Sisterhood fighters. That they surrendered to a bunch of women would be a horrible disgrace to their manhood. Yet, these women were armored and they were not. Alice could read their cold calculations on their faces. The captain finally reached a decision. He yelled, "Charge!" Immediately, the hundred rushed forward to do battle.

Alice yelled, "Flank left, right." The sounds of steel being drawn from scabbards echoed in the open courtyard before the barracks. One of her regiments began running to the right side of the enemy line, while a second regiment flanked to the left. Alice and two other regiments braced for the charge. Seconds later, the sounds of clashing steel upon steel echoed throughout this city block. The battle had well over two hundred onlookers by now, most cheering the Santi. Alice didn't hear them; her full concentration was upon the men in front of her, as she feinted, parried, and delivered deathblow after deathblow.

Two minutes later, with the expected Sisterhood efficiency, the fighters moved from body to body, making double certain each heart had been cut open. "Well that's that. Looks like no prisoners from here," Alice said. "Casualty report?"

"Cassie's got a broken arm. Lots of minor cuts, Commander."

"Get her back to the Fortress and into the infirmary," Alice ordered.

Sam commented, faking a great alarm, "Oh darn, we have a broken arm as a result of the battle. They have one hundred dead, but we have a broken arm." She poked him in his ribs.

"Come on; now we must deal with the priests." Quickly, her regiments reformed, and they then marched toward the main rectory where the Bishop stayed. However, the Nunnery was on the way, so she stopped there first. Barging in, she arrested the Head Nun and her assistant. Next, she had a thorough search done, looking for more of those nasty metal devices. Her troops found a half dozen concealed in a closet.

"Put her in one," Alice ordered. The Head Nun protested and struggled, but soon was encased with the metal ring forcing her mouth open, just as she had done to so many women. "Bring them along," Alice said, and several picked up the nasty devices.

Next, she barged into the Rectory. Here the Bishop was saying Mass over the meal he and his fellow priests were about to eat. "Sorry to interrupt your meal, Bishop, but you and your men are all under arrest for High Crimes against the People of Pieta."

He screamed, protested, swore, spat, and cursed at her. Finally, she said, "Put him in one of those devices too." Now he really screamed at her, something about recalcitrant women and Bad Marks. Two minutes later, Bishop Theophilus was encased with a ring forcing his mouth open. He was escorted out to join the Head Nun, who was likewise quite helpless.

"Take them back to the caravel. Chain them all securely. Okay, next, Regiments One and Two fan out and search all the other churches. Regiment Three you have the list of key people, go find them and bring them to Central Park. Regiment Four, take up your assigned key positions around the city, but stay alert for trouble. There could be many angry local supporters of the Holy Paladins, who are looking for retribution. Keep order. You three are with me; we go to Central Park." Sam and Johnny went with her as well. If the key personnel could be located, the hands of power would be officially shifted to them this afternoon.

An hour later, the regiment returned, escorting a number of men, mostly the nobles who had ruled before Justinian took the city. Additionally, a representative of each of the many guilds had been brought to this meeting. Alice stood on the musician's platform. "Alice Augato, the Santi Fortress Pieta Garrison Commander, in case you don't know me by now. At this time, Pieta is once more a free sector. General Tassos and all his nearly four thousand men are dead. They chose to attack the Santi and paid the ultimate price! Additionally, all the priests and nuns have been arrested and will be dealt with by the Santi. We give you back your sector. At this time, I would like to have the Fortress Commander speak with you. Willomena Stone." She stepped down amid a large round of applause.

Willomena had the far more difficult task. "We would like at this time to give control of Pieta Sector back to you. However, just to who do we give control back appears to be somewhat of a problem. As I understand your history, the nobles gave away control of the sector in the first place. Should we give it back to the very ones who bargained it away? I fear if we did so, the lives of you nobles and your families would be in severe jeopardy. Many citizens have been terribly harmed by the results of your actions; undoubtedly, many will seek retribution."

"Worse still is that there is no government or facilities currently in existence, no city guards, no one to guarantee the safety of anyone. In short, we are facing a crisis of management. While we Santi could take over control of Pieta, such is totally against our policies. We do not and never will desire to rule over you. Don't even consider asking us to do that."

"Officially our solution is to turn over the control of Pieta to the Guilds, representing all the various trades and skills so needed in running an economy. We know that some of you served on the High Council before the Centurions came, and thus have some ideas of how things could be run. Guildsmen begin your organizational activities yet this afternoon. Know that the Santi will back you and provide any support that you might need until you are back on your feet. We will deploy forces on the border with Bonilla later today, with more coming in the ensuing weeks ahead, guarding against any attempted retribution by the Holy Paladins of Bonilla, just as we have done for Solamina. Later when you have rebuilt your forces, you can then take over border patrols."

"Now I know that the nobles are likely fuming over this handover of power. This is the only way that we can minimize local retribution against you and your families. Many will want you dead, particularly so if you regain the power of control over their lives. We cannot play personal bodyguard to each one of you. However, if you are seen as providing monetary support in the reconstruction of Pieta, that may go a long way toward appeasing the many who feel that you betrayed them. No guarantees, though, but your actions will be watched closely, on that you can count. Unlike Solamina, Barcella, and Zargarb, you retain most of your original population and certainly most of your funds. These other sectors lost everything and are yet struggling to return to prosperity. I say to you, now is the time to use those funds wisely, something the other three sectors lack."

"Alice will have a regiment of Santi patrolling the city streets day and night until you get city guards organized and ready to take over that task. From experience in the other freed sectors, one problem that will appear almost at once is retaliation. Many who have suffered greatly will be seeking revenge against those whom they believe collaborated with and supported the enemy. In Zargarb, five hundred were killed by vigilante squads for this reason within the first week of freedom. Likewise, Solamina and Barcella. Our forces cannot be everywhere, so be advised that this is likely to occur. We will do all that we can to prevent or stop it, but you know your people better than we do."

"Finally, to you Guildsmen, if you need advice and assistance or have questions, my husband, Sam, is an expert in such matters. Feel free to call on his services at any time. I know that he would love to lend you a hand working things out for the betterment of all Pieta. Any questions?"

Many wanted to know the details of the defeat of the Holy Paladins, but she told them that those who were involved would soon be passing through Pieta. She promised to have some discuss the events with them at that time, neatly sidestepping the situation. Several nobles wanted to pay for

Santi protection, but she refused, but agreed to have Santi patrolling their section of town heavily. "You reap what you sew," she added. "In the future, perhaps you ought to be more careful of what you sew."

The head of the Dock Workers Guild asked if Sam could help them get started right now. This leadership-ruler move had come as a shock to them. He agreed, and they all adjourned to find a reasonable location to begin the huge task of reconstruction. Sam knew that this whole decision to turn control over to the guilds was fraught with problems. Yet, he, as did his wife, could see no other reasonable course to follow at this time.

Chapter 23 Check

"What?" cried Jenna. She had just heard the news from Bregia, West Reach. It was April 1, 642 and we were all celebrating the great news that Pieta had been freed and that the Holy Paladins were wiped out at the walls of Solamina. Paulette, who had just been contacted by Lucinda West of Fortress Bregia, was near tears.

Holding back her emotions, which had just gone from elation to the pits, repeated the message. "A flotilla of ships from Megalos had just landed at Bregia, delivering five thousand Holy Paladins, that had already taken over Bregia, besieging our fortress there, and were moving out towards other towns."

"Are they actually fighting at the moment? Are they in any imminent danger of being captured?" Jenna asked Paulette.

"No, she says that they are surrounded, but they have not yet attacked. She has one hundred-fifty fighters in the fortress, along with fifty support personnel. Most of the enemy fighters are moving out heading north towards Nuadilan and Amathon."

"Okay, tell her to keep us informed, we'll see what we can do from here," Jenna requested.

"Damn, Tegid is there!" Lilly Ann exclaimed, growing more worried about his safety by the minute. "They are headed for him!"

"Mommy, let me help. I'll contact Tegid and his people. Let Paulette handle the other communications," I volunteered. Tegid was my son from last lifetime, and I still felt responsible for him. I knew that Lilly Ann would definitely appreciate my assistance. Jenna gave me the most grateful look I'd ever seen her give anyone. Lilly Ann just hugged me.

I relaxed and made contact with Tina Fairwell, Tegid's Communicator. *Hi. Lizzy Ann or Ket Bethany here. We have a very serious problem. You are all in danger. Please link us up with Tegid and the other Guardians right away.* I had tried to put a little time into the delivery of my message to soften the impact. I sensed her growing concern as one by one Tegid, Henry, and Rosamund Blackwater were linked into us.

Hi everyone. Hi Tegid. It's me, Lizzy Ann. I have some very bad news, terrible news actually. About the Holy Paladins. Fortress Bregia just reported in that they are under siege. A whole lot of ships have brought an estimated five thousand Holy Paladins to Cymry. They've already captured Bregia. Lucinda West reports that most of their army has ridden up the north road toward you guys. I think you have maybe two days before they get to Nuadilan.

I won't repeat their wild reactions, especially Tegid's. I let them vent their surprise and anger for a time. The real question was what to do about it. I decided to make a unilateral decision without asking anyone else. Time was critical.

Look Tegid, if we had a month's notice, you could prepare. When I had to defend the towns, I had nearly six months warning that the attack was coming. You have two days.

The Grande Council of Kings should be told, and all the kingdoms can then mobilize. Together, we can drive them out, Tegid suggested.

Nice idea, but there is no time for that. Two days at most is all you have, Tegid. Two days. Once they arrive, your towns will be surrounded and there is nothing much we can do about it. You will be trapped like a rat in a box. Our whole strike force is in Solamina right now, as you know.

I want to fight them, he pleaded.

I know you do. We all know you do. Tegid, will you listen to me, please? You have to buy us time. No time to react is precisely what the Holy Paladins are counting upon. Land and strike quick like a viper, before they have any time to react. You have to buy us and everyone else on Cymry more time or everything will be lost. I tried to give him some goal to work toward in this mess.

At last he said, *What must I do?*

Several things that will require an enormous effort on your part, but I think you can do it. Let all the townsfolk know what's coming. Tell them that anyone who wishes to escape, we will help them resettle. Get Leann Finn and all her workers out of the town. Make a mad dash to the Santi Fortress at Fergus's place. Pool all your soldiers to help protect the evacuating people. Get everyone you possibly can up into the Highlands. That land is far more defensible. From there, have them travel further north and then come down to the eastern coast in Moyrath, where the Lir River meets the coast at Westonheath. That's Axeman country, and I don't think the Holy Paladins will gamble on attacking them. We will have many caravels there waiting to bring everyone safely to the mainland.

You and all the forces you can muster on such short notice hold up in Fergus's new fortress. Send out messengers to all the kings, requesting military support at once. I know they are pledged to come to your aid, but if and when remains to be seen. We will send everyone we can find over to you via that same route, from Westonheath up the Lir and through the Highlands. You simply must buy everyone some time.

Okay, that sounds like a reasonable action to take, Lizzy Ann. You know, little girl, it is very hard to be thinking of you as a little cousin making all these calls for Jenna.

Don't think of me as a little girl, son. Think of me as your pop. Get the heck out of there or I'll tan your hide! How's that? Everyone laughed.

Bring all valuables and for heaven's sake get Leann Finn and her crew of longbow makers out of there. We must not ever let the art of longbow making fall into these evil men's hands. Do I make myself clear?

Yes, pop, perfectly. We'd better get going on this. You've given us a mountain to move with only a shovel with which to do it. We dropped the connection. I then told Jenna, Adam, and the others the plan. I found out that Calgary, Mont Blanc, Velona, and d'Grange had all been notified. Their leaders were at this minute attempting to organize various strike forces with what remained of our Santi fighters and the local City Guards.

Just then, Elona came rushing in, accompanied by her Circle. "I've requisitioned all caravels that are in port that we've got that can sail immediately, well as soon as some are unloaded. I must stay here in Velona to coordinate things, but my Circle wants to go and lend a hand. However, I have some concerns that I would like to discuss with you, Jenna."

"Thanks for the ships. Go ahead ask," Jenna said, looking very haggard.

"Do you think that the Holy Paladins will come charging out of Bonilla or Vito, like they did in Pieta? Are we seeing some kind of well-coordinated series of attacks? We only have a regiment patrolling the Barcella border for Jovanna. Do we dare send more of our forces over to West Reach?"

"I simply do not know, Elona. We've heard nothing from the Vito or Bonilla fortresses that would suggest that they are massing for a counter strike in Barcella or here."

"Okay. Then, I propose to substitute our City Defense Force personnel for the Santi Fortress personnel, freeing them up to head to West Reach. That would make about two battalions worth," Elona declared. "However, if we do see a buildup or a counter strike coming, I would request that you send in as much of the returning Strike Force as is in the vicinity. My city forces are not well armored or trained to stop cavalry; they are used to defending the walls."

"You have my word on that. If there is any threat to Velona, I will put all returning forces on it, the whole Strike Force, if need be," Jenna swore.

That satisfied Elona, who then changed the subject, "Has anyone heard from Tegid? How's he holding out?"

Everyone looked at me, and I made a girlish grin, "I have. He's trying to evacuate everyone into the Highlands. I hope he can get to Fergus d'Aine's new fortress. The Highlands are much more defensible. I told him we would be bringing in forces up the Lir River and evacuating people that way too. I asked him to bring Leann Finn and all her longbow makers."

"Well, done, Lizzy Ann," Elona said, giving me a little hug.

Jenna made one request, "Alton, I think that you should stay here with Elona. I feel uncomfortable with all you Guardians leaving her alone. I know the attempts on her life happened years ago, but who knows, maybe we've a traitor somewhere in our midst. I'm personally asking you to stay behind and watch over her, please?"

"How can I refuse you Jenna? I dearly wanted to go, but you have a valid point. We barely survived that one traitor. I'll stay behind." Jenna gave him a thank you hug.

The afternoon therapy sessions were cancelled, and everyone set to work trying to work out the logistics behind such a rapid mobilization of so many disparate secondary forces. Even if we could load all the main Strike Force there in Solamina today, which we couldn't, not enough caravels were there; worse, they wouldn't be able to land at the Lir River for at least two weeks, given good winds. We had to make do with what remained, juggling security with the needed relief forces. Time, we needed time. Even if we could somehow set sail today for the Lir and Westonheath, from there, the forces would require another week to ten days to get to Fergus, there at the southern edge of the Highlands.

Around suppertime, Paulette received another communication from Lucinda. "Lucinda has just had a meeting with a Bishop Hercule Thopolos and a General Hellas Konas. She wants to replay that meeting for you." Jenna gave her the okay, and one by one, we were all Mind Linked to Lucinda in the fortress tower of Bregia.

We watched as two men, accompanied by six guards, walked up to the gates of the fortress. One wore the sky blue robes of the priesthood, the other wore the typical pieces of armor that the Centurions had always used. The taller soldier announced, "Bishop Hercule Thopolos and General Hellas Konas are here to see the Santi fortress commander." We watched as her husband, Hector Romerez, the Fortress Commander, Sue Ellen Leeds, their Healer, and Lucinda, accompanied by a group of Santi fighters walked to the gate.

"I'm Hector Romerez, Bregia Fortress Commander. How may I be of service?" he was being tensely polite. We could feel what he really wanted to say, but didn't. "What the hell are you doing?"

"I am General Hellas Konas, leader of the Second Army of Holy Paladins. We are here at the request of Bishop Hercule Thopolos. We do not have any intentions whatsoever of attacking your fortress or the Santi, which may be here on this island. Forgive what must appear to be a siege of your complex. I ordered it for the safety of my men, while they were most vulnerable unloading at the docks. I assure you that they will be removed later this evening, after the last ship has been unloaded. Ours is a mission of a religious nature, not one of conquest. Bishop," he indicated for the forty year old, rotund man to make his speech.

"Yes, religious in nature. Our Church of Jehosanity has been thriving here in West Reach for many years. However, for a long time, primarily here in Layamon, two local perversions of our Holy Religion have been upsetting our parishioners with their corrupt, vile perversions of our Blessed Scriptures. Our parishioners have repeatedly begged our Pope for some assistance in the removal of these perversions. His Holy Eminence has finally consented and sent General Hellas to see to it that these vile, perverted religious beliefs are ended."

"Specifically, here in Bregia and other nearby towns, the local shamans preach idolatry of Nature, some ancient pagan worship. This must stop and the people must learn the truth of Lord Jehosa, for their sake of their souls. Additionally, there is this Church of the Blessed Holy Mother that has sprang up a little further north of here around Nuadilan. These particularly perverted people have blasphemed our Lord and Savior, Jes Amir, the Holy Son of Lord Jehosa. These vile people are perverting this spiritual Son of God into a flesh and blood man! If that was not enough, they claim that the man was married, to a prostitute with long hair, it is said, and that they begat many children. These unholy people actually worship that supposed woman! Total heresy, total perversion. The Pope will not stand for that heresy and gross misrepresentation any longer. The perversions must be stopped. The General is here to see that it does indeed stop. I assure you that as soon as it has been stopped, the General and his men will be sailing back to Megalos."

"You realize that on this island people believe in freedom of religion, freedom to worship as they choose. Those towns may put up a fight. Their kings will undoubtedly go to war with you over this. There is a Grande Council of Kings here on West Reach. One of their founding principles is if one king is attacked, all the others will bring their armies to his defense. You may be starting a war against every kingdom on West Reach," Hector pointed out.

"Oh, I believe the Council of Kings will see reason. I have already sent a messenger to them requesting that I be allowed to address them. I see no need to fight all the kings' armies. We do not want to conquer the island, but make no mistake; we will do so, if that is what it will take to eliminate this horrid blasphemy of our Holy Religion. Anyway, I've taken up far too much of your time. I bid you good day." With that the brief conference was ended; the two men turned and left, heading back into town.

Lucinda then sent, *Since we didn't react with force, already over half of the besieging men have left. Still, we cannot leave the fortress, should we desire to. What do you make of this and what are our operating orders?*

Jenna had no immediate orders for them; just continue to monitor the situation. I went ahead and contacted Tina and replayed the lengthy message from Lucinda. I had her then set about warning all the priests of all the churches in the four towns. My advice was to have the priests leave at once. I was certain that they would be merely killed outright when the Holy Paladins took over. Tina agreed to relay the message and orders, and I broke the connection and began to eat my rather cold supper.

Adam was talking, "Two battalions from Velona is fabulous. Probably one battalion from Calgary, Southway, and Mont Blanc. Possibly one from d'Grange. Still bad odds, sixteen hundred against five thousand, and with so few Guardians and Healers. Perhaps some of us should go as well; I could lead them. I don't know whether to order the Healers back from Solamina first or as many of our crack troops. If Tegid could stall them long enough until we got everyone back, we could make a descent showing."

"Well, I stand corrected," Lilly Ann spoke up. "I was not in favor of doing a lot of recruiting, expanding our fighters as greatly as some of you wanted. I always hoped the Pope would eventually see reason. As Ket always used to say, "There is no reasoning with an insane man.""

Suddenly, I choked on a mouthful of food. The sudden Mind Link from Tina and her emotional screams took me by complete surprise. While everyone looked at me to see if I was okay, tears formed in my eyes. I blurted out, "Tegid's been assassinated! They are trying to save his life right now. Henry killed the assassin; it was one of Tegid's own captains!"

"Oh good god! No! No, not Tegid!" wailed Lilly Ann, as dismayed and shocked as I was. She had raised him from a babe as her own son.

"Damnable bastards!" cursed Adam.

"Hank, I was so afraid that something like this would happen, I should never have let him go," Jenna began crying.

"Vile swine! May an earthquake level their entire island!" swore Allan.

Beth Ann and Paulette merely began crying. Curt, Lilly Ann's youngest son now twelve, promised, "Mommy, when I get a bit older, I am going to do down there and kill that evil Pope myself! I will get us revenge for my big brother!" His little sister, Linda Sarah, just cried.

At last, Jenna asked me if Tina was still there. "No, mommy. She was so upset that she could just barely reach me. I saw that she and everyone were just covered in blood. Rosamund was bending over Tegid. She was probably trying to save him.

Beth Ann came over to my chair, "Lilly Ann, can you put me into direct contact with Rosamund please?" I agreed. One of my more useful abilities lay in the unusual manner in which my rogue telepathic capabilities operated. As long as I knew the person, I could locate them anywhere on Tarra. This time, the locating was not difficult; she was near the place we had chatted earlier. However, I knew that she must be working like mad on Tegid, and I dare not startle her. This was the gentlest mind touch that I could recall doing. Slowly she became aware that I was linking up with her. I whispered, *Lizzy Ann here. Beth Ann wants to join with you. Okay?* She agreed and I finished the link.

I was about to get a hold of you Beth Ann, but Tina's too upset right now to make the connection. You are the absolute best Healer that I know of, and I really need you here right now. Look at this. Beth Ann was now looking through the eyes of Rosamund. Since I was maintaining the link, I also saw what they were sharing. I felt the gentle tug of Paulette joining me, and shortly thereafter, Lilly Ann, Jenna, and the others, all of whom were being very quiet, mentally that is, thinking no thoughts, suppressing all emotional reactions to what they were seeing. They had to or it would have disturbed the two Healers at work.

Poor Tegid. He lay on the floor of his Great Hall, surrounded by an enormous pool of blood. Tina and Henry were grasping the arteries and veins of his left arm near his shoulder. The sword wound had all but severed his left arm from his shoulder. Only the topmost muscle still held it attached. The Healers were trying to save his arm. However, the decision had to be made, and Beth Ann had no real choice. *It has to come off if you are to save him. If only you could have somehow stopped the bleeding, we might have stood some chance, though with all the nerves cut, it would have been a useless arm. Leave as much skin there to cover it as you can. The tricky part is going to get that artery closed off. That's the first action.* At this point, the others backed out, leaving the Healers to do their work.

Quietly, everyone left the dining room, leaving me and Beth Ann to do our work without interruptions. I heard Jenna whispering, "At least he is still alive, Lilly Ann. There's still hope."

It was very late at night when we finished up. Beth Ann tucked me into bed, saying "Thanks, looks like we may have saved him." She gave me my good night kiss.

Somewhere in that dreamlike state just before waking, it came to me what we should do. At breakfast, I again made contact with Henry this time. *He's alive, barely, unconscious. Lost a lot of blood. Very iffy situation, Lizzy Ann. What else did you want to know?*

Here's what I want you to do. Pretend to the rest of the world that he is dead. You can show his arm and even bury that in a ceremony; make it convincing. Then, get him back to Fergus's fortress in secret. Continue with the mass evacuation, but make sure the priests all know that if they do not leave, they will be most certainly slain. If there is one spy, there are more. I want the enemy to believe that Tegid is dead, that their assassination plot has worked. Once Tegid is safe with Fergus, go to the Council of Kings, claiming to be Tegid's regent. Do what you can to get the various kings to commit to battling the invaders.

Clever and diabolical, for such a little girl, he praised me. *This way we will find out their full plans. I'll see to it. Leann Finn is supposed to be bringing up her many wagons this morning. I hope we have enough time to get everyone out. Contact you later.*

When I finished, I saw everyone was looking at me over the breakfast table. "Well?" Jenna prompted me.

"He's still alive, but unconscious. I'm having them pretend that he is dead, and they are going to give his arm a funeral today."

"What on earth are you doing?" mom asked. So I explained what I was having Henry do.

Lilly Ann jested, "Watch out, Jenna! You have one very sly rascal on your hands." Everyone chuckled.

I smiled. Still I wanted to know whether all this was just an excuse to get Tegid assassinated or whether it played some role in the Holy Paladin's overall plans of conquest. I was beginning to think that his assassination was more because he was the king over the four towns, which had the largest Churches of the Blessed Holy Mother in them. In fact, whoever was king there would have been assassinated was my current suspicion.

Later during the morning meeting, we received news that d'Grange had just sent several caravels over to Westonheath. By tomorrow, they would have an entire battalion ready to head up the Lir River. Most of the fighters had come from the fortress tower protection units and were not field combat ready. Still, any fighters on the ground were invaluable right now.

Later that afternoon, Tina gave us all a Mind Link view of the mass exodus. Henry had conducted the hasty funeral as planned, and many grieving people paid their last respects for their king. Tina was sitting on her horse, which was on the high ridge north of Nuadilan, she was looking back down at the town. Amathon could be seen in the far distance. Lines of people, carts, wagons, and horses trailed off as far as one could see. Near the town, I could see mounted cavalry. Henry pressed every available fighter into duty protecting the rear of the caravan from any surprise attack from the Holy Paladins. Tina estimated that over half of the towns had left. That also meant half had chosen to stick around. I feared for their safety, especially when Tina said that four priests refused to leave, but had gone underground to service their flock, as they put it.

That evening, Henry gave us a full report. The assassin had also that strange marking on his arm, an inverted number eight. The assassin had been one of Tegid's trusted captains of his guards and had used the confusion of the situation with everyone going in all directions packing, to make his fatal lunge at Tegid. The only thing that had saved Tegid's life was the split second timing and reactions that the monk had drilled into him all those years that he had been training here at the estate. Tegid had very nearly gotten out of the way of the thrust aimed at his heart, but the blade had caught the inner edge of his shoulder. Its forward motion had nearly severed his arm, however. Henry had reacted swiftly, and the assassin was dead before he could recover his footing after his mighty forward thrust.

Leann Finn and nearly fifty of her bow construction company had packed up nearly everything, and her wagons were leading the exodus. With luck, the leading wave of the evacuees would reach the Highlands tomorrow night and arrive at the d'Aine lands the next morning. Already, Fergus had sent out one hundred cavalrymen to help provide security. Another two hundred were expected tomorrow. The fortress garrison from the Santi highlands fortress had already arrived and were now with those watching the rear of the caravan, where most there were on foot, having fallen behind the riders and wagons. Still, five hundred could not stop five thousand, if the Holy Paladins chose to attack the stragglers.

I didn't believe that they would. It all depended upon what those who chose to remain in the four towns decided to do. If they opened the gates and allowed them inside, they would head for the churches, perhaps even burning them down. If they chose to barricade the gates, then they would have to assault the fortified cities. I rather hoped that would be the way it played out, for it would buy us much needed time to get our forces there.

I felt sorry for those who chose to stay. This time, there would be no Blessed Holy Miracle that would save them, as I had done before when, as Ket Bethany, I and my wife, Caitlyn, took over rulership of her towns. If they were praying for such deliverance, they would be very disappointed. I realized that that was the liability of using our "super powers." It gave the normal man, who saw these as godlike powers in action, completely false ideas. Here these townsfolk believed that they had experienced a divine miracle with that huge lightning storm so many years ago, which had ended the enemy's attack on Nuadilan.

I felt a bit guilty that I had created that effect, the Divine Miracle of Lightning, which had saved Nuadilan so many years ago. I wondered if there was anything that I could do to help them. I knew that they had worked very hard to build their new stone church, replacing the older wooden one. It was a great work of art, I thought. If they go there to burn down the churches, how could I stop them from burning this beautiful new one? Suddenly, I had an idea.

Instead of running out to play with the other kids after supper, I went over to Lilly Ann. "Can we go talk someplace in secret?" I whispered into her ear.

She gave me a grin, expecting one of our silly children's games, yet she played along. We walked over by the flowers next to the side of our building away from other's ears. "Okay, what's the big secret?" she asked.

"I need your help. It is a small thing, but you are the master of illusions; you are the Judger and I am not very good at them at all. A blue light is the best I can manage. Here's what I want to do." I whispered into her ear for a couple minutes.

"Oh you cannot do that. Oh, I see, oh, that is an awful trick to play, but you are right, it just might work. You had better not say anything about this to your mom. She might not approve, but I certainly do! When do we do it?" I now had a solid co-conspirator.

"When I go to bed tonight, I'll slip off and see if I can find their army. If I can, maybe I can guess when they will get there. When we do it, I want you here to kind of make sure I'm okay."

That night, as I let my little body drift off to sleep, I floated up and away. West Reach is only a short distance away, relatively anyway. However, when I am outside my body, my concept of spatial distances is still not so good, but this time, I noticed that it was better than it had been. Perhaps that had something to do with the therapy assist I had gotten some time ago from Jes or the Guardian of the Anuir in the Red Desert. I found Nuadilan and fought to keep all my memories from flashing through my mind, distracting me. Next, I began moving down the road from there heading toward Bregia on the coast. I was looking for a large encampment of troops. I soon discovered that it was impossible to miss. Hundreds of campfires were still smoldering; tents littered the landscape; part of a farmer's field was wiped out. My guess is that they would reach Nuadilan midmorning. Satisfied, I drifted back beside my sleeping body's head.

Next morning, I told Lilly Ann that our time would be midmorning. She said that this morning was just going to be one of coordination of reports and issuance of orders, so she could sneak out for a time. While I often sat in on mommy's meetings, this morning I told her I wanted to play outside for a while. Instead, I ducked into my room and lay back down on my bed. A little while later, Lilly Ann came in and shut the door. She said, "I told them I needed a little time for myself, upset about my son. Are you ready? What exactly do I do?"

I relaxed and shot over to Nuadilan, hovering high above it. Next, I Mind Linked Lilly Ann to me so that she could perceive all that I did. Already, the sky blue tunics were riding upon the town. As I expected, first they were completely encircling the town. I focused in on the gates. Ah, all the gates were open. That was a good sign in some ways, because those that remained behind were not intending upon starting a fight in which so many of them would be killed. Now a party of riders was heading toward the southern gates, so I zoomed in closer so that I could hear any conversation.

I recognized both the Bishop and General in this initial vanguard, surrounded by a dozen fighters. They rode in through the gates. The few people who were about mostly tried to ignore these new arrivals. The General asked directions to the six churches and received them. Now more of their soldiers began entering as well. Evidently, they were intending to hit all the churches at the same time. Interestingly enough or perhaps, I shouldn't have been surprised, the two leaders went to the huge, new stone cathedral, leaving the other five old wooden churches to his subordinates.

I stayed with the two leaders, hovering over them as they approached the magnificent building. Quickly, they all dismounted, and several men ran into the nearby rectory, where the priests and their small staff had lived. They returned saying that everyone was gone. The General began questioning several bystanders who had come to see what was going on. "Oh they all fled two days ago. Half of the town went with them."

Further interrogation yielded similar stories from nearly everyone. The only new detail was that the priests were seeking sanctuary somewhere in the Highlands, and that the Santi were promising to protect them there. The Bishop then began his well- rehearsed speech. "I am Bishop Hercule

Thopolos of the Church of Jehosanity. I have come to destroy these vile priests here who have been filling your minds with false teachings, outright lies about our Sacred Son of God, the Great Messiah. He was not of mortal flesh and he certainly did not indulge in fleshly matters. He was never married. This false woman who your blasphemous priests have said was his wife and bore his children is a total figment of their wild imaginations. She does not and never did exist. We know the truth; we have the Holy Gospels written by the hands of the Ten Disciples of the Great Messiah."

"Repeatedly our Holy Pope has asked, even begged, your priest to cease and desist from filling your minds with utter falsehoods and lies. Yet, they have not. Your foul priests have left us no choice but to burn down all of these false houses of Lord Jehosa. We will build you new, magnificent stone cathedrals in which you all will learn the Sacred Truth of Lord Jehosa that your very souls shall be allowed into Heaven, the Holy Kingdom of Lord Jehosa. Now stand aside while we torch this unholy, pagan structure."

Now, Lilly Ann.

All those standing within two hundred feet of the church, which was now at least fifty locals as well as thirty enemies, believed they heard a loud, disembodied voice speaking from the sky above them. "Touch not this Holy Cathedral of the Blessed Holy Mother."

This completely unnerved everyone. The locals began shouting prayers and thank you's toward the sky, believing once again that divine intervention was at hand. Again, the Bishop shouted, "Burn this pagan, house of Lucifer to the ground!" Several men began lighting torches, while others carried buckets of oil.

Wham! A lightning bolt slammed into the ground right before the men with the torches, causing them to drop them as they crashed into the ground. The booming voice said, "Touch not this Holy Cathedral. You have been warned!"

Suddenly, a shimmering wall of flames appeared in front of the massive oaken doors of the church. I shaped the flames into the shape of an ancient old man's face, complete with full beard. I made the flames look as if the fires were speaking. "Do not touch this church! Bishop Thopolos, dost thou not recognize the face of thy Lord Jehosa when thou dost see it?"

Many other people were running to this church now, as the flames from the other five burning churches broke the otherwise silent town. All stopped and stared at this Holy Miracle of the Burning Face there before the doors of their most precious church.

The Bishop rubbed his eyes and stared at the flames. One stupid Holy Paladin went and put his hand in the flames. Instantly, his clothing burst into flames, and he began wildly dancing about screaming in pain, while his companions tried to pat out the flames.

"But My Lord Jehosa, this vile church has been spreading blasphemy, falsehoods, and utter lies to all of these hapless villagers. It must be destroyed; your Holy Pope has so decreed. Is that not your orders to His Holiness?" The Bishop was completely confused.

I realized that at this instant in time that I had a choice to make. I could launch into a speech about the truth of their perverted religion. Probably those hearing this would believe it utterly. However, convincing only this one Bishop would not bring down the Megalos Church. They'd just excommunicate him and send in another Bishop to burn the church down. My goal was to save this building.

The booming, bass voice, at least that is what they thought they heard, said, "Dost thou consider that the stones and mortar of this Holy Church preacheth the blasphemy? Nay, the Church is but stone. Only men speaketh the words which so offendeth thee. Thy quarrel is not with the stone but with men. Taketh thy grievance unto the men, not unto this stone. For I sayeth unto you this day, this Church of the Blessed Holy Mother is sacred unto me."

"I have taken these villagers and those of the nearby three towns unto my bosom. Many of my followers worship me here. This be'st the Holy Temple that they, with their own sweat and blood, have builteth unto me and within these walls I dost dwell. Once more I sayeth unto thee, toucheth not this Holy Church. Harm it not or thee and all thy followers shall face the terrible wrath that I, Lord Jehosa, shallst bring down upon all thy churches in Megalos, beginning with your huge cathedral in Constanza City."

I purposely dropped that name, because the Bishop would not believe that anyone living here on West Reach would even know the name of their holy city in Megalos. "This House of Lord Jehosa I proclaimeth to be sacred for all time. Preacheth what thy will within these walls, but harmeth it not. Thus speaketh the Lord Jehosa." Poof! At that instant, I cancelled my flames. The Holy Image vanished, leaving only a brief after image in many eyes, but a burned image in many, many minds.

The Bishop fell to his knees and began praying. "Thy will shall be done, oh Blessed Lord Jehosa."

We didn't stick around to listen to more of his drivel. I returned to my bedroom, breaking the Mind Link. As soon as I open my eyes and sat up, Lilly Ann looked at me, and we both started laughing hysterically. It was so funny that this supposed holy man would believe such a spectacle. Yet, we both knew that no harm would come to this monument to the Blessed Holy Mother. Yes, their priests would begin indoctrinating the people there with their perversion, but in the end, such would be useless. Twice now, the people of Nuadilan had received a Holy Miracle from apparently Lord Jehosa himself. Nothing these priests would say could ever dissuade them from what they knew. She and I danced around my bedroom, laughing. At last, still chuckling, we rejoined the meeting.

Jenna, upon seeing our jovialness, asked, "What's going on you two?"

"Oh nothing, mommy. We just saved the new stone Cathedral in

Nuadilan from ever being damaged by these men from Megalos. We gave them a new Holy Miracle, nothing much."

"You did what?" her jaw dropped. Everyone in the room stopped what they were doing and stared at us. I didn't want Lilly Ann to get into trouble, so I told them all that we had done. Soon, they were laughing as well.

Lilly Ann added, "People often see what they want to see, what they expect to see, what they think they see, but seldom actually observe what they are truly seeing. Judger's rule!" She laughed again. Mommy wanted to say, "Don't you ever do anything like that again!" Her motherly instincts were kicking in, so she didn't. She knew better. Instead, she gave me a big hug and kiss.

"You all see that? Don't mess with my little girl or she'll get you good!" We all laughed once more. Then, it was back to the sober work at hand.

In the middle of the afternoon, Tina reported in to us, via Paulette. They had arrived at the new Santi fortress in d'Aine, Fergus's capital city. So far so good, Tegid's body had been secreted inside and only the Guardian Santi knew that he was still alive. However, we now knew the magnitude of the problem we were facing on the mass evacuation. Henry and Fergus estimated that close to forty thousand men, women, and children were on the move. Such huge numbers would rapidly overwhelm Fergus's ability to handle them. Jenna advised them to continue to head toward the Lir River and port town of Westonheath.

"What are we going to do with forty thousand immigrants?" Jenna asked, rubbing her arms in her hair.

After supper, Tina again contacted us. First, Tegid had regained consciousness, which the Healers took as a good sign. Second, Archdeacon Abban Rynn had come to see her. He was the elder Church of the Blessed Holy Mother.

Abban explained that most of those who were making the Holy Exodus, as he now called it, were of Juda Arad descent or had actually emigrated to West Reach from there many years ago. Some still practiced the Old Religion, as he called it, but most had adapted to the modern version as preached in his church. Long familiar with religious suppression and the Holy Paladins, these people desired to find a new location where they could begin life anew without much chance of these Megalos maniacs bothering them, a place where religious freedom could be practiced. Perhaps only a few thousand were local Layamon evacuees, such as Leann Finn and her closely-knit group of longbow makers. According to Abban, these were staunch supporters of King Tegid and the Santi. They knew they would be most likely killed or forced to work for the invaders.

Abban had asked Tina to ask Jenna if there was a place for them to relocate. Hence, Tina had forwarded this on to Jenna. This was the topic of our next morning's meeting. Allan came up with the solution. "Let's give them a large section of the Langdoc region. We have already established five fortresses long the northern edge, stretching eastward from Mont Blanc nearly fifty miles. However, there are so few people in that region, and we could let them take their pick of locations."

"Leann's group can settle in Southway, just north of Mont Blanc. There they would be protected by Southway to the north, Calgary to the west, and Mont Blanc to the south. There couldn't be a safer location."

His solution was quickly adopted, but I also saw his other reasons for resettling nearly forty thousand in the Langdoc region, more workers for the stone industry. In turn, he would have more stone for building more fortresses and towers, something Allan still passionately continued to do.

More preparations had to be made, but I went outside to play. Moving what ship where, delivering what to whom and when, these things did not interest a girl of six or me, for that matter. The cool April evening with the early blooming flowers I found more interesting. Indeed, quite a lot of the women who were still staying with us, some still receiving therapy from Jenna and me, joined me. Of the forty-seven women who had lost their arms during that massive wave of rescue operations last year, forty were still staying with us. Over half had been artists or performers. During their long recovery and training period here at the estate, a strong bond of comradery had developed among these women from the five different sectors. That evening they started the first of the Kick Ball Wars with me, forty to one were the odds. We all had a ball until it grew too dark to play.

The mid-morning report the next day was ominous. Fergus and the rear guard had at last encountered the first wave of Holy Paladins. Rather, the paladins rode up the north roads looking for the fleeing townsfolk. They found the tail end, those who had no choice but to walk on foot to escape these vicious men. However, they also found Fergus, his battalion of fighters, and a mixed battalion of fighters hastily grouped together from the four town's defense troops. The eight hundred were all mounted, and most wore chain mail armor and carried longbows as well. Arrayed two riders deep, they completely held the high ridge overlooking the road below them as the sky blue enemy riders approached and halted, surveying the situation.

Fergus signaled his bag pipers, who began the Highland War March. The nasal sounds of the pipes pierced the valley below. The paladins could not avoid hearing the tune. At the same time, Fergus gave the signal for the archers to notch arrows. Eight hundred men drew back their bows, pointing them at a forty-five degree angle upwards. Fergus measured the distance the night before, the enemy was now at the extreme range of the bows. If they charged his position, he wanted to have the opportunity to get off a large number of volleys before he ordered his men to charge down the hill into a deadly melee.

His move worked; the paladins halted their long column. Presently, three riders began riding forward; one carried a white flag. Fergus signaled his men to lower their bows. Taking three companions, he rode down the hill to meet their parley. He rode up to them, bagpipes still playing.

"We are looking for a number of evil priests who preached vile blasphemy at the disgraceful Church of the Blessed Holy Mother. These priests are wanted by the Holy Church of Jehosanity of Megalos for high crimes against our religion. Said priests have fled the four towns behind us. We have reason to believe that they are among those people ahead of us. Let us pass; we have no quarrel with you, only the wicked priests."

"I am King Fergus d'Aine and my kingdom starts here, laddie. I have given those honorable, worthy priests temporary sanctuary in my fortress. You are not welcome here. Go back the way ya came. You'll not be allowed into the Highlands. While you're at it, laddies, take your foul, evil, perversion of Jehosanity with yea. Tis not welcome 'ere," Fergus said in his thick Highlander accent.

"You'll regret this," the Holy Paladin captain threatened.

"Not as much as yea will laddie if yea takes one more foot into my kingdom!" Fergus retorted. "Many of my fine young laddies here are veterans of the Line. We fought against your foul Emperor Justinian and soundly defeated his mighty legions. Your fighters pale in comparison to those of Justinian. Bring them on, and yea'll get a good taste of Highlander steel, the finest in all the lands." Fergus was just edging him on, hoping for a fight. However, the captain thought better of it. He had perhaps only a thousand men behind him, not good odds, especially since Fergus had the high ground and the archers. He wheeled his horse around and ordered his men to return the way that they had come. Fergus commented, "Well, laddies, I guess there'll be no fighting today. I was sure hoping he'd 'a started something!" He rode back up to the top of the ridge line.

Late in the day, a dispatch rider found Fergus. The message called for a meeting of all the kings in Brea, the Grande Council of Kings. The Bishop wanted to address them three days from now. Henry would go along with Fergus and represent King Tegid's four cities, which meant that Henry would have two votes instead of just one. Although the d'Aine forces kept watch at the edge of his kingdom, the Holy Paladins did not attempt to enter it. However, a small party with the Bishop was allowed to pass, but were accompanied all the way to Brea, where the council met.

This year, the leader of the Council was King Cathal of a small southern Layamon kingdom. He called the meeting to order and allowed the Bishop to speak to all the assembled kings. The Bishop gave his predictable speech, detailing the many blasphemes, lies, and falsehoods that these local priests had committed. "I say unto all of you mighty kings, we are not trying to conquer a single kingdom here in West Reach. We are only after stomping out the heathen, pagan worship of this pretentious whore. We will not attack any of your soldiers, unless we are attacked first. We will only then defend ourselves."

King Lachlan Laird, the founder of this council, spoke up. "Many of the older ones here actually knew the Blessed Holy Mother and her children. Many have seen with their own eyes the miracles she performed. Then, there was the Holy Deliverance Miracle when Nuadilan was about to be overrun by two armies from the south. I say that what you are saying is the falsehoods, so it must be that you are the liars."

"Ah good king," the Bishop hated women in power. However, he tried not to sneer at her. "Any woman can come into a village and claim to be the wife of the Great Messiah. What was her proof? How can a purely spiritual being have relations with a fleshy woman? Nay, it cannot be. Did you ask for proof of her claims? I think not. Perhaps she cast a pagan charm upon all of you, enchanting you to believe her. Who can say? Certainly not I."

King Cathal asked, "And you swear that your men are not going to harm anyone but these aforementioned priests of the Blessed Holy Mother?"

"I so swear. That is our sole purpose for coming to West Reach. We will leave as soon as we can guarantee that these wicked men are not allowed back to resume preaching their evil messages. We do not want to start a war with any of you, just these vile priests who have been continually perverting our religion, selling your souls to the devil Lucifer, nothing more."

Cathal, concluding that the Bishop had finished, asked him to step outside, while the council deliberated. "It is clear that they are not starting a war with anyone of us. I say we let them be. Once they have left West Reach, our priests can then do as they please."

Henry fumed, "You don't know these vicious men! They routinely cut off women's arms just because the women will not go along with their perversions. Once you let them stay on Cymry, believe me, they will not leave! You have this one chance to unite and throw them off the island."

"Aye, laddies, he's right," Fergus spoke up. "These men, especially their priests, cannot be trusted. Nay, they say and promise one thing, but do the opposite. Their own pope swore that they would stop mutilating women. Yet, they continued to do so in secret using diabolical torture mechanisms. I got them stopped at my borders. I say we unite and drive them back into the sea."

The kings argued for over an hour. Since these Holy Paladins were not in most of the kingdoms, the final vote was 23 to 10 in favor of allowing the Bishop to finish his work and then leave. Henry and Fergus were fuming over the decision, with some talk of pulling out of the Grande Council of Kings entirely.

On their way out, King Lachlan Laird took the two aside, "May I have a private word with thee?" She took them into a side room where they could not be overheard. "I know that we have not always seen eye to eye. Indeed, the Magician did not trust me; perhaps he had the right to do so. Yet, I am ever a seer. I am the bearer of the Sacred Talisman, given to visions of the future. I voted with you to save the Grande Council of Kings. We have failed. You are right. They will never leave. Like a wild turkey, they will begin to gobble us up, one kingdom after another."

"I and several other kings are behind you. I ask you plainly, can you muster enough army to defeat these vile men and throw them into the sea? If so, I will join with every soldier I have in my kingdom."

Henry answered her, "Truthfully, King Laird, at this time, the Santi has nearly all of its main army away in Solamina, where they have just defeated an army of many thousands of these Holy Paladins from Pieta. It will take months to get them all back over here, assuming that we can even find a port, which will let us disembark. We have a battalion down by the Lir waiting to assist the evacuees. Several more are en route to provide security. As I said, these are garrison troops, not our main fighters."

"It is as the vision showed, then. We are doomed. Answer me this, is it also true that they have been cutting off the arms of women in the Sea Princes?"

"Unfortunately that is so. Jenna, our Supreme Commander, still has some forty-seven women staying with her that are recuperating still. Many others, she has found new homes for in other places. Yes, it is horribly true, very sad, particularly because so many of these fine women were noted artists, painters, sculptors, even performers. Very sad indeed," Henry explained.

"Again, the visions do not lie. Then, today marks the beginning of the end for us on Cymry. Before you go, I have a box that I wish you to take to Jenna. Can she read our language or does she have someone who can do so? I am sending along a message for her."

"Yes, I believe that her daughter can read your language."

"Good. There is one final thing that I need from you. Here, this is our Sacred Talisman, handed down from the dawn of time to the Seer chosen to lead our people. In the not so distant future, my kingdom will come unto utter ruin. The unending line of Seers will end with me. This talisman must under no circumstances ever, I do mean ever, fall into the hands of those from Megalos! You will know the time of our destruction. At that time, go to the Standing Stones, Fergus knows the place of which I speak. There, when the moon is full and rising, the stones will guide you to the talisman. Take it; keep it safe at Mont Blanc. My visions show that you have much of great value hidden away there in underground caves. One distant day, one of our children will come seeking it, give it to him or her. Will you do this for our people?"

"Yes, King Laird. You have the sworn word of the Santi. We will do this thing for you," Henry swore before her. It was the only honorable thing to do, he later explained to Jenna.

"Thank you sir. If you will follow me, I have a heavy box for you to take to Jenna for me." They followed her through several hallways and into her throne room. Beside her beautifully carved throne lay a well-made box about three feet in length and width, two high. "Here is the key to give to Jenna. Please do not open it until she is present." She handed Henry the key.

It was a heavy box indeed. Both men were required to carry it outside to their horses. King Laird loaned Fergus a packhorse with a special saddle on which to attach the box securely. She waved farewell to the two as they rode off, accompanied by several of his men-at-arms. King Laird knew that she would never see them again. She sighed; her visions had never yet been wrong, though now, she dearly wished it could be so. Nearly a month later, she received a letter from Jenna, thanking her profusely and promising her that they would do as Henry had promised her. It was personally signed by Jenna, in her large, crude letters. It was also signed by many others in various writing styles that brought tears to King Lachlan Laird. She knew of those who had signed this letter. She treasured it more than her kingdom, which she knew was doomed.

"Well, laddie, tis just us," Fergus commented to Henry as they rode home to the d'Aine kingdom. "I'm sure thankful that you Santi built one of your fortress complexes near my castle! We may yet be standing alone against all these vile cowardly men."

"Aye, that we may be. Yet, we have allies, King Fergus. We are not as alone as you might think. We should be joining the exodus I think, bringing up the rear."

"My men will flank far and wide across the Highlands. If they try to do an end run to get around d'Aine, we'll give you plenty of warning."

"Thanks, I think the d'Grange Battalion ought to be nearing the front of this incredibly long line of evacuees. I wish it had not come to this, however."

"Aye, laddie, tis a sad day in the Highlands."

With the threat of war now unlikely, our efforts became one of resettlement of the forty thousand people. Yes, it was a massive effort to get so many ferried across the waters from West Reach to Calgary. A month was needed to accomplish the task. As expected, Leann Finn and around two hundred of her associates fell in love with the Greenway and settled in a southernmost village called Backwater, only twenty miles from Mont Blanc. Here she set up her longbow factory, only on an even grander scale.

The vast majority moved out into the Langdoc region. This sparsely settled region was ideal for these Arad descendants who, with our help, began forming villages. However, their spiritual leader, Archdeacon Abban Rynn, spent many, many hours discussing private plans with Allan, before they actually picked the locations of their new settlements. Allan would not share their private discussions with us, however. "All in good time," he continually replied. Not even his wife, Beth Ann could get him to say more. This was a mystery that we would have to wait to unravel.

On the last day of October, Henry arrived at our estate bearing Tegid, who was very much alive and on the mend. I noticed right away a huge change in his personality, his manners. Gone was all his enthusiasm for life. Gone was his fun-loving vigor. I could not even get him to play ball with me. Mostly, he just moped in his room. At last, Jenna insisted that he allow her to use her therapy on him. "What's the bloody use, Aunt Jenna? I'm mostly useless for life. I should have listened to you. Now I've lost my kingdom, my brother's kingdom, and my arm. It's pretty damn pointless."

While others tried to coax him out of this mood, Jenna didn't bother, saying only, "Okay, Tegid, I do understand. Now here's what I want you to do." She was off and running. He'd been unconscious for nearly three days, so it took a considerable time to go completely through this trauma, uncovering every small detail, all the pain, all the unconsciousness. As Jenna expected, once he had thoroughly discovered the entire trauma, his attitude had not changed much. She asked him if he had an earlier image of some similar trauma in his mind. After some coaching, he found it.

Another day later and I had my son back. Tegid came laughing from his room. He found me, picked me up with his one arm, and spun me around in circles. To this day, I don't know what he found in therapy. Jenna would not betray his confidence. All I cared was that the old Tegid was back. He then decided that he would be called King Diget I. The forty thousand who he had ruled cheered wildly when King Diget I returned to their new villages, bringing with him a small army to aid in their defense. These people knew firsthand what keeping your mouths shut meant; his secret ancestry would be safe with them.

At last, Jenna had time to examine the very heavy box from King Laird. Of course, she had Hank open the lock for her. We all were standing around waiting to see, especially me, a very curious six year old girl. Inside were wedged into tight stacks gold coins with a central smaller box that contained a pouch of gemstones. A letter lay on top of the pile. When it was counted and the value of the gems estimated, the box contained nearly five hundred thousand gold coins worth!

I read the letter to Jenna.

Dearest Jenna Rose Weston,

My kingdom is ending. The visions have never been wrong. The Grande Council of Kings failed to act. Hence, our doom is at hand, fast approaching.

However, I know that there is Good in this world. In my visions I have seen what I believe to be you, a victim yourself, helping all these women from the Sea Princes who have lost their limbs, providing them a sanctuary from the world in which they can survive. I verified my visions with one of your Guardians who used to be with the King of Nuadilan. After I knew the true situation that so many women are facing, I myself tried to imagine life the way that they have no choice but to live. I was mortified beyond words. It seems to me that you must be a Heavenly Goddess from the Annwn visiting here upon Tarra.

With my kingdom facing its death here shortly, I have decided to set up an endowment fund in memory of our kingdom of Brea, Ruadan. The box contains the entire accumulated wealth of Brea. It is given unto you for the sole purpose of providing lifetime support and care for all the women who come unto you for their survival. While they may no longer have arms, hands, or whatever, they shall not want for anything else. The funds are yours to use as you deem appropriate for their care.

Please share this letter with these women. I, King Lachlan Laird, wish each one of them to know that there are still decent, honorable, caring, loving people on Tarra. I wish that I could do more, but time will not allow it, as I must now ride our kingdom into its extinction.

You all have my fondest love and highest respect,

King Lachlan Laid, Brea, Ruaden, Cymry

When I finished reading it, Jenna was crying, so were many others. While I still blamed Lachlan for inciting the two kings into attacking Nuadilan when I was their king, this side of her I had never seen before. Her generosity was unparalleled. Jenna immediately sent for all the women still here under her wing, so to speak. One by one, they all filed into the room, gaping, gasping at the contents of the box. They too cried after I finished reading them the letter. Jenna insisted on dictating a thank you letter immediately. I wrote what she wanted said, translating it into the Highlander dialect. When I finished and read it back to her and she was satisfied, she insisted on personally signing the letter. Many were still crying as they watched her fumble to make the large, blocky letters of her name. Each one of the other women insisted on adding their names at the bottom. I helped them as much as possible to manipulate the quill.

November 642, brought some quiet time and only one crisis. Now that I was seven, I decided to ask mom what I had wanted to learn for these last seven years: how do you move objects without using your body? She and I were alone in the kitchen, and the day was done, but we both wanted some hot chocolate brought up from the Spice Islands in the distant southern waters off the coast of the Southlands. I decided now was the time to ask her.

"Mommy, I'm old enough to get some training. I'm seven."

She looked at me rather surprised and said, "Why, so you are. My how does time fly around here. Yes, but you already know most everything. As far as I am aware, Lizzy Ann, you remember all your skills. Have you forgotten something?"

"No, mommy. I remember everything just fine, but there is one new skill I really, really, want to learn how to do." I used my little kid smile and pleading eyes. How could anyone resist?

"What is it that you want to really want to know? How to cast the Judger spells that Lilly Ann knows, perhaps?" She was wracking her mind for what it was that I might desire to learn.

"Mommy, I want to learn how to move things like you do, without using your body. After all, you are the only one who knows how to do it. I want to be the second person who can do it. Please mommy, I'll work very hard at it. I'll do everything you tell me to do, please mommy."

"Ah ha, so it was you who were peeking in my mind when I thought no one was around and was moving things. I thought so, but I never was sure of it."

"Well, yes, I thought if I saw how you did it, then I could do it too."

"It didn't work, did it?"

"No, I don't understand why, though."

"It is a skill that a spiritual being can do. Jes Amir taught it to me, but only after I had faced up to the real reason that I stopped myself from doing that kind of thing. If you are unable just to do it, then my opinion is that you probably think that you have a good reason not to be able to move things without a body. Nevertheless, I think that we ought to try it and see what happens, but you must promise me that if we don't succeed, you will not be terribly upset with yourself. It took all the skill of Jes to get me to undo my decisions that I made so long ago never to do it again. It may be that you will have to learn it from him."

I was so excited that I could hardly sleep that night. For the next few weeks, we trained in the afternoon, which was when the therapy sessions had been held. Since we had exhausted our patients for now, it was prime time for me. We started out small. "See that tiny dust mote there on the table. Look sideways; catch it in the sunlight. Yes, that spec. That is what we want to move. Now I want you to decide to move it over to here. Let me know when you have made the decision." I did. "Okay, now go ahead and move it."

I strained every muscle in my body trying to get it to move. It did not budge. Suddenly, I began laughing, realizing what I was doing. I was still holding onto my little body and somehow trying to work through it to get it to move. I floated out and over the dust mote and looked down upon it. "Yes, that's a better position," mom said. "Now go ahead and decide to move it and then move it."

Still nothing happened, except I had the strangest feeling coming over me. It was as if I knew that I should be able to move it, but was holding back for some unknown reason. The harder I tied, the more I felt this strange sensation. I tried for an hour to no avail, except now I had some kind of greyish mental mass building up all around me. I was ready to give it up as impossible. "I just better not do it, mommy," I said dejectedly. Jenna looked at me with her stern face. "What?" I asked her.

"Where did that remark come from?" she asked without answering me.

"I just better not do it?"

"Yes."

"Oh, oh!" I realized it was connected with or coming from this greyish mental mass that was all around me. "I see something grey." I replied. That was all Jenna needed. We were off and running, so to speak. Next thing I knew, there I was smack dab in the middle of a bloody execution! "I'm someplace that has grey stone walls, giant castles with neat looking pinnacles rising into the orange sky. Weird looking. I'm being brought up to the castle. I'm in a cage on wheels. Everyone is jeering me. I think they think I did something bad somehow. I see someone looking out of a tower window, down on me. I think I know him. I think it is my brother. Why is he doing this to me? They are chopping my head off! Then, all goes black and I float away."

She had me go back over it several more times. Slowly, I began piecing the events together. Our father was the king, but he just died. My brother was first in line and would have gotten the throne, but I was more popular than he was. On the other hand, he had control over the army. "His eyes meet mine as he looks down on me, as if to say, 'So long, it's all mine now.' As they are chopping my head off, I realize what he is doing. I get very angry just as the axe is falling. I pick up the head, which is bouncing over the cobblestones. I hold it high in the air. Then I'm swinging it around, poking its face into the executioner's face. He is freaking out. I dance it about all the spectators' faces too. I'm enjoying this. I am flying the head up to my brother's window now. He goes crazy, flailing his arms wildly. I see my lovely sister there. I didn't see her before. She looks terrified. I'm frightening her something awful. She is panicking and jumps from the window. Oh, good god no! I watch her fall and see the awful bloody mess on the ground below me. I feel horribly guilty. I don't mean to harm her. I swear to myself. I'd better not do it again. I let the head fall and smash into the ground. I'd better not do it again!" I began laughing. "I'd better not do it again." I laughed even harder now. That ended this day's session.

The next day, when mommy asked me to move the dust speck, by golly, it moved! Yes, I was thrilled. Gradually, she kept on making the objects larger. I could move one tiny grain of sand. Now I knew I was getting somewhere with this. Next, she put a small pebble on the table, asked me to decide to move it, and then move it. This was much harder! The more I worked at it, the more difficult it became. I was not noticing it, but that black energy mass, which used to cause me to go insane when I let loose a huge volley of lightning bolts in a dire emergency, had activated once again! Suddenly I couldn't see anything except blackness and that pebble. Using all my will power, I commanded it to move. What happened next I found out later.

According to Lilly Ann and Beth Ann, who came running when they heard Jenna yelling, chairs were flying in all directions. They each managed to catch the oil lamps that went flying in their direction. The bed was attempting to make an unscheduled flight across the room, but Jenna was holding it against my violent attempts at throwing it wildly around the room. Jenna asked, "See if you can snap Lizzy Ann out of whatever she is in. I have to keep the bed from flying around." Both women began shaking my small body, to no avail. Finally, in a panic, Lilly Ann gave me a sharp slap across my face. The sting reached me at last. I felt something besides this mass of blackness. I opened my eyes, and the whirlwind died down.

"Mommy, I'm scared," I said, more than a little frightened. I had just done it again, gone temporarily insane as far as the world was concerned, locked into my own frightening memories, which I could not see, just the blackness of it all.

"Are you all right, Lizzy Ann?" Lilly Ann asked very worried about me. Beth Ann immediately gave my body a thorough examination, in case I had somehow injured myself.

"I'm okay, just scared," I said meekly, figuring this would be the end of my training.

"What the heck just happened, Jenna?" she asked, not getting a satisfactory reply from me.

"We are in a training session. It appears that the training has brought the real reason that Lizzy Ann cannot do what she desires into focus. It has made its presence known, rather dramatically, don't you think?"

"Yes, but what training?"

"Moving things like I do," Jenna replied.

"Whoa, that is far too dangerous a thing for me!" declared Lilly Ann. Beth Ann agreed with her twin sister.

"We need to continue, but I can see that we are going to need to use a different room, one that doesn't have anything in it. Let's see; come on Lizzy Ann, I know just the room." I followed her meekly. The twins followed me into an empty room, which had at one time been used as a bedroom. However, no longer needed, its contents had been moved elsewhere. Jenna had Beth Ann bring a blanket from the infirmary and spread it out on the floor for me to sit on.

"There now, this time there is nothing that she can throw around, I hope. You two are welcome to stay and watch. It might be a good idea, because we are in for a tough one here." After making sure that I was comfortable, she had me find where this thing with the black mass started or began. I had no idea, but gave it my best shot. As I re-contacted the blackness, once more it took over control of me, I began screaming over and over, "I'm insane!" at the top of my lungs, which must have startled the entire estate, because soon a number of others came to see if everything was all right.

She had me go through it repeatedly, without much luck, other than my screaming subsided to yell of "I'm insane." I was literally surrounded, encased within the black mass; I felt as if I were truly insane. On the tenth time thorough it, I saw a flash of a picture before the blackness came over me. I realized something vitally critical about this whole blackness thing: it was a lie! "Mommy, it's a lie; that's why it has gone black on me. It's not the truth! I saw something for a second in it, so it's not all black."

"Very good, honey. Now let's go back to the beginning of it one more time."

"I'm not behaving the way they want. There are three physicians there, no mind physicians, not real healers. They come at me with this needle that is somehow hollow and attached to this vial of greenish stuff. They poke me in my arm, and the stuff goes into me. I begin to feel funny, weak. I know they are turning me into one of the mindless zombie women I've seen around this place. I protest and try to move my body, but it is becoming almost numb! I am trying to scream but my body doesn't work anymore; it just lies there. I am above it, I get really, really, really mad at them for doing this to me. I began picking up chairs and smashing them against the walls. I am throwing everything in the room around like mad. They are screaming, 'She's gone insane. She's insane. There is nothing we can do for her now. She's just insane.' I smash everything in the room into small pieces. Oh, then I grab the three men who did this to me and threw them into the walls, over and over and over. Blood is everywhere, covering everything. While I am pulverizing them, some man comes in and cuts my body's throat. 'She's insane. Nothing can be done for her. She's just insane,' he says. I agree with him cause I suddenly see everything in the room all broken into little pieces; their heads are not recognizable anymore. I must be insane. I cannot control myself anymore. Then, it all goes black, and I float away."

Mommy said, "Very well done, Lizzy Ann. Now, let's go back to the beginning of it once more." We were off running through it again. Each time I went through it, describing all the details, I found more little things becoming clearer to me.

"You know, mommy, every time I've been in a situation where I see everyone around me trying to kill me or my friends, this thing somehow triggers. All those times when I went temporarily insane with the lightning bolts, this was lying there behind it, but I couldn't see it. It was just one big black mass."

Mom just said, "Very good observation. Now let's go through it one more time."

I got about half way through it and started laughing. "Oh I meant to do what I did all right! I created just the effect I desired. It's just after that I denied having done it. 'Oh I'm just insane.' What a good excuse for my behavior! Only after I denied what I'd done did it all go black on me. Isn't that interesting?" I laughed long and hard over this bit of silliness. Naturally, mom ended the session for today.

The next day marked the beginning of the renewal of my spiritual ability to move things. Mom began small, moving a rock about the table and up in the air. Now I saw that it was just drill. She insisted on my developing pinpoint accuracy with my placement of objects. After another week, I could balance a plate on the end of a darning needle! The next week we worked on larger and heavier objects, until I could lift our carriage, spin it around, and placed it precisely where I wanted it located. The next week, she had Allan bring in one of the heavy stone blocks that had arrived from the Langdoc stone quarry. It was destined to be shipped out along with the rest of the blocks on their way to Barcella. By the end of the week, I was whipping that block all around the grassy knoll, standing it on its edge, and generally having fun with it.

During this last week with the stone block, I had many observers peeking at me from inside the warm building. It's not every day one sees flying stone blocks doing a dance. I think everyone in the estate saw me at one time or another during the week. At the end of the week, mom gave me my final pass on the subject. She explained, "It is now just a matter of drill. I don't think there is any limit on how large or heavy an object can be. If it is heavier than this stone, you might need to drill some before you master its total control." I couldn't imagine anything larger or heavier, so I was satisfied.

"Now there are two of us who can move things, mommy! Isn't that just grand?"

"Yes, dear, but what did you have in mind moving?"

That took me by surprise. I honestly didn't have an answer for that one. I'd only wanted the ability. Now that I had it, what was I going to do with it? I figured time would tell.

A week later, we received news from Isla Roca that Helas Taxos had completed his education in how to tell if an action was harmful or not, based upon the good it would do to the Seven Aspects of Life. Now I had to live up to my promise to him. Further some two hundred or so other prisoners had also arrived at the point in time where their next step was to begin to make amends. Jenna had a new problem for us to solve: how to handle their many amends projects.

Ideas were few in coming at our meeting. Several hours later, Allan came up with an idea. "Look, most of these men were fighters, strong, able bodied workers. Most of their crimes were against the population of the sector in which they were stationed, not so much against an individual person. Perhaps their amends project could be doing something to benefit the whole sector. If you concur with this idea, then I have just the projects for them to do." We had no objection, so Allan outlined his plan. "One of the biggest barriers to expansion in the sectors is their infernal road system, spoke and rim roads. It makes transporting of goods awkward and inconvenient, unless it is solely to and from the main city. I propose that we have them build a new, more logical road system here in Velona, a grid system."

"We could house them here under guard; we have more than enough Santi to keep them from attempting to escape or worse. Finally, Velona could have a better system of travel throughout the whole sector. If it works out and becomes popular, then we can propose similar new road systems for the other less populated sectors. The new roads will open up more country for settlement, perhaps easing the crowding in Velona proper. Of course, we would need to discuss this proposal with Elona Po first."

A week later, several caravels brought some two hundred prisoners from Isla Roca to our estate, where they were housed in a secure section under a very heavy watch. During the next two years, they built a paved road that ran from the northernmost fortress along the Barcella border straight down the line, connecting all the other fortresses and ending at the Centurion made coastal road. Four other north-south roads were built at approximately twenty-mile intervals apart, skipping the already existing north-south spoke road coming from Velona. Next, three cross roads were built running the width of the sector, all going nearly straight east-west. One by one, ten new towns sprang up at some of these intersections.

When the crews finished the project, all two hundred and six petitions to be allowed back into society were approved. Further, they knew that they couldn't return to Megalos and chose instead to continue their road constructions. Jovanna needed new roads, and the whole bunch began to build similar roads in Barcella, only now they were paid for their labors and were welcomed wherever they went, known as the Master Road Builder Crews. Interestingly enough, five years later, these same men were rather well off financially, at least twenty times better paid than when they had been Holy Paladins.

When the caravels arrived with these men, one was Helas Taxos. He was brought to the manor house for therapy sessions. Mom had six guards standing just outside the empty bedroom in which I worked with the general. I looked at Helas for the first time. I saw a thin, gaunt shell of a man. He had lost weight; the nightmares still plagued him, though they were now far less severe. "We meet at last, general, or should I call you Helas?"

"Helas, please. Calling me general reminds me constantly of, well, you know, all that I have done. You are so young."

"Body is. I'm not. Now let me read your extensive writeup here. You've listed out all the specific harmful actions you can recall doing?"

"Yes, all that I can remember doing. I'm ashamed that there have been so many. Yet, I have been feeling a lot better since I wrote them down as I was instructed by Father James. The nightmares have lessened since then. You can read them?"

"Yes, I am fairly fluent in your language, Helas. Give me a few minutes to read this many pages so I'm more familiar with you." He waited patiently, but I noticed that he had both fingers crossed. He knew this was his one and only chance to ever be rid of his insane nightmares. He had been working toward this meeting for several years now. Helas hoped against all hope that he could be cured.

"Okay, I've looked these over, Helas. Thank you for having disclosed them. Now then, shall we begin?" He was more than ready. "I want you to close your eyes and return to the time when you first began to rape the young maiden, Ariana." We were off and running through a lengthy series of rapes. He found that he had extremely vivid mental images of them. I did not expect these to erase, however, because he was not the one experiencing trauma, rather he was the perpetrator. After two runs through, I asked him if there was an earlier time something like this had happened.

What a wonderful thing for a young girl to be running out of another — a long chain of rapes! Ah well, I kept doggedly at it. The second day of running out the many times this man had forced himself off on others, he finally replied, "Well, that was the last one. That was the first time I bedded a woman." His idea was "now that's all handled."

However, since nothing had yet erased and he was not cheerful, I asked, "Take a look, and see if there is an earlier time something like this happened." It took a good deal of prodding and coaxing, but finally he said that he saw some tiny, little image, surrounded of course with a lot of blackness and that it probably wasn't real anyway.

Two hours later, it was really real to Helas! He had been a young woman who had been repeatedly raped, beaten, and had later died from the infections given to her from the brutal men. For most of that time, he thought he must have been one of the men doing the raping. It came as a total shock to him finally to realize he was the woman! Unfortunately, while he did a tremendous amount of yawning, the traumas did not erase; he was not yet cheerful: shocked, yes, cheerful, no.

The next day we found an earlier one. Nearly a century ago, he had been a Centurion commander during the invasion of Zargarb. He had vivid images of that famous battle where a few hundred Sisterhood women, led by Isabel, had withstood and halted the advancing Centurion army, the only ones to prove effective in combat against them at that time. These women had killed nearly his entire legion, before they finally captured the last standing woman, Isabel. His general had ordered her hands cut off so that she could never fight them again. He had been the one who did the deed, had followed orders, and had raped her several times, before leaving her to die on the mound of dead bodies. My own memories of our rescue of Isabel came back to me. Here was the man who had done that horrible deed to her!

Now I could see now how vital this therapy was! He had not gotten this handled back then, and here he was nearly a century later still doing similar actions!

I swore to myself that I would see this one to its very end! We spent a day working this incident. It reduced in intensity somewhat, so I asked for yet another earlier one. Then, I hit pay dirt, so to speak! He found a small image of a woman, and we began to run through it, re-experiencing all that had gone on in this one. Almost at once, he began shaking and fidgeting, and then he began screaming loudly. After a few minutes, he began crying and then passed out for some time. As Jenna had, I kept asking, "Okay, then what happens?"

Eventually, the unconsciousness passed by, and he continued to move through it to the very end. After a couple more passes, it began to make sense to me. "I am a young woman with long, lovely hands. I was rather obsessed with my hands, long nails, and rings on each finger. Nobleman's daughter, I think. Dad wants me to marry this pig of a man. I refuse. He tries to kiss me, and I gouge his eyes out. Dad curses me; everyone's against me. Next day, an army of men shows up, kills my father, and are coming for me. Everyone is now against me. I lock myself in my bedroom. They smash my door down and come after me. Dozens of them; everyone is against me. They tie me up to my bed, spread eagle. I am screaming and screaming, but that only makes them do it harder to me. Leave me alone, I cry out. Everyone is against me. We're going to teach you to put a man's eyes out, bitch, they are saying to me."

"They wave this knife in front of me now. They are going to cut off my hands! No, I scream and scream, not my lovely hands! Anything but them, I beg and plead, but everyone is against me. Whack them off, boys, one attacker says. It's as if I am in my hands, somehow trying to protect them. I screamed at the top of my lungs; the pain is so horrible! Too horrible to bear. Then I'm in my hands; somehow I move into them, and the pain is gone. I move my hands. I can move them! There is my body up there lying on the bed, half-naked, and bleeding profusely onto the bed and floor. I'm not in it. I'm in my hands on the floor! I'm going to get even with them, and I make my hands go for them, fingers crawling across the marble floor. They are spooked and run out of the room, but I keep on moving my hands slowly across the floor. I'm going to strangle them as soon as I can catch them. They are all against me. I cannot get to them. I cannot move my fingers fast enough. I finally gave up. There is nothing I can do. I've lost everything. Everyone is against me. I float up and out of my window. Oh, I am bringing my hands with me. I am still connected to them! I see the man who chopped them off down below. I drop my hands down on him and begin to choke him. I'm doing it! I am actually choking the man who did this to me! I did it! I got even with him. His eyes! Terror beyond all terror in them. Serves him right. He dies, but cannot make a sound! I drift up into the sky."

Helas stopped yawning now and began laughing. "I did it. I actually did it. Everyone was against me, but I did do it! I did it to her Ariana. I knew I did it, so she could do it to me. Oh god! No wonder I was spooked!" He roared with laughter, "I did it. I did it. Me, I did it." He continued to laugh even harder. "Oh god! I am a spirit! I can see the back of my head!" I noted that Helas was now sitting about a foot behind his head looking at it. Interesting, I thought.

Quietly, when I got a chance, I said, "Thank you, Helas. That's all for today."

He, of course, continued to laugh and added, "Sure, sure, but I did do it. I've been doing it to myself too! All along!"

The general got a solid night's sleep that night with no trace of his nightmares. No further trace of them ever appeared after that. I decided that his therapy was done, as far as I was concerned. We'd eliminated the nightmares and perhaps a lot of his insane urges to harm women. Mission accomplished. Only now what do we do with him? That was the next problem. How was he going to make amends, particularly to Ariana and the other women he had indirectly harmed in Zargarb?

Helas helped us with this one. He requested that he be allowed to work heavy construction on all the various Laird Art Foundation projects. This he dutifully did until the twin palaces where finished. Thus, in a small way, he helped build the facilities for all the women who had been so mistreated by his church. What surprised me the most was all during that time, he studied all the religious documents he could find, including copies of the recently published Ten Gospels of the Disciples of the Great Messiah. When he at last had his re-entrance into society approved, he became a minister in the Velona clergy, accepting only the lowliest posts in the poorest parts of town. He spent the remaining years of his life trying to convince others of their spirituality. He'd seen what he actually was and wanted others to realize just who and what they were.

Thus, we had at last proven that our new method of handling those who are causing harm actually worked. We were able to rehabilitate them, no small feat in my opinion.

Chapter 24 A Whimper, Not a Bang

During the early winter of 642, the Holy Paladins began making their stronghold moves, beginning with Nuadilan. Our fortress in Bregia kept us notified of all incoming traffic. Indeed more boatloads of Megalos people arrived, priests, a few head nuns, and a number of scholastic teachers. Shortly after their arrival, Bishop Thopolos posted a public notice all over Nuadilan. In effect, it said that everyone must attend Sunday Services or suffer punishment. Their operation had become more sophisticated. Each person attending received a token as they entered. At tax time in the fall, each person turned in their tokens. If they were short more than a few, their taxes were ten gold coins, whereas everyone else paid only one.

I thought this was an improvement. It was better than beating the non-attenders or cutting off their appendages. Slowly, they expanded the towns in which enforced attendance was mandatory. The expansion was based upon the arrival of sufficient numbers of priests.

In Nuadilan, our old hilltop fortress was turned into a religious center. Here the Scholastic University was established, again with enforced attendance of all children less than twelve years of age. The Bishop launched a program to get more single women to join their Holy Nuns, under the pretext of helping and aiding others who were less fortunate.

By late spring 643, the entire Layamon region was under the thumb of their control, having slowly encroached into the other kingdoms. Interestingly, they did not venture north of the Danaes River into Tewdwr region, because they could not master the thick accent these people spoke. Besides, they didn't find anything there of much value, just a lot of coastal fishermen. They did not venture into the dense forests of the Moyrath zone on the eastern side of the island either. Towns there were rare, and the forests offered many opportunities for being ambushed. Fergus d'Aine and our Santi fortress there at the gateway to the Highlands also completely blocked their passage into the Highland region.

Mid-April 643, Bishop Hercule Thopolos walked into the office of General Hellas Konas. He was expected. "Ah there you are at last, Bishop."

"You have news for me? Are we any closer to removing that vile Lucifer's Spawn from her throne in Brea?" The Bishop hated utterly any woman who held power, and King Lachlan Laird epitomized his hatred. She had to be eliminated. How remained the real question with Fergus d'Aine totally blocking the passage of his army into the Highlands. If he ordered the General to move thousands of men through Fergus d'Aine's kingdom, then that would trigger a war, probably uniting all the kingdoms against them.

"Yes, I believe that we have a solution. Several months back, I sent out a number of recon parties into Tewdwr, following the edge of the Ath

Mountains. One has found a way that we can get an army of sufficient size in there by climbing the Ath and sneaking in from her rear. They will have to climb in on foot, however. Once into the valley of Brea, then there remains the small task of somehow breeching her heavily fortified city."

"So there is a back way into her valley! Ah that is the best news I have had in a long time."

"We will begin operations as soon as the Mano del Dio representative arrives next week. He will come along with us and get the gates to her fortress opened for us to enter. We will attack at night. I plan to send only a hundred riders north to the location at a time, spaced a few days apart. I don't want to raise any suspicions. Also, they will not be wearing their tunics. I don't want the Highlanders to know for sure who conducted the raid. Bishop, you finally get your wish. Tonight, you will see the first hundred paladins move out, heading north."

"Excellent, excellent. Remember, these people in Brea are pagan worshipers of the very worst kind, praying to strange, ancient non-existent deities. The Church will not say anything about the numbers of non-combatants your men slay. They are, after all, utter pagans, hardly worth bothering about."

"I'm glad to hear that, Bishop. No matter how careful one is, always there is some collateral damage to be expected in such a clandestine operation. My men will be grateful not to have to concern themselves with sparing all villagers. A month from now, Bishop, King Laird will be a figment of history, long forgotten with a few years." The Bishop smiled from ear to ear. This assignment was working precisely according to the Pope's carefully crafted plans, though the Bishop strongly suspected that the Mano del Dio played a major role in defining those plans. He did not consider the new Pope to be wise enough to have devised this whole operation himself.

May 1, 643, Prelate Herodotos arrived at the large Holy Paladin encampment in a long, narrow, but grassy valley of the Ath range. General Konas had brought him here along with the last hundred men. Over a thousand paladins were now ready to make the long climb into the upper Ath. A week of steady climbing brought them to a narrow pass, beyond which lay the fertile valley of the kingdom of Brea. In the center of the grasslands lay the wooden stockade walls surrounding the major town. Here they paused until nightfall. As soon as it was dark, the men began jogging toward the fortress. With luck, they would arrive close to dawn. Prelate Herodotos led the way, carefully eyeing the fortress, looking for sentries and guards.

Around five in the morning, they arrived at the walls. Positively primitive, thought Herodotos; a child could break in here. He checked his special weapons; all were in place. He threw a rope over the timbers, caught it on the spiked tip of a log, and tightened it. Hand over hand he climbed to the top, peering cautiously over the top. About five feet below the top, a wooden walkway allowed archers a clear line of sight. Two men were on sentry duty not too far from his position. Wearing all black clothing, the nearly invisible form slipped over the top and onto the walkway.

He had not been noticed. Next, he crept up on the first sentry. Timing was critical. Two throwing daggers whizzed past the first guard's head, hitting the second twice in his head. That man slumped to the ground. An instant after that, the second guard's throat was slit open, and he too slipped to the ground. Herodotos paused to see if anyone else had noticed. None had; all was silent in the early dawn twilight. He moved to the gate and examined how it opened. A minute later, King Lachlan Laird's western gates were wide open, and the General's men ran in to do their job.

Startled from a deep sleep, King Lachlan awoke, bolted up in bed, heard the sounds of battle, and jumped out of bed. Still in her nightgown, she grabbed her sword from its sheath. No time to don her armor, she spoke softly, but hastily and insistently, to her bed mate, Dwyn, her late brother's wife, whom she shared her bed with ever since her brother's death a number of years ago. "Dwyn, the time I spoke of has come to pass. Now I order you to fetch Cerys and get her to safety in the hills. Remember, no matter what happens, you must get Cerys to Mont Blanc somehow, some way. The future of our people depends utterly on your getting Cerys to Mont Blanc! Do you understand me?"

Dwyn, frightened from the noise of combat nearby, got up, and put on a robe. For months, she had listened to the doom predicted by her lover, Lachlan. A hundred times, Lachlan had told her what she must do, flee in the night, and take her daughter, Cerys, to safety. Still, Dwyn had never been beyond the borders of Brea, and Mont Blanc was to her some mythical place — on some other continent, whatever that meant. "Take the knife," Lachlan exclaimed. Dwyn had already forgotten it. "And the purse," she added. "I'll guard the door until you get Cerys out the secret door. Move, we don't have much time!"

"But," poor Dwyn was so frightened that she couldn't remember what she wanted to ask. Holding the two items, she rushed into the adjoining room. Already Cerys was awake, a frightened ten year old girl.

"Mom, what's going on? Are we under attack?" she asked, already putting some clothes on, unlike her mother, who still wore her robe.

"Yes, doom, come on; we have to get to the tunnel right now before it's too late." She grabbed her daughter's hand and pulled her back into the master bedroom. Lachlan blew both of them a farewell kiss. She had already opened the secret door, which led into a dark tunnel. Dwyn paused, saw Lachlan's stern look, and dragged her daughter into the dark opening.

"Mom! I can't see!"

"Feel our way, I guess," Dwyn replied, not having any other ideas. That she should light a lantern escaped her; terror overwhelmed her reasoning. Behind her she heard Lachlan shutting the door, and then she heard someone kicking in the master bedroom door. Steel upon steel reached their ears, but the two kept on feeling the black walls and floor, moving pitifully slowly down Lachlan's escape tunnel. After an eternity, they spied a faint light ahead. At last, they reached the end of the passage. Here another concealed door opened onto an alley. If they exited, they would be right in the middle of the fighting. Dwyn couldn't bring herself to open the door yet. Instead, she looked out through the tiny crack. Men were running in all directions, stopping to fight anyone who dashed outside of their homes, indiscriminate killing was more like the scene. Dwyn was petrified. She could not move even if she had wanted to do so. Cerys merely clung on tightly to her mother.

"Ah Laird at last!" exclaimed General Hellas. He had just smashed her door into pieces and entered to find King Laird standing in her nightgown, sword poised for battle. Around her neck hung a strange talisman.

"You beast! You will never get away with this," she cursed him, and their swords clashed in a resounding bang. She had the upper hand; it was her bedroom. Twice her bade made contact with his flesh. For the first time in his long career, General Hellas was in a true, to the death match with someone who may just be better than he was! His body was still near the doorway, effectively blocking other men from coming to his aid.

Just then, the talisman began glowing. He saw her eyes drifting off to some other place; a smile graced her face. He made a desperate lung at her, since she was obviously distracted. She didn't attempt to parry his blow. His thrust sliced deep into her chest; with effort he pulled the blade out and then swung a deathblow, severing her head. The talisman still glowed and then completely vanished from sight, as if it had never been around her neck. Since nothing else happened, he shrugged it off as the play of light in this dimly lit room. He called out, "Laird's dead! Secure the town!" Holding her head in his left hand, he walked out of the room. For some time, he continued to hold the head up on display, especially unnerving the few of her loyal fighters who continued to fight his men.

In a half hour, the sounds of battle ceased. General Hellas ordered, "Burn this town to the ground, and let's get out of here. Has anyone found the treasure room yet?"

While men scurried to carry out the order, a captain reported, "Sir, the treasury room only contained this small bag. I guess King Laird was nearly broke." Hellas spat on the ground, not even a respectable profit from this venture. He threw the head inside her building and began walking to the gate that he'd entered. Flames sprung up like small dots in the early morning light. A half hour later, most all the buildings were burning, and the small army of men began their long walk back to the Ath mountains.

Bodies lay everywhere, in the streets, in the alleyways, and even inside some homes. However, many had actually been able to flee the attack, throwing open the other gates. Their forms could be seen running in all directions from the burning Brea. Smoke eventually forced Dwyn out of her hypnotic trance. Coughing, she stepped back into the blackness. She realized now that she had no clothes, no food, no nothing. "Cerys, you hold this knife and purse. I have to go back to get some clothes and food for us. If I do not return, you know what you must do; go to this Mont Blanc place."

"Yes, mom, but you've got to come back! I don't know where it is! I'm scared, mom! Can I come with you? Don't leave me, please mom," she begged.

"No, you stay here. If they catch me, then they won't get you. Remember what your aunt has told you many times. You must get to Mont Blanc; the entire future of our people is depending upon you now. I know that neither of us know what Aunt Lachlan means by this, but she made us swear to it. I'll be quick." She gave her daughter a kiss and felt her way back the long, dark passage.

She carefully opened the door, saw no one, and came back into the master bedroom. She shrieked when she saw the headless body of her king and lover. She vomited. Presently, she found clothes, but the smoke began seeping into the room. She forgot about planning, just grabbed an armful of her clothes, and some for Cerys. She could not get to the panty because of the fire nor could she get any water skins. At last, the smoke was so heavy that she had no choice but to go back into the escape tunnel.

Soon she reached the other end, where Cerys was coughing from the acrid smoke. "We've got to get out of here," she managed to say while coughing. She smashed through the outer concealed door, and the two found themselves in a back alley. All around them buildings were raging infernos. Dwyn held onto her daughter's arm, while her other arm held tightly the bundle of clothing. They stepped out onto the main street and gasped, so many dead bodies! Cerys began crying. Dwyn wanted to as well, but kept on pulling her daughter along, stepping around their fallen townsfolk. At last, covered in soot, hair singed, the two rushed through the northern gate, free from the blazing Brea. They just kept running across the grasslands for quite some time. At last, out of breath, Dwyn staggered and fell to the ground. Cerys landed on top of her, still clinging to her mother for dear life.

They looked back at their beloved home, Brea. The entire town was totally engulfed in flames. Both began crying; they had just lost everything that had meant anything to them, including their protector Aunt Lachlan. After some time, Cerys complained, "Mom, I'm hungry."

There was nothing Dwyn could do about that. Instead, she said, "Come on; we must reach the safety of the hills. Maybe we can find some early berries up there." She wasn't hopeful of that however. Dwyn began to think that the two of them would probably die of starvation out in the wilderness of the Ath.

Five days later, the paladins finally reached the meadow where they had left their horses. They were tired, very hungry, and nearly exhausted. However, General Hellas was now in very bad shape. Because of the steep climb required to ascend the Ath, all healing supplies had to be left here with the horses. The two deep wounds Lachlan had landed were now infected and he was running a fever. Still he was better off than fifty-one of his men, ten of whom died during the descent. Their wounds were worse than his were. While men prepared hot food for the nearly thousand men, others began attending to the wounded, beginning with the General. Even Prelate Herodotos examined his wounds, though he didn't tell the General that he was actually dying, that their skill in healing battle wounds was insufficient to treat the General. The next day, the small army broke camp, riding slowly back to Nuadilan, and then on to Bregia.

Along the way, General Hellas Konas died from his wounds, along with forty-one of his men. At least he received a proper burial. Prelate Herodotos presided over the hasty funeral. The Bishop, of course, was elated that they had at last eliminated the major barrier to his conquest of West Reach, at least the part of the island that he was concerned with, anyway. To the Bishop, generals were replaceable. That, however, did not prove to be the case. He was not replaced for over a year.

May 20, word reached us at the estate of the attack on Brea, the killing of King Laird, and the burning of the entire town. Fergus had taken a scouting party there the day that the news reached him. His subsequent report was grim indeed. His men had at least been able to give the many dead a proper burial, well a mass grave site at least. Brea was now a burned out shell of a town. There were no signs of survivors in the town, although trails in the grasslands suggested that many had indeed been able to flee the carnage. The attackers, Fergus discovered, had come from Tewdwr, scaling the Ath range. No clues remained as to the identity of the butchers, though many of us felt that it had to be the Holy Paladin's work.

"Mommy, remember our pledge to Lachlan?" I piped up at the big meeting. "We promised to go to the standing stones for her."

"I know, Lizzy Ann. I'm trying to figure out who I can send."

"I'll go," I volunteered. "I do know where they are at."

"It's much too dangerous, Lizzy Ann. Who knows, there could be more of these evil men lying in wait. I'm going to ask Fergus and the Guardians there with him to do the deed. He knows the place as well as you do."

Three weeks later, Fergus reported they had the talisman safely secured. It only appeared when the full moon rose. He said it was spooky. They'd spent an entire week searching every inch of the standing stones and found nothing, but the moment the rising full moon struck the stones, there was the talisman lying against one of the stones, opposite the rising moon.

Now, it was safely on its way to Mont Blanc. Thus, we had kept our word to King Lachlan Laird.

Early June of 643, we also received news that we had dreaded: more women were being mistreated in the remaining Occupied Sectors of Bonilla and Vito. We had the secret letter that the Megalos General had failed to burn, which said that the recalcitrant women were not to be mutilated, nor encased and left as before. Rather, the new plan was to put them onboard a ship and send them back to Megalos, where they would be kept encased and imprisoned indefinitely in the newly built underground and secret prison beneath Constanza City.

Ever since we had translated that letter, the Guardians of both Bonilla and Vito fortresses had kept a vigilant eye out for any signs of such activities. Until now, nothing unusual had been seen. Today, word came from Bonilla that during the night, at least ten, maybe more, metal-encased women had been secreted on board the Slow Poke, a ship whose new destination was Megalos. Interestingly, it carried no cargo manifest. It had sailed at high tide.

"Damn those priests and their idiot pope!" exclaimed Jenna. "Now what do we do? I can't stand by and let those poor women get to Megalos. That's signing their death warrant!"

"Some are going to be in as bad a shape as the ones we've already rescued," Beth Ann added. "It's been a couple years since we made that wide ranging rescue operation. Undoubtedly, they just began a new prison somewhere else, probably within the main city so that they could be easily transported to the docks."

Only Allan seemed unperturbed by the news. "Are you willing to give my plan a try now?" he asked coyly. Ever since we had received that secret letter outlining their new plan to ship their prisoners down to Megalos, Allan had been devising a foolproof plan to rescue the prisoners. Until now, no one paid his wild scheme any mind.

"What are the options that we have?" asked Jenna, recovering her composure.

Silence.

"Mine," Allan finally said softly, a twinkle in his eye. Personally, I was totally in favor of his plan the first time that I heard it several years ago.

"Well, all right then. How soon can it be executed?" Jenna gave in, for she had no other real choices, if she wanted to rescue the prisoners.

"A Planner is always ready with his plan," Allan teased. In fact, he had been secretly working on it for over a year now, working out the details, and arranging the proper personnel and special equipment — all done on his own initiative. "I believe it can begin operations within a week."

"Okay, then go to it. I expect results, mind you. This is a costly plan," she agreed.

"I'm on my way to Point Bleak immediately," he replied, kissed his wife, and left humming a tune.

He returned a few days later, even more cheerful. However, we had just received word that the Slow Poke had just docked in Vito. Our Guardians there were on a twenty-four hour alert, using the far seeing eye to observe if other prisoners were loaded onto the ship. The next morning, we received news that indeed at least a dozen women wearing the damnable metal torture devices were secretly loaded onto the ship in the dead of night. So far, none of the enemy had the slightest idea that their nefarious activities had been detected. That was in our favor, however.

Allan advised, "The crew is ready to depart at high tide tonight. The Communicator is one of our new recruits, Sammy Welts. Protector Jason Farthington is there along with his Healer wife, Cathy. The captain is old Henry Freeze. They need one night to handle the transformation, once they are out of sight of land and other ships."

"Okay, Paulette, relay the news that the Slow Poke has picked up another dozen and will likely sail at high tide tonight," Jenna ordered. Turning to Allan, she said, "Are you sure this will work?"

Allan grinned like a cat, "Sure, Jenna my dear. It can't fail." She doubted that. His plan was totally wild, totally crazy. No one would believe it. She sighed, hoping that all would go well.

On board the Sleepy Hollow, Captain Henry Freeze, a young man in his twenties and an able seaman, yelled to his crew. "Yahoo, we finally get to do it! This plan of Allan's in just so wild — gang this is going to be fun! Get ready to sail. Bosun Thad, take us out into the sea south of West Reach, outside the normal shipping lanes to Bregia. Tomorrow night we transform! Yahoo!" All twenty of his crew let out their own war hoops. These men were all handpicked over a year ago by Allan, chosen for their dash and daring. Even the three Guardians were only sixteen and very willing to try new and wild things, as only the youthful can envision. This operation required a certain dash and daring that mature folks would lack.

During late afternoon, Sammy received the message that the Slow Poke has set sail from Vito. The ship was one of the obsolete Megalos cargo ships that was both slow and not very maneuverable, a perfect target for this new, sleek caravel of the Santi, normally based at Point Bleak. During the day, the crew watched the southern tip of West Reach drift off behind them, as they sailed south by west. By nightfall, they were far off any normal shipping lanes. The sails were dropped, and the ship came slowly to a halt in the water. Many lanterns were lit, and every member of the ship became extremely busy.

First, all the main sails were replaced with black ones. The lovely, hand-carved maiden in the bow was replaced with a black dragon, whose open mouth appeared to be shooting fire, but it was just red paint. The port and starboard placards that read Sleepy Hollow were replaced with two that read Black Dragon. More importantly, four large ballistae, which shot spears instead of quarrels were attached to the foredeck. Finally, most importantly, four huge catapults capable of throwing balls of fire were mounted strategically on the rear main deck and on the poop deck, where the captain normally stood. Cathy added the final touch, lowering the Santi del Dio flag and raising their new flag, an impressively large one at that. Across the white fabric was a large black dragon with a skull and crossbones in its mouth, as if it were eating the remains of a person.

Satisfied that everything was now shipshape, all went below to change into their new costumes. A little while later, the Bosun called out to the Captain, who had returned on deck, "All set, Captain Swallowtail. Shall we set sail?"

"Aye, aye, Bosun Pugnose. Unfurl the mainsails. Look lively me lads! We've a ship to catch and rob!" exclaimed Captain Swallowtail. "Set a course south by east, Pugnose!"

"Aye, aye, captain!"

Captain Swallowtail went below to his chart room once the ship was under sail. He needed to plot the intercept course. It was mostly guess work, but then this ship was at least three times faster than the Slow Poke. He wanted to intercept the Slow Poke just as it left the Med Sea, veering south along the Red Desert. An hour later, satisfied with his calculations, he grabbed his far seeing eye and went on deck. "Here, Pickledfeet, take this to the crow's nest with you. Keep a sharp look out. We should intersect Slow Poke in two days or thereabouts."

Meanwhile, Cathy went from crew member to crew member handing out bits of jewelry, mostly made of gold and gemstones. While not expensive, it added to the illusion that these men were indeed thieves of the sea. She put the most expensive piece around Captain Swallowtail's neck. He griped, "I look like a woman."

"No, you look like a cutthroat thief who will steal even a helpless woman's broach!" He grinned and saw her point.

The Black Dragon arrived at the interception point well ahead of the Slow Poke. For an entire day, the caravel sat motionless in the waters off the coast of the Red Desert. Several other ships came by but gave her a wide berth! The Black Dragon looked spooky and dangerous to the other captains.

Finally, the cry came from the crow's nest. "Slow Poke ahead. Ten miles off."

"Look lively lads; raise the main sails. Show time begins!" hollered Captain Swallowtail.

Sometime later onboard the Slow Poke, the bosun called out, "Captain, what's this ahead of us? Looks like big trouble!"

"Curses, what are they doing? They are cutting across our bow! Damn that captain ought to know better. We are the slower ship; we have the right of way. Holy crap! What was that?" A huge flaming ball flew through the sky, narrowly missing the bow of the Slow Poke, splashing and sizzling into the waters off her starboard side.

The Black Dragon sliced across the bow of the Slow Poke, missing her by mere feet. Everyone could see every detail of the Black Dragon. Twenty men were manning four huge ballistae, but even scarier were the four flaming ball throwers! Captain Swallowtail called out as they passed by, "Heave to and be prepared to be boarded by the pirates of the Black Dragon! If you do not heave to, the next shot will land amidships!"

Now, the Black Dragon had to come around in a tight circle to catch back up. It tacked sharply to starboard and circled around the stern of the Slow Poke, coming nearly broadside, but a few feet away. "Are yea going to cooperate and heave to and be bordered or do we need to burn you out?" yelled Captain Swallowtail.

The captain of the Slow Poke had no choice but to issue the orders to drop the main sail. What else could he do? One hit from the flames and his ship would be on fire, a catastrophe when at sea. The ship was their lifeline; it had to be protected at all costs. It was more valuable than a human life to those on board. The Black Dragon also dropped its sails and nudged in closer to the Slow Poke. As soon as the ships were mere feet apart, six crewmen jumped onto the Slow Poke and moored the two ships together. Captain Swallowtail and Bosun Pugnose stepped grandly on board, their short swords drawn ready for action. Also, fifteen of his crew scampered onto the Slow Poke as well.

"Captain Swallowtail and Bosun Pugnose of the pirate ship Black Dragon," he introduced himself to the Slow Poke's captain. "We are pirates, if you cannot tell. We stole this ship and made the late captain walk the plank at sea. His bones lie at the bottom with the sharks. We are here to take your gold and valuable cargo, whatever that may be. Stand aside while my men search your ship. Once we have your gold and any cargo worth stealing, we will be on our way, and you, my fine captain, can be on your way, less a bit of gold," he chuckled sneeringly.

"But we carry no gold or valuable cargo, just making a return run to Megalos," the captain tried to explain.

"Ah, that's what they all say, 'We ain't got no cargo.' Well, look at this," he said touching the brooch around his neck. "Took it off a pretty young lass who said that very thing. Found it in her trunk. Let's see what me men can find. Search every inch o'this ship, lads. Bosun Pugnose, you make sure they doesn't miss a thing."

"Aye, aye, Captain Swallowtail. But can't we please make one of these men walk the plank? We ain't had any fun fer weeks now. You know how the lads just love to see 'em walk the plank."

"Ah, we'll see. Business first; fun, second. Hop to it Pugnose!"

The Slow Poke captain grew more fearful by the minute. This talk of walking the plank unnerved him. He assumed he would be the chosen plank walker!

A short while later, Pugnose came back to report. "Damn it, Captain Swallowtail, I tolds you she was ridin' high. No damn cargo; only got these two paltry money bags! No valuable cargo, sir. But we did find something else, captain, they's hauling a bunch o' women prisoners. The crew's been asken' if we can take them. You know they'd have a lot of fun with 'em. What-da-ya say, captain, cain't we steals'm prisoners? They's won't mind its."

"What do you mean no cargo? Just prisoners? Damn our rotten luck! Hell, take the prisoners; the men need something to take their minds off our not getting any loot. Get'em aboard and in the cargo hold. We'll have a fun time tonight!" Captain Swallowtail spoke with authority.

Slowly, the frightened, half-starved women, wearing nothing but rag sacks for clothing, were brought on deck by the crew members. "What's with these bindings? You got the keys?" asked Captain Swallowtail. He already knew the answer, but he just wanted to hear what the captain would say, since he was now a part of the diabolical scheme of the Pope's.

"No keys, they don't work no more, so we were told. Can't get them off. Feed them in pig's troughs, that's what we were told." the captain answered, beginning to hope that these pirates would forget about walking the plank.

Bosun Pugnose replied, "Don'ta matter much, not fer what me crew's gonna do with them tonight. Don't need no hands fer that," and he laughed sadistically and convincingly. "Look lively lads. Don't drop any'o them overboard or yeu'll not get one to play with tonight. Lively now lads." The now even more terrified women had to be physically lifted from one ship over to the other ship and carried down into the cargo hold.

As soon as the last woman was transferred, Captain Swallowtail opened one of the money pouches and handed the Slow Poke captain a gold coin. "Now yea cain't say that I left yea all penniless. Pleasure doin' business with yea, yes, mighty fine unexpected business at that. Me men thank yea mightily," and he snickered sadistically and hopped back on board the Black Dragon. The mooring lines were dropped, and the two ships drifted apart. Soon the Black Dragon had set her sails and swiftly left the Slow Poke behind, they headed due west.

Onboard the Slow Poke, the captain and her crew breathed a huge sigh of relief. His bosun said, "I though sure they were going to make you walk the plank, Captain."

"Me too. Okay, set sail once more for Megalos. Guess we don't have to worry about that messy cargo anymore."

As each woman was carried into the cargo hold, each was placed on a soft cot. Cathy went from woman to woman, covering each up with a warm blanket. She dare not say anything until they were underway once more. At last, Captain Swallowtail poked his head down into the cargo hold. "It's okay to talk now. We are out of range from them. We'll transform late tonight."

Now Cathy and the other two Guardians began explaining and examining their patients. She said, "Ladies, you are now safe at last. We are not really pirates, but Santi del Dio, who have come to rescue you and get you to safety. Encased in the metal devices with gag rings in their mouths, they couldn't speak, but their tears spoke volumes. "It's all right now. I am a Healer. First thing we want to do is to examine your bodies to make sure nothing needs emergency treatment. Next, we are going to get you all fed proper, nutritional food. As far as the torture devices go, we are under orders not to try to remove them here at sea. We don't have the proper tools or expertise to safely get them off you without harming you. So be patient with us for a few days until we can get you to the safest place on Tarra."

The physical examinations went swiftly. Malnutrition had taken its toll, more so on these women than ever before. Only two had other diseases transferred to them from men, and these two had to be treated at once. Next, hot, warm food was prepared and turned into a slurry that they could swallow. Instead of lying on the floor and slurping like pigs, they ate with some dignity, being spoon fed by many hands. When they had eaten their fill, next each woman was given a warm bath and cleaned up, something that had not happened for years. Their matted hair proved most troublesome and took a good deal of time to handle. Finally, each woman was helped into a clean set of real clothes, not the sacks they had been forced to wear for so long. Cathy was doing everything she could to make these women feel like real human beings once more, insisting on giving them back some of their lost dignity.

It was midnight before she finished up with the last woman. Now the cargo hold became one of activity once more. The women watched, and the crew began lowering the heavy ballistae and the giant catapults into the hold, lashing them securely opposite of the cots. Next, the heavy black canvas sails were swapped with the normal white sails, which also had huge red fleur-de-lis crosses on them, signature of the Santi. A few hours later, the ship was once more under full sail, transformed back into the Sleepy Hollow. The crew changed back to their normal clothes. At dawn, any passing ship would see nothing but another normal Santi caravel, one of many plying the waters in and around the Med Sea.

However, this time the ship could not dock at Velona. Too many eyes would see the special cargo being unloaded. Suspicions would be raised. Secrecy had to be maintained for future rescue operations. Hence, they put in three days later at Point Bleak. There, the women were transferred into three waiting coaches. A Guardian rode in each to help the women inside as needed. On July 1, they pulled into the estate; the coaches had traveled nearly non-stop.

As usual, Jenna was there to greet the women, along with the many others who had been victims of this nightmare torture. True, when they saw so many armless women, they became more than a little frightened. Nevertheless, Jenna was a firm believer in the truth of a situation. She did not lie to these frightened women. Their prognosis did not look promising, because we all suspected that they had been encased like this for far too long a time.

Jenna had gathered six Healers to help out, along with a number of strong blacksmiths who had performed their miracles before, cracking open these devices without harming the women. Jenna gave her usual lengthy speech, which by now she had down perfectly. This time was a bit different because the other fully recovered victims were also present. They wanted to see what happened and wanted very much to be with their fellow victims at this crisis point in their lives, when their encasements were broken open. They had experienced it themselves and could relate to what the women would feel. Hence, Jenna had allowed them to help.

"First, let's divide you into your sectors," Jenna asked. "Bonilla over here and Vito over there. Quickly the women moved to their areas. "Now I will be quite frank with you. We've handled nearly a hundred other who were imprisoned as you are now. The length of time, we've discovered, is a key factor. Let's begin with Bonilla. I want any of you who have been encased like this for less than a year to step forward." No one did, though I rather suspected this might be the case. Perhaps Jenna did also.

"Okay, now those who have been like this for less than two years, please step forward." Three women did. Carefully, we helped each one to get onto the stone floor and in to the proper position. Carefully, the blacksmiths positioned their bars and gave a whack. As expected, the thin casings that held the head harness in place cracked, and the rings were removed. Each expressed their gratitude for this small action. Next came the decisive moment. A pair of precisely placed blows caused the casings that held their arms rigidly up and across their backs to shatter in the front and back, allowed us to gently slide off this diabolical restrain. Many gasps and shrieks echoed in the room, frightening the poor woman.

"What's wrong? What's happening? I can't feel my arms," wailed the first woman who had been freed. Everyone stared at a pair of crossed matchsticks, which had been arms.

"I'm afraid they have basically died on you. Get her over to the bed very carefully; do not touch her arms; they will shatter," Beth Ann ordered. "Here, I want you to see the others; that will give you an idea of what yours look like," she explained to the now terrified woman, who was in a near panic.

Crack, the next woman was freed, but with similar results. The original woman now gasped at the sight as well. She now understood what hers looked like. Ghastly. Crack, the third was now free, but not much better than the other two. As expected, all the women were now crying uncontrollably, presuming their arms were just as bad, how could they be worse? Jenna picked three more women who had been encased even longer. Their arms looked far worse and were extremely fragile. One cracked in several places as she was being lifted up from the floor.

While the six Healers began their work, Jenna explained that the dead arms would have to be removed. However, there was one small benefit: there would not be much pain involved. Mostly a stinging sensation while they were being stitched up. There nerves were already non-functional in their arms.

While the surgery was being performed, the blacksmiths worked on freeing the other women's ring gags. That was at least a positive action. The sobbing, petrified women were grateful to at last close their mouths and to speak, though few said anything. Many just watched the surgeries and moaned to themselves. Jenna was very glad that the others who had undergone this sometime back remained quiet. Each had Jenna help them erase the trauma they had undergone and knew from their own experience that anything they would say at this time would have lasting value and might even hinder their therapy sessions later on. Time enough for pep talks once the horror and shock wore off. Indeed three women did go into shock, nearly passing out.

Instead, the others attempted to help the Healers with any action they could perform, such as fetching more blankets, bandages, and relaying messages to the other staff who were handling the boiling of water and so on. Yes, the infirmary was a beehive of activity. An hour or so later, the six Healers had finished with their patients, who had had time to grapple with their situation. Now they were helped up and the other armless helpers took them over to the far side of the infirmary where their beds would be for the time their bodies needed to heal. They began chatting softly to these six women, trying to be as encouraging as they could, based upon their own experiences. Jenna kept an eye on them, however, just in case they made matters worse. However, they had the opposite effect; they actually calmed down considerably and finally began to relax, something they had not been able to do in years. One by one, they dropped off into a deep sleep.

Approximately every hour another six were freed and helped to the surgery beds. With thirty-two women to handle, the Healers worked non-stop for six hours. It was after supper when they finally finished the last two. At first, Jenna had the notion to box up all these dead arms and send them to the pope in Megalos, but then she realized that doing so would blow the cover of the pirate ship, which would likely be needed again.

While we ate supper, she had Beth Ann give a report on how the women were faring. "The surgeries went as well as can be expected. No complications there, since their arms were already numb and mostly dead, no blood circulation or very little. All those bruises you see are symptoms of scurvy, which also is causing their gums to bleed, and it's why their teeth are nearly falling out. It's probably why they are so weak too. My guess is that they have not been getting a balanced diet, very low on fruits and vegetables, would be my guess. I am hoping that if we can get enough fruits into their systems, their teeth may recover. But honestly, as it stands, their teeth are in the worst shape of anyone I've ever seen. We may have no choice but to remove them; boy will that ever add to their awful situation. I'll wait on that until the last possible moment after we've tried everything possible."

"Interesting, I never knew that lack of fruit could be so deadly," Jenna commented. "Do everything you can for them. Lizzy Ann, looks like we have our work cut out for us once more." I nodded, grim work indeed, but most rewarding too. If they had any chance for any kind of a life after this ordeal, the trauma had to be erased. Failure to do so would lead to an even worse nightmare for them, one which would follow them into all their subsequent lives on Tarra.

It took them fully two weeks to recover their physical health, sufficiently that we could begin therapy. However, the other armless women hovered about these thirty-two like mother hens during that time, telling them how utter fabulous this promised therapy actually was, how they were now getting along quite well, how some had even begun to create decent paintings once more. Mostly, many insisted that if they had a choice, they should get the little girl to do their therapy, claiming she got fabulous results, as if Jenna's results were somehow not as good. Indeed arguments broke out about who was better, Jenna or me. Jenna's patients claimed that Jenna was terrific, while mine claimed that I was terrific. Either way, the new women felt encouraged.

They were even more encouraged when they were allowed to get up and go for walks, always escorted by one of the other women, who showed them how to use their feet to open the doors and many other little things. Some tiny bit of normalcy returned to their lives, yet it did not touch the awful feelings of hopelessness these women felt. That could only be relieved by therapy sessions.

When Beth Ann finally released them for therapy sessions, I again donated my mornings, so that I could handle two, while mom handled one in the afternoons. Based upon our previous experiences, we estimated one week's worth of therapy per patient would be needed, some more, some less. We two faced three months of solid work without a day off. It would be the middle of October before we would have finished with this group of patients. On July 15, we began the first three women.

One thing that we did learn from them was where they had been kept imprisoned within Bonilla and Vito. This information we passed along to the Guardians in our fortresses. From now on, they would keep a close watch on those two locations. They promised to attempt to find out how many women might still be imprisoned there.

This year was going down as the whimper year. Layamon fell under the control of the Pope without so much as a fight. Brea and King Lachlan likewise were gone; no major battles fought. I did not like how this year was going, not one little bit. Could anything else go wrong?

Chapter 25 Shattered Security

Early fall had come, the trees were barely starting to turn colors, the air was crisp, though not yet cold. Jenna and I were down to the last twelve patients who still awaited their therapy sessions. Yes, while they still felt horrid, they had seen their other twenty companions change so drastically for the better, that they now greatly wanted to experience this miracle that Jenna and I were creating.

It was the evening of September 26; dinner was done, and we were all outside playing kick ball, well at least some of us were hard at it, Jenna, me, the other children, and most of those who had completed their therapy. It was a time for simple fun and games; we left all our cares elsewhere. If you didn't concentrate on the ball, you'd end up being it and then had to try to kick the ball and bang it into another person. No one wanted to be it, except mom and me. Having nearly everyone outside either playing or watching or merely sitting and chatting is what probably saved us.

Suddenly out of the corner of my eye, I saw something dark dropping to the ground far across the open field by the barrier wall. It stood up; it was a man. I yelled to mom. Instantly, the game stopped. Not one man, but over fifty of these dark forms came over our walls! In less than a few seconds, they came running at us, pointing crossbows at us. Twang. The first bolt whizzed by Jenna, who snatched it and dropped it to the ground. Everyone else just saw the bolt stop mid-flight and fall to the ground. Instantly, people began screaming. The Guardians yelled for everyone to run into the main building. No one needed a second order. Jenna screamed, "Older children, look after the younger ones and the women. Move!"

A hail of quarrels came flying at Jenna and me, the two lone targets out on the open grassy knoll. However, she and I knew what to do. Out of our bodies, I followed her lead, snatching flying quarrels, and dropping them on the ground. That lasted all of a minute. While crossbows can deliver a solid initial punch, they take forever in a combat situation to reload. These men merely dropped them, drew their swords, and rushed towards us, giving us time to back up and form a sort of battle line.

No clouds meant no lightning bolts. Lilly Ann and the others began dropping fire sheets upon individual attackers. However, we were greatly outnumbered. Jenna became furious, and I continued to follow her lead. She picked up the man who was closest to her and flung him high into the sky. Who knows where he landed, but it was a long way away from here. I did the same. I found it so trivial to pick up such a light object. Unfortunately for that man, I forgot that he was as light as he was. When I threw his body, we discovered many weeks later that he had landed ten miles away to the west!

We had a dozen Santi guards on the premise. However, three were killed before the attack actually began. They had been watching the main gates. The attack came from all sides, which meant that many other men we couldn't see had climbed over the walls behind the housing complex and were now coming through the buildings at our rear, scaring the people rushing inside, forcing them to retreat outside. Fortunately, the Santi fighters hastily formed a barrier line between them and everyone else. Each fighter ended up taking on three or four of these assailants. Grim.

One got too close to mom, and I saw her body get stabbed. That did it now I became just as furious as mom! I concentrated and picked that man and two others and threw them miles away. Then, I got four more, then five. Mom saw what I was doing and began to get several at one time herself. We were still back-to-back, but her wound must be serious. I felt her body slowly sinking to the ground. I wanted to staunch the wound, bandage it, anything, but I couldn't, the men just kept coming at us! It was as if they were under orders to kill Jenna! Six went on the next toss, then seven, then eight. Now I was throwing those who were already in flames, only these looked like Roman candles as they lit up the sky. Jenna stopped throwing bodies. I feared that I had lost her. Now I really got mad and concentrated even harder. I heard cries of pain, shrieks of terror, but paid them no mind.

One benefit of not being inside your head is that you can see in all directions at once. Well, as I've said, my sense of direction is not so good this way. Yet, I continued to increase the numbers I was grabbing. Suddenly, I realized that I was merely wasting time this way. I picked the men up and held them about fifty feet above the ground. I continued to pick them up and bunched them into an ever growing mass high in the sky. Another ten, another ten, another ten, most were in flames, but I added them anyway. Several minutes later, I could see no more bodies to grab. I looked around; so many of us were on the ground! Yet, I saw no more attackers. Everyone heard this seven year old girl say, "Bye, bye, evil men; have a nice fly." I took the entire massive pile of men floating helplessly fifty feet above the grassy knoll and gave them a huge toss, far out to the west. We later learned that the mass landed over two miles away, smashing down several olive trees in the process of landing. None survived the fall, however.

Beth Ann rushed to Jenna. "Someone help me get her into the infirmary immediately. Lizzy Ann, can you put pressure here to stop the blood?" Mom was covered in blood from a deep wound to her chest. I did as Beth Ann asked; only I did it without using my body, just my new skill, which worked with pinpoint accuracy, so much better than trying to use my hands. As Allan and Hank struggled to carry her into the infirmary, I noticed both of them were bleeding as well. I applied pressure to their arm wounds as well.

Just then, Paulette, who had been spending the night with her husband and family in Velona proper attempted to contact Jenna. Finding that she could not, she latched onto me. *What's happening? I can't reach Jenna.*

We've been attacked. She's hurt very bad. Bleeding a lot. Hank's hurt too, so is Allan. And many others. I sent to her.

Good god! I'll be there as fast as I can! Elona Po has been attacked; some have been killed, don't know who though. God, this is a disaster. I'm coming! She broke contact.

The nine Santi fighters who were not killed at the gates were all badly wounded, as were Hank, Allan, Lilly Ann, and Adam. Only Beth Ann and myself were uninjured Guardians. Beth Ann was used to crises that involved healing. "Lizzy Ann, I know that you are not prepared for this, but I have to use you. I need to ascertain the state of the other wounded right away. I want you to continue to keep your mom's blood from seeping out. Can you do that?" I promised. She dashed quickly to the other patients. Hank and Allan were in the best shape. She explained, "I will put an emergency bandage on you two so that you can carry the wounded Santi fighters into the infirmary where I can see how badly they are injured."

"Wait a minute, Aunt Beth Ann. I can bring them in faster and easier than they can," I blurted out. The many women had recovered from their fright and began clumsily to bring in the needed bandages and supplies that Beth Ann would need. Thank goodness for their help. However, they witnessed the injured Santi apparently floating into the infirmary and being laid gently onto the available beds.

"Good god!" Beth Ann exclaimed as she saw the nature of their wounds. "Okay, Hank, Allan, you to get a temporary patch up so you can get started on the others." She took bandages that one of the armless women held between head and shoulder and tied up their arm wounds. Two minutes later, the two men dashed off to deal with the badly injured fighters. "Okay Lizzy Ann, go take care of Lilly Ann and then Adam in that order. Have some of our many helpers bring you what you need."

"Okay, is mom going to make it?" I asked.

"I think so, we stopped the blood loss, and she is not bleeding from her mouth, good sign, but we need boiling water. Oh no, I forgot about that!"

"It's coming," called out Curt, Lilly Ann's son. "We kids are minding the stove. Have some shortly!"

"Are all you kids okay?" Beth Ann called out. They were, thank goodness for that small detail.

Lilly Ann had gone unconscious on me. I went to work. At least, I had not forgotten how to stitch someone up. I never was a terrific Healer, but at least I knew what I was doing with sword wounds. In thirty minutes, I had her all fixed up properly. Paulette arrived and began aiding Hank and Allan, so I tackled Adam next.

He was in a lot of pain from a serious leg wound. He had the presence of mind to tie his belt on it to slow the loss of blood. Now his strength failed, but I was there in time. I tightened it and set to work. Sometime later, I finished him. "There you go, all done." He whispered thanks and passed out. How he could have stood all that pain, I don't know.

Hank lost one of the Santi fighters; she had lost too much blood from her five wounds. However, the three of them had just finished up with the remaining eight. Hence, Paulette and I went to work on those two, which were a whole lot easier: clean the wound, sew it up, salve it, and bandage it. Our many helpers were exceedingly observant and helpful. Indeed, over half were already in training as Guardians. Every time I needed something, I found one of the women right there with the bandage, or the soak rag, or whatever. We all worked together as one very large team. Finally, we finished and went to see how mom was doing.

Beth Ann explained, "She's alive, that's all I dare say at the moment. She's breathing on her own and with luck, will recover. We all cheered and looked around at ourselves. Here was a room mostly filled with armless women and very bloody Guardians. Beth Ann yelled out, "Very well done, all of you! Without your incredible help tonight, we would have lost most of these patients. You owe yourselves a big round of applause — well stamp your feet any way!" and she did just that. Soon the infirmary echoed with the sound of many stamping feet. "You make a fabulous team, thank you," she added.

I noted, "Well, at least they didn't get our cooks; they were all off shopping." Everyone laughed at my silly remark, a tiny bit of brevity in an otherwise nightmare situation.

Paulette brought us back to worry once more, "I haven't been able to contact Elona's Communicator, Sally, all night. I'm going to head back into town and see if they need help."

Adam tried to get up, saying, "I'll go with you." His leg gave out, and he fell back on the bed.

"I'm in the best shape, I'll go. Only you all look after my precious wife," Hank volunteered. The two headed for the stable to saddle up a second horse.

"Should we clean up the mess now?" asked one of our many helpers.

"Yes, that would be terrific if you can manage it. We should cleaned up and then begin inspecting our work," Beth Ann replied. She and I began to scrub up, but it was hopeless, for we were covered in Jenna's blood. We stripped out of our clothes and headed for the bathhouse. After a quick bath, we climbed out only to find two women holding a towel between their heads and shoulders for us. "Thoughtful as ever. Thank you," Beth Ann complimented them both, who smiled.

Wiping our hair and in clean clothes, we returned to the infirmary. Already the women were on their butts scrubbing away with their feet. If any of the new women thought that they were now completely helpless, they were totally convinced otherwise! I saw most of them in there pitching, trying to figure out how the others were doing it. Beth Ann and I smiled at each other and went to check on mom.

She was breathing easier now, which I took as a very good sign. We made our rounds of the other patients. Only Adam needed further attention; in his valiant attempt to get up out of bed, he had managed to pull a couple stitches loose. I fixed him back up and ordered him not to get out of bed. "If you need something, just ask one of the many helpers here. They are quite capable of helping you, if you hadn't noticed." Several who were scrubbing the floor nearby gave a little chuckle at my remark.

Shortly after that, Paulette contacted me. *Hank and I will not be back tonight. We're needed here. Elona's still alive, but barely. Albert, her Planner, didn't make it. The others in her Circle are pretty badly wounded. Mary's in the best shape and really needs our help tonight. They killed over twenty-five attackers. Her guards eliminated another thirty before they breeched their defensive line. The Santi were wearing their chain mail, unlike ours, so they came out of it with mostly bruises. I'm sending ten to help guard you tonight.*

I relayed the news to everyone else. We were indeed a somber bunch that late night. Finally, I said, "I'm starving. Aunt Beth Ann, can you make me something to eat?"

"No, go get the older children to do it. In fact," she didn't get to finish her sentence. In walked all the many children, carrying trays of hot cocoa, tea, biscuits, cheese, and even a pile of cookies! They, too, had been busy doing what they could. "Well I'll be! Thank you, all of you. I am sorry that I forgot all about you kids." Quickly, they all began going around handing out mugs and treats to everyone.

Damien, my youngest brother, and Curt, Lilly Ann's youngest son, began pestering us with questions. Damien asked, "I know Aunt Lilly Ann and the others were causing all the flames that we saw and we all know that mom could toss a man, but what about all the rest? Mom was unconscious when all the evil men were just floating in that massive pile. Who did that? That was a very neat trick! Curt and I want to learn how to do that, don't we?" Curt nodded.

"Well, I'd like to know who our attackers were and how did they get to us?" Beth Ann asked. "Well, yes that was an awfully convenient way to end the attack. I'm sure it wasn't your mom who did it."

Now all the other women began asking about the incredible, unbelievable things that they had witnessed. One said, "How do men go flying through the air? Where did all those fires come from?"

"I can answer that one, though I expect quite a few of the others who have been here this past year can also answer that one," Beth Ann answered. Nearly forty heads nodded. For the benefit of the thirty-two newer arrivals, she explained that most Santi here were Guardians and that they could conjure flaming sheets of fire, lightning bolts, and ice sheets. "However, what else we saw tonight is beyond everyone else here, except Jenna. She is the master of moving objects. I saw her pick up the first one and throw him a long way away. This gives us a completely new meaning to combat! There is only one other possibility that could account for the incredible display that we saw." She looked at me, and I grinned sheepishly.

"Yes, mom has taught me how to move objects too. I only recently passed my final test. When mom went unconscious on me, I got really, really angry. I just started piling them up in that big ball. I just made a big kick ball out of those bad men and then gave the ball a big kick. I think that they flew a very long way, though."

Another woman asked, "We saw the wounded Santi fighters floating into the infirmary. Was that your doing?"

"Yes, no one else could carry them safely. They were too big for Curt and Damien. I had to do it."

Another asked, "Are you a goddess?"

"No, but I am almost eight years old though," I said quietly.

Another woman said, "See, I told you that you should get your therapy from her!" Several women chuckled.

"Don't worry," I realized that the three women who were in the middle of their therapy sessions might be concerned because Jenna was so badly wounded. "I'll cover for mom tomorrow. Everybody continues to get their sessions, only I'll probably have to do some after supper for a while too."

At this point, the regimental commander walked in on us. "Everyone okay?" she asked.

Beth Ann gave her a full report, especially sad because of the four that had died defending us. "Well, you can sleep in peace tonight. A full regiment of Santi is now guarding the estate. Another regiment is looking after Elona and her crew. Bad business, these assassination attempts. Tomorrow, we will see if we can figure out who they were, where they came from, and if there are more of them to slay. What I don't understand is just how they knew where to attack and when? They caught everyone completely off guard."

"Inside job," Beth Ann speculated. "Probably we have one or more spies around here too. Thanks for watching over us. We ought to get to bed; it has gotten very late. I'll stay up with all the patients."

Several of the women countered. "Beth Ann, why don't you leave that to us. We can watch over them, and if they need anything or anything looks not good, we can come wake you. You are exhausted."

Beth Ann smiled, "I won't argue with your offer!" She gave them some specific instructions on what to watch for and then ushered all the rest of us into the main house. I hit the sack almost at once, tired, satisfied, but very sleepy.

The next morning, the reports began coming in to us. Mom was barely conscious, which was great, I thought; she was going to make it. For the morning briefing, only mom and Lilly Ann were not present. Additionally, three Healers from other Santi units showed up and checked on all the patients. All during the day, dead bodies began showing up; Santi units went to retrieve them when the locals reported finding them scattered all over the western landscape just north of Velona. I really had been a bit carried away with my body tossing, I discovered.

Our attackers were indeed from Megalos. Every body had the telltale bronzed skin color, indicative of living so far south. The Santi, we discovered, had sent out various patrols during the night, looking for additional attackers. While they did not find any more, they did discover from whence they had come. Apparently, a Megalos ship had beached west of the city and unloaded several hundred attackers. The Santi stormed the ship at dawn, killed everyone on board, and burned the ship. No incriminating evidence was discovered, however.

Our discussion this morning was on how to find the traitors in our organization. There could be no doubt that these men had been fed key, critical information about our headquarters and about Elona's habits and routines. "Look, they attacked us in the evening when we are all together as families. They had to know that," Beth Ann said defiantly.

"I hate to bring this up," Adam countered, "but can you imagine what would have happened if they had attacked us at say midnight when we were all asleep? I daresay none of us would be around this morning. It could have been a lot worse."

"Well, they didn't," Beth Ann answered. "Maybe they do not know where we all sleep or who is who just by sight. They only went directly after Jenna, but she is the only one without hands, a dead giveaway, if you ask me. If we are all together, then she could be easily found. If they had to go room to room, they might have missed her. However, you are right; if they had come when we were asleep, probably all would have perished."

"As I see it, the real questions are: one, how do we ferret out the spies among us and two, what kind of a response do we give to Megalos?" Allan broke in, trying to get us back on the case at hand.

"Well, we can't just go after anyone with bronzed skin color," Adam replied. "There aren't any in Velona. It's crazy if we no longer know who in our own organization we can trust!"

"The only certain way is to have Jolina check every one out," Beth Ann suggested. "That means she would have to check many thousands of people, almost undoable."

They continued to banter around ideas, getting no real handle on just how we might ferret out our spies. At last, I piped up, "I know a way we can do it." All eyes suddenly focused on me. I was sitting as usual quietly in the corner.

"Look, first we get the Guardians we can trust the most to get Jolina and her family taken to some secret location that only we know about. Then we spread the word widely and harshly to everyone in the organization here in the Velona Sector that we know that there are traitors among us and that we are going to bring in Jolina, the soothsayer, and interrogate every single person who has any connection to us all. Further, we say that anyone caught lying will be immediately beheaded. Make it sound like we are going to deal out very harsh justice at once."

I continued, "We make as if we really mean business. However, we tell them that it will be a week before she can get here. Then, we keep an eye on people. I know that if I was a spy and I heard all this, I would attempt to sneak out of here. So that's what I think the spies might do. All we have to do is catch them in the act of fleeing. I suppose that we could then have Jolina check those few people, just to make doubly sure. What do you think?"

"Diabolical, that's what I think," Adam chuckled. "From the mouth of a little girl even," he teased me. Since no one had any better idea, we decided to go with mine. The first step of getting Jolina to a safe place was easily handled. She and her family made a visit to Mont Blanc. Next, we brought in all the brigade and regimental commanders and briefed them on the Spy Project, as we came to all it. These were all veterans of the Line, completely trustworthy, in our opinion. Their biggest concern was their ability to track down those who fled. For starters, we suggested having someone monitor the gates of the city at night, noting who left and their direction of travel. Each day, bed checks could be done to see if everyone was still present. We agreed to begin making the announcements when we received word that Jolina was safe at Mont Blanc.

Later the day following the assassination attempts, for security reasons, the Healers decided to bring all the wounded here to the estate from Elona's buildings. The Healers wanted everyone together to make their jobs easier. Moreover, the estate was more easily defended. From this point on, we had a full regiment of Santi fighters around our perimeter throughout the day and nighttime hours.

Then it was into therapy sessions for me, handling three therapy cases through most of the rest of the day. I did find one thing particularly curious however. All three women ran through their traumas much more rapidly than ever before. The two that I had been treating had a certain pace as they re-experienced these tragic events. Today, that pace nearly doubled! What could account for such a significant change, I wondered. Could it have been the events of last night? Surely, that would have only added more traumas, not less. The only other change that I could identify was that they had seen me do some amazing things. Could that be playing a factor? If so, how? I had no real answer, except I was happy about it. They would complete their therapy much more quickly.

During the supper break, I saw all the new additions to our infirmary. I went to see how mom was doing and saw Elona lying on the bed next to hers. I found them both conscious, but very weak. I told them about our plan to ferret out the spies, and they smiled. Mom whispered, "Good girl." I also noticed that many of our women were hovering around the patients; they were determined to be as useful as possible. I teased mom, "You've now got the whole estate looking after you!" She and Elona smiled again.

On my way out, one woman caught up to me and said, "We'll all play with the kids tonight so you can run your therapy session. That way they won't miss you." I gave her a hug and my thanks.

A week later, everyone was out of the infirmary, excepting mom, Elona, and a couple of wounded Santi. However, they were now sitting up in bed and more active. Still most wore bandages, and we must have looked like the walking wounded. Yet, now we were ready to put the Spy Project into motion. Adam gathered every one of the staff here at the estate together and gave them the preplanned warning about bringing in Jolina to check on everyone, including our cooks. I know that some felt rather upset that we would doubt their honesty, but that was the drawback of my plan. I must admit that I was not expecting the result that we got later that evening.

I had finished my therapy session; it was dark, and I went to the kitchen to find something to eat. Lilly Ann and Beth Ann were already there, along with one of our cooks, Aline. She was sobbing. I was obviously interrupting something serious. Beth Ann saw me and motioned for me to come on in and sit with her. "Aline has just admitted her part in the assassination plot to us, Lizzy Ann. She is from Vito, originally. Back in Vito, she has a young niece named Alaina, who is twenty-one. It seems that the Holy Paladins have taken her prisoner and are using her to force Aline to cooperate with them."

Poor Aline, I always liked her; she frequently gave me an extra cookie when no one was looking. She wailed, "I didn't know anyone would be hurt. They told me that they put Alaina into one of these horrid metal cases, just like the poor women who you have rescued, the ones who have lost their arms because of it. They said if I didn't give them the information they wanted, they would poor hot metal in the locks, and she'd stay that way until she died!" Now Aline really began to sob uncontrollably.

Lilly Ann added, "She told us the name of the person here in Velona who had contacted her and had given the information to, so I'm going to see that he is taken prisoner tonight. I'll be back in a bit. You two stay with her, please."

I had an idea, "Aline, please can you tell me about your niece? Where did she live? Is she married? Any idea who has taken her?"

She described where her niece had been living, though it had been a long time since she had seen her. She didn't believe that she had yet married. Unfortunately, she couldn't provide much useful information. I didn't remember who the Communicator for Fortress Vito was, so I Mind Linked to Paulette and asked her. Dropping that connection, I relaxed and expanded outward searching for Elvire Evarte.

Hi, Lizzy Ann here. Is this a good time to chat?

Oh yes, we heard about Jenna and Elona. How is your mother doing? And Elona?

I told her that they were both sitting up now and doing better. Then, I explained the situation. Somewhere in the city of Vito, Alaina Onore was being held captive in the damnable metal cases. I told her all that I knew about the young woman, which was not a whole lot to go on I knew. *Can you please see if you can locate where she was living and find out if anyone knows if she has actually been taken prisoner? If so, see if you can find out where she might be being held for me, please?*

Oh, I'm sure that Gervaise Genoa will love this assignment. He has been so bored of late. We'll get back to you as soon as we know something.

"Aline, we are going to see if we can find Alaina. If so, we will rescue her somehow. Don't you worry." I tried to put her mind at ease somewhat. She had betrayed us and gotten many of us wounded and some killed, yet she was only trying to prevent her niece from becoming another victim. I only wish she had come to us when they initially contacted her about it.

"Oh thank you. I know I don't deserve it, but for my niece, I thank you. May I go home? I need to get some sleep. I've been up since five this morning you know, fixing your breakfasts."

Beth Ann also felt sympathy for her and told her to go home and get some sleep. We'd worry about all this tomorrow. When Lilly Ann came back, she was annoyed with her sister having let our traitor just go home, but there wasn't anything she could do about it now.

The next morning, the body of Aline Onore was found washed up on the public beach. She had not gone home. Instead, she had tied a number of stones into her dress and jumped off the pier. Jenna was furious with Beth Ann the next day. "How could you just let her go home like that? Can you imagine the guilt that woman must have felt when she came to work and found out the all the damage her information had caused? No wonder she felt she could no longer live!"

"Well, I am a Healer, not a Judger or Wid," Beth Ann defended herself. "I felt sorry for her, and she didn't show any signs of wanting to kill herself." I was sad that we had lost our forty-five year old breakfast cook. She had always, until now, treated us as if we were her family. Interestingly enough, later that day a package came for Jenna. Inside was a box with a hundred gold coins and a short note from Aline, which said basically that this was all she had and could never make up the awful damage that she had done. Beth Ann and I both realized that we should not have let her go home that night.

Lilly Ann reported at the morning meeting that the spy had been captured. His last words as he was being carted off to Isla Roca, were, "You'll never find her niece. She'll lose her arms just like all the rest!" I swore to myself that was not going to happen!

I continued working three patients each day. During the second week, when I checked up on mom, there she was giving Elona a therapy session, erasing the recent trauma from her. I found out from all their helpers that Jenna was systematically helping every one of the wounded in the infirmary. Thus, I excused myself from the morning briefings and gave mom some therapy sessions in the early morning, before she got going on the others. She thought it was rather funny at first, her baby daughter giving her a session, but it worked out well for both of us.

An interesting side note: all those who had therapy sessions, which erased the recent trauma, healed in twice the expected time. In three weeks total time, both mom and Elona were back at their normal routines. I resolved that in the future, whenever anyone around me suffered any kind of traumatic event, I would give them sessions right away so that they could heal twice as fast.

A week after I had contacted Fortress Vito, Elvire contacted me. *Gervaise has had some luck. He used a cover story that her aunt had left her a dowry for her marriage, and that he was trying to locate her to give it to her. People were most helpful. He finally located where she was living. She had moved twice from the original location. She and several girlfriends had taken a house together. You are right; several weeks ago, she was abducted. The Holy Paladins busted in their door late at night and had taken her screaming out of the house. They believe that the men knocked her out, because once outside their home, her yelling ceased. No one has seen her since then. It's been about a month now that she was abducted. He is now trying to figure out where she might be being held.*

I thanked her profusely. She promised to keep me posted on Gervaise's progress.

Gervaise Genoa was thirty-three, with black hair and moustache, and he still cut a dashing figure. He had a playful mind and considered himself the luckiest man in the world. The lovely, powerhouse of a woman, the blonde Jeanne, the Santi Fortress Commander, had given him her hand in marriage a few years ago. Both were madly in love with each other. They discussed his findings about the abducted Alaina Onore. She said, "We must get her out of there before she loses her arms like all the others, Gervaise. Just tell me which building she is in, and I'll take a squad and bust in there and free her!" He loved it when she talked defiantly like this; her lips took on that special look; her eyes sparkled; her cheeks flushed with that pink glow. He gave her a kiss instead.

"Okay, three buildings are the likely locations. I need to get in there and see for myself. I need a way to get in there and be allowed to look around. I would guess that she would be held in the basement. From all the information the Santi have shared with us, normally the nuns and their trainees are on the main floors. All the nasty stuff apparently happens down in the basements, so that's where I need to begin looking," he explained.

"I have it," Jeanne replied, "a sewer inspector has access to everyone's basements."

"Brilliant. I shall become a Vito sewer tomorrow morning. I love you!" and he gave her a big kiss.

Next day, Jeanne helped him dress in soiled clothing so that he looked the part. She put some smelly remains from their chamber pot into his hair for added realism. "Take a bath before you return," she jested, wishing she could go with him.

He went up to the first building, the main Nunnery building in Vito, which had long ago been the Sisterhood Inn in Vito. He presented his forged papers, claiming he needed to inspect the sewer connections in the basement. One whiff of him and the Head Nun did not question him further. She had one of her assistants show him to the basement. He poked around looking for the various drains and generally acted out his new role for the benefit of the assistant. He did find a pile of newly made encasement devices, but they were all covered in dust and had not been touched in some time. Satisfied this building probably did not hold Alaina, he thanked the assistant and left, heading for the next possibility.

"I'm here to inspect the sewers," he told the priest who answered his knock on the rectory building, home to all the priests. He showed the forged papers, but again, one whiff of his odor, and the priest led him at once into the basement. Nothing was here either, just piles of unused, worn out junk, all covered in dust. He told the priest, "Better clean this junk up, you know it draws rats." The priest thanked him and assured him it would be taken care of at once.

These two buildings were fairly close to each other. The last possibility was closer to the docks. It was their storage facility, where cargo being delivered to the Church was temporarily stored before it was sent off to all the various churches scattered throughout the sector. "Here to inspect the sewers," he again presented his papers. "Just need to see the sewers in the basement."

The rough looking man said, "Hey, we are really busy right now, moving lots of boxes down in the basement. New shipment came in and all that. Can you come back in say an hour? We should be done by then. We don't want to accidentally drop a box on you while you are on the floor examining the sewer, now do we?"

"Oh sure, I have to check other buildings. I'll drop back in a couple hours, is that okay with you?" It was and he left, highly suspicious of this building. He looked around and saw no one else in the vicinity. He leaned against the side wall, pretending to tie his shoe. His ear to the wall, he listened for the sounds of workers moving boxes around. All was silent.

"Fishy, fishy in a brooke, what do we have here e?" he muttered cheerily to himself as he set off to find another nearby building to inspect to kill time and make it believable.

He inspected two nearby warehouses and then returned a little over an hour later. "Right this way," the rough looking long shore man said, and he led him to the basement. Gervaise began his inspection, crawling along the floor, examining the drains very closely. In fact, he was examining the signs on the floor. He saw what appeared to be scrape marks. He spied a pig trough, a metal pan about two inches deep. This one had water in it. He also saw a bit of blood from the corner of his eye. He concluded that she must be being held here.

"All ship shape as we say in this business. Thank you sir," and Gervaise allowed the man to show him to the door. He visited the bathhouse before returning home.

"So when do we bust her out of there?" asked Jeanne as soon as he told her what he found.

"Tonight, I do believe that we shall pay them a visit, my dear. Bring your sword. We need a clever plan. I want to snatch her without giving away that we know about this place. I suspect that they have been holding other women here at various times as well, probably before they loaded them onto the ship several months back. If they don't suspect anything, then we will know where they keep their prisoners in the future and can rescue more. Now all we need is a good disguise. We need a way to bring her out the gates at first light without anyone suspecting anything. Probably have to bring her out in a wagon or cart, something like that. If she is encased, she cannot be seen."

They thought about this for a time. "I know," Jeanne hit upon it, "the flower women! They are always leaving with their little donkey carts at first light, delivering flowers to the outer towns nearby. There would be plenty of room to stash Alaina in the back of the cart."

"That's a good one. Wait a second. It's only women who drive them, not men."

"No problem, we will just have to turn you into a flower woman for a time," Jeanne grinned. "I'll go see about renting a cart right now. Back in a little while." He tried to object, but she left in a rush. She stopped by the kitchen and made a hasty outfit change. Ten minutes later a poor looking young woman in worn out leathers walked out of the fortress gates and into the gates of Vito. Jeanne wandered the streets looking for a likely flower stall. Late afternoon, she found the perfect cart, already half filled with greens. For a gold piece, the owner was very willing to loan her the cart for one day. Jeanne promised to return it here by tomorrow night. The flower woman had just made a week's earnings, so she was more than pleased with the deal.

Next, she had to get Gervaise fixed up to look like a down-on-her-luck flower girl. He moaned the loss of his prized moustache. In a half hour, he did indeed look like one of the many flower girls he'd often seen about town. The long plain dress with many patches really added to the effect. The bonnet hid most of his facial features. They wrapped their swords and his other tools into bundles, which looked much like flowers nicely wrapped up, and headed into Vito. The gate guards paid them no attention. It was getting dusk, and now they had to kill time. Gervaise wanted to make his move around midnight. After walking for a half hour, they arrived at the flower stall; there was the promised cart waiting for them. No one was around, so they hopped into the back and pulled the canvas over themselves. Now they lay back and waited as the hours passed by.

When Gervaise estimated it was around midnight, the two crept out and climbed up on the buckboard. He slowly drove the donkey cart down to the docks. As they rode along, both women acted as if they were about to fall asleep any moment. The ruse worked fine, the few passersby thought nothing of these women returning home late. He parked the cart in the dark alleyway behind the warehouse. They grabbed their bundles and headed for the main door. It was locked as expected. Gervaise cast his blue light and picked the lock in thirty seconds. Both ducked quietly inside, she had her sword drawn and ready.

Their first action was to search the main floor quickly for signs of anyone present. It was deserted. This was going to be easier than he expected. They stole quietly down to the basement, using only his blue light. He went to where he'd seen the pig trough. Sure enough, there was a young woman totally encased lying on the floor asleep. Beside her was an empty trough; presumably she had eaten. The water trough still had some water in it.

"Alaina," Gervaise whispered. "Alaina, are you Alaina?" The woman woke up; her frightened eyes looked at the strange blue light. She heard a man's voice but saw two flower women instead. She couldn't speak, of course, but she timidly nodded, hoping they wouldn't hurt her.

"Good. We are Santi here to rescue you. Your Aunt Aline sent us. Are there any other women here with you?" She shook her head no.

"Okay, let's see if I can get this contraption off of you." She shook her head as if to say no. As he put the blue light close to the key holes, he saw what she meant. "Damn they have already jammed these locks so they cannot be removed." She began crying. "There, there, we will get them off you in due time. Now, here's what I want you to do." He explained their plan, and she shook her head yes, she understood. They helped her up and then the three went back upstairs.

After making sure no one was outside, they opened the door and walked into the alley. After getting her into the cart and covered up with the canvas, Gervaise went back and re-locked the warehouse door. "That'll give them something to ponder," he muttered to himself. Then, he and his wife climbed back on the cart and began to drive very slowly back to the eastern gate. They pulled up near the gates off to one side and whispered to Alaina, "Now we wait until they open the gates. Couple of hours. Take a nap." Both Santi dozed.

Around five in the morning, others began arriving at the gates, ready to begin their day as well. Many were farm hands off to tend the nearby fields. Others were flower women, off to pick the day's flowers from the hills outside Vito. Soon the guards arrived, marching in step. The gates swung open, and one by one, the throng passed through, and no one said a word to the two flower women on the little donkey cart. They drove north until they were out of sight of Vito and the other people who had left. Now they doubled back and entered the Santi gates around six in the morning, mission accomplished. Jeanne was a little annoyed that she did not get to cut up someone; she loved battles.

Once safely inside, they undid the canvas and helped her out. "We are going to take you to the infirmary where our Healer, Flavie Jensen, will check you over to make sure you don't need any healing right away. We'll be back after we change out of these filthy clothes." He introduced her to Flavie, who like a mother hen, took her in her arms and led her inside, chatting calmly to her all the way.

First, however, the two returned the cart to its owner, entering the north gates this time. An hour later, wearing their usual Santi clothing, they went to the infirmary to check on Alaina. They found her looking much more presentable. Flavie had washed her, dressed her in better clothing, and even worked a bit on her hair, which was matted beneath the metal straps that held the ring in her mouth. Alaina looked somewhat better, at least more relaxed and relieved, though still in misery of course. The other Guardians came to visit as well, and Flavie introduced the fortress commander, Donat Evrarte, and his wife, Elvire, their Communicator.

Donat explained, "The Santi have rescued over a hundred women who have been encased as you are. We are under orders not to try to smash you out of these horrid devices because we might really cause you more harm, like breaking all your teeth or worse. Instead, we are ordered to send you to the Santi headquarters in Velona. There they have successfully gotten every woman out of this encasement without harming them any further. We are preparing the caravel right now and will have you there in just a few more days. You will be freed of this torture probably the very day that you arrive there. Just hang in there a little while longer. You are a very brave young woman, Alaina." She wanted to smile, but couldn't; emotions got the better of her, and she cried instead.

Flavie asked, "Would you like for me to go with you to Velona and be with you all the way?"

Alaina nodded profusely. "You got it. I'll go pack a few things. Be right back. Don't let her out of your sights, everyone," she teased. Again,

Alaina wanted to grin, but couldn't.

A week later the two arrived at our estate. Jenna was able to greet her in the infirmary. I must say that the shock of seeing so many other women who had been tortured as she was and then to see the results, threw Alaina into a panic! Beth Ann tried to explain to her that the loss of arms came only after they had been encased for years at a time, and that those who had been like this for a short while ended up perfectly fine.

A few minutes later, the blacksmith removed the ring from her mouth. Then, we laid her on the stone floor to remove the arm constraint. She whispered repeatedly, "Please, not like them, please, please. I couldn't live like that." She was now crying, though the others who were watching kept quiet. A couple minutes later, the device was destroyed and her arms freed. "Ouch, that hurt. Oh, my arms are so stiff and sore, I can hardly move them." Gently, she was able to lower them to her sides. "Am I going to lose them?" she wailed.

"No, you are in the best shape of anyone we have freed! Come on, to the bath for you. We have a warm bath, and I will start your physical therapy in the warm waters. We'll have you back to normal in a few days, I hope," Beth Ann cheerily told her. As she led her out of the infirmary to the bath, a dozen others volunteered to help and followed the two.

"Gosh are we ever so happy that you didn't lose your arms like we did!" one chatted away.

After they were gone, mom told me to go fetch the box Aline sent her. I did so, but wondered what she had in mind. How would she explain what Aline had done to save Alaina? A couple of hours later, they returned, and I noticed that she had also eaten a bit as well. She seemed in much better spirits, though her arms still were stiff and very sore.

Beth Ann introduced her to Jenna and explained who she was.

"You, you are the leader of all Santi?" she asked in disbelief, staring at her missing hands.

"Yes, a leader does not necessarily need hands, but come sit my me. I am still recovering from the assassination attempt." She then explained what had happened here at the estate with the sneaky night raid.

"Now the reason that the Holy Paladins knew when was the best time to strike us, when I would be out in the open, was because of your Aunt Aline. She was trapped. They captured you so that they could get her to give them that information. That's why you were abducted and tortured so they could force your Aunt, who loved you dearly, to betray us to save you. Unfortunately, Aline could not live with herself after she found out what they did with the seemingly useless information that I am always outside playing with all the many children after supper. She thought the information they wanted which would save your life was trivial. Yet, when she discovered that they tried to kill us all, she couldn't live with her guilt. She loved us all too. However, she did leave you this. It is all the money she had in the world, and she wanted you to have it so you could get a fresh start in life. Remember her as a brave woman who would do anything to save her niece from such tortures." Alaina cried, and Jenna held her in a hug for some time.

Mom then explained that she could not safely go back to Vito and why that was so. She gave her usual speech about being able to stay here at her estate as long as she desired. Further, she promised her therapy sessions to eradicate the recent trauma that she had suffered. "Since I am feeling better now, and I'll begin your sessions tomorrow," Jenna suggested. "Beth Ann, why don't you get her a room and then take her to the supper table. I need to rest now a bit."

Beth Ann wisely gave her a room to share with one of the other Vito women who had lost her arms. This way, Alaina could become more comfortable around them and could learn from them. It took a couple of weeks for Alaina's arms to return to normal. During that time, we learned that she was a musician, playing the lute and harp.

Once Beth Ann pronounced Alaina fit and Jenna finished her therapy, Jenna had Hank bring her Bard Tal's old lute that he had left here when he got his new one. While Hank handed it to Alaina, Jenna explained, "This belongs to Lilly Ann's oldest son, Tal, who is running his own music group. It's his old one, so he won't mind you playing around with it. How about practicing up a bit and then playing us all some music? We certainly do not have enough music around here, that's for sure." The joy on her face shone like a light. She promised that she would do just that as soon as her arms and fingers were working properly.

The first of November, Jenna was back to battery, ready to resume operations. The very first thing that she did was call for a meeting of everyone, including all those who were staying here on the estate. "Hi everyone, I'm officially back on duty. I'm happy to also announce that every woman here has had her therapy sessions and I'm very proud of everyone. The progress that you have made is phenomenal. Well done to all of you." Much foot stomping echoed everyone's appreciation. She continued, "As you know, a while ago my estate was breached, and we were attacked by hundreds of assassins. Never in the entire time that I have lived here has such a breach of security happened. I have always felt safe here. Not any longer. During my long recovery period, I have given this much thought, and I want to share that with you today and get your opinions as well. Even though we now have a hundred fighters standing guard outside the walls day and night, we cannot continue like this. Yet, that is not the only problem we are facing. Simply put, we are rapidly running out of space here in this estate." She was right; we had to hold this meeting in the infirmary because this was the only space large enough to hold us all.

"As much as I love this estate, it is time I feel to build us a new estate, one that is much larger, more to our unique needs, and one that is much more secure for us all, without having to have so many guards on duty all the time. Besides, Velona continues to expand. When Hank and I first came here, we had a nice five-mile ride in the open country to reach the walls of the city. Now the city has expanded to within a mile of our walls. There are plans to expand all the way out to our walls in the next few years."

"Does anyone have any objections to us building ourselves a new estate, a much larger one?"

Of course, there followed a good deal of discussion. Everyone backed her idea of moving, just adding a bit here and there, asking just how far out we should move and so on.

One of our rehabilitated painters stood and spoke for all her companions. "Jenna, we too have been discussing what we all want to do. As you know most of us are or were artists or performing artists. Now some of us are in training to one day become a Guardian we hope, though I have to say that we unanimously agree that we are now one hundred percent Santi del Dio. Yet, we want to push on with what we consider our driving force in life, the arts."

"What we've decided that we want to do is to build wherever the new estate is located one huge arts building, in which we can all have a spacious, well lighted studio, and a center for the performing arts. In addition, we want to build a similar huge arts center in Velona, where we can encourage young people to become artists themselves, where dances can be held, plays performed, and where the arts are thrust forward as the spearhead of civilization. We believe most strongly that when a culture loses its artists, it is a doomed culture. We want to resurrect the fine arts and provide the means to make them thrive as never before."

"I'm not done yet," she exclaimed. "We also want to build these centers in all the other freed sectors as well, though perhaps not as big, because they are not as populated as Velona is. We don't know if it would be accepted or not, but we'd like to do this as well in Calgary, Southway, and Mont Blanc at least. Have I forgotten anything?" she asked her fellow artists. She hadn't.

Alaina, tears streaming down her cheeks, said, "This is utterly incredible that you would want to do this for us artists. I have to be a part of it, if you'll let me."

She replied, "Certainly, we could use another pair of hands around here." All the women laughed, and even Alaina began to see the humor as well. She swore that she would dedicate her life to helping anyway she could.

Jenna replied, "I cannot think of anything more profound than what you have proposed. I say let's all do it as fast as we can!" Everyone in the room cheered loudly for several minutes, including me.

Allan stood up and added his thoughts. "Ladies, gentlemen, children," he sounded very formal. "If I could be allowed to add my art to yours, that is, beginning a school of architecture in one small section of the arts building, then I would be totally willing to design and oversee the constructions of everything."

He received instant approval. He figured he would, so he went on, "I'll let you in on a secret. A Planner and architect such as me must always be ahead of the needs and demands of his clientele. I've known that we are very short on space for the last six months, and I have been searching for a new suitable location. I believe I know the perfect location and I happen to know that it can be purchased for a fair price and soon. Just a mile further north and west of here is the Dumont Estate. Lord Dumont is getting old and has expressed a strong desire to move into Velona proper. None of his children wants to take over the estate, because it is far too large an enterprise. The estate is around six hundred and forty acres in size, about a mile square. This estate is only a little over five acres."

"The manor house was built of brownstone back in the hey days of early Velona history. It is a landmark building, which ought to be preserved. I know that it only has one hundred fifty bedrooms in it." His voice sounded quite depressed, as if this was a huge barrier. He was teasing, of course.

"What?" exclaimed Jenna. "You're joking; that's nearly triple what we have here and then some!"

"No, it has one hundred fifty bedrooms. Its dining room is large enough to allow all of us to dine together. It is two hundred feet long and one hundred wide, three stories tall."

"Wow!" exclaimed many women in unison.

"There is an attached kitchen and pantry building. It used to house the vineyard workers as well as the Dumonts. Unfortunately, it has a down side. It is in great need of repairs inside, but the outer walls are fine. There is a small duck pond not far from the front. Besides renovations, all we need to do at once is construct a better wall around it. There is plenty of space for your huge fine arts building. Pick a spot."

"Further, with security in mind, we shouldn't hold huge dances on the estate. But why not take this estate here and rebuild the huge Velona arts center/dance hall here? It's close to the city, and there would be more than enough space. We can reuse all the stone from these buildings so the dance hall can be up and operational sooner. Once built, we could all just walk over here for the dances. However, before you make any decisions, you all need to visit the Dumont estate and see for yourselves if it will do."

"Allan, I could kiss you!" exclaimed Jenna, and she did, much to his embarrassment. Suddenly he became worried that all the women would follow suit! Fortunately they didn't!

"Can we go see it now?" I piped up, just as excited as everyone else was.

"You bet. Let me go warn him that he is about to have more company than he has had in years. Shall we?" We cheered and urged him to go arrange it at once!

Not twenty minutes later, he rode back into the estate. We were still discussing all these new plans and ideas when he returned, saying, "It's all arranged. He was overjoyed finally to have someone truly interested in buying it. When he heard it was us, he even lowered his price! Will you beautiful women care to join me in a nice morning walk? It's a bit chilly out, so we ought to wear a light jacket."

Twenty minutes later, the whole crowd was ready to go. We had to help put heavier walking shoes on many women and help them with their coats. Over a hundred of us paraded across the countryside to see this estate. Allan had understated the site!

The manor house appeared even larger than any of us imagined, stately, brown stone, with typical old style red tile roof. I couldn't count the number of chimneys! While much of the land had once been vineyards, most was overgrown with weeds. The land was rolling with so many possibilities for development that we would have a tough time deciding upon what to do next. Yet, the huge home was in need of repairs.

The inside was ornate woods, lots of mahogany and beautifully carved. Yet, in contrast, the rugs were filthy; the hanging tapestries looked the worst for wear; the windows had not been cleaned in years, and there was an odor in many places on the first floor. His wife had been an invalid for the last few years and had recently died. We chose not to ask about the odor.

The layout of the first floor was ideal for our use. The front half, two hundred by fifty feet, held an entry room, an enormous dining room running half the length of the front, and a huge sitting room nearly as long. Back of these ran an enormously long hallway the length of the building. Here were fifty bedrooms, including a huge master bedroom. The upper floors held room after room, nearly all identical in shape and size. Most had old beds in them, long worn out. Much of the furniture had been already sold or taken by his children.

Jenna bought it on the spot! Hank returned later that evening with the funds and a very pleased Lord Dumont moved his few remaining things into his new small home in Velona. He had finally gotten the albatross off his neck, as he saw it.

The flurry of activity during the next two months was something to behold. How Jenna could keep track of all the thousands of details I surely do not know, but that was a skill that mom most definitely had, always had for that matter. She commandeered two regiments of mostly idle Santi fighters and put them to work on our new estate. First, it was out with the junk, and then came a massive, thorough cleaning, which had not been done for many years. While all this was going on, she sent many of her Circle into Velona on a massive shopping spree, purchasing new beds, linens, towels, drapes; the list seemed endless.

While this was going on, Allan hired a work crew of top wood workers who began the necessary repairs along with altering all the doors to Hank's specifications. That kept many craftsmen at work in Velona just trying to keep up with the orders! Even more exciting, Allan drew up some ideas for the placement of two new buildings, the massive Fine Arts building and our new infirmary. The infirmary would be one story and large. The manor house front faced due east, the new infirmary would lie just behind it and to the north. Our pond lay just to the south and east of the front. Thus, the women chose a spot not too far from the manor house to the south such that the front of the new building faced the pond. Allan and the women decided on a formal garden look that would stretch from their new building out and beyond the pond. What they could not decide upon at first was the design of their new building, but there was no rush on that detail.

For security, the low stone fence that surrounded the estate would have to be replaced with something that provided us with significant protection. We could not have regiments of guards on duty. However, Jenna realized that we would need a significant security detachment for a place this size. Beside, housing was already becoming a problem for the regiments. Hence, Allan designed a barracks and stable which would accommodate up to two full regiments of guards. However, Jenna had another idea. Since this was going to be the new headquarters of the Santi del Dio, why not go all the way? She had him redo his thinking and allow for four complete regiments to be housed at the far end of the estate, nearly a mile from the manor house.

The first major construction began almost the very day that we took possession. Allan insisted that a large, heated bath building be built right away. It would be located behind and adjoining to the southern rear of the manor, allowing everyone easy access to it. There would still be space between it and the kitchen and panty buildings, which also sat behind the manor house. Jenna insisted that every building be made from stone to avoid fire hazards. Scouts exploring the land nearby discovered the original quarry from which all the brownstone for the manor was cut. Allan then continued to use the same stone for the new construction, which made a perfect blend.

By the time that we all moved into the new quarters in mid-December, all traces of the overgrown vineyard had been removed. The many Loremasters and their apprentices had several months to plan massive landscaping projects. At the time of our move, Jenna had also hired two more cooks and two stewards whose duties were simply shopping for daily supplies and keeping the panty well stocked. Additionally, she hired two seamstresses and a weaver. This pleased the women who now would be regularly getting new clothes. We women definitely enjoy frequent new digs. All the hired women were already Santi; many were ex-Sisterhood non-combatants.

The last week of December, construction began on the outer walls. Allan chose contrasting grey stone. The walls were going to be fifteen feet tall with an archer's walkway all along the perimeter. Cradled against the northeast corner would be the massive barracks. The huge stables would run along the northern wall from the barracks about a third of the way to the manor house. At the same time, the main entrance was chosen to be in the middle of the eastern wall. From here, a cobblestone drive was laid that ran in an enormous circle up to the manor house and around and down to the stables, on to the barracks, and finally rejoining itself near the entrance.

At the old estate, now called the Rose Dance Hall and Arts Center, all the existing buildings were dismantled, with much being reused, either here at the new place or as part of the new construction there. Allan simply moved the bath building to our new location. By May, the new dance hall was ready for operations. It was a single story stone building that could accommodate over a thousand dancers at one time. A small kitchen and pantry were connected to the rectangular structure at its rear, where our bathhouse used to be. This way, the existing cobblestone drive way was not altered, only it now led to the entrance of the dance hall. Plenty of parking space for the carriages existed on our old grassy knoll.

The most fantastic aspect of the new building was that all the voluminous perennials that Hank and Jenna had planted over the many years they lived here were left untouched! When it opened in May, the flowers were spectacular, adding to the attraction and ambiance.

The women finalized their design for their Laird Foundation Fine Arts Center at our estate in May as well. Allan and the women had the most fantastic looking drawings I'd ever seen. When it was done, two nearly identical palaces were connected by a walkway connecting to their second stories. Yes, it had barbicans on it, and you stood nearly twenty feet above the grounds below; the view of the formal gardens would be breathtaking from up here. The first floor of each palace had huge windows, semicircular at their tops, all allowing all the daylight possible to enter this first floor. The palace nearest the manor was their painting studio. Its companion further south was the art show room, in which formal art showings would be held and art purchases made. The second floor of the second palace held an enormous theater, while the first building held other art studios for pottery, ceramics, weaving, and so on. The third floor held smaller music studios in the first building, while the second building had a giant party area, which opened out onto a massive open aired patio, suspended twenty feet above the ground by enormous columns, ornately carved. This patio extended across the entire backs of the two palaces, allowing one to cross between buildings way up here as well as the walkway connecting the second floors.

However, per everyone's needs, Allan designed it so that it could be built one story at a time, allowing the artists to begin using their new studios as soon as the first floor of the first building was finished in late summer.

The entire complex would not be finished for at least five years, however. When it was done, there was not a single structure like these twin palaces in existence!

Finally, by December of that next year, the smaller scaled version at our old estate was ready for use by Velona artists, at least the first floor was ready. Another two years were needed for its completion.

Life definitely took a wonderful turn for the better for all of our women artists in residence. The genus of that change began when we held the grand opening of the Rose Dance Hall in mid-May. All of us, including me, had new, fancy satin dresses made especially for the gala opening. By now, news of the impending Fine Arts constructions and what all that meant for the many artists of Velona had spread widely. At the grand opening, two thousand people at least attended. In hindsight, I ought to have realized what was about to happen, but at the time, I was only eight years old and had no real thoughts about guys. Hundreds of artists attended and our women artists found themselves the center of attention, not only for the arts but also as women. I've never since seen so much flirting going on at one time and place! During the year, many a romance began. Yes, for all of us, 644 turned out to be one of the happiest times of our lives.

Chapter 26 The Dance

The afternoon of the Grand Opening of the dance hall here in early May of 644, we women were fussing with our new dresses and our hair. All of us were excited about this first dance in our new hall. How would it be received? Would any calamities occur? The Santi regimental commanders promised that they would have everything under control, but would our dresses be okay? How about our hair?

Hair, all the women had decided many years ago to let their hair grow as long as possible. They thought that the long hair accentuated their unusual appearance. I had to agree with them fully. Every one of them looked positively radiant, beautiful, and striking, especially when they wore these new dresses with their long hair sliding down their slim sides. More than one hundred women had picked their choice from the twenty possible colors for their new dresses. We looked like a pastel rainbow.

Into the fussing came a familiar voice, "Hello in there. Anybody here to welcome us back?" I heard the teasing voice of Bard Tal! I raced to the front door and jumped into his arms.

"Glad you are here! Just in time. The big dance is tonight. You are coming, right?" I fired off.

"You bet, dad, I mean, Lizzy Ann." He fumbled, but we both knew what he meant, I had been his dad before I got this new body. "We've timed it perfectly, if only we can have a quick bath and some rooms where we can change. New dress?"

"Yes, we all got new dresses. You just have to see this new place, Tal! It's already fantastic only it'll be even more so as things get done!" Then, I saw the others, "Oh, hi Zita, Lia, Angus, Sam. Oh. . ." I stopped short; five others were standing behind them.

"I've added more musicians, Lizzy. These are Liam and Kayley Lainn from Amathon. They've immigrated to Southway and ran into me. He plays the dulcimer, and she, the flute. This is Ian Mac Taggard from the Highlands and is a wicked percussionist! Basil and Addie Broadford from Southway. Both are dancers, but Basil also plays guitar. Gang this is Jenna's youngest, Lizzy Ann, the one I've been telling you about. She may look small, but from what I've been hearing, you have outdone your mom." He was referring to the attack on our estate last year.

Just then, Lilly Ann and Jenna came walking by. "Tal!" his mother exclaimed and the two hugged tightly. He then hugged Jenna too. Another round of introductions had to be done.

"Back for the big dance?" Lilly Ann asked, knowing it was.

"Yes for sure. We thought we might get a chance to show you what we can do now, but there is another reason we are here. Now is as good a time as any." He had his arm around Lia's waist. "Mom, I've come to ask your blessing on my wedding plans and to ask Jenna if she will conduct our ceremony. I'm madly in love. I've already asked Lia for her foot in marriage."

"I sent off a boy and get back a man," Lilly Ann jested. "Seriously though are you two sure about this?"

She needn't have asked. I saw her radiant, beaming face. Lia said, "I sure I'm sure."

Lilly Ann merely hugged them both together as one. "Er one more thing. Angus and Zita are betrothed as well. He already has his parents' approval. We hoped it could be a double wedding."

Now more congratulations were given all around. Jenna asked, "Are you in a rush or do we have time to plan a wedding? I do hope that you will stay around a while. We have a lot to show you; our resident artists have enormous plans which are beginning to blossom, like the dance hall tonight."

"Well, we wanted to talk with these artists, Aunt Jenna. It may be that we will be around quite a lot, if that's all right with you?"

"Fine, now let's show you around quickly, and let you get cleaned up. We've all got these new satin dresses to fiddle with, and we want to look our best tonight," Jenna replied, a twinkle in her eye as she spied Hank walking her way. More introductions and announcements later, I took them on a tour. I got them some unused rooms at the far end of the hall and left them going into our new bathhouse.

The large group had no more gotten into the warm waters, when six women entered carrying a bunch of towels between their heads and shoulders. One said, "Hi everyone. We brought you some towels. Just yell if you need something. Everyone's getting ready, big night you know." They were already wearing their new satin dresses and looked delightful. Several chorused, "Thanks! You look stunning!" The six blushed and made a hasty exit.

During the next few hours, the most frequently asked question was "How do I look?" The men had already heard that enough and were waiting in the large sitting room. At last, it was time to go. Seventy-five armless women were under our care and Jenna was the mother hen. "Remember ladies whom you are going with, watch out for your group, and make sure that your entire group is in the coach when it's time to return. Golly, I dare say you make a knock-out group of young ladies! You all look positively lovely tonight!" Mom meant it too.

We needed seventeen coaches to take everyone over the relatively short distance. Those of us with hands helped those without into the coaches. I noticed that Tal and his group now wore their fancy costumes, so they too looked all dressed up. Also, I observed that he now had three identical wagons. He'd left with one, but now had three. At last, I climbed in beside mom and her coach led the way. Of course, a squad of Santi fighters rode out in front of the long line of coaches. Hank and mom were already sneaking a loving kiss, so I watched the countryside pass by.

We were nearly the first to arrive. Only the musicians and the cooks had been there before us, setting up their instruments and preparing the drinks and snacks for the affair. Jenna and I stood by the door as the other carriages came up and dropped off the passengers. Jenna kept reminding them, "Remember, if you need some assistance, don't be bashful about asking someone with hands." She was worried about her flock and how they would interact with so many other people. After all, they had only infrequently been out in public; mom was definitely worrying tonight. It was such a big affair, and I knew that she wanted it to go righter than right for her women.

Me, I just thought each one with their long hair cascading over their shoulders onto their long satin dresses looked picture perfect. I knew that in these tight, form-fitting dresses, fancy hose, and snugly laced shoes that they would not be able to use their feet, as they were accustomed to using. Perhaps that was what bothered mom so much. I wondered if my nearly non-existent breasts would ever look as good as theirs, such thoughts a young girl can have.

Now the carriages from Velona began arriving, and soon the place rapidly filled up. Jenna found herself with Isabella Callisto, the elected Chairwoman of the Arts, who was going to make the first official speech tonight, dedicating the dance hall to Jenna. Both needed to be on the musician's stage at the far end of the hall. Tal had been there talking to the band of a dozen players for some time. As they approached, with me quietly following them, Jenna said, "Oh Tal, got a minute?" He stopped chatting and moved to her. "I've someone you need to meet. This is Isabella Callisto. She is the Chairwoman of the Arts. All the others have elected her to be the spokeswoman for their foundation. She is the one to speak to about this whole arts situation. Isabella, this is Bard Tal."

"Very pleased to meet such a beautiful young woman of the arts!" Tal replied and gave her a hug. "May we talk later on, Isabella? We have heard just incredible things that you are supposedly planning."

"Sure, I've just got to get this affair going. After that, it will probably be too noisy around here. How about tomorrow morning?"

"Perfect. My group has a little surprise for all of you tonight as well. It may effect what we have to discuss tomorrow. By the way, Isabella, you look stunning!" She blushed and said thanks. Just then, she got the signal to begin the dance. She and Jenna stepped up onto the edge of the stage.

Tal discovered why she had been elected the spokesperson. She was trained in the theater and could speak clearly and most importantly project her voice across the vast space of the dance hall.

"May I have your attention please?" At once, silence fell. "I am

Isabella Callisto, the Chairwoman of the Laird Foundation for the Arts. It is my pleasure to dedicate our new hall here tonight. This is only the first and smallest of the arts projects that our organization is establishing and building not only here in Velona, but in all the other free sectors. Very soon now the huge arts studio and performing arts centers will be built here, so that we artists of Velona will at last have the facilities with which to create the very best art on Tarra." The roar and clapping was nearly deafening. If there ever was any doubt about its acceptance, there was none now.

"We all have come tonight for fun, so I will keep this short. We, the free artists of Velona, have built this dance hall for everyone to use and enjoy. We wish to dedicate it to the one being, without whom this hall would never have been created, the one person, well actually there are two, Elizabeth Ann, you come up by your mom." I flushed but did as told. "Without the incredible skills and abilities and dedication and love for their fellow men, we women would not be here tonight. Yes, you cannot help but notice that we have lost our arms. Normally, that would have been the end of our lives; we all certainly thought so at the time. Yet, these two, Jenna and Elizabeth, did something for us that gave each one of us back our lives, our goals, our freedom, our ability to create. So tonight, we wish to dedicate and name this public dance hall the Jenna Rose Weston Freedom Dance Hall!" The round of applause, whistling, and yelling was deafening. We took the liberty of stepping off stage, and I made sure that Isabella got safely down the steps.

Now the band began to play, and the dance was formally underway. Hank swooped up Jenna, and they were off onto the dance floor. Almost at once, a young gentleman approached Isabella. "Excuse me my Lady. May I have this first dance with you?" He bowed low. She consented, slightly unsure about being asked to dance so quickly.

I was heading to the drinks section, but I didn't get that far. Both my brother, Damien, and Lilly Ann's youngest son, Curt Thomas, corralled me, asking for a dance. Curt suggested, "Hey Damien, why don't you ask my sister, Linda. She'll be glad to dance with you. I think she has her eye on you." Damien headed off to find her.

Curt was five years older than me. At our ages, this seemed a very big difference. "I asked him why he wasn't asking the girls his own age."

"Mom said I was supposed to see that you got to dance." I grinned. I knew that he really wanted to check out some of the young women his own age. After all, in another year, he would be of age. After this first dance, I sent him off on a quest to do just that.

Lilly Ann caught me next, "Come dance with me. Hank is supposed to be keeping Jenna occupied so she can't keep fretting over our women. Look, they are doing just fine. Every one of them already had at least one dance partner and that is a good sign indeed. If you want to dance with your dad, you are going to have to wait a little while."

"This is fine, Aunt Lilly Ann. Really it is. I think they look just super with the way they have let their hair fall down over their shoulders. Besides, I'm sure that they are all very happy with everything tonight."

"The real test comes at intermission, Lizzy Ann, when everyone takes a break and has something to drink and a snack. In this getup, they are not going to be able to do either by themselves. It's one thing, Lizzy Ann, to be a flower on the dance floor and quite another to be so utterly dependent upon another to feed you. No, the only thing that I am worried about is how they will be able to handle that. On the dance floor, they are close to a normal person, but at the dining, their handicaps will be most pronounced. You may have some additional therapy sessions to deliver after tonight. That's what scares me. Here's the plan. You and I are going to monitor our women during the break. If we see one getting very upset and embarrassed by it, we are going to escort them discretely outside until they recover. Hank will meet us there and look after the ones we bring out so we can dash back inside to rescue others. It's all arranged."

"Aunt Lilly Ann, you are basing your predictions upon what we have seen with all the men we helped during the bloody Crusades' aftermath. Yes, without our therapy, I would completely agree with your extreme concern. What you are missing is that part of what we eradicated is that which would have made them so extremely uncomfortable in social settings. I am almost willing to bet you that you won't have anyone to escort out of here."

"We'll just see about that," she said determinedly.

When the intermission came, I saw that Tal and his group were setting up on the stage, moving everything back. That could only mean they would also be dancing for us. However, I had to stick with Lilly Ann, who moved us closer to the many serving tables, where many mugs of ale were neatly arranged, along with trays of goodies to eat. I wanted to sample lots of the goodies, but was being forced into active service.

We watched as Isabella and the young man who had been dancing with her approached the table. "Shall we share one mug and one tray?" she said coyly.

"Ah, that would give me great pleasure, my Lady. Forgive me, but I am uncertain what to do."

"Well, for starters, put some of those cookies and a bit of that cheese on the plate for me and add what you want," she replied. He did so and helped himself to a sampling of ten different goodies. Oh, I wanted those goodies so badly! "Okay, Amido, poke a bit of the cookie into my mouth. Hum, that is good! Try one of those yourself!"

Soon they were each sampling what the other was sampling. "Hold the mug up to my lips, Amido, and I'll take a sip." He did so, "Thanks, try some yourself." He did. Soon, he thought nothing of the whole thing, and they were chatting about the arts. It seems that he was also a painter. Periodically, he offered her a bit of this or that and she gobbled it down.

Sometimes she suggested he try one that she liked. Well, she wasn't having any problems, so Lilly Ann moved us on down the line.

Finally, I said, "Now can we go get some goodies before they are all gone? No one needs rescuing." At last, I filled up a plate, but she would not let me have any ale, however. I had to have the children's punch. Ah well, I tried.

While we were eating, suddenly Lilly Ann flushed red. "Oh I get it! It's what Beth Ann suggested. Well, she ought to know; she's the flirt in the family."

"Get what?"

"They have made helping them eat into an intimate, flirting thing. The men are falling all over themselves to be helpful, even though they haven't a clue what the women need. I guess I really am an old foggie."

"If your attention is not on yourself but on the others around you, then you can see what needs to be done and get it done. If your attention is inward, everything collapses in upon you. Our therapy got them over any desire to look inward, so they are all focusing outward. Makes a giant difference, Aunt Lilly Ann, don't you think?"

"It's hard thinking of you, an eight year old girl, as an all knowing Wid!" she teased me, but I thought that there might be some truth in her jest. Now Bar Tal was introducing his group, so we moved as close as we could to the stage. I was having a hard time seeing around all the bigger people, so Lilly Ann picked me up so I could see.

I listened, ". . . Traveling Musicians. Tonight, we pay honor to Jenna Rose as well. You will see a small sampling of our normal, full-length show, but I promise you that soon you can see all of it. We are going to play a sampling of popular tunes from Velona first, then from West Reach, and finally from the Greenway. We combine music with dancing for your entertainment. One and a two and a three and a four."

They played songs that I knew from around here on all sorts of instruments. Zita, Lia, and Addie danced as a trio using the dance patterns that we all had been using. It was indeed good and well done. Next, the songs from West Reach brought back all sorts of memories, especially with the golden voice of Lia, who sometimes sounded like an instrument, so well did she blend. The bagpipe and drums of the Cross Swords dance featuring Zita and Basil brought yells and cheers.

They played several Greenway tunes, and Basil accompanied the three women in the jumping style dance. This was new and novel to most here, and their performance nearly brought the house down!

"For our last number, we dedicate this song to my father, wherever he may be. Dad, Lia found the words to it." Kaylee began to play the bass flute. It was my favorite lament! Then, Lia's voice, so low for a soprano, floated in over the bass flute. I got chills down my entire body. "My love is lost, lost to me, gone to the depths of the lonely sea. . ." If the music was not enough to swamp your emotions totally, the interpretative, modern dance done by Zita and Basil would totally captivate your attention, riveting it upon the two intermingling forms! She leaned over backwards, his arm beneath her back. I thought that she was about to fall over, when his other arm came over her chest. Then next instant she was flipping over backwards! She made a pleading run and dash at him throwing herself into the air; then he caught her, pivoted her around, setting her gently on her feet. Tosses, throws, catches. Wow! This was a showstopper. The audience here in the dance hall responded with a thunderous applause, wild yelling, whistling, and cheers. The noise did not die down until Zita, Kaylee, and Basil had taken their tenth bow! Bard Tal certainly had learned how to captivate an audience and create a living work of art centered on the music.

Tal, who was Caitlyn last lifetime, my wife and a competent musician with our Cymry Minstrels, had just gone ten giant steps beyond the music that we had made so many years ago. I was speechless. He had blended music and dance into a unified, inseparable whole, something that had never been achieved before on Tarra. I realized that he was not kidding me when he said his goal was to be the most famous bard in the world. The rest of the evening was anti-climactic for me. Our musicians were down right dull in comparison to Tal's group.

When we all finally got home around ten that night, all talk centered around two topics. "He kissed me!" This was followed by many chats. It seemed to me that over half of our women had been passionately kissed this evening, the discussion of which did not die down for days. Naturally, Beth Ann was right there in the middle of all the chatting. I guess being only eight years old accounts for why I didn't pay all that much attention to it. Rather I was more interested in the second topic. "Tal, Zita, Basil, Kayley, Lia, (pick a name), that was utterly incredible! The tones, the movements, I've never seen anything like it, so utterly descriptive movements!" On and on came similar comments from nearly everyone. This, I was keenly interested in hearing. (Okay, so I am just a little biased.) Everyone was so much more interested in talking about the night, that it took us with hands until nearly midnight to get them out of their confining clothes. (For once, mom completely forgot about my bedtime.)

Around midnight, mom, Lilly Ann, Beth Ann, Hank, and I sat around the far end of the dining table, along with Tal and all his crew. They still had not changed from their performance costumes. We were finally relaxing and eating a late night snack and sipping hot cocoa. Lilly Ann was speaking, "Tal, Zita, Lia, Basil, Kayley, all of you, that lament was so beautiful, so moving. It brought tears to my eyes. I'm so proud of what you have all accomplished."

I noticed that in their form-fitting costumes with fancy tapping shoes, both Lia and Zita couldn't use their feet to eat. Instead, I watched, as Tal would instinctively know when Lia wanted something and either put it in her mouth or hold the mug so she could sip. Neither would look at each other while doing this, both keeping their focus on the conversation and us. I found that pretty incredible. Then, I noticed that Fergus and Zita were doing pretty much the same thing. I knew immediately that their matches were made in heaven, that they were perfect for each other. I wondered if mom also saw how seamlessly these two couples had become.

I hadn't been listening to the conversation and picked it up again. Mom was saying, "Well, how about Sunday? We can do it outside by the pond." Both couples kissed each other.

"Perfect!" exclaimed Lia.

"Lizzy Ann, will you be our flower girl?" Zita asked. Now I knew what they had been talking about while I was not paying attention. I grinned and said I'd love to do it.

The next day, I cleverly followed Tal and Lia around, eager to eavesdrop on their plans. I really wanted Tal to stay here with us; the prospect of more delightful and fabulous entertainment was my objective. I quietly sat at the breakfast table being completely inconspicuous while people came, ate, and went, just waiting for Tal to come. At last, he and his entourage came in to eat, and shortly afterwards, Isabella entered, accompanied by several others, whom I knew were the other various elected directors of specific arts. They sat across from Tal's group.

I ought to mention that one of Hank's inventions was the tall bar stool type of chairs. When sitting up higher, the women could use their feet far more easily to eat and drink. I noticed that both Zita and Lia made good use of these chairs, as of course did the other women. Isabella said, "Tal, I'd like you and your group to meet some of my directors. You see, I am the organizer of the overall actions, but these women control and direct their specific areas. Each one was at one time very qualified to do so, only now we all have to learn new ways of doing or performing our respective arts. This is Chelo, our Director of Dance. Lucia, Director of Painting, Arcelia, Director of Theater, Ramira, Director of Ceramics, Drina, Director of Music, Mayte, Director of Writing."

After the introductions were finished, Isabella continued. "After last night's incredible performance, we all wish to extend an offer to become a part of our establishment, Artists in Residence, you might say. Let me explain what we are doing and planning." She launched into a lengthy discussion of what it was that they were doing, not only here in Velona, but also all across the Santi controlled lands.

When she finished, Tal began, "We'd love to join up, Isabella. I must be honest with you, though. When we heard about your grand plans, we all just could not believe it! Lia and Zita thought that this would be the absolutely greatest thing ever to come to Tarra! So yes, we have been working very hard getting our routines down, just so that we could impress you enough so that you would allow us to join and help spread creative art to the world."

"However, there is a selfish second reason why we came back here. We, ah, er, would like to audition some of your dancers and singers. You see, we would like to add a whole lot more dancers and a few more singers as well. After seeing all the Greenway dances live in all sorts of towns and villages in the Southway and Calgary, we want to put at least a dozen more on stage during those numbers. In addition, if any have the desire to do creative interpretations as Zita does, we desperately want to get those women to join up with us. Can you imagine the visual impact of four of them? Mind blowing, I say. Of course, we also would like to find at least another male dancer to balance them, to say nothing about adding more musicians. I apologize if this seems so self-centered. We can understand if you don't want your performers to join us. Good dancers and singers are invaluably rare."

"Four expressive dancers!" exclaimed Chelo in disbelief. "Zita, you are unbelievable as it is, but four? We'll have to provide earplugs to dampen the applause! Honestly, counting myself, we have six dancers here at the estate. However, already I've had a number of inquiries from dancers who live in Velona and want to join our dance studio once the building is ready for operations. I dare say, Zita, none of us are in your league, not even remotely."

Zita blushed at the compliment, but explained, "I didn't start out this good. Hours and hours of practice. Plus, it takes a very good partner too. I can't begin to tell you how many times I've lost my balance and fallen on my butt. Basil and Tal just make me get up and try it again. They don't even help me up even," she teased them both. "No, seriously, we want to see if any have the right feel for music and dance. If they do and want to work very hard at it, we'll take them on."

Drina volunteered, "In the music department, I have ten of us ex-musicians. We have it the hardest — our loss, you see. The painters have adapted well; so have the dancers. Even Ramira has got some of the ceramic makers back to battery more or less. But a musician without arms? About all we can do is to hold a stick in our mouths and beat a chime! We are devastated in our field. I've been trying to convince them to use their voices. However, we have mostly concluded that about all we can contribute is encouragement to the real players and provide them with instruments, facilities, and opportunities. Pretty pathetic, I know."

Isabella added, "Their morale is the lowest of any of us, Tal. Even the two sculptors are discovering they can still do a little bit of their art, usually on a very small scale from what they were used to doing. We all have been working with the musicians to try to figure out ways and means, but as Drina says, how do you play instruments without arms?"

"Show them Tal!" insisted Lia, interrupting Isabella. "Come on; show her."

"Okay, back in a couple minutes," Tal said mysteriously. "Angus, come lend me a hand."

While they were gone, Lia explained, "Tal and I, well we have been thinking about this situation for ever so long now. During our travels, we visited just about every music shop we could find. One luck day, we came across an instrument import from the Southlands that we had never seen or heard before."

"Right, and the second that Sam and I heard these," Kayley exclaimed, "we were totally enthralled! Wait until you hear these!"

"So Tal ordered several different sets. They are supposed to be delivered here in a few months," Lia went on. Just then, the fellows came in carrying a huge set of bamboo tubes tied into a long line. Some were as big around as my arm, and they varied uniformly in length. The contraption stood on a wooden base and was played standing up.

"Behold, bass pan pipes from the heart of the Southlands," Tal proudly announced. "Mind you, we are still trying to figure out how to play these. It takes at least two to play anything on them. Have a listen. Kayley, Sam, give them a little taste of what these amazing pipes can do."

Kayley and Sam stood side by side. Tal counted them in. Wump, wump wump. That's the best I can do to tell you how they sounded. Low, breathy tones echoed in the dining room, strange and yet incredibly beautiful sounds, totally enthralling. Before they were done, the dining room was half-filled with people who heard these most unusual musical sounds and had come to see and hear for themselves. When the two played their last notes, they wavered their breath pressure so that the ending notes seemed to waver in pitch, creating a fabulous sound indeed. The place cheered when they finished, and everyone talked at once, wanting to know what these were, where they came from, and all about them.

Finally, Tal continued with Drina, "They come in all sorts of sizes, so I ordered the lot. I was hoping to find ten here who might like to learn how to play these and join us, but we need at least two. We just have to have two to play these bass pipes! Aren't they just magnificent?"

At once, five women moved over to the pipes. "Let me try them." "No, let me." "No, I was here first." "But I told you about them, I go first."

Kayley began laughing, as she stepped back. "You all can have a try. Here, let me show you what Sam and I have figured out so far on how to play them."

For the next half hour, these melodic, low, resonate notes echoed through the dining room, while Drina and Tal chatted about them. Finally, Estela said, "Come on, Drina, you give them a try." She didn't waste a second in obeying, but she had been restraining herself, as a good director ought to, she felt. Wump. She made her first note; her eyes sparkling with pure joy.

Later Tal explained that some were very high pitched, small ones, usually hand held. However, that would be easily altered merely by mounting them on a pedestal like the bass ones were on. All the six women could then play; no longer were they constrained to voice only. Thus, Bard Tal made his reappearance at our estate here in May of 644.

"Oh mom, I nearly forgot. King Diget I wanted me to deliver his letter to you," Tal said as he gave Lilly Ann the dispatch. "He wanted to drop by but he's really too busy right now."

After thanking him for bringing it, she opened it and read.

Dear Mom,

I just wanted to let you know that I am doing very well as King Diget I. I have discovered or learned something profound — just don't laugh please. A leader leads. Duh, I never really understood that until now. I have nearly forty thousand here with me, and we are having the times of our lives designing and building our new towns and all. I've never had so much fun ever. I just wanted you to know that I've stopped being a warrior and have started being a leader. Too busy right now to come for your grand opening of the dance hall.

Give everyone there my love, especially Jenna.

Love,

King Diget I

Lilly Ann smiled and chuckled to herself. Later, she showed the letter to Beth Ann and to Jenna. I, well, I read it over her shoulder.

What of our enemies in 644? Over in Vito, Flavie was very upset to learn the dismal fate of the women that were rescued. She and Elvire decided to attempt to alter the Holy Paladin's use of these horrid devices. Elvire based her plan on what little she knew about similar mental suggestions used in the distant past. "We will start with the two most likely ones calling the shots," she explained to her co-conspirator, Flavie. They did not let anyone else in their group know exactly what they were doing, just in case it did not work.

At night, when everyone else was in bed, they stole away into the deserted kitchen. Here they worked their plan. Elvire made contact with Hagne Andros, the Head Nun in Vito, and then a bit later on, with Bishop Fotios Kourgos. What they did, a telepath should *not* do. Once she had made a link into their minds, she and Flavie began implanting dream-like sequences of images. Horrid images of women encased just as the rescued women had been. Only this time, the two made it seem as if it was Fotios and Hagne who were encased.

After running this sequence for many nights, they then added the horrifying scene in which someone cracked them out of their torture devices. Indeed, Flavie had witnessed the extreme emotional distress these women had undergone. Thus, she helped create vivid, painful, upsetting image sequences, always ending with the nun or priest discovering that they now had no arms left! Each night, they left the two with feelings of utter terror and total helplessness, similar to what they imagined their poor women had felt.

Two months after they had begun their campaign of mental intimidation, Flavie asked, "Elvire, how will we ever know if all this is actually doing anything? It's been fun, but I am really getting tired of being up so late, night after night."

"I don't know, but it does feel good to be getting back at them, even if it is only in their dreams," the Communicator replied.

In the rectory, Bishop Fotios was having one of his recurrent nightmares about the recalcitrant women. He'd been having these now for some time. He'd quietly asked their physician for some sleeping powders, but they didn't help at all, and the nightmares seemed even more real after taking the powders. Tonight, he woke up in an awful sweat, just as he often had been doing for weeks now. The dreams were so real! Sweat trickled into his eye; he reached up to wipe it off on his sleeve. Nothing happened! Panic struck him. He tried to move his arms, but they did not move! Awkwardly, he got out of bed and tried to shake them, but they just dangled uselessly at his side. He tried to open the door of his room to go get someone to call for the physician, but his arms would not move; he couldn't open his own bedroom door. His stomach knotted into a tight ball of utter panic! He tried to use his feet to open the door, but the knob refused to budge and he fell down.

He tried to use his arms to get up, but they still didn't move. It was an awful struggle just to get up. Now he began calling out loudly, hoping to wake someone. Finally, another priest came to see what was the matter. Shortly afterwards, he woke everyone else up and sent for their physician.

Sometime later, he said to him, "I can't move my arms! What has happened to me?"

He examined his patient thoroughly, but could find nothing physically wrong with the Bishop. "Have you taken a fall recently?"

"No."

"Perhaps you just slept on them wrong somehow. I bet they will be just fine in the morning" He gave the Bishop some sleeping powders and helped him back into bed. "I'll sleep in the spare room, Your Holiness, in case you need me. Now get some sleep. I'm sure you will be fine after a good night's sleep.

When the roosters began crowing, the Bishop awoke, feeling refreshed; the nightmare of last night was gone. His panic had evaporated. He moved his arms to pull the covers back and to begin getting up. Nothing happened! His arms still would not work! Bam! Back came the horrible panicky rush from hours ago. He yelled out loudly. The physician came rushing in to see what was wrong, once more examining him thoroughly by the light of day, in case he missed something during the night. Again, all seemed just fine with the arms.

The Bishop had to suffer the indignity of having one of his priest help him go to the bathroom and then the even worse disgrace of having them feed him like he was a mere baby. The calamity that had befallen their Bishop became the topic of conversation that day. The physician tried numerous remedies, all to no avail. At last, the Bishop confessed about the horrible nightmares he had been having. Of course, the physician only thought that the Bishop may have gone insane, crazy at best.

At the nearby Nunnery, Hagne was undergoing her own nightmares. She began to feel sympathy for the women whom she would order locked up for the night. Worse, though, every day now, her arms had been growing steadily weaker. She continued throughout the daytime hours to see her own arms as matchsticks, just skin and bone, not the rather plump arms that she had. Around the time that the Bishop awoke to find his arms no longer working, Hagne's were steadily becoming weaker. Now she could barely open her own door, eating took her three times as long as the other nuns. When questioned about her health, she had brushed it off saying it was just old age catching up with her. She told no one about the awful dreams, however. She discovered that the only thing that helped her was to order the six women released earlier than normal each morning. Only then did her arms begin to recover somewhat.

When his fellow priest missed his mouth slightly, spilling the porridge down his chin, Bishop Fotios, seeing the image of himself sitting at some table with no arms and being fed by ugly women, finally reached a decision. "Helmas, take down my next Bishop Order of the Day. From now on, we will desist from using the Mano del Dio's metal devices to restrain our recalcitrant women. All are to be freed from them this morning and the devices put into storage somewhere. This method has not yet worked well, so we must find a better method of getting these women to begin to earn Good Marks. See that this order is relayed to Hagne at once and see that it is carried out."

"Yes, Your Holiness, I have it written. It only needs your signature, oops." The Bishop glared at him. "I'll just put your seal on it. That will have to do for now. You can sign it later when you have recovered, Your Holiness." He left to carry it out.

"Hagne, here is the latest Order of the Day," he explained to the Head Nun, who was still at the breakfast table, working very hard to get her arms to feed herself. They moved only very slowly.

"Would you be so kind as to read it to me, Father?"

He did so and it brought a sigh of relief to her face. "We will do so immediately. I am so glad that we do not need these Mano del Dio devices any more. I'm sure that we can find better ways to help these women learn to earn Good Marks."

He left and went to their special warehouse, where those who had repeatedly failed to comply and who had hot metal poured into the locks on their devices, were kept. It was expensive just to run a ship all the way to Megalos with only a couple of prisoners onboard. Hence, the Bishop had ordered that these women be temporarily housed here in this warehouse close to the docks until enough of them had been accumulated to warrant the expense of shipping to Megalos. There were four such women being held here, he discovered. He gave the guard the Bishop's orders and left.

Much later that day, the Bishop received the news that the locks on the four could not be opened, and what did he want done next? Already he had some feelings returning in his arms so he was a little upset with this message. He ordered that the women be well fed at least and ordered a message be composed to the Bishop in Bonilla to see if between them there were enough prisoners to justify hiring a ship to send them to Megalos.

When Elvire next touched the Bishop's mind, she discovered all that had been happening. The two stopped their nightly sessions, but then contacted the Bonilla Communicator and explained what they had done. She agreed to try it on the Bonilla Bishop. She found that the implanting of images worked even faster on Bonilla's Bishop and Head Nun, due in part to both having heard of the malady, which had infected Bishop Fotios. That he had also sent along a query about the numbers ready for shipment to the Mano del Dio also played a part. Here in Bonilla, five were in storage awaiting shipment to Megalos.

Thus, on December 1, 644, all use of the torture devices quietly ended in both sectors. That night the five women were loaded onto an empty ship bound for Vito and then Megalos. The news was relayed to headquarters, and the Black Dragon was notified that another rescue mission was underway. Once the women were shipped off, both Bishop Fotois and Head Nun Hagne slowly returned to normal. It had been one horrible nightmare for both of them.

On December 10, the Black Dragon once more attacked the ship bound for Megalos, just off the coast of the Red Desert. The nine women were rescued and brought to our new estate. Again, Jenna and Beth Ann gave their speeches to the terrified women, while all the other women stood nearby. However, these nine were very lucky. They had been encased only for a few months. While their arms were sore and had atrophied, they did not lose them, for which they were eternally grateful. Still, mom and I had more therapy sessions to perform during December and early January.

Only then did Elvire finally relay to headquarters what she and Flavie had done. While one cannot condone the use of telepathy in such a manner, the outcome was highly praised. No longer would women be losing their arms to this barbaric practice. That was something we all took as a positive thing.

However, in mid-December, one tragedy did occur in Vito. It began with the arrival of a Mano del Dio Prelate, Acos Daxous. Gervaise saw the black coach of the Mano del Dio being unloaded from a Megalos ship.

Knowing this could well spell trouble, he sent more than the usual number of Santi fighters into the city on shopping trips, where they would listen to the local gossip. The Santi were a common sight in the city anyway, often out shopping, adding to their overall economy.

Acos ignored the welcome from Bishop Fotios; he headed straight for the General's headquarters. His business this trip was with Hamion Akedon. "To what do I owe this visit?" asked Hamion, when the Prelate was shown into his main office.

"Ah good General Akedon. Good to see you again. It has been far too long, has it not?" Acos said covertly. The general nodded. "This time the Mano del Dio brings a new device which can be used to extract key information from our enemies. My men are even now setting up this new machine in a warehouse close to our ship. I need to obtain key information, and I need your help."

"How may I be of assistance?" the general politely asked, thankful he was not being reproached for whatever. He couldn't think just why the dreaded Mano del Dio would be after him, however.

"Capture me one of these Santi fighters you have around Vito. Female, preferably. Then, I will show you how we can easily extract the information that we desire. Bring her to Warehouse 1B as soon as possible. We are on limited time. I must leave soon for Megalos."

"As you wish." Acos turned on his heels and left quickly. Haimon walked to the door to get his aides. As he passed by where Acos had stood, he spied three tiny drops of blood on his floor. He made a note to get someone to clean in here. Haimon issued the order, and one aide left to get it carried out. A few minutes later, an orderly came in and scrubbed the floor. Haimon always insisted on a neat, clean house. Clean hands make a clean life, was his motto.

Pina Bella was a Santi fighter from Vito. Twenty-two years old now, she hated these Holy Paladins for what they had done. She had been living with her family until that fateful night when she had her fourteenth birthday party. That night, the Holy Paladins had come knocking on her father's door, demanding that he give Pina over to them. Her mother, overhearing this, had secreted her out the back window, telling her to run away fast. She had delayed, fearful of everything. Instead, she snuck around to the side of their home and had seen the men kill her father. In the fight, the lantern had been knocked over and fire quickly began burning their house. She wanted to run inside to rescue her mother and little brother, but the men just stood at the front door, blocking all passage. Evidently, they were waiting to catch her as she tried to run out of the burning building. Finally, the flames were too intense, and they themselves left. She'd tried to go inside, but the fire was too hot. She ran to the rear window from which she had jumped out, but the smoke was so thick she couldn't even see the window. Her family had perished that day. She did the only thing she could think of doing, she went to the Santi fortress for help.

That was nine years ago now. Today, she was a well-trained fighter, just itching to do battle with these cowards of men, the Holy Paladins. However, as yet, no battles had developed. She was following Gervaise's orders to go shopping today and had been listening to the street talk. Yet, she heard nothing about the Mano del Dio's visit. She had purchased a new pair of shoes, however, and was walking back toward the gates when something hit her in the back of her head. Everything went black.

In Warehouse 1B, General Haimon stood beside Prelate Acos, who was explaining the use of this new device. "It is called a rack, our latest invention for obtaining the truth from someone. See, we tie their legs down there. No take off her mail first, are you entirely stupid?" he cursed at one of his helpers. Quickly, Pina was stripped of her prized chain mail, but she was still unconscious. "Now then, we tie her legs down there, just so. Good. Now we tie her hands together and then tie them to this ring up here. Yes, she is stretched out fine. Perfect. Now begin cranking until she is stretched good and tight." The clanking sound of gears echoed in the warehouse. Haimon watched as her form was slowly being stretched out taut. "Now strap her legs into position to the table and put the chest belt around her. Make sure it is good and tight. We don't want it slipping on us." Finally satisfied that she was secure to the new device, he then ordered, "Now toss some water onto her face and wake her up so that we can begin to get the desired information out of her."

Pina screamed when she awoke to find herself being tortured by the Mano del Dio. Her body was strapped tightly to some table; her arms hurt and were being pulled tightly over her head. She twisted to see what they were tied to but could only glimpse her hands. "All right Santi. You will tell me about your plans to attack Vito."

"We don't have any such plans," she said honestly, becoming terrified. She was so helpless. What would this man do to her?

"Wrong answer. One click, please." She saw a man turning a large spoked wheel and felt her arms being pulled even tighter. Then a click sounded and the machine stopped. "Make this go easier on yourself, Santi. Just tell me what I need to know. Tell me about the Santi plans to attack Vito."

"But we haven't any," she pleaded.

"Wrong answer! One click, please." She screamed in pain as her arms felt as if they were being torn from her body. She passed out again from the pain.

They tossed more water on her face, and she was conscious again. "Tell me about the Santi plans for attacking Vito!" He yelled at her.

"We don't have any," she shrieked in terror and pain.

"Wrong answer! One click, please." Again, she screamed in pain as again her arms felt as if they were being torn from her body. Once more, she passed out from the pain. Once more, she was woken up with cold water being thrown on her face, coughing for breath. "Tell me about the Santi plans for attacking Vito!" He yelled at her again.

"We don't have any," she said softly.

"Wrong answer! One click, please."

The pain now was excruciating. Just as the man was about to turn the wheel, she screamed out, "No! Wait. Yes, attack. We are attacking Vito."

"See, General Akedon; now we are getting results. Santi, tell me where you are going to attack."

"Nowhere in particular," she replied unable even to think because of the intense pain in her arms and shoulders.

"Wrong answer! One click, please." Again, she screamed in pain and passed out. Again, she was awakened by cold water on her face. He yelled at her again, "You are going to attack at Binder's Crossing, right?"

"No." she whimpered, her pain befuddled mind tried to recall where Binder's Crossing was located, somewhere up Spoke Road #3 she thought or was it #1?

"Wrong answer! One click, please." Again, she screamed in pain and passed out, only to be awakened by the cold water on her face. He yelled at her again, "You are going to attack at Binder's Crossing, right?"

"Yes, yes, yes, Binder's Crossing," she screamed, hoping this would satisfy him and end this horrible nightmare.

"Now tell me when the attack is to occur, in the spring?"

"No," she could barely hear her voice; she was rapidly losing consciousness again. Spring? What about spring? She liked the springtime.

"Wrong answer! One click, please." This time her screams were bone chilling and at an incredible volume. Her arms, which were long ago out of their sockets, came popping off; the machine broke, and her arms went flying three feet beyond the table. Blood gushed out splattering on the immaculate general and on Acos, who screamed, "Stop that blood immediately!"

The machine had malfunctioned. This was not supposed to happen. Quickly, his men tied large bandages across her shoulders, temporarily halting the blood flow. "Well, the machine is not supposed to rip their arms off. Yet, this field test has been satisfactory. We have the information that we desired to confirm. The Santi will be attacking Vito this spring, General, up at Binder's Crossing. I suggest that you take appropriate countermeasures. Clean this mess up. We need to set sail in an hour. Get this malfunctioning piece of equipment onboard by then. That will be all General."

Haimon needed no further urging. He ran all the way home, greatly desirous of a bath! That was the most disgusting event he had ever witnessed. "Fool. He should leave the intelligence gathering to us professionals. He only heard what he told her to say. Stupid Prelate! There's not going to be any attack. We are on particularly friendly terms here with the Santi. They handle all our profitable trading. Idiot Prelate! I'll just have to order a new uniform, this one is hopelessly contaminated."

"What do we do with her?" asked one of his men.

"Oh hell, I don't care. She's as good as dead anyway. Just dump her body on the pier as we depart," Acos said, wiping the blood from his face. He walked out and headed onboard his ship, confident of his report to the Supreme Prelate: "The rack works, but needs some improvements."

Gervaise was heading back toward the docks. He had been called into Vito on business, a shipment of gold needed to be sent northward. As usual, the Santi would escort it safely there. As he came past the docks, he saw the Mano del Dio ship tacking out to sea. "Good riddance," he muttered. Then, he spied the form lying on the empty docks. He rushed over and saw that it was one of his Santi fighters. Her arms were missing as was her chain mail. Crude blood soaked bandages covered her shoulders. "Good god, what happened to you, Pina?" He picked her up and began running down the streets heading for the gates. After passing a number of side streets, he came upon several Santi who were riding their horses home. He commandeered one. The fighters lifted her up to him, and he galloped through the streets, accompanied by the others, who acted as escorts, swords drawn.

He galloped straight to the infirmary, yelling for Flavie. She came running, as several others gathered around him, taking her from his arms, and carrying her inside. "Good god, what happened to her?" Flavie asked.

"Don't know. Just found her lying on the docks, just after the Mano del Dio set sail. Ten to one they had something to do with this!"

Flavie set to work; a frantic scramble to save a life ensued. Meanwhile, Elvire contacted Paulette to report this savage attack. For a time, messages flew back and forth every few minutes. Flavie reported that Pina had lost so much blood that she didn't know if she would make it. She was having a hard time stopping the blood loss.

Beth Ann ordered Pina to be brought to our estate as soon as humanly possible. Thus, as soon as Flavie had finally managed to get the bleeding stopped and something resembling a patch up done, they carried her on a stretcher onto their caravel. Flavie went along with her patient, continuing to care for her patient, though she didn't hold out much hope that the poor woman would live to make it to Velona. The ship's captain pulled out all the sail on the ship, determined to set a new speed record between Vito and Velona! This caravel would fly there or else sink, so strong was his determination after seeing the patient being brought on board. Indeed, he did set a new speed record, arriving there in just over three days!

Somehow, Flavie managed to keep Pina alive during the voyage, though the woman never regained consciousness. However, all during the voyage there, Beth Ann had Paulette make Mind Links to Flavie. Beth Ann had every Healer in the Santi looking in on the patient, examining her wounds, in a valiant attempt to determine a proper course of treatment should Pina actually live long enough to get to Velona. No one had ever seen such wounds before, so many theories flew by Beth Ann, who ultimately would have to pick from these proposals and work her best magic. The consensus was, however, that Pina would not survive the boat trip.

Pina surprised all the Healers and was still breathing as the coach galloped through the streets of Velona that night. Less than a half hour after docking, her stretcher was carried into our new infirmary, which was all ready for the operation. Lights blazed so that Beth Ann could see as well as possible, here in the middle of the night. Water was boiling and ready; her instruments, all laid out. Bandages were piled nearby. This would be Beth Ann's greatest healing challenge ever.

She took a deep breath as the woman was gently placed onto her table. Flavie looked utterly exhausted. She had not slept in three days for fear her patient would need something. She was covered in blood herself. "Flavie, go take a bath, get into some clean clothes, grab a bite to eat, and get some sleep."

"No I must stay and help. You will need help," Flavie insisted.

"But you are asleep on your feet, and I have all the help I can use here with me," Beth Ann declared. Indeed the Guardians were all present, along with several dozen of our other women.

Jenna added, "Come on; I'll show you. You have worked a miracle to get her here and alive. They were predicting she would not even get here. You've earned some sleep. Let Beth Ann take over for a time." Flavie allowed herself to be led away. She was so terribly tired, and this had been so utterly horrible for her.

"I'm getting too old for this, Jenna," she said and felt it.

Three hours later, Beth Ann came in from the infirmary, having done all that she could for Pina. Now it was up to her body to heal or not. "What did they do to that poor woman?" she asked. "I'd swear that someone had literally pulled out her arms!"

"Is she still alive?" asked Flavie. "Yes, that's what I though too, but the amount of force needed to do such a thing is unimaginable, well maybe if you used horses to pull her."

"She's still breathing, thanks to you, Flavie. You did a great job on the arteries and veins. I only added a bit to them. I pieced together the remnants of flesh still connected and added a bit from her legs to it. I hope it works out."

"Thanks, I'm off to bed, now," Flavie stated with a very big yawn.

After she left, Jenna asked, "Think she'll make it?"

"Iffy, very, very iffy, could go either way. I know that everyone must know what happened to her as soon as possible. I have Paulette watching over her now. If her body does die, Paulette will make the Mind Link with her and find out. I don't dare try that until she has awakened on her own."

Jenna thanked her and went to bed herself.

Pina did not awaken the next day either, but Beth Ann saw definite signs of healing beginning to occur when she changed the bandages. On the second day around noon, the entire estate knew that Pina had regained consciousness. A hideous, loud, high-pitched scream tore through the infirmary and into the manor house. Beth Ann had been in the room when Pina awoke and screamed. She later explained that the scream was not from the shock of seeing her condition, but she was still convinced she was being tortured; she was still in the incident for a bit.

Rushing to her bedside, Beth Ann spoke soothingly, "There, there, Pina. You are safe now. It is all over. You are here at the Santi main headquarters in Velona in our infirmary. I am the Healer here. It's okay; you've had quite an ordeal."

Pina looked around her. This place was not that horrible machine. A woman was looking down at her, not that evil faced man in black. She sighed deeply and tried to move her arms to sit up. Nothing happened. She glanced at her sides and saw nothing, and then moved her head to look at her hurting shoulders. Again, she screamed, this time from shock, not stark terror and pain. She cried and cried for some time. At last, she blubbered, "I got to go pee really bad." Beth Ann helped her up and somehow she managed to hit the chamber pot, before collapsing in Beth Ann's arms. She was incredibly weak and could not stand. Nearly fainting, she laid back down and cried some more. Soon, Beth Ann began feeding her some warm broth, which she gulped down, realizing that she was starving.

"A healthy appetite, that is very encouraging, Pina," Beth Ann complimented her. After she had eaten all that the Healer would allow, she again fell asleep, tears still seeping down her cheeks. Beth Ann wiped her tears and tucked her in before reporting to us.

Each day, Pina regained strength. By the third day, she was eating solids once more. Beth Ann gave Jenna permission to discuss what had happened to her, guessing that she was probably strong enough to withstand the questioning. Pina could not remember too much of what had happened to her. One minute she was walking in the street and then next minute she was tied to this machine and the Mano del Dio man kept asking her about some non-existent spring Santi attack. She had agreed with him hoping to end the torture — not much to tell. She had no memory of how her arms had come to be missing.

With the information relayed, Allan took it upon himself to do something. He contacted the Black Dragon again relaying the key information of what he wanted done. A week later, he received the report. They had, of course, resisted, and were made to walk the plank. The ship was then allowed to continue on to Megalos, less its cargo, which was dumped at sea. Only now did Allan make his report to the rest of us. Jenna was furious at Allan for acting without telling her. He claimed that if anything had gone wrong, he wanted to be able to assume full responsibility, so that none would fall on her. She eventually was mollified, though she would rather have had the Mano del Dio man at Isla Roca, where he could have been questioned.

The first week in January, Jenna began Pina's therapy sessions, knowing that this one was going to be rough. We all knew that from the first session, which started out normally, but the wild, piercing, horrid screams at the top of her lungs shocked everyone of us! It was so loud that I had to put my hands over my ears! Every few minutes, another one came even louder than the first. Then came a big one, similar to the first one we heard when she regained consciousness. Then, stark silence. How could Jenna sit there beside her and face this, I wondered. That took an awful lot of pure guts.

Yet, Jenna did persist. Three more times that afternoon we endured the screaming cycles as we began calling them. I will say that the last time they were no longer as loud as that first series. When they ended for the day, Pina had finally realized how she'd lost her arms, but she was exhausted after having re-experienced the trauma four times.

The next afternoon, the therapy continued, complete with sound effects, though they were becoming noticeably less in volume. By the end of the week, the screaming had stopped much to the relief of everyone here at the estate. Yes, mom looked very ragged at the end of that week. "It's reducing, Lilly Ann, thank god for that," she told me as we headed off to supper.

Pina still refused to leave the infirmary bed even though Beth Ann had said she should move around some now. She refused to eat with us. It was my turn to go feed her. Encouraged with what mom had said about it was at least reducing, I carried in the tray.

"Hi Pina. Brought you supper. Hope you like it. Chicken and dumplings in a special sauce."

"You'll have to feed me," she said tearfully, being reminded yet again how helpless she now was. "I don't know why you all bother with me."

"I like your hair," I said, unable to think of any reasonable reply. She smiled a little.

"Now I cannot even brush it anymore, but who cares anyway. They've taken away the one thing in all this world that kept me going these past fourteen years."

"Wow. Can you tell me what it was?" Curiosity got the better of me.

"Revenge. This isn't fit for such a young girl. I should probably just let you feed the baby and shut up."

"Oh, I've seen lots here, really I have. Here have a bite," I put a bit into her mouth. "You know the therapy mom's been giving you?" She nodded. "Well, I've been doing it to at least half of the others that you've been seeing around here. I can understand revenge."

"No, it's not for this," she said, tears flowing again. "It's my folks and family."

"Tell me about that."

"I just had my fourteenth birthday party. It was night and the Holy Paladins came to abduct me. While dad stalled them, mom shoved me out the window. They killed dad, set fire to our house, and stood there watching the place burn waiting for me to come running out. Mom and my little brother died in the fire. That's why I joined the Santi, knowing that one day, if I became a good enough fighter, I would at last get a chance to fight them and give them what they deserve. Now they've even taken that away from me."

She began crying again, so I just snuggled up to her, put arms around her, and said, "Thanks for telling me that." After a time, she wanted to eat some more and I continued to feed her. When we were done, I left and told mom what she had just told me.

"Yes, I know that is there to be handled, Lizzy Ann, but it is good that she is willing to at least talk to another about it. We'll get it all erased in time. Pina has had more than her share of pain and trauma."

After a few more days of the therapy, Jenna was satisfied that she had gotten all the horrid torture confronted and finally asked Pina the question, "Now is there some trauma that happened earlier that is similar to this?"

Immediately, Pina went into her childhood incident, where the abduction was foiled at the expense of her whole family. Again, Jenna had her re-experience and go through that awful happening many times, each time working her to get more details, what she smelled, what she saw, and what she heard. However, after working this one for two days, Jenna was not getting the result she desired, still no laughing, still no realizations, and still no release of trauma and emotional pain. Reluctantly, she decided to explore further and asked her if there was something else that happened even earlier than this one, which was similar in nature.

"No not really." So Jenna had her run through this one once more, and then asked her about something earlier. "Well, I see some silly picture, but it isn't real though."

"Well that's okay. Let's go through it and tell me what is happening as you go along."

"Well if you insist. I see this guy standing over some woman. He has a knife. There's blood everywhere. That's all."

"Very good. Now let's go back to the beginning once more and go over it again."

"Oh this man is having an argument with his wife. They are yelling at each other. She throws a pot at him and hits him in the head. Damn, Jenna, I'm getting a headache now. Do we have to continue this right now?"

"Thanks for telling me about the headache. Let's continue with this and see what happens. Continue going through it please."

"Well, after that, he is mad and holding his head. He chases her around the room. 'You can't get away with this, you know. I'll get even with you sooner or later.' He runs around the kitchen after her. He sees a butcher knife and grabs it. Now he corners her. God this is awful. He chops off her hand! Blood flies all over the place. The woman shrieks loudly. My head hurts real bad. That's all."

"Very well done. Now let's go through it once more. Tell me everything that you hear and smell."

"You know I think this might be Zargarb sector, from the way the houses all look adobe-like. Cannot be real. I've never been in Zargarb. Anyway, there is this man who's having an argument with his wife. Ah, her name is Fiona. Yes, Fiona. She's has very short blonde hair, stands around five-nine, but she is well built; she looks stronger than the man does. Anyway, she throws this flowerpot and hits him in the head, right here where my head hurts now. He gets angry and he yells at her, 'You can't get away with this, you know. I'll get even with you sooner or later.' He yells it several times, as they are running around the kitchen table. He can't get to her. She's too fast for him. Then, I see this butcher knife. I grabbed it. Damn you Fiona, I'll get even with you! I chase her some more, and whack, I swung the knife down hard onto the table. I cut her hand clean off her arm. Blood flew everywhere. She screams wildly and runs out of the house into the street. God, what have I done? I said to myself. Oh god, Jenna, what did I do? I — that was — oh my god, I did that awful deed! I cut off my own wife's hand. Oh dear god, now I do deserve to die! I feel very sick at my stomach. I've done what they — oh no!"

"Very good on spotting that. Now let's go through it one more time."

"I came home from a tough day at work," she began adding more details this run through. "You can't get away with this, you know. I'll get even with you sooner or later. I screamed that at her over and over as I ran after her. I knew that I'd never let her get away with it. I just knew it in my very bones that you can't get away with it. I'd get revenge somehow." She continued to describe the chase and the bloody scene until Fiona ran out of the house holding her arm. Then, Pina yawned heavily. "Somehow I knew revenge had to come. You can't get away with this. Sure enough, I came home about a month later and was drunk as usual. I got drunk every night after that, and was lying on the bed when Fiona came in. She had a sword in her good hand; her other arm was still bandaged up. She didn't say a word but came up to me and cut my head off. I just lay there and let her do it. You can't get away with this, you know."

Jenna ran her through it a number of times, yet even this one didn't fully erase either. Following our well-marked guidelines, she asked for yet another earlier trauma that was similar. "Oh, well I do see something really large and red here. It's huge. Oh, I see a very bloody mess and a woman lying in the dirt." Jenna had her go through this one.

Slowly the pieces began to fall into place. By the third pass, Pina had most of it viewed. "I was around twenty-one. My boyfriend got very drunk and tried to have me whore his three buddies. I refused and slapped him in the face. I gave him a black eye. He got teased about it the next day and came to our place quite drunk. We argued and he got really mad and told me that my place was to be seen and not heard. It was just like what we've always heard life was like way back then, you know how awful women were being treated like dogs or objects. Well I told him I wasn't his whore. He got even madder, and he drew his sword to teach me my place. Before I knew it, he'd cut off my arm just at my elbow! God the pain, it was so like this time. I hurt so. I was bleeding all over everything. Red, everything was red. He threw me out into the street. I passed out. When I awoke, I was in a Sisterhood safe house. My arm was all bandaged up. I was safe. I became a Sisterhood fighter and I swore that one day I would get even with him. I just knew that I would never let him get away with cutting off my arm. Then, one day, I got my chance. I found him alone, stumbling home half-drunk. I walked up to him and cut off both his hands. He bled to death in the street, however. I finally got even with him."

"Getting revenge, getting even drove me on for so many years, but after I took it, I felt totally sick at my stomach over what I had done! Now I was no better than he! Oh god, what have I done? I am no better than he is. I had to get revenge, but then I am no better than he is. What a horrid paradox I ran into. There was no way out!" She started to laugh. "Jenna, no way out! I got to have my revenge. Look, he cut off my arm for no good reason. But in getting revenge — that made me just like him, I was no better a person than he was!" Now she was really laughing hard. "Get it? Got to get revenge, you can't get away with it, but getting it makes me no better than him! No way out! There was no way out of the circle!" Now Pina was laughing so hard she could barely talk.

"No way out. I've never ever had any way out. All these years, no way out! I have to get revenge, but getting it makes me into what I needed to get revenge from." Pina now had to sit up, she was laughing so hard. "Get it? No way out! That's why everything. It just keeps on happening to me, because there is no way out!" She continued to laugh long and hard.

"Jenna, Jenna, I feel so relieved. So light. So free. So everything. No way out. Stupid me. All these years. No way out. Free. Free at last. Like a thousand pounds has been lifted off of me!"

She continued to laugh long and hard. Jenna just sat there smiling at the young woman. At last she calmed down enough for Jenna to say, "Thank you very much. You did a good job. Well done indeed. That is all the therapy for today."

"Right. I can't take any more right now." She laughed some more.

"Come on. I think I smell supper waiting on us. Dine at my table with us?"

"Sure, if it is not any trouble. I guess someone has to feed you and all the other women I keep seeing around here. Have they all had their arms ripped off like me?"

Jenna led her towards the large dining hall in the adjoining building. "No, they suffered in a very different, though no less horrid way than you did. It's no trouble. Actually, we have learned new ways to take care of our needs here. You are welcome to stay here as long as you desire. You may find that there is much the other women here that are like you and me can teach you. We'd love your company. We still have our feet. You'd be amazed at just how useful feet can be for things other than walking."

When the two walked into the very full dining room, everyone gave her a cheery welcome. Pina was still laughing and trying to explain everything to anyone who would listen, which was nearly everyone present.

After dinner, Beth Ann wanted to change the bandages. Just between you and me, based on all of Jenna's other "miracles" in the past, Beth Ann wanted to see how the healing was going after the therapy. To her utter amazement, her wounds had fully healed, pinkish skin was now quite healthy, and there was no longer any need for bandages. Beth Ann was floored, because this should not have happened for weeks yet. "Well, no more bandages for you, Pina!"

"Well, that's something I guess. Less trouble for everyone."

"Actually, now you can have a real bath. Come on. I promised Lizzy Ann that I'd wash her hair tonight, so we may as well do yours too. Lizzy Ann really likes long hair, always has, but come to think of it, so do all the other women who've lost their arms. They seem to find the long hair adds to their mystique. The guys at the dances sure do love it too." She chatted all the way to the bathhouse, where I was already nice and pink.

"Gosh, you do have a huge bath! I thought it would be a tub. Oh, this is really good. I do need a bath!"

"Come in, Pina, water's nice and warm. We'll get you cleaned up in no time, and you can use your feet to scrub our backs," I said.

During the bath, Pina told us all about what she had discovered during her therapy session. "I do really feel badly over what I did to my wife, Fiona. Golly, that sounds so strange, you know, my wife, and all."

"I once knew a Fiona who was in the Zargarb Sisterhood," I mused. I described her to Pina.

"That's her! That's Fiona, my wife! But how could you have known her?"

I launched into my usual we are all immortal spiritual beings explanation. "A lifetime ago, I knew her. She became a very famous person in the Zargarb sector."

"She did? Tell me about her. What did she do? I felt so guilty over what I had done to her, you know. No way out." She laughed hard once again.

I relayed all that she had done and how the Great Messiah, through the prayers of the great disciple Bandar Dero, had healed her, growing her a new hand. "She was living proof that one can turn one's life around and do really helpful things for others. You don't have to be stuck in what you are calling no way out. The way out is to do as you have just done, let go of the past trauma and decisions and start out fresh, helping others as best you can."

"That is the best news that I think I have ever heard. Fiona actually overcame what I could not. God, she was one fantastic woman. Well, if she can overcome it, so can I!" Pina said more determined than ever. She gave another long laugh, "You know revenge makes an awful bed mate!" We chuckled along with her. Pina laughed again and said, "You know, I never ever really wanted to be a fighter! Back when I was thirteen, I saw this dance troupe at the carnival, which came to town, and I wanted to be a dancer. I always dreamed of being like those women, but certainly not a fighter. Guess I don't have to be a fighter anymore!" She laughed once more.

"A dancer? Really? Well, tomorrow I'll get Tal to show you a little something about dancing. Pina, you have certainly come to the right place to stay!" I replied. I thought with all her fighter training, she should be a natural for Tal. Besides, she was now also a member of the Laird Foundation.

The next day, Tal and his group gave Pina a short sampling of their dance routines. Actually, it was just another practice session. They had added musicians: Drina, Estela, Pili, Nina, Reina, and Juana, who played panpipes or sang. Additionally, Pili, Reina, and Nina doubled as dancers in the Greenway estampes. Plus Chelo, Juana, Camila were exclusively dancers, very expressive dancers. Additionally, today they were also auditioning several male dancers from Velona as well.

Pina was astounded at what she saw. Zita insisted that Pina join her, and she did. "Just be careful of your balance. That's the hardest thing to adjust to, Pina, it is much tougher to keep your balance with no arms to throw out. I can't tell you how many times I've fallen. And I'll warn you now that these guys here don't give a darn if you do, and they won't help you up afterwards either," she teased Angus. With her extensive fighter training, Pina caught on quickly. Afterwards, Tal begged her to join up. He needed not have begged, because she would have given anything to become a part of this incredible group of performers. He also hired the young Velona dancer Phillepe Reamau. Finding competent male dancers was becoming a problem, Tal discovered.

Chapter 27 Closure

May of 648 came. Yes, we actually had six years without any major issues! Growth and prosperity abounded within the Santi organization, the Sea Prince sectors (excepting Vito and Bonilla), and the Laird Fine Arts Foundation. A brief recap is in order.

The Fine Arts constructions in Velona were finished. The Laird Foundation now has over two hundred artists in residence throughout Velona alone. Never in the history of Tarra has so much really quality art been produced! From paintings, to sculptures, to frescos, to ceramics, to music, even to books, artists are thriving as never before. Demand has steadily been increasing and this year the Laird Foundation actually expects to make a substantial profit beyond all expenses!

Christina, the third woman of the Three Roses, is now the most widely read novelist. Mayte, the Director of Publications, cannot keep up with the demand for her books. We have even printed an edition of the Ten Gospels of Jehosanity, the original versions, not the perverted ones from Megalos.

Music and dance have become the thing to do in Velona on Friday and Saturday evenings. At these times, Bard Tal presents two evening concerts each week. The one on Saturday night is a public dance, where they play mostly popular dance music. On Friday nights, they give a performance of their art, the blending of music, song, and dance. These have become gala affairs, and every attendee comes dressed as formally as they can. It's quite a spectacle observing all the very fancy clothing being worn by the audience. Of course, the recital is always sold out and it's rare for them not to have to play at least six encore pieces just to satisfy the audience's raving demands. Both of these are held in the new music hall here at the estate.

On the same two nights, public dances are held in the Rose Dance Hall at our old estate. Here, local musicians play and the public can come and dance and have a good time. These are informal and usually the hall is packed to capacity. Because it is so popular and free, there has been talk of constructing another one on the other side of Velona.

What of all our women who formed the Laird Foundation? Only a handful are not now happily married. Many already have children. At least half their husbands are also involved in the arts in some capacity. All of them live here at the estate. Yes, we still have plenty of unused rooms available, especially on the third floor. The Laird Foundation twin palaces are a magnet for artists and people. It is truly something to behold. Allan has recently been drawing up plans for an entire subdivision of small homes for our women and their families so that they can have their privacy and yet still be within a short walking distance of the palaces, where most of them spend their days.

Velona now boasts a milestone in population, a half million citizens! No Sea Prince sector has ever had that many people in it. Elona is now encouraging folks to immigrate to the other sectors! She is rapidly running out of space in which to build new towns and still maintain the necessary farmland to support everyone.

The Santi fighter groups have doubled. Yes, we now have two entire battalions of strike forces. Even the supporting personnel have doubled. In addition, because of the large number of fortresses being built along the borders of the recently freed sectors, we have quadrupled the number of garrison forces, adding ours to the smaller numbers of local sector forces who are stationed at these outposts.

At Mont Blanc, the Planners there have built a second walled town, adjacent to the totally secure Santi fortress. Here, the town is more open to the public. The Laird Foundation Fine Arts Building and Museum has become an incredible draw, a tourist attraction never before seen on Tarra. Rea Helios now has all her father's many fine pieces of art on permanent display there, as well as her own large collection of paintings. Fifty artists in residence thrive at that center.

Similar buildings now exist in d'Grange, Barcella, Pieta, Solamina, and Zargarb sectors. Each of these is now playing a major role in artist revivals in those sectors. Heavy emphasis is on paintings, music, and dance.

King Diget I now has five towns very well established in the Langdoc region. In fact, they are doing so well, that as of the last two years, they are seeing fair numbers of Greenway folks immigrating to their towns, escaping the tyrannical kingdoms that the Greenway evolved into, with the exceptions of Calgary and Southway, of course.

Allan finally showed me a map of the greater Langdoc region. On it, the key Fortress towers or new stone cathedrals were marked. "Okay, Lizzy Ann. Here's your puzzle for today. I've marked Mont Blanc on the map here, There's Middleton's Great Church. And there are the five new cathedrals of Diget's new towns, Drillon, Dion, le'Ours, Kunigunde, and Colombe. I will give you a clue. To complete the mystical pattern, five more must be built within the region. First, find the pattern. Second, place dots where the new five landmark structures must be built. You are supposed to be a Wid, so see if you can figure out Diget and my interesting puzzle. It has historical and religious significance. That's all I am going to say!"

"Oh, here, you may have these two tools. This compass draws circles, and this ruler draws straight lines. Bye, bye, Lizzy Ann." Allan left me with a real puzzle. What possible plan had they dreamed up? I stared at the large map for some time, trying to see any patterns. I saw none.

At last, I fiddled with the ruler. I noticed that Mont Blanc, le'Ours, Dion, and Drillon lay in a perfectly straight line. I drew it in lightly. Hey, so did Middleton, le'Ours and Kunigunde. I drew in that line. Also Middleton, Dion, and Colombe formed a line as well. Nothing connected Mont Blanc, Middleton, and Drillon however. Hey, I had not used the compass. Knowing Allan, he would not have given me the compass if it was not somehow needed. But what and where to draw circles?

Ah, would a circle connect the three outer towns? I fiddled with the compass and found that if I got the right radius, eureka, all three, Mont Blanc, Middleton, and Drillon all lay on the circumference of the large circle! Hey, they were evenly spaced as well! But also the two lines emanating from Middleton also intersected the circle. If I drew a line connecting these two points, it formed a peculiarly familiar triangle! Ah, what if the Mont Blanc, le'Ours, Dion, and Drillon line was the bottom of another similar triangle? Quickly, I sketched in the two missing sides. Now Mont Blanc and Kunigunde were on one line while Drillon and Colombe lay on the other side.

I stared at the design and it hit me. I was looking at two inverted triangles contained within a circle. The interlocking triangles comprised the old druwid symbol that we in the Lightning Circle took as our special mark. Also, this same symbol played a prominent role in the original Arad version of Jehosanity, and was also the symbol of the Blessed Holy Mother! Quickly, I put in little circles where the missing five landmark buildings needed to be located. Then, I went to find Allan.

"Ah, you have given up this soon, Lizzy Ann? It's only been a half hour," Allan teased me.

"I don't know; come and see what I have marked." I played coy with him. After all, I was now thirteen, nearly of age. Boys and men now interested me, more so than in the past.

He took one look at the map and said, "Darn, this was my big mystery! You were supposed to take hours and hours at it and never figure it out!"

I grinned. "What do I win?" I teased him.

"This, you rascal," and he gave me a big hug and kissed my forehead. "Diget and the priests wanted to make a permanent monument to Jehosanity, one that would stand long after they were gone, one that would be here even if the land was overrun by the Holy Paladins. It will be their ultimate joke on the Megalos folks, if they conquer this land. The cities will forever mark out this concealed bit of reverence. Pretty clever, don't you think?"

"Yes, ingenious indeed. I don't think many will actually be able to figure it out, though."

"That's the whole point of it, the ultimate joke, the ultimate mystery, the ultimate temple to the real Jehosanity and Blessed Holy Mother." I agreed that it did meet these requirements, but I just hoped that the Holy Paladins never got here.

In the two Occupied Sectors, life was still tough. However, no more women were being horribly mistreated, so we took that as a positive sign. Our fortress commanders in Bonilla and Vito continued their reports that the Holy Paladins were continuing to build up their numbers. Worse still, now nearly half of their men were clad in chain mail! Ever this ominous sign lingered in the backs of our minds. Slowly they were becoming as difficult to conquer in battle as we Santi were. We were losing our combat advantage. Still, they made no threatening overtures to either Pieta or Barcella, our prime concerns.

In West Reach, the entire Layamon region was in the tight grip of the Holy Paladins. However, Tewdwr remained Tewdwr, with its thick accent and dislike of large towns and formal governments. The Megalos folks left it alone. In the Highlands, Fergus had united all the kingdoms there into a solid group. Thus, the Holy Paladins did not dare push into the Highlands, risking a major war in the process. Further, at the requests of the local woodmen kings, the Axemen expanded their presence along the eastern coast down to the border with Layamon. Again, the Holy Paladins left them strictly alone, for they were very formidable opponents, with nothing to be gained by conquering them.

Whatever the plans of the Pope and the Mano del Dio, no signs of them could be seen here up north. Peace and quiet remained now for six years. Hence, I thought that this would be a perfect time for me to take some time off and finish one dangling obligation that I had made thirteen years ago. Besides, once I was of age, I expected that Jenna would give me some kind of permanent assignment and taking an extended leave would be more difficult.

"Mom, it's time I ought to go see if I can find those people who cared for me last lifetime. I refreshed her memory of this, because we had not spoken of it for thirteen years now. I needed to find the island of Eyrarbakki, located in the Vest Sea, wherever that was. My rescuers were a fishing village family. Hitra, a young girl of twelve then, would be twenty-five, likely married with a family of her own. Her older brother Voss would also probably be married with his own family. Would their father, Orebo and his wife, Vasteri, still be alive? It was likely, only thirteen years had passed. To them, I appeared in a Hero's Funeral Boat and could only have been a great Tewdwr Hero of some kind.

However, I had promised them that one day a young girl would return to thank them properly for all that they did to save my life. I needed to fulfill my promise made thirteen years before. I intended to bring them metal tools, including axes, leather supplies, sewing supplies, and of course seed grain as well as grains to eat. These were items in short supply there, at least when I was there thirteen years ago.

"Lizzy Ann, as much as I would like to say no, I have to say yes; but, okay under the conditions I dictate. Is that agreeable with you?"

I sighed, and I had expected to have to debate the issue. "I agree, mom. What kind of condition?" I suddenly wondered what she might have in mind.

"You can take the Black Dragon. There has been no more need of it for years now, I know for a fact that they are tremendously bored with making cargo runs. This whole pirate thing has gotten them a feel for action. Loading grains is hardly that. In case of trouble, Captain Henry has a very large crew, plus many older adults."

"That would be perfect, mom." Jeesh, I was thinking she would be making some unusual restrictions.

"That's only for starters. I want to send along some others with you. I have my reasons. I must make some arrangements first."

"Thanks! I'll start packing now. I'd better make a list of things to take along as cargo too. Thanks mom."

"Don't thank me yet," she teased, "I haven't finished picking your companions."

I rushed off to tell Linda Sarah, Lilly's youngest daughter. She and I were the same age and had become fast friends. It seems these last five years that we went everywhere together. "Did your mom say who else she is sending?" she asked.

"Well, no, not yet. I think she is going to pick some." Linda dashed off to find mom. I predicted that she would beg to tag along. After all, she was in her last year of Judger training, nearly done.

A while later, she came dashing back in to my room. "Guess what? I'm going too!" We held hands and jumped around the room. Together we both began packing and chatting away. She and I then began making a list of what trade goods to take along. Not for trading mind you, they would be the gifts that I brought.

The next day, mom called us into the spacious study. A number of others were already there. "Hi Benet, Emil, Tonia, Cedric," I said as we bounced into the room. "Oh," I noticed our two out of town guests who had been staying with us for the summer, Andre and Leknova's youngest, the twins Renzo and Rosina Pazzio le'Gouer. "Hi you two. What's everyone doing here?"

Mom said, "These will be accompanying you. Benet Donegal will be the Loremaster; he may find many new plants and animals to inventory." (Benet was Beth Ann's youngest and was eighteen.) "Emil Amir will act as one of your personal Protectors." (Emil was Justus's youngest son and nineteen, much older than Linda and me.) "Tonia Po Woodgrove will be your Healer." (Elona's youngest daughter was fourteen and had her mother's hair and eyes; everybody said so.) "Cedric Dietz will be the Planner, though I'm not sure how much planning will be needed, but still there might be some quaint structures for him to study, since this is an unknown land you are seeking." (He was the son of Mary Dietz, Elona's Healer.)"

"I have gotten permission from Andre and Lenkova. Our twins from Zargarb are going along as well. Rosina is a Communicator and Renzo is a Protector." (They were both fifteen.) "Lenkova wanted them to come to Velona to broaden their horizons. I think that this fits that rather nicely — exploration into an unknown land."

"Golly we have a whole bunch going. I hope you're not all disappointed. I'm only going to thank these people. The hardest problem will be finding them," I explained.

"One more person must go with you," Jenna stated flatly. "I have sent out a request for the very best linguist that we have in the Santi organization. While I know you Communicators can make do reading other's mental images and concepts, I just think that going into unknown lands, you should have the very best linguist that we have, although I freely admit that I don't know who that might be. I left orders for whoever that may be to drop by here this morning, so I expect that we'll soon know the identity of the last person."

"One more thing, I had Elona check with her many Axeman friends about the location of this island called Eyrarbakki or at least the Vest Sea. She found out that over on West Reach in the northernmost village called New Volks, in our language, there is a retired seaman known as Red Reif. According to her contact, this man probably can give you sailing directions, at least to the Vest Sea. So that is your first stop, New Volks."

"Fabulous mom!" I gave her a hug.

"Now then, have you two gotten the list of items you want to take to give to the people there?"

Linda handed her the list. "Well, why don't you chat and work out how soon you want to go and all that, while I get this list to Allan?" She left and we did just that. Everyone was very excited to be going on a voyage into the unknown. We chatted like mad would be the proper description.

We were talking away, when Natale Angela walked in from the front door. "Oh, hi Natale, come on in," I said as I recognized the young woman who had lost her arms some years back. I had performed her therapy sessions. She was one of the few women who was still single and was twenty-four now, with beautiful, long, curly blonde hair and pale blue eyes that captivated one's attention. "Have a seat. I am off to find an island called Eyrarbakki, located in the Vest Sea, wherever that may be. All these are coming with me. Mom either doesn't trust me or more likely she wants me to be really well protected." The others giggled. They already knew Jenna's orders: Look after her or it is your head that will roll! I didn't know this until we were at sea, however.

She came in, sat with us, and soon joined in on the conversation. Speculation ran wild about where this unknown island might lie. Finally, mom returned. "Oh hi Natale. I haven't seen you for some time. How's everything in Velona? I know that you were studying in the city for the past what's it been now, years?"

"Yes, Jenna. Oh, I was told to report here this morning. I have no idea why. They said that you requested the best linguist in the Santi. I feel a little embarrassed by such a description. I'm good, but the best? Surely there are others that are better." She was being modest. I knew from having done her therapy.

"Oh! Oh my," Jenna faltered for an instant, but recovered. "Well I asked for the best. I want to send a top-notch linguist along on this voyage. We know that they speak a very different language on this island, and I wanted the best chances for good translations. I guess you are it."

"You want me to go with everyone here? To this Eyrarbakki? Me?" Natale said very surprised by the idea.

"Well, you don't have to go. This may well be a long sea voyage and might be rather difficult for you," mom was attempting to give Natale a way to gracefully back out of the assignment.

"No, I would just love to go! New languages! Wow, that is a linguist's dream! Oh," she then realized the real situation. "That is if you all don't mind having me along. I mean like this, no arms. I will probably need assistance with many things. I don't want to be a bother, so you won't hurt my feelings if you think I shouldn't go. I mean this could be dangerous and all that. It's just that I owe so very much to Lizzy Ann for what she did for me that I would do anything to help her, but I cannot ask that of all of you."

"Natale, if you are willing to go with us, then I would be very upset if you didn't get the linguist's golden opportunity!" I stated determinedly. "What do you all say?"

Everyone else agreed with me. We were all druwids, all Santi. We knew how much discovering something new in our own fields would mean to us. None of us could ever deny that to her as long as she was willing to go. "That's settled! You are with us!" declared Linda proudly, and she gave Natale a hug. "Glad you are with us."

"Well, then that's all settled," Jenna stated. "The cargo should be assembled in two days. You can leave at high tide, according to Henry. He would like you to come aboard the day before and get settled in before the cargo is loaded. Something about living arrangements for a long voyage, so you had all better get packing!"

"Linda and I are already packed, mom. We will go back with Natale and help her get packed too. She can spend the night in my room. See you all later today when we get back," I said. Natalie had come in a carriage, so we two rode back with her, chatting all the way. She had never been on a long boat trip before and had no idea of what to bring. Indeed, she was as excited about the trip as we were.

"Oh, I am so glad that you all don't mind my coming along," Natale explained. "This is a dream for a linguist, you know, meeting a new people who speak a different language. It's like the opportunity of a lifetime. I'm the luckiest linguist around! I hope I'm up to the task. Say, how do we know about these people anyway?"

We were stuffing clothes into her travel bag, and I said, "Let's talk about that one when we are underway. It will take a lot of explaining, and the others don't know how we do either."

"Oh a mystery! I'm game. I'll wait. Do you think I need to take the party dress and stuff?" she asked. A woman shouldn't be without something to look fancy wearing, so we took it. She had two sacks. The one that held her everyday clothes and items she insisted on carrying herself. "Just loop it over my head — watch the hair though. Thanks. I'll carry my own load as much as possible." I grabbed the other sack with her dress outfit in it. We got back into the carriage and headed back to the estate.

A few hours later and after lunch, we were all ready, so I decided we might as well go a bit early. If we found out that we were just in the way, then we agreed that a shopping we would go. I'm not so sure that the fellows liked that idea, however.

It took us a half hour to say goodbye to everyone. We had an awful lot of well-wishers. Around two in the afternoon, we rolled up at the docks. Men were in the process of loading some large crates into the hold of the Sleepy Hollow. Emil and Benet went ahead to see if we ought to board just now. Presently, Emil and Captain Henry Freeze waved for us to come on ahead and board. We gathered up our many sacks and walked up the gangplank onto the caravel.

"Ahoy, Lizzy Ann," Henry welcomed me aboard. "Before we go below, let's have a discussion about the accommodations. "Jason, Cathy, and Sammy are in town shopping, along with most of the Santi. We're beginning the loading of your small cargo. We have poop cabins for eight, two per room. One is the captain's cabin."

"Who normally has the others?" I interrupted him.

"The three Guardians have two along with the Santi lieutenant. The two Santi sergeants share the last one. The rest share the forward crew cabins. We have seven crew members and thirteen Santi on board. Since we don't have enough cabin space, we are storing the cargo in the center of the hold and setting up temporary hammocks along the port side. The starboard side you can use for exercise or whatever, unless you want the girls on one side and the guys on the other side. They are all willing to vacate their cabins, of course, but we will still be short a couple, since you number nine."

"No, I don't want them to give up their cabins for us. The hammocks will do fine for us. This could be a long voyage, so I think we ought to have exercise space. It's probably best for us all to bunk in one place."

"Very good, ma'am. I'm sure the others will greatly appreciate your kind gesture. There is one more thing that I must insist upon during the voyage. It's because you've got an armless companion. Keeping your balance on a rolling ship can be challenging at times even if you have hands. Plus, the stairs are a bit steep to go from the poop cabins down into the hold. Thus, I insist that one of you always be at her side, just in case of trouble, especially when going up or down the stairs. It might seem easy while we are motionless here at the dock, but once underway, I always tell them to hang onto the rope rails when going up or down, safer that way." We all promised to look after Natale.

He took us below so we could see the arrangements. Indeed, the fifteen-foot descending stairs from the poop cabins down to the floor of the cargo hold were a bit steep, but the steps were wide. Benet went first, just in front of Natale, who climbed down just fine. Along the port side, nine hammocks were arranged in a line. Pegs would hold our sacks. Also, a sea chest was bolted to the floor close to each hummock. We could hang sacks or stow them, as we desired. "Oh, I like this, I can get in and out by myself," Natale said as she sat on her hammock. "Perhaps one of you will put my sacks in the chest. I can manage things better from the floor than this swing."

We spent a few minutes stowing our gear and then began nosing around. They had their clever Black Dragon transformation material stowed at the front of the cargo hold, with the supplies I was bringing in the process of being stacked behind them. Beyond this lay the galley and tables. A pantry adjoined it on the starboard side. Just beyond the galley, we could see the crew quarters. We were still poking around when two women Santi fighters found us. "Hi I'm Angel Hatfield and this is Mary Beth Blackstone. Santi sergeants and gun crew leaders. Glad to see you all made it. Why didn't you want our nice quarters? Passengers are supposed to take our cabins."

"We want to be together and not to force you all out of your cabins. We'll be fine down here," I said. I introduced everyone.

These two women were from the Greenway and in their twenties, with short brown hair and eyes. They explained that they both loved archery, especially the longbow. They joined up as archers originally for some fun and travel. However, both just loved all this free traveling and wouldn't trade their jobs now for anything. In fact that was pretty much the opinion of all those onboard. Somewhat later, we met Bill Weatherspoon, the oldest on the ship at thirty. He was in charge of the Santi force here.

Bored, we then went up on deck to watch, standing near bow, out of the way of the busy crew, who used a large rope and pulley system to lower the heavy boxes down into the hold. While we were watching, the three Guardians drove up in two wagons, loaded with more boxes and barrels. They had been shopping for provisions. They were planning to be gone for four or five months and wanted a good supply of food.

They came to meet us all after they crossed the gangplank. "Hi ladies," Cathy said. "I brought you each a rose to welcome you aboard." She began handing out the fragrant red roses to each of us.

"Here, I'll put yours in your hair," I said as she handed one towards Natale.

"We are so glad that you picked us for this trip," Cathy continued. "We were so utterly bored it's not funny. Oh, I should introduce us. I'm Cathy Farthington, your Healer, though I hope we don't need any of that this trip. My husband, Jason, Protector, and Sammy Welts, Communicator." All three were in their early twenties. I introduced my party to them.

Jason said, "Hey, Natale, wait til you see what I brought for you. Ah, they are loading it now." He had brought her a tall chair, to replace the usual sized ones. Now she could eat with far less effort. She thanked him for this thoughtfulness. "We aim to please," he teased everyone.

After supper, I decided it was time to fill everyone in on the mission. Captain Henry also joined us, as well as the three Guardians and the three Santi leaders. "Gang, this mission is to find a specific island and deliver these goods to them. We are looking for the island of Eyrarbakki, located in the Vest Sea, wherever that is at. As some of you know or possibly have speculated, last lifetime I was Ket Bethany."

"Not *the* Ket Bethany!" exclaimed the twins in near unison. "The one who our folks admire so greatly?"

"Yes, that's me. I know your parents, Andre and Lenkova very well, two fantastic people," I replied.

"And before that she was my mom," Linda Sarah blurted out, "Bethany Madelyn Amir, the wife of Jes Amir, the Great Messiah." The exclamations of surprise told me that most had not known this detail.

"Okay, since all my past lifetimes are being exposed, I was first Elizabeth Stanton, leader of the Lightning Circle. Okay? I've been around a lot, it seems."

"No kidding, I didn't know all this. Incredible, gang, no wonder Jenna was so insistent on us keeping Lizzy Ann safe this trip!" put in Cedric.

"Wait a minute," broke in Natale, "I've been sort of taken with the Church of the Blessed Holy Mother. Does this mean you are hearing my prayers?" She flushed slightly.

"No, they have built up a whole religion around that lifetime of mine. I had nothing to do with it. Natale, you can keep right on praying; religion is a very personal thing between you and the Creator, whomever you decide that is from your own viewpoint."

"Anyway, back to the point of all this. You all know or have heard the story of Ket's assassination in West Reach when he was on his way to the Council of Kings." Everyone had. "Well, thanks to my sister Fianna, they gave me a traditional Tewdwr Hero's Funeral, sending my body off on a small boat upon the western ocean. Everyone, including myself, believed the body to be quite dead. I know that I thought so and went and picked up this new one that you are calling Lizzy Ann. However, quite a long time later, I came to. I awakened from the dead. I have no other way to describe it. The boat landed on this island that we are seeking, Eyrarbakki. Two children found me, Hitra, a young girl of twelve then, but she is now twenty-five, perhaps even married with her own children. Her older brother Voss went for help when the boat beached on their shores. Their parents, Orebo and Vasteri nursed me back into the land of the living. Well, sort of anyway. My whole left side was nearly paralyzed. Still their kindness I will never forget. Their island is iced in and snow covered at least half the year. Finally, when spring came, they gave me provisions and helped me make a sail and I left there bound on another mission."

"You've all heard how Jenna went down to Megalos to give them her warning, threatening to show the world the contents of the Journal of the Mano del Dio. Ever wonder how she came into possession of it?" Now that I mentioned it, everyone had wondered just how Jenna had it. "Well, when I killed the assassin who killed my body, from his mind, I accidentally discovered the existence of this journal and where it was kept in a secret location in Megalos. That was my mission when I left this island, to sail to Megalos and steal it for us. I got the job done somehow, though the body died a second time shortly after I stole it and hid it for the Santi to come and get."

"I promised this unbelievably kind family that one day, a young girl would return to their island with thank you gifts for their kindness. Yes, I already had this body, so I knew it would be me coming, as a young girl. That's what we are doing, repaying that very kind family. I'm sorry if you expected some grand battle or something, but this is just a thank you trip, assuming that we can even find this island."

"Well, I think that is truly a very worthwhile thing to do," Natale was the first to comment. "We need more kindness in the world." Others added their ideas as well, all favorable. Natale then asked, "But they spoke a strange language, right?"

"Ah yes, it took me several months to learn enough to communicate with them. We did it with a lot of pointing and gesturing, you know, 'Me, Ket. You?'" I pointed to myself and then to Natale, who understood at once.

She then asked the critical question, "Do you still remember some of their language?" I knew what she desired.

"I haven't spoken it in thirteen years, but maybe I can remember enough to teach you all a few words. It will help if we can all say a little bit in their tongue," I explained. "Remember, that was thirteen years ago and another lifetime. I might be completely wrong in words and pronunciations. Yet, it is a place to start."

"I look forward to learning it. How soon can we begin?" asked Natale. She was the only one who was ready to start immediately! I chuckled and said that we would once we were under way and had some idea where to sail. She was disappointed, but took it in stride.

The next day, we set sail, and we stood on deck to watch Velona slip slowly behind us. It was an inspiring sight to say the very least. For two days, we sailed up the coast, past d'Grange with its trio of tall fortress towers, and then slipped over to the West Reach side, with its lush green forests passing by on the port side. Cathy made everyone take her herbs to counteract any motion sickness, so for once no one got green sick. Yes, with the rolling ship beneath her, Natale did have a harder time keeping her balance, but then so did we, for none of us had our sea legs as yet.

It was night when we slipped into dock at the Axeman town of New Volks, Ny Hem as they pronounce it. The next day, the crew slid out the gangplank and our party walked onto their docks, where a number of the burly Axemen had gathered to watch us. It was not often that a foreign ship docked here. Natale insisted in going with us. I began to try to remember the little bit of their language that I had learned last lifetime. I was so rusty that the men on shore rather stared at my silly sounding speech. Natale bumped me and said, "You just told them that you are a fish. Let me try." She said rapidly, "Få tag i pensionerad sjöman Red Reif?" Our mouths nearly dropped off in total surprise.

"Ya, taga du," one man replied, motioning us to follow him.

"He says he will take us," Natale explained, though it was rather obvious he was.

"You are darn good," I complimented her. "When we meet Reif, I'll let you do the talking. Just try to get as good a set of directions as possible, please." She smiled, thinking to herself, naturally! As we walked through the streets, people stopped and stared at us, especially Natale, who didn't pay them any attention.

A small log cabin, barely twenty feet square, stood at the top of a small hill that overlooked the ocean. Nautical objects were plastered over its front. A pair of oars stood vertical on either side of the door. The man knocked and when an old man with white hair and beard opened the door, spoke rapidly to Reif. The old seaman smiled and said, "Komma, komma," motioning for us to come in.

Since we were too many to fit in his small place, I asked Natale, Linda, and Emil to come in with me. The Axeman and the others stood outside, trying to hold some kind of conversation. At once, Natale began talking to Reif, who chatted with her. I didn't get a word of what they were saying. Finally, Natale explained, "He asked what happened to my arms. I told them that they fell off. He thinks I was in a big battle, so I let him think that. I'll tell him what we are after now." Again, she began chatting away, but this time I recognized two words, Eyrarbakki and Vest.

He took out a pipe, lit it, and motioned for her to come over to his desk, which held all sorts of maps. "Skapa kopia?" she asked.

"Nej, här eder," he said, handing it to her.

"Tacks," she replied. "He's giving us this map. Can someone take it please?"

"Here, give him this with our thanks!" I took the map and handed him a small bag with some gold coins in it. She translated; he smiled, looked in the bag, and then really thanked us, beaming broadly. We said goodbye and left, escorted back to our ship. Henry at once set sail, not wanting to stay too long in this foreign port.

Once he saw that the Sleepy Hollow was clear of the dock, he left Bosun Thad to get us underway, and everyone went below to examine the map, where Natale explained what Reif had told her. "They didn't have too accurate a map. We are to sail northward toward that large island called Landsätta Stump. He said to sail around up there until we find it. After that, follow this line of islands to the west. They call this the Vest Sea. Eyrarbakki is the last island on the map."

"Very well done indeed, Natale!" I praised her.

She smiled, replying, "See how useful a linguist can be?" We all agreed with her. She had already proven her worth!

Once he had studied the map, Captain Henry showed us a surprise. "Here are the latest versions of the Nicolo Helios inventions. This device tells us the direction of north. This device can be used to measure star angles, and this one keeps track of time, twenty-four hours at a time. The other mariners and I have worked out a navigation system by which we know where we are located when out of sight of land. Also, we have these scaled down far seeing eyes. The regular ones, we can't hold steady on the ship, but these smaller versions work great."

All eight of us spent the next week learning how all this was done. It was revolutionary. As long as the Captain kept accurate records in his log, at any time we could sail back at full steam with certainty that we would arrive where desired. Only Natale was not interested in these devices and their use; instead she spent her time sunbathing, getting a good tan. For a week, while we sailed northwards, we studied and learned to use these and to navigate with them. If only there existed accurate maps, sailing would be revolutionized.

After a week, the sound of "Land Ho!" came from the crow's nest. We slowed down now, since we were in unknown waters. Who knows what boulders lay beneath these waters, ready to rip our bottom open? Soon we all saw the small island ahead. It was not the major island we had hope for, though, only a mile in diameter. Yet it had a beautiful red sandy beach with bright blue, still waters in it that lapped gently onto the smooth shore. Uniformly, we decided to lay anchor and go explore this small island. Inland a ways were some trees. Four dingys were lowered and most everyone went ashore.

Benet, the Loremaster, said, "Okay, I am going exploring. Anyone want to go with me?"

I looked at the beautiful water and beach and said, "I'm going swimming. Anyone want to go with me?"

About half went with Benet, including the Captain, the others, but mostly we women, just had to try out the beach. Normally, at home when we swim, we have on only our underwear at most. Often, everyone just goes nude, since after all we all share the same bathhouse. Quickly we all stripped and splashed into the warm waters. Oh, this was heavenly. Natale whispered to me, "Lizzy Ann, I used to be a good swimmer, but now, I don't know if I dare."

'Well, let's see if we can figure it out, shall we? Probably, you can float all day on your back, paddling with your feet, if nothing else. Let see, shall we? I'll be right here so if you get into trouble. I'll help you out." She bravely waded out further and then pushed on onto her back. As I watched from her side, she swam on her back and did well, I thought.

"I'm doing it!" she shouted, pleased that she could still enjoy the warm waters. I thought that she was extremely brave for insisting on doing things that she might otherwise not ever attempt again. "Lizzy Ann, if I give in to it, I am lost. I just have to keep trying to do things for myself somehow, someway. The alternative is just too awful to contemplate. I am alive and I want to live life and enjoy it. I cannot do that if I sit around in a chair all day and let others do everything for me. I cannot live like that."

"I couldn't agree more with you," I replied.

"That's one reason this trip is so important to me; I'm being forced to do many things that I otherwise might not even contemplate trying, like swimming again," she explained.

"Hey, can I ask you a personal question," Linda Sarah broke in, "I've been meaning to ask you this before, but never had the right time, you know, it's personal." We paddled to shallower water and sat down on the sandy bottom, the waters lapping at our chests.

"You see, Natale, Elizabeth and I are only now starting to take an interest in boys," she giggled. "We probably ought to chat with Beth Ann about things — you know how big a flirt she is. Anyhow, we haven't yet; we haven't got the courage to ask her about things. Anyway, we've noticed that when all of you go to the dances in your fancy, form emphasizing dresses, you look stunning, and the men really pay close attention to all of you. By now, nearly all the others have gotten married, and we were wondering why you hadn't gotten married, because we both think that you are prettier than many of the others who have. Were just wondering, well, I was really wondering," she said honestly. I was only a little curious. "Please don't tell us that we will understand when we get older, because everyone keeps telling us that."

"Ah, it is not me that you are really asking about is it Linda Sarah?" Natale grinned. "I've seen the way that you are stealing glances at Cedric!" Linda turned beet red and muttered something about she was trying to keep it a secret.

"Okay, yes, the guys fawn all over us. I haven't gotten married, though I've been asked twice by two men. I want to marry just the right man. So many of the other women are artists, and many their husbands are also artists; they then have much in common. Also, there is the small matter of love. I'm only going to marry someone I truly love, period. Yet, it's worse than that for me," she sighed.

"Oh, not because of no arms, it's not that. I mean I have a sharp mind. I'm a linguist. I love to learn new languages and speak with those who speak it. I've always wanted to travel and meet new people. Either the men I've met at the dances don't have a keen mind or they don't like anything that I like. I am probably doomed never to find love, but that's okay if I can travel and learn new languages and speak with those people — well, if I can do so every now and then. That's why this trip means so very much to me."

"As far as you and Cedric are concerned, make eye contact with him, see if he returns it. If he looks away, he's not interested in you. If he does, then try smiling at him and see what he does next. I suppose that you really ought to talk with Beth Ann. We all know that she has an incredible knack with men. You are really talking to the wrong woman about these sorts of things."

"Hey, gang, look at this!" Benet yelled as his group was returning from their exploration of this small island. "I've found a new kind of turtle!" He was holding it for us to see. We all waded ashore to peek at his find. It looked like a turtle to me, but I didn't say anything. He was certainly happy about it and was wondering if he could bring it back with us. In the end, he left it on the island. Benet decided to call this Turtle Island, because there were dozens of them up by the trees. After the turtle discussion, the rest of the party took off their clothes and joined us for a relaxing swim before we headed back onboard the caravel.

During the next week, Captain Henry gave us all little chores to do each day, designed to keep the caravel in tiptop shape. Swabbing the cargo hold floor was the chore that I liked least. However, Natale enjoyed this one, because we had all the time in the world to do the chores, and given time, she could actually do this one herself.

The third week, we spotted the large island which we hoped would be Landsätta Stump. In order to be sure, since the rest of our voyage depended upon finding this island, Captain Henry sailed entirely around the island, which must have been fifty miles in circumference. We spied several villages near the coast as we passed by. Now we were at last on the map of Reifs. Since there was no scale on the map, how much further we had to sail no one knew. Captain Henry explained that now we did what he called island hopping. He often did this, he explained, when navigating about the Spice Islands.

Natale asked him about these islands, and the two had a lengthy chat.

He ended by saying, "You really ought to visit them sometime. You might find their language interesting. I can only understand a few words, just enough to make trades." I noticed that Natale was looking at his eyes and he, hers, while they spoke.

The next day as we were sailing along, going slowly because we were in unknown waters, we spied a school of fish. Captain Henry suggested that we all go fishing, and if we caught any, the cook would prepare them for our supper. Fresh fish sounded much better than the salted meat we had been getting. Thus, soon eight lines went into the water. "Hey, how about me?" called out Natale. "Maybe I can fish too." Oops, we had forgotten about her. Quickly, Emil fixed her up a pole and baited a hook for her. "Thanks," she smiled, and pushed the hook over the side and held on to the pole with her feet, more or less sitting on it.

Benet got a tug on his line. "Hey, got one. Here's what you do when they nibble. You give the pole a tug like this, makes the hook grab. Then you just walk it back like this, and the fish comes up. One of you catch it in the net for me?" Emil did so. "Hardest part is getting the hook out, by the way. We used to sneak off and go fishing when mom and dad were busy," he explained.

"Good going, Benet," yelled Captain Henry from the helm. He was steering for a time. "You are going to need a lot more than one for dinner," he teased. Well, we had all afternoon, I thought, but I noticed that he was also watching Natale. She apparently had a tug as well. Using her feet and butt, she manage to give it a tug and then scooted and leveraged the pole back towards the middle of the deck, until her foot-long fish came flopping onto the deck.

"I got it!" Emil pounced on it. "Good catch, Natale. Yours is two inches larger than Benet's is. She's got the lead for the biggest fish caught today."

"Nice catch, Natale!" Henry called out. Now we had a game going: see who could catch the biggest fish. Of course, I wanted to know what biggest meant: the longest or the heaviest. We argued about that one for a while.

Over supper, with more fish than we could all eat, Natale said, "Well, I did something today that I've never done before in my life: fish. I rather like it, but I know that I can't possibly bait the hook or take it out. Glad you are all able to do that for me. That was fun."

Captain Henry smiled at her and said, "You know, it's a shame that we're not off the western coast of the Red Desert about now. There is one interesting fish there;
it's called a swordfish because it has a long pointed beak or whatever it's called. Looks like a short sword, but when you fry them, oh my, it tastes like a steak, marvelous, just marvelous. However, the fish is huge and hard to catch. Friend of mine caught one couple years ago. Four of us stopped our caravels for the evening; one fish fed us all."

"Yes, I remember that," Jason added. "Best fish I ever had!"

"I'll second that," Cathy put in. "Little things like this you never get when you are stuck on land. Landlubbers, we all call you folks." They chuckled, but we didn't get the joke.

We were going slowly through the chain of small islands. Captain Henry, along with our help, prepared a detailed map for future use by all the other mariners. This, everyone thought was great fun, charting unknown lands. We were really enjoying our trip! Then, I asked a very stupid question. We were all staring at the large map of Tarra with the usual shipping lines drawn in along the coasts. I asked, "What's out here?" I pointed to the blank areas out beyond about fifty miles from the coast of the Southlands. "Or out here?" I pointed to the open space west beyond West Reach.

"No one knows," Captain Henry replied. "Some ignorant folks claim the world is flat and that when you sail too far from land, you fall off the edge of the world, much like falling off a table top. However, those of us who know navigation — we know that cannot be true. Tarra must be round."

"Why?" asked Natale, having never given this any thought before. The world always looked flat to her.

"Because — oh it's easier to show you than to try to explain it, Natale. Pretend that these two cups — remind me to take them back to the galley." Both had very dry tea stains along their sides; he'd forgotten to return them for some time. "Okay, now get your eyes down at the level of the cups here on the table. Pretend that these are two galleys many miles apart. What do you see?"

"I see two teacups," she said, evidently not grasping his idea.

"Right, you see the whole teacup, the whole ship coming towards you don't you?"

"Well, yes. Obviously."

"Now I am moving this ship really far away. What do you see now?"

"I still see the teacup, but it's smaller," she replied, still squatting down.

"Precisely what you should see if the world was flat. Now, if Tarra is a big ball, then the sea is actually curved, so when this teacup is this far away, it would be lower, like this. Now what do you see?" He was holding the cup half below the table.

"I see the very top of the cup," she replied. "Say, I've seen that several times already! When we were starting out, we'd see ships in the distance, but only their tops until they got closer."

"See, you too have seen evidence that Tarra is round, not flat." She thought about that one for a while.

"No one knows what's out there, Lizzy Ann. Mariners are terrified to sail out of sight of land for fear of getting utterly lost! However, now with our new gadgets here, we can always find our way back!"

I said, "Yes, I remember that typhoon that we got caught in down south of the Southlands when we were evading the trireme. We were blown terribly off course and had no idea of where we were. However, we used what the captain said was dead reckoning and with my help and insistence, we managed to get back to the Red Desert. I still wonder what is actually out there?"

"Could be anything," Henry replied, "or nothing at all, for that matter. No one knows. It's the same thing with you landlubbers. You ask what is beyond the Kathos Mountain range and across the Desert of Desolation, where nothing lives. The answer is the same: no one knows."

"So we could sail out into this unknown area and then get back using our new tools," I thought aloud. "We could find out."

"What if there are new lands and new people with new languages?" put in Natale. "I'd sure like to go and see for myself! What a great opportunity we have! When we get back, I'm going to see if I can convince the Laird Foundation to finance me a caravel to go exploring for new worlds!"

Captain Henry looked at her as if he'd never seen her before. "It's terribly dangerous, Natale. We've had nothing but perfect sailing weather. Just wait until we hit our first big storm. In the winter, storms get bad out here. Then you'll change your mind! Sometimes the blow gets so bad we cannot keep on our own feet and have to tie ourselves to the helm! Ships caught in huge storms have been known to sink, sending their crews to a watery grave."

"Yes, but we all die of something sooner or later. I bet they all died doing what they loved to do and that is what matters most. At least I think so," she replied.

Henry gazed into her eyes and grinned, "Wow. You are one hot landlubber! You are right; we'd rather go down at sea doing what we love than to rot in a bed on land, but you'll change your mind after the first big blow that we get."

"Land Ho!" interrupted our conversation. Another island appeared ahead of us, this one was much larger than the other smaller islands. It was not the one we were looking for however. This one was on the map, drawn as if it was about a quarter the size of Eyrarbakki. It was inhabited. We saw several small fishing boats not too far from land. A few smoke clouds curling into the blue sky suggested villages or hamlets lay inland as well as on the coast.

As we drew near one small boat, Natale yelled to the man in the boat. She pointed to the island with her foot. He nodded and said, "Lund. Lund." She turned to Henry and said, "Mark this island as Lund; that's what he called it. His is a dialect of Volksholm, probably an old form of their language. I'd guess that these people came here a very long time ago, before the current changes in the Volksholm language occurred. Good guess anyway."

"You know that you are pretty incredible, don't you, Natale?" he complimented her and she smiled. He marked the name on the map. "Okay everyone, we are two small islands from our destination! If the scale of the map is remotely right, we may sight Eyrarbakki in two more days!" Our spirits grew, nearly there!

In late afternoon, the skies grew ominously dark to the west and south of us; the winds were coming from that same direction. "Captain, a blow is com'in," the bosun reported.

"Take her due south until it hits, and then head her into the storm. Batten down the hatches, boys; we've our first blow this trip!" He turned to us and explained, "Big storm is heading our way; probably be on us in a few hours. With these small islands dotting the sea around here, I can't chance running aground during the blow. We head swiftly south, putting some miles between us and the island chain. Once the blow hits us, we must head into it or we risk capsizing or becoming swamped. It's going to be a rough ride for a while, but the Sleepy Hollow is a good ship; she'll ride it out. What I need you all to do is go below and lash down anything that is loose. We don't want anything moving around down there. Double check the cargo lashings. My crew will triple check it shortly. Get moving; we got about an hour before she hits."

We all went below. Already the cook and his helper were latching everything up into the cupboards, tying them shut. Carefully, we inspected everything and tied up the water buckets and mops we used to swab the deck. Everything seemed in good order, so we then checked on all the lashings that held the cargo firmly in place. Again, nothing appeared loose. We noticed that the caravel was bobbing more now. Walking was becoming more difficult. Several crew members came down and suggested we spread our legs out wider, more stability. Quickly, they rechecked all the cargo, the galley, and our areas. The captain's whistle sounded, and they dashed back up on deck. We felt the ship pitch and turn, undoubtedly turning into the storm. Now we could hear the thunder and heavy rain drops pounding on the deck above us.

Soon the caravel was really moving about. We struggled to get to our hammocks. "Woo, hoo!" exclaimed Natale as she barely kept her footing. "Some ride!" She was just as excited as the rest of us. Linda and I helped get her into her hammock, and then we struggled to get into ours. Twice I was thrown off balance and dropped to the deck. Finally, I made it in to the swinging hammock. We watched as most of the crew, soaking wet, staggered down from above decks, heading to their hammocks in the bow. "Nasty ride eh?" one said as he passed.

Captain Henry had tied himself to the helm. All the sails were stowed, except for one small jib used for steering. The bosun had tied himself to the foremast, ready for any emergency. The last crew member coming down shut the watertight doors of the poop deck. As he passed, he called out, "Stay alert for any water dripping down. Holler if you spot any. Should be ship shape, but blows can stress the joints. May need repairs tomorrow." He staggered on down to his hammock to ride it out with the rest of us.

Now the full noise and fury of the storm hit us. The Sleepy Hollow was no longer sleepy! She creaked and groaned, as she rose and fell in the huge waves. We heard thunder and lightning outside, and it sounded close to the ship. Rain pelted the deck and sides of the ship. Worse were the sound of the waves crashing over the main deck, dripping down the sides, and falling back into the ocean. It was a wild ride, but not nearly as bad as the typhoon that I rode out in Pietro's Folly.

"Lizzy, ah, do we need to try to control the weather," Emil asked, his voice sounded a bit shaky. "We are really rocking about."

"Hey, relax everyone; this is just a blow, not a typhoon. I'll let you know if we run into something that is so bad that we need to intervene with the weather. You don't hear any mast cracking; they did during the typhoon. This is just a small storm, so we just ride it out." I tried to calm their fears. After all, only one small oil lamp stood between us and utter blackness in the cargo hold. It can be a bit frightening and disorientating rolling around like this in the dark.

"I, ah, see water dripping down!" Natale broke in, an urgent tone in her voice. "It's not a big leak. Do we worry about it now?" We looked at the leak; the main deck was leaking a little. We yelled the warning to the crew who said to ignore it unless it became a big leak.

Sometime later, Benet told us that the storm was lessening, that we were through the worst of it. Everyone relaxed. A couple of hours later, the crew began climbing out of their hammocks. The bosun opened all the hatches, allowing sunlight once more to illuminate the hold. "Ya dry down there? We's soaked up here. All crew on deck."

We got up and Linda commented, "Well, looks like we got some water to clean up down here." Natale, Linda, and I began mopping up, while the guys and the others went topside to lend a hand. Soon the noise of wooden hammers thumping away on the deck over our heads rattled us. They were putting more oakum into the cracks between the planks that had opened up during the blow. No serious damage occurred, just a little messy below decks. Later, we went on deck to watch the view and get some fresh air. The backside of the distant storm was silhouetted by the late afternoon sun, looking breathtaking.

"Wow, what a view! You don't see that in Velona," Natale commented.

"No Miss, you sure don't," the voice of Captain Henry came from behind us. He had gone below to change out of his soaking wet clothes. He was still drying his hair as he came back topside. "Views like this make going through a blow worth the trouble, isn't it?" We couldn't agree more, staring at the view for nearly a half hour.

"So Miss Natale, how'd you like our little blow there?" he asked, as she continued to gaze at the view.

"Well, except for the little leak, when I got worried, I liked it, like being rocked in a cradle. Of course, I would have a different opinion if I had to walk around during it. I know I couldn't keep my balance at its height. However, Captain, you stayed on deck all the time, didn't you, steering the boat?" He nodded. "Well, if it's not a bother, sometime I'd like to be on deck and watch the storm rage around us, though I would have to have someone lash me to something. I couldn't possibly stand up during it, but then I suppose that isn't wise, in case something happened, I'd just be in the way. Still, I'd love to experience a blow once."

"You got it, Miss Natale! As long as it's not a serious one, we can manage. Of course, if it's a typhoon, then you are right, things can get dangerous topside, masts cracking, yardarms falling, and all that. Well, now I wonder where we are. Okay, you landlubbers, here's your next test; find out where we are and where we need to go to get back to the island chain, so we can continue onwards."

Oh boy, we had a challenge. All eight of us dove into the navigation problem, chatting amongst ourselves, trying to reckon how long we had sailed and in what direction. A half hour later, I reported our findings to the Captain, who compared them to his. Benet won the contest. While we were all within a couple miles of each other's position, his agreed precisely with Henry's. He gave us all a pass on the test. We set sail, heading back to our last position in the island hopping line. By nightfall, we were back on course.

Two mornings later, the call came, "Big island dead ahead!" Everyone rushed on deck to catch the first glimpse of Eyrarbakki! There it was, just as I remembered it. Only it was much larger than I had thought. The center of the island had tall mountains; the tops still held a little snow pack. "If this is the island, their map scale is all wrong, the island is much bigger than the map suggests," Benet commented. I agreed with him. Now I had to try to find the right southern beach. Around ten, we began sailing close along the southern shoreline. Initial estimates put the circumference at nearly a hundred miles around.

The crew was busily doing continuous soundings. They carried a rope with a lead weight attached to one end to the bow and dropped it down. Slowly the weight sank to the bottom, as they walked along the deck towards the stern. Every few feet a knot was tied in the rope, indicating the depth. When the weight hit bottom, the crew member would call out the depth. We dare not get let the depth get to less than ten feet, fifteen preferably. The bottom was still around twenty-five, so we were okay at this distance. I used the handy far seeing eye to study the slowly passing island, looking for anything that I could recognize.

"Can you just let her drift?" I asked Henry. "When I came here, I just drifted in with the currents." He only had the spinnaker up, and he accommodated my request by dropping it and hoisting one small jib to help steer. Even more slowly the island moved beside us. Okay, we moved, not the island, but it looked that way to us.

Finally, I recognized the beach. "That's got to be it! Over there, that one." Slowly we steered toward the cove or bay. The shape of the land matched my memories from thirteen years ago. Only as we drew closer, there were now four homes scattered along this piece of coastline. There was Orebo's dwelling just as I remembered it, but now three more lay to the north and east of it, in an arc around the lovely beach. We spied a small dingy not too far from shore. Slowly, sounding constantly, we made for the beach. When we were closer to the small fishing craft, I could see a boy perhaps eight years old out fishing. I yelled to him "Orebo? Vasteri? Hitra? Voss?"

Relief filled me as he yelled back and pointed to the houses! "We found them!" I called out, but need not have, since everyone had already decided that.

We anchored about five hundred yards off shore, unwilling to chance bottoming out. Since so many of us would go ashore, Henry ordered the skiff lowered. It had a small sail and could carry twenty passengers. An hour later, we climbed down the side and into the small craft. Henry draped his body around Natale, providing her support as she climbed down the rope ladder into the skiff.

As we began sailing toward the shore, a crowd of some twenty men, women, and children had gathered on shore waving at us. We waved back. I was excited. As we drew very close, I spied all four of them. No mistaking Orebo and Vasteri, however they had aged. He now had grey hair, while hers was lined with streaks of grey. Voss had become a tall, well-built man. His arm was around another woman whom I did not recognize. Ah, there was Hitra, she had really grown up from what I remembered of her. A tall, thin man stood beside her and she held a baby in her arms. Ten children were scampering around chatting and pointing to us. Yes, for these people, the arrival of such a huge, giant ship was a spectacular event in their lives. He had told me that such ships seldom came here to Eyrarbakki.

After we landed, I said, "Natale, you are with me. Here we go." I helped her out of the skiff and everyone on shore looked at us. I walked up to Orebo and said in their language as best I could remember it, "Welcome Orebo." He replied but I didn't get his meaning. Natale caught several words.

"Give me a couple minutes, will you Lizzy Ann?" I agreed and watched her. She began pointing with her foot to him and spoke a word in Volksholm. He corrected her pronunciation slightly. She pointed to me and said another word; again, he said it slightly differently. For ten minutes, she pointed to objects, made motions with her body like walking, running, and so on. Each time the two exchanged words.

"Okay, I think I have enough figured out. What do you want to say?" she asked me.

"Thirteen years ago, you saved the life of a Tewdwr Hero who came to you beach in a funeral boat. How's that for starters?"

"Oops, I haven't gotten to the numbers yet." She began saying the words, stopped and drew thirteen lines in the sand with her foot and added, "år." She went on. He repeated what she said, the two coming to an agreement on what she had said. From broad smiles on their faces, I knew that they remembered the Hero they had saved. The other three were explaining it to their children, so I also knew that Voss, Hitra, and Vasteri also grasped what was being said.

"Now what?"

"The hero, Ket Bethany, said that one day a young girl would return, bringing you presents to properly thank you for saving the hero's life and helping him return to the mainland."

"Oh boy, that's a challenge. Here goes." Natale began translating, occasionally pointing her toe at me. Not only Orebo, but the others began nodding and whispering among themselves, so I suspected that she was getting the idea across.

"I am Bethany and I have brought the thank you presents for you. We will begin unloading them now."

"Bethany, I like that better than Lizzy Ann," Natale smiled at me and then worked on trying to get this message across to Orebo. He grinned and nodded yes.

He shook my hand, welcoming me, saying crudely, "Bethany." Soon, I was shaking hands with Vasteri, Voss, and Hitra. Then, they all wanted to shake hands with everyone. Natale tried her best to let them know everyone's name, and we all tried to keep track of the others' names. I'm afraid we didn't do such a great job of that however.

Orebo said several more words, and all his people began cheering. I made out one word, förpläga. Natale said it back to him, and he made eating motions. "Ah, förpläga!" she exclaimed. "Feast, they are going to give us a feast. I think they are all excited about having a feast for us."

One little girl of Hitra came up to Natale and said something, touching her side with her hand bashfully. Vasteri said something to Natale, who had to have her say it a couple times before she understood. She flushed, but sat down to be at eye level with her and said, "De här droppa åstad."

The girl looked confused and pulled down on her own arms. "Nej de här droppa åstad."

Hitra asked, "Duga många kvinna ha nej bestycka?" Natale became more embarrassed.

"What're they asking, Natale?" I asked her.

"About my arms. I tried to explain that they fell off, but I think they think that many or our women don't have any arms."

"Say you are a hero who lost your arms in a fight. That's not too far off; we think you are a hero, and it was a different kind of fight," I suggested.

She tried to explain that. The girl brightened up, saying to the others, "Svärd, svärd! Hjälte!" while making swings with an imaginary sword. Hitra leaned over and gave her an understanding hug. Her daughter hugged her leg. Natale smiled in relief. Only now, they were overly sympathetic towards her, as if she might be in pain. Ah, well, she went on trying to figure out their language and translating away.

While the skiff made trip after trip unloading the many boxes I brought, the locals began preparing for the feast. The men began making a large bonfire, while the older women began fixing a large slab of meat to be roasted. Each time a new batch of cargo was set on the sand, Natale and I would attempt to explain what it was, while Orebo and Voss opened them. They loved the new shiny axes for chopping wood. However, Natale was hard pressed to explain the difference between the seed for planting and that for cooking and eating. Eventually, Benet went through a long sequence of actions showing the planting of the seed through its harvest. I think that they finally understood.

It was near nightfall when the last of the crates had been unloaded. The women really appreciated the sewing supplies and all the cloth. At last, we were starving, and the food was ready. We sat on logs around the large bonfire. I helped Natale get hers into a better position for her, while Linda cut everything up on her plate. Of course, the entire group had to stare as she ate with her feet. She again had to try to explain why she wanted to feed herself and not have someone else feed her. Yet, she did it without embarrassment, even poking a bite towards one of the young girls sitting near her, showing them she could feed a child if need be. Everyone chuckled and seemed to enjoy this little show.

After dinner, Henry brought out his map, which showed this island. "Miss Natale, can you please ask them if they know what lies out here beyond Eyrarbakki. More islands?"

"Orebo?" Natale began, pointing her toe to the map, trying to figure out how to translate this request. The two of them had a lengthy discussion before she grasped his full meaning. Finally, she explained to Henry, "That's rather interesting. He says that once a man called Rolf Nosebeak, or something like that, not sure of his last name, sailed further west. After more islands and an open sea, he came to Vihreä, which I think means a green land. He says that it is a large land."

Once the meal was finished and Henry satisfied with his new information, I had Natale translate a bit for me. I found out that there were four extended families now living in this cove. When the two children had married, some of their families decided to come here as well. No sooner had we figured all this out than Vasteri and several other women began singing us their songs. Soon the children joined in as well. I wish Bard Tal could have been here; he would have had a ball with this. After nearly an hour of songs and clapping, it was time for bed. We explained that we would sleep on our boat. A half hour later, we were all onboard, heading for the galley and a bit of tea before bed.

While we were all sipping our tea, Benet pulled out a surprise. "Gang, what do you make of these?" He laid six green pebbles onto the table. They looked like green rocks to me.

"Hey, those are uncut emeralds!" Captain Henry noted. "We mariners often come upon uncut gemstones when trading with other people. When they are all polished up, you have probably found yourself a hundred gold pieces worth there, my friend."

"Hey, they were all over the place where the little brook runs down to the sea," Benet explained.

"Ah ha! Profit time!" exclaimed Henry. "Tomorrow, let's see if we can open up a trading deal with these people here. A cargo of supplies for bags of emeralds? Miss Natale, can you translate that reasonably well?"

"Hum, probably, if you bring along one of them so I can show them what we want," she replied.

"Terrific, Miss Natale! By the way, you are hired! The way you handled the translations today was utterly amazing! You, ma'am are a genius! I need you here with me when we encounter new people. Gosh, you made that look easy! If it had been just we mariners, we would still be working out the introductions! Sometimes it takes us a week to get anywhere. You are hired any time you want a job!"

"Yes, thank you very much, Natale," I added. "That was simply amazing. How did you pick up their language so quickly?"

She beamed, "Well, first I spent a few minutes ironing out the key fifty or so words that I needed to know, like the names of the objects, a few action verbs, and things like that. Actually, it really helps to know modern Volksholm, because this is likely an ancient form of that language. Often, though, my pronunciation was slightly off."

"Fabulous job, Natale, just incredible," I replied.

"I think that we ought to take a closer look at these Volksholm folks. It appears that their mariners have already explored far to the west of here. I'd sure like to know what is out there," she replied. Actually, we all did. However, now we were all facing the sad fact that tomorrow we would have to sail home.

"Do we really have to sail back tomorrow?" asked Rosina. "This has become incredible fun. I wish we didn't have to go back so soon."

As it turned out, we didn't right away. When we made the trading deal with Orebo, he told us that there was a large port city on the northern coast. They would greatly desire to establish trade for these great axes and for grain and cloth. After arranging to swap more goods with Orebo later in the year for a bag of the green stones, we sailed around the island. We found the town of Bakki, with perhaps five hundred people. They had a small dock, which would handle one boat. We sounded all the way in, not sure how deep the waters were. We just barely made it.

Once more, Natale worked hard on the translations, but we succeeded in opening up a new trading partner. We promised one large shipment of axes, grains, and cloth bolts in exchange for uncut emeralds and gold nuggets, which their women wore as decorations. These nuggets were found in some of the inland streams. In essence then, Captain Henry explained what we had done here. The exchange, if it occurred, would net the caravel that delivered the goods and received payment something like a three hundred percent profit. This was a tidy sum, plus if all went well, at least one shipment per year could be made. He estimated the net profit to be close to a thousand gold coins, one of the best deals yet. Of course, the locals figured they got the better end of the deal, trading a few nuggets and a bunch of rocks for the goods. I guess it is all in how you looked at it.

Thus, we set sail for home a day later than expected. Captain Henry was not constrained to go slow, and he put up all the sails. We flew along. None of us really wanted the trip to end, Natale most of all. We all spent a lot of time discussing this very thing during the swift trip home. Rosina asked me, "Bethany, you are a key Santi. Can't you do something so that we can all stay together and go exploring?" I had convinced them all to start calling me Bethany now. I much preferred that to Lizzy, which sounded childish to me.

"Please, Bethany, after all Jenna will listen to you," Linda added.

"Don't forget little me, I want to be part of this too," Natale added.

I laughed, "You, Miss Natale," I mimicked the captain, "are indispensable. You don't have any choice! If we go exploring, you come too!" She grinned from ear to ear, even though it was a tease. "All right, does anyone not want to go exploring?" Not a soul wanted to stay at home once we got there, not even the Santi who were the caravel's protection squad.

"Okay, then we best work out all the convincing arguments we can use," I suggested and began making a list of them. We would be opening up new markets for trading goods, yielding very good profits, if this first excursion was the norm. We would be solidifying the maps of Tarra. We would be finding new lands with perhaps new ideas, tools, foods, and materials to share. We would be refining the newly developed navigational aids, which we could then share with all the other caravel captains. We would be having a whole lot of fun. Oops, we couldn't use that one as an argument; we all laughed at that.

When we returned, everyone met with Jenna and her crew. Captain Henry summarized the results we had obtained. That one ship would return with one thousand gold coin net profit was jumped upon immediately! I told them about how well we were received and that I had now fulfilled my old promise, ending that long-standing loose end. Captain Henry then spent considerable time outlining just how incredibly valuable Natale had been in making this work out so fabulously well for the Santi.

Finally, I took a deep breath and told mom what we all had in mind. I rattled off our list of the benefits to the Santi and to the various trading countries. "Besides, mom, everything is now quiet with the church in Megalos. We ought to take advantage of this to expand, don't you think? Besides, if trouble develops, we can return at top speed, which is darn fast in that caravel." Finally, I raised my hands and brought them down, signaling all the others. In unison, everyone said, "Please Jenna, we all want to do this."

That cracked up her whole group! "Oh brother! How can I refuse all of you?" she asked cheerily. "But are you all sure that you really want to do this? It can be dangerous you know. Besides, the twin's parents might not approve of this." Renzo and Rosina's faces fell.

"I have an idea about that mom," I broke in. "Why not appoint all of us to be a new Circle, the Explorer's Circle, and include Natale and the whole crew of the Sleepy Hollow as well. It would not have to be a permanent Circle necessarily, just for however long we are off exploring. I'm sure that Andre and Lenkova would go along with that. We need Captain Henry's experience, Natale's great skill with languages, the protection of the Santi fighters most likely, and the older Guardians as well."

"I will okay it if Natale trains someone to be able to handle the trade with your new island later this summer, if you get it okayed with Andre and Lenkova, if Henry gets the map update to the mariner's guild so that others can easily retrace the route to deliver the goods, and if the necessary modifications to the caravel are made so that you all have proper housing for such a long voyage. Finally, remember that I may have to call upon you when emergencies arise here."

"Thank you mom!" I gave her a huge hug. The others jumped for joy and hugged her as well.

What I found interesting in the next month were the modifications being made to the ship. A set of cabins were added below the poop deck cabins, so that everyone now had a permanent room, albeit small and two to a cabin, with the portholes for air at a high position, so that water would not splash inside. Even the crew's quarters were rebuilt, giving them a private cabin. All the doors were modified so that they were double hinged and not be a barrier for Natale. Yet, each had a sliding bolt mechanism that could be operated easily by hand or foot when the doors needed to be shut, as in a violent storm. In addition, we had one large chart room where we could work on the detailed maps of our trips.

Word spread rapidly about the new Explorer's Circle. A few days later, I was called in for a special meeting with Jenna. Drina, the Director of

Music was present along with one of our musicians, Mireio, who sang beautifully. Her husband was also present, a guitarist, Roberto Milienne. "I'm going to let Drina speak first; she has requested this meeting with the Wid of the Explorer's Circle, Bethany." Mom had adapted well to my name alteration, short for Elizabeth.

Drina cleared her throat, "Lizzy, I mean Bethany, since you are going off on a lengthy exploration for new, uncharted lands, undoubtedly you will encounter music and song from these places. We've heard about all the songs that Vasteri sang for you. If only you had a musician or two with you, they could have brought back some of that music to share with the rest of the world. The Laird Foundation would like to remedy this by sending along two musicians with your group. They do not necessarily need to be official Circle members. However, they need the chance to hear and bring back the music and song and perhaps even the new instruments that you may uncover. We realize that this may be an imposition upon you and your Circle, but we are willing to pay for their keep."

"Drina, that would be fabulous indeed. The only reservation I have is that this is could be a long and dangerous voyage. The musicians would need to be seaworthy. I mean, once we are five hundred miles out in a strong blow, there is no turning back. They need to be able to adapt to life on board a ship," I replied.

"We rather guessed that might be a strong consideration. That's why we've asked Mireio and Roberto. Both have been on long voyages and have had no major problems with ship life. They are good musicians as well, though not up to Bard Tal's stature, mind you. At first we thought that you might not accept them because of Mireio's situation, but Natale is part of your group, so we would like you to consider these two."

I looked at Mireio; she was twenty-four with the typical long blonde hair of our women. Her eyes told me everything I needed to know. I saw in her the same thing I saw in Natale's eyes, a desperate desire to be part of this group. I looked at her husband and saw a similar desire. "Okay, then they can come along. However, there are two conditions. One, they must consent to be part of the Explorer's Circle and two, they do not need to use Laird Foundation funds to pay for anything. You women need your funds for everything else. We Santi cover expenses for our Circles. This is a very loose knit Circle anyway. What say you?"

Mireio jumped up for joy and rushed over for me to hug, since she couldn't hug me directly. Roberto followed shaking my hand vigorously. "You don't know what this means to us both," he said, but I had a very good idea. Drina was all smiles.

"Probably Mireio ought to chat with Natale to find out what to bring and all that, since she has had some good experience," I suggested. "Mom, looks like we need to add one more cabin to the caravel. I'll let them know this afternoon."

On August 1, 648, the Sleepy Hollow slowly tacked out of Velona. The Explorer's Circle began its maiden voyage of discovery of new lands and new trading partners. I was beginning a life that I always wanted — to be at sea — well, I had dreamed of being the captain, but I'm settling for being the Wid, the leader of this very large Circle of explorers.
The End.

A Favor to Other Readers

How about helping other readers? Many readers rely on reviews to make the decision whether to buy a book. You can help them make their decision by leaving your opinions and viewpoint in a short review of the positive things of this book. Writing the review and expressing your opinion only takes a few minutes, and other readers will appreciate your efforts.

Click this link: Volume 5 Power Plays
scroll down to Customer Reviews; click on Write a Review, and enter your review. Thank you.

Author Information

Visit My Amazon.com Author Page
Vic Broquard Author Page

Follow My Blog
Vic Broquard's Blog

Follow Me on Social Media
Facebook
Google+
LinkedIn
YouTube

Other Books by Vic Broquard

Without Warning (fantasy)

The Trident Series: (fantasy)
> Volume 1 The Trident and the Book
> Volume 2 The Trident and the Scepter
> Volume 3 The Trident and the Resurrection

The Adventures of Elizabeth Stanton Series: (science fiction)
> Volume 1 The Evolution of the Path
> Volume 2 The Great Messiah
> Volume 3 Of Kings and Queens and Troubadours
> Volume 4 Chaos in the Aftermath
> Volume 5 Power Plays
> Volume 6 Age of Exploration
> Volume 7 Abducted
> Volume 8 The Emperor and Empress
> Volume 9 A Job Worth Doing
> Volume 10 Degradation
> Volume 11 The Second Crusade
> Volume 12 When Worlds Collide
> Volume 13 Dark Ages

The Lindscy Barron Series: (fantasy)
> Volume 1 The Rod of the Apocalypse
> Volume 2 The Board of Governors
> Volume 3 The Crown of Moses
> Volume 4 Dominus for President
> Volume 5 The National Health Care Program
> Volume 6 States Justice
> Volume 7 Cross and Double-cross

Zoran Chronicles Series: (fantasy)
> Volume 1 A Dragon in Our Town
> Volume 2 Dragons, Power, Courts, and War

Planet of the Orange-red Sun Series: (science fiction)
> Volume 1 When Kingdoms Fall
> Volume 2 Dark Ages
> Volume 3 Age of the Towers
> Volume 4 Difficillis Exitus
> Volume 5 Age of the Lords
> Volume 6 The Renegade Tower

www.ingramcontent.com/pod-product-compliance
Lightning Source LLC
Chambersburg PA
CBHW081131020726
47504CB00010B/2041

* 9 7 8 1 9 4 1 4 1 5 3 7 5 *